DEREK NICHOLLS

WITH MAGIC IN HER EYES

CORONET BOOKS
Hodder and Stoughton

Copyright © Derek Nicholls 1990

First published in Great Britain in 1990 by Hodder and Stoughton Ltd

Coronet edition 1991

British Library C.I.P.

Nicholls, Derek
  With magic in her eyes.
  I. Title
  823'.914[F]

ISBN 340 55124 0

Printed and bound in Great Britain for Hodder and Stoughton Paperbacks, a division of Hodder and Stoughton Ltd., Mill Road, Dunton Green, Sevenoaks, Kent TN13 2YA (Editorial Office: 47 Bedford Square, London WC1B 3DP) by Clays Ltd., St Ives plc.

WITH MAGIC IN HER EYES

'I say! Look there! That gel. She must be Leander Flamsteed, the one they're all talking about.'

She was distinctive enough in her working clothes of breeches, riding boots and shabby canvas jacket, with her long, golden hair gathered by a crimson silk bow at the nape of her neck. Not in the least put out, she favoured the group with a radiant smile.

'Good Lord, yes!' It was a fruity voice that must have been nurtured on port. 'Isn't she a bobby-dazzler? Who are those two fellows with her, I wonder.'

Leander provided the information. 'This is my father,' she called out, indicating Giles by laying a hand on his shoulder. 'And this, gentlemen, is our jockey, Mr Izzard.'

Peter shrivelled with embarrassment; Giles, half afraid of the consequences, had no idea what to make of the situation. But the moment turned to gold: the flushed faces in the grandstand were subdued by awed respect, the hats came off, Leander gave them a wave and passed on her way like a queen. For the first time on a much broader stage than Cannings Ambo, her allure and *élan* had worked the magic. Giles always remembered the episode and was confident that it was the sign of truly great things to come.

**Also by the same author,
and available from Coronet:**

THE BLUE RIBAND

About the author

Derek Nicholls was born in Birmingham and educated there and at Durham University. His grandfather was a racehorse trainer in Co. Kildare, Ireland, and the author has been a racing enthusiast from an early age. His first novel, THE BLUE RIBAND, was published to acclaim and was shortlisted for the Boots Romantic Novel of the Year Award. WITH MAGIC IN HER EYES is his second novel. HEIRS TO ADVENTURE, his third novel which carries the story of Latimer's Barn to the present day, is published soon in Hodder and Stoughton hardcover.

For

David Dyer

who was with me when I first discovered
Wiltshire in 1956 under the somewhat less than ideal
conditions of National Service
and has been a good friend ever since

Author's Note

The village of Cannings Ambo does not exist, but if you drive along the A4 road from Marlborough to Calne you will see at least two locations that would be ideal. Both are on the left-hand or south side of the A4 between one and two miles from Marlborough.

It follows, therefore, that the village's inhabitants, Hawksworths, Flamsteeds and all their employees and friends are imaginary. They do, however, encounter many real people including, for example, the legendary John Porter and the great jockey Morny Cannon, one of whose sisters was to become Lester Piggott's grandmother.

Mention must be made of Mary Alice Douglas, who was headmistress of the Godolphin School at Salisbury from 1890 to 1920. I am grateful to Miss Elisabeth Hannay, the headmistress at the time of my visit to the school, and Commander Julian Loring, the Bursar, for helping me to understand Miss Douglas's remarkably enlightened approach to the education of girls. The Godolphin School continues to be a delightful establishment and will be entrusted with the education of Cannings Ambo's young ladies for generations to come.

Finally, my special thanks go to Nick Sayers and Anna Powell of Hodder and Stoughton. It was Nick who planted the idea for the history of a racing stable in my mind when I had barely started writing *The Blue Riband*, and the finished product is a good deal better for Anna's efforts.

Derek Nicholls

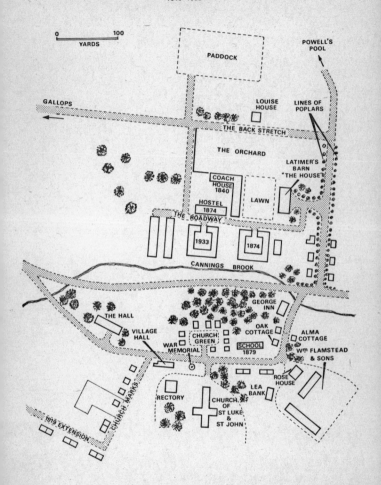

LATIMER'S BARN
1840–1939

0   100
YARDS

PADDOCK

POWELL'S POOL

GALLOPS

LOUISE HOUSE

LINES OF POPLARS

THE BACK STRETCH

THE ORCHARD

LATIMER'S BARN "THE HOUSE"

COACH HOUSE 1840

LAWN

HOSTEL 1874

THE BROADWAY

1933

1874

CANNINGS BROOK

THE HALL

GEORGE INN

OAK COTTAGE

ALMA COTTAGE

VILLAGE HALL

CHURCH GREEN

WAR MEMORIAL

SCHOOL 1879

Wᵐ FLAMSTEAD & SONS

ROSE HOUSE

LEA BANK

RECTORY

CHURCH OF ST LUKE & ST JOHN

CHURCH MARKS

1919 EXTENSION

CHAPTER I

1840

'God created it for thoroughbreds!'

Lord Francis Rashleigh first saw the tiny hamlet of Cannings Ambo on a peerless evening in early May 1840. A long and tiring day that had included his first journey by railway failed to dull his interest, and the ruin that the locals had always called 'Latimer's Barn' enchanted him.

"Hugh Latimer was a priest in these parts, my lord," his host, Jasper Beresford, explained as they dined. "That was before he became Bishop of Worcester and a martyr, of course."

"A sad business, sir, a sad business!" Rashleigh was quite content to let his ignorance give the impression that he believed it might have happened last month rather than three hundred years ago.

"He was much loved round here," Beresford continued. "He disapproved of the tithe system and took the barn out of commission long before the Reformation."

"An exceptionally sound policy, sir." Rashleigh paused to wash down a mouthful of beef with a whole glass of wine. "I am most struck by the heath to the south of the pile. Excellent, quite excellent."

Beresford was certain that his luck had turned at last. He had never regarded the ruin as anything other than an eyesore; now, this lordly idiot from Kent was poised to buy the whole estate because of it.

The Cannings Ambo estate, some two miles west of Marlborough, had been confiscated for the Church in 1537. After two years during which it was plain that the administration of Henry VIII had no idea what to do with the land, the local squire grabbed it, and it had remained in the family ever since. For nine generations an adequate living had been obtained, mostly from sheep-farming. Then, in 1793, everything began to change. Motivated by patriotism, the comparative nearness of a vulnerable coastline and a thirst for adventure, many

1

young men went away to fight Napoleon. Those who came back, and had all their limbs intact, also had money in their pockets and an inclination to carry on exploring.

The year following the start of war, 1794, Parliament passed a Bill giving approval to the construction of the Kennet & Avon Canal, linking the Thames at Reading with the Avon at Bath. The line of the canal passed only a few miles south of Cannings Ambo, and once the enterprise commenced under the Scottish engineer John Rennie, designer of the new London Bridge, there was plenty of work for the asking. Twelve men from the estate joined the teams of navvies helping to dig ten miles of cut before being employed on the spectacular flight of twenty-nine locks that lowered the canal 250 feet through Devizes. Much of the work was back-breaking and the hours long, but it was no worse than looking after sheep, and there was money every Friday night. When the canal opened in 1810, only two of the twelve came back.

Nevertheless, for a while it seemed that the old ways might return; in reality, what appeared to be stability was stagnation, and when Jasper Beresford inherited the estate from his father in 1832, the final blow had already fallen. It came in the form of a self-opinionated dynamo of a man in a stove-pipe hat. Isambard Kingdom Brunel was bestriding the north-Wiltshire Downs in search of a route for the London to Bristol railway. The men from Cannings Ambo were not navvies this time: they worked as blacksmiths, repairers of machinery, and, from a base in the small village of Swindon, supplied food and drink to the work-gangs. Jasper Beresford's own younger brother, Horatio, spent two years with one of Brunel's assistants before moving to Birmingham where he set up his own factory to produce the nuts and bolts to hold the line together.

It was the end. Sheep-stealing was the only activity now carried out with any consistency across the estate, income from rents dwindled to a miserable trickle, and in 1832 Jasper Beresford's wife died giving birth to their son. Gradually, but inevitably, he became certain of only one thing: the estate must be sold. When he was free of worry and had his hands on money, Beresford would decide what to do next.

Lord Francis rose with the lark next morning, surprising Jasper Beresford, who thought his guest had eaten and drunk far too much to be putting on a vigorous early-morning show. In no way deterred by his excesses of the previous evening, and faced with a day in the open air on horseback, Lord Francis made a hearty breakfast.

During the course of the meal, Beresford's son, Peveril, was led in to be presented to His Lordship. Eight years old with a long, pale face, sorrowful grey eyes and a mass of fair hair that made him far too pretty for Rashleigh's taste, the boy stood, stared gravely, said, "How do you do, my lord?" and was then taken away by Beresford's old housekeeper.

"Fine-looking boy," Lord Francis said with no attempt at sincerity and looked round for more food.

Outside, they encountered what appeared to be Beresford's other servant; he was, in fact, the pot boy from the George Inn, borrowed and bribed for the occasion. Climbing astride Beresford's own hunter, Rashleigh glanced disdainfully at his host's mount. He would never have given the time of day to such a poor-looking creature, and saw that Beresford's affairs were indeed in a bad way.

Lord Francis already had a fair idea of the lie of the land. The estate comprised almost exactly two thousand acres and was a near-rectangle some three miles long by one mile wide. Lying along a line north–south, it extended from the River Kennet to the boundary of the downland parish of Cannings St John, and was bisected by a rutted lane connecting the London–Bath road to Cannings St John and a string of regularly-spaced hamlets meandering towards Devizes. The village of Cannings Ambo was to the east of this lane.

Apart from the church, the largest building was The Hall, built by an extravagant Beresford in 1698. Since the death of his wife, Jasper Beresford had retreated into one corner of it. Inspecting the rear of the house from the vantage point of a horse, Lord Francis noted the signs of neglect and decay. Weeds were flourishing between the cobbles of the stable yard; all but one of the six loose-boxes had obviously not been used for some time and their doors were rotting; the windows of the house were filthy and many were cracked.

They rode towards the church. When it was built between 1390 and 1400 it had been proportionate to the needs of the community; now it was ridiculously grand. Lord Francis took careful note of the huge Rectory, inhabited, he imagined, by an importunate wind-bag who was forever bemoaning his lot and casting covetous eyes at a man's purse. Opposite the church were six ramshackle houses on one side of a green. Beresford almost volunteered the information that there had been many more before the canal and railway, but they had been abandoned, then demolished for firewood and road-mending materials by those who had been forced to stay. He thought better of it; the unkempt desolation was there for all to see.

At the corner where the village street began to curve back towards the lane there was what had once been an elegant double-fronted house. Jasper Beresford looked mournfully at what he regarded as the greatest tragedy of all.

3

"Rose House, my lord," he said. "My factor used to live there."

"Oh? And what became of him, sir?"

"The railway. I understand that he is an important official at Temple Meads in Bristol."

"Really? Well, well!" Lord Francis spared the very briefest of glances for the house and fixed a jaundiced eye on The George Inn, a hundred yards ahead.

"An evil-looking place," he growled.

"I fear so, my lord."

"Where the devil do his customers come from?" Rashleigh looked round, clearly implying that the place was deserted.

"The worst elements of Marlborough, my lord. And Cannings St John. They have no inn there."

Despite the intensity of Lord Francis's stare, there was nothing to be seen through the windows of The George as they rode past; filthy curtains and shutters barred the view.

"I may have to do something about that place," His Lordship said ominously, thus raising Beresford's hopes: he was going to buy.

Rashleigh reined in his horse at the end of the lane and studied the view to the west. Apart from the old ruin that so fascinated him, there was nothing. This had been the province of the sheep. In the background, running parallel to the lane, a ridge climbed steadily from the London–Bath road towards Cannings St John. The skyline, crystal-clear today against a perfect blue sky, was bare and featureless save for a large cluster of trees about a mile from the shell of the barn.

"Powell's Wood, my lord," Beresford explained in response to the brief sparkle of interest. Rashleigh nodded, not in the least concerned about who Powell was or might have been. "There's a big pool in those trees, a most unusual feature on the Down. It's fed by an artesian well of great antiquity. Very good water, although the stream serves us well, of course." Rashleigh nodded again. He had noticed the Cannings Brook, passing close to the ruin on its way to the River Kennet at the foot of the valley.

Far more interesting to him was the stretch of open downland to the south. For the most part it was practically level; after a mile it rose gently. Galloping over it as fast as Beresford's horse would go, Lord Francis found the ground very much to his liking and smiled with private satisfaction. Concentrating on putting up a good show as a horseman, Jasper Beresford left Rashleigh to his thoughts.

With an hour to rest the horses while they ate the bread and cheese from Beresford's saddle-bag, they were out all day. Rashleigh insisted on riding round every inch of the eight-mile boundary of the estate,

4

a journey that took them from the edge of Cannings St John, to the ridge past Powell's Wood, down to the River Kennet and into the lush meadows behind the church of St Luke and St John at Cannings Ambo. Eventually, Beresford gave up trying to draw honest attention to shortcomings: Lord Francis's disinterest in such matters was monumental. Instead, he was obsessively concerned with the safety and seclusion of the place, demanding repeated assurances that the area was not infested with thieves and vagabonds. In mid-afternoon, while they were on the highest point of Cannings Down, Ezekiel Huish, the carter from Devizes, trundled noisily along the lane on his weekly round; producing a pocket telescope, Rashleigh observed his progress with glowering suspicion.

At last, when it was six o'clock, and Jasper Beresford was close to dropping with exhaustion, they returned to the ruin. Lord Francis gazed with joyous speculation at the huge expanse of well-drained turf to the south of it, then made an astounding pronouncement. "I shall turn this into a most splendid house!" He roared with laughter at the expression on Beresford's face and said, "Come, sir! Let us make a bargain."

"You wish to purchase, my lord?"

"I do, sir. What shall we say to a price?"

Jasper Beresford squirmed. "Three thousand guineas, my lord. That was the figure in the advertisement."

"Yes, yes. Quite so, sir. My view is that a guinea an acre would cover it. Two thousand guineas. So let us meet half-way. What do you say to two thousand five hundred?"

It was, Jasper Beresford supposed, inevitable. No one else had bothered to show an interest in the sale, but pre-ordination did nothing to soften the blow. He cared deeply about the estate. There had been a time when he imagined he might make it work. Now he knew differently.

"Very well, my lord," he said wearily.

"Capital! Come, sir, let us shake hands on it!"

After they had done so, Beresford asked, "Forgive me, my lord, did I understand you to say that you would be making *this* into a house?" He indicated the barn, in the shadow of which they were standing.

"Indeed you did, sir! It will be excellent, quite excellent. Precisely what I have always had in mind."

"I see. Does that mean you will not be using The Hall?"

"Just so! Your house is excellent, of course, but it lacks the amenities I need. It has no potential."

Beresford took a deep breath and grasped the nettle. "Would you consider renting The Hall to me, my lord?"

Excited by his prospects, Rashleigh was inclined to salve his conscience over the hard bargain with a magnanimous gesture.

"You wish to remain at The Hall?" he asked.

"Yes, my lord. My son and I are . . ."

Lord Francis cut him short. "You shall, sir, you shall. As to rent, I will not hear of such a thing! You will be my honoured guest for as long as we both live. Simkiss, my man of affairs, will see that it is all drawn up to your complete satisfaction."

"My lord!"

"Think nothing of it, my dear fellow, think nothing of it! You are fulfilling my dreams, so I must do right by you in return."

As they walked their horses the hundred yards or so to the lane, Jasper Beresford wondered how best to satisfy his curiosity. The man who was taking over his estate had ignored the village other than to regard it as a likely intrusion into whatever he was planning. There was nothing for it but to ask.

"Might I know what you propose to do here, my lord?"

Rashleigh halted to gaze at him in outraged disbelief. "*Do*, my dear sir? What am I going to *do*? I shall keep the finest horses, the very finest, and they will win famous races. Look!" He flung an arm grandiloquently towards the land over which they had galloped. "Look at it, sir. God created it for thoroughbreds! Has that never occurred to you? That will make the greatest training ground in the realm."

Long before he had any hope of receiving the deeds of the estate through the proper legal channels, Rashleigh set to work.

A contractor from Calne began using teams of shire horses to move tackle and materials up to the barn while Lord Francis sat down in Jasper Beresford's library and drew a plan of what he wanted. The roofless barn measured sixty feet by one hundred and twenty, with massive walls that were sound up to a lofty seventy feet. The eaves of the new roof were to be forty feet above the ground and the surplus stone would be more than sufficient for the new stable and coach-house.

The men from Calne erected scaffolding and set to with a will. Their progress, together with the posturings of Lord Francis Rashleigh, was followed with hawk-like vigilance from The George Inn.

Only a place like Cannings Ambo as it then was could have accommodated and tolerated Eli Munge, landlord of The George. The family name had probably been Monger originally, but Eli's father, who had fallen drunk and dead in a ditch at Ogbourne Maizey during the great equinoctial gale of 1819, always insisted on Munge, and his disgustingly eccentric son was more than happy to follow his example. Eli was about thirty-five, but was taken for sixty any day of the week except Tuesday when he shaved. A squint in his left eye and a mouth that sagged to the right made him immediately alarming to all but a handful of drinking cronies. Jasper Beresford was not alone in believing that one or both of these unprepossessing afflictions might be nothing more than perverse affectation, as was Eli's ranting obsession with the possibility of a French invasion led by the ghost of Bonaparte.

Joseph Barnfather, nearly seventy, was a member of the inner circle. One evening at the beginning of June, he brought the latest news to The George.

"His Lordship's down again, gold weskit an' all. He'm driving they lads from Calne summat cruel," he reported.

"They'm plain daft for putting up with it," was the opinion of Gabriel Densham.

"Ah, but jus' you wait," Joseph went on. "Every man jack of 'em gets ten golden sovereigns extra if the job's done to time."

"And when will that be?" Gabriel wanted to know.

"He'm moving in at Michaelmas."

"Never!"

"'Arry Irons reckons those boys of his'n'll do it."

"Was that Parson Proudfoot I seed up there this post meridian?" Gabriel asked.

"Ar, 'twas. He was a-telling His Lordship as how he wanted a new roof."

"Is he getting one?"

"Reckon not, Gabriel. His Lordship told Parson not to come trespassing and cadging on his land."

Gabriel Densham thought this hugely funny. "'Tis all his land now," he said. "If he've a mind to be like that he can chuck old Proudfoot out of his pulpit."

So far, Eli Munge had not spoken. This was perfectly normal. His taciturnity was a by-word. Now he uttered. "Ar!" That was all. Not a syllable more. But his clique found it eloquent.

"Us'll all have to watch us Ps and Qs now, dost reckon, Eli?" Joseph Barnfather asked.

By way of confirmation, Eli Munge produced a look of searing malevolence.

The building work proceeded well. The barn was equipped with windows and a hipped slate roof, pitched elegantly low. A magnificent staircase of the finest oak was constructed up to a landing and first

7

floor. The joists for the new floor were massive timbers, each sixty feet long, the full width of the barn, eighteen inches wide and two feet deep. There were to be eight splendid bedrooms, together with smaller and entirely separate rooms for the servants, to be reached by a utilitarian staircase at the west end of the house.

Using stone from the upper superfluous reaches of the barn's original walls, an L-shaped block, with boxes for ten horses, was to be built fifty yards from the house. Between the house and the stable a massive lawn was to be laid, and nearly an acre of the best turf on Cannings Down had already been earmarked for this purpose.

Rashleigh's wife, Dora, rendered dire and bitter by twenty years of childless marriage to a barbaric fool, sat patiently in the family home at Strood in Kent, listening to the inflated stories of progress. She was certain that, as well as horses, Lord Francis intended installing a mistress at this incredible-sounding place in Wiltshire. It was a prospect to which she looked forward fervently, hoping that the arrangement would take him out of her life for at least eleven months of the year.

After a week in July during which his bombast brought her to the verge of madness, Rashleigh took himself off to Newmarket to find horses and a man to take charge of them.

William George Frederick Cavendish Bentinck, third son of the fourth Duke of Portland, was engaged on a crusade. It had occupied him for the last ten years and would last until 1846 when he sold all his bloodstock, withdrew from racing completely and concentrated on politics until his untimely death in 1848.

The main thrust of his policy was to rid racing of the crooks and twisters who had gathered round it like moths to a candle since the earliest days. In this he was utterly ruthless, pursuing a line first taken by Sir Charles Bunbury who had made Newmarket untenable for King George IV in 1791, when he was still Prince of Wales.

Bentinck was aloof, arrogant and high-handed. Habitually, he did things that would have caused him to have anyone else warned off Newmarket Heath. Everyone understood this and accepted it; none but the most mean-minded or criminally inclined ever doubted that the good of the Sport was his prime concern. Bentinck's methods had to match the inventive evil and chicanery of the times.

Rashleigh had been in Newmarket barely an hour before Lord George, watching from his window above the High Street, knew the purpose of his mission.

The Rashleighs had always been scoundrels, causing untold trouble wherever they appeared. Under no circumstances was this latest specimen of the pestilential family to be allowed a chance of entry to racing. Within the hour, the story was on its way: no one who valued his living would sell Rashleigh decent horses, or work for him.

The stable was ready by the end of August. Two weeks later the last piece of wallpaper was fixed in the house, men came to lay carpets, and a team of seamstresses set to work on curtains. The arrival of waggon-loads of furniture plunged Lord Francis into a state of high excitement, and he raced around adding to the natural chaos with an endless torrent of contradictory instructions concerning the placing of every single item. From breakfast until supper he worked himself and everyone unfortunate enough to be near him into a state of total panic.

Miraculously, without anyone really understanding why, it all came right. On 15 September Lord Francis took up residence at his new country seat. He was joined by a group of servants he had collected from Marlborough and the surrounding villages, mostly bribed away from perfectly good employers by means of a little cash in hand and high-sounding promises. The avid but largely unseen band of spectators thought that this was the end of the matter: the new squire was in place, the excitement was over, he would now settle down to fool around with his horses.

Then, at Michaelmas, the feast of St Michael and All Angels on 29 September, Arabella Fenton, a raven-haired beauty with lascivious eyes, came to become the mistress of Latimer's Barn.

Eli Munge and his cronies saw her arrive. The carriage, Lord Francis's finest, with the baggage cart following at a respectful distance, had been spotted coming down the main London–Bath road by Gabriel Densham's son who raced across the fields to deliver the news to The George. Galvanised into activity, the inmates, including half a dozen hard cases from Cannings St John, hurried up the lane in time to see the carriage turn in through the new gates. Arabella Fenton was somewhat taken aback by their sudden appearance and befuddled boggling, but she smiled radiantly and waved.

"Be that Lady Rashleigh, then?" one of the group asked.

"No, her bean't."

"How do 'ee know?"

"Real ladies don't look like her."

"Her'm an whore!" Eli Munge pronounced with damning finality.

In the carriage, Arabella Fenton asked Lord Francis, "Who are those men, my love?"

"Villagers," Rashleigh replied grimly. "You will not be seeing them."

On the whole, Arabella thought this a good thing: quaint though they seemed, there was a vague air of menace about them. A city-dweller used to the best that money could buy, Arabella found Eli Munge and his clique disturbingly suggestive of an earlier, less civilised era. She fixed her attention firmly on the house, finding it much more to her taste.

Two days later, her illusions were destroyed. Ten poor-looking horses and two seedy men arrived at dawn after a three-day trek from Newmarket. At once, her lord and master flung himself into preparing the animals for racing and her life became a misery.

CHAPTER 2
1859

'I have a mind to try my hand at that'

On a May morning of uncertain weather, one of the Stringfellow brothers questioned if it was worth leaving The George to watch the flight of Rashleigh's latest mistress.

"How many's this, then?" Walter demanded.

"Fourteen," his brother Jack replied.

"No, you'm wrong, 'tis fifteen," Gabriel Densham said.

Malachi Stringfellow, the senior member of the trio of ne'er-do-wells who posed as farmers in Cannings St John, agreed. "Ar, you'm right, Gabriel. There was her from up north, Jack. You missed 'un when you went down Salisbury way summer before last."

"Her with the buswams, by God!" Walter's eyes glazed at the memory. "Now her were summat! I don't reckon this 'un's worth it."

But Eli Munge had stopped dispensing ale and was leading the way. They *always* watched Rashleigh's fancy bits make their departure: Joseph Barnfather, laid to rest three years since, God rest his soul, would never forgive them if they let the tradition of nineteen years lapse.

After the lady's departure with her outraged brother, Lord Francis locked himself in his library with the brandy and assessed his situation.

It was lamentable.

In nineteen years, Latimer's Barn had provided periods of pleasure, fleeting happiness, disturbance and uproar as one mistress after another had departed and not a single success on the Turf. There was no point in avoiding the truth: his horses were consistently below par and his selection of men to train them had been disastrous.

Not that he had ever been allowed to buy horses of any merit or employ capable men. When Lord George Bentinck died in 1848, Rashleigh hoped that he might find greater favour with the new order at the Jockey Club. But on the day that Admiral Henry Rous assumed command at Newmarket, Rashleigh's fate was sealed for all time. An edict was issued declaring him to be an unworthy person with whom to do business: it was entirely unofficial, but Rous's reputation as a martinet ensured that no one who valued his livelihood would consider defying it.

Financially, matters were at crisis point. Latimer's Barn had swallowed all but two thousand pounds of Rashleigh's fortune, and there was no hope of credit. At this low ebb, the fact that he was loathed throughout the county assumed significance. It had started over the case of Seamus O'Malley in 1841. Seamus, fifteen at the time, had broken a leg in a fall from a foul-tempered horse. Scarcely pausing for thought, Rashleigh had dismissed him without a penny: but for the goodness of the Catholic priest in Marlborough, Seamus would have been destitute as well as crippled. After that, Rashleigh's name was mud.

Although he was perfectly capable of comprehending the scale of the problems facing him, the state of Rashleigh's health prevented all attempts at a constructive solution. His sturdy body had stood up well to the abuse of food and drink and his dangerous-looking complexion was no worse than it had been twenty years ago.

Within the last eighteen months, however, his rapacious indiscretion had taken him too far. On his way to York races, he had availed himself of a London prostitute's services. The girl, now dead, infected him with syphilis.

Doctor Palfreyman, ever mindful of the disgraceful affair of the lad with the broken leg, had no sympathy with Rashleigh. Visiting The George one night, he had gone so far as to tell Eli Munge all about it, stressing that the disease was incurable and fatal.

Lord Francis knew this. The signs and symptoms were already ominous.

"Is something wrong, Francis?" Beresford asked when Rashleigh found him pottering round the garden at The Hall.

"No, Jasper, merely my age!" Rashleigh smiled ruefully, trying to make light of his condition.

"Do you wish to talk, Francis?" Jasper asked as he detected Rashleigh's true state of mind.

"Er . . . yes. Yes. I would like that."

But when they were settled indoors, Lord Francis was in no hurry to get to business. He spoke about the fine weather and the perpetually vexatious issue of his wife's health. Even when he did come to the real issue, he was less than frank.

"I have to go to Kent," he said. "Things are not as they should be in Strood."

"I'm sorry to hear that," Jasper said mildly and waited for enlightenment.

"Yes," Lord Francis said vaguely. "Yes, indeed. I may be away some time. Do you suppose you could keep an eye on the estate for me, Jasper?"

"Of course, with pleasure."

"You might be a good fellow and collect the Midsummer rents."

Jasper looked alarmed. It was barely a week since he had finally finished gathering the Lady Day instalment. "You intend being away that long?"

"It may be necessary. Yes, I imagine so."

"What about racing? The season has only just begun."

Lord Francis nodded, then his face was illuminated by a flash of sardonic humour. "I fancy it will proceed perfectly well without my contribution," he said. "It always has done!" He paused to look round the sitting-room in which he had spent so many happy hours. "When my man has driven me to Swindon tomorrow, I shall instruct him to place himself at your disposal with the carriage and horses, of course. A fellow in your position needs a good conveyance. And there's another thing."

"Yes, Francis?"

"Company, Jasper, you should have company. How long's that boy of yours been gone?"

"Thirteen years."

At the age of fourteen, Peveril had gone to Birmingham to work alongside his Uncle Horatio in his engineering works. The expectation was that he would eventually take charge.

"You've been cooped up on your own for too long, Jasper. Company and creature comforts, they're the thing. Now, listen to me: you know Lucy Miller, my assistant housekeeper?"

"Yes, I do."

"A very pleasant young woman."

"She is indeed!" Jasper responded with enthusiasm.

"Aha! There you are. Not such a dried-up old stick after all, are you? In less than two months, that woman will be looking for gainful employment."

"Really?"

"Really, Jasper. Furthermore, she would look very kindly upon an offer from you."

13

"Good heavens!"

"That's set you pondering, eh? Think on it."

"Yes, I will."

"She's twenty-five, Jasper, and she's thoroughly genuine." There was a final self-mocking flourish. "And she's clean. I haven't laid a finger on her."

Three days later, Rashleigh visited his lawyer, Simkiss, and made a will. Once the business was done, using two press-ganged witnesses, Rashleigh strode across the street to a tavern, where, before leaving Rochester, he became thoroughly drunk.

At the front door of his house, he found his wife and a group of local worthies on the point of departure for a fund-raising luncheon that he had promised to attend. Ignoring his wife's remonstrations and the semi-embarrassed greetings of her guests, Rashleigh ordered his carriage to the back of the house.

Little more than a minute later, there was a gunshot. Using a powerful sporting weapon, the sixth and last Baron Rashleigh had blown his head off in the summer-house.

Like so much of his life, his death had a certain awful style.

John Flamsteed, fourth-generation wine merchant of Greenwich, was astounded by the communication he received two weeks later from Simkiss.

Sir,

I beg to inform you that you are a beneficiary under the terms of the will of my recently deceased client, Lord Francis Rashleigh. His Lordship died on the 14th ultimo in circumstances which, I regret to say, were bizarre and tragic.

Very shortly before his death, His Lordship, while setting his affairs in order, confided to me that he owed you a sum in excess of £1,700 for wines supplied by your good self. Unable to meet his obligation with cash, he nevertheless wished to make amends for his oversight and to repay your kindness over many years of which, sir, he spoke with great warmth. Accordingly, he has bequeathed you a property and land in the county of Wiltshire.

What is known as 'The Cannings Ambo Estate' lies to the west of Marlborough and consists of some 2,000 acres with, as I understand the matter, a range of fine dwellings. This is now all yours with the exception of a property known as 'The Hall' which Lord Francis has willed to a Mr Jasper Beresford. From my perusal of the plans and deeds, I conclude that

14

*the messuages involved, some five acres, do not detract substantially from
the extent and value of your estate.*

There was a great deal more, and John Flamsteed's attempts to
make sense of it met with little success. He took the letter to his
wife, Mary.

"How amazing!" she said. She had never approved of Lord Francis,
and considered her husband foolishly lenient over the amount of credit
he had extended to the scoundrel. "What will you do, John?"

"Why, sell the place, of course. It's no use to us."

"Will you go and see this Mr Simkiss?"

"I hardly think it necessary, my dear."

"He suggests it."

"H'm. Yes, he does. No, I think not."

A week later, John Flamsteed and his eldest son, Giles, travelled to
Rochester. Giles was twenty-five, courteous, loving and dutiful: but
in his mild-mannered way he was implacably persistent, and usually
got what he wanted. He said they should talk to Simkiss.

After an hour with the solicitor, when he had a grasp of the scale
of the Cannings Ambo estate, Giles made a suggestion.

"Father, I really do feel that we should go down to Wiltshire and
inspect this place."

John Flamsteed looked perplexed. "Whatever for, my boy?"

"Surely we ought to have an idea of what it *looks* like. Mr Simkiss's
maps are excellent in their way, but I'm sure they don't tell us anything
like the full truth. There seems every chance that this estate may be
worth a good deal more than seventeen hundred pounds."

"Without The Hall?" John Flamsteed asked. "That strikes me as
being by far the best property."

"No, sir, oh no," Simkiss insisted. "Latimer's Barn is the best.
Lord Francis had a wonderful piece of work done on that."

"You've seen it?" John Flamsteed asked mildly.

"Er . . . no, sir. No. I have never *actually* been to Cannings
Ambo."

John Flamsteed's smile suggested that his point was made, while
Giles was equally convinced that *he* was right. "That is all the more
reason to go, Father," he said.

"It can only be for the best, gentlemen," Simkiss agreed. "If you
were to contact Mr Beresford at The Hall, I am sure he would
render every assistance."

Father and son debated the point all the way back to Greenwich.
At last, John Flamsteed bowed to the inevitable. "You have set your
mind on seeing this place, Giles?"

15

"Yes, Father, I have."

"Very well. Could you go alone?"

"You don't wish to?"

"No, not really. I'm far too old to be gallivanting."

Giles smiled. His father was fifty-one.

An exchange of letters with Jasper Beresford took eight days and Giles Flamsteed set out for Wiltshire with a sense of adventure, thinking that his mission might take a week.

No one considered that his wife of only two months should have gone with him. Sarah was completely happy in the close-knit, well-ordered bosom of her new family, settling comfortably into one of the houses round the courtyard that had been home and business premises to the Flamsteeds for over a century.

Giles was away for ten days and there was an air of expectation as they gathered to hear his report.

There were six round the dinner-table, John and Mary, Giles's younger brother, Ralph, who was twenty-three, his sister Elisabeth, aged seventeen, Sarah and Giles himself.

From the moment of his return, three hours ago, Mary knew that something had happened to Giles in Wiltshire. He was excited: it was heavily concealed, but she saw it. She said nothing, waiting patiently until he was ready to speak.

When Giles did set about describing the Cannings Ambo estate, two things were immediately obvious. What he had seen was very much to his liking, and he had found Jasper Beresford helpfully congenial. Deeply shocked by Rashleigh's suicide, Jasper had been consoled by the gift of his beloved Hall and by Lucy Miller, about whom Lord Francis had been precisely right. Although meeting him for the first time, Giles realised that life had recently become infinitely sweeter for Jasper Beresford.

Giles's account was scrupulous and a shade long-winded. Reactions round the table varied. John Flamsteed listened attentively; Sarah was bored; Ralph found it tedious, yet remained watchful, waiting for the moment to ask his question; Mary and Elisabeth were, for different reasons, fascinated. Both detected something akin to love in the way Giles spoke of the village, the Kennet Valley and the Downs; Elisabeth attributed Giles's enthusiasm simply to a novel experience whereas Mary knew that something far more serious was afoot.

At last, Ralph was able to ask his question.

"How much is all this worth?"

Sooner or later, this was what he asked about everything.

"That's difficult to judge," Giles replied blandly. "Many of the buildings are in poor heart. The land is fit only for sheep and the price of agricultural land has fallen over the last ten years because people are moving away to live in towns."

"How much?" Ralph persisted.

"I believe it's worth two thousand pounds."

John Flamsteed was visibly relieved. "We want seventeen hundred to balance the books," he said.

"Presumably we shall have to pay an agent to act for us?" Ralph's avarice was becoming blatant. It usually did.

"Yes, if it goes on the market," Giles said. "There is an alternative." He paused. "Would you consider selling the estate to me, Father?"

John Flamsteed was momentarily rendered speechless; Mary and Elisabeth exchanged knowing looks; Ralph leaned forward with an expression that seemed almost predatory. Sarah was no more than mildly surprised; she looked briefly at her husband before returning her attention to a slice of roast beef.

"You want to buy it?" John asked when he eventually assimilated what Giles had said.

"If I can raise the money."

"Why?"

"I'd very much like to own and work a place like that."

"But, Giles, what about the business, *our* business?"

"You have Ralph." Giles turned to his brother. "How does the idea strike you?"

"What are you suggesting?" Ralph asked, his desire to have the thing straight causing him to sound suspicious.

"That I go to Cannings Ambo and leave you in line to take over the business from Father."

Giles knew what the answer was to be. Ralph would do anything to gain control of Flamsteed & Sons, bottlers and purveyors of fine wines since 1747.

"I think I could manage that." Ralph used a lofty calmness to cloak his excitement.

Giles smiled, nodded and turned to his father, oblivious of Sarah's growing interest.

"I'm sorry to spring this on you, Father," he said. "Seeing Cannings Ambo has made me realise that my heart isn't truly in our business. Yes, I know I might have seemed to be making a fair job of it, but that was because I couldn't bear the thought of letting you down. Now that Ralph has shown himself capable, you can manage without me."

Ralph nodded smugly: John Flamsteed looked far from certain.

"What on earth will you do down there?" John asked. "Farming?"

"No, I think not. Mr Beresford advises me that the days of trying to get a living off the Downs have gone and may never return. There is another idea that appeals to me." Giles betrayed his nervousness with a pause. "My Lord Rashleigh set the place up as an establishment for the training of racehorses. I have a mind to try my hand at that."

There was a nerve-jangling crash as Sarah's cutlery fell across her plate. When Giles looked at her, he found that she was gaping at him in horror.

Sarah spent two days coming to terms with the unbelievable fact that Giles was perfectly serious, her dismay increasing by the hour.

Sarah Winstanley, as she had been until two months ago, was the eldest of five daughters of a Rotherhithe shipping merchant who did extensive business with John Flamsteed: over half the wine put into Flamsteed bottles was imported in Winstanley vessels. Sarah, a girl of striking, dark beauty, had caught Giles's eye the very first time he visited her father to arrange a shipment. All was joy in the Winstanley household when he began to pay court to her and his proposal of marriage was awaited with bated breath.

Giles was a desirable catch. Tall and strong, with fair hair and blue eyes ever willing to register humour, he was undoubtedly good-looking and Sarah was fond of him. But once she had been to Sunday-afternoon tea in Greenwich, she was armed with more powerful reasons for accepting him. Successive generations of Flamsteeds had deplored ostentation; nevertheless their life-style was revelatory and precisely to Sarah's taste. In two short months, she had assumed much of the Flamsteed style and manner as well as their name, and looked forward to the day when Giles was in charge of one of the most respected wine merchants in the country.

Now, while attending to what had seemed certain to be a rather boring piece of business connected with a long-standing debt, her husband had plunged the future into anarchy.

Sarah went to Rotherhithe to enlist her mother's support. However, when she had listened to the story, Molly Winstanley delivered a most unpalatable verdict.

"I can see that you may find it inconvenient, my dear, but it's your duty to stand by your husband."

"*Duty*, Mother! Duty! Is that what *you've* been doing all these years?"

"Sarah, stop that, at once! Giles is a good man. You were very lucky to get him."

Sarah's colour rose dangerously and the truth burst out of her.

"I was lucky to become a Flamsteed. And I mean a Flamsteed of *Greenwich*, not some dead-and-alive hole in Wiltshire!"

"Oho, so that's the way the wind goes, is it? Well, my lady, you've made your bed and you must lie in it."

Stunned by the uncompromising attitude of the woman who had always pandered to her every whim, Sarah's mood changed abruptly. Tears were the weapon now. "Whatever will become of me, Mother? I married an upright man of substance, now, overnight he decides to become involved with racehorses. *Racehorses*, Mother! We shall be mixing with the dregs of society."

"Don't be ridiculous, child! Racing is the sport of kings and the nobility."

"Yes, men like Lord Francis Rashleigh. Fine reading his exploits make! And I do *not* want to be imprisoned in Wiltshire."

"What's wrong with the place? Do you know anything about it?"

"No, but it must be awful."

"I am certain that it will be pleasant enough with Giles beside you."

Deprived of the sort of comfort she had expected from her own mother, Sarah went to Giles's parents.

"It's certainly a great shock," John Flamsteed agreed. "I won't try and pretend otherwise. But Giles has a right to choose his way of living. And I wouldn't be in the least surprised if he made a real go of it. He's a very determined young man, you know."

"And I believe Wiltshire is such a *pretty* place," Mary said. "I shall look forward to visiting you in the country, Sarah."

Although it was a foregone conclusion that talking to Elisabeth would be equally unrewarding, Sarah still did it. Utterly devoted to Giles, Elisabeth thought his decision was quite the best thing for years.

"Isn't it exciting?" she said. "So very *brave* of Giles. He's sure to be a great success. My goodness, Sarah, you must be thrilled."

There were two people to whom Sarah did not talk.

Ralph Flamsteed was habitually almost hostile towards her and actively discouraged conversation other than that dictated by social necessity. He had been like it from the start and Sarah believed it was because he lusted after her.

And not once did she consider raising the matter with her husband. Instead, she sulked and Giles ignored her. He was very pleasant about it, but grappling with the difficulties of Cannings Ambo left him no time for her self-inflicted misery.

Days passed and nothing more was forthcoming from Giles. John, Mary and Elisabeth found this unexceptional; it was the quiet way

19

that Giles always went about things. While Sarah began to persuade herself that the madcap scheme was dead or dying, Ralph became anxious, unnerved by his brother's silence.

One evening, when they were working late in the office, Ralph asked, "How are your plans for this place in Wiltshire progressing, Giles?"

"Not too well, I fear. There are difficulties." Giles looked downcast.

"Oh? What sort of difficulties?" Ralph made a great effort to appear disinterested.

"Money!" Giles said ruefully. "I can't find enough to finance the scheme."

Ralph's anxiety was turning into alarm. "How much do you need?" he asked.

"Well, Ralph, I have to take the view that it may be some time before I can produce a profit, so I need a float for safety. I reckon I'll need two thousand in my pocket *after* I've paid Father, and that's the bare minimum."

"You're looking to raise four thousand?" Ralph said. The only statement that Giles had made during the preceding days was to insist on paying his own valuation of two thousand pounds for Cannings Ambo rather than the seventeen hundred required to clear Rashleigh's debt.

"Yes, and I don't have much of a start. I've never taken anything out of the business, you see. I've always followed Father's example of ploughing the profits back in. That new bottling shop in Leather-market Street cost a pretty penny. The truth is, I've only a few hundred, Ralph. I was hoping to raise money from the bank, but they won't look at the venture. You know what old Hamilton's like – he nearly fainted at the idea."

"I see. I thought you were really set on the scheme."

"I am, Ralph, I am! It's the money that's short, not my will."

"I wonder if I could help." Ralph made it appear that he was thinking aloud. "Perhaps *I* could lend you the wherewithal."

"Or you could buy me out of the business," Giles responded with a child-like simplicity that came close to making Ralph lose his temper. By all accounts, many of the Flamsteeds had possessed this seemingly naïve approach to life; a great many people had discovered, to their cost, that it was backed by an iron resolve. Their grandfather was the last to exhibit the trait that was growing strong in Giles.

"There would have to be a formal agreement to that effect," Ralph said.

"Of course." Giles smiled. "I don't imagine you would have

difficulty finding the money. With your prospects, Hamilton will fall over to oblige."

"How much?" Ralph asked.

Giles considered it. "We're talking about a price for Flamsteed and Sons," he said. "Five thousand pounds seems fair to me."

"Not to me," Ralph protested.

"Oh, I think so," Giles said quietly. "Think of it, Ralph, five thousand and you have all this to yourself."

Ralph set about finding the money the following morning.

A week later, the five thousand pounds was handed over in Bank of England notes, and Giles signed a paper renouncing all title and claim to his father's business, upsetting Ralph by insisting on having a signed copy of the document for himself. The transaction was kept secret from John Flamsteed, who, with very mixed feelings, accepted two thousand pounds from Giles in return for the deeds of the Cannings Ambo estate.

When Giles deposited the remaining three thousand pounds from Ralph in the bank account that he had recently transferred to Marlborough from its hiding-place in Dartford, the balance stood at well over eight thousand pounds.

Renowned for his honesty and straightforwardness, Giles had deceived his brother without a vestige of compunction: nor did he ever suffer remorse. His awareness of Ralph's grasping greed went back twenty years to the nursery. It was perfectly right and proper that Ralph should pay a fair price for the easy benefits he was to reap in the years to come, thus providing Giles with a substantial buttress against the hazards of his new life.

Because of Ralph's nature, deception had been the only way to achieve justice.

Giles was in no hurry to move to Wiltshire.

During June and July he spent a total of three weeks on his new property in order, as he said, "To make proper arrangements and put things to rights." He seemed not to mind when Sarah rejected his invitations to go with him to Cannings Ambo on the grounds of trumped-up minor illnesses, and went ahead with his plans as though nothing of any great seriousness was involved.

Both Sarah and Ralph began to believe that the project was faltering. One viewed the possibility with hope, the other with fear and rage.

The announcement came out of a clear blue sky without any warning.

In the course of a family dinner at the start of August, Sarah seemed in rare good spirits, chattering nineteen to the dozen with Mary and Elisabeth about the latest trends in ladies' fashions. When all the talk of new fabrics, bodice-lines and the fall from favour of the crinoline had finally petered out, Giles smiled at Ralph.

"It's all settled and arranged," he said. "Latimer's Barn is ready for us." He turned to Sarah. "We shall be going on the tenth, my dear, a week tomorrow."

Mary thought that Sarah was about to faint.

At the age of fifty-one, Jasper Beresford had been granted a new lease of life. After faltering at the initial shock, he grasped his good fortune with both hands and became rejuvenated.

After receiving the letter from Simkiss, it took three days for Jasper to appreciate fully that The Hall was his again. Then, intoxicated by euphoria, he approached Lucy Miller. She responded at once to his offer of employment, wasting not a minute in showing that she placed the broadest interpretation on the arrangement. Within a week she had swept aside the neglect that had built up since the death of Jasper's old housekeeper three years ago; once The Hall was clean from top to bottom, she turned her attention to the well-being of the man himself. Lucy showed that she was a remarkably enthusiastic instigator of wanton romps in Jasper's bed: nothing was demanded in return except their mutual gratification.

Initially, the joy of The Hall's reacquisition was offset by worries over the ownership of the estate. Obviously these wine merchants would sell to the highest bidder to make good what Rashleigh owed them. However, the moment Jasper set eyes on Giles, he knew that the rest of his life would not only be safe, but blessed. The two men were ideally suited to each other: Jasper saw that Giles was deeply concerned about the careful long-term development of the estate, Giles realised that Jasper was the man to help him with this. They became firm friends on the spot.

The many hours they spent together in planning the future produced a massive improvement in self-esteem; Lucy Miller's ministrations boosted the process. Thus, when Jasper met Giles and Sarah from the train at Swindon, he stood proud, had a healthy glow about him and wore a new suit in the very latest style. His greeting of Sarah left her with no option than to abandon the sulks.

"Mrs Flamsteed, ma'am, it is a great honour to meet you. My goodness, your husband did not exaggerate."

"In what way, Mr Beresford?" Sarah asked, intrigued.

"Your beauty, ma'am. Mr Flamsteed spoke so highly of it, I have to confess that I thought he might be gilding the lily somewhat. But he wasn't. My word, he wasn't!"

As Jasper Beresford helped her into the carriage, Sarah was radiant. In addition to the flattering welcome, she rather liked the carriage. It was the vehicle that Rashleigh had given to Jasper; newly painted in dark green with the fancifully inaccurate but very decorative Beresford crest emblazoned on the doors, it was very stylish. Quite as good as anything in Greenwich.

There was no welcoming committee to spoil the pleasure of the drive over the Downs. Eli Munge and his cronies had been threatened with the direst consequences if they turned out to gawp.

"You'll be hearing from the squire in due course," Munge had been told by the newly authoritative Jasper. "He has many good ideas for the village, so be on your best behaviour. There's to be no more of your lunatic goggling, d'you hear? You've disgraced Cannings Ambo for long enough."

As they passed up the drive, Sarah's face indicated that she was pleased with the house. Its size and elegance were not at all what she had feared; it made the houses round the courtyard at Greenwich seem quite modest.

A thought struck Giles as they arrived at the front door. "I know what that drive needs, Jasper. Trees! It looks so bare."

"What would you say to poplars?" Jasper asked.

"Good!"

Jasper reached for his notebook.

"Now, my dear," Giles said, turning his attention to Sarah, "you will find our house in something of a turmoil. I fear Lord Francis allowed it to become a mess. So, I've had it gutted, and we can start afresh."

Inside the entrance hall, Sarah was confronted with bare floors and walls. The carpets and curtains had been taken away to be burned, the wallpaper stripped. Giles allowed no time for her astonishment to turn to dismay.

"Once you've given the word, Sarah, this will be put right within days. I have men coming tomorrow to show you carpets, fabrics and papers. Make your choice and it will be seen to."

"I'm to decide how it will all look?" Sarah gasped, her eyes widening at the thought.

"Absolutely!"

"Oh, my dear!" She was completely disarmed.

"Now, Mrs Flamsteed," Jasper said, "you can't live here until it's finished, so you and your husband are to be my guests at The Hall.

While you are with me you must select your servants. I will arrange for you to interview suitable prospects."

Giles saw that Sarah was already won over.

The whirlwind began after breakfast on Sarah's first full day at Cannings Ambo. By the middle of the afternoon, she had carried out a full inspection of Latimer's Barn, made her choice of carpets and decor for the most important rooms, selected a cook and found a housekeeper. She returned to The Hall to find her first social caller.

Lady Priscilla Hastings, decorative in a rather obvious way, was the wife of Sir Ambrose Hastings, fifth baronet and one of Marlborough's leading lights. Priscilla was over-conscious of what she deemed her position to be; nevertheless, Sarah was flattered by her visit and promised to accept the invitation to tea at the Hastings's house in Marlborough.

The afternoon following, it was the turn of the co-doyenne of local society, Mrs Alexandra Fandine-Browne. She was thirty, tall, stunningly attractive and utterly self-assured. In addition to her glorious mane of auburn hair that shone with vitality, expressive brown eyes and fine figure, Mrs Fandine-Browne had a radical outlook on life. All in all, Sarah found her a little intimidating.

Jasper explained the background of the two ladies. "The Hastings family have been in Marlborough for well over a hundred years. They own several farms and pieces of land round Savernake Forest. It's a funny sort of estate – I suppose it's grown over the years, a bit here and a bit there. Sir Ambrose is a good deal older than Lady Hastings and possibly a little out of touch with modern thought."

"Do they have children?" Sarah asked.

"Yes, indeed. Arnold is the heir. He's away at Eton, I think, and they have a daughter of ten called Charlotte."

"And what of the Fandine-Brownes?"

"Fish of a very different kettle! They are newcomers, and I can't for the life of me see what they're doing in Marlborough. Mr Fandine-Browne is a financier. He arranges venture capital for all manner of companies and seems to spend most of his time in London or the North. They, also, have two children."

When Giles returned that evening, saddle-sore and weary from the unaccustomed exertions of a day riding round the estate, Sarah told him of her new-found friends as a prelude to seeking a favour.

"My love, I fear that I may have made a mistake with the choice of wallpaper for the dining-room. Do you suppose I might change my mind?"

"For me, you may do whatever you please, my dear," Giles told her. "But we shall have to see what Harry Irons has to say."

"Who is Harry Irons?"

"He is the man in charge of operations. At the rate he and his fellows set about the job yesterday morning, I fear he may be finished by now."

"Oh dear!" Sarah looked tragic, inspiring Giles to put a comforting arm round her.

"Don't worry," he said. "If he has started that room, he can strip it off and start all over again."

"Will he do that for you, my love?"

Giles laughed. "Sarah, I have the impression that Mr Irons will do anything for me!"

Giles was right.

"Look 'ere, lads," Harry Irons had already told his men, "this y'ere's a real gentleman and he means business. He bean't anything like that bugger Rashleigh what we had to contend with so us'll do our best."

And Harry was as good as his word. Now nearing seventy, he left a great deal of the work to his sons Jim and Bill, but insisted on supervising the redecoration of Latimer's Barn himself. When everything was complete inside an incredible ten days, Giles was delighted.

"Well done, Harry," he said as he paid for the job and handed out bonuses. "It looks a picture, it really does."

"Ar, 'tis summat like now. This is what us should have had in the fust place."

Later that day, Harry Irons moved his men to The George. Whether Eli Munge liked it or not – and Giles had been unable to form an opinion – the place was going to be fettled. The rebuilding of Cannings Ambo had begun and it would not be long before some wag suggested that Harry Irons should move his outfit to the village and have done with all the travelling from Calne.

Giles and Sarah, together with their domestic staff, took up residence on 1 September. Two days later they gave their first dinner party at which Sir Ambrose and Lady Hastings, the Fandine-Brownes and Jasper and Lucy were the guests.

Thrilled with her magnificent new home, now all light and airy prettiness, Sarah sparkled. She found Sir Ambrose, who had been born in 1799 and served as an ensign at the action around La Haye Sainte during the Battle of Waterloo, a charming old gentleman. His wife was not nearly such fun: Giles suspected that Priscilla Hastings spent most of the evening disapproving of Lucy's presence.

Gilbert Fandine-Browne, a dark, supercilious man with a slightly sallow look and an inability to relax, came close to making Sarah feel uncomfortable until she entertained herself by trying to guess how much older than his ravishing wife he was. Her final estimate of fifteen years was very accurate.

When Fandine-Browne noticed the labels on the wine bottles, he unbent a little and said, "I see you take your own medicine, Flamsteed."

"There is no better wine," Giles declared. "I trust you have it at home?"

"Of course!"

"Nothing to do with me now," Giles said without a hint of regret. "However, perhaps I can look forward to being of service to you in the matter of horses."

"Ah, yes." Fandine-Browne eyed Giles keenly. "You are setting up a training establishment, I understand."

"That is correct."

Sarah saw that Fandine-Browne did not find the idea at all outlandish and Sir Ambrose nodded approvingly.

It was such a successful evening that the church clock was striking the quarter before midnight when the carriages were called to take the guests home. As they stood at the door for their farewells, Giles realised that Sarah was standing very close to him, transmitting an affection that he had never known before.

Thus far, inhibitions and ignorance had made their love-making a great disappointment. That night, everything was different, yet even as the barriers collapsed to reveal that Sarah was capable of insatiable desire, Giles half-suspected that it would prove a rare if not unique event. He did not allow the discomforting premonition to impair his repeated responses to his wife's passion; for three hours he did his utmost to satisfy her, for once casting aside the habitual delicacy of his approach.

When blissful exhaustion finally overcame them, they both had a profound awareness of what had transpired. The massive walls of Latimer's Barn had been host to a multitude of events throughout nearly five hundred years of chequered history, but despite the efforts of generations of young swains and Lord Francis Rashleigh, it was the first time a child had been conceived within them.

CHAPTER 3
1860

'Leander isn't a girl's name!'

Charles Darwin's *Origin of Species* was published in 1859, but the full-blown furore over it did not get under way until the spring of the following year. The conflagration was triggered by a book with the innocuous-sounding title of *Essays and Reviews*, one of whose seven authors was an Oxford professor called Baden-Powell, the father of the man who was to win fame as the defender of Mafeking and founder of the Boy Scout movement. As blithely unaware of the controversy as he was of all other current affairs, Giles Flamsteed set about the never-ending task of learning how to be a trainer of racehorses. The men who enabled him to do so were Jasper Beresford's brother, Horatio, and Caleb Jackson, fifty, wracked with arthritis and generally considered to be long past usefulness.

On an evening when the autumn of 1859 was chilled with the winter to come, Sarah complained bitterly of turning out to dinner at The Hall, dreading the meeting with Horatio Beresford who was spending a few days in Cannings Ambo.

"He will be astonishingly common," she declared, sulking into the dressing-table mirror. "These people in trade always are. And Birmingham! Have you *heard* them?"

"Remember that Horatio is a Wiltshire-man," Giles pointed out mildly. Although he refused to encourage her almost incessant peevishness by saying so, Giles was, for once, inclined to agree with his wife's prejudices. He believed that Birmingham was indeed a foul place, revoltingly filthy, and teeming with philistines who had atrocious accents and a disgustingly naked obsession with making money.

So, Horatio came as a revelation.

An absolute gentleman to his well-manicured fingertips, Horatio was the very antithesis of the popular conception of an industrialist.

From the tentative beginnings of his first workshop in 1840, he had progressed to the point where his new factory in Aston, known as Alma Works, employed sixty men, all highly skilled, their training and education paid for by himself. Beresford Engineering was pioneering the manufacture of machine tools, and Horatio's own design of lathe was in great demand. Sarah was entranced by him, and, at her insistence, he went into some detail about his enterprise, his Wiltshire origin still evident in the quiet enthusiasm of his voice.

Because of the need to explain so much to Sarah, it was some time before Horatio was able to turn to the matter that had tickled his fancy the moment Jasper wrote to him about it.

"Now then, Mr Flamsteed, you intend setting yourself up as a trainer of racehorses?"

"Yes, sir."

"Do you know anything about the job?"

"No."

"Have you got any horses to train?"

"No, sir, not yet."

"But you're keen."

"Yes. I intend to succeed."

Horatio looked as Giles speculatively. "Look here, Mr Flamsteed," he said after due consideration, "I've reached the stage in life where I think I'm entitled to a bit of fun. I've no real interests apart from the factory and I'm a crusty old bachelor." He smiled self-deprecatingly. He was approaching fifty, two years younger than Jasper, and bore his years well. "I've a fancy to own racehorses. How many animals can that place of yours take?"

"Ten, sir."

"Right, this is what we'll do. On condition that you find yourself a good man, someone who knows horses inside out and top to bottom, I'll buy you ten animals and you can find out how to train 'em. How does that strike you?"

"Wonderfully well, sir!" Giles could hardly believe what he was hearing.

"And I'll pay you two sovereigns a week to look after each horse."

"I have calculated that thirty shillings would suffice," Giles protested.

"No, it won't! Listen to me, young man. Don't start off thinking you're going to cut corners: you must always aim high. Always! If you miss, it's easy enough to lower your sights a fraction, but if you start off in the gutter it's the very devil to get the standard up. Two pounds it shall be and you'll do the job properly." Horatio grinned and his tone softened as he went on, "I've always thought the world

28

of this place. Do you remember what it was like when we were lads, Jas? The ruination of this estate fair cut me up, but I reckon you could be the coming thing, Mr Flamsteed. With a bit of help and a lot of luck, you're the man to put things to rights round here. Well, what do you say? Are we in business?"

Giles took a deep breath, looked Horatio squarely in the eye and said, "Yes, Mr Beresford. We are."

"Remember what I said," Horatio told him as they shook hands across the table. "Find yourself a good man."

Once the luck began to run, it gathered momentum to such an extent that there was barely time to worry about the problem before it was solved.

Towards lunch-time the following day, Giles was in Marlborough High Street after a visit to his banker. Like everyone else abroad that foul morning, he was well-muffled against the wind and rain, and not looking where he was going. Neither was Doctor Palfreyman; they collided outside Morrison's bakery.

"I beg your pardon, sir. Ah, Flamsteed! Faugh! What weather, eh? How is your good lady?"

"Excellent, thank you, Doctor. Expecting a child seems to suit her wonderfully."

"It mostly does, Flamsteed. They all thrive on it. I must pop in and see her next week. Look here, I was just about to go over the road to warm myself up." He pointed to the Ailesbury Arms. "Come with me."

Giles needed no second bidding. They scuttled across to gain the shelter of the covered entrance to the yard where London to Bristol coaches had changed horses day and night for over two hundred years, and shook the worst of the rain from their capes before going inside. They were soon seated before a blazing fire with glasses of mulled claret, Palfreyman smacking his lips in appreciation of the first taste.

"Better," he declared, "much better. Look at that!" He pointed to his boots, already steaming. "Anyhow, Flamsteed, how are things with you? Made any progress with this racehorse lark?"

Giles recounted his conversation with Horatio, Palfreyman nodding eagerly as he did so.

"Horrie Beresford's a damned good sort," the doctor said. "He wants to see that estate up and doing again, so go to it, my boy, go to it!"

"I have to find a good man who knows all about horses," Giles said.

"Well, of course! Stands to reason. Make sure you listen to Horrie. He knows what he's talking about."

"I don't doubt that, Doctor. The question is, how do I find the right man? I've no idea where to start looking."

Palfreyman gaped at him. "No idea? Bless me! Why, outside, of course. Right on the other side of that wall unless I'm mistaken." He pointed, leaving Giles none the wiser.

"I'm sorry, I don't understand."

"Caleb!" Palfreyman said. "Caleb Jackson. He's your man. What he doesn't know about horses isn't worth knowing. He's been here thirty-five years to my certain knowledge."

"Er . . . who is he?" Giles asked.

"You don't know?" The good doctor shook his head in sorrowful disbelief and proceeded to put Giles straight.

Caleb Jackson had started work in the stables of the Ailesbury Arms as a lad of fourteen in 1823. In the final glorious decade of the stage-coach before the coming of the railway, he had looked after sixty horses, keeping them in a condition that soon became a legend over the entire route from London to Bristol. His teams worked as far east as The Bear at Hungerford and over the difficult west-bound leg to the Lansdowne Arms in Calne. The occasions when they weren't up to the job could be counted on the fingers of one hand, and it was an accepted fact that visiting horses were always the better for a night in Marlborough.

Now, it was nearly all over. In the past month, only five coaches had passed down Marlborough's broad High Street, Caleb's team was reduced to twelve and he spent most of his time waiting for someone to pluck up the courage to tell him to go.

They found him in the stables, working on the strained fetlock of one of his charges with an ointment of his own preparation.

"How d'ee do, Caleb?" Palfreyman said. "This is Mr Flamsteed who's going to do something with Cannings Ambo."

Caleb Jackson got to his feet with arthritic difficulty. "I heard about that," he said.

"Mr Flamsteed wants a first-rate man to get him going," Palfreyman went on. "How are you placed?"

"It's all finished here, sir."

"You can go to Mr Flamsteed, then?"

Caleb nodded, turning to Giles. "I'd need two things," he said firmly.

"Yes?" Giles knew that he sounded too eager.

"A place to live."

"Of course. Are you married, Caleb?"

"Not any more." His face betrayed nothing. Giles was conscious of the resolute jaw-line and the strength in the grey eyes.

"You'll have a choice," Giles told him. "There are good quarters above the horses, and there are cottages in the village when I've had them put in order."

"The other thing is Seamus," Caleb Jackson said. "He'd have to come with me."

"Who is Seamus?" Giles looked to Palfreyman for guidance.

"Yes, Seamus. Quite right!" The doctor nodded his approval. Giles knew that, whoever Seamus was, he was coming to work at Latimer's Barn. "Seamus O'Malley, Flamsteed. He was a young boy at your place when that bounder Rashleigh started up. The poor devil broke a leg and His Lordship chucked him out."

"Good God!" Giles was appalled.

"Oh, yes! And that was only one of his charming little tricks. I did the best I could for the lad, but his leg's never been right – and you've had him ever since, Caleb?"

"That's right. Eighteen years." Caleb turned to Giles. "Seamus sometimes isn't all that good on his feet, Mr Flamsteed, but he's a wonder on a horse."

"You think I should have him?" Giles asked, purely as a matter of form.

"I do. In any case, you don't get me without Seamus. I look after him."

"Very well. What do you say to two pounds a week and all found?"

Caleb's face registered that it was an astonishingly good wage. "Thank you, sir. I'll come. Seamus will have thirty shillings."

"Good. When will you come to Latimer's Barn?"

"Two weeks next Monday," Caleb Jackson replied. "That gives me time to put things right here – I wouldn't want to leave without doing that." He paused. Looking at Giles, he detected his nervousness. "Don't worry, Mr Flamsteed, Seamus and me will see you right. And thank you. Thank you kindly, sir."

Caleb Jackson touched his forelock and Giles knew that he had taken the first real step into a startlingly different world.

Horatio insisted that Caleb and Seamus must accompany Giles and himself to Newmarket in search of horses.

"What use are we on our own?" he asked Giles. "Do you know one end of a horse from another?"

"No."

"Exactly! From what I'm told, the place is packed solid with rogues,

31

all waiting for the likes of us with open arms. We shall watch and learn while Caleb and Seamus do the business."

Sarah, who had been listening with mounting unease, asked, "How long will you be away?"

"No idea, ma'am," Horatio replied cheerfully. "As long as it takes. A week, ten days? I don't know."

"What about your factory? Can you afford to neglect it for so long?"

Giles knew that Sarah was trying to invent reasons why they should not buy horses for him to train. Unaware of such subtleties, Horatio had the answer.

"There's no danger of neglect, Mrs Flamsteed. Jas's boy Peveril will keep things in good order."

So, with Sarah sulking furiously as she waved half-heartedly, they set off on the adventure.

Newmarket put the fear of God into Giles.

Throughout his first day there, he was convinced that he had made one of the greatest blunders of all time. Everything was on show and, good or bad, it was all carried out with magisterial assurance. *This*, the town seemed to be saying, is how it is done: what on earth makes you think you can compete? Even Horatio was fazed.

The place seemed packed with sharp-faced men who had an air of frenzy or desperation about them. They were of all types, in all conditions – drunk, sober, taciturn, vociferous, down-at-heel, elegant – all seeking a fortune, not next year, or next month or even next week, but now, today, this very minute.

They saw string after string of horses exercise on the public gallops, watched over by the trainers, autocrats to a man, the lads put on their mettle and best behaviour by fear. At night, they heard the same lads hell-raising in the town's taverns, fighting, roaring abuse at each other and laying hands on any wench foolish enough to go anywhere near them.

And they saw the men who owned and governed Newmarket. Some were aloof, others irascible and arrogant and some had the languid indifference of tenth-generation aristocracy. The common factor was isolation: outsiders approached at their peril.

Giles was an outsider.

Worse, he and Horatio were regarded as dangerous eccentrics because they took Caleb and Seamus, mere lackeys, everywhere they went. Not that they were necessary: even Giles was perfectly capable of deciding for himself that all the horses they were shown were worthless.

"Do you suppose that we ought to forget this silly idea and crawl back home?" Giles whispered to Horatio as they dined on the fourth evening.

Horatio took the point with a grim nod. "Let's wait and see what happens tomorrow," he said. "You never know, it might be better."

They went to Westley Hall at Six Mile Bottom half-way between Newmarket and Cambridge, where, so the rumours went, a recently widowed lady was seeking purchasers for her late husband's blood-stock. The stories proved to be true, they were made extremely welcome and shown sixty horses, nearly all of whom brought smiles to the faces of Caleb and Seamus.

Eventually, after several hours of inspection, Horatio was presented with ten which Caleb said he could buy with complete confidence. There were four colts and six fillies, all two-year-olds reckoned on the 1858 ruling that every horse's birthday was to be 1 January. Horatio staggered Giles by producing over a thousand pounds in notes to pay for them on the spot. The thought that his friend had been strolling round Newmarket with *that* concealed about his person was almost enough to induce hysteria.

However, they had ten horses to take back to the sane secrecy of Wiltshire, and Seamus had begun Giles's education by explaining how a good horse should look, how it must have a bold eye and all that could be deduced from the way it walked.

When they set out with the horses on what was to prove a leisurely three-day journey back to Cannings Ambo, Giles was unaware of a vital piece of acumen in Caleb's choice of horses – although he was soon grateful for it. Knowing that they would be facing enough problems without the menace of a group of animals unable to stand the sight of each other, the shrewd old ostler had picked ten who seemed to have grown up together and had no collective faults other than occasional flashes of infectious high spirits.

Sarah found pregnancy a loathsome business.

Once the first few weeks of morning sickness had passed, her condition evolved according to the blandest textbook account: there was never a whisper of trouble. Sarah was outraged when Doctor Palfreyman told her that it was all going extremely well and there was nothing to worry about. The unspeakable wretch then passed the information to Giles.

Not, it seemed, that Giles would have taken the slightest notice if she had been at death's door. Once the horses arrived, he worked the most ludicrous hours, winter and the restricted span of daylight notwithstanding. The stable and its work became very obtrusive, especially when two young lads came to join in the learning. Peter and Paul Izzard were identical twins whom Giles took from an orphanage in Swindon with the intention of providing them with a home and a living. They were an irrepressibly cheerful pair of fourteen-year-olds who annoyed Sarah by waving and shouting greetings to her whenever they saw her.

The need to provide good meals for Caleb, Seamus and the two youngsters led to confrontation. Giles felt that Sarah's cook should do the job on top of her other duties, but Sarah was having none of it.

"Really, Giles! I will not have Mrs Bayliss running round after those people outside."

Giles did not like her tone. "What you call 'those people outside' are a vital part of our future, Sarah," he said.

"I suppose you may be right, Giles, though I fail to see how. In any event, you must find another way of feeding them."

The answer was Lizzie Shaw, pretty as a picture, albeit somewhat untidy and slovenly. Doctor Palfreyman brought her from a village between Cannings St John and Devizes, explaining that there had been difficulties, but a good home and firm guidance would soon straighten her out. He was right. Whatever Lizzie, who was eighteen, had been up to in the past was soon put behind her. When she was not cooking wonderful meals for the lads or helping out in the stable, she worked so hard as a housemaid that even Sarah was forced to admit her worth. Seamus had a magical influence on Lizzie; within days of arriving, she fell under his spell and began to smarten herself up.

The issue of food for 'the people outside' was the only one upon which Sarah spoke out. She suffered Giles's other foibles in silence.

There were two that she found particularly irritating.

She could have screamed at the interminable reports on the poplar trees. Jasper had arranged for two hundred saplings to be planted along the drive. Meticulously placed at intervals of thirty feet, they extended the line of the driveway towards the distant ridge of Cannings Down as well as bordering the circular area at the front of the house. Giles inspected them every day at precisely two o'clock and hardly ever failed to comment on their success. For Sarah, they were nothing more than twin ranks of sticks and twigs, five feet high and dormant if not dead in the winter.

Then there was the way he began to speak of his property. 'Latimer's Barn' was used in a grandiose way to encompass house, stable, and, for all Sarah knew, the hundreds of acres of desolate-looking downland that were supposed to be useful as gallops. Where

34

they lived became 'The House' – and the capital letters were writ indelibly large every time Giles spoke of it. Maddeningly, first Jasper, then others took up the affectation.

At least once a week, Sarah took her dissatisfaction into Marlborough for afternoon tea at the Hastings or Fandine-Browne houses. Following her departure from one such visit at the end of February, it emerged that her two acquaintances had divergent opinions.

"That woman is becoming very tiresome," Alexandra Fandine-Browne said, exasperated by over two hours of Sarah's petulant self-pity.

"That's a very harsh judgement, Alexandra," Priscilla Hastings declared in the rather grand manner she frequently favoured, unaware that it aged her by at least ten years. "I think Sarah is in a most difficult position."

"In what way?"

"Being wrenched away from a comfortable situation in Greenwich to be deposited in Cannings Ambo cannot be pleasant. I imagine the winter has been very trying for her."

"Winter? We haven't had a proper winter!" Alexandra was scornful. "There's only been one decent frost."

"True, but we have had a great deal of rain and fog. That can be most depressing. And we must allow for her condition, of course."

"You would think that she was the first woman ever to be pregnant! I'm told it's proceeding quite smoothly."

"She's awfully young," Lady Hastings pointed out. "That husband of hers needs to take more care of her instead of spending all his time with those horses. As a matter of fact . . ." her tone became confidential ". . . I'm not at all certain that he knows what he's doing. I told Ambrose as much only yesterday."

Alexandra seemed to find the idea that one would discuss such matters with a husband extraordinary. Recovering from her surprise, she smiled. "On the contrary, Priscilla, I think we can assume that young Mr Flamsteed knows *exactly* what he is doing," she said. "He gives me the impression that he is *very* competent."

There was something in the way she said it that caused her companion to stiffen accusingly.

"Alexandra, you haven't . . . have you?" Although she sounded scandalised, there was a prurient gleam in Lady Hastings's eyes.

Alexandra laughed, holding up her hands in a gesture of reassurance. "No, Priscilla, I have not. I fear that Mr Flamsteed is far too preoccupied with his horses to be concerned about any other sport."

And if Giles had never taken very much notice of Alexandra Fandine-Browne before spring came, she, along with everyone else not directly connected with the stable yard, ceased to exist once the horses began to work seriously.

It was all trial and error, without a clear idea of what success looked like. Caleb and Seamus were supposed to be the experts, but even they were soon marching through completely uncharted territory.

To make matters comically worse, nothing could be achieved until the Izzard twins, who had never sat on a horse, were taught to ride. Seamus did this, starting them off on the placid old gelding that Giles used as a hack. Confident that they had mastered the art, they were soon out in the vast expanse of Cannings Down, trying to ride the racehorses, and promptly began falling off. Amazingly, they never hurt themselves; March, sunny and breezy, was bringing the splendid resilience back to the turf and they seemed to bounce on it, always coming up laughing. The horses, who loved the twins, usually stopped and waited for them to remount.

Lady Hastings, a frequent visitor to Latimer's Barn, sometimes took Sarah out on the Down in her carriage.

"I must say, it looks dreadfully chaotic to me," she said one day, as they watched the Izzards falling off while Caleb and Seamus, riding with them, were trying to get a group of four horses cantering together.

"It's a shambles," was Sarah's sour comment.

"I expect they will eventually decide what it is they're supposed to be doing," Lady Hastings said with overdone tolerance.

"I doubt it!" It was one of Sarah's days for sulking.

At least she had the consolation that Giles had found a new obsession, one that he kept to himself. The poplars were forgotten. Now, tutored morning, noon and night by Caleb, it was horses' legs. Whenever Sarah saw him, it seemed that he was always either feeling or peering at a part of some animal's leg.

When he began to study them closely, Giles decided that the leg of a horse was the most improbably impractical thing: the more he looked at them, the more spindly and delicate they became, surely incapable of withstanding the jarring strains of galloping. He buried himself in books on the subject, learned how to diagnose the slightest problem within the complex ligament structure and became an expert on strapping and poultices. And he was a fanatical advocate of the efficacy of cold, running water. Any animal who walked painfully was taken off to the Cannings Brook to stand in it for an hour or more.

At first, Sarah dreaded being subjected to lectures on his new-found enthusiasm. Giles, firmly of the opinion that she would not understand or care, kept quiet and her relief was profound.

By the end of April, the Izzards were staying on their horses and something like a routine was being established. Inspecting the horses one morning, Giles felt that they all looked well, his only concern being that they were possibly too sleek and overweight.

"Are we working them hard enough?" he asked Caleb.

"I don't know," was the frank answer. "There's a lot of folk gallop them all day and every day: they even wrap them up and make them sweat. That don't seem right to me. It wears a horse down to no good purpose."

"Is that why we saw so many poor specimens at Newmarket?" Giles asked.

"That would be a good enough reason." Caleb paused. "There's one sure way to find out how we're doing."

"Race one?"

"That's it. Now this fellow looks right enough." Caleb pointed to a handsome chestnut colt, just returning from an easy six-furlong spin on the gallop with a grinning Peter Izzard still firmly planted on him. Horatio had named the horse The Beresford Lathe after his own invention, and the animal appeared mightily pleased by the honour.

Lizzie Shaw, skirt hitched up as she helped to muck out one of the boxes, cocked an expectant ear. Was this going to be what they had all been waiting for?

"All right, Caleb, we'll try him."

Giles selected a race at Salisbury, the nearest racecourse to Latimer's Barn. The Wilton Plate, run over a mile for a piece of fine porcelain and a purse of thirty-five sovereigns, looked as good an opportunity as any from Giles's position of complete ignorance.

On the momentous day, they set off from Latimer's Barn at six in the morning. Sarah, thrown into nervous decline by the fact that her pregnancy had, at long last, started to show, remained steadfastly asleep and knew nothing about it. The Beresford Lathe was in a box pulled by two magnificent draught horses, hired for the day from a firm of hauliers in Marlborough. Caleb drove while Giles rode alongside on his hack. They stopped to rest the horses and have breakfast at an inn near Upavon, yet still covered the twenty-five miles to the racecourse by noon, giving Giles three hours' breathing-space before the race. He had to discover how to declare his horse: there was also the matter of a jockey to be found.

At first sight, both tasks seemed impossible. There were a handful of honest faces scattered among the hundreds milling around outside the weighing room and offices, but they belonged to disinterested, unapproachable men. Those who actively sought to catch Giles's eye all reeked of avarice or chicanery. Admiral Rous, tightening his grip by the day, was acutely conscious that much remained to be done before everything connected with racing was both honest and safe.

Giles was experiencing the first gnawings of despair when a tall old gentleman of commanding demeanour elbowed his way through the crowd and bore down on him.

"It's young Flamsteed, is it? I'm Protheroe. How d'you do?"

Colonel Protheroe, one of Rous's most formidable and trusted representatives, was master of both Salisbury and Bath racecourses. He sported luxuriant mutton-chop whiskers and a royal-blue top hat; his penchant for horse-whipping rogues was a by-word. "That your horse?" he demanded, nodding at The Beresford Lathe.

"Yes, sir."

"H'm! Looks a good sort. Plenty of condition. Needs a race, I'd say. This your first?"

"It is, sir."

"Right, come on. I'll show you the ropes."

A couple of minutes later, Giles saw that declaring a horse to run was like so many other things: easy, once one knew how.

"Have you got a jockey?" the colonel asked.

"No, sir. I must find one."

"Will you take advice?"

"I need it desperately, sir!"

"See there." Protheroe pointed out of the window to a group of jockeys hanging around outside the office. "They're all looking for work. I take it you want your horse back in one piece?" Giles nodded. "Go for the chap over there on the right. See? That's Dan Goakes. He's a bit over the hill now, but he's been very good in his time. Got a lovely pair of hands. He'll do right by you and your horse."

The one thing above all else that Giles remembered about that day in years to come, was the look of startled gratitude on Dan Goakes's face when he was offered the ride. They had a good look at The Beresford Lathe, Dan made friends with him, then went into the shed provided for jockeys, still unable to believe his good luck. He took with him the racing silks and cap in Horatio's newly registered colours; Lizzie Shaw had run them up and they were as near perfect as made no matter.

Giles and Caleb had a glass of beer and a meat pie, watched the first two races, both of which set off a fight in the Silver Ring, and realised it was time to saddle their own horse. The Beresford Lathe looked a picture as he moved off to the start, obviously happy with Dan Goakes.

"That's a fair sight," Caleb said quietly.

"Ye . . . es." Giles was having the greatest difficulty believing that it was anything to do with him.

The Lathe ran very well, but seemed to tire at the end, finishing ninth of twenty. When Giles got close to him afterwards, he was alarmed by the horse's stertorous breathing and discomfort.

"What the devil's wrong with him?" he asked Caleb.

"That's all right. Don't worry. He's blowing. We didn't have him fit enough."

Dan Goakes nodded eager agreement. "He went at seven furlongs, sir, and I didn't push him." Giles had seen it and was very grateful. "If he'd had a couple of good gallops over the last week we might have had a chance. He's a good horse."

"We've been too soft with him?" Giles asked Caleb.

"Looks like it."

Giles gave Dan Goakes a guinea. "I shall want you to ride for me again, Dan," he said. "Where can I find you?"

"Turvey's Farm at Lynchetts, sir."

"That's not far from us, is it, Caleb?" Giles asked.

"Three or four miles across country."

Giles thought hard for a few moments. "Tell me, Dan, do you do much with horses now?"

"Not a great deal, sir. As a matter of fact . . . well, to tell you the truth, I haven't had any proper work for two years."

"Come and see me next week," Giles said. "I fancy you and I can do business."

Dan fled into the jockeys' shed before his luck had a chance to turn sour. Giles turned to Caleb, as impassive as ever. "Well, did I do the right thing?" he asked.

"You did." Caleb considered it and the utterly incredible happened. He smiled. "But now, you've got a pregnant wife, a cripple, two lads that are nothing more than children, *two* has-beens and that flibbertigibbet Lizzie to support. By God, guv'nor, you're going to have to do well!"

For the first time, Giles realised how very happy Caleb was to be at Latimer's Barn.

For Dan Goakes, his young wife, Jennie, and their three-year-old daughter, Ellie, life at Lynchetts was wretched. Jennie's sister and her alarmingly anti-social husband had only taken them in on sufferance, out of grudging pity for Ellie. After eighteen months, frayed tempers and abysmal living conditions in a single dank room at Turvey's Farm had brought the uneasy arrangement to the brink of ruin. And Jennie was expecting another child.

There had been idle talk about the new man at Cannings Ambo: Dan had already suggested that he might go and ask for a job, but even when invited to do so by Giles, Jennie Goakes expected nothing.

"He's a city gentleman playing games," she said scornfully. "What will he want with the likes of us? Save your time, Dan, he'll have forgotten all about you."

Jennie's sister was pessimistic, too. "They say his wife hates it. He won't be staying long."

It made sense, and Dan half-believed them. But he had an advantage over the gossips and clung to it: he had met Giles Flamsteed and seen the look in his eye.

On the morning that Dan walked the four miles to Latimer's Barn, it poured with rain and he turned up like a drowned rat. Inside half an hour, he had been dried out, given breakfast and offered a job.

"I must have someone here who can work these horses properly, Dan," Giles told him. "So the job is yours." He paused to grin ruefully. "To be perfectly honest with you, we also need a man who knows about racing and all the wrinkles."

Before accepting, Dan told Giles of his present parlous position: barely had he finished, when a cart driven by Seamus set out to Lynchetts to fetch Jennie, Ellie and their pathetically few belongings.

Two significant things occurred while Seamus and Dan were away.

Allowing peevishness to get the better of her, Sarah found that she had blundered badly.

"Are you intending to employ that wretched man?" she asked Giles.

"Yes, my dear." His tone was mild.

"Really, Giles, this is too much! You seem determined to fill the place with scarecrows and misfits."

"My judgement is that we need Dan Goakes very much, Sarah. Our good intentions are no substitute for hard experience. I suggest that you do your best to relax until our child is born. After that, you will find that you have plenty with which to occupy yourself in The House. The yard is *my* province."

He was perfectly pleasant, yet there was a new iron determination beneath the words. Sarah realised that something had happened to Giles: he was no longer a dilettante.

The second event concerned Giles's announcement that Dan

would have one of the cottages on Church Green. Lizzie Shaw promptly set off with the Izzards to select the dwelling with the soundest fabric. By the time a bewildered Jennie arrived in the evening, the place was spotless, a fire was roaring up the chimney to drive away the unseasonal cold and damp, and the first lot of furniture from Lord Francis Rashleigh's left-overs had been moved in. What finally made Jennie burst into tears of wonder and gratitude was the delicious-smelling stewpot that Lizzie had left simmering on the hob.

The gang of misfits had started to weld themselves into a family.

It took Dan two weeks to bring about a complete revolution, simply by refining what Giles and Caleb had already done.

In the middle of May, Giles hired the van again and they went to Bath, this time with two horses. Trapped in Birmingham by a series of business meetings that Peveril was nervous of handling on his own, Horatio missed seeing how his first prize-money was gained. One of his fillies finished third, yielding the stupendous sum of nine pounds seven shillings and sixpence. After paying the entrance fees and transport costs of the two horses, there was a profit of eighteen shillings and fourpence on the day.

When Giles, Caleb and Dan struggled wearily back to Latimer's Barn at one o'clock in the morning, Seamus and Lizzie were waiting up for them. They celebrated as though they had won the Derby. Sleeping only fitfully that night, Sarah was almost certain that Giles was so misguided as to invite the revellers into The House, albeit only as far as the kitchen. Outraged, she feigned sleep when eventually he came up to bed; after her lesson over Dan Goakes, she made no mention of her displeasure.

Two weeks of fine weather and hard work followed. The Beresford Lathe worked well, lost a little weight and was, according to Dan, crying out for another race. With her time drawing near, Sarah seemed calm and in good spirits, having decided that motherhood was going to suit her. The day before The Beresford Lathe returned to Salisbury, Doctor Palfreyman had ventured the opinion that she would be delivered of her child in a week or ten days. Happy with this, Giles set off early and with high hopes on the first day of June, 1860.

This time, Horatio was waiting for them on the racecourse. After two days of negotiating sales of his machinery in London, he had travelled down to Salisbury the previous evening by the London and South-Western Railway, spending the night in an hotel.

Their horse was running at three o'clock in the best race of the day,

The Godolphin Stakes, and while they ate lunch, Horatio astonished and delighted Giles with the information he had acquired.

"Interesting family, the Godolphins." Horatio sounded as though he was airing knowledge of long standing. "Sidney Godolphin was a Cornishman who became Queen Anne's Lord High Treasurer. Sounds a good job, eh? While he was about it, he got himself made an earl and helped to start Royal Ascot. His son imported an Arab stallion in 1733 – The Godolphin Arabian. You'll have heard of him?"

Giles pretended that he had and asked, "What's the connection with Salisbury? Why have they got a race named after them?"

Horatio grinned. "I don't know! One of the family founded a school for girls here. It might be that."

The race was over a mile and a quarter. Dan's suggestion that the colt might be suited to a longer trip proved brilliantly successful. With a furlong to run, it seemed that any one of five horses had every chance of capturing the prize, but when Dan asked The Lathe for a final effort, it came in handsome measure. Twenty years after Lord Francis Rashleigh's original idea, Latimer's Barn produced its first winner. Caleb smiled, Giles and Horatio found that they were hugging each other.

As Giles paraded the hero of the hour in the ring provided for the winner, he was conscious that many members of the crowd were looking at him in a new way. The wine merchant from Greenwich might have to be taken seriously, they seemed to be thinking.

Colonel Protheroe bustled up, nodding vigorous approval. "Well done, Flamsteed," he called. "Damned good show. That horse is a credit to you."

"Thank you, sir."

"I believe you've just upended a big betting job." The colonel chuckled. "My spies tell me that the favourite was backed to lose over two thousand pounds."

"Two thousand!" Giles was incredulous: it was as much as he had paid for the estate.

"There are some very funny people about, Flamsteed," the colonel said. "I expect you'll find out soon enough. Be on your guard, there's a good fellow. They tell me you've taken Dan Goakes on."

"I have. He seemed precisely what I wanted."

"Very good! He deserved some luck. Tell me . . ." Colonel Protheroe was suddenly hesitant ". . . this animal's name – what does it mean?"

Giles smiled. "The owner, Mr Beresford, is an engineer. He manufactures machine tools in Birmingham and has patented his own lathe."

"Ah. I see. Decent sort, is he?"

Giles felt light-headed. The question indicated that he had already been accepted to the point where his opinion was sought. "Most certainly, sir," he said and beckoned to Horatio, who was on the other side of the ring, refusing an offer of more than three times what he had paid for the distinctively named colt.

Colonel Protheroe and Horatio inspected each other and formed favourable impressions.

"You've a good horse there, sir," the colonel told Horatio. "And you appear to have found yourself a very talented young man for a trainer."

Horatio made sure that Giles remembered this as they wended their happy way back to Cannings Ambo. He rode on the box of the van alongside Caleb, eager for a few days with his brother and a good look at all his horses before returning to Birmingham. When they stopped at an inn near Pewsey to enjoy a drink in the cool of dusk after a broiling day, Horatio pulled Giles's leg with great gusto.

"Well now, Mr Flamsteed, how does it feel to be a talented young man who's just had his first success?" Then, as Giles blushed, Horatio's tone changed. "No, it's very good, very good indeed. One hundred and seventy pounds in prize-money and only your fourth attempt."

"Thank you," Giles replied. "Do bear in mind that *I* didn't do all that much. I have a team."

Caleb and Dan exchanged a look. Now they really did know that they were part of something very unusual.

"Well said, sir!" Horatio beamed. "Now then, this is what we shall do. I intend making you a present of ten per cent of all my winnings, and I'll look to you to distribute it fairly as you see fit."

"With the greatest of pleasure, Mr Beresford!"

At exactly the same time, a gathering of a very different nature was taking place fifteen miles away to the south-west.

Branksome Lodge was completely isolated in the fastness of Salisbury Plain between the tiny hamlets of Chitterne and Orcheston. As if that were not enough, the original builder had gone to great lengths to hide the uncompromising edifice in a fold of the Downs. It had an air of the nefarious long before the Association got their hands on it in 1845.

There were four of them, Baxter, Cooper, Sixsmith and Wrigley. They owned horses, fifty all told, housed in mean, jerry-built boxes, and had installed Captain Sullivan to do their bidding. No one seriously believed the authenticity of Sullivan's rank, but it was never openly questioned except in the distant safety of Newmarket. Strangers who lost their way on the Plain, and strayed too near the gallops, were shot at. A pedlar was killed in 1854, yet nothing had ever been proved, especially after his body was taken ten miles to be dumped in a drain.

The Association used every trick permitted by the still-imperfect rules of racing. Their horses were never named and they themselves used pseudonyms in their capacity as owners. There were at least thirty-two assumed names in regular use with Branksome Lodge horses.

The money came from gambling, as much as £20,000 in a good year. On most racecourses in the south of England, the Association had hirelings to smooth the way to rule-breaking; despite the efforts of Colonel Protheroe, Salisbury and Bath were their special fiefdoms.

But times were changing. Admiral Rous was relentless and the policing of the shires was improving. The Association recognised that in ten years they would probably be finished; they intended to make hay while the sun shone, the prospect of extinction sharpening their greed.

Investment on their horse in the Godolphin Stakes had been massive and confident. The Beresford Lathe's convincing victory was a devastating blow.

"That man Flamsteed cost us two thousand pounds," Cooper said. Like all those present, his sour looks were not improved by the effects of strong drink.

"Three thousand, more like," Sixsmith corrected. "He went off at six to four."

"Two to one in the Silver Ring," another added.

"What the devil does the man think he's playing at?"

"Nothing. Forget it. That was a flash in the pan."

"No it wasn't. I warned you about that one the first time we saw him." Captain Sullivan was quite pleased. Every so often, he liked to see his masters thwarted and out of pocket.

The four glared at him with substantial ill will. It was true. In April, when Giles had first turned up at Salisbury, the captain reported that he was something absolutely out of the ordinary and meant business.

"He can't be allowed to do that on our course," one of the confederates grumbled.

"Quite right. Let's have some action!"

"What do you recommend, gentlemen?" Sullivan helped himself to another liberal measure of their brandy. "What's it to be this time, eh? The needle? Fisticuffs? Or something a little more drastic, perhaps? How about a knife in the back?" He smiled mockingly round the table. "Have a care, my friends. Young Flamsteed seems to be the apple of that old devil Protheroe's eye. And did you not notice something else today? The good colonel never let me out of his sight, and you, Mr Sixsmith, were followed everywhere by his new spy. He even watched Larkins putting that second lot of bets on."

The intensity of the audience's loathing increased. Captain Sullivan was making a very annoying habit of being right.

Reaching Cannings Ambo at midnight, Giles was aware that something was afoot even before Eli Munge materialised at the entrance of the driveway. Instead of being no more than a silhouette against the mid-summer night sky, The House was alight: there seemed to be lamps in nearly every room.

Eli Munge was alone. For an occasion such as this, he had summoned what had to do service as his best behaviour, leaving the Stringfellow brothers slumped in various corners of The George. Moreover, his approach to Giles included a vaguely respectful gesture towards his forelock.

"Mr Flamsteed, sir, you'm a father," he announced.

Looking towards The House, Giles saw that someone with a lantern was hurrying down the driveway.

Anxious to provide more detail, Eli Munge forgot himself and reverted to normal. "Ar! 'Er dropped 'un this morning, round 'bout ten o'clock."

Giles, urging his horse forward, failed to hear him.

Lizzie Shaw was jigging up and down at the back door with Mrs Bayliss hovering behind her. Whatever else had happened, Lizzie's priorities remained rock-solid. "How did The Lathe do, sir?" she asked.

"Eh . . . oh, yes . . . he won," Giles replied, precipitating Lizzie into a gleeful dance that threatened to unhinge Mrs Bayliss's already dangerous nerves.

Giles blinked as he saw Alexandra Fandine-Browne sitting calmly at the huge kitchen table. "Congratulations," she said. "Your very first winner *and* a daughter on the same day."

She was, Giles realised in that instant, an astonishingly handsome woman.

"A daughter?" he echoed, looking dazed.

"Yes, and she's perfectly lovely so you mustn't be disappointed. Men are supposed to want sons aren't they? I didn't get to hear of this until after lunch, so I thought I'd better come over and see what

45

I could do to help. I fancy I've calmed things down a little." She glanced pointedly at Mrs Bayliss.

"But . . ." Giles overcame a tendency to splutter. "Doctor Palfreyman said it wouldn't happen for a week or more."

"Pooh! That was only a guess. They never know with any exactitude. Palfreyman attended your wife, by the way. One of the Izzards rode over to Cannings St John for him. Mother and child are both doing well." After the merest of pauses, Alexandra added, "And don't allow yourself to be persuaded differently," in a marked manner.

"Good. May I see them?" Giles asked with great diffidence.

"My dear man! Of course. I will come with you to see that she is ready for you."

Half-way up the magnificent staircase, Alexandra stopped and laid a hand lightly on Giles's arm. "I am *so* pleased with your great triumph at Salisbury today, Mr Flamsteed. There will be no stopping my dear husband now. He is quite determined to have horses of his own."

Giles was kept waiting for some time outside the bedroom while Alexandra made preparations. When he was finally allowed in and she had slipped away, he found Sarah resting against a huge pile of freshly plumped pillows. She was a little pale and drawn, but very proud of herself, the hair that Mrs Fandine-Browne had brushed so expertly, cascading over the pillows.

"Well, my love," he said awkwardly, "this is a business and no mistake. How are you?"

"Somewhat weak," Sarah murmured contentedly. "It *was* rather frightening."

"Yes, to be sure. Good gracious, what a way to behave as soon as my back is turned. Dear me!"

He had not noticed the bundle cradled in the crook of her arm. Now, the child stirred and gurgled and Giles was overcome with a mixture of wonder and alarm. When he picked the infant up he discovered that her face was smooth and creamy-white, not red and puckered. She had a tuft of blonde hair in the centre of her head and he saw that her eyes were blue, exactly like his own.

"My word, isn't she beautiful?" he said.

"Do you really think so, my dear?"

"I do indeed. You have produced the most beautiful child ever, my love. There is not a shadow of doubt of it."

Sarah glowed with fulfilment.

Suddenly, as he held his daughter, an idea so powerful came to Giles that its brilliance made his mind reel. It had the absolute, perfect rightness of the sunrise.

"We shall call her Leander," he announced.

"Leander?" Sarah was baffled. "That's very strange."

"Not at all, my dear, it is a wonderful name." Giles tried it out. "Leander Flamsteed! Yes! And we shall have Elisabeth, too, for my dear sister."

"I don't think I like that," Sarah said, her good humour disappearing rapidly.

"You will soon grow used to it, my dear."

"But . . ." Sarah's face screwed up with petulance as her objection came out in an eruption. "Leander isn't a girl's name!"

"It is now," Giles said and produced the bland, seemingly naïve smile that told Sarah the game was up. "Leander Elisabeth Flamsteed, born on the day we turned out our first winner!"

The Reverend John Shepherd was young and inexperienced, having replaced Parson Proudfoot as vicar of Cannings Ambo only that spring. It was the first baptism he had ever carried out, a fact he betrayed in his nervously liberal use of water. However, his mellifluous voice was steady as he pronounced, "Leander Elisabeth, I baptise thee in the name of the Father, and of the Son, and of the Holy Ghost. Amen." And Leander Flamsteed took not the slightest notice of the water trickling down her back and gazed with solemn curiosity into John Shepherd's eyes, perfectly aware that something of great importance was taking place.

Her godparents, Horatio, Jasper, Elisabeth and Alexandra Fandine-Browne watched happily, unaware of Sarah's brooding dissatisfaction.

Five months later, in November, Sarah's perception of her predicament worsened.

On the very day that Gilbert Fandine-Browne decided to buy four racehorses and Jasper offered the stables at The Hall as their home because there was no room for them at Latimer's Barn, Sarah discovered that she was pregnant again.

And it was obvious that the hard-nosed Fandine-Browne was hardly pursuing an idle dream. After The Beresford Lathe had shown the way at Salisbury, the Cannings Ambo companionship of misfits had produced the winners of seven more races.

CHAPTER 4

1861

'He might like to try dynamite . . .'

It was clear that Elisabeth was already taking charge. She assumed responsibility for ushering the guests into the uncomfortably large sitting-room while Giles walked to one of the windows, looked out at his stable and felt disgusted with himself. After the trauma of the last seven days, that seemed the only emotion left to him.

Sarah's second pregnancy had proceeded as smoothly as the first and she had gone into labour during the evening of 12 July. Doctor Palfreyman, dining at The Hall with Jasper and Lucy, was at Latimer's Barn within ten minutes, and the child, a boy, was born three hours later.

Then Sarah started to bleed. And scream.

It was the only time Giles ever heard a noise that permeated the whole of the vast, solid house.

For twenty minutes he stood at the foot of the stairs praying for it to stop. When it did, he remained rooted until Doctor Palfreyman came down: his shirt was blood-stained, his face leaden.

"I'm very sorry, Flamsteed," he said. "There was nothing I could do." He put an arm round Giles, to steady himself as much as to offer comfort. "Come on, we both need a drink."

Lizzie Shaw, for once distracted from the stable and Seamus, took temporary charge of the thirteen-month-old Leander and the baby, whose name was William.

Now they had all come to the funeral, but Giles was preoccupied with the thought that he should have been at Goodwood. Months of work and planning were lost; Caleb and Dan had offered to take the three horses, but Giles decided against it. Some sign of respect was necessary.

They had been to the church and the graveyard and were back at The House for the protocol of a little light refreshment and awkward conversation. Just as Giles had expected, Sarah's parents waited only half an hour before edging to the door, making twitterings about the afternoon train from Swindon. Mr and Mrs Winstanley and their daughters had come to the funeral because they had no choice. While satisfying form, they felt under no obligation to show sympathy towards Giles whose wretched estate they regarded as the prime cause of Sarah's death.

The others followed soon after the Winstanleys. The Fandine-Brownes went first, then Sir Ambrose and Lady Hastings; Jasper and Lucy slipped away ten minutes later. Finally, Doctor Palfreyman detached himself from a bottle of whisky and trudged off, looking very much as though he was still blaming himself for the tragedy.

Giles faced his mother and father wearily. The first phase of the conversation was so utterly predictable that he thought he might as well start it himself and have done with it.

"Well, Mother, things are going to be very difficult for me now."

"You *must* think of the children, Giles. I know it's a terrible thing to lose a wife, but Leander and baby William need a mother."

"One option is for me to stop all this nonsense here and return to Greenwich," Giles said.

Mary Flamsteed smiled gently and nodded; Giles did not see her gesture of hope. He was studying Ralph.

There was one reason why Ralph had come all the way down to Wiltshire, and it had nothing whatsoever to do with paying respects to his dead sister-in-law. He was there to grasp every opportunity to ensure that Giles did *not* return to Greenwich.

"What a pity there's such a conflict of interests, Ralph," Giles said quietly.

"No, that isn't true." John Flamsteed was in a hurry to stifle conflict before it took a hold. "We have discussed this, Giles, and Ralph is perfectly willing to have you as a partner."

"That's uncommonly decent of you, Ralph," Giles said. "What would I be doing? Washing bottles?"

"Don't be ridiculous!" Ralph snapped. "I'll find something for you – although God knows, Giles, you aren't in any position to dictate terms."

"*Position*, Ralph?" Giles appeared to be mystified. "What on earth do you mean by *position*?" While Ralph was groping for an answer that would not let his parents into the secret of the bargain he had struck with Giles, his brother provided it for him. "My position is that I own two thousand acres of Wiltshire. I love it very much and there are already a dozen people who depend on me for a living. I came here to train racehorses and that is exactly what I am going to do."

49

Giles was his customary self, speaking in a relaxed way, yet no one doubted that he meant what he was saying. "There is another possibility, Mother," he said. "The children could come to live with you."

"Yes, that would be nice." Mary's face was alight.

"I have no doubt that you would make a wonderful job of looking after them, enjoying yourself immensely while you were about it."

"Of course I would, my dear."

"Yes." Giles sighed wistfully. "But they belong here, Mother. One day this place will be theirs and they must be brought up to love it and understand their responsibilities."

"Giles, how can you hope to look after the poor little mites?" Mary asked. "You surely cannot intend to employ some dreadful woman who will beat them?"

"Definitely not, Mother!" For a moment, Giles displayed fierce passion. Back to normal again, he said, "I was wondering if Elisabeth might care to look after them."

"Exactly what I was about to suggest!" Elisabeth sprang out of her chair to stand at Giles's side. "I shall begin at once."

Ralph was furious. "Elisabeth, I refuse to allow you to involve yourself in this ridiculous affair," he said. "You have important duties to perform for me in *our* family business."

"Book-keeping, Ralph," she replied, coolly dismissive. "That's all it is, that and pandering to your every whim. Anyone can do that for you." She smiled ironically. "Providing you paid them, of course. Only *I* will do it for nothing."

"Don't be absurd, Elisabeth!" Ralph's voice rose as anger took command of him.

"Ralph, please! This is a house of mourning," John Flamsteed said in a futile attempt to calm his son.

"No, Father. We have to put a stop to this or it will be our ruination. You are not to think of leaving us, Elisabeth. I expressly forbid it!"

"Forbid it, Ralph?" Mary thought her daughter was shaking with rage: the truth was that she was trying not to burst out laughing.

"Yes, I forbid it!"

"Ralph, you amaze me," Elisabeth said. "You really do amaze me. You can forbid until you are blue in the face, but I am staying here. This is my home now. Will you get that into your head?"

John and Mary looked on in amazement, asking themselves why they had never noticed the strong similarity between Giles and Elisabeth. There was the same total determination masked by blandness.

"What do you think will become of you if you incarcerate yourself in

50

this god-forsaken hole?" Ralph demanded. "What are your prospects? Will you marry some grubby yokel or become an old maid?"

"I have no idea, but I am confident that I shall fare no worse here than slaving away in your counting-house." Elisabeth's chin tilted up dangerously. "It may be *you* who needs to think of his prospects, Ralph. If you persist in adulterating the claret with third-rate dregs, you may be the one with trouble, not I."

John Flamsteed's face darkened. "What's this about . . ." he began, but Giles cut him short.

"That will do, Father. You will have to discover what Ralph is doing to your business at some other time. Elisabeth has made up her mind, and that is that. You must excuse me for a while, I have horses to see to. They will not wait while we argue."

There was to be one more disturbance before Giles could resume the comfort of his routine. In high dudgeon over losing the battle for Elisabeth, and badly rattled by her allegations about his ethics, Ralph insisted upon returning to Greenwich that day. Seamus had to leave his work in the yard in order to drive him to Swindon. As Ralph was climbing into the carriage, Giles had a final word with him, and this time, there was no sign of mild courtesy.

"It's your business, Ralph, but be *very* careful how you conduct it. Father will not take kindly to having his standards abandoned, let alone abused. Neither will I!"

There was no response other than a final venomous look.

John and Mary Flamsteed stayed at Latimer's Barn for three days. They showed great interest in the horses, spent time at The Hall where Lucy and Mary exchanged recipes and views about the upbringing of children. Greenwich, Ralph and Sarah were never mentioned.

Inevitably, there was tension at the time of their departure; Giles and Elisabeth calmly turned their backs on it and went about their work, Giles in the stable, Elisabeth in The House. They had already made changes. Giles had vacated the bedroom in which Sarah had died and moved to one with a view of the yard at the eastern end of The House. Elisabeth was directly across the corridor in a room with access to the nursery.

On the evening that their parents left, Giles and Elisabeth made themselves comfortable in a small sitting-room adjacent to the library. Never used very much previously, it was to become their lasting favourite. For nearly an hour there was companionable silence as Giles studied official Jockey Club publications and Elisabeth knitted for William.

Then she sensed his gaze on her and looked up.

51

"What is it?" she asked, for he seemed in no hurry to express his thoughts.

"I think we shall be all right," he said.

"I'm sure we shall."

"The children adore you already."

Elisabeth smiled. "Poor little William doesn't have much choice, does he?"

"True! But Leander isn't easily pleased. She has a mind of her own which she uses all too often."

"She does indeed. May I ask you something, Giles?"

"Of course."

"I want to get rid of Mrs Bayliss."

Giles considered it. He had never liked the woman, but wanted more information. "Why?"

"She isn't our sort of person." Without Elisabeth's wide-eyed simplicity it would have sounded dreadfully arrogant. "She isn't 'of the faith'."

"What on earth does that mean?" Giles laughed.

"It's a Lucy Miller expression. It means being completely devoted to the idea that Latimer's Barn and all that therein is is the most wonderful thing ever to happen – well, in Cannings Ambo at any rate."

"Is that what they say?"

"Yes, Giles, it is."

"Well I'm dashed!" He paused to think about it. "No one could ever accuse Mrs Bayliss of thinking that."

"I'm told that there are at least two positions vacant in Marlborough that would be much more to her liking."

"And are you also told whom we might employ in her place?" Giles asked with a smile.

"Of course! Lucy Miller says that there is a young woman called Bertha Bradley who would be splendid."

"Very well, see to it."

Giles returned to his papers and silence. After a few minutes, Elisabeth had another question.

"Giles?"

"Yes?"

"You and Sarah weren't happy, were you?"

There was no question of his being angry; nevertheless, Elisabeth became alarmed at the time it took him to respond. He seemed to be digging very deep indeed for the answer.

"No, Elisabeth, we weren't," he said at last, looking and sounding very sombre.

"What would have happened?"

"I don't know. I often wondered. It was a great worry. She hated this place. I'm afraid there would have been difficulties."

Elisabeth nodded and went back to her knitting. They both knew what she had come close to saying, and they both knew that the topic would never be raised again.

Ten days later, two of the horses that had been prepared for Goodwood each won a race on the same day. It happened on the almost perpetually wind-swept racecourse at Lansdown above Bath and represented a considerable feat of training.

A mild celebration at Latimer's Barn coincided with an evening of black hatred at Branksome Lodge. The members of the Association were livid. Both Giles's victories had demolished projected betting coups: indeed, one of the Association's horses had been drugged to make sure it won and carried a wager of a magnitude not even they could afford to lose.

"This has gone beyond a joke," one of the confederates stormed. "It's getting out of hand. Flamsteed must be stopped. One of those animals today belonged to someone called Fandine-Browne – it seems he has another owner!"

"I spoke to Flamsteed," said Sixsmith, who had been on the course. "I tried to suggest that we might come to an accommodation."

"That wasn't awfully clever of you," Captain Sullivan drawled. "How did you get on?"

Sixsmith shook his head, stunned by what had transpired. "I tried to be discreet," he said, scowling as Sullivan sniggered. "But he didn't understand me. He just sniffed and walked off. Left me standing!"

"He understood you, never fear," Sullivan said. "I expect you disgusted him, Mr Sixsmith, sir. Flamsteed's quite a prig apparently: he wouldn't take kindly to a shifty individual like yourself."

"Never mind that," Sixsmith snarled. "We need action. See to it, Sullivan."

"You wish me to consult Daphne."

"You'd better do more than consult! Get something organised and accomplished, damn you!" A bag containing fifty sovereigns was dumped on the table. "That should cover the expenses."

Sullivan scooped up the bag, laughing at the malicious looks he received. "Thank you, gentlemen. I shall attend to it without delay. It is an even *greater* pleasure doing business with Daphne than with yourselves."

She called herself Mandrake.

Her real name was Daphne Isherwood-D'Eath, she was twenty-four and the daughter of a marquess. She lived in a pleasant house on the western edge of Amesbury, estranged from her family on terms dictated by herself.

Three months before her twenty-first birthday, her father and elder brother fell foul of her by arranging her marriage to the heir to a dukedom. Daphne considered the husband-to-be so repellent that she could not bear to be alone with him and refused to countenance the match. The Marquess, hopelessly ignorant of his daughter's character, threatened her with the direst consequences if she did not assent to his wishes.

Daphne's response was breathtaking. She would, she said, publish a fully documented account of her father's disgusting private life unless she was granted a thousand pounds a year to go her own way. The Marquess, who represented a Lincolnshire constituency at Westminster and hoped for high office, decided to keep his ambitions alive by complying.

Daphne set about building her defences the day she arrived in Amesbury. She had the great good fortune to encounter a couple of down-and-outs recently released from prison after serving twelve years for petty theft. They made a comfortable home in the stables at the rear of her house and soon recruited three more comrades in misfortune. So it was that the two men hired by Daphne's lunatic brother to kill her received the most dreadful beating when they attempted to break in. One subsequently died from his injuries and Daphne sent a most severe letter to her father.

Shortly afterwards, Captain Sullivan came into her life.

He was thirty and perfectly presentable on a good day when he was off the bottle. The Association had a cast-iron certainty going which he advised her to back when they encountered each other at Salisbury races. She did, recklessly, reaping huge rewards at odds of ten to one.

It was a good start to a friendship that subsequently flourished on their mutual love of danger. Daphne's Desperadoes, as Sullivan whimsically called her bodyguards, were soon in action, first to frighten away an idiot farmer who persisted in grazing his sheep on the Branksome Lodge gallops despite being shot at, then to wreck the house of a Salisbury busybody who periodically called for an investigation into the Association's affairs.

Sullivan placed a high value on her friendship, and was never happier than during their all too infrequent meetings. Unfortunately, Daphne refused to crown the relationship with her sexual favours: she laughed at his suggestions, telling him to take more exercise and cold baths.

He always arrived after dark: as usual, he whistled a brief snatch of 'Lillibulero' as he rode down the alley into the stables. A dim figure stepped forward to take his horse and the word was passed. "All right, lads, 'tis the captain."

As ever, she was glad to see him.

"Captain Sullivan, what a pleasant surprise! Come in, come in." She took his riding cloak, gave him a glass of sherry that was too refined for his tastes and sat him down in a comfortable chair. "Now, what brings you here? There is a game afoot?"

"Yes, ma'am, there is."

"Where?"

"Cannings Ambo."

"Oho!" She leaned back in her chair and gave him a searching look. "And what has Mr Flamsteed done to upset your friends?"

"You're well informed, ma'am."

"What else is there at Cannings? Dear old Jasper Beresford and a fine church. Your masters cannot have taken exception to them."

Sullivan nodded. "Flamsteed has been sending out winners. It seems he might amount to something."

"And your Mr Sixsmith wants a stop put to it?"

Sullivan shifted uneasily. He always regretted letting that name slip during one of their early conversations. "Yes. There's forty sovereigns for your men."

"That will buy you a very great deal of trouble, Captain. I don't imagine that it will take much to crack Flamsteed's nerve – he's recently lost his wife, you know."

"Yes, I heard."

"What's the matter, Captain? You appear to lack stomach for this one."

"Truth to tell, ma'am, I do. Flamsteed seems a decent chap to me. And talented, very talented." Sullivan acknowledged the attribute he lacked with honest sadness.

"Somewhat arrogant, by all accounts."

"Some say that."

"But not you, eh?"

"I don't know!" Sullivan's face betrayed a mixture of conflicting emotions. "To hell with it. Just do the job!"

"Oh, I will, Captain, I will. You and your friend Mr Sixsmith may rely on it."

The attack came at two o'clock in the morning, four nights later.

In the instant at which Giles was woken by the noise of shattering

55

glass, his impressions betokened a catastrophe far worse than the reality of daylight subsequently exposed. Pandemonium reigned and his bedroom was lurid with the glow of arson.

They had fired the stores of hay and straw behind the stables. By the time Giles got outside, Caleb and Seamus were already at work trying to beat it out, while Lizzie, in her night-dress and barefoot, and the Izzards brought water from the Cannings Brook. Bertha Bradley was racing to fetch help from the village, Elisabeth, hugging Leander and William close to her, watched from a bedroom window.

Giles quickly saw that things might have been a lot worse. The horses had gone, presumably released before the fire was started: the selection of the most important task was simple.

"Fight the fire," he shouted. "We'll worry about the horses later."

It was a perilously close thing. New deliveries of bedding and fodder had been made the previous week, and Giles had taken advantage of a discount offered by a friendly farmer to order vast quantities. Even after the Reverend Shepherd, Jasper, Lucy Miller and Dan Goakes were on the scene and working like mad things, it still took over an hour to be sure that the stable and coach-house were safe.

When they all trooped into The House, their faces streaked with sweat and smoke-black, to attack the bucket of tea brewed by Bertha Bradley, Elisabeth told Giles that all the ground-floor windows were smashed. It was worse than that: many of the glazing bars had been reduced to matchwood.

Bill Irons was disgusted when he saw the damage. He and half a dozen of his men were gutting and renovating the cottages on Church Green and were staying in the village until the job was complete. Offended that Bertha had not thought to drag him and his lads out to help with the fire, Bill inspected the damage in grim silence.

"Well, Mr Flamsteed, sir, some bugger's taken against you and no mistake," he said.

No one argued with him.

When it was fully light, Elisabeth spotted two of the horses grazing contentedly near the trees surrounding Powell's Pool. Doctor Palfreyman reported three wandering around in the vicinity of Cannings St John and Eli Munge found another in the water-meadows near the River Kennet.

By lunch-time, all but one of the horses had been recovered and found to have come to no harm. When darkness fell again with the stench of burning persisting in the air, there was still no sign of the tenth, and everyone saw that Giles was worried sick. The missing animal was The Beresford Lathe, now a four-year-old and destined for stud at the end of the racing season. Caleb, Seamus and Dan, not wanting to talk about it, slipped away quietly.

When Elisabeth returned from the nursery after putting the children to bed, she found Giles slumped across the kitchen table, fast asleep. She sat with him until half past eleven when he woke, blinked and smiled.

"Are you hungry?" she asked.

"Ravenous. Breakfast would be nice."

"Sixteen hours late!"

"How are the children?"

"They've been as good as gold. Leander is fascinated by the windows."

"No wonder!" Bill Irons had been forced to rig tarpaulins over the wrecked windows until he could track down suitable materials to effect a proper repair. Stretching and standing up, Giles said, "I shall be fifteen minutes."

He came back washed, shaved and wearing a clean shirt.

"You think they will come again?" Elisabeth asked as she set a heavily laden plate of ham and eggs before him.

"Yes. I imagine they will have found out they didn't do all that much damage."

"And what do you propose to do about it?"

"I don't know. Give myself the satisfaction of shouting at them, perhaps."

"Oughtn't we to have sent for a constable from Marlborough?"

She saw from his look that he wanted to resolve the matter himself.

He was in no hurry: he enjoyed his meal, then equipped himself with a stout stick. "Stay close to Leander and William," he instructed. "And bolt the door after me."

"But the windows, Giles, they can get in that way."

"Not without cutting themselves to pieces on their own broken glass," Giles replied. "That's why I told Bill Irons to leave it."

The night was moonless. Giles remained near The House for a while to allow his eyes to adapt before setting off to the stable. As he came to the end of the path round the lawn, Caleb fell into step beside him. He, too, had a stick.

"Seamus and the boys are on watch," Caleb said softly.

"And me!" Startled, Giles looked up in the direction of the whisper. Camouflaged in a dowdy old coat, Lizzie was on the roof of the stable.

"She's got a pile of stones and brick-ends up there, sor," Seamus whispered from his hiding place.

Giles found that he was feeling better.

By unspoken consent, he and Caleb walked back towards the front of The House. They stood for several minutes in the centre of the drive's gravelled turning circle, sniffing at the night and wondering what to do for the best.

Giles's stomach contracted as he heard the first faint sounds. Looking closely at Caleb he saw that he was enduring the same sensations. A group of men were advancing up the drive without much pretence at stealth.

Their shapes were visible now. As Giles was drawing breath to issue a challenge, a leading member of the group darted towards him.

"My God, Dan, you gave us a fright!" Giles gasped, relief flooding over him.

There were fourteen of them. Bill Irons and his six lads were clutching off-cuts of timber and pick-axe handles; Jasper had a sword-stick; Eli Munge and the Stringfellows, stone-cold sober and deadly earnest, were encumbered with a collection of apparatus of which Giles could make no sense, particularly since they hung back. Doctor Palfreyman had his shotgun.

"What on earth are you going to do with that thing, Doctor?" Giles asked.

"Use it, of course. What a damned silly question!" There was a belt packed with cartridges round Palfreyman's waist, another across his chest like a bandolier.

"We'm not having this, Mr Flamsteed," Bill Irons announced, his attempt at a whisper coming out as a fierce croak. "They buggers have got to be learned, good and proper!"

There was a growl of assent from his men and the Stringfellow brothers: Eli Munge muttered something about the village looking after its own.

"Now, you must deploy your forces, Giles." Jasper had never been so excited in his life. "Tell us what we should do."

Two of Daphne Mandrake's men always stayed in Amesbury to protect her and the house. The first raid on Latimer's Barn was carried out by the other three. Dissatisfied by what had been achieved, she decided to invest a few of the Association's sovereigns in four extra ruffians.

They gathered shortly after midnight near an inn at Beckhampton Crossroads, six miles to the west of Cannings Ambo. Their orders were to burn down The House and they received them from Daphne who was leading the expedition in person. Dressed from head to toe in black and mounted on her mare, Lady, she guided them along an ancient bridle-way that kept well clear of the London to Bath road, bringing them to Cannings Ambo by the side of the river and up the Cannings Brook.

When they reached Latimer's Barn at a few minutes before two o'clock, the seven men went about their work at once, moving swiftly across the lawn to The House.

In the centre of the lawn, three of them paused in order to light torches, stumps of wood impregnated with pitch and bound with oil-soaked rags. The consequent flare of light enabled them to see and be seen.

There was a line of men in defence of The House; at a shout, more came running. Giles had split his forces to deal with an attack from either front or rear. The men on the lawn froze, unsure of the strength against them. It was a moment of indecision on all sides.

Doctor Palfreyman fired both barrels of his shotgun.

He was standing in the dark shadow of The House's western wall, and, as Giles had made him promise, discharged the weapon harmlessly into the air. Not knowing that, the attackers turned tail.

"Right, lads," Bill Irons roared, waving his pick-axe handle. "Let's have 'em!"

As Bill led the charge, the doctor reloaded with expert rapidity and fired again. Rampaging across the lawn, Bill Irons's warriors let out blood-curdling roars.

Out of sight behind the stables and coach-house, Daphne was in no doubt that the plan was going hideously wrong. She smoothed a calming hand along the mare's neck and wondered what to do.

The marauders, confused and panic-stricken, ran straight towards the stables, the three torches abandoned on the grass giving out an eerie light. Doctor Palfreyman kept blasting away demoralisingly with his shotgun, while Lizzie was pelting bricks and stones down from the roof. One of the four men hired for the night was hit on the head. As he keeled over and slumped to the ground, Lizzie lost her footing and slithered off the roof, adding screams of excitement and anguish to the wild cacophony.

Giles had seen enough.

"Stop!" he roared, fearing a lynching now that the raiders were surrounded and outnumbered. "Take them and lock them up."

The authentic voice of authority brought calm; it even caused the doctor to cease fire and made Daphne stiffen. The game was over and lost, it was time to slip away quietly. Instead, a final mad desire for adventure caused her to wheel the mare round and urge her forward into the remains of the fray. At the back of her mind, there was a vague hope that she might create enough of a diversion to enable some, if not all, of her men to escape.

It damned nearly worked.

The sudden appearance of the mare and her ominous-looking rider surprised everyone, particularly Bill Irons and his men, who seemed frightened by the massive horse. Judging the situation in a fraction of a second, Daphne pulled a revolver from an inside pocket of her cloak and fired two shots over the heads of the crowd. While a number of the gang made a run for freedom, Bill Irons was convinced that this startling new participant in the drama was hell-bent on murder.

There was a moment of ugly fear.

Then the world turned upside down.

From the eastern side of the lawn, there came a blinding flash and an ear-splitting explosion. Eli Munge had discharged his ancient fowling piece, a horrendous weapon with a bore of one inch and a barrel so unwieldy that a forked rest was needed to prop it up. A hail of lead pellets, nails and tacks clattered on to the stable roof and a second, similar weapon was fired by a Stringfellow. The mare reared, nearly unseating Daphne, and she dropped her revolver as lead shot entered her right shoulder.

Now it really was time to go. Hurt and badly unnerved, Daphne dreaded what Latimer's Barn might have in reserve. Regaining control of Lady, she galloped off past the stable into the safe darkness of Cannings Down.

"That was a woman!" Bill Irons said, hardly believing what his eyes had seen at the last moment. "Her was riding side-saddle."

"It was," Giles agreed. "And I'm certain that last broadside hit her. Who fired it?"

"Malachi Stringfellow," someone replied.

Giles surveyed the scene by the glare of the torches, still alight and burning holes in the lawn. Eli Munge was being helped to his feet; the recoil of his preposterous but terrifying gun had knocked him flat. Seamus had his arms round Lizzie, comforting her after the fall from the roof. Months later, Giles was to realise that this was the birth of the romance that culminated in their marriage. And the six attackers, completely cowed and defeated, were gathered round their unconscious comrade.

"Lock them up in the feed store," Giles commanded. "I'll talk to them when it gets light. And will someone shift those blasted torches before they ruin my lawn completely!"

*

60

The mare, Lady, stood eighteen hands high and was eight years old. Before Daphne acquired her, a succession of owners had attempted to hunt her with a pack of staghounds over Exmoor. Immensely strong, Lady could be temperamentally vile, and they had all given up in despair or rage. But Daphne fell in love with the mare the minute she spotted her in Shaftesbury market and the feeling was returned fulsomely. Each found the other the most loyal and rewarding being she had ever encountered.

Once clear of the stable, Lady made a wide turn to the south, settling into an effortless stride that took them over the mile of Cannings Down that Giles used for training gallops in under three minutes.

They paused at the Cannings Brook while Daphne caught her breath and moved her shoulder gingerly in an attempt to assess the damage. The thick cloak had afforded some protection; nevertheless, the pain and burning sensation were severe, and she could feel the blood-soaked silk shirt clinging stickily.

"Take me home, Lady," she said. "And don't be too long about it."

It was fifteen miles and they had never been that way before.

Lady set off with unerring confidence. She went straight across country at her own pace. By turn, she covered two miles at a loping canter, then walked for a mile, increasingly showing signs that she was capable of carrying on the cycle for ever if need be. Daphne's one concern was that the inevitable bumps exacerbated the discomfort of her shoulder.

The only delay was caused by the obstacle of the Kennet & Avon Canal. Rather than use Pewsey Bridge where they might be heard or seen even at that hour in the morning, Daphne took the mare east until they came to the isolated Bristow Bridge. After that, there was nothing but the emptiness of Salisbury Plain save for crossing the old Devizes to Andover turnpike.

They reached Daphne's house in little more than two hours, at half past four, and her two men were by her side at once.

"Give Lady the best feed she's ever had," Daphne told one of them as he helped her down. "And, Tom, go and fetch Doctor Stanton. Not that miserable old busybody Codington, I *must* have Stanton."

Giles went to the feed store at six o'clock. He was accompanied by Bill Irons and his lads, still with their cudgels. There was no need for the escort: fearing that the most serious charges were to be laid against them, the captives had no desire to cause further trouble.

Almost immediately, Giles established that four of the men, including the one knocked senseless by Lizzie, were no more than casual hirelings for the night.

"Who put you up to this?" he asked the other three.

One of the trio took the plunge. "Captain Sullivan, sir!"

"Ah!" Giles nodded, accepting the half-truth. "And might Captain Sullivan be connected with a Mr Lauderdale?" he asked.

The spokesman was genuinely mystified by the pseudonym.

"What about Gilchrist?"

Again, blank faces.

"Sixsmith?"

"Yes, sir, I have heard that name mentioned."

"Very well." Giles surveyed each of them in turn. He did more than memorise their faces, he looked into their souls, and they all squirmed at the scrutiny. "After thinking about it, I have decided not to have you taken in charge," he said. "You are free to go. It will be a very different story if any of you as much as set foot on my land again. Is that understood?"

They all nodded, their faces registering disbelief and dawning elation as the prospect of a long prison sentence or deportation miraculously vanished.

"Go on," Giles commanded. "Be off! Get out of my sight. All except you." He pointed at the man whose head Lizzie had broken. There was congealed blood in his hair and he still had a dazed look. "Do you have a home to go to?"

"No, sir."

"What's your name?"

"Nathaniel Thomas, sir." He was, Giles judged, about twenty-five.

"Well, Nathaniel Thomas, you had best stay here until the doctor has had a look at you. Can you see that he gets some breakfast, Caleb?"

Caleb nodded, in no way put out at being told to look after a villain.

Later, as Giles finished his own breakfast, his second in eight hours, he said to Elisabeth, "I think I shall offer that young man Thomas a job."

She grinned. "Now he really *is* a misfit," she said. "What will you do with him?"

"I believe he would make an excellent night-watchman."

Elisabeth burst into peals of laughter which did not stop until something outside caught her attention.

"What is it?" Giles asked as she stared out of the window.

"A horse has just wandered in from the Downs," she said.

The Beresford Lathe was giving the impression that he had not been away for more than ten minutes, but was still rather put out not to find a feed waiting for him.

Unable to control his desire for news, Captain Sullivan went to Amesbury that afternoon. Without the faintest idea that it was to be his last visit, he flung caution to the winds to arrive in broad daylight.

His welcome was frigid. Daphne, her right arm supported in a sling, looked haggard. It had taken Doctor Stanton over an hour to remove the twenty-seven fragments of assorted metals from her shoulder, during which time the pain was excruciating.

As her account of the night's work unfolded, Sullivan's unease turned to disappointment and finally horror.

"For God's sake, Daphne, was there nothing you could do?" he demanded.

She glowered at him. "Flamsteed had an army guarding Latimer's Barn last night, Captain! There must have been at least twenty of them and they had guns – including two dreadful things that were more like field artillery."

"You should have made a job of it on the first night when you had the element of surprise."

"Yes, I should, shouldn't I?" Daphne said bitterly.

"What am I to tell Mr Sixsmith?"

"Really, Captain Sullivan! *All* my men are taken, I have been shot, and the only thing you can think of is your bloody Sixsmith!"

"I shall have to tell him something," Sullivan persisted. "He wants Flamsteed stopped."

Daphne smiled sardonically. "He might like to try dynamite. That's what I think it will take. In any case, it's up to him now, I'm finished."

"He'll want his fifty sovereigns back."

"*Fifty?* My word, Captain, your commission is heavy. If I were you, I'd pay him."

"What are you going to do?"

"I propose taking very good care of myself, Captain, and you would be well advised to do the same. My guess is that we are in danger from both Sixsmith and Flamsteed. You will go now, please, and you are not to come here again. I still have two good men and they will be warned against you."

Captain Sullivan understood.

Two hours later, Daphne discovered that Giles Flamsteed was even more remarkable than she had imagined. Her three men came back, footsore from the long walk, but free and unscathed.

"We said it was Captain Sullivan wanted it done," her faithful Sam told her. "You was never mentioned, miss." He paused to rub his chin. "You know, that Mr Flamsteed's a real gent – why was we trying to do him down?"

Lawrence Stanton's confidence had taken a battering since he came to Amesbury three years ago. He saw himself as one of the new men, a graduate with honours of Edinburgh University's world-famous School of Medicine, a man who, if God spared him, would be practising the healing science and art into the twentieth century.

That was before he went into what was supposed to be a partnership with Doctor Codington, who proved to be a professional incompetent and a tyrannical skinflint. Now twenty-seven, Lawrence was paid a pittance and had given up trying to raise the question of his status within the practice.

There was a powerful reason why Lawrence Stanton did not pack his bags and move on: he was hopelessly in love with Daphne Mandrake. He knew that the time would come when he had to face facts, but for the moment there were his dreams, now fanned by the memory of the morning on which she sent for him. For much of the time that he had been dragging lumps of metal out of her delectable flesh, she rested her head on his shoulder.

Daphne was aware of his feelings for her and found him attractive. She also knew that he would never pluck up courage to call on her, so she waited, dressing the wound herself each day, noting that Lawrence had done a good job and that she was healing quickly.

After two weeks, she sent Sam to fetch him in the evening.

"I thought it wise for you to take another look at my shoulder, Doctor," she told him when he hurried over straight away.

"Of course, Miss Mandrake. I have been concerned about you."

"Have you? How kind of you." Daphne unbuttoned her linen blouse, pulled it loose from the skirt waistband and cast it aside. "Now, Doctor Stanton, what do you think?"

"I . . . er . . ." He advanced cautiously to peer at her shoulder, now almost completely healed. "That is very good, Miss Mandrake, very good indeed." He bent to take a closer look. "There will be a scar, I fear. To be honest with you, there will be several – a cluster of small ones, you understand?"

"It cannot be helped," she sighed and gazed into his eyes.

He was flushed, barely retaining his composure. Above the waist, she wore only a flimsy silk shift and his reaction to the creamy swell of her breasts and the finely sculpted cleft between them was barely controllable. When she reached out a hand to his face, there was nothing he could do except snatch her into his arms.

The unmitigated fury of their hunger left them breathless and light-headed.

Part of Lawrence Stanton wanted to believe that this was a passing moment of delirium that would disappear without trace the instant he went back to his room in Codington's miserable abode. But as the skirt fell in a swirl at her feet and it was obvious that the knee-length shift was all she wore, the fever took command of him and he was tearing off his own clothes. With the shift gone, he was given tantalising glimpses of her nakedness as she lunged about the drawing-room grabbing cushions from chairs to hurl on the floor. She dragged him down to the makeshift bed in an embrace that surprised him by its sheer animal power.

"Now, Doctor Stanton," she gasped, "love me!"

He took possession of her with a swift mastery that delighted her: she would never have imagined him capable of such a thrusting assault. As he set about impelling them towards ecstasy, Daphne was finally released from the nightmarish events at Latimer's Barn and began to see a new, idyllic and safe way ahead.

After they had basked in their afterglow for several minutes, she said, "I always knew that not keeping servants would turn out to be a wise thing."

He smiled nervously, starting to doubt what was happening to him.

"You didn't ask me how I received this shoulder wound," Daphne said.

"I thought it none of my business."

She nodded in appreciation of his consideration. "That was very good of you, Lawrence. But there are certain things you need to know about me. As a matter of fact, there are a lot of things I have to tell you."

"Why?"

"Because we are to be married. I shall make you a very good wife. I promise."

Although he did not have a horse competing, Giles made a special point of attending the next race meeting at Bath.

It took him an hour to track down the person he was looking for, largely because of evasive action by his quarry.

"Good afternoon, Mr Lauderdale," Giles said when they were at last face to face. "Or is it some other name today? You were

Lauderdale when you suggested that we might take it in turns to win, but your horse in the first race belonged to someone called Gilchrist. Confusing, is it not?" Giles smiled. He was at his most bland.

"What do you want, Flamsteed?"

"I thought I would give you some advice. As you may have heard, I've had trouble at my stable. If anything like that ever happens again, I will have you warned off Newmarket Heath and ruined. I trust we understand each other, Mr Sixsmith!"

Watching from his office window, Colonel Protheroe saw Giles walk away from the encounter as though nothing but the vaguest pleasantries had been exchanged. Sixsmith's scowl told a very different story.

CHAPTER 5

1868

'She's very together'

At ten minutes to six on a magnificent June morning, Giles walked out to inspect the gallop. Half a mile ahead of him, bent to deal with a fault in the turf, was Nat Thomas, one-time drifter and casual criminal, now a symbol of the changes taking place in Cannings Ambo.

Eli Munge had died in 1862. No sooner were the arrangements made to give him a decent funeral, than people came from far and wide to make application for the tenancy of The George. It was a phenomenon that took Giles completely by surprise; it seemed that under his stewardship the estate was acquiring a reputation and that people wanted to be part of it.

"Choose carefully," Elisabeth told him. "This is a big opportunity to shape the future."

"We want our sort of people – 'of the faith'?"

"Of course!"

To be sure, Giles involved Elisabeth in the selection process, not that it was difficult. Martin and Vicky Foxton, a young couple from Newbury, stood head and shoulders above the rest. Disowned by her parents for supposedly marrying beneath her, Vicky was looking for happiness and security, and was prepared to work all hours to achieve those goals. The whole-hearted support of her personable husband was plain to see, and they moved in the day Bill Irons and his men finished giving The George a very thorough going-over. On their first day, Martin Foxton threw the Stringfellow brothers out, telling them not to come back until they had acquired some clean linen and manners. Within weeks, The George had developed into a place where Caleb Jackson could be found most evenings.

Alfred and Margaret Wesley were out of the same mould as the Foxtons. They came from Devizes two years later, in 1864, to take over a three-acre smallholding in Church Marks that had been a neglected, weed-infested mess for as long as Jasper could recall. Inside a year, Alfred and Margaret were turning out enough produce to supply the village and run a stall in Marlborough market every Thursday.

Also in 1864, Doctor Palfreyman announced his retirement at the age of seventy-one, and put his practice up for sale. This was universally seen as bad news and greeted with dismay. The blow was softened to some extent when it became known that Palfreyman would be staying in his house at Cannings St John and playing a full part in local affairs.

As soon as Daphne heard about the opportunity, she knew that it was precisely what she, Lawrence and their baby son, Charles, wanted.

Daphne and Lawrence Stanton married within a few weeks of first becoming lovers. Having made a form of peace with her family and absolved her father of the need to make any more payments to her, Daphne used her real name for the ceremony. Doctor Codington was amazed by the whirlwind romance and extremely annoyed when Lawrence took up residence in Daphne's house, thus depriving him of the services of a day-and-night dogsbody.

Three of Daphne's protectors, those who had taken part in the abortive raid on Latimer's Barn, left her. She understood their desire to attempt a new life outside Wiltshire and gave them a generous sum of money to provide them with a start. The other two stayed and Lawrence was happy enough with the arrangement; men on tap to do his bidding were a welcome addition to the great transformation his life underwent.

Daphne came to love her husband very much, feeling a little safer with each uneventful day that passed. The local people, with whom she had always been on good terms, and who now regarded her with increased respect, kept her informed of the rumours concerning Branksome Lodge. Early in 1862, Captain Sullivan disappeared, with, it was suggested, a fair amount of Association money. Thereafter, a succession of men seemed to be in charge of the place, none of them lasting long.

Daphne's biggest worry was that she had no idea how much Sullivan had told Sixsmith about her. Usually, she worked on the pessimistic assumption that Sixsmith and his cronies knew where she was and could, therefore, act at any time their vindictiveness got the better of them. Escape was necessary.

After three years of attempting to find a suitable way, the announcement that Doctor Palfreyman's practice was for sale came as manna from heaven to Daphne. What safer place was there than Cannings Ambo, where, as she knew to her cost, they looked after their own?

As she had expected, Lawrence objected.

"Daphne, my darling, I cannot possibly afford to buy my own practice yet. In fact, at the current rate of progress, I doubt if I shall ever be able to."

"How much do you think he will want for it?"

"Five hundred at least, even without the house."

"Lawrence, I have money. We must use that."

He was difficult for two days, then accepted. He was, she knew, heartily sick of Codington and would do almost anything to get away from him.

Since becoming a doctor's wife, Daphne had bought a carriage, and one of her men drove them to Cannings Ambo. The journey evoked eerily uncomfortable feelings in Mrs Stanton: she remembered the night when, as Daphne Mandrake, Lady had brought her home over approximately the same route. Feigning interest in the countryside, she looked round constantly, searching for a recognisable feature of the way she and Lady had gone.

There was worse to come.

"No point in staying here," Doctor Palfreyman said when they found him in the garden of his slightly ramshackle house in Cannings St John. "Giles Flamsteed wants a word with you. He's the squire down the road." After he had climbed into the carriage and they were on their way, Palfreyman told them more. "The fact is, we're trying to arrange matters so that I only sell to someone he approves of. There's no need to worry, he's a very good fellow. You'll like him."

And ten minutes later, Daphne found herself being driven up to the front door of Latimer's Barn. Her heart was in her mouth; she had given Lawrence a great deal of information about herself before their marriage, including a passably accurate account of how her shoulder had come to be damaged. She had not, however, mentioned the locality of the escapade. It was a time for summoning up the degree of nerve she habitually displayed before she encouraged Lawrence to change her life.

Giles, strong and good-looking, more or less as Daphne had come to imagine him, was charming. He and Lawrence took an instant liking to one another, and Giles made no secret of the fact that he found Daphne agreeably attractive.

"I want a doctor *here*, in the village," Giles explained. "That's very important for the community I'm trying to build."

"That would suit us wonderfully," Daphne replied with a demure smile.

"Excellent! There are a number of houses that might be suitable,"

Giles went on. "They all need renovation, but that can soon be put in hand once you have made your choice."

Daphne would very much have liked to live in Rose House, the large, graceful building on the bend between the church and the entrance to Latimer's Barn. Regretfully, Giles told her that this was not possible since, although he had no specific plans for the place yet, he felt certain that it was destined to play an important part in the future of his family. Almost opposite Rose House was an equally fine if slightly smaller residence with five bedrooms, a large garden and good staff quarters over the stable.

"I won't sell it to you because I want to keep the whole estate in one piece," Giles explained. "But you can have it rent-free. You can go whenever you like, but if I want to get rid of you, I have to give two quarters' notice. How does that seem?"

"Very fair indeed," Lawrence replied. "I think we should be responsible for repairs."

They shook hands on it. Giles had a word with Doctor Palfreyman, and the sale of his practice took place half an hour later over a glass of sherry in the library of Latimer's Barn.

Returning to Cannings Ambo two months afterwards, Daphne and Lawrence found that their house had a new roof and bathroom and was in the process of being decorated from top to bottom. Under the supervision of Alfred Wesley, volunteers had rescued the garden and the women of the village were ready to start making curtains. The house gained a name, Oak Cottage, in honour of the two fine specimens that flanked its entrance, and a brass plate announced that Doctor Lawrence Stanton, MB, was in residence.

Daphne had travelled a mere fifteen miles, but hoped and prayed that her past was irrevocably left behind. Her two men and the mare went with her to Cannings Ambo. Tom and Jim, hard-working and ever-willing to oblige, were soon accepted as natives of the village, and Daphne's excursions on Lady became part of everyday life. Whenever she saw Giles, he raised his hat and smiled a greeting. For the first time in her life, Daphne Stanton became an insider, part of a fellowship.

As he made his leisurely way down the gallop towards Nat Thomas, Giles counted the measure of his estate's new vitality. It lay in the number of babies delivered by Lawrence Stanton: two each for Martin and Vicky Foxton, Seamus and Lizzie, Alfred and Margaret Wesley, and a daughter for himself and Daphne. During the same four-year period, there had been only one death, an old lady of eighty-two at Cannings St John. After fifty years of decline, the estate was growing once more.

And the Victorian spirit of progress and enterprise had touched Giles's corner of Wiltshire. In 1864, the Great Western Railway arrived in Marlborough with a branch line from Savernake where there were connections for Bath and all stations to London. By walking his horses two miles to the railway station, Giles had vastly improved transport facilities at his disposal, and Horatio was able to reach Cannings Ambo from Birmingham in under four hours.

Nat Thomas straightened up respectfully as Giles approached. "Good morning, sir," he said.

"'Morning, Nat. Another fine day."

Nat Thomas had been trustworthy since the day Giles set him on. Seven years later, Elisabeth still commented on it.

"You are incredible, Giles! You disapprove of gambling, yet you take the most awful risks with people. And you always win!"

Nat spent every night in or near the stable with a loaded shotgun at his side. When Caleb was up and about, generally at half past five, Nat set off to walk the gallop, replacing divots, filling rabbit holes, ensuring that there was nothing to damage the horses as they worked. After finishing this chore, a task he had suggested himself, he took himself back to bed. Refusing all offers of accommodation in the village, Nat had set up home in a derelict shepherd's hut at the furthest limit of the level part of the Down, nearly a mile and a half from the stable. From time to time, Giles made it his business to look in and check that Nat was taking care of himself. The place was always snug and clean; occasionally there was a suggestion of a woman's recent presence to indicate that Nat sometimes garnished the lonely life that suited him for most of the time.

"Ascot will be very nice if this weather holds," Giles said.

"Are we doing anything, sir?"

"I hope so. You'll see for yourself in a few minutes."

They walked on for a hundred yards, Giles joining in the inspection of the turf. When he looked back towards the stable, he gave a grunt of satisfaction.

"Here's the first lot now."

There were five racehorses with Caleb alongside them on a hack. Leading them was a chestnut colt of exceptional quality. Bred by Horatio at a makeshift stud farm in the grounds of his house near Lichfield in Staffordshire, the three-year-old heralded a new era for Latimer's Barn. A son of The Beresford Lathe, New Invention, so called to celebrate another remarkable advance in machine-tool design by Horatio, had placed the name of Giles Flamsteed in the front rank of trainers.

Five weeks ago, he had won the Two Thousand Guineas Stakes

at Newmarket. On that memorable day, Giles was given further cause for satisfaction; for his epic run along the Rowley Mile, New Invention was ridden by Peter Izzard, now in his second year of replacing Dan Goakes who was finding the struggle to control his weight to race-riding limits slipping beyond him.

While the horses moved into a circle to trot and canter as a prelude to galloping, Giles reconsidered the problems that New Invention's triumph had given him. No sooner was the colt past the winning post than established and would-be owners were clamouring for Giles to train their horses. They all had to be refused: with the stables at The Hall full, Giles was looking after sixteen horses and could take no more. Horatio raised the issue during his visit at Easter, before New Invention had catapulted Latimer's Barn to prominence.

"You need to think of expansion, Giles. The place isn't going to be big enough for you soon."

Giles had deflected the idea; now, he was less certain.

"Here they come, sir," Nat said.

Three horses were on the gallop, moving towards them. Two, ridden by Seamus and Dan Goakes, were setting a good pace in front while New Invention cruised along behind with a grace that seemed almost languid. After five furlongs, New Invention's rider let him off the bit, and, within a few strides, he surged ahead of his two pacemakers with contemptuous ease.

Nat Thomas looked awestruck as the colt swept past, only a few yards from where he and Giles were standing. But striking though the colt was, it was his rider who made the greatest impression: it was Leander, a week after her eighth birthday.

Giles smiled at the look on Nat's face. "Yes, she's very together, isn't she?"

It was Giles's latest phrase, something he had picked up at Newmarket. It described a rider who was completely at one with a horse, an integral, attuned, flowing part of him. No one deserved the description better than Leander.

She had started riding at three. Giles bought her a pony, put her on it, and that was that; Elisabeth added the tailoring of riding breeches to her skills since, from the outset, there was never any question of Leander Flamsteed riding side-saddle. She had begun riding the horses when she was six, rapidly attaining a standard that impressed even Caleb. A year later, a miracle happened.

When New Invention first came to Latimer's Barn, he was lazy and seemed rather stupid. He would not buckle down to serious work and gave the impression that he had no idea what was expected of him. No matter who sat on him, he would not go. Purely as a last desperate measure, without hope of success, Giles agreed to let Leander try.

The results were startling, encouraging the belief that Horatio had provided them with an animal of quite exceptional ability. It was several weeks before New Invention could be persuaded to gallop for Peter Izzard as well as Leander, but once that difficulty had been negotiated, his winning career began.

Nat Thomas slipped away to his hut and Giles waited for Leander to bring the colt back.

"You were quite right, Father," she said, drawing level with him. "He wouldn't have been any good at Epsom. Anything beyond a mile and he's done for."

She was referring to Giles's decision not to run New Invention in the Derby, unpopular in the village and with the experts of the racing press, who always considered themselves better judges than the trainer.

"There's no point in knocking a good horse up," he told her. "I believe you can break a horse's heart by expecting too much of him. He nearly kills himself trying to achieve the impossible, then feels terrible because he knows he's let you down." He saw that she was taking it in with all the seriousness of a lesson; she would, he knew, never forget it. "But he's brilliant over a mile," Giles went on. "No one will get anywhere near him at Ascot."

William was waiting at the stables; he always was, and Giles knew that it was very brave of him. Although he was terrified of horses, William turned up without fail to help Leander dismount and take the saddle off. All horses, apart from thoroughgoing rogues, loved William and would never hurt him, but William could never understand that. Leander had tried to teach him to ride on a pony that the village children used every day: after three attempts, she gave up.

It made not a scrap of difference to their relationship. They were utterly devoted to each other and nothing would ever change that. One extrovert and confident, the other shy, they were contrasts that complemented each other. With Leander's blonde hair and pale blue eyes and William's brown colouring they were like dawn and dusk, hope and contentment.

Despite the constant warmth of Leander's love and assurances, William still worried about being such a duffer. Only a few days ago, Giles had overheard part of a conversation that had been extremely revealing.

"It doesn't matter, William," Leander was saying. "As long as one of us is good with horses, Father will be all right, and we shall be able to keep it going."

"What about me?" William asked.

"There'll be plenty of things for you to do."

"It's got to be here. I don't ever want to go away, Lea." That was what he always called her, pronouncing it, 'Le-ah'.

"Of course you'll be here, silly! Latimer's Barn will become very big and important and terribly famous and we shall have to look after it. We shall be ever so busy!"

Giles crept away, careful not to make a sound.

Everyone had breakfast after the first lot were back in their boxes and feeding. Then, while Giles rode out with the second lot, Leander and William went to school. This was held in a specially equipped room in The House, and was for all the children of Cannings Ambo. Elisabeth presided, helped on most days by Daphne Stanton. Giles had thrown his enthusiastic support behind Elisabeth's idea; anything that helped to make The House the focal point of the village was sure of his backing.

The horses from The Hall were taken out as a third lot which kept everyone busy until half past twelve when Giles looked forward to half an hour with Elisabeth over lunch. Today, however, there was an intrusion: Sir Ambrose Hastings was waiting to pay the training fees for his two horses, a task he carried out with punctilious regularity, although Giles always feared that he had another motive for his visits.

Marlborough tittle-tattle attributed a wide range of motives to Sir Ambrose's decision to become a racehorse owner. The one finding most favour was that he hoped for a boost in his social standing. When he first came to Latimer's Barn in 1865, this seemed plausible. Gilbert Fandine-Browne had created a crisis by moving his six horses to a Newmarket stable and the arrival of Sir Ambrose was greeted with relief, not questions.

But now, with Fandine-Browne back, and incessant pressure on yard space, Sir Ambrose was content to let his commitment drop to only two horses, and, when he insisted on his tour of the stable, he took barely any notice of them.

Instead, he admired New Invention at great length.

"Are you sending him to Ascot, Flamsteed?" Sir Ambrose asked eagerly.

"Yes, sir. We think he should do well."

"So does everybody else, I expect." Sir Ambrose smiled ruefully. "Tell me, what do you know about Blamire? Belongs to Lord Guildford. I think Markland-Davies trains him at Newmarket."

"No, sir, I am not familiar with the animal."

74

"What about Lady Esmerelda? Now she's supposed to be *very* hot."

"She won a good race at York last month. Beyond that I know nothing about her."

"Oh!" Sir Ambrose was disappointed. "They say you're not a betting man, Flamsteed."

"No, Sir Ambrose, I am not. I regard it as a game for knaves and fools."

By heavy-handed emphasis that he knew ran the risk of offending his patron, Giles turned the statement into a warning.

Until the next landmark of the day, Giles worked in the library, writing letters to finalise the arrangements for transporting New Invention to Ascot and looking for future races that might suit his horses.

At four o'clock, Elisabeth came in with a tea-tray and the post, which rarely reached Cannings Ambo until the middle of the afternoon. They settled down to read letters: Elisabeth had one from an aunt, Giles was glad to see a long missive from Horatio.

Elisabeth's pleasure soon disappeared. Giles ignored her the first time she said, "Oh dear!" but when it came again with much more feeling he looked up.

"What's wrong?"

"The latest news about Ralph," Elisabeth replied. "It seems that things may be getting very bad."

"What's happened *now*?" Giles asked gloomily.

For the past two years, Ralph had been in sole command of Flamsteed & Sons. Mary had died in 1865 after a long struggle against cancer and John followed her in 1866. He contracted what appeared no more than a minor chest complaint and simply gave in to it, lacking the will to live without Mary. Left to his own devices, Ralph used every trick to maximise his profit: as inevitably as the price of Flamsteed wine crept up, its quality declined.

"He's lost two more contracts," Elisabeth said. "One of them is Bartley's."

"Bartley's!"

Giles was appalled. The arrangement to supply wines to a chain of shops in London was the biggest piece of business that John Flamsteed had ever secured. The contract had run for twenty years and in its heyday had been worth three hundred dozen bottles a week.

"The usual reason?" Giles asked.

"Yes." Elisabeth consulted her aunt's letter. "Poor quality, too expensive and insolence in response to complaints or suggestions."

Giles knew it all only too well.

"And it seems that Ralph's engagement has come to a sudden end," said Elisabeth. "Aunt Florence says she was far too nice a girl, anyway."

Giles smiled. "Well, she would, wouldn't she?" Aunt Florence Crosby, their late mother's sister, had a long-standing and somewhat notorious lack of affection for Ralph.

"Is there anything we should do?" Elisabeth asked.

"What, about Ralph?" Giles considered it for a few moments before shaking his head. "No, he wouldn't take the blindest bit of notice."

Elisabeth nodded sadly. "Poor Father," she murmured. "What does Horatio have to say for himself?" she asked, making a determined effort to brighten up.

"He's reminding me to think of expansion," Giles replied.

"Are you going to build a bigger yard?"

"Yes, in my own good time. He also suggests that we need a proper stud farm and that it ought to be in this area."

"Is that a good idea?"

"Yes, it is. Our present arrangements are quaint, to put it mildly."

"They produced New Invention."

"Indeed, but what about when *he* retires to stud? If we have the right facilities, he should be a very popular stallion – say forty mares a year."

"At what sort of fee?"

"At least fifty guineas."

"My word!" Elisabeth's eyes opened wide as she appreciated the possibilities.

"Quite! Horatio points out that we should be looking at this as a business proposition rather than a hobby, and he's absolutely right."

"And where might this stud be?" Elisabeth asked with a strong suspicion that Giles already had well-developed plans.

"Cannings St John."

"Whereabouts? I can't think of anywhere suitable."

"The Stringfellows' farm would make a good start."

"Could you persuade them to sell it?"

"I don't see why not. They haven't made much pretence of farming the place for the past few years. I think that for a thousand pounds and a good house in the village we could do business."

"More work for Bill Irons."

"That's right." Giles looked again at Horatio's letter. "He's reminding me to send the children to Lichfield for a holiday."

"You'll never get Leander to leave New Invention."

"Don't be so sure. I think she'd go to look after William."

"He will love it, of course. He can't wait to get inside Horatio's factory and find out how it all works. Do you suppose he'll ever stop being frightened of the horses?"

"He'll grow out of that eventually, but he'll never be fully at ease with them." Giles was unconcerned. "He's very good with his hands."

"He is! Do you know, he's always mending things about The House?"

"And in the yard, too. I found out from Caleb the other day that William saves us a small fortune in tack repairs. He's forever going round looking for something to do, and I don't think it will be all that long before he starts *making* things. You'll see, once Horatio's given him a shove in the right direction, he'll be turning out all sorts of contraptions."

Giles looked at his watch and prepared to stir himself for evening stables, his last official duty of the day. "Is John coming to see you this evening?" he asked.

"Yes, he said he would look in."

"That's nice." He smiled at her and she was momentarily bashful.

"And you?" Elisabeth asked. "Is this one of your nights for going to The Hall?"

"It is."

"Try not to be back so late. You work very hard, Giles, and you must have plenty of sleep."

"I'll do my best, dear, but you know what Jasper's like when he gets talking."

At six o'clock, Leander and William heard the distinctive rattle of the vicar's dogcart coming up the drive from the Devizes Lane.

"It's the Good Shepherd," William said, using the name bestowed on him by Doctor Palfreyman.

Originally, the epithet was no more than an attempt at witticism, but John Shepherd had proved himself worthy of it.

"He's coming to see Aunt Elisabeth," Leander announced.

"I think he wants to marry her."

"Of course he does!" Leander regarded it as self-evident. "And she thinks very highly of him. She's only waiting for us to get more grown-up."

William looked glum. "He's awfully old."

"Don't be so silly, William! He's thirty-five. That's only a year older than Father."

"How do you know?"

"I asked Father. Aunt Elisabeth is twenty-six."

"What will become of us?"

"We shall stay here and be happy. Aunt Elisabeth will only be going to the Rectory, and in any case, they won't marry until I'm old enough to look after you and Father. That will be in about two years, I think."

Giles, who liked John Shepherd very much, and had long accepted him as a future brother-in-law, sat with him and Elisabeth for nearly an hour. Because he kept himself fully abreast of social and scientific developments, John was a valuable window on the world for the busily preoccupied Giles. For months their talk had been of the increasing formation of trades unions, Giles agreeing with John that they were urgently needed as an instrument for improving the lot of working men and women, especially in the lamentable textile mills of the North. Now, unions were banding together into a Congress, the inaugural meeting taking place in Manchester even as they spoke.

"Will they achieve anything, John?" Giles asked.

"Probably not. This will be a talking-shop for the parade of high ideals. Hopefully they will establish the procedures."

"And do something next year?"

"Let us hope so."

Despite the fact that Giles eventually had to tear himself away from the conversation that ensued, Elisabeth noticed that he went off to The Hall with a hint of jauntiness in his stride. She smiled indulgently to herself, having come to terms with it. Giles was entitled to his pleasures and it all seemed harmless enough. For his part, Giles hurried on his way in the firm belief that his sister had absolutely no idea what he was about.

Lucy Miller had prepared an excellent supper of cold meats and salad which the four of them, herself, Jasper, Giles and Alexandra Fandine-Browne, set about with gusto. Immediately, they were bringing each other up to date with the latest gossip: who had a new hat; who had finally abandoned the crinoline; who had been taking umbrage at whom. For several minutes it was light-hearted until Alexandra introduced a more serious topic.

"I keep hearing strange stories about Ambrose Hastings," she said.

"Oh?" Giles showed only mild interest, Lucy was all agog.

"It seems that things are disappearing from his house."

"What sort of things?" Lucy asked.

"Very valuable items – gold, silver, paintings."

"I presume that Sir Ambrose has reported the matter to the proper authorities," Jasper said. He was proud of being a member of the County Watch Committee.

"No, he has not," Alexandra replied. "Priscilla is quite vexed about it."

"So I should think," Giles said. "What on earth can be happening?"

"He's hocking the stuff, of course. Really, Giles, you can be quite simple-minded sometimes." Alexandra's smile contradicted the apparent harshness of the words. "The wretched man is in financial trouble. You need to watch out for him."

"I don't believe it," Giles said. "Dash it, he came to The House today to settle his account – bang on the nail. He's never late."

"Just a moment." Jasper was looking anxious. "Haven't we heard stories about his land? Who was it, Lucy?"

"Bill Jarvis when he came past at Easter."

"Yes, that's right. Bill's an old friend," Jasper explained to Giles. "He's a forester up in Savernake and he always calls in when he goes down to Urchfont to see his mother. Last time he was here, he told us that most of the Hastings land was getting into a shocking state."

"In what way?" Giles asked.

"It's a peculiar sort of estate, as you probably know." Giles nodded. "Parcels of land here, there and everywhere. Bill said that the farms and smallholdings are getting nothing spent on them and the coverts have gone to wrack and ruin because all the gamekeepers have left. No wages, apparently."

"This is most odd," Giles said. "Whatever can be going on?"

"Scandal!" Lucy said gleefully.

Giles shook his head dismissively: he disapproved of rumour-mongering.

Prompted by his stuffy attitude, Alexandra and Lucy pulled faces at each other and began clearing the supper things away. While they were in the kitchen, Giles began to tell Jasper about his idea of turning the Stringfellow farm into a stud. Jasper, very much in favour of the idea, had several suggestions to make, carrying on even after Alexandra had come back into the dining-room to remain standing and looking impatient. Eventually, she was forced to interrupt.

"Come along, Giles," she said gently.

Jasper smiled apologetically. "Forgive me," he said. "I get carried away by your schemes to revitalise the estate."

"I know, and I appreciate it," Giles told him. "We shall return to the topic very soon."

In the hall, Alexandra took his arm and led him towards the stairs.

Half-way up, he stopped. Directly ahead of them, the evening sun was streaming through a window to make her hair look even more splendid. She smiled at his look of admiration.

The beauty and irony of it was that it had all come about as a result of her husband's stupidity and arrogance.

At the end of the 1865 racing season, Gilbert Fandine-Browne had, completely without warning, taken his horses away from Latimer's Barn. Giles's initial reaction was to suspect the influence of the Association, still reputed to be active despite a number of set-backs and increased probing from the Jockey Club. However, when it became known that Fandine-Browne was using a Newmarket stable, not Branksome Lodge, Giles forgot about Sixsmith and his cronies.

Fandine-Browne soon discovered that his horses did no better at Newmarket, rather the reverse in fact, and during 1866 Giles's reputation was greatly enhanced by prestigious victories at Royal Ascot, Goodwood and Newmarket.

Giles began receiving letters in January 1867. At first, Fandine-Browne was brusque and officious: Giles would be so kind as to make arrangements to receive the horses back into the yard. Then, after the position was made clear to him, Fandine-Browne resorted to half-hearted pleading, all to no avail.

It was at this point that Alexandra saw the opportunity. Laying claim to influence with Giles, she was given *carte blanche* by her despairing husband.

Alexandra contacted Jasper, knowing that he *did* carry influence with Giles. During the course of her first visit to The Hall, Alexandra discovered a staunchly sympathetic ally. Sensing Lucy Miller's great warmth and singular approach to life's problems, Alexandra took her aside and laid her cards on the table.

"To be perfectly honest with you, my dear, I don't give a tinker's cuss about my husband's horses. I know there is no room for them at Latimer's Barn, and that seems to be the end of the matter. What I *am* looking for is the chance to make Giles Flamsteed my lover. You see, Lucy, my husband is rarely at home these days, and when he is, he's *completely* unsatisfactory. Quite apart from my feelings in the matter, I fancy Giles would benefit, don't you?"

Lucy accepted this hypothesis zestfully, realising that Alexandra was a woman after her own heart. She tackled the matter in her customary style, head-on, telling Jasper the position straight out.

"What ought we to do?" he asked.

"They're short of peace and quiet," Lucy replied. "What you might call 'facilities'." She gave the word a fastidious quality and stared solemnly at Jasper.

He mulled it over. He had no difficulty in accepting the garnished version given to him by Lucy, that Giles was anxious to bed the admirable Mrs Fandine-Browne, and appreciated that both her house and Latimer's Barn were out of the question as a venue. Was this the point at which he could do Giles a favour that might be a small recompense for all the good he had done in Cannings Ambo? Jasper rather thought it was.

"There's the blue room," he said vaguely, trying to have Lucy believe that he was doing no more than thinking aloud.

"Lovely! That's *such* a nice room. They'll be very comfortable in there."

Jasper's face was a picture.

So was Giles's when Alexandra told him.

Their first encounter made it obvious to Alexandra that Giles had enjoyed no sort of life at all with Sarah. Saying nothing, she persevered, and it was not long before her expert tuition evoked the most satisfying responses.

Purely by chance, Alexandra's husband gained what he wanted. As Horatio and Sir Ambrose Hastings, coincidentally and for different reasons, reduced their numbers of horses, there was room for Fandine-Browne's animals. Two of them had already won races and everyone was pleased.

The blue room was at the back of The Hall with a view of Cannings Down and Latimer's Barn. When they went in, Giles noticed that Alexandra's bag was unpacked, with the clothes that she would wear to return to Marlborough tomorrow hanging in the wardrobe.

They undressed slowly and deliberately; there was a feeling of calm single-mindedness about their actions, and they never took their eyes off one another. When she was completely naked, Alexandra stood before him with pride, reading the expression in his eyes.

"Yes," he assured her. "You are magnificent."

"So are you," she replied. "It must be all that healthy fresh air and exercise." She picked up a bottle from a table at the side of the bed. "See, the new oil I ordered from Paris. It arrived yesterday."

Giles took the crimson bottle from her. It held about a third of a pint and had a florid, verbose label, not one word of which he could understand. When he pulled out the cork and sniffed at the contents, his eyebrows rose and he whistled.

"My God, Alex, this smells like a Mesopotamian whore-house!" he said.

"So I should hope! That cost over two pounds, I'll have you know."

"Let's find out whether it's worth it."

When Giles drew the bedclothes back, he found that she had placed two large towels on the undersheet in readiness. With a knowing look, Alexandra stretched herself out on them, flat on her back.

"Proceed," she instructed.

Giles sat on the edge of the bed and poured a quantity of the oil on to her stomach, watching in fascination as the viscous liquid formed a pear-shaped pool, then remained quite static, simply rising and falling slightly with her breathing. When he started to spread the oil, massaging it into her, the palms of his hands bore down with firm gentleness, his fingers splayed out, probing.

Gradually, responding to Alexandra's sighs and movements, Giles's ministrations became more wide-ranging. Long, sweeping strokes up her thighs with his hands meeting in the lush web of her pubic hair made her squirm and moan sensually. When necessary, he applied more oil, scarcely interrupting the fluid caresses that were having a mesmeric effect on both of them.

After five minutes, he moved to kneel astride her thighs, his fingers toying with her shoulders. She smiled up at him and waited. Very slowly his hands began to encompass the sumptuous breasts of which she was so proud. Through half-closed eyes, she saw that he was in control of himself: one of her cherished secrets was that her breasts sometimes drove cool, calm Giles Flamsteed mad with desire and the consequences were always most gratifying.

Alexandra waited a long time. He seemed so perfectly content with his stroking and kneading and she felt so blissful that it seemed a sacrilege to disturb him.

But her need for him finally became overpowering. Alexandra reached for the bottle and smeared her hands liberally with the oil, enjoying the expression on his face as she reached out to anoint his loins. She lingered over his penis, hard and powerful, until a look of fierce intensity tautened the lines on his face.

"Now, Giles, now! I want you," she said.

She took him into her with a silky suction, her arms and legs embracing him with such comprehensive strength that their bodies were clamped together, immobile. There was no urgency and barely any movement, but deep within her came a fluttering that took them off towards fulfilment. At the inevitability of his climax, Giles gave a series of stabbing lunges and was rewarded by the transfiguration of Alexandra's face as she joined him in paradise.

Minutes passed. They were still entwined.

When Alexandra finally opened her eyes, she asked, "Is that what you mean by 'together'?"

Giles grinned. "Not really," he said. "What I call 'together' isn't anywhere near as good as that."

Half an hour later, as the sun sank below the trees surrounding Powell's Pool, their passions caught fire again. This time he took her with a searing vigour that made her cry out in delight. Ascending the stairs with a pile of freshly laundered sheets for the linen-cupboard, Lucy heard the sound of their wild turmoil and smiled to herself. It was, she reflected, high time that Jasper exerted himself to that extent. She resolved that he would be inspired to do so within the hour.

Giles woke soon after dawn and reached for his watch. It was ten minutes past four and he slid out of bed to dress. Alexandra stirred briefly, sighed, and was fast asleep again as soon as he had kissed her.

Leaving The Hall without making a sound, Giles went through the grounds, crossed the Devizes Lane and Cannings Brook, approaching Latimer's Barn from the south-east towards the lawn.

With three weeks to go until mid-summer, the morning was vibrant with a joy of life that magnified his own sense of sparkling well-being. A sudden thought struck him. As usual when he came back this way from The Hall, he felt precisely like Lawrence Stanton so often looked as he went about his rounds. Did that mean that Daphne was as thrillingly uninhibited and passionate as Alexandra? As Giles secretly knew, she was capable of anything. He smiled at the thought and hurried on.

Nat Thomas, near the end of another night guarding the stable, was unsurprised to see him.

"Good morning, Nat," Giles said, returning his greeting. "Everything in order?"

"Yes, sir. A quiet night."

Giles looked across to The House and the peacefulness indicating that all within were still asleep.

"Come on, Nat," he said. "You've time for a cup of tea before you do the gallop."

CHAPTER 6

1875

'Let's give them some quality'

A small but vociferously self-important minority in Marlborough claimed that Latimer's Barn was a den of iniquity.

The story was started by Sir Ambrose Hastings's widow, shortly after his death in 1870. With a singleness of purpose that most found distasteful, Priscilla Hastings insisted that her husband had died in disgrace, and whenever anyone succeeded in losing sight of the fact, she reminded them.

Six months before Sir Ambrose died, information was laid before the Jockey Club concerning gambling debts that he refused to honour. When proven, such a charge was regarded as the most heinous crime an owner could commit, and Sir Ambrose was warned off Newmarket Heath, a punishment that barred him from attending all race meetings and ended his career as an owner.

Giles was furious with himself for ignoring the danger signals that had so frequently been brought to his attention by Alexandra, Jasper and others. Sir Ambrose, who had never gambled in his life, became an addict shortly after acquiring his own horses. Curiously, he always backed other people's animals, armed with what he foolishly imagined was the accurate information his privileged position gave him. Thus it was that whatever disasters befell him, he had to maintain his position at Latimer's Barn; so long as he had access to other owners, Sir Ambrose lived in hope of recouping his losses. When all his capital was used up, he stripped the house of treasures.

Hand-in-hand with the vilification of her husband, Priscilla Hastings put it about that Giles Flamsteed was the true guilty party: he was the hardened gambler who had encouraged Sir Ambrose. There were few who accepted the slur. As Alexandra pointed out, if Giles *did* place bets, he – and anyone who enjoyed his confidence – would be far more likely to win than lose. There was also the evidence of the Izzards, popular visitors to Marlborough, who were often asked how much gambling went on. Their answer was always the same: very, very little. The guv'nor disapproved of it strongly. If Caleb, Seamus or Dan Goakes wanted a small flutter when they went racing, they had to do it while Giles's back was turned.

Advised by Alexandra that the uproar was no more than a storm in a teacup, Giles was interested only in the man who had impeached Sir Ambrose. At that time, well over ninety per cent of betting on horse races took place on the course during the day of the race. Apart from a daily gathering in Hyde Park and the gambling saloons of Newmarket, off-course bookmaking was virtually non-existent, if only for the simple reason that lack of information on starting prices made it a cumbersome business.

Yet Sir Ambrose had fallen foul of a bookmaker in Bath, a man called Selwyn about whom next to nothing was known except that he never went near a racecourse. Giles was convinced that Selwyn, apparently devoid of forenames or initials, was the assumed name of a man connected with the Association.

Despite Priscilla Hastings's efforts, most of Marlborough's interest was centred on Sir Ambrose's heir, his son, Arnold.

The sixth baronet was twenty-five at his succession to the title and had spent most of the past seven years away from home. He reappeared with a wife of only a few weeks; she was attractive enough in a starchy, self-conscious way, and was rumoured to have brought enough money to the marriage to stave off the immediate problems.

Sir Arnold was not popular. Sourly arrogant, convinced that the world owed him respect and a living, he soon undermined what little sympathy his mother had drummed up. Most significantly, his sister Charlotte, four years younger than him, left home for London within weeks of his arrival in Marlborough. She was to be trained as a nurse at St Thomas' Hospital where the School of Nursing was under the personal supervision of the revered Florence Nightingale. Although everyone admired her purpose, it was assumed that Sir Arnold had much to do with her going.

Charlotte Hastings was accompanied by Victoria Fandine-Browne, Alexandra's daughter. Giles was surprised by the news.

"Victoria has had this in mind for some time," Alexandra told him. "She's a good girl and will do well at St Thomas's." As a rather wistful afterthought, she added, "I shall miss her, but it's probably best that she goes away."

It was one of those days when Giles was taking no notice of subtleties that did not concern the yard.

By the spring of 1875, Priscilla Hastings had only three supporters other than her son and daughter-in-law. They were Mrs Dallow, a retired solicitor called Andrews, and Elias Cooper, a Nonconformist minister with a vitriolic outlook on life and a raving obsession with fornication, hell-fire and damnation.

As far as the people of Marlborough were concerned, these three were entitled to their opinions, but should not expect anyone else to take them seriously. Latimer's Barn was harmless: it generated business. When they visited the town, the staff were well behaved and the stables had brought distinction to the area. Many expected that great fame was waiting round the corner after the building of the new yard the previous autumn. Live and let live was a good principle.

But not for Emily Dallow.

Samuel Dallow, her husband of twenty years, was rarely easy in his mind about his decision to marry her. For some years he had been of the opinion that he could have made the transition from street-trader in Swindon to being Marlborough's grocer without her two hundred pounds and so-called help. At forty-six, he was still personable enough to cut a dash with the lissome young women who served in the shop, whereas Emily, puffed up on chocolates and self-righteousness, had become a fat, boring tyrant.

Samuel never imagined that things could be worse, that what his wife called 'the expedition' to Cannings Ambo would lead to ruin.

He had no idea why they were going. The previous morning, something had thrown Emily Dallow into a fury; she had stormed out of the shop to see Mr Andrews, and had not come back for two hours. Still quivering with rage when she returned, she remained mercifully silent.

Andrews collected her in his carriage at half past eight in the morning, and off they went to give Giles Flamsteed a piece of their minds. All that Samuel had gleaned was that they were not taking Elias Cooper with them; he had refused to set foot anywhere near the abode of Satan.

Knowing nothing about stable routine, the expedition reached Latimer's Barn at ten past nine, quite the wrong time to find Giles. Bertha Bradley and Lizzie O'Malley were the sole occupants of The House and gave the two busybodies short shrift. Mr Flamsteed was in the yard; no, it was not possible to disturb him.

"You could try looking for him," Lizzie suggested. "But don't expect him to be pleased to see you. This is his busiest time."

The building programme of the previous autumn had changed the appearance of Latimer's Barn quite dramatically. The most striking feature was the new forty-box yard directly to the east of the lawn. Working to a design prepared by Giles himself, Bill and Jim Irons had employed thirty men in the construction of a handsome brick and slate building which was one hundred and fifty feet square. Running parallel with the coach-house was a hostel to provide luxurious quarters for the twenty-three new lads that Giles had taken on when the yard was filled with horses within days of its completion, to give the stable a total capacity of fifty animals.

Unsure of their ground, Mrs Dallow and Mr Andrews made their way to the arched entrance of the new yard which faced the lawn. Passing inside, they found themselves in a world of esoteric bustle; the second lot of twenty-five horses was being prepared to go out on to the gallop. Large though the quadrangle was, it seemed packed with activity as horses were brought out of their boxes for saddling.

Recognising Caleb Jackson who was supervising the operation, Andrews scuttled up to him and said, "We are looking for Mr Flamsteed, my good fellow."

Caleb favoured him with an expressionless stare, then eyed Mrs Dallow, waddling to catch up.

"Over there," Caleb said, pointing to one of the boxes.

All that Andrews could see through the open top half of the door was the rump of a horse, but Giles suddenly appeared, straightening up from the crouching position in which he had been examining a suspect fetlock.

"Mr Andrews!" Giles was not pleased. "And Mrs Dallow. What are you doing here?"

"We have come on a mission of the utmost gravity and importance," Andrews announced, oblivious to the frigidity of the welcome.

"Indeed?" Giles leaned on the lower half of the door, making no attempt to move.

"Quite so." Andrews bent forward to become offensively confidential. "Do you suppose that we could go indoors, Flamsteed? Far better to discuss such matters in private." He looked round the yard with unconcealed distaste.

"No, Mr Andrews, we could not!" Giles replied curtly. "I have a hundred thousand guineas-worth of horseflesh waiting for me. State your business."

Andrews exchanged a look of unease with Mrs Dallow: perhaps this was not going to be so easy after all.

87

"This is an errand dictated by duty," Andrews began sanctimoniously. "We are here as representatives of the good people of Marlborough." Giles stared at him, his face immobile. "We have a problem, a difficulty – what I see as a dilemma. To put none too fine a point on it, Flamsteed, your daughter."

"My daughter? You mean Leander?"

"Precisely. Quite so."

"Why do you consider my daughter to be a *dilemma*?" Giles sounded perfectly calm. Andrews became confident.

"We are, of course, sensible of your most awkward circumstances. Raising children without a wife and mother is fraught with danger."

"What is your point, Mr Andrews?"

"The point is the unladylike behaviour of your daughter."

"Really?" Giles seemed astounded. "You can cite examples?"

"Indeed I can. Your daughter comes into Marlborough once or twice a week for provisions. She frequently creates a disturbance. Only yesterday, she was most outspoken to a group of lads who had done no more than call out a few pleasantries to her."

"Do we know who these young men were?" Giles asked.

"The Birketts, I believe."

"Ah, I see." Giles's manner changed with such sudden ferocity that Andrews took a step backwards. "The Birketts are a gang of foul-mouthed ruffians, Mr Andrews, and well you know it. The probability is that what you call 'pleasantries' were crude abuse and that my daughter was merely standing up for herself."

"There may be something in what you say," Andrews conceded, earning a critical glance from Mrs Dallow. "I think the problem stems from the fact that your daughter persists in coming into the town on her own. This is a very provocative act, you know. The lads are bound to be incited."

"Are you suggesting that a young woman may not go alone into this town, in broad daylight, without constituting a provocation? Can this be true? Of the town of which you claim to be so proud?"

Mrs Dallow felt that it was time to launch an attack from a new angle. "We also have to consider the question of those quite indecent breeches she wears."

"Who are 'we'?" Giles asked, quiet again.

"Mr Andrews and myself."

"Madam, it is none of your business what my daughter wears!"

"It is when it creates a sensation in the town."

"Then I suggest you put the town to rights. And there is one other thing you can do."

"What is that?" Andrews asked.

"In future, you will keep your interfering, trouble-stirring noses off my property!"

"I must say, Flamsteed, you are behaving abominably," Andrews complained waspishly. "We came here with the best of intentions."

"Sir, what you parade as your best intentions are a load of meddlesome, hypocritical twaddle. Now get off my land before I set the dogs on you."

Their retreat was the more ignominious for the twenty-odd pairs of eyes that watched them go: all the lads had stopped work to listen, and their hostile stares crushed even Andrews's monumental arrogance.

After they had disappeared through the arch, there was a moment's silence, then Giles, apparently addressing the ground at his feet, said, "Really! The trouble you get me into." But the warmth of love was in his voice.

Leander came up like a jack-in-the-box. She, too, had been inspecting the colt's fetlock, but had remained crouched behind the door, unseen, but privy to all that was said.

She was almost fifteen and the bud of burgeoning womanhood was about to burst. It was, without a shadow of doubt, to be a most glorious flowering. Although her blue eyes and blonde hair were breathtaking enough, it was the broad forehead and fine structure of cheeks and jaw that set the seal on what was already an outstandingly beautiful face. And there was one other thing: she smiled with her eyes. She did so now, and Giles found himself looking into azure pools that danced and shimmered with mischief.

"Did you really tell those Birkett louts off?" he asked.

"Yes, I did. They won't forget it!" she replied and her chin tilted up, a characteristic gesture of bold self-assurance.

"Well done!" He kissed her.

"Father?"

"Yes, darling?"

"We haven't got any dogs."

"What?" Giles looked blank.

"You said you'd set the dogs on them. We haven't got any."

Giles grinned. "No more we have," he chuckled. Suddenly aware of the continuing inactivity in the yard, he roared, "Don't stand there like a dumb show. Get those horses out!"

William missed all the fun with Andrews and Mrs Dallow. He and his constant companion Jim Goakes, the son to whom Dan's wife, Jennie, had given birth shortly after their arrival in Cannings Ambo, spent the day at The George.

Jim was in the same boat as William. At fifteen, he was no longer terrified of horses, but no one expected him to be able to make a living with them. Their shared phobia had drawn them together in Elisabeth's schoolroom and they had gone on to discover that they had far more useful and constructive things in common. Encouraged by Horatio and using magnificent tool-sets provided by him, they had turned themselves into expert carpenters. That day, their job was to make a set of kitchen cupboards for Vicky Foxton.

William heard all about the morning's high jinks when he came home to have tea with Leander in their own private sitting-room. This jealously guarded symbol of their semi-adult status had been Elisabeth's bedroom until she married John Shepherd in 1872.

"That Mrs Dallow is a very bad lot," William said when Leander finished her tale. "I think she may try and do us harm."

Leander considered the point briefly. "She may try."

"Aren't you worried?"

"Not in the least."

"She's a powerful person, Lea."

"She *imagines* she is. She has a vile tongue, that's all. Mrs Fandine-Browne will take care of that."

"Oh." William was aware that the Fandine-Browne influence was now paramount in Marlborough. "Why will she?"

"Mrs Fandine-Browne thinks highly of Father."

"Really? I didn't know."

"She does. Believe me."

And with that, William knew he had to be content.

Mrs Dallow might not have ruined her husband's business if she had kept her mouth shut about the abortive expedition to Latimer's Barn. Silence, however, was the last thing that occurred to her.

Priscilla Hastings, one of the first into the shop the following morning, received an outraged account of what had transpired. Still seething with anger, Mrs Dallow fulminated at great length, embellishing the story so as to make Giles appear an unmitigated ogre. During her performance she was unconcerned about the group of customers gathering, impatient to be served. Eventually, one of them interrupted the tirade.

"Mrs Dallow, am I to understand that you and that dreadful man Andrews went to Mr Flamsteed's stable and had the gall to tell him how to manage his daughter?"

An ominous silence fell over the shop. The speaker was Mrs Spooner, wife of the bank manager. Her eyes were inimical at the best of times: now, they were like gimlets.

"Yes, Mrs Spooner, we did!" Emily Dallow declared proudly.

"How utterly stupid of you!" Mrs Spooner was contemptuous rather than annoyed.

"It's high time someone took a stand against Flamsteed," Priscilla Hastings said. "He is an unprincipled crook. He ruined my late husband. Everyone knows that."

Mrs Spooner surveyed her with icy disdain. "And who, pray, is doing the ruining now?" she asked. "What has become of the small fortune your son received for enabling that idiotic wife of his to call herself a lady?"

The observation was quite improper, based as it was on her husband's conjugal gossip about the Hastings finances. It was also entirely accurate. Having delivered the blow, Mrs Spooner swung round and stalked from the Dallow emporium.

When Guy Mallender and his pretty wife Hester arrived in Marlborough the previous year and opened a grocery shop, even their few well-wishers had prophesied failure and Guy Mallender now agreed with them. The fact that his premises were directly opposite the Dallows' had proved to be a disadvantage, and a demoralising one at that. The only pleasure shared by Samuel and Emily was the daily gloat at their would-be opponent's discomfort as he struggled to exist on a handful of customers.

Guy Mallender saw Mrs Spooner leave Dallow's. As usual, he was at his counter looking cheerful, trying not to worry about Hester and the baby son they now had to support.

Mrs Spooner was across the High Street and into his shop before he knew it. She slapped a list on the counter and was looking round the shelves.

"Pay attention, Mr Mallender," she said. "In order to keep my custom you will have to improve your stock. Should you require it, I am sure my husband will be pleased to offer the assistance of a loan."

Numbed, Guy realised that Mrs Spooner was smiling at him and that her cheeks were slightly dimpled. Rushing to offer her a chair, he saw that two more ladies had left Dallow's and were heading towards his door with great determination.

Until Alexandra arrived near the end of a frighteningly successful day, Guy Mallender remained ignorant of the reason for the spectacular shift in his fortunes.

"You see, Mr Mallender, the real heart of the matter is Leander Flamsteed," Alexandra said when she had finished her explanation.

"Between you and me, Mrs Fandine-Browne, I think she's a wonderful young woman," Guy said fervently.

"Indeed, and most of the town agrees with you. They may not

want to admit it because she is *rather* unconventional, but secretly they admire her, and they won't have her attacked, least of all by that dreadful woman over the road. Now, Mr Mallender, I take it that you can deliver?"

Watching with ferret-faced anxiety from his upstairs parlour, Samuel Dallow already suspected that the days of gloating were over.

Giles was told all about the great grocery battle by Horatio.

Two years ago, on his sixty-third birthday, Horatio had surprised everyone by retiring from the day-to-day running of Beresford Engineering. He was, he said, getting under Peveril's feet and the time had come for him to return to his childhood home to concentrate on enjoying himself. Once a month he spent a few days in Birmingham, but the major purpose of these visits was to keep in touch with old cronies, loyal friends of thirty or more years. Peveril got advice if he asked for it, otherwise he was left to do things his own way. For the greater part of his time, Horatio lived in a self-contained suite of rooms at The Hall and involved himself in everything that happened in the village.

Every Sunday morning at eight o'clock, Giles and Horatio set off in a carriage to visit the stud at Cannings St John. After a pretence at hard bargaining, the Stringfellow brothers had been glad to be rid of the farm and have money in their pockets. They still lived in the remains of the old farmhouse. There were only two of them now, Jack's body having been brought back from Southampton on the Latimer's Barn feed cart the previous autumn. A confounded nuisance to the very end, he had suffered a heart attack while attempting the impossible in a whore's bed.

As they bowled along the Devizes Lane, Horatio told Giles about the boycott of the Dallows, adding additional gossip that he had gleaned from a visit to Marlborough.

"The talk is that Arnold Hastings has received a very stiff letter from Spooner."

"Why?" Giles asked.

"Spooner's threatening to call in loans if Hastings doesn't put his house in order."

"Do you suppose Mrs Spooner has had anything to do with that?"

"Of course! Just get yourself ready."

"What for?" Giles was puzzled.

"To be blamed. The Hastings clan are going to say that everything is your fault now."

"I shall look forward to it," Giles laughed.

The stud, covering a hundred acres, had provided yet more work for Bill and Jim Irons, who freely admitted that their company was growing in direct proportion to the requirements of Latimer's Barn and Cannings Ambo. Separate boxes for stallions, mares and foaling had been constructed, along with two houses, one for the manager, one for the groom. As Giles pulled the carriage up in the courtyard that was nicely framed by the houses and stallion boxes, Seamus O'Malley came bustling out to meet them.

"Now then, Seamus," Horatio called. "How is everything?"

"Fine, sor, fine. How are yourselves, gentlemen?"

"Very fit, Seamus," Giles replied.

When all the work to prepare the stud was finished, Giles faced up to the problem of finding the right man to run it. Although only two miles from Latimer's Barn, the isolation of the stud put it in another world, and Giles saw at once that a man who was less than totally competent and trustworthy would turn the place into a shambles or thieves' kitchen within weeks. It was two days before Giles spotted the ideal solution, right under his nose. Seamus was approaching fifty and the aches from his deformed leg were giving him increasing trouble in the arduous environment of a racing stable.

It was Lizzie who saw the sense of the idea and persuaded Seamus that, far from being put out to grass, he was being given great responsibility. From the very beginning, two years ago, Seamus had loved the job and performed it to everyone's satisfaction. Paul Izzard, having married a girl called Polly, a maid from the Fandine-Browne household, volunteered to be the groom, and his partnership with Seamus was a happy one.

A fixed routine governed Sunday mornings at the stud. First, Giles and Horatio went to look at the two stallions, The Beresford Lathe and New Invention, now aged eighteen and ten respectively. After that, they walked to the far side of the stud to make a fuss of the six mares that Horatio kept for breeding. Like the stallions, the mares had all spent two or three years at Latimer's Barn and always expressed great pleasure when Giles came to see them.

Then it was breakfast in the kitchen of Seamus's house. Everyone joined in the meal, Paul and Polly, Lizzie, and her two daughters, Lizzie and Brigid. Patrick, Seamus's twelve-year-old son, was the only absentee: since the opening of the new yard, he was one of the Latimer's Barn lads.

It was a family occasion, a time when Giles passed on information about the stable and heard what had been happening at the stud. This week, there were four winners to talk about while Seamus waited quietly to come out with the pearl of the news.

"I believe we've had a visit from the gentleman you've been expecting," he told Giles. "Friday it was."

"What was he calling himself?" Giles asked.

"Mr Clare, sir."

Giles and Horatio chuckled.

"What did he look like?" Giles wanted to know. "Tall, thin, dark hair, very pale?"

"No, sir. Quite a portly gentleman with a ruddy face."

"Ah! Him again." Giles nodded. "Let me explain. Our friends in the Association are keeping a close watch on us. I'm not absolutely sure, but they seem to have picked up a couple of new members. For some peculiar reason, they are using the names of colleges at Cambridge University. Mr Downing and Mr Emmanuel have been following us round at Newmarket for the last two years, now Mr Clare turns up here." As a grim afterthought, Giles added, "And there is Mr Selwyn, the bookmaker, of course. Go on, Seamus."

"This Mr Clare came up from Devizes way with a very nice carriage. His driver seemed a decent enough chap."

"He was very hungry, though," said Lizzie, who had given the man something to eat and pumped him mercilessly.

"He said he had a mare he was thinking of sending to New Invention next season," Seamus went on. "Wanted to know if he could have a look at him to see if he was sound."

"Satisfied, was he?"

"Oh yes, sir. Then Paul came out with what you told him to say."

"Go on, Paul," Giles prompted.

"I made out I was speaking out of turn, letting the cat out of the bag. I said we knew his first two crops hadn't been up to much, but things were going to change this year. And he said: 'I hear that Mr Flamsteed has a very good one down the road in his yard.'"

"Marvellous!" Giles slapped his thigh and smiled broadly.

For months, the whisper had been going round that Latimer's Barn had a son of New Invention who would sweep all before him. Spending several days in Bath's best hotel, Doctor Palfreyman had blundered affably round clubs and taverns singing the praises of the wonder horse. "A Derby winner from the instant his dam dropped him!" he would declare. At the same time, one of Horatio's engineering friends from Bristol, a man known to have helped Brunel correct the design of the Clifton suspension bridge, had been trying to track down the elusive Selwyn with a view to placing a one-hundred-pound bet on the animal whenever it first ran. The talk had obviously spread and gained momentum.

"So, I agreed with him," Paul went on. "He asked me what it was called, and I told him it hadn't got a name yet. 'That's very unusual for Mr Flamsteed,' he says, and I agreed with him. 'I've heard that Mr Flamsteed and Mr Beresford have had a very sharp dispute over what to call him,' says I. 'As things stand he may have to go out first time without a name.'"

"What did he say to that?" Giles asked eagerly.

"I think he swallowed it, sir," Paul replied. "I said the horse hadn't been too good – trouble with his forelegs – but you were hoping to race him soon and he was doing a stiff piece of work next Tuesday."

"And?" Giles was on the edge of his chair.

"He asked what time it would be, and I said about eleven, after the second lot. Then he said: 'How might I recognise the animal?' Very casual he was! I said it was easy, he's a great strapping bay without a mark on him and, in any case, Miss Leander will be riding him."

Giles had one last question. "Did this Mr Clare recognise you, Paul?"

"Yes, he did. He thought I was Peter." Although they were now thirty, the resemblance between Paul and his increasingly famous jockey brother remained uncanny. "I told him who I was and that I worked for Mr Beresford now, sir, not you. I let him think there'd been trouble."

It was widely believed that the stud belonged wholly to Horatio; in fact, he and Giles owned it jointly.

"I told the driver that we were very happy to be working for Mr Beresford instead of you, sir," Lizzie said.

"Well done, Lizzie!" Giles thought for a few moments. "I think we'll have a go at it," he said to Horatio.

"I don't see why not," Horatio said. "You'll never get a better chance and we've nothing to lose."

They talked about it as Giles drove them back to Cannings Ambo in time for Horatio to attend John Shepherd's morning service at the church of St Luke and St John.

"So it's settled," Horatio said as he got down opposite Church Green. "You'll work the lad on Tuesday?"

"Yes. I think you'd better come and watch."

"Oh, I will, never fear." Horatio winked.

'The lad' was one of a pair of two-year-old colts by New Invention being trained at Latimer's Barn. He belonged to Giles, Horatio having made a present of him as a token of his gratitude for the new life Giles was breathing into the estate.

"It's about time you had a horse of your own," Horatio said. "And that one might more than pay for his keep."

As the colt grew and was schooled, the highest hopes took shape around him. Big, strong and beautifully athletic, he had an equable temperament, and, Leander asserted, immense reserves of courage. From the moment he came into the yard as a yearling, he was hers; she looked after him and always rode him out to work.

"He's the best horse we've ever had," she told Giles and he saw no reason to disagree with her.

The other New Invention colt was a very different kettle of fish. Amiable to the point of near-idiocy, he favoured the quiet life. He never actually refused to work because he knew it was expected of him in return for his comfortable quarters and high-quality food, but he did no more than was necessary to avoid disgrace.

"I shall be very surprised if he enhances your reputation as an owner," Giles told Horatio after they had watched his early efforts on the gallop.

"He's a good-looking fellow, though, isn't he?" Horatio said fondly.

He was indeed.

In fact, he looked very like his infinitely more talented and determined contemporary. They both had New Invention's head and his characteristic way of carrying it, and they both had the massive chest development of their maternal grandsire. Their dams, two mares from whom Horatio had been breeding for five years, were daughters of an Ascot Gold Cup winner.

To a casual observer, especially at a distance, the only difference between the two bay colts was the white star on the forehead of the one that belonged to Giles.

Neither of them yet had a registered name and no one outside Latimer's Barn realised that there were two New Invention colts in training there. Moreover, Mr Clare had been so taken with all the stories, that he had not bothered to ask Paul Izzard the name of the wonder colt's dam.

The coach came from the direction of Devizes and halted on the lane about half a mile from Cannings Ambo. There were three men in it. Giles was amused to see that they and the driver went through an exaggerated pantomime of pretending that there was something wrong with a wheel.

He made them wait.

The second lot were clear of the gallop at ten minutes to eleven, but the spies in the lane had to occupy thirty minutes with their

96

concern over the supposedly damaged wheel before they had anything other than the vast, thousand-acre emptiness of Cannings Down to watch.

When it finally happened, it was all very businesslike. Four horses trotted out of the yard and moved briskly towards the gallops. Peter Izzard led them on Abbots Bromley, an easily recognised four-year-old of proven ability: last year he had finished second in the Two Thousand Guineas and gone on to win good races at Goodwood and York. A couple of useful-looking three-year-olds followed. They were ridden by Dermot O'Grady and Connor Daly, two very experienced lads who were part of the new contingent at Latimer's Barn. Dermot was known as 'Carrot' and the brightly coloured hair that inspired the nickname flared in a shaft of sunlight that broke through an overcast sky.

Last came Leander on a bay colt, obviously on his toes and impatient to be at it.

Beyond the circle on which the horses cantered to warm up, a measured six furlongs had been laid out along the gallop; white marker posts were fixed at furlong intervals. Giles and Horatio bumped along a strip adjacent to the gallop in an old phaeton, a relic of Lord Francis Rashleigh's era. When they reached the last marker, Giles stood up to wave his hat.

Abbots Bromley and the three-year-olds set off at a furious pace. The bay seemed to have been left standing, unsure of what he was supposed to be doing. Leander had him on a tight rein which she maintained for almost four furlongs. Keeping an eye on the coach, Giles saw that one man was using glasses while another stared at an object in his hand.

"Stop-watch!" Horatio growled.

It was over the moment Leander gave the bay colt his head. Inside three strides he produced an utterly annihilating turn of speed. From five lengths in arrears he took the lead, stretching it to seven or eight lengths before Leander began pulling him up, long before they reached the final marker.

"She didn't touch him!" Horatio enthused.

"She isn't even carrying a whip," Giles pointed out. "She never does on this one. Now it's our turn to do a bit of acting."

As the phaeton followed the horses back to the yard, Mr Horatio Beresford appeared to be having a most heated quarrel with his trainer. The men on the Devizes Lane, avoiding the arousal of suspicion by moving off too quickly, took it all in.

When Giles hurried into the concealed safety of the yard, Leander was attending to the bay colt. Standing on a box, she was using soap and water to remove the patch of boot polish from his forehead. The white star was emerging once more.

"What did you think?" she asked.

"Very good," Giles replied. "I think you're right about him."

"I know I am, Father! Did you see the way he went on once he hit the front? That's the sign of a *really* good horse."

Much as he loathed them, Giles left the marker posts in place lest the spies returned and found significance in their removal. Of one thing he was certain: it was the first time he had ever staged a race on the gallop and it would be the last.

The posts stayed there until winter when Nat Thomas was told to take them to his hut for firewood.

Giles and Horatio travelled to Bath the day before the race to stay with Digby Protheroe, the son of the old colonel, who had taken over where his father left off. One of the reasons for the offer of hospitality at his house in Claverton was that he was trying to persuade Horatio to become a steward, either at Bath or Salisbury, preferably both.

"Fact is, Beresford, we need men like you, chaps with backbone and the time to do a decent job. We're smoking the scoundrels out, but there's a devil of a long way to go."

Giles smiled at how very like his father Digby Protheroe had made himself sound.

Horatio was flattered, and was only holding out so as not to appear indecently eager to accept an honour for which many men would have sold their families.

"Talking of scoundrels, Digby, we may have something of interest tomorrow," Giles said.

"Oh? What's going on, eh?" Digby Protheroe leaned forward to peer at him with fierce curiosity, just like his father used to.

"I have a feeling that there is going to be some very heavy betting on my horse," Giles told him. "The Association may have decided that he cannot be beaten."

"That lot!" Digby Protheroe came close to spitting. "Mind you, Giles, there's been a hell of a lot of talk about this animal. At least three men to my certain knowledge have been going round trying to back him to win a fortune – a *very* large fortune I might say."

"Really?" Giles seemed mildly surprised. "You know, I wonder if there hasn't been some confusion here. Between ourselves, Digby, we do have a very fine New Invention two-year-old who will probably turn out well, but that isn't the fellow we're running tomorrow. To be honest with you, this one's a bit of an idiot. We're only trying him out to see if there's any hope of teaching him the rudiments."

The bookmakers set up their pitches at noon, two hours before racing began, and the business for the Batheaston Maiden Stakes for two-year-olds, third on the card at three o'clock, began at once. Immediately, at least ten men were flitting about with bets of fifty and one hundred pounds on the horse now registered under the name of Alma Works.

"Bloody funny name for a horse," someone grumbled.

"It's what Beresford's factory in Birmingham is called," a well-informed punter said.

"No wonder Flamsteed didn't like it."

"Didn't he?"

"Apparently not. He and Beresford had a terrible row about it."

Eventually, however, people accepted that after The Beresford Lathe and New Invention, Alma Works made sense.

The race itself was unimportant compared to what happened afterwards. It was reported at length in *The Times* the following day.

The mere idea that an unknown horse, running at a fairly obscure racecourse, should be backed to lose over twelve thousand pounds was noteworthy enough in itself. That the animal should then prove totally disinterested in justifying this massive confidence was tragic for its supporters, but not particularly exceptional.

What *was* sensational was the riot that flared up after the race to produce conditions in which bookmakers required a police escort and two men were stabbed to death. The editor of a Bath weekly journal, who supplemented his income by working as a stringer for the national press, sent a full account by electric telegraph to London and John Delane of *The Times* gave the story twenty-six column-inches.

In the midst of the uproar, Giles was calmly unscathed, widely recognised as blameless. During the hysterical making of the book on the race, while the odds about Alma Works were plunging from twenty-five to one to even money and less, a number of people had distinctly heard him say that the frenzy was ill-advised, that Alma Works was on trial and was unlikely to do well.

Digby Protheroe, however, was sniffing at something. "I'm damned if I know how you've done it, Giles, but you've given the Association a fearful drubbing," he said. "At least ten thousand pounds of all that betting was their money. And they've started sticking knives in each other, damn it. The deuced thing is, you don't seem to have broken any rules."

"I haven't," Giles said, at his most bland. "I promise you that I haven't, Digby."

Five minutes later, while trying to find Caleb and Dan Goakes,

Giles unexpectedly came face to face with Sixsmith. He looked dreadful. The poorer by four thousand pounds, he had seen one of his confederates stabbed to death and another badly wounded by the very men they had hired to place the bets. Desperate to save his own skin and acutely conscious that the police investigation of the riot would mean the end of the Association, he was still trying to organise the waylaying and robbery of several bookmakers.

"Flamsteed!" he snarled. "Tell me, how did you do it? That horse wasn't held up, was it? It really is useless."

"What on earth are you talking about?" Giles asked.

"That won't wash with me, Flamsteed. I'll find out, and while I'm doing it, I've something for you to be thinking about."

"And what might that be?" Giles asked courteously.

Two days later, Giles completed the documents to register the name of his own New Invention colt, the one with the white star. He chose Bellerophon, the son of the King of Corinth who slew the monster Chimaera with the aid of the winged horse, Pegasus.

Then, he set off to Oak Cottage to talk to Daphne. He found her picking flowers in the garden. As he had hoped, she was alone.

"There's something I think you ought to know," he said quietly, taking care to be gentle.

"Oh!" She was tense, much of her colour and natural gaiety gone.

"Understand that I am only telling you this because I imagine you must have been very worried." He paused to gather his thoughts. "I ran into a man called Sixsmith at Bath races the other day."

Daphne's hands trembled as she clutched the flowers.

"Purely out of spite, he told me the most amazing story about you," Giles went on. "It was how you organised the attack on the stable back in 'sixty-one." Daphne was ashen, completely at a loss to understand Giles's broad grin. "The evil swine was quite taken aback when I told him that I'd known ever since you and Lawrence came to live here."

Daphne gaped at him. "You knew?" Her voice was barely audible.

"Yes."

"How?"

"Your mare."

"Lady?" The memory of her wise and gallant companion who had died two years ago was starting to fade.

"Yes. I never forget a horse, Daphne, especially one that big that I'd seen ridden across my lawn. All I had to do was to find out how long you had owned the animal."

"And you didn't expose me?"

"Why on earth should I? We had some inquiries carried out."

"We?"

"Horatio and me. Horatio is very good at finding out things. Once I knew the sort of existence you'd had, I could see how you were trying to rebuild your life – and making a damned good job of it. In any case, if I'd had you arrested, I would almost certainly have lost a good doctor!" They both smiled. "Now look here, Daphne, remember what I said: I'm only telling you this because of Sixsmith. He made me realise how worried you must have been."

"Thank you, Giles. That's very good of you." Her composure was returning rapidly.

"Now you can tell me something I've often wondered about. Did you get hit when old Eli Munge and the Stringfellows let those terrible fowling pieces off?"

She smiled. "Yes, my shoulder." Her hand went up to it involuntarily. "As a matter of fact, that's what brought Lawrence and me together."

"There! Look at the good that came out of it." He took her arm. "Let's go inside for a cup of tea and I'll tell you of the *immense* misfortune that has befallen Mr Sixsmith and his colleagues."

Bellerophon made his debut at Ascot, winning the most valued two-year-old race of the great event by six lengths.

This success, coupled with the excitement of her first visit to the Royal meeting, caused Leander to make Giles do something about what William called 'the big book', left lying in a corner of the library since Giles had yielded to the curious compulsion to buy it from a stationer in Salisbury about eighteen months ago.

It was a huge commonplace book, made up of half a ream of best quality Elephant-sized paper folded and bound to form 960 numbered pages measuring twenty-three by fourteen inches. With its marbled covers and leather spine, it weighed over ten pounds. Giles intended that it should be used to compile a record of life at Cannings Ambo, but had never found the time to start the work.

Using gentle but persistent nagging, Leander made Giles gather together all the jottings and diary notes that he had made since 1859, and they sat down with William to assemble a chronological list of events. That occupied them for several evenings, and Giles had to be reminded of things he had forgotten, such as the laying out of the orchard.

While the new yard had been under construction, it was William who had conceived the idea of the orchard, which now occupied a two-acre rectangle to the immediate west of The House and lawn. Once the ground had been prepared, William and Jim Goakes had assisted Alfred Wesley in the planting and staking of nearly three hundred apple and pear trees.

Once the draft of important events had been agreed, Leander sat beside Giles as he began copying it into the great tome, painstakingly employing his very best handwriting.

"This needs a name," she said, tapping the book.

"You're right." Giles thought for a moment or two. "What is it that William calls it?"

"The Big Book."

"Well, that seems about right, don't you think?"

Leander nodded her approval, then smiled. "With capital letters, *of course!*"

"Naturally!" Giles laughed at her affectionate fun-poking; his predilection for capital letters, first evidenced in 'The House', was now a well-established source of humorous comment.

"Make sure you write everything down about Bellerophon," Leander instructed.

"I thought we'd agreed only to put the important horses in here," Giles protested.

"So we did, and Bellerophon *is* important. Very important indeed."

Giles did as he was told.

Seven years ago, it had been said that Leander believed New Invention was the best horse ever to set foot on earth. She still retained a special place in her heart for him, and there was always an element of joyous reunion in her visits to see him at the stud, but her feelings for his son eclipsed all that had gone before.

And it was mutual.

"Look at that!" Giles said to Caleb one morning as they watched the second lot come back to the yard after work. At the back of the string Leander had dismounted from Bellerophon to give him an easy walk and was not even bothering to lead him: he followed her like a pet dog, his muzzle never far from her shoulder.

Giles smiled, seeing that Caleb was both impressed and disgusted. "I suppose they know what they're doing," Caleb grumbled.

'They' were Leander, Conn Daly and Carrot O'Grady, who seemed to have formed a close-knit fellowship with the express purpose of training Bellerophon, sometimes implying that, for them, the rest of Latimer's Barn hardly existed. Conn and Carrot, both aged about twenty-five and badly hard-bitten by experiences before they joined Giles, adored Leander; neither would have turned a hair at the need to die for her.

Their methods, often unconventional, soon yielded further fruit when Bellerophon followed his Royal Ascot victory with an even more convincing performance at Goodwood. After that he went to York and won the Gimcrack Stakes. Leander's concern then became finding one more race in which her pride and joy might round off his two-year-old campaign.

"I don't think there's one good enough," she told Giles. "It's no good running him against mediocrities."

While considering this and all the other details of managing a racing stable, Giles kept a careful watch on events in Marlborough, aided by reports from Jasper and Alexandra.

At the Dallow shop, business was bad and getting worse. After the initial surge of customers to Guy Mallender, it seemed that enough might remain loyal to the Dallows to enable them to carry on. Both Emily Dallow and Alexandra had other ideas, however.

Emily Dallow's hatred of Giles and everything connected with Latimer's Barn grew by the day, and it became impossible to buy a pound of sugar from her without first listening to a stream of vituperation. The atmosphere in the shop was made infinitely worse by Priscilla Hastings, who, apparently no longer at ease in the house that now belonged to her son, spent most days with Mrs Dallow, stoking up her invective.

The widely publicised betting fiasco involving Alma Works was taken by Priscilla Hastings to be final damning proof of what she had been saying for years: Giles Flamsteed's encouragement to place bets produced ruinous consequences. She preached this illogical creed with monumental disregard for the results of the Jockey Club investigation into the Batheaston Stakes affair which had exonerated Giles from any suggestion of blame.

At the same time, Alexandra was tireless in her praise of the service provided by Guy Mallender. "The quality of *all* his goods is absolutely first-class," she told waverers. "And I think you will find that his prices are a little lower than *elsewhere*."

By the middle of August, Samuel Dallow was at the bank, asking for a loan. Much of his stock, left on the shelves for a long time, was bad or suspect: he needed money to re-stock so that he could launch a counter-offensive. Egbert Spooner, mindful of his dear wife and her likely reaction if he relented for an instant, turned him down with a finality that left no room for future hope.

"And I understand that Spooner is getting annoyed with Hastings,"

Jasper told Giles. "I wouldn't be surprised to see him foreclose the mortgage."

"What mortgage? Hastings owns everything, doesn't he?"

"Not any more: he put some of the property up as a security for a loan."

"Dear me!"

Oblivious of Marlborough's squabbles, petty issues that she thought had no bearing on life at Latimer's Barn, Leander busied herself with Bellerophon and the search for another race for him.

She found it one afternoon as she and Giles sat in the kitchen, waiting for five o'clock and evening stables.

Idle for once, Giles watched as Leander scanned the latest edition of the *Racing Calendar*, the official voice of the Jockey Club, organised and published by the Weatherby family who had acted as the Turf's civil servants since 1773. Giles suppressed a smile at her expertly rapid scan of the densely printed pages: his daughter was incapable of embroidery and virtually all other socially acceptable feminine achievements, but she extracted the essence of this complicated document faster than most girls of her age could thread a needle.

Suddenly, her face lit up and she reached for a pencil.

"That's the one," she said. "Let's run him in that."

"What?"

"A new race at Newmarket in October. It's for two-year-old colts and fillies and they're calling it the Dewhurst Plate."

She passed the *Calendar* to Giles who studied the paragraphs she had marked.

"H'm. Yes. They certainly seem to be looking for quality. Can we have him right for it?"

"Yes!"

"It won't damage him?"

"No. I promise."

Leander knew that Giles was always at great pains to avoid overtaxing a horse, especially a young one. "He'll get fed up and miserable if we don't give him something else to do before winter," she said.

Giles was still undecided.

She gave him the very best of her smiles, her eyes quite enchanting. "Come on, Father," she urged. "Let's give them some quality!"

A Mr Gee, owner of the Dewhurst stud in Sussex, had suggested the race to the Jockey Club, putting up three hundred sovereigns to supplement the stakes money.

He had hoped for excellence and was richly rewarded. Apart

from Bellerophon, the other eight runners had won twenty-three races between them. Not knowing this, Bellerophon turned the first running of the Dewhurst Plate into a procession.

A week later, when they were ensconced in their sitting-room for the evening, snug against the advance of autumn, William suddenly said, "Everyone is talking about Bellerophon."

"How do you know?" Leander asked.

"Jim told me. It's in all the newspapers."

"What are they saying?"

"That he will win anything we choose next year. Jim's going to back him for the Guineas."

"He mustn't do that," Leander said firmly. "Bellerophon probably won't be any good at a mile."

William looked disappointed. "So what *will* he do?"

"Further," Leander said with simple, rock-solid assurance. "And remember, we have to get him through the winter and train him on."

"What does that mean?" William asked.

She started to tell him.

William settled contentedly to listen. He knew that he would not understand most of the points she was about to make, but her knowledge astonished him and he loved her dearly.

CHAPTER 7

1876

'Everything will be within our grasp!'

They – the experts and fanatics, the crooked and the straight – talked about Bellerophon all through the winter of 1875–76. The decision eventually reached in smoking-rooms, clubs and public houses all over England was that his victory in the Two Thousand Guineas was so much a foregone conclusion that it seemed almost a shame to take money from the bookmakers.

The idea that he would fail to win for the blindingly simple reason that he did not take part in the race was never given a moment's thought.

Yet that is precisely what happened.

Ample warning was given. Bellerophon was entered, but Giles notified Messrs Weatherby and the editor of *The Sporting Life* of his decision to withdraw eight days before the race. Nevertheless, confusion reigned in the betting market, and when the Viscount Dupplin's excellent colt, Petrarch, ran out the winner, his supporters were rewarded with the munificent odds of twenty to one.

No explanation was given of Bellerophon's non-appearance at Newmarket; Giles saw little point in trying to explain that he had seen enough of the colt's work to know that Leander had been right. A mile was not Bellerophon's distance and that was the end of it. He might have disarmed public outrage and bewilderment by saying that the horse had pulled a muscle or was coughing, but such a pacifying subterfuge never occurred to him.

Ten days after the Two Thousand Guineas, Bellerophon went to Salisbury and raced over a mile and a half. The opposition was mediocre and he won it in a canter with less effort than he had expended in a casual trial spin at home three days before the race.

He raced next on 1 June.

It was Leander's sixteenth birthday.

It was also the day that Latimer's Barn won the ninety-seventh renewal of the Derby Stakes, the Blue Riband of the Turf.

Through all the years ahead, Leander never forgot a single detail of the glorious afternoon that heralded the start of the great times.

For Giles, the most memorable few moments came during the previous day.

Bellerophon travelled from Wiltshire to Epsom Downs in a horse van attached to a succession of railway carriages. Once they reached the racecourse, Caleb, who had defied his worsening arthritis for the occasion, Conn Daly and Carrot O'Grady set about making their colt comfortable in the stables.

Giles, Leander and Peter Izzard walked the course over which the race was to be run.

They had never seen anything like it. Nothing at Newmarket, Salisbury, or any of the other courses with which they were now so familiar was any preparation for this terrifying horseshoe-shaped track that was, apart from the last three furlongs, in a state of constant turmoil. It twisted, climbed, and, worst of all, descended so sharply to the famous Tattenham Corner that it seemed impossible for a horse to gallop down it and stay on his feet.

"We'll never get round here in one piece," Peter Izzard said, voicing the same defeatist thoughts that had enveloped Giles.

"Stuff and nonsense!" Leander replied. "Ninety-six horses have won this race, and a lot of the others must have made a fair job of it." And she kept talking, gradually lifting spirits.

There had been racing that day, and although it was long since over, not all the spectators had dispersed. Several hundred remained in and around the grandstand, participating in the ritual of annual reunion or hoping to see something of significance for the morrow. From one group, an utterance delivered in an affected drawl emerged.

"I say! Look there! That gel. She must be Leander Flamsteed, the one they're all talking about."

She was distinctive enough in her working clothes of breeches, riding boots and shabby canvas jacket, with her long, golden hair gathered by a crimson silk bow at the nape of her neck. Not in the least put out, she favoured the group with a radiant smile.

"Good Lord, yes!" It was a fruity voice that must have been nurtured on port. "Isn't she a bobby-dazzler? Who are those two fellows with her, I wonder."

Leander provided the information. "This is my father," she called out, indicating Giles by laying a hand on his shoulder. "And this, gentlemen, is our jockey, Mr Izzard."

Peter shrivelled with embarrassment; Giles, half afraid of the consequences, had no idea what to make of the situation. But the moment turned to gold: the flushed faces in the grandstand were subdued by awed respect, the hats came off, Leander gave them a wave and passed on her way like a queen. For the first time on a much broader stage than Cannings Ambo, her allure and *élan* had worked the magic. Giles always remembered the episode and was confident that it was the sign of truly great things to come.

Leander slept in Bellerophon's box that night. Conn and Carrot were outside, propped against a bale of hay resting on the door. It was assumed that the Association was finished, but there were other villains about: anyone wishing to get at Leander and the colt would have to climb over two dead bodies first.

They all woke at five o'clock on the morning of Derby Day. Almost at once, Leander took Bellerophon out to walk and trot round the course, allowing him frequent stops to inspect his surroundings. The Downs were already a seething mass of humanity: thousands of people had arrived during the night to grab a good position in the centre of the course or near the rails of the home straight. Many of them were travelling folk, gipsies and those involved with the huge fairground that was springing up. Leander had a good view from Bellerophon's back and was smiling and waving at the crowd for most of the way.

Returning to the stables, Leander found that Conn, Carrot and some of the lads with the other horses had conjured up a fire on which they were cooking breakfast and brewing tea. While they ate, she told them that overnight showers had left the course in perfect condition.

"The turf here is almost as good as our own," was her final high commendation.

Giles, Caleb and Peter Izzard, having spent the night at an inn near Chessington, had difficulty finding a way through the throngs jamming every road and by-way to the course and did not arrive until nine o'clock. Giles wore a new suit of black frock-coat and striped trousers in which he contrived to look simultaneously elegant and wretchedly uncomfortable. Peter Izzard was green with apprehension.

Eventually, when it was noon and Horatio had finally negotiated the crowds, Caleb led Bellerophon out for a stroll round the stable enclosure and Conn brought two buckets of water to the box. He and Giles stood guard while Leander removed all her stable clothes, washed, and emerged looking as pretty as a picture in a flower-patterned dress that Ellie Goakes had made for the occasion. Horatio's admiration turned to uproarious laughter when he saw that she was about to slap a broad-brimmed hat on to her head.

"Not yet, my lovely," he chuckled. "We'll get the straw out of your hair first!"

Lunch was at a reserved table in one of the marquees, and the people who appeared to have come to Epsom for a social occasion rather than to watch the races, got on Leander's nerves. She felt a little better after Horatio, sensing her irritation, gave her a knowing grin.

At long last, the fifteen runners for the Derby were paraded in the paddock, and there was something to occupy her mind. While Conn led Bellerophon round, Giles, Leander and Horatio were rubbing shoulders with lords and ladies, the great and the good, some men whose integrity was renowned and others who could not be trusted an inch.

Not in the least overawed, Leander looked around her with open curiosity and soon found a strong-faced man in his mid-fifties staring back at her. His attire was immaculate but sombre, relieved only by the incredible shine on his boots and the wonderful flower in his buttonhole. When he pulled the rug off Viscount Falmouth's Skylark and assisted Fred Archer to mount, Leander realised that she was looking at Matthew Dawson, the great Newmarket trainer who despised money and was crushingly outspoken about his famous jockey and one-time protégé.

After the horses left the paddock, there was a long wait while they traversed the Downs to reach the start. They were out of sight for most of this time and even when the race was under way the first few furlongs of it were invisible from the grandstand. Not that this deterred a contingent of overwrought know-alls from making the most incredible pronouncements at the top of their raucous voices.

When the horses finally came into view, they were on the descent to Tattenham Corner and Bellerophon was last. Using the binoculars that were Horatio's birthday present, Leander saw that their colt was bowling along without a care in the world whereas Peter Izzard looked grimly worried. Skylark and Fred Archer were lying second behind a horse called Julius Caesar: Forerunner was moving up fast on the outside.

Fred Archer carried the money and good wishes of a sizeable part of the crowd, and there was concerted cheering as he urged Skylark forward to take the lead. Leander saw that the excitement was to be short-lived. "Archer's horse is nearly finished," she told Giles calmly. "He isn't going to get the trip."

And sure enough, within a few seconds, the groans indicated that Forerunner had overhauled Skylark and was looking a convincing leader as they swung round into the home straight.

For a few moments the crowd enjoyed a great struggle between Forerunner and Julius Caesar who appeared to be leaving the rest of the field for dead. At first, only Leander and Horatio saw that Peter Izzard no longer looked worried and had Bellerophon moving to devastating purpose. Of all the people on Epsom Downs that afternoon, Giles was one of the last to realise what was happening, and then not until Bellerophon had taken the lead with just under a furlong to run.

"My God!" Giles muttered. "He's going to win it . . . he is! He's going to win the damned thing!"

The gap widened visibly as Bellerophon lengthened his stride and went away like a champion. Completely unmoved, Leander watched with great concentration. She was still observing how Peter kept him going until they were well past the finishing line, trying to assess how much stamina was left, when Horatio lifted her clear of the ground and she became conscious of the din.

Joyous bedlam reigned for five minutes. Leander had no idea what happened to her: did she walk, or was she carried to the winner's enclosure? Was her father really so stunned that for a while he looked positively ill? And surely Horatio did not have tears in his eyes?

No, it was real enough. She was sixteen years old and the winner of the Derby was trying to eat her hat.

Suddenly, the hundreds of people who were jostling to snatch a view of Bellerophon fell silent; an invisible hand opened a path through the packed ranks, and there he was, His Royal Highness Albert Edward of Saxe-Coburg-Gotha, Prince of Wales, Earl of Chester and goodness knows what else.

The Prince patted Bellerophon's neck and smiled at Giles. "Very well done, Mr Flamsteed," he said. "A very nice horse. A credit to you."

"Thank you, Your Royal Highness." Giles bowed. "As a matter of fact, my daughter is mostly responsible for him."

"Ah, yes, so I have heard."

She curtsied as Aunt Elisabeth had taught her when she was a little girl. Then Leander Flamsteed and the Prince of Wales looked each other up and down.

Her face remained dutifully expressionless, yet there was something about her that Albert Edward found discomforting: she made his imagination play the strangest tricks. "So, you're Teddy, are you?" she seemed to be thinking. "H'm. Not much, really. I'm taller than you, and aren't your arms short? I know you're going to be King one day, but *I'm* Leander Flamsteed!"

"Yes. Charming. Very nice," His Royal Highness said, and, having seen quite enough of the eyes that could become disconcertingly grey when she was perplexed or irritated, turned and went back to his party.

As the crowd round them began to break up and a group of newspapermen closed in on Giles, Leander and Conn took Bellerophon back to the stables. Conn and Carrot washed him down, Caleb prepared a feed fit for an emperor and Leander hurried in to the box he was occupying; stretching up on tiptoe, she brought the pigeon basket down from the high windowsill.

"Now, Lucifer, are you going to be a good boy today?" she asked, reaching inside the basket to bring out the plump, slate-coloured bird. Cupping him in her hands, she checked that the tiny roll of paper was still in place inside the rubber ring on his leg: it had been there for over an hour, ever since Bellerophon went into the paddock. Walking clear of the stable buildings, Leander threw the pigeon into the air and watched as he rose, circled twice, then set off towards the west.

Seventy minutes later, it was Jim Goakes who caught the first sight of Lucifer as he came into Cannings Ambo past the church tower. Jim and William were waiting in the loft of the coach-house, staring out of the skylight constructed for this very purpose.

"Come here!" William urged through clenched teeth. "Don't you dare play games today!"

Having arrived over the village, Lucifer did not always come straight home. Especially when he returned from Newmarket, he had the annoying habit of flying up to the ridge of Cannings Down and roosting for an hour or more in the trees surrounding Powell's Pool. Today, however, he flew straight in, landing on Jim's outstretched, seed-laden hand to set about gorging himself.

William was shaking as he reached for the piece of paper. He had no idea what the final arrangement had been. Was Leander sticking to her usual habit of releasing Lucifer only to announce a victory, or had she complied with his plea to send a message whatever transpired?

"Come on, come on!" Jim Goakes urged as William became flustered and fumbled with the rubber ring.

At last he had the roll of paper, only to drop it on the floor where it lodged in a crack between the boards. Forgetting Lucifer, they both scrabbled for it, and it was Jim who finally revealed the message:

BELLEROPHON DID THE BUSINESS

William was speechless: he alone knew exactly how much it had

111

meant to Leander. It was left to Jim to relay the news to the lads waiting anxiously below.

"We've done it! Bellerophon's won the Derby."

Paul Izzard, who had come from the stud to await the news, detached himself from the cheering, dancing scrimmage and set off like a stag to take the news round the village. In his excitement, he forgot Giles's strict rule about the lawn and went careering diagonally across it.

It was out of the question for Bellerophon to travel back to Latimer's Barn that day. The crowds would have prevented a passage to the railway station before seven o'clock, far too late to embark on a seven-hour journey. So, with the resolve to set off at six the following morning, Leander settled down for a second night in Bellerophon's box.

She did so blissfully. Her wonderful boy had delivered handsomely and, as she drifted into sleep, she had fragmentary perceptions of what this would mean for the future.

In Cannings Ambo, William lay in bed, unable to sleep and sharing her joy. He remembered what she had said as she was leaving for Epsom.

"He can do it, William, I'm sure he can. And if he does, everything will be within our grasp. Everything!"

"I suppose there will be no limit to the man's conceit now," Priscilla Hastings declared.

"There never was!" Emily Dallow replied.

"The devil looks after his own."

"We shall be well out of it," Emily Dallow declared, making a virtue out of necessity.

A week after the Derby, they were passing their final verdict. These matters were dealt with much more easily now that so very few customers interrupted their conversations.

It was the last week in which the Dallow shop would attempt to do business under its old colours.

When Samuel Dallow had bowed to the inevitable and put it up for sale two months ago, he had expected the worst and it duly happened. Prospective buyers, who came from as far afield as London and Exeter, took one look at the turnover figures and disappeared. The asking price was reduced slightly, then lowered sharply: all to no avail.

Acting on his wife's instructions, Samuel Dallow refused Guy Mallender's initial approach.

112

Two days later, Guy made another offer. "Look here, Mr Dallow, what about if I give you the original asking price plus two hundred pounds?"

"Need my wife know of that?" Samuel asked, congratulating himself on the prescience that caused him to conduct this second discussion in Guy Mallender's shop, well away from Emily.

"Not from me," Guy replied. "What you tell her is strictly your own affair."

And so the deal was struck. With what Samuel Dallow was prepared to admit receiving from Guy Mallender, he was able to buy a promising-looking shop in Swindon. It was far less grand than what he was leaving, but there was the massive consolation of a secret nest-egg amounting to more than five hundred pounds. One day, Samuel Dallow promised himself, he would put it to good use.

The Hastings family were also on the move.

Sir Arnold and his wife, Augusta, now had three children. In an endeavour to secure some sort of future for them, he had put the estate up for sale and was buying a dairy farm near Chippenham. Thanks to a bank manager more amenable than Spooner, a bridging loan made the move imminent, leaving the Marlborough estate in the hands of an agent.

Priscilla Hastings was putting a brave face on the distasteful prospect of living on a farm. Making the most of the last few opportunities to blacken the name of Giles Flamsteed was a help.

"Did you see that dreadful man when he came out of Mallender's yesterday morning? He actually had the gall to raise his hat to me. Imagine that! After what he did to my poor Ambrose."

"Shameful!" Emily Dallow agreed, sharing the delusion that half of Marlborough was still listening to them.

While they railed, the object of their odium was sitting down to lunch in The House with Horatio. Giles had an important point that he wanted to make and saw no alternative to a direct approach.

"I think you should have a share of the Derby prize-money," he said.

"Why?" Horatio looked annoyed.

"Damn it, Horatio, do you know how much that race was worth?"

"Five thousand five hundred and seventy-five pounds fourteen shillings," Horatio snapped promptly. "What about it?"

"You *gave* me that horse."

"Bloody hell!" Giles found himself confronted not by the mellow son of Wiltshire, but by a reincarnation of the pugnaciously self-willed man who had made a success out of decades of cut and thrust in Birmingham.

"I gave you that horse as a present, Giles, and that's the end of it."

"But . . ."

"But nothing, listen to me! I hoped he might turn out useful. I'll admit I never thought he was going to be *that* good, but even if I had, it wouldn't have made the blindest bit of difference. What that horse has done is all down to you and Leander – and those two lads, of course. So let's hear no more about it."

"I'll always be grateful to you," Giles said, knowing that he was beaten.

"That's fair enough as long as you do it quietly." Horatio's vehemence was ebbing as quickly as it had flared up.

"Do you know where that race left me?" Giles asked. Horatio shook his head, inviting enlightenment. "After all the entry fees and expenses have been paid and I've given out a few presents, I'm left with five thousand pounds."

"A useful sum," Horatio chuckled.

"It's two and a half times what I paid Father for this estate," Giles said.

"Is it, by God!" Horatio looked vastly impressed. "And you've got his stud fees to come yet. That's going to amount to a pretty penny given the luck."

"Yes, and you *will* have half of that," Giles said triumphantly.

"Harrumph!" Horatio grudgingly acknowledged the joint owner-ship of the stud and all fees. "But you're set up for the rest of your life."

"Yes, I know."

A thought occurred to Horatio. "You haven't finished winning money with that horse yet."

"Oh?" Giles was surprised.

"Leander's got ideas."

"What?"

"I hear she's got her sights on the St Leger."

"Well I'm blowed!" The news came as a complete surprise to Giles.

"Keep your eyes and ears open and you'll see what I mean," Horatio said. "She was talking to those two lads after the second lot this morning. They're plotting something."

Giles laughed. "You're right, I must pay more attention to what she's doing."

"Well, it isn't as though she can't be trusted. You're a busy man – and I'll bet you're worrying about Caleb."

"I am," Giles admitted ruefully.

Caleb was now sixty-six and his arthritis became more troublesome by the week. His retirement was planned for the end of the year: the difficulty was finding a replacement. Giles had spoken to Dan Goakes, who, well content with his lot, had been scared witless by the thought of becoming head lad and the responsibility involved.

"You're going to have to hunt round for a man," Horatio said. "Be careful!"

"Don't I know it!" Giles said with great feeling. "How am I supposed to find the right man?"

"Oh, I daresay you'll manage it." Horatio prepared to impart a nugget of fresh information. "While you're about it, be on your guard against that brother of yours."

Giles looked at him keenly. "What do you know?" he asked.

"Nothing much," Horatio replied airily.

"Come on, Horatio, I know you too well. You keep your ear very close to the ground. What's going on?"

"It's said he's in trouble. Business is poor and he's fouled up with some customers who are bad payers. He might be thinking of trying to raise money by going public, but that won't wash. He's too much of a risk."

"Oh dear!"

"See!" As Giles looked wretched, Horatio pounced. "That's what I'm afraid of. You could be a soft touch because you care about the family name."

"Ralph knows where he stands with me," Giles declared firmly.

"Make sure you keep it that way. Your brother has turned into a thoroughly bad lot. Give him a couple of thousand and he'll be back for more inside a month."

A few days after Bellerophon's Derby victory, Latimer's Barn returned to normal as the excitement faded.

But both Giles and Leander were aware of the change. What now passed for normal was at least one grade higher than before and the difference was evident in all departments of the stable's life. The lads were smarter, keener, a minute or two sharper into their work, and the horses picked up the new sense of purpose. Moreover, as if by some innate system of communication, they seemed to sense that one of their number had achieved something truly great and, with the exception of the ever-likeable but useless Alma Works, wanted to emulate their illustrious companion.

Shortly after Royal Ascot, when their reputation received a further boost from two good winners, Giles noticed Leander give a fierce

115

nod of approval as they watched the second lot prepare to leave the yard for the gallop.

"Well?" he asked.

"The place is starting to look something like," she replied.

"Hasn't it so far?"

"You know what I mean, Father," she said, dazzling him with a smile.

"Tell me what you think we ought to do with Bellerophon," Giles prompted.

"That's obvious! The St Leger."

"You think he'll handle the extra distance?"

"Yes. We'll try him at Salisbury first."

The bookmakers offered no odds on what was perceived as a public training gallop for Bellerophon; the ease of his effortless stroll over a mile and three-quarters was carefully noted, and everyone knew where his next race would be.

Doncaster was justly proud of its Town Moor racecourse, home of the St Leger since 1776, which meant that the Northern Classic was four years older than the Derby. During the first week in September, the warm-hearted locals made no bones about being more interested in the increasingly famous Leander Flamsteed than in the distinguished horse she brought with her. In the event, both proved very much to Yorkshire taste.

When Leander went into the paddock, arm-in-arm with Giles, one of the observers declared: "That lass is reet gradely," and a cheer of approval for the sentiment was raised.

Once the race was under way, Bellerophon gave generous proof of his worthiness as a champion. He took the opposition by storm on the turn for home and for the next thousand yards gave a demonstration of graceful power that sent the crowd wild with joy and put him past the winning post ten lengths clear of his nearest rival. There was never the slightest doubt of his getting the extra distance; indeed, the further he went, the better he got. As the very proud owner, Giles was the richer by four thousand eight hundred pounds.

The enthusiasm that Leander and Bellerophon aroused on Town Moor was such that it was four o'clock, nearly an hour after the race, before she could slip away to release the pigeon, Lucifer. His best line of flight to Latimer's Barn was a route of one hundred and seventy miles, and he flew it splendidly in four hours fifteen minutes. Jim Goakes took the news to The George while William ran the other way to The Hall.

Jasper was thrilled.

"That's it, nothing can stop Giles now," he said to Lucy. "He's

116

put Cannings Ambo on the map and no mistake about it. By God, I'll bet Horrie's pleased!"

Horatio had gone north with Bellerophon's escort.

Lucy went to the kitchen. Returning to the sitting-room half an hour later, she found that Jasper had dozed off; he often did at this time in the evening.

But when she tried to wake him, one of his arms swung lifelessly from the confining support of the chair.

Lucy was most struck by the expression on Jasper's face: happiness was tinged with surprise. Lawrence Stanton commented on it, too. His theory, eagerly accepted by Lucy, was that the heart attack had been so sudden that Jasper was left with time only for curiosity.

William went to Marlborough railway station the following afternoon to meet the party returning in elation from Doncaster.

One look at him told Leander that something awful had happened. William stressed the point by hurrying straight past her without a word as he made for Giles and Horatio at the other end of the train.

Both men were visibly shaken by what William had to impart, but, from the very beginning, Giles took it badly, very badly indeed.

"Father thought the world of Jasper," Leander said to William later. "He once said that we'd never have got started here if it hadn't been for Jasper."

After two days, Horatio was seriously worried by Giles, who stayed away from the yard and never mentioned Bellerophon's St Leger victory. The opportunity to state his point of view came as they left the Rectory after making the funeral arrangements and Horatio did not waste it.

"Look here, Giles, it's a damned shame about poor old Jas, but you must get a grip on yourself," he said. "He went out like a light and he died a happy man. That doesn't happen to many."

"Are you sure?" Giles desperately wanted to be certain.

"Yes, I am. He'd heard about Bellerophon and Lucy says he was as pleased as Punch. And you know how happy he was at what you were doing with the village."

Giles nodded, accepting this. "He wasn't much of an age," he insisted.

"He was sixty-eight," Horatio replied. "It's within three per cent of what the Bible gives us." He smiled. "That's not bad tolerance for engineering on this scale." He waved an arm to encompass the solar system as well as Cannings Ambo.

"A hell of a shock, though, Horatio," Giles said.

"Of course it was! That's the way things are. Do try and cheer up, old man – Peveril gets here this afternoon and it won't help him if you're acting like a wet weekend."

Four days later, there was a bigger congregation in the church for Jasper's funeral than the village had seen for many a long day, with over thirty people coming out from Marlborough as a sign of the close ties building up between village and town. Giles noticed only one thing that seemed not quite right: although Peveril was clearly saddened by his father's death, he nevertheless gave the impression of detachment, as though he was only an onlooker instead of an integral part of the proceedings.

It was the same the following day when they discussed the well-known contents of Jasper's will.

The provisions were very simple. All the money went to Lucy while Horatio inherited The Hall on the strict understanding that he willed it back to Giles. This arrangement, agreed over a period of several years, suddenly struck Giles as potentially unfair.

"What do you have to say about this, Peveril?" he asked. "Do you fancy you might want to come back here when you've finished with Birmingham?"

"Er . . . no, I don't think so. I'm happy enough with the house in Lichfield and I've never been all that keen on the village, to tell you the truth."

"It's a beautiful place," Giles said.

"And getting better all the time," Horatio added.

"Oh, I agree," Peveril replied. "But I grew up here in the bad days. Before Rashleigh we had no money, and when we were solvent it meant tolerating his appalling behaviour."

Giles saw that the conversation was putting Horatio in a bad mood. The vagueness of Peveril's plans for the future had directed attention to the one thing about him that Horatio did not like: at the age of forty-four, Peveril remained a bachelor. There was no heir to Beresford Engineering.

Steering the talk into safer waters, Giles asked, "Did you hear what Guy Mallender told me about the Hastings estate, Horatio? Apparently no one has shown the slightest interest in buying it yet."

"I'm not surprised, at that price," Horatio growled. "Who's going to pay six thousand for that collection of run-down rubbish?"

"The house in Marlborough is very nice," Giles protested.

"That's as maybe – what about that ridiculous hotchpotch scattered round Savernake? Oh, no, it's going to be the very devil to get rid of."

*

118

One of Alexandra's two anxieties was new.

After his departure from Oxford University, which had been premature and cloaked in secrecy, her son, Rowland, spent four years amusing himself in London, hardly ever condescending to visit Marlborough. Things were different now, however.

A year ago, in October 1875, the week after Bellerophon won the first running of the Dewhurst Plate, there had been a crisis concerning Rowland. Gilbert, badly rattled by it, had passed it off as simply another business worry and refused to divulge the merest scrap of information: Alexandra's instincts suggested that her son was implicated in something startlingly bad.

This impression was reinforced when Rowland began to work for Gilbert in a somewhat menial yet well-paid capacity.

"It will be to his advantage to learn a profession," Gilbert said. "Especially under close supervision."

As a consequence, Rowland was frequently in Marlborough with little to occupy him. He was twenty-five, good-looking and very eligible; despite all this, he continued to show no interest in young women. Alexandra also noticed that Victoria, loving every minute of her demanding work at St Thomas' Hospital, never once inquired after her brother's well-being.

Rowland's time at Eton had given persistent trouble in its later stages. On two occasions, a flurry of hectic activity with much coming and going had left Gilbert in the foulest of moods for over a month and caused Alexandra to conceive a theory so unspeakable that it appalled her. After the initial shock of the terrible thought, it had proved possible to push it to the back of her mind and keep it there.

That was until Rowland began paying frequent visits to Latimer's Barn.

His reasons seemed genuine enough. Following the great expansion of the stable and success at Ascot in both 1874 and 1875, Gilbert Fandine-Browne now had twelve horses in training with Giles. He encouraged Rowland to visit them, watch them at work and report on progress. It was, Alexandra thought, precisely the sort of thing a son might do for a father, carrying out a pleasant duty while preparing himself for the day when he had horses of his own.

It looked so innocent, but Alexandra was plagued by the thought that she should warn Giles. Warn him of what, for God's sake? Her own outrageous assumptions? That was utterly out of the question. Even thinking about it paralysed her with embarrassed fear, so how could she bring herself to speak about it?

With varying degrees of success as the weeks and months passed, she forced herself into the belief that nothing could possibly go wrong.

Alexandra's other source of disquiet was permanent and tangible. She hated it, but at least she was able to recognise and come to terms with it.

She was forty-five years old, and, according to everything she read and heard, ought to consider herself well into middle age, with senility lurking round a none too distant corner and the joys of youth irredeemably lost. She had no sensation of this; within herself she felt much as she had always done, and when she stood naked in front of a full-length mirror, she could not be anything other than pleased at what she saw. Still, she dreaded the day when Giles might find her attractions waning and the cocoon of hedonism they had built with such loving enthusiasm was placed under threat.

Following Jasper's death, she was uncertain what would become of the 'facilities' at The Hall; before there was a chance to resolve the matter, a stomach infection struck at Latimer's Barn, badly affecting every horse. For nearly a month, Giles worked day and night, not simply to get his charges better, but in a desperate bid to save their lives, so virulent was the disease. Reliant on Lucy for news, Alexandra learned that the only possible cause for comfort was the safety of Bellerophon. After the St Leger, he had gone to the stud at Cannings St John and was spared the affliction.

At last, all was well again. The horses were weak, but they all survived and their recovery was measurable by the day. Meeting Horatio in Marlborough High Street, Alexandra was delighted by the news and his invitation.

"We've had a damned upsetting few weeks, haven't we? It's time we got things back on an even keel again. When will you be coming to visit us, my dear?"

Lucy, determined to make the best of life without her beloved Jasper, laid on a splendid dinner at The Hall. Afterwards, Alexandra and Giles found themselves bundled upstairs to their neglected blue room. Despite his gaunt appearance after the strains of the past few weeks, Giles spent most of the night giving convincing proof that Alexandra's charms remained potently unimpaired.

That same evening, Leander and William, who had fought alongside Giles against the sickness that had ravaged the yard, also set about regaining their habitual routine.

"We must look at the Big Book first," Leander decreed. "I haven't had time to see what Father has written about Bellerophon."

They went to the library, hoicked the book on to the table and settled down to read.

Leander smiled at the typically prosaic entries Giles had made. 'Bellerophon won the Derby,' was followed by, 'Leander thinks he will get fourteen furlongs.'

"Dull as ever," William grumbled.

"You know Father hates people who get over-excited about horses," Leander said. "There's an enormous amount of pretentious blether spouted . . . I say, look at that! He's put 'St Leger' all in capital letters."

"Quite extravagant!" William smiled.

Without thinking, Leander turned a page to reveal the comments on Jasper's death. They stared in amazement. Giles had written an unprecedented forty-seven lines, by far the biggest entry to date. It was an obituary, and as William and Leander read it, the rightness of it emerged powerfully, most especially at the end:

Above all else, Jasper Beresford loved this estate of Cannings Ambo. For much of his life, he fought what must have seemed to him a losing battle to save it from partition and ruin. Latterly, we three Flamsteeds have been able to start doing things that gave Jasper heart. We must continue that work, always remembering that the health of the estate will depend upon us being able to populate it with decent people and give them fulfilment. That is our duty.

After reading it a second time, Leander gave a firm nod. "That is absolutely right," she said. "We must work to that when it's our turn, William."

CHAPTER 8
1877

'No one touches my family!'

Daphne Stanton first noticed Michael Pilgrim at Jasper's funeral as everyone was filing out of the church. Then, apart from realising that he was one of Giles's lads, she had no idea who he was. For an instant, at a distance of twenty yards, Daphne and Michael looked at each other. Never had she seen such haunted misery allied to what seemed like pleading.

"God! What *is* wrong with that boy?" Daphne thought.

Much later, she felt desperately ashamed of the way she had allowed it to slip from her mind once she was at The Hall toasting Jasper on his way.

Michael Pilgrim was fourteen. He had come to Latimer's Barn from the same orphanage that had produced the Izzards fifteen years ago. Giles selected him for his eagerness, his charm and his physique: unless he grew quite phenomenally or ran to fat, Michael Pilgrim was made to be a jockey. As soon as he began riding lessons, he displayed immense natural talent and Giles congratulated himself on having made a good choice for the future.

Giles half expected that Michael might have problems settling into the robust community of the yard, the possible stumbling block being his looks. Michael was pretty: there really was no other word for it. Not only did he have the face of an angel, it seemed to have been produced by a sculptor with an eye for the aesthetic.

Sure enough, Michael did receive some ribbing from his new, less beautiful companions. However, his ability to laugh at both his critics and himself made mocking him a very poor sport, and his horsemanship was soon earning admiration. Conn Daly, the most audaciously exciting of the gallop riders, took Michael under his wing, and Giles relaxed the special watch he had been keeping; the only problem the boy would face now was mild jealousy from those of his comrades who had seen themselves as future jockeys.

The gaiety began to ebb out of Michael Pilgrim around the middle of 1876 when everyone in Cannings Ambo was cock-a-hoop at Bellerophon's Derby triumph. Conn sometimes asked Michael what was wrong, only to be fobbed off with stories of headaches and other vague ailments. Some days weren't so bad, others were terrible; the day of Jasper's funeral was one of the worst.

When the horses began to work for the 1877 season, Dan Goakes was particularly aware of Michael's vagaries, but he had more than enough on his plate without going out of his way to find trouble. On the strict understanding that he was to be replaced at the very earliest opportunity, Dan bowed to the inevitable and allowed himself to be cajoled into acting as head lad following Caleb's retirement. His priorities were doing his best with a demanding job and making sure that Giles did not go too long before looking for a permanent man: he had no time for a brilliant but moody boy.

The sudden emergence of an horrendous crisis left everyone deeply shocked.

At half past four on an April afternoon, Conn was on his way back to evening stables from Oak Cottage. For several months he had, with the permission of Lawrence and Daphne, spent the free part of his afternoons with Sally, their housemaid. Confident that romance was flowering, Daphne repeatedly urged John Shepherd to call the banns and have done with it.

Rather than follow the road, Conn always took a direct line from the back garden of Oak Cottage straight to the yard. The hundred yards or so to the Devizes Lane were through a lush beech wood. It was in the middle of this that Conn found Michael Pilgrim, sitting against a tree and sobbing his heart out.

"What's the matter, Michael? Michael!"

Conn knelt down alongside his friend. Getting no response, he took him by the shoulders to shake him; in cringing away, the boy lifted his face.

Conn was appalled. There was an ugly cut less than an inch below Michael's left eye. Fresh blood was seeping from it and the eye was already closed, the lid and surrounding flesh badly discoloured.

"Who did this, Michael?" Conn's voice was soft, almost gentle enough to conceal his anger.

Still getting no reply, Conn was momentarily at a loss; he looked towards Latimer's Barn, then back the way he had come from Oak Cottage. His mind made up, he hauled Michael to his feet.

"Come on, this way."

"Where are you taking me?" Michael cried.

"To see Doctor Stanton. You need fixing up, my lad."

"No! Please, Conn, no! Let me alone."

The first few paces were a struggle. Michael was so determined that Conn had to drag him, using a degree of force that he knew was probably harmful. Then Michael gave in. As they went on, Conn had the strong impression that submission was accompanied by infinite relief.

Shocked by Michael's appearance, Lawrence Stanton left his tea at once and guided the boy into his consulting-room. Conn went with them to explain how he had found Michael.

Beneath his jacket, Michael's shirt was so badly torn that it was practically dropping off his back. When it did fall away, a mass of bruising was revealed, some of it clearly several days old.

Lawrence's face became very grim indeed. "Would you wait outside, please, Conn," he said. "I want to give Michael a thorough examination."

It took thirty-seven minutes. Conn sat nervously in the hall, counting each one by the long-case clock. After five minutes, Michael cried out three times in pain, then there was the soothing murmur of Lawrence Stanton's voice, followed by Michael's, disjointed at first, gradually getting more fluent.

Eventually, Lawrence came out, closing the door behind him.

"Conn, I want you to run and fetch Mr Flamsteed for me," he said.

"He'll be doing evening stables, sir."

"Never mind about that, Conn. You tell him that this is desperately important and that he's to come at once. I'll patch Michael's eye up while you're away."

For most of the fifteen minutes that Lawrence took to explain matters, Giles was thunderstruck. Pulling himself together, he insisted on going over it all with Michael, now comfortable in a bed that Daphne always kept prepared for an emergency. Initially, Michael was painfully embarrassed at having to speak of it, but this soon passed. The realisation that his ordeal was over loosened his tongue.

"Well?" Lawrence asked as they stood at the foot of the stairs afterwards. He could see that Giles's mind was made up.

"I'm going into Marlborough. Now!"

"I'll come with you."

"Well done, Lawrence!"

One of Daphne's men prepared the carriage and drove them: they reached their destination at half past seven.

The Fandine-Brownes were about to start dinner. Their butler did his best to keep Giles and Lawrence on the doorstep, mindful of the fact that there were house guests, important people from London. Disturbed by the noise, Alexandra hurried from the dining-room to be taken aback by Giles's mood.

"We wish to speak with your husband and son," Giles said sternly. "At once, if you please. The business is of the utmost gravity."

Alexandra was to ride out the subsequent chain of events with great courage, but in that instant she was sick with fear. She knew that her nightmare had come to pass.

Gilbert Fandine-Browne was very annoyed when he faced Giles and Lawrence in his study.

"What the devil is it, Flamsteed?" he demanded. "I can't be bothered with horses *now*."

"This is not about horses," Giles snapped. He paused to look searchingly at the son. Yes, it was all there in the face, cruelty, perversion, and, possibly worst of all, arrogance. Giles delivered his thunderbolt with cold fury.

"Mr Fandine-Browne, your son has been sodomising one of my stable lads. According to the boy, it has been going on since last June. The most recent of these disgusting acts was this afternoon."

Lawrence Stanton was momentarily stunned by the way Giles expressed himself. Surely a more cautious approach was called for? But Gilbert Fandine-Browne was also shocked and his involuntary reaction put the issue beyond doubt. Giving his son a look compounded of anger and disgust, he said, "You damned fool! You promised me . . ."

Too late, he stopped, his face betraying his feelings.

"Ah!" Giles glared at him.

"Now look here, Flamsteed, I'm certain that this isn't as black as you think," Gilbert Fandine-Browne said. His manner had changed. He was conciliatory now, attempting a man-of-the-world style. "You know what these boys can be like. I expect this lad of yours encouraged my son. It happens all the time, you know."

"Absolutely not, sir!" Giles's statement resounded like a gunshot. "My lad was a completely unwilling partner in this sickening business. Doctor Stanton here has examined Michael and found him to be in a woeful condition." He pointed at Rowland Fandine-Browne's right hand, on which there was an ornate signet ring. "I presume that is what cut his face. No, Mr Fandine-Browne, it won't wash! Your son has been bullying Michael Pilgrim into complying with his revolting depravities. If he did not, a trumped-up complaint was to be made to me – insolence perhaps – and Michael was afraid I would get rid of him. Since he came from an orphanage and *was* very happy at Latimer's Barn, he thought he had no alternative but to comply. Once he found out what was expected of him, he was too afraid to tell anyone."

"Utter nonsense. A pack of lies."

Giles stared at Rowland Fandine-Browne in disbelief. Under the circumstances, a denial was the last thing he had expected.

Taking advantage of the hiatus, Gilbert Fandine-Browne moved swiftly to his desk and sat down. "I think we can deal with this quite amicably," he said. "What do you suppose the boy would say to fifty pounds?"

The words scarcely registered with Giles; he was too preoccupied coming to terms with the fact that Fandine-Browne had reached for his cheque-book and pen. Misreading his expression, Fandine-Browne amended his offer. "Seventy-five pounds perhaps . . . no, I think one hundred would be more like it, don't you?"

He was happy with this. The pen was poised.

"Tell me, is this how you have always done it?" Giles asked quietly. "Pay them off and no more trouble until the next time?"

Rowland Fandine-Browne detected, and reacted to, a new quality in Giles's voice. He seemed about to say something, but was left speechless by Giles's sudden move out of the room. Surprised by the turn of events, Lawrence Stanton had to run after him.

"Take us to Kennet House," Giles ordered Daphne's driver. "I want to see Colonel Thompson."

Colonel Thompson was the man in charge of Marlborough's infant, but immensely keen and effective, police force. His superior, the Chief Constable of Wiltshire, was a firebrand ex-cavalry brigade commander and Digby Protheroe's brother-in-law.

Thirty-six hours later, Rowland Fandine-Browne was arrested and charged. He went before magistrates within the hour to be remanded for the County Assizes; bail was refused and he was taken at once to Trowbridge Jail. As a panic-stricken Gilbert Fandine-Browne dashed to London to consult his lawyers, Marlborough seethed with rumour and counter-rumour.

That evening, Alexandra had herself driven to Cannings Ambo. She was dreading the encounter with Giles, but knew that she must make her peace with him at the earliest possible moment.

As luck would have it, Giles was at The Hall when she arrived. He came straight out with the vital question.

"Alexandra, did you know that damned son of yours had those proclivities?"

126

"No, my dear, truly, I didn't *know*. But I must confess that I had my suspicions."

"And what the devil does that mean?"

To Alexandra's great relief, Horatio intervened to break up the encounter at the front door. "Give the poor woman a chance, Giles. Come along, my dear, let's get you sat down. You must be feeling awful."

Once she was at ease and had sipped gratefully at the glass of brandy Horatio cajoled her into accepting, Alexandra recounted the fears that had preyed on her mind during the past ten years. As she told of the mysterious crises at Eton, Oxford and in London, Giles saw that she merited sympathy, not censure. Because of the freedom of spirit that made their relationship possible, Giles was apt to forget that Alexandra was part of a household governed by rigidly conventional principles and values. Gilbert Fandine-Browne, though complacently glad to be rid of sexual responsibility for his wife, was a stiff-necked autocrat who would see it as his duty to deal with his son's disgusting behaviour and keep it heavily shrouded from delicate female sensitivities.

"The town is in uproar as you can well imagine," Alexandra concluded. "The general opinion seems to be that Rowland deserves all that will happen to him, but some are rather shaken by the severity of your line, Giles."

He nodded understandingly. "So I imagine. However, I will not have Latimer's Barn or anyone belonging to it abused."

Alexandra smiled sadly. "I think they realised that – they certainly do now, at any rate!"

"What about you, my dear? Where does all this leave you?" Horatio was deeply concerned.

"Goodness only knows! Gilbert is going to have a terrible time, of course. I rather think that he expects to be ruined."

"He should have acted years ago instead of covering it up," Giles said. His manner was without a trace of sympathy.

"Have you seen anything of public opinion?" Horatio asked Alexandra. "Are they turning against you?"

"From what I heard this afternoon, they feel sorry for me," Alexandra replied.

"Good!" Horatio looked approving. "If that doesn't carry on, you must come here for help. Promise me you will."

"Yes, I will. Thank you, Horatio." Alexandra closed her eyes for a moment or two. "I know that it's going to be dreadful, but I'm *so* glad it's all out in the open. Things will be resolved now."

"Oh yes, things are going to be resolved all right," Horatio said grimly, exchanging a look with Giles. "I hope you're not too fond of your son."

"Fond of him!" Alexandra was suddenly herself again. "I've always thought he was the most detestable creature I've ever come across!"

Gilbert Fandine-Browne was under no illusions: it was bad.

The lawyers with whom he had done business for twenty years made no secret of their unease.

"We do not much like the sound of this, sir. From what you say, the prosecution case is formidable – and *very* distasteful. Juries don't care for this sort of thing, you know. And there is a great deal of respect for Flamsteed these days."

Nevertheless, they promised to do their best.

The speed at which the news spread, and the reaction to it, came as a very unpleasant surprise.

That afternoon, only two days after Rowland was arrested, Fandine-Browne called at a bank in Poultry. It was one of his regular sources of money to be re-lent as venture capital at his normal mark-up of one per cent. Setting his problems to one side, he took his seat in an ante-chamber while the clerk went to inform the general manager of his presence.

"I am sorry, sir, Mr Thornton cannot see you today," the clerk said, returning after an unusually long absence.

"But I have an appointment," Fandine-Browne protested.

"No, sir, you are quite mistaken."

The clerk raised an expressionless face in a gesture of defiance and Fandine-Browne saw that argument was useless.

An hour later, he suffered similarly ignominious treatment at another bank with which he had done business for many years.

Michael Pilgrim remained at Oak Cottage. Lawrence Stanton was adamant that he should have complete rest in peaceful, enclosed surroundings. As well as the mental unpleasantness Michael had suffered, there were injuries about which Lawrence refused to be specific.

Oak Cottage saw important comings and goings. Senior county police officers made several visits to interview Michael, and they were followed by the Queen's Counsel who was to act for the Crown. To Lawrence's relief, Michael not only learned to cope with his eminent guests, he did so without falling into the trap of self-importance.

Throughout a spell of wonderful weather in May, the patient spent most of his time in the garden of Oak Cottage where his constant companion was Caroline, the eleven-year-old daughter of Daphne and

Lawrence. Conn saw them for a few minutes each afternoon when he looked in on Sally and smiled quietly to himself at the protective wall Caroline had constructed around Michael. She allowed Conn five minutes to talk about the stable, then he had to go away.

Five minutes was plenty. The good news about Latimer's Barn did not require even that much each day.

All the horses were fit and seemed to be working well, but they were not winning any races. Conn told Michael that it was a complete mystery, although he knew full well the cause of the trouble. Under poor Dan Goakes, the routine of the yard was breaking down; confusion reigned over who was supposed to be doing what, people got in each other's way, tempers frayed and the fraught atmosphere infected the horses. In the absence of a sound regime, Leander's actions sometimes made things worse. Brilliant with individual animals, her priority needs for her particular favourite could increase rather than reduce the chaos.

Painfully aware of the muddle he was causing, Dan Goakes knew that Giles had taken no steps to find a head lad: there was much talk among the lads about his uncharacteristically bad temper and a big problem supposedly devouring his time and energy.

While Dan was screwing up his courage to put his foot down, the miracle happened.

Out of the blue on the loveliest of those May mornings, Abraham Merriweather appeared.

Leander found him in the Devizes Lane at half past six.

He was standing alongside a cart on which his wife, children and worldly goods were laden. He guessed at once who she must be; there was surely only one young woman in the whole of England, let alone Cannings Ambo, who was so dazzlingly beautiful, dressed like that and marched so frankly up to strangers to discover their business.

Fifteen minutes later, when Giles went out to investigate the noise of the cart trundling up the drive, he was amazed by the sight that met his eyes.

"This is Mr Merriweather, Father," Leander said as though announcing someone of considerable rank. "He has brought his family all the way from Yorkshire to look for a job."

Giles found himself studying a man in his late thirties, with fair hair, grey eyes and a weather-beaten face that was full of strength. About five feet seven or eight tall, he had the stance and bearing of a born horseman. There was something immediately reassuring about him.

"Good morning, Mr Merriweather," Giles said, holding out his right hand. "I'm Giles Flamsteed."

"Abraham Merriweather, sir." His firm handshake was confirmation of great character.

"I see you've met my daughter," Giles said.

"Yes, sir. A very great privilege."

"You've come from Yorkshire?"

"I have, sir. I lost my job, you see."

"Where were you?"

"With Major Bruce-Peters."

"Really?" Giles was impressed. The major, who had died the previous autumn, had kept good horses at Malton, between York and Pickering, for over forty years. "How long were you with him?"

"Twenty-four years, sir. I started when I was fourteen."

"What's gone wrong?"

"The major's son, sir. Him and me don't see eye to eye about the way to treat horses."

"But you were good enough for Major Bruce-Peters?"

For answer, Abraham Merriweather took a letter from his jacket pocket and handed it to Giles. It was a reference from Bruce-Peters, glowing with praise.

"Why have you come all this way for a job?" Giles asked. "Surely Newmarket would have been much easier for you?"

Abraham Merriweather, not a man short on confidence, shuffled uncomfortably. "Well, sir, it's like this . . . there's been a lot of talk about you and . . . well . . . the fact is, you're said to be the best guv'nor there is for man or horse."

"I see." Giles did his best to keep a straight face, even when Leander winked at him, and took another look at the reference. "You were the major's head lad for six years," he said.

"I was, sir."

"How many horses?"

"Thirty, sir."

Giles passed the letter back and inspected the cart. Alice Merriweather sat on the driving seat with her youngest son, John, still only six months old. Albert and young Alice, four and three respectively, were perched atop the great pile of furniture, clothes and household linen. They all smiled back at him, frank, open faces, glowing with health and sheer good nature.

"How long has it taken you to get here?" Giles asked.

"Twelve days, sir. The weather's been very kind to us."

Giles came to a decision. "Right, breakfast, Mr Merriweather. Bring your family inside for something to eat."

Leander sensed that he had made up his mind. Confirmation came as they finished the meal.

"The only house I can offer you at the moment will be a little bit cramped," Giles said. "But it's snug and comfortable – it was fettled only last autumn, and I daresay you'll manage until I can get you something more suitable."

"Does that mean there's a job for me, sir?" Abraham asked, exchanging a look with Alice.

"It does indeed, Mr Merriweather," Giles replied and made no effort to elaborate.

Five hours later, when work was finished, half a dozen of the lads helped to move the Merriweathers into the last vacant cottage on Church Green. Giles came down to see that they wanted for nothing and was pleased that Alice appeared delighted with her new home. Satisfied that all was well, he took Abraham into the garden.

"I suppose you spent a fair bit of your savings on that horse and cart, Mr Merriweather?"

"I did, sir."

"And what are you going to do with it now?"

"I'd best get rid of it."

"I could use that for work around the estate. How much did you pay for it?"

"Fifty-five pounds, sir. That includes the harness and tack."

"Right, let's take it back to Latimer's Barn now and I'll give you the money."

As they settled into bed that night, with the children fast asleep, Abraham and Alice Merriweather agreed that all the stories must be true: Giles Flamsteed was a very good guv'nor indeed.

Three nights later, Abraham was completely baffled.

Giles had still not mentioned any specific duties to him. All that Abraham had been expected to do so far was to stroll round Cannings Down with his new master while the horses worked, and act as a spectator at evening stables.

"Yes, I know it sounds funny," Alice agreed when Abraham voiced his disquiet, "but Mr Flamsteed strikes me as a man who knows what he's doing. He's got something up his sleeve, Abraham."

Alice was right.

On the fourth morning, Giles turned to Abraham after the first lot left the yard and said, "There is probably a great deal of room for improvement, Mr Merriweather."

"That might be true, sir," Abraham replied cautiously.

Giles smiled. "I know it is! We've acquired some very sloppy habits this year. I expect that you have one or two ideas you'd like to see put into practice?"

"There are a few suggestions, sir, begging your pardon."

"H'm." Giles nodded and stared at the ground. "Well, you'd better get cracking, Mr Merriweather. I'm appointing you head lad. You'll have five pounds a week and a decent house as soon as I can get one built. Oh, and you'd better start sending your children to school in The House – it's very good, my sister and Mrs Stanton run it."

Abraham was still shaken when he went back to Church Green for lunch, but Alice was full of admiration for Giles.

"That's what he intended all along," she said. "I was talking to Jennie Goakes this morning. Mr Flamsteed has been trying to find a head lad for six months."

"Then why didn't he come straight out with it?" Abraham asked.

"And what would you have done if he did?" Alice wanted to know.

"Run a mile," Abraham confessed.

"Exactly! So what does Mr Flamsteed do? He gets us moved in and buys that horse and cart off you. You've got to accept the job."

"Alice, my dear, I can't be head lad of a place like this! It's in the same class as some of those places at Newmarket."

"Oh yes you can!" Alice was eleven years younger than Abraham, loved him dearly and was determined that he should succeed, even if that meant getting behind him and shoving. "Let me tell you this, Abraham Merriweather. I had a dream about Cannings Ambo last night, and do you know what? We've come to stay. There's going to be Merriweathers helping to run this place in a hundred years and more. So, you'd better make a job of it, my lad!"

Abraham always did what Alice told him.

Within forty-eight hours of his setting to work, the yard was once more running with the quiet efficiency that had been the hallmark of Bellerophon's great year. Abraham knew all the lads and horses by name and had already developed his own shrewd ideas on their strengths and weaknesses. At the end of his second week, Peter Izzard rode two winners on the same afternoon at Bath, and Conn was bribing Caroline Stanton with sweets to let him have ten minutes with Michael instead of five.

"This Merriweather's a bit of a stickler, but he's damned good," Conn told Michael. "He's found out all the dodges and put a stop to them, and he's straightened the horses out – you should see the way they smarten themselves up when he's around."

"What about Dan?" Michael asked.

"Never better! He's like a dog with two tails. Mr Flamsteed has put him in charge of taking horses to the races and he loves it!"

"What does Miss Leander think of Mr Merriweather?" Caroline asked Conn.

"She approves," he replied, grinning at her astute grasp of life's realities.

That was it then, Michael thought.

"Give Gilbert his due, he made a good job of it. No one will ever know for certain what was in his mind."

Although Alexandra saw that Giles was finding their conversation difficult, she went on uncompromisingly. "And he appears to have left his affairs in remarkably good order – especially in view of the circumstances."

There was, Giles supposed, one immediate benefit: as time passed, Alexandra had inevitably attracted odium on account of her foul son. Her husband's death now made her the object of sympathy.

Four days previously, Gilbert Fandine-Browne had left London on an evening train to Liverpool in order to keep an appointment with one of the few business associates remaining loyal to him. He never arrived at the Adelphi Hotel to take up the booking for his room.

The standard routine check on the train following its arrival at Lime Street Station revealed his abandoned luggage on the rack of a first-class compartment. The mystery of his disappearance was unsolved until the following morning.

At first light, a plate-layer found his body lying alongside the track at Norton Bridge, five miles north of Stafford. Then the greater mystery presented itself: was it an accident, was he pushed, or did Gilbert Fandine-Browne deliberately jump from the speeding train?

"We shall never know," Alexandra told Giles. "The police appear to have decided that no other person was involved."

Giles looked dubious, but Alexandra's daughter, home for the funeral, made it plain that debate was an intolerable luxury. "There seems no point in speculating about this unfortunate incident, Mr Flamsteed," she said and Giles knew that he was meant to shut up. Now twenty-four and working in the operating theatre of St Thomas' Hospital, Victoria Fandine-Browne was a frighteningly self-assured young woman.

Later, while Victoria was making tea, Giles shuffled uncomfortably and asked Alexandra if Gilbert's death gave her financial worries.

"No, Giles, I am very well provided for," she replied. "I shall discharge all Gilbert's debts and still be extremely comfortable."

"I suppose your son would have inherited in the normal way of things?"

"No doubt!" After a slight pause to adjust her mood, Alexandra asked, "What do you think we ought to do with the horses?"

"I can arrange for them to be sold."

She thought about it. "Couldn't I take them over?" she asked. "Does the Jockey Club have anything against women owners?"

Giles furrowed his brow as he went over the relevant laws of racing in his mind. "No, I think they're fairly liberal-minded in *that* respect," he said. "In any case, you could always adopt an assumed name."

"Oh, I hope that won't be necessary. We must preserve the Fandine-Browne reputation!"

It was a bravely ironic remark; her son's trial took place the following week.

To provide support for his ordeal in the witness-box, Michael Pilgrim was accompanied by Giles and Daphne, who took rooms at an hotel in Trowbridge for the duration of the trial. Lawrence attended only for the morning that was necessary to present his medical evidence.

Giles saw at once that a *cause célèbre* was in the making. That part of the court set aside for the press was packed solid: it seemed that the editor of every local and national newspaper had sent a representative and that they were looking for sensation. Giles never rid himself of the idea that for this reason alone the case was kept going for five days, whereas, in his opinion, two would have sufficed.

The prosecution case was massive and meticulously prepared. Michael was the main witness, but the Chief Constable, ruthless in his resolve to secure a crushing conviction, had spared no effort to root out corroborative evidence. Boys from Swindon, Newbury and Marlborough itself were produced; their fathers swore they had been given sums of money to overlook certain outrages perpetrated by the prisoner upon their sons. And a whole day was spent considering the reasons for Rowland Fandine-Browne's precipitate departure from Oxford University.

The man in the dock had an appalling time.

Of all that he had to endure, the worst was the constant, everlasting glare from Giles, who seemed never to take his eyes off Fandine-Browne, and the expression on his face was implacable.

"We are a family at Latimer's Barn," Giles had said. "No one touches my family!" He wrote it in the Big Book and he spent five days transmitting the sentiment to Michael Pilgrim's persecutor.

Each morning, the newspapers printed graphic accounts of the previous day's proceedings. Nowhere were they read more avidly than at Broadleaze Farm to the south-west of Chippenham. Priscilla Hastings savoured every word of fact, opinion and innuendo.

"Well, here's a pretty mess!" she declared. "The Fandine-Brownes! You see, this man Flamsteed ruins anyone fool enough to come into contact with him."

"You're surely not suggesting that Rowland is innocent, are you, Mother?" Sir Arnold asked. He was rather pained at having the thing raked over across his breakfast table.

"He may not be totally innocent, but he is nowhere near as guilty as this!"

That particular intellectual somersault was too much for Sir Arnold. "How can one be partially guilty of sodomy?" he asked. "And it appears that the lad from the stable was not the only victim."

"All perjury!" his mother insisted vehemently. "Flamsteed has put them up to it. That boy Briggs, for instance: his father is a great friend of Mallender, the wretch who drove the Dallows out of business."

To Arnold's discomfort, his wife joined in.

"You talk about victims – how would you describe poor Mr Fandine-Browne?"

"The London and North-Western Railway Company have admitted the possibility of an accident," Arnold said.

"Nonsense! The unfortunate man was hounded to his death – and well you know it, Arnold!"

From the earliest days of her marriage, Augusta Hastings had espoused her mother-in-law's causes; nowadays, she did so with a fervour approaching fanaticism.

Returning to *The Times* to read of the latest developments in the Balkans where Russia and Turkey had been at war for five months, Arnold was unaware that he had at least one thing to be grateful for: his wife and mother remained ignorant of the fact that Giles and Alexandra were long-established lovers. Given *that* piece of information, their speculative flights of fancy might have taken them into the stratosphere.

Giles was grimly satisfied when he returned to Cannings Ambo from Trowbridge. The jury were out for less than ten minutes to reach their verdict, and the judge handed down the maximum punishment without pausing for thought. Rowland Fandine-Browne was sentenced to penal servitude for life.

Tired and feeling somehow unclean, Giles was given a most unwelcome piece of news by Leander after she had greeted him in her usual effusive manner.

"Uncle Ralph's at the Rectory. He arrived on Wednesday."

"Oh? What's he after?"

It was an adult question and the seventeen-year-old Leander produced a completely adult answer. "Money! He claims he's worried about us, of course."

In fact, Ralph Flamsteed's professed interest was in his nephew,

John Shepherd, now four and growing strong after eighteen months of very indifferent health. For a while, his parents had worried themselves sick over him, especially since, as time passed, he seemed fated to be the only child. However, now that Lawrence Stanton had found the right tonic, young John was progressing famously.

"What did Elisabeth think about him turning up out of the blue?" Giles asked.

Leander pulled a face: her aunt had said several surprisingly strong things about Ralph's unexpected and most unwelcome arrival.

The following day, a Saturday, Giles worked normally until lunchtime, then he went to the Rectory.

Ralph was not ill, but neither did he look well, and he had the disturbing demeanour of a tense man pretending to be at ease. Using the simple expedient of talking only about neutral topics and ignoring his brother's jittery condition, Giles remained unaffected.

By Sunday afternoon, Ralph had no option other than to come out with it. A stroll along the gallop alone with Giles to counteract a good lunch at The House seemed the only chance he was likely to get.

Impatient to have done with it, Giles helped him. "And how is the business, Ralph?" he asked.

"It's doing very well, Giles, very well indeed. I've introduced a few Spanish lines that seem to be popular."

"Good! I'm pleased to hear it."

"There are one or two problems, however."

"Really?"

"Yes. The warehouse needs a new roof, and I should be thinking of investment for the bottling plant."

"Very wise."

"But at the moment, I'm having liquidity problems."

"Talk to the bank."

"They won't help. Hamilton's retired and the new man thinks I'm being too ambitious."

Giles said nothing.

"So, I'm stuck, you see," Ralph was finally forced to say.

"Dear, dear!"

"But I'm sure you could lend me the money, Giles."

"No, Ralph!"

"Giles!"

"No!"

"Ten thousand, that's all it needs."

"Ten thousand!" Giles stopped dead in his tracks, gaping at Ralph, aghast at the magnitude of the mess he had created. "Ten thousand! For God's sake, Ralph, what have you been doing?"

"That's none of your business!"

"It is when you come here asking for a king's ransom. And while we're about it, let's have the truth, eh? You don't want the money for improvements. You're trying to paper over the cracks so that Coopers and Smedhurst might believe you're worth buying out."

"How do you know about that?" Ralph's face was grey.

"I keep myself informed," Giles said, deliberately lofty. Secretly, he raised a hat to Horatio's intelligence service, as accurate as ever.

"Look here, Giles, I gave you seven and a half thousand to set yourself up in this place."

"Ralph!" Giles almost burst out laughing at his brother's powers of self-deception. "You *paid* me *five* thousand for my inheritance. We have papers to prove it. They were drawn up at your insistence. Do you remember?"

"Don't you care for the good name of Flamsteed any more?" Ralph shouted, abandoning all pretence at logic.

"Yes, I care very much." Giles was angry now. "I work night and day for it. But Flamsteed means horses now, not our father's business that you have driven into the gutter. The only 'liquidity' problems you have is the filth you've been putting in bottles these last eighteen years! I'm astonished that you've managed to get away with it for so long."

Ralph was left standing as Giles strode back to Latimer's Barn.

On Monday morning, Elisabeth was overcome by distinctly unchristian feelings as she watched Ralph leave the Rectory in a carriage for Swindon. After his failure with Giles, Ralph, with unmitigated gall, had tried to borrow money from her, creating an ugly scene when she refused.

"May the good Lord forgive me," Elisabeth said, "but I don't think I ever want to see my brother again."

"After the way Father dealt with him, I don't think you will," Leander assured her.

Throughout the 1860s, a band of romantics who dreamed of an England that never really existed, had devoted much time and energy to castigating the railways as an aesthetic and social menace. Yet not even the eloquence of men like John Ruskin had the slightest effect on the march of progress, and Sir Arnold Hastings was glad of it.

Broadleaze Farm had a dairy herd of three hundred cows and the Great Western Railway was capable of getting their milk to London by four o'clock each morning. After six months of sending part of his output to the metropolis, Hastings now had the chance of a contract with the London Co-operative Society that would take all the milk he could produce at a penny a gallon more than his best current price.

So it was that he boarded a Bristol to London train at Chippenham that morning and settled down to compose himself for the critical negotiations ahead.

Twenty-five minutes later the train halted at Swindon, and, after an unsuccessful search for an empty compartment, Ralph Flamsteed became Hastings's travelling companion.

The two men took no notice of each other beyond the exchange of looks customary between strangers when one is spoiling the other's privacy. Ralph, obsessed with the thought that he had left something behind in Cannings Ambo, checked through his bags while Hastings gazed fixedly out of the window as the train accelerated out of Wiltshire.

Against the optimism of the forthcoming milk contract, Hastings found himself setting the continuing difficulty of finding a buyer for the abandoned property and estates round Marlborough. Only the previous day, a letter from the agent had recommended lowering the asking price by £1,000 and Hastings reflected bitterly that, were he to secure the Co-operative Society contract, the extra profit on a quarter of a million gallons of milk would be needed to make good this shortfall in his expectations. In round figures, that was two years' work.

Beyond Didcot, he shook off his gloom and noticed his fellow-traveller.

Ralph, too, was assessing his position. Having taken a file of papers from a small suitcase, he was recalculating his future in the certain knowledge that help would not be forthcoming. As he finished with each sheet of paper, he laid it on the seat beside him, the seat opposite Sir Arnold Hastings. Even though they were turned top-to-bottom from his point of view, Hastings found no difficulty in deciphering the distinctive letter-head of Flamsteed & Sons on some of the papers.

Surreptitiously, he studied Ralph. By stretching the imagination, there was a family likeness, so, without knowing why, Hastings took the plunge.

"Excuse me, sir, are you Mr Ralph Flamsteed?" he asked.

Ralph's reaction was slow and suspicious. "Yes, I am," he replied at last. "What of it?"

"Your brother used to train horses for my father."

"Ah, I see." Ralph's manner became more friendly. "And do you have horses at Cannings Ambo?"

"Good God, no! It ruined my father."

"Did it? Did it really?" Ralph looked at him speculatively. "My brother's establishment seems to be ruining a great many people. Whom do I have the honour of addressing?"

"I beg your pardon – Hastings. Sir Arnold Hastings. I inherited my father's title."

"Yes, indeed. I recall reading about your father's sad case. How did that end?"

"I repaid everything, but it came close to finishing me." Hastings paused. "You implied that others have come to grief through association with your brother?"

"Absolutely! Look at the Fandine-Browne affair."

"Yes." Hastings's tone indicated that he remained unconvinced on that score.

"And myself, of course," Ralph added quickly, as if it were of no consequence.

"Yourself?"

"I lent Giles ten thousand pounds to start him up in that venture, and I've never bothered with repayments." Pleased with his performance as an out-and-out liar, Ralph warmed to his theme. "Sadly, things are different now. Between you and me, Hastings, my business is in trouble – I'm sure you appreciate how hard things have been these last two years. So, I want my money back. As a matter of fact, I've just been to ask for it."

Ralph Flamsteed stopped and assumed an air of distress.

"What happened?" Hastings asked impatiently.

"He refused to acknowledge the debt. As good as had me thrown off his precious estate."

"Surely not!"

"He did, and that's as true as I'm sitting here."

Arnold Hastings was much impressed. His wife and mother were right: Giles Flamsteed was indeed an unprincipled rogue.

They talked eagerly for the remainder of the journey and were in no hurry to part when the train reached Paddington.

"I say, how long are you staying in town?" Ralph asked as they walked down the platform.

"For the whole week, I think. There is some ticklish business to transact."

"Why don't we have dinner at my club one evening?"

"That's very good of you, Flamsteed. Thank you."

CHAPTER 9

1880

'That young man on a bicycle'

The evidence of progress was plain to see.

Built and opened in 1879, the village school between Church Green and Oak Cottage was Giles's anticipation of the following year's Education Act which stipulated that all children must have access to a school. Rather than make youngsters struggle to and from Marlborough, Giles spent nearly five hundred pounds on a graceful, well-equipped building. Elisabeth and Daphne, who ran it, knew that there was a strong element of what was now called 'estate philosophy' behind the altruism: Giles was a firm believer in self-sufficiency. In the same way that it fed itself and looked after its sick, Cannings Ambo must also provide for the young, enabling them to grow up as part of a large family.

A splendid new house stood at the entrance to the drive of Latimer's Barn. It was purpose-built for the Merriweathers, who now had a fourth child, Letitia, born at a few minutes past midnight on Christmas Day 1878, when the church bells were ringing and the waits were singing carols outside The George.

There were also new tombstones in the churchyard.

Doctor Palfreyman and Caleb Jackson had gone in 1878, the doctor at the ripe old age of eighty-five, Caleb at sixty-nine after an all too short enjoyment of his richly deserved retirement. Both received special mentions in the Big Book for their part in the stable's early development.

Malachi and Walter Stringfellow died within a few months of each other in the following year. No one was able to determine their exact ages, although the scrappily incomplete parish records of Cannings St John suggested that Malachi was born in the year of Trafalgar.

But now, in the spring of 1880, after two years in which Latimer's Barn had turned out a consistent stream of good winners, all eyes were fixed eagerly on the future, with one aspect of it commanding especial attention.

It was Piers Prideaux, youngest brother of the Duke of Laverstoke, who finally caused Horatio to let off steam on a subject that had nagged at him and several others for some time.

After a year of manufacturing excuses to visit Latimer's Barn at weekly intervals, Lord Piers proposed marriage to Leander on her twentieth birthday. He was thirty years old, handsome, kind and surprisingly wealthy for an aristocratic younger son.

Leander thanked him nicely, kissed him on the cheek, explained that she was unable to return the affection he felt for her, and left him in no doubt that he had been turned down flat.

The natural charm with which Leander handled the matter was polished by practice: Piers Prideaux was the sixth suitor she had rejected in as many months.

"Now then, what's to be done, eh?" Horatio demanded when Giles informed him of the latest unsuccessful supplicant. "I told you they were going to be at her like bees round a honeypot. She's the most attractive girl for miles around."

"She's the most beautiful girl I've ever seen," Giles said proudly.

"Right! So what are you going to do?"

"I don't follow you, Horatio, why should I have to *do* anything?"

"Well . . . I . . ." For once, Horatio was at a loss for words.

"Do you think she was wrong to refuse a bit of a title?" Giles asked. "Are you afraid the Duke might be upset?"

In all honesty, Horatio knew that he could hardly use that possibility as an excuse for his agitation.

Desmond Aubrey Hubert Prideaux, sixth Duke of Laverstoke, had become a patron of Latimer's Barn with the opening of the new yard in 1874. Now forty-two years of age, his classically aristocratic features and bearing gave a completely erroneous impression of haughtiness. Desmond Prideaux was a philanthropist from the old eighteenth-century landed gentry, but his estate to the south of Chippenham and Calne, fifteen miles from Latimer's Barn, was run in a way that proved His Grace to be in the vanguard of Gladstone's reforming liberalism.

Eaton Mandeville, over three thousand acres of lush park- and farm-land, was famous for its magnificent Tudor mansion, gardens and follies – there were supposed to be fourteen of them. Recently, the Duke had set up a model farming experiment and acquired notoriety in certain circles by banning the hunt from his land. This side of his character was responsible for his choice of racehorse trainer: Desmond Prideaux sent his horses to Giles because of the suspicion that they were not being treated right in Newmarket rather than their conspicuous lack of success.

But the Duke of Laverstoke was no airy-fairy dreamer, and was perfectly capable of telling his brother to get a grip on himself and look for a more suitable wife, one who desired nothing more than pampered idleness. Knowing this, Horatio switched to the real nub of the matter.

"Whoever marries Leander is going to have a say in running Latimer's Barn."

"It's likely that he'll be the next trainer," Giles replied, showing that he was aware of the point Horatio was struggling to make.

"There you are, then!"

Giles smiled affectionately at his friend's turmoil. "I think we can assume that Leander appreciates this," he pointed out gently.

"Have you spoken to her about it?"

"No."

Horatio scratched his chin in search of comfort. "Well, I must say, she's always been a credit to you," he admitted.

"She's never come within a million miles of letting me or Cannings Ambo down," Giles said.

"So you're going to trust her to pick the right one."

"Yes – assuming she wants a husband."

"I imagine she will."

"So do I." Giles gave Horatio a look that acknowledged Leander's loving, passionate nature.

"She seems to have a soft spot for Rupert Timberlake," Horatio said with obvious disapproval.

"Oh, she likes him," Giles replied, "but there's nothing serious in that."

"H'm!" Horatio needed convincing.

The Timberlakes were a funny lot.

Marlborough's problem was finding out how many of them there were and where the money came from.

They had bought the Hastings estate in the spring of 1878 after a winter of fierce haggling. Godfrey Timberlake, thought to be aged about sixty, occupied the house in Marlborough with his sons Rupert and James. There was no sign of a wife and mother. Godfrey's elder brother, Cuthbert, took up residence in a lodge at the Hungerford end of Savernake Forest, and had at least two sons and a daughter spread round the various components of the estate, presumably living in the least run-down houses. Additionally, there were persistent reports of more brothers, cousins, step-daughters and mysterious hangers-on.

Timberlake money was purported to come from industry in Yorkshire and the area round Newcastle-upon-Tyne; there was talk of involvement in a Carlisle brewery, Derbyshire coal mines and fishing at Grimsby. Later still, the grapevine picked up whispers of interests in newspapers, canned foods and chemicals. Giles and Guy Mallender tended to dismiss the stories as over-embellished fantasy, but, in due course, Horatio's contacts in the world of business reported that most of the stories were true.

After the Timberlakes had been in Marlborough and Savernake for a year, with minimal social contact between themselves and the townspeople, Leander came face to face with Rupert in the High Street one afternoon.

"I say, are you Miss Flamsteed?" Rupert asked eagerly.

He was twenty-five, tall and decent-looking: she rather liked him. "Yes, I am," she replied. "And I'll lay odds that you're one of those frightful Timberlakes!"

"I'm Rupert, son of Godfrey," he laughed. "Why are we frightful?"

"Only because *they* can't find out anything about you and you seem to be in trade up to your necks."

"Is that all?" He looked and sounded disappointed. "So, you're the famous daughter of Cannings Ambo?"

"I am. Are you interested in horses, Mr Timberlake?"

"Very much so."

"You should come and see us. I'll show you our stable. It's very impressive."

A few days later, Rupert Timberlake agreed with her. "Amazing, Miss Flamsteed, truly amazing," he said after she had spent an hour conducting him round the yard. "Now you and your father must come to dinner with us."

Once Leander's condition that William must be included in the invitation was met, she set about persuading Giles.

The evening was a great success. Godfrey Timberlake was delighted and a little flattered to have the famous Giles Flamsteed and his daughter sitting down at his table, and proved charming. Nevertheless, an iron will and formidable temper lay beneath the veneer; even Leander was made to feel that she had poked her nose where it was not welcome when she asked after the whereabouts of Rupert's brother, James.

"Away. On business," Godfrey Timberlake told her with a sharp edge to his voice.

For most of the time, however, he was very agreeable, and William had an astute comment to make when he and Leander were back in their own sitting-room at Latimer's Barn.

"That man Timberlake would be pleased if you married his son, Lea."

"Do you think so?" She was surprised.

"I'm sure of it, but I don't think the idea has occurred to Rupert yet."

"Let's hope it never does," Leander said wearily. "Rejecting unsuitable young men is such a miserable occupation."

She need not have worried: Rupert Timberlake was much too sensible.

The more he saw of Leander, the more he liked her. He could easily have allowed himself to become captivated by her looks, exciting independence of spirit and brilliant style, and, like many another red-blooded male, would have given his eye-teeth to bed her. But even if he were able to conquer his aversion to marriage, he could see insurmountable obstacles. She expected the very highest standards and no one, absolutely no one, would be allowed to come between her and Latimer's Barn, or, to a lesser extent, that brother of hers. Somewhere, there must be a man capable of meeting Leander Flamsteed's requirements, and a very lucky fellow he would be, but not for an instant did Rupert Timberlake entertain any illusions of himself in that role.

His sensible attitude paved the way for them to become friends. They were often to be seen together in Marlborough and Cannings Ambo, and Horatio was not the only person who jumped to the wrong conclusion. Half of Marlborough was convinced that it was only a matter of time before the wedding was announced.

In all his twenty years as a trainer, Giles had never handled a really top-class filly. There had been dozens of exciting promises and as many failures; worst of all was a tragic daughter of New Invention who stumbled and broke a leg on the way to the start of the 1874 One Thousand Guineas.

Ophelia never really looked like improving on the dismal record.

When she first entered the yard as a yearling, Giles soon feared that he had guided the Duke of Laverstoke into paying a fearsome 1,750 guineas for an animal that was to prove worthless. Her sire was Hermit, the winner of the 1867 Derby, and if looks were anything to go by, Ophelia was destined to be unbeatable.

Instead, she was the most nervous, highly strung animal that anyone at Latimer's Barn could ever remember. Literally frightened of her own shadow, she was terrified of other horses, and, for the first few weeks, only Leander could go anywhere near her without provoking hysteria.

Breaking and schooling the filly was a nightmare. Long after her contemporaries were out on the gallops, Leander and Conn still had her on the lunging rein twice a day.

"I don't know what we're going to do with her, Miss Leander," Conn said after a series of frustrating days. "I've never seen one this bad before."

"We aren't giving up, Conn," Leander replied fiercely. Now married to his Sally and living on Church Green, Conn seemed to be much more serious-minded, and inclined to worry these days.

A week later, Giles shook his head disconsolately as he watched their vain attempts with the filly and said, "It's no good, she'll have to go. I'll talk to His Grace."

"No! She's staying here," Leander said. "She's very talented and she's going to be outstanding."

Not since Bellerophon had anyone even considered arguing with her when she was in *that* mood.

Ophelia first raced in August, at least three months later than the other two-year-olds. The result was embarrassing, particularly for her partner, Peter Izzard.

No longer could any Tom, Dick or Harry get on a horse and ride in a race: jockeys were now required to have a licence. This vital document could be rescinded for a wide range of misdemeanours, thus making the interruption or end of a jockey's career a very public disgrace. Failing to ride a horse to the best of one's ability was a serious offence, and Peter half feared that Ophelia's astonishing performance might make the stewards think twice about his integrity.

It was bad enough getting her down to the start, but at least it was an operation that could be planned and controlled. What was likely to happen when the starter lowered his flag to set them racing was anybody's guess.

As the others set off on the five-furlong dash, Ophelia, positioned well to the rear by prior arrangement with the authorities, stood stock-still. When she was fully satisfied that there was no danger of her getting anywhere near another horse, she condescended to run. Peter Izzard would long remember the jeering as he finally passed the main body of the crowd; their suggestion that his mount was a premature entry in the next race was mostly good-natured since no one had considered Ophelia worth a bet.

The race was at Salisbury, where Horatio, who had long since surrendered to Digby Protheroe's bombardment and become a steward, was not a member of the panel of three on duty that day. Horatio saw this as a good thing.

"I say, Protheroe, I'm glad not to be involved in any deliberations on that fiasco," he said.

"There aren't any," Digby Protheroe assured him. "Both Giles and His Grace warned us about her temperament."

Peter Izzard's relief was not without apprehension; Leander had made it plain that a single failure would not discourage her.

Ophelia took part in two more races in 1879: or rather, she was entered for them, paraded round the paddock, then provided a talking-point and amusement for the spectators. Peter was profoundly grateful for the second occasion, when she spared him the ribald comments of the crowd by refusing to do anything at all. She remained placidly cropping grass, twenty yards behind the start, until Leander arrived to lead her back to the van and the safety of her box at home.

The Duke of Laverstoke came to Latimer's Barn frequently, but his end-of-season visit in October had special significance. He gave each of the lads two gold sovereigns and began to formulate plans for the following year.

He tackled the question of Ophelia at once.

"Don't you think, Mr Flamsteed, that I should get her out of your sight and leave you a box free for an animal you *can* train?" he asked. "There's no difficulty, you know – I'll take her to Eaton Mandeville and my sister Harriet will potter round on her and turn her into a pet."

Giles squirmed. "That is what *I* would recommend, Your Grace, but my daughter insists that she can do something with her."

"Does she, indeed?"

"Yes. I have to say that it's rather difficult to agree with her in this instance."

The Duke looked at Leander who contrived to be resolute while giving him one of her brightest smiles.

"All right!" His Grace's mind was made up. "I'm of the same mind as you, Mr Flamsteed, it looks hopeless. But I'm not going to be the one to say your daughter's wrong. We'll keep Ophelia going for another year."

During the relatively mild winter of 1879–80, not a single day passed on which Leander did not do something with the wayward filly. For several weeks it was all kept secret: Ophelia was only taken out on Cannings Down during the lunch break or in the ever-shortening afternoons, when everyone was occupied with other things. At the end of November, Giles became aware that a second horse, ridden by Conn, was becoming involved in the clandestine training sessions. Once Christmas was past, Abraham Merriweather was drawn into the conspiracy: at first, he dreaded being questioned by Giles, but soon discovered that the master he revered was content to let his daughter go about things in her own way.

At the end of April, Ophelia travelled to Newmarket to compete in the One Thousand Guineas. There had been no question of risking a preparation race, and Giles's heart was in his mouth during the parade round the paddock and the canter down the Rowley Mile to the start.

Leander squeezed his hand and whispered, "Don't worry, Father. She and Peter know how to do it."

Sticking to the procedure established in her previous attempts at racing, Peter held Ophelia back at the start, well away from the other horses. But once the flag came down, everything changed. It was so dramatic as to leave everyone on Newmarket Heath blinking with disbelief – everyone, that is, except Leander who had planned it and Peter Izzard who was doing it.

Ophelia surged forward with tremendous power and zest to lead the field within the first ten strides.

Glad that she had at least made a show of it this time, Giles was certain that the filly's spectacular burst of speed would soon fade away. It did not. At the furlong distance Ophelia still had a lead of two lengths, and when Peter asked her for a final flourish it was soon apparent that the rest were run ragged: Ophelia passed the winning post six lengths clear of her nearest rival in a new record time.

"Well, Miss Flamsteed," the Duke of Laverstoke said as he stood in the enclosure with his first Classic winner, "you were right, weren't you? What have you done to her?"

"She doesn't like having other horses anywhere near her," Leander explained. "She *detests* it! There are a few at home she can just about tolerate, but strangers send her crazy."

"Hence this performance of dropping herself out last year?"

"Yes. What we've managed to do over the winter is to persuade her that she doesn't have to be *behind* – there's a perfectly safe place in front. She's got the speed and the stamina for it."

"What do we think of this, Mr Flamsteed?" the Duke asked, smiling broadly.

Giles shook his head. It was clear that he was prouder than ever of his daughter.

Five weeks later, Ophelia repeated the performance, this time over Epsom's fearsome mile and a half in the Oaks, the day after the Duke of Westminster's colt, Bend Or, won the Derby. Her accomplishment

147

was the finest example of courageous front-running that most people could recall, and the filly regarded for over a year as useless had won five times her substantial purchase price in only two races.

At that stage, Giles and the Duke of Laverstoke were content to rest on their laurels, thinking only of Ophelia's future as a brood mare.

Leander had other ideas. She kept the filly at work, and on Sunday afternoons, the young man on a bicycle started watching her.

His first appearance was on the second Sunday in June. He was coming along the lane from the direction of Devizes and stopped to stare as she cantered past about half a mile from him. He was still there fifteen minutes later when Leander took Ophelia back, this time at a sharpish gallop.

Precisely the same thing happened the Sunday after; later in the week, Horatio commented on the march of progress.

"I saw a young chap on one of those new safety bicycles the other day," he said. "Here, in the village! Lovely machine. Made in Birmingham, of course."

"Cannings Ambo has all the modern gadgets," Giles said with a facetiousness that Horatio failed to pick up.

"Oh, no. I don't think this fellow's a local. I haven't seen him round this way before."

Leander remained silent.

The bicyclist was there again the next Sunday, even though she delayed riding Ophelia out for nearly an hour. This time, there was no question of his simply happening to be passing; he was waiting, leaning on his machine and looking very relaxed about it all.

William was annoyed when Leander told him.

"What a cheek! We'll get something done about him if he carries on like that."

"Don't be silly, William." Leander was laughing. "He's perfectly harmless. If he turns up again I'm going to ask him what he's doing."

"Be careful, Lea! You never know, he might be trying to abduct you or the filly."

"In broad daylight? And what about his gang? Where are they lurking?"

William looked truculently dubious.

Sunday came round again, and sure enough, there he was. Leander turned Ophelia away from the line of the gallop and set her walking across the downland towards the bicyclist.

It was obvious what she intended and it took nearly five minutes to close the gap between them. The young man had every opportunity to jump on his bicycle and go, but he stayed, perfectly still, waiting.

The closer she came to him, the more Leander liked what she saw, and she noticed that Ophelia showed no fear of him, so much so that she walked to the very edge of the turf where it merged with the half-metalled surface of the lane and stopped only two feet from the stranger.

Not in the least put out by the advantage of height she had over him, he smiled and she found herself smiling back into a face that was frank and friendly.

"Good afternoon, miss," he said. "I reckon you're Leander Flamsteed. Am I right?"

"Yes. How do you know?"

"Everyone knows you. You're famous."

"Am I? And who might you be?"

"Steven Hawksworth," he replied. "That's Steven with a 'v' instead of a 'ph' because the parish clerk made a mistake when he registered my birth and we never bothered to put it right."

Smiling at his quaintness, she asked, "Well, Steven-with-a-v Hawksworth, why have you been watching me?"

"Because I think you and that filly look very beautiful together. As soon as I came out on my new machine, I saw you, so I kept coming back."

Inclining her head at the compliment, Leander found that its unaffected directness caused her to recognise a kindred spirit.

"This is Ophelia," she said, running a hand down the filly's sleek neck. "She's the winner of the One Thousand Guineas and the Oaks."

"I thought it might be."

"Why did you think that?"

"The special treatment you give her. They say she's very difficult."

"*Was* difficult," Leander said. "She's very good now, as you can see. Do you take an interest in racing, Mr Hawksworth?"

"I like to keep myself informed. The men on the boats talk about it a great deal."

Leander dismounted, ducking under Ophelia's head to face him. He was a fraction under six feet tall with straw-coloured hair, pale blue eyes and a face glowing with healthy vitality. She guessed, correctly, that he was twenty-four; she also thought that Steven Hawksworth was no more capable of duplicity or unkindness than of riding his bicycle to the moon. His Sunday-best suit, however, was not a success: it had been cobbled together by a tailor concerned only with

149

giving his customers what they thought they wanted as quickly and cheaply as possible. Nevertheless, Leander was acutely aware that he had a strong, pleasing physique and decided that he was the most attractive man she had ever met.

"Boats? What boats?" she asked.

"On the canal. My father builds and repairs them."

"Oh, are you the Hawksworths at Pewsey Wharf?"

"Yes." He seemed immensely pleased.

"You see, Mr Hawksworth, I've heard of you, as well. So, you work with your father?"

"As you do, I believe."

"My word, Mr Hawksworth, you are well informed!"

It was, of course, far too soon for him to be able to comprehend her expressions and nuances. Her tone and the brightness of her eyes led him to fear that she was mocking him.

"No, no, Miss Flamsteed, all this is common knowledge. I assure you that I have not been prying. Your stable has been very famous for some years – particularly since you won the Derby."

He was rewarded with a smile of exquisite radiance that turned his knees to jelly. "Of course," she said. "Please don't think anything of it. You must understand that Bellerophon was our *first* Derby winner. We intend repeating it as often as possible."

They both laughed.

"I must take Ophelia back for a feed," Leander went on. "Abraham gets anxious if I keep her out too long on a Sunday – it upsets his routine."

"Who's Abraham?" Steven asked.

"Mr Merriweather, our head lad. He's wonderful. He came all the way from Yorkshire on chance because he wanted to work for us."

"Does he live in that new house at the entrance to your drive?"

"Yes. Father had it built specially for him. Come along, you can walk with me."

Instead of going straight across the turf of the Down to the yard, Leander followed the lane. It was a mile to the drive and she set an easy pace, thus allowing nearly twenty minutes of conversation. Aware of what she was doing, Steven Hawksworth made the most of the unexpected golden opportunity.

When they arrived, he was dismayed to find Abraham working in his garden so that he was subjected to a most searching scrutiny.

"That's Mr Merriweather," Leander said unnecessarily. "And look! Do you see the little one?" A tiny girl of eighteen months, with dark hair and eyes like coal-black jewels, who had been playing with a pile of stones, jumped up to squeal with delight and wave excitedly when she saw Leander. "That's the newest Merriweather. Her name is Letitia – but everyone calls her Tish, of course. Isn't she beautiful?"

"She is, very beautiful," Steven agreed and Leander saw that he genuinely meant it.

"Thank you for your company, Mr Hawksworth," she said. "It has been a great pleasure talking to you."

"Thank *you*, Miss Flamsteed. Perhaps I shall see you again next Sunday?"

"Perhaps," she said and led Ophelia away.

Despite Abraham Merriweather's stare, Steven Hawksworth watched her until she was out of sight before he mounted his bicycle and rode off.

When they were alone together in their sitting-room that evening, Leander stared at William in a way that made him feel most uncomfortable.

"What, exactly, did you imagine you were doing this afternoon?" she asked eventually.

"Er . . . nothing. Whatever makes you think I was doing anything?" he asked in an attempt to establish his innocence.

"Oh, William, really! You were skulking with a pair of binoculars." She thought it was funny.

"How do you know that?" he asked, looking rather put out.

"The sun caught them when I was riding across towards Mr Hawksworth. Later on, I saw you crawling along by the brook. You were stalking us."

"Well . . ." William was burrowing into his chair, willing himself to disappear. "I thought I should keep an eye on you."

"Whatever for?"

"He may have been connected with the Association."

As part of what he considered a full and proper upbringing, Giles had given them an account of the difficulties that had beset Latimer's Barn.

"That lot were done for and finished *ages* ago."

"We don't know that for sure, Lea."

"Even if the Association does still exist, I can assure you that Mr Hawksworth is nothing to do with it. He didn't try to ravish me or make off with me, did he?"

"You sound disappointed!" William accused, quite inaccurately.

"Don't be silly, William!" She jumped up to kneel at the side of his chair, taking his hands in hers. "It's very sweet of you to worry, but there really is no need for it. Mr Hawksworth is very nice –

and funny. Do you know what he insisted on telling me straight away?"

William shook his head.

"His name is Steven – spelt s–t–e–v–e–n, not *ph*. A mistake was made when his birth was registered. Now isn't that a droll thing to go round telling people?"

"Yes, it is. Where does he come from?"

"Pewsey Wharf. He works in the boatyard with his father."

"Oh, *those* Hawksworths!"

William and Jim had been re-roofing Alfred and Margaret Wesley's house in Church Marks. The new timbers were brought by canal from Reading to Pewsey, where William and Jim collected them with the cart used by Abraham Merriweather in his move from Yorkshire.

"I say!" William was brightening up. "Does this Mr Hawksworth of yours build boats?"

"Yes – although from what he was saying, the business seems to be dying out. It's mostly repair work these days."

"But he's an expert carpenter?" William asked eagerly.

"I imagine so. However, he is not *my* Mr Hawksworth, William."

"You like him, though."

Leander smiled. "Yes, William, I like him."

"I'm told he was here again yesterday," Elisabeth said as she welcomed Giles to one of his regular Monday lunches at the Rectory.

"Who?"

"That young man on a bicycle."

"Oh. Was he?"

"Now, Giles, don't be vague," his sister chided. "Horatio is saying it looks serious."

"What on earth do you mean, Elisabeth? Serious? How?"

"Romance, my dear."

"Surely not!"

"I have no idea. I've never seen them, but almost everyone else has. Both Alice Merriweather and Lizzie O'Malley are convinced that it's going to lead to something."

"They must be mistaken!"

Nevertheless, Steven Hawksworth was invited to tea in The House the following Sunday.

Leander rode out to meet him on a hack that afternoon, and he smiled knowingly as she approached.

"I guessed Ophelia might be resting," Steven said.

"She won't be doing much else now," Leander replied.

Two days previously, the filly had won the Champion Stakes at

Newmarket, and Leander now agreed with Giles and the Duke of Laverstoke that her racing days were over. Arrangements were already in hand for her to be moved down the road to the stud.

Although Steven was brought into The House at his instigation, the occasion was an ordeal for Giles who had no idea how to set about evaluating a potential suitor for his daughter. Had the object of his scrutiny been overawed and lapsed into frozen politeness, tea would have been a disaster. But Steven Hawksworth did no such thing: his outgoing nature, coupled with great respect for a man who had taught himself to train racehorses, ensured that he and Giles were soon chatting like old friends, allowing William no chance to introduce the subject of carpentry.

Once the rapport between Giles and Steven had been established, Leander worked hard at separating them. She felt sorry for her father, who looked quite crestfallen when she dragged Steven away at five o'clock, but she was determined.

Steven was shown round the yard in a most comprehensive manner, being taken into each box and introduced to its occupant. He thought he was being afforded a great privilege; in reality, Leander was giving him an examination.

He passed it with distinction. Steven loved horses, and, with the exception of two animals who were sick and listlessly below par, they all recognised his feelings and reacted accordingly.

Satisfied, Leander became aware of the time and was hopping about like a cat on hot bricks. "I must get ready for church now, Mr Hawksworth," she said, preparing to dash back to The House. "Will you come with us?"

"Er . . . yes . . . with pleasure, Miss Flamsteed."

Steven did his best to conceal his misgivings: being shown the stable was one thing, attending Evensong with the Flamsteeds was a fish of a very different kettle. As he feared, they had their own boxed-in pew set at right angles to the nave and the congregation could get a good look at him. They all knew who he was, if only by repute: finding him in the Flamsteed pew was a surprise that unleashed a flood of curiosity that was nerve-wracking despite its intrinsic politeness.

There was, however, a consolation to help him through the ordeal. It was the first time that Steven had seen Leander in anything other than her riding gear. He had already decided that she was the most beautiful woman he was ever likely to set eyes on; now, in a cream dress with grey and pink trimmings, she was breathtaking. And during the singing of the last hymn, 'For all the Saints who from their labours rest', there was a moment he knew he would never forget if he lived to be a hundred.

At the words, 'But lo! there breaks a yet more glorious day', Leander turned to him and smiled from beneath the broad brim of her hat.

He remembered her eyes as he set out to cycle the seven miles back to Pewsey in the balmy late-September dusk. There had been a great, glowing warmth in them together with fleeting suggestions of both companionship and mischief. He came to think of it as magic: there really was no other word for it.

On the first two Sundays in October, Leander went out on foot to meet Steven at prearranged times. There was no talk of returning to The House. Instead, they enjoyed perfect Indian summer weather, and Leander learned to ride the bicycle, reducing Steven to helpless laughter by her effective but ungainly mastery of the machine.

"You look infinitely better on a horse, Miss Flamsteed," he said between gasps of mirth.

"So I should hope, Mr Hawksworth," she replied grimly. "So I should hope! I've been sitting on horses since I was three. In any case, this miserable thing has no soul."

On the third Sunday of the month, Leander finally allowed herself the luxury of looking forward to Steven's arrival. Latimer's Barn had produced another winner of the Dewhurst Plate, and she was confident that he would want to hear all about it.

But the weather was dreadful that Sunday. After lunch, Leander donned a heavy waterproof cape and trudged along the Devizes Lane almost as far as Cannings St John. Steven did not come and when she returned after two miserable hours, her attempts to look unconcerned were only partially successful.

It was the same the following Sunday; after a week during which she had repeatedly displayed unprecedented signs of nervous irritability, Leander made no show of concealing her feelings.

"That's it," she said to William. "He won't come again."

"I'm sure he will, Lea. You can't expect a chap to cycle miles in this weather." He was shocked by the helpless deflation that had overcome her.

"No, it isn't the weather. I expect he's gone to London or Bristol."

"Why? What for?"

"He needs to find work. The Hawksworth business is in fairly bad shape."

"It can't be. There must be hundreds of boats to be repaired on that canal."

Leander shook her head with the vigour of despair. "No, William.

Traffic on the Kennet and Avon is bad and decreasing all the time because the owners are driving business away."

"That's lunacy!" William said angrily. "Why should they do that?"

"The owners of the canal are the Great Western Railway Company, William. They've had a controlling interest since 1852 to make sure that it can't compete with them."

William was silent for a few moments, mulling over and failing to understand his first encounter with the more ruthless subtleties of business. "So you think Steven Hawksworth may have gone away to look for work?" he said.

Leander sighed. "He spoke of it. Several times, in fact. He said he had to make a way for himself in life and the chances in Pewsey seemed pretty poor."

"And you think he won't come here again?"

"No, I'm afraid not."

"You could write and ask him."

"Of course I couldn't." She smiled ruefully at the realisation that some things lay beyond even her unconventional reach.

William stared at her sombrely for several moments. "You're very fond of him, Lea, aren't you?" he said quietly.

She made no reply and her face remained expressionless but for a slight twist of her mouth.

CHAPTER 10

1881

'Your very good friend, Leander Flamsteed'

The winter that took a grip on England during January 1881 quickly became the worst disaster in living memory. Cannings Ambo was only one of hundreds of villages in which intense cold and shortage of food put life in danger.

At Broadleaze Farm, near Chippenham, Priscilla Hastings died from the aggravated effects of bronchitis. She was fifty-nine and the ten sterile years of her widowhood had been consumed by myth and hatred.

The weather delayed her funeral. Clearing the snow-drifts around the farmhouse was merely the back-breaking prelude to finding a vacant plot in the churchyard and hacking a grave in earth frozen rock-solid to a depth of two feet. When the miserable ceremony did finally take place, Ralph Flamsteed was a reluctant mourner.

After selling Flamsteed & Sons to Cooper and Smedhurst in 1878, he had been kept on as a so-called general manager. In reality, the job was nebulous and in July 1880, it disappeared altogether. Increasing his capital by selling the houses in Greenwich that his great-grandfather had built, Ralph cast around for a means of earning a living.

He was helped and influenced by Sir Arnold Hastings. Following their chance meeting on the train and subsequent dinner, the two men had become friends, often visiting each other. Augusta Hastings gave Ralph a very warm welcome. After hearing of the stories he told about Giles she acted on him in a most pernicious way: more and more, Ralph Flamsteed began to believe the outrageous tales he concocted about his brother.

It was Arnold Hastings who spotted the shop and house for sale in Chippenham Market Place and urged Ralph to buy. Surprisingly, the town was without a decent wine shop and the one-time drapery store seemed ideal. Unoccupied for a year after half a century of neglect, the premises needed attention and while this was in hand the homeless Ralph was installed as a guest at Broadleaze Farm. The initial arrangement was for a fortnight, but towards the end of the second week, the snow came, marooning Ralph in a house made grim by death.

The first fall of snow was a blizzard that lasted for thirty hours.

When it stopped and the wind fell, Cannings Ambo was quiet and completely isolated. Inside the hour, scouting parties found that a drift up to fourteen feet deep, and extending over several treacherous acres, blocked access to the main road and Marlborough. By a freak of nature, however, the south-easterly gale had swept the Devizes Lane almost clear, allowing an easy passage to the stud. Beyond Cannings St John, the snow was impenetrable.

Giles and William joined with Horatio to organise the village; Leander, Abraham Merriweather and Conn were in charge of the horses.

There were two items of good fortune.

On the day before the blizzard, enough feed to last into spring had been delivered at Latimer's Barn. After Leander had made a careful inspection of the various stores she was confident that, whatever else happened, the horses would not go hungry.

Nat Thomas living to tell the tale was the second piece of luck. Because the snow started at three o'clock in the morning, he was at the stable, not in his hut. When Leander walked to Cannings St John to see how Paul and Seamus were coping, Nat's home had disappeared without trace. The lower slopes of Cannings Down and the gallop were unrecognisable beneath a white blanket whose surface had been whipped into crescent-shaped peaks and troughs by the savagery of the wind. The hut, fourteen feet high at the roof ridge, did not reappear for seven weeks.

Apart from those two happy chances, everything else was dreadful.

Leander made her first visit to the village two days after the snow stopped and found herself confronted by a fantastic sight. A way had been cleared past The George and Oak Cottage as far as Church Green, where the cottages had snow up to the bedroom windows, but The Hall and Church Marks were still cut off. William, near to dropping after forty-eight hours' continuous work, took her to the top of the church tower to view the problem.

"We *must* get down to Church Marks by tomorrow," he said.

Leander sensed the desperation in his voice. "Why? What's wrong?" she asked.

"Food."

"Oh. Is it bad?"

"It is, really." William was doing his level best to damp down any suggestion of alarm. "There's a fair bit of flour at The George, but we need vegetables. Horatio thinks Alfred and Margaret will have plenty in store."

Church Marks was opened up the following afternoon; rum punch was served to celebrate the meeting of William's diggers with Alfred and Margaret Wesley, their son, David, and daughter, Amy, who had been digging their way out. Immense relief greeted the discovery that Horatio was right: there were indeed plentiful supplies of vegetables in the smallholding's store sheds.

Now, under a sky that was clearest blue all day and lit by a full moon at night, came the wicked embrace of a bitter frost. The Cannings Brook and the wells became useless. At Latimer's Barn, water was produced by melting snow and ice in the huge copper boiler used for making the horses' Saturday evening treat of bran mash; smaller boilers at The Hall and Oak Cottage kept the village supplied with water.

William and Jim Goakes made two sledges. After four days of frost with the snow fields settling and becoming firm, they set off towards Marlborough with Carrot and three other lads. The four-mile round trip took nine hours and they were half dead with exhaustion on their return, but they brought back two sides of beef, half a pig and several assorted crates of luxuries to a well-deserved hero's welcome.

That night, the sky clouded over and there was fresh snow by morning. It was the first of several such falls spread out over the next five weeks. Although none was anywhere near as bad as the first onslaught, there were always at least three men at work with shovels somewhere in the village.

They adapted and worked together. Nothing was easy and much was very nearly impossible. Martin Foxton caught pneumonia; he was nursed safely through the crisis by his daughters Ann and Bella, assisted by Lucy Miller. Conn's wife, Sally, was safely delivered of a baby girl; it was a difficult birth in the middle of the night, but for Lawrence Stanton it came as a welcome relief from dealing with chilblains, frostbite and sprains. On their third trek for supplies from Marlborough, the sledge party caused panic by going missing overnight after losing their bearings in the white wasteland at dusk. They turned up an hour after dawn, none the worse for their circuitous slog over fifteen miles.

The horses had the best of it. They never went short of food and their stables were the warmest place in Cannings Ambo. A few animals were restive until arrangements could be made to walk them each day, but, like the humans, they learned to put up with a curtailed life-style.

As the relentless weeks ground by, the greatest sufferer was Leander. Watching the horses grow fat and lazy, she became irritable at not being able to get them working. Abraham Merriweather watched her and sympathised.

"It's no good, Miss Leander," he said as they warmed themselves up with hot tea one morning. "You won't get the better of nature. We'll be able to start when the good Lord is ready and not before."

"Well I wish He'd hurry up, Abraham! We've got a Two Thousand Guineas winner getting fat, idle and bored."

Abraham was surprised. "I didn't know you thought he was *that* good."

"I do! Definitely! But he'll be ruined if this carries on much longer. We must win Classics, Abraham. It's the way to get people talking about us and build up our reputation."

Impressed by her fervour, Abraham thought that like many an ill wind, the appalling conditions seemed to be doing some good: at least she had stopped fretting about that young Hawksworth chap.

One morning, as Leander was talking to Conn and Carrot outside the tack-room, she felt water dripping down the back of her neck. She looked up and her face was illuminated by the happiest smile anyone had seen for a long time. The spots were from a cluster of icicles on the eaves.

Progress was painfully slow for the first twenty-four hours while the thaw struggled to establish itself. Then, as soon as the Cannings Brook was unfrozen, the first tentative rivulets turned into a raging torrent. It rose six feet in a night, seething up over the Devizes Lane near The Hall and sending a foot of muddy water streaming through the ground floor of The George. Between the village and the main road, great tracts of land disappeared under water, and the normally indolent River Kennet burst its banks, bringing chaos to Marlborough.

A week later, with the floods subsiding, the March winds began the drying process and the gallop was soon fit for use. Latimer's Barn and Cannings Ambo emerged unscathed and followed Leander's headlong dash back to normal.

There was one change. Nat Thomas never returned to the hut; he was more than happy to make his home in the stable loft at The Hall.

Leander was, of course, perfectly right. The colt that she favoured, victor of the previous season's Dewhurst Plate, was put through the most rigorous work programme when the weather finally lifted and duly won the Two Thousand Guineas.

He was a fine bay by the ever-reliable New Invention, and the Duke of Laverstoke called him Trapezium.

Once that was safely out of the way, Leander set to work on the two-year-olds, intent on getting them fit and keen to race. The youngsters responded extremely well, exhilarated by the most wondrously intoxicating spring that Leander had ever seen. From earth that had been buried for weeks beneath snow, frozen solid, leached by flood and looked to be all but dead, a glorious profusion of life sprang up under the influence of the early-May sun and a few gentle showers. Nature, it seemed, was wasting no time in making amends for the dreadful winter and Cannings Ambo was a fragrant riot of vigorous new growth. Hawthorn and horse-chestnut blossomed with what seemed reckless profligacy, and the hedgerows were thick with yellow weasel snout, lady's mantle and common garlic. People stopped, stared and smiled at the sheer beauty of their surroundings.

But the finest display of all was in the orchard at Latimer's Barn. Giles had often grumbled that the three hundred trees had put on good growth, but never yielded blossom or fruit. Now, at last, the blossom came, great clouds of it in pink and white with the most delectable perfume.

Steven Hawksworth was transfixed by the sight of Leander in the middle of it.

That Sunday morning at the end of May was his first chance to return. After eight months, and with the filly Ophelia gone to stud, he had no idea what Leander's routine would be, so he simply got on his bicycle and pedalled furiously.

As he admitted to himself afterwards, he had the luck of the devil. Without the faintest inkling of what he was going to do or say, Steven arrived to find William talking to Jim Goakes outside Abraham Merriweather's house. William transformed an impulse into a great occasion with a broadly welcoming smile and one simple sentence.

"I told her you'd be back!"

It took Leander some time to react to William's excited calls. She and Bathsheba, the stable cat, were in the orchard to round up Bathsheba's kittens, fathered by a handsome tom who had appeared at The Hall during the blizzard and was now in permanent residence with Nat Thomas.

When she did peer through the trees, the sight of Steven Hawksworth, smiling and waving with awkward self-consciousness, came as a shock. She walked towards him slowly, using the necessity to duck under blossom-laden boughs as a delaying tactic, grabbing time to compose herself. Steven thought she was not pleased to see him: William knew the severity of her control.

"Mr Hawksworth!" she said, extending a hand. "How very nice to see you again."

"Good morning, Miss Flamsteed." He found that he was trembling as he took her hand. "You are looking extremely well, if I may say so."

"Thank you." She surveyed him critically. "Have you not been well?"

His face, without the colour she remembered, was slightly pinched and he had lost weight.

"I had influenza. It was the very devil to shake off, but I'm feeling much better now that I'm back home."

"Ah! So you *did* go away?"

"Yes, to London."

"What was it like?"

"Awful!"

Quietly, without them noticing, William slipped away: Leander had made no attempt to withdraw her hand from Steven's anxious clasp.

Giles greeted Steven like a long-lost friend when Leander brought him into The House to share their lunch and wanted to know all about his experiences in London where, it seemed, the difficulties caused by the harsh winter had been every bit as great as those faced by country-dwellers.

At the end of the meal, Leander wasted no time in taking Steven away.

"I expect you would like to see Trapezium, our Two Thousand Guineas winner, Mr Hawksworth," she said.

"Yes, indeed, Miss Flamsteed."

"He's a very, very nice horse. Unfortunately, he doesn't get the Derby trip."

After only five minutes with Trapezium, Leander and Steven slipped away up the extension of the drive towards Cannings Down, chatting as they went. Leander told of the way the village had kept going during January and February, Steven gave a few details of his wretched period in London.

"Will you try again?" Leander asked.

"If I do, it certainly won't be in London! It's an impossible place. Gerald wants Father to spread into other areas. We could do anything involving carpentry – it doesn't have to be boats."

Leander simply expressed polite interest: she knew that Gerald was Steven's elder brother and that he also had a younger sister, Henrietta. They seemed a close-knit, loving family. While Leander listened to the ideas for extending the Hawksworth business, she guided him towards Powell's Pool.

"My word, this is a pleasant spot," Steven said as they passed through the screen of trees and came to the water.

"I like it." Leander sat down on a fallen tree trunk. "It's very private. No one except me ever comes here."

Steven hesitated, then joined her on the makeshift seat, careful to keep a respectable distance between them. The climb in the warm afternoon had made him uncomfortable; he ran a finger round the inside of his shirt collar, attempting to ease its starched grip on his neck. Leander thought he was probably still feeling the after-effects of the influenza.

"It's my birthday on Wednesday," she announced. "I shall be twenty-one."

"Is there to be a party?"

"Yes, and you must come. It starts at lunch-time and goes on all day." She smiled. "Father is arranging for a marquee on the *lawn*. Imagine that! He's going to allow people to walk on his precious lawn!"

"It's a very special occasion."

"I know, but the lawn! What an honour!" Her eyes sparkled as she thought about it. "You will come, won't you, Steven?"

It was the first time either of them had used a Christian name.

"Yes, I'd like that. I could be here by six o'clock."

"That will do. It won't end until ten."

"I'll do my best," he promised.

She was satisfied and they fell into a companionable silence. When Steven broke it, his eagerness to make his point had an element of bravado.

"Leander is a very nice name. I like it."

"Thank you. So do I – I'm sure lots of people don't like their names. It was Father's idea. I don't think Mother cared for it."

Sensing the slight strain in the extremely rare mention of her long-dead mother, Steven made a remark that was never intended to be serious. He was showing off, demonstrating his classical knowledge.

"Your namesake swam the Hellespont every night."

Leander laughed. "My namesake was a man!"

"Even so, I think you should be a strong swimmer." Steven's flippancy took command of him.

162

"I am!"

"Are you?"

"Of course."

Steven was not sure whether he believed her or not. His look was interpreted as disbelief by Leander and she reacted immediately. Jumping to her feet, she said, "Turn round!"

"What?"

"Turn round. Face that way." She pointed away from the pool, towards the village.

He did as he was told, swinging his legs over the tree-trunk to turn his back on her. Mystified and a little intimidated by Leander's imperious attitude, Steven sat and stared into the trees. A passing breeze stirred their tops; a dog barked in the village. The rest was silence until she said, "Don't look round."

"I wasn't intending to," he retorted.

More silence.

A great splash frightened Steven half out of his skin. Whipping round to find the surface of the pool disturbed and no sign of Leander, he was convinced that she had somehow fallen into the water and was in desperate danger. Then he saw her clothes lying on the ground, one of the pretty, distinctive dresses made by Ellie Goakes and a number of items of underwear.

She swam underwater to the middle of the pool, sixty feet from the bank; as her head bobbed above the surface, she grinned and smoothed her hair back. "There!" she called. "I told you. I *can* swim!"

"Er . . . yes . . . so I see."

Steven was spellbound, taking in her dramatic gesture only with the greatest difficulty. When she began to swim again, powerfully and gracefully in a wide circle, it was possible to appreciate what the pile of clothes intimated: she was quite naked.

Not that he was able to see her all that clearly. The sun was in his eyes and played tricks on the water. Once, for the briefest of moments as she was still, all the fleeting, half-perceived impressions fused to give a vision of desirable loveliness that acted on him like a physical blow: then she was churning up the water again and there was nothing but the coruscating games of the sun.

"Do you believe me now?" she called after five minutes.

"I never doubted you."

She laughed. "I'm sure you did. I'm getting out. Turn round again!"

In what seemed to be no time at all, she was sitting beside him, dressed save for the petticoat she had used as a towel. She pushed it under the tree-trunk. "I shall have to take that back home tomorrow morning when there's no one about," she said, chuckling at the thought of being seen carrying an undergarment. That special light danced in her eyes.

"You come here every morning?" Steven asked.

"Most days in summer, yes. That's how I taught myself to swim when I was a little girl."

"You really are most remarkable, Miss Flamsteed."

Although they stayed by the pool and talked for well over an hour, the formality brought back by Steven after they had apparently set it aside robbed their conversation of lustre. Continually fanning out her hair to dry it, Leander found that he persisted with the 'Miss Flamsteed', leaving her with no alternative to 'Mr Hawksworth'. It was annoying.

When they returned to The House he seemed uneasy, anxious to be away. Realising that there was no point in asking him to accompany her to church, Leander made a last attempt to shake him out of his stuffiness.

"Remember Wednesday, Steven," she urged. "I shall expect you at six o'clock."

"Yes, I shall do my best to be there."

She watched him ride down the drive on his bicycle. Before turning into the Devizes Lane, he stopped and waved: like so much about him in the last two hours, it lacked conviction. One thing was certain, Leander decided. During the course of what should have been a most pleasant afternoon, Steven Hawksworth had turned into a very nervous young man.

"Botheration!" she snorted and stomped off to get ready for Evensong.

Wednesday was splendid and memorable.

Cannings Ambo's most important event since Bellerophon's Derby, five years ago to the day, was favoured by magnificent weather and a huge turn-out of guests. The Duke of Laverstoke and his Duchess came to celebrate the twenty-first birthday of the talented and singularly beautiful young woman who had already given them the winners of two Classic races and proved thoroughly enchanting in the process. As she helped them to champagne and a selection from the lavish buffet, Leander whispered an earnest message.

"I wonder if I might ask Your Graces to tread carefully on the grass. My poor Father fears that it will wear out with all these people trampling on it."

"Come to Eaton Mandeville, my dear," the Duke said. "I don't

164

know how many acres of lawns we've got and you can walk all over 'em to your heart's content." He then executed a few paces of heavily exaggerated mock tiptoeing across the hallowed turf.

Giles, with Alexandra at his side, watched the performance happily.

"You can be very proud of her," Alexandra said.

Her tone made Giles solicitous. Nowadays they were largely successful in forgetting her son and husband. "You have Victoria," he said. "She's doing wonderfully well."

It was true. Victoria Fandine-Browne was now an operating-theatre sister and as Alexandra smiled at the thought, Giles emphasised the point with a reassuring squeeze of her hand.

Afternoon became evening and the perfect day continued unblemished. Only William noticed Leander's mounting anxiety at six o'clock, anxiety which turned to resignation when she knew that Steven Hawksworth was not coming.

The substantial Marlborough contingent of guests, including the town band who had made a fair fist of playing entr'actes and quadrilles, left with Guy Mallender at half past nine, and others soon followed. When Giles slipped off to The Hall with Alexandra, Lucy and Horatio, Leander bade the stragglers goodnight and went indoors on William's arm.

"I had a feeling he wouldn't come," she confessed.

"Why?"

"It seems I may have frightened him the other day."

Secure in the knowledge that William would not dream of asking questions, Leander allowed the full extent of her disappointment to show.

The day after the birthday party, a sour-looking man alighted from a London-bound train at Chippenham and hurried down the hill from the station. A stranger to the town, he nevertheless knew exactly where he was going and how to get there.

But for Ralph Flamsteed, who was making a show of dusting and rearranging bottles, the wine shop was empty. The man made no pretence of being a customer.

"Mr Flamsteed?" he asked curtly.

"Yes."

"There's talk that you have been ruined by your brother."

"Oh?" Ralph looked at him mistrustfully, noting that the man was probably no more than thirty despite his crabbed appearance.

"My father suffered a similar fate – as did Sir Ambrose Hastings, I believe."

"Ah, yes." Ralph Flamsteed nodded. "And your name?"

"Sixsmith."

"I see." They stared at each other in silence for a few minutes before Ralph asked, "Do you have something in mind, Mr Sixsmith?"

"Yes, I do. There is a way to recoup some of our losses. At the very least it will put your brother out of pocket and cause him great inconvenience."

The malicious glee that animated Ralph Flamsteed's face faded as a thought came to him. "Why come to me?" he asked suspiciously.

"Because I need help to finance the venture." Sixsmith's face was distorted into a bitter grimace at this unpalatable fact. His father's gamble on Alma Works and the catastrophic repercussions had brought penury uncomfortably close. "We shall have to hire three or four men and pay them to keep their mouths shut. It isn't all that great an expense, but I can't afford to stand it on my own."

"You expect a good profit?"

"Very much so."

Without further thought, Ralph went to the shop door, locked it and turned the sign to CLOSED. He and his visitor then retired to a back room.

It was three hours before Edgar Sixsmith returned to the railway station, leaving Ralph Flamsteed trembling with excitement at the reckless plan in which he had agreed to involve himself. As well as putting up nearly two hundred pounds for the scheme, he had offered to find a place where a stallion might be safely hidden. He was confident that Augusta Hastings would overrule any scruples her husband might have about the use of Broadleaze Farm.

That summer, William made up his mind about Rose House.

"It's time that place was put right," he told Giles.

"Well, it's yours to do what you like with. Do you have any plans?"

"We'll get it fixed up first."

"And then?" Giles was sure his son had ideas of long-term significance.

"Let's wait and see," William replied. His smile was slower and less brilliant than Leander's, yet it had the same confidence.

A thorough survey of Rose House revealed that the building was more run-down than had been supposed. The worst fault, the one that needed curing before anything else was done, was the rotting roof timbers. William and Jim Goakes decided to do the job themselves, beginning with the removal of the existing roof. When the new timber was ordered, the same arrangements that had proved satisfactory in the past were used: the supplier was in Reading and delivery was to be by canal to Pewsey Wharf.

As William and Jim were setting off one morning to fetch the first load, Leander stopped them in the drive.

"Are you going to Pewsey?" she asked William.

"Yes."

They were impatient to be away; she had to think quickly.

Two Sundays had passed since her birthday and there had been no sign of Steven Hawksworth. Whatever foolishness was in command of him had to be stopped. Now.

"Wait!" she cried and dashed back to The House.

William and Jim considered the possibility that she was playing a joke and would not come back: it was, in fact, less than five minutes before she returned, slightly breathless, holding out an envelope to William.

"You'll be going near the Hawksworths," she said. "Give this to Steven."

Nodding, William put the envelope carefully in a jacket pocket.

Two hours later, when the cart had been positioned alongside the crane, William left Jim to look after the loading while he strolled to the other end of the wharf in search of Steven. He found him without difficulty in the boat-yard's main workshop.

"Oh, hello, William." Steven was friendly but sheepish. Nervousness made him betray his main concern. "How is your sister?"

"She's very well. She asked me to give you this."

Steven looked bewildered by the plain envelope on which Leander had not had time to write his name.

"Go on," William urged. "See what it says."

While Steven was opening the letter and reading it, William was staring round at the splendid tools in the workshop.

"I'm blowed if I can understand this," Steven muttered. "I'd best look at a Bible."

Intrigued, William followed him, going into the house without waiting for an invitation and finding himself in a kitchen where a still pretty woman of about fifty was rolling pastry on a table nearly as big as the one at Latimer's Barn.

"Mrs Hawksworth?" William asked politely. "I'm William Flamsteed from Cannings Ambo."

"Are you, now?" She gave him a big smile. "You'll be Miss Leander's brother, will you?"

"Yes, I am."

"My goodness, our Steven's been getting himself in a fearsome mix over her."

"Oh dear!" William was genuinely sorry. "I've brought him a letter."

"I see." Rebecca Hawksworth's nod conveyed a wealth of meaning. "Maybe it will sort him out."

"Oh, I should think so, Mrs Hawksworth," William said firmly. "My sister is a great one for sorting things out."

Steven wandered back into the kitchen with the Bible he had been given twenty years ago at Sunday school; he was still searching through it. William saw him find what he was looking for. As Steven read a few lines, a look of complete stupefaction spread over his face; he looked again, then sagged into a chair, incapable of speech.

William and Mrs Hawksworth exchanged looks. In response to her nod, he took Leander's letter from Steven's hand. They read it together.

Dear Steven,
What on earth are you doing? Have you taken fright? There is no need to. See Ruth 1, verses 16 & 17.
Your very good friend,
Leander Flamsteed.

Then they looked at the Bible.

. . . for whither thou goest, I will go; and where thou lodgest, I will lodge: thy people shall be my people, and thy God my God: where thou diest, will I die, and there will I be buried . . .

The kitchen was silent as William and Steven's mother looked at each other with wide eyes. Eventually, Steven found a shaky imitation of his voice.

"What do you think of that?" he asked.

William grinned at him. "I reckon you've found what you were looking for," he said.

"Eh?" Steven was utterly lost.

"You wanted another job, didn't you?" William asked. "Well, you've got it! You're going to be Leander's husband and help run Latimer's Barn."

"Marry Leander?" Steven looked ready to pass out.

"Don't you want to?" William was going to be very annoyed at the wrong answer.

"*Don't I want to!*" Steven came back to life with a vengeance. "Of course I do! I think she's the most wonderful person on earth and I love her dearly. But I'm never worthy of her!"

"She appears to disagree with you," William said calmly. "If you take my advice, Steven, you won't argue with her. It doesn't do to argue with Leander. And I wouldn't waste any time letting her know how you feel about her. You've done enough messing about."

"Perhaps I should come back with you," Steven suggested.

"I think that might be wise," William smiled.

But it was over an hour and a half before they finally got away. Mrs Hawksworth insisted that William and Jim should join in the family lunch, and everyone had to be told. Steven's brother and sister, Gerald and Henrietta, were pleased, although they pulled his leg mercilessly. Their father, a solid, dependable-looking man to whom William took an immediate liking, seemed quite perplexed by the news. As Steven eventually set off with William and Jim, his bicycle on top of the cart's load of timber, George Hawksworth was still somewhat dazed.

"They say that Miss Flamsteed turned a duke's son down last year," he said to his wife.

"'Twas only a *younger* son," Rebecca told him. "He wasn't a patch on our Steven."

Much of the journey back to Latimer's Barn passed in silence, William being content to leave Steven in peace with his turmoil of thoughts.

Warned by Conn, who had been keeping a firm look-out for the cart's approach, Leander went to the front door of The House to meet it. Steven climbed down, reached for his bicycle and stood looking as though he wanted the ground to open and swallow him. After turning the cart, William and Jim, both stupendously po-faced, departed to unload their timber at Rose House.

Leander walked towards Steven. She was, he thought, looking severe; it made her seem more beautiful than ever. Seeing that she had no intention of speaking first, he took the plunge.

"I came because of your note, Miss Flamsteed. It had a profound effect on me."

"Steven!"

"Er . . . yes?" He was startled by her tone.

"Do you love me?"

"Yes, I do! Most definitely. I love you with all my heart."

"Then for God's sake stop calling me 'Miss Flamsteed'!" She smiled and her tone softened. "You said I had a nice name, use it!" He nodded vigorously. "Now, where have you been? Why didn't you come to my birthday?"

He squared his shoulders and told the truth. "I wanted to desperately, but I didn't think I was good enough for you."

She nodded. "We must put a stop to that. Come!" Taking his arm, she piloted him into The House. Passing through the vast entrance hall and along a short corridor, she pointed to a door.

"My father is in there," she said. "Go and ask him for my hand." As he gaped at her, she added, "You've got about ten minutes before he goes out to evening stables. Go on, get on with it!"

Giles blinked as Steven blundered into the library. "Hello, Steven, I didn't know we were expecting you today."

"No, sir . . . I . . . that is . . ."

"Yes, my boy, what is it?"

"Sir, your daughter has told me to ask you for her hand in marriage." The words came out in a rush.

"Has she, by God!"

"Yes, sir."

As Giles stood up, a happy smile was spreading over his face. "So, she's made up her mind, eh?"

"It seems so, sir."

"Well, well!"

It occurred to Steven that he ought to say something on his own account. "I love her very much, sir, and I'll look after her."

"I know you will, Steven. My word, you're the luckiest man alive."

That was all very well, and Steven felt ten feet tall, but when they sat down to dinner two hours later, the bombshell landed.

"Steven, the time will come when you are in charge of Latimer's Barn," Giles said. "You will also have a big say in running the estate, so we shall have to think about getting you ready."

It was a perfectly sensible remark based upon Giles's view of the future and the need to provide smooth continuity, but for Steven it came as a shock. While he was trying to adjust to the idea, Leander and Giles began discussing his transformation into an expert on racehorses.

"Don't worry about it," William whispered.

"It sounds frightening," Steven said. "I've been assuming that you and Leander would run the place when your father retires."

"Not me," William replied. "At least, not the stable – I'm hopeless with horses."

"I don't know *anything* about them," Steven said with a hint of desperation.

"You've got natural talent."

"Who says so?"

"Leander! You'll be all right. Look at the tuition you're going to get." William waved a hand at his father and sister.

By the time Steven left to pedal back to Pewsey, William's assurances were making him feel more confident. Leander detected the change in him when she went out to see him off. As they stood and smiled at each other, she thought that there was every chance he might be persuaded to give her a small kiss. He did very much more; in the twilight of a beautiful day close to the summer solstice, her betrothed drew her to him with arms that were every bit as strong as she had hoped, and kissed her with an energy that kindled a new impetus in her body.

"It seems to me, Mr Hawksworth, that we really shall be able to make something of you," she said. In an effort to control her breathing, she sounded very serious, but as ever, her eyes told the true story.

As Steven mounted his bicycle, she said, "Oh, there's one thing I may have forgotten to mention."

"What's that?"

"I love you, Steven Hawksworth. Don't you forget it."

"I won't. Goodnight, Leander."

He kissed her again.

A few minutes later, Giles laughed as Leander wandered back into The House. "You look as if you're floating on air," he said.

"I surely am," she replied, nestling into the support of his arm.

"I suppose you want this in the Big Book?"

"Definitely!" She was alert at once. "Let's go and do it now while it's fresh in my mind. I'll tell you what to write."

Steven sang and laughed all the way back to Pewsey. Apart from the kisses with their promise of the delights that lay in store, what he wanted to cherish was the way she had rounded off the short letter that had changed his life. "Your very good friend, Leander Flamsteed."

He repeated it aloud, over and over again.

Looking back on it ten years later, Steven came to the conclusion that it must have been rather like being absorbed into a royal or noble family.

A week after the betrothal, which Giles insisted on announcing in *The Times*, Steven moved to Cannings Ambo to take up temporary residence in the Rectory as a guest of John and Elisabeth. This followed the first full meeting of Flamsteeds and Hawksworths at which the only minor difficulty had been Leander's insistence on an early wedding. Even Rebecca Hawksworth's rock-solid equanimity seemed in danger when she discovered that she had only until the last Saturday in August to prepare for the great day. Henrietta and Gerald, both entranced by Leander and utterly at a loss to understand how their brother had won her, eventually managed to persuade Rebecca that she would be able to cope.

George Hawksworth had no objection to parting with Steven at such short notice. "There isn't a great deal of work on here, Mr Flamsteed," he said. "And from what you tell me, you want to get him started on something useful."

So, Steven went to the Rectory.

The day after, he took Leander to London on the train. They were away for fourteen hours and returned wearily footsore, but it was worth it; the women of the village were soon clamouring to see the diamond ring from Bond Street that now adorned Leander's left hand.

After that, it was work.

Inasmuch as he had ever thought of it, Steven imagined that training racehorses was something less than a *proper* job. Leander disabused him of that notion within the hour.

"You'll start at the bottom and learn everything," she said. "Absolutely *everything*."

She meant it and Steven found himself plunged into fifteen-hour days of mucking out, riding lessons, feed theory and practice and the study of equine anatomy and ailments. Nothing was neglected. Steven spent a week at the stud and was delighted to find that Ophelia, now in foal to Bellerophon, remembered him from the previous year's Sunday-afternoon encounters. By using his carpentry skills to fix some shelves for Lizzie and teaching Paul to ride the famous bicycle, Steven assured himself of an everlastingly warm welcome in Cannings St John.

Above all else, Leander insisted that Steven should get to know everyone in the village and the stable.

"That's the most important thing," she drummed into him. "They aren't just faces, they're people, our friends, and we all depend on one another."

Most of them were courteous and helpful. However, Steven sensed that one or two of the older lads resented him. He was able to appreciate their point of view: the idea of a boat-builder moving into a senior position at a racing stable in addition to his great good fortune in capturing the heart of the delectable Leander Flamsteed was bound to upset some. Steven kept his mouth shut, was cheerfully courteous and worked harder than ever.

172

Every minor problem had a massive compensation: the time when he made his first correct diagnosis of a pulled muscle, or the day Leander said that he could now be seen out on a horse without disgracing the stable, and the excitement of going to the races with Dan Goakes, especially when they had a winner.

Three days before the wedding, George and Rebecca Hawksworth celebrated the thirtieth anniversary of their marriage and a party was held at Pewsey. To their great annoyance, both Giles and Leander were unable to come: they had to take three very special two-year-olds to race at Newmarket and were not expecting to be back in Cannings Ambo until midnight on the day of the celebration.

William attended, not only as a representative of his family, but as a member of the Hawksworth work-force. No sooner had Steven gone to Cannings Ambo than William persuaded George Hawksworth to let him work in the boat-yard for a few weeks to refine his carpentry skills and pick up expert advice. Both parties to the agreement had done well out of it: working without pay, William's efforts on three boats were a help to the yard and had taught him many new tricks.

It seemed that the entire population of Pewsey had come to the party, and to accommodate them all, huge trestle-tables were set up in a partially-cleared workshop. Very early in the proceedings, William became fascinated by a shy, dark-haired girl called Ruth Burgoyne. Miss Burgoyne, daughter of a corn merchant and a close friend of Henrietta, quite forgot her natural reticence at having one of the famous Flamsteeds to herself and found William totally charming. It was half past one in the morning before Steven could persuade them to part.

William now had a bicycle identical to Steven's and they rode the first mile to Cannings Ambo in silence, each wrapped in his own thoughts. Then William said, "Miss Burgoyne is a very nice young lady."

"I've been waiting for you to say that," Steven chuckled. "She's fairly timid as a rule."

"I didn't find her so at all."

"So I noticed!"

A moment later, Steven swore as his front wheel hit a pot-hole.

"We ought to have lights," William said. "I can barely see the way."

After two more bone-jarring encounters with bad faults in the road, they slowed down and drifted into fierce concentration, finding that their eyes gradually became accustomed to the pitch-darkness of the night.

At last, after a difficult fifty minutes, they came into Cannings St John, free-wheeling down a gentle hill, travelling smoothly and silently over an exceptionally good surface. Automatically, they looked towards the stud, recognisable only as a dark outline of shapes against the sky. They both saw the brief flash of a light in the stallion yard and they both felt the same stab of suspicion.

"Stop!" Steven whispered. "Quietly."

They did so, placing their bicycles gently on the grass verge.

"Perhaps one of the horses is sick," William suggested.

"Why aren't there any other lights?" Steven asked. "No, this looks wrong. Come on!"

They climbed over a fence, blundered through Seamus's garden and worked their way round to the entrance of the stallion yard. At first, everything seemed to be in order. Then they heard a faint metallic jingle, a series of clicks and an undecipherable oath. The lamp was briefly uncovered once more and there was a glimpse of at least three men huddled round a door. One of them was trying to pick the padlock.

Steven took a deep breath and shouted, "What the devil is going on here?" only to be dismayed as William dashed away from him, lost in the darkness.

The silence was frightening.

"We have you marked," Steven shouted, hoping that his voice sounded steadier than he felt. "Come out!"

Shuffling footsteps seemed to be making their way towards him. Steven edged away from them, acutely conscious of villainy.

Suddenly, the night was shattered. William was hurling bricks, first through Seamus's bedroom window, then Paul's. And he was shouting fit to raise the dead. There was a light: and another. Paul was calling out.

Somewhere to Steven's left a man said, "Run for it, lads. The game's done for!"

Instinctively, Steven flung himself at the voice. The man was knocked flat with Steven on top of him. He cried out in pain and rage. "Bill! Give us a hand. Here! Blast your eyes, over here!"

The lamp was uncovered and, as William raced back into the small yard, he saw that there were four men: one of them had a knife and was moving towards Steven. Swerving wildly, William raced full-tilt at him, bemusing the man into defencelessness; he was wide open to the punch in the stomach that left him doubled up in agony.

Another of the men leapt out of the darkness, swinging an iron bar. Steven saw it coming, twisted and raised his right arm in a futile attempt to protect himself. The bar struck midway between shoulder and elbow: they all heard the bone break.

Joined by an associate, the man with the iron bar turned on William.

At that moment, the yard was flooded with light.

Seamus was carrying a lamp as well as a shotgun. Lizzie, her two daughters and Polly Izzard had lamps; Paul Izzard only had a shotgun. Without hesitating for a fraction of a second, he used it.

The iron bar clattered to the ground and the scoundrel responsible for Steven's injury was clutching at his own arm.

"We've three barrels left between us," Paul said. "What's it to be?"

As the four men were rounded up and locked in an empty box, New Invention and Bellerophon, badly disturbed by the gunshot, were kicking frantically at their doors and Seamus went in to them. The padlock safeguarding Bellerophon was troublesome; a broken skeleton key was jammed in it.

"For goodness' sake," William said to the women and girls who were mesmerised by the four villains, "see to Mr Hawksworth. He's hurt."

Steven, now sitting with his back against a wall, smiled wanly as the ladies, all in night-dresses, gathered round him.

"I think my arm's broken," he said. "It's quite painful."

As Polly knelt down to comfort him, he fainted.

Lawrence Stanton did an excellent job on Steven's arm after William had bicycled into Cannings Ambo to rouse him, but Steven was not at all pleased with the state he found himself in.

"Fancy having to get married in this condition," he grumbled to Horatio.

"Bit of a nuisance," Horatio agreed. "Look on the bright side."

"Oh, and what might that be?"

"My lad, that arm makes you a full and honoured member of the most exclusive club I've ever come across. Marrying into it's fair enough, I suppose, though I daresay there's some wouldn't accept it. But getting wounded stopping a gang making off with Bellerophon – well, that's a different matter altogether." Horatio smiled broadly. "That animal is sacred, you know."

"Is that really what they were trying to do?" Steven asked, still disbelieving the planned outrage.

"They've confessed, damn it!"

They had indeed. Leander found no difficulty in talking Giles out of showing leniency to this gang, and they had been handed over to the County Police who charged them with several serious crimes.

"What on earth did they think they were going to do with him if they did get him away?" Steven asked.

"God knows! Ransom him back to us? Get him over to South America? One thing's for sure, if it hadn't been for you and William, the swines would probably have taken him."

Steven was conscious of the exceptionally high esteem in which he was now held by all. No one doubted that Leander had chosen the right man to be her husband. The warmth of the few originally against him was almost overdone.

And Leander was euphoric.

"Just look at her!" Elisabeth said to John Shepherd. "She adores him."

John smiled mildly. "Well, my dear, he hasn't made a bad start, has he?" he said.

The expectations were immensely high. Everyone wanted her to be the most beautiful and exciting bride ever.

Leander did not disappoint. When she entered the church on the arm of the stupendously proud Giles, the huge congregation, men, women and children, all gasped in admiration.

The dress, worked on for weeks in the utmost secrecy, was Ellie Goakes's masterpiece: she herself always insisted that she never made anything quite so good again. Ellie was also responsible for Leander's hair, which looked like a golden cloud and was crowned with a wreath of wild flowers.

But what really set the seal on it was Leander's radiant exuberance. Deciding at the last minute not to wear a veil, she allowed all to see that no bride had ever gone to the altar with such enthusiastic confidence.

Rising to meet her, Steven and Gerald were visibly moved by what they saw. Once she had taken her place on Steven's left, alongside his good arm, she brought him back to life with the most special of her smiles and nodded to the Good Shepherd to begin.

At the appropriate time, she held his right hand, grinning when he was unable to muster a strong grip.

"I, Leander, take thee, Steven, to my wedded husband, to have and to hold from this day forward, for better for worse, for richer for poorer, in sickness and in health, to love, cherish and obey, till death us do part, according to God's holy ordinances: and thereto I give thee my troth."

A little later, as John Shepherd finished his address to the congregation with ". . . I pronounce that they be man and wife together, In the name of the Father, and of the Son, and of the Holy Ghost. Amen", he looked into Leander's eyes and she knew what he was thinking. He was thrilled at having performed the marriage ceremony for the first child he ever baptised.

When they sang Leander's favourite hymn, 'For all the Saints', her strongly distinctive soprano was joyously audible throughout the church, causing members of the congregation to look at each other and marvel. There was no doubt that Cannings Ambo's princess was delighted by her new status and name.

Afterwards, when Steven had made a fair job of signing the register with his left hand, he and his wife posed patiently outside the church while Guy Mallender struggled with his apparatus. Guy was a keen amateur photographer with much good work to his credit, and had pleaded to be allowed to take the pictures. Today, of course, his equipment was temperamental, but the job was eventually done and Mr and Mrs Hawksworth walked through a happy crowd to their carriage, driven by Michael Pilgrim who had won the yard lottery for the privilege.

Food and drink for all had been laid on at The House and the festivities were soon under way, no one minding that the bride and groom were restricted to a brief attendance because they had a train to catch. Much to Steven's surprise, they were going away, not just for one, but for two whole weeks. Never imagining that it would be possible to separate Leander from the stable, Steven had discovered that she was actually insisting on a honeymoon.

Once they were changed into travelling clothes, it was William who drove them to Savernake station. There, he embraced them both and entrusted them to the care of the Great Western Railway.

Giles, who had been extraordinarily pleased with himself all morning, became pensive as he waved them off from Latimer's Barn.

"What's the matter?" Horatio asked.

"Well . . . I was wondering how Steven will cope," Giles replied. "You know . . . with that arm."

"Don't worry," Horatio advised, looking sagacious. "If that daughter of yours can't deal with such a simple matter, she's not half the woman I think she is."

George and Rebecca Hawksworth did their best to keep straight faces.

The best suite at the Imperial Hotel, Torquay, added another layer to Steven's awareness of his new circumstances. His own family were comfortably well-to-do, but luxury on this scale was probably beyond them, even for a very special occasion. Not that Steven had the faintest idea what it was all costing: the two weeks was one of Giles's wedding presents.

It was very grand, frighteningly so.

Completely in her element, Leander behaved as though the whole magnificent edifice had been built and equipped especially for her. Seeing that Steven was rather fazed, she took effortless command, issuing instructions about their luggage, the serving of refreshments in their rooms, the newspapers that were required and a host of other matters. In response, the manager, flanked by two hand-rinsing minions, went gladly through the hoop of, "Yes, Mrs Hawksworth . . . of course not, Mrs Hawksworth . . . whatever you say, Mrs Hawksworth."

Mrs Hawksworth! It still came as a shock to realise that this dazzling creature really was his wife.

Dinner was brought up to their suite that first night, to be served at a table in a huge bow window overlooking Torbay. Once the meal was over and the two waiters had cleared up and left, Leander said, "I think we should get ready for bed, sweetheart. It's been a long day."

While she slipped away to the bedroom, Steven remained in the window, watching the outlines of the bay disappear into the deepening dusk. He basked in the memories of the day and tried to pretend that he was not falling prey to nervousness.

To one side of the palatial bedchamber there was a bathroom, on the other, two small dressing-rooms. It was from one of these that Leander eventually summoned him.

"Try the bathroom, Steven. It's marvellous. We must have one like it in The House."

He smiled: he was getting used to the capital letters.

Ten minutes later, wrapped in a huge bath-sheet, he sallied forth.

Leander chuckled. "You look like a Roman emperor – except I'll bet they didn't go round with their arms in a sling!"

He tried to laugh with her, but the breath caught in his throat. She was wearing a white lace peignoir that had come from Paris under the auspices of Alexandra Fandine-Browne.

Moving towards him, she parted the robe and let it slip from her shoulders to the floor. The tantalisingly elusive vision of Powell's Pool was now presented to him in all its substantive glory.

"Well," she said quietly, "will I do?"

She knew the answer. His face was eloquent. So was his body. When she unwound the towel, his manifest arousal brought a new, intense look to her face.

"Come along," she whispered. Easing out of his one-armed embrace, she guided him towards the bed.

There was a moment in which Steven's total lack of experience nearly got the better of him; Leander saw him teeter on the brink, but was rewarded by his relaxed surrender to her resolution as she made him lie comfortably on his back, the broken arm safely supported on his chest.

"Don't worry, I've had some advice on how we should set about this," she said calmly.

Steven, who had spared his father the embarrassment of giving instruction, goggled at her. "Who from?" he asked.

"Daphne Stanton."

"Did she offer it?"

"She didn't take much persuading. She was very helpful."

"And what did you discover?"

"Oh, all sorts."

"I can imagine," Steven said weakly.

"The main thing is that we're supposed to enjoy ourselves. *Both* of us!"

She was on the bed now, swinging herself astride his hips. Despite the allure of her body, Steven found himself entranced by her eyes. The magic was very potent indeed. Tonight, it was sheer sorcery.

He gave himself up to it.

They became addicted to the steamer trips. Every other day, they were at the landing-stage for ten o'clock, eager to be off to Brixham, Kingswear or Dartmouth. Once, they sailed all the way round Start Point to Plymouth and caught a train back.

At other times they listened to band concerts, sat in the extensive hotel gardens, or strolled along the promenade after dinner. The weather was consistently kind.

On the only morning that they took breakfast in the dining-room, a retired general waylaid them to ask if his horses might be trained at Latimer's Barn. He was promised every assistance.

Two activities preoccupied them above all else.

They talked endlessly. Unconsciously revelling in a companionship that caused passers-by to stop, stare and smile, they held conversations that shaped the rest of their lives.

And they made love.

"We're getting better at it all the time," Leander said on their last morning. As usual, they had woken to the rapturous stimulation of each other's presence. "Hurry up and get that arm mended so that we can make a real job of it!"

179

When it was time to return to Cannings Ambo, Steven was a new man. In two weeks, Leander had implanted a calm confidence that made him believe everything was possible. For the rest of their lives together, they never felt the need for a conventional holiday; their work at Latimer's Barn was reward enough. But they always remembered every moment and event of the two weeks that had made them one.

On a morning in November, a week after the four who tried to abduct Bellerophon were sent to prison for ten years, Ralph Flamsteed's stomach contracted as Leander walked into his shop.

"This is a pleasant surprise," he said with nervous lack of sincerity. "My goodness, you *do* look well. Married life must agree with you. I was sorry not to be able to come to your wedding."

Leander ignored the oblique complaint about the fact that he had not been invited and stared at him, allowing a silence to hang ominously between them.

"To what do I owe this unexpected pleasure?" Ralph was forced to ask.

"I thought you might help me."

"Of course!"

"I am seeking the whereabouts of a man called Sixsmith – Edgar Sixsmith. I'm told you know him."

It was difficult to tell whether his unhealthy pallor actually worsened, but the look in his eyes was enough.

"Sixsmith? Sixsmith, you say. No, my dear, I don't recall anyone of that name."

"He was the man who organised those ruffians we had put away last week," Leander said. "They squealed like stuck pigs to try and save their skins."

"Oh. I see. Yes."

"You don't know him?"

"No."

"You've never met him?" Leander's voice grew harder with each question.

"No."

"And you didn't give him two hundred pounds to help him organise that outrage?"

"No! Absolutely not! Good heavens, what a thing to suggest! Really, Leander!"

She looked at him contemptuously. "You and I both know that you are a liar," she said. "Now listen carefully, *dear* Uncle. My father knows nothing of this, and that is how it will remain. However, if

180

the merest hint of suspicion ever attaches itself to you again, you will have *me* to contend with. Do you understand?"

He stared at her in frozen silence.

"Leave Latimer's Barn alone," Leander told him. "Otherwise things will go very badly with you. Next time you will lose a damned sight more than two hundred pounds, I promise you." She paused, fixing him with an even more unnerving look. "I suppose it's too much to hope that you will ever stop running round telling lies about Father," she said and walked out of the shop.

The moment she was gone, Ralph Flamsteed locked the door and scuttled into the back room where he poured himself a large measure of brandy with hands that shook. Two things had put the fear of God into him.

The first was Leander's attitude. Her husband and father, who thought she was looking for curtain material, would not have believed that she was capable of such terrifying menace.

The other was her failure to provide any clue as to the source of her information. As Leander left Chippenham on the train back to Calne, she was pleased by this, knowing the effect it would be having on her uncle.

A couple of weeks ago, Charlotte Hastings had paid one of her increasingly rare visits to Broadleaze Farm. While there, she had overheard Ralph Flamsteed complaining to her brother, Arnold, about the disappearance of Sixsmith and his two hundred pounds. Knowing that the four men taken at Cannings St John had named Sixsmith as the instigator of the plot to capture Bellerophon, Charlotte had passed the news on to Victoria Fandine-Browne, who promptly told her mother.

Alexandra thought carefully before she acted. Eventually, she spoke to Leander rather than to Giles, convinced that this was the most effective course of action: Ralph Flamsteed would have agreed with her.

William was waiting at the Lansdowne Arms in Calne with a carriage. They had lunch, she told him what had passed between her and their lamentable uncle, and he nodded approvingly. Then they made an early start up the main road towards London to ensure daylight for the return journey to Cannings Ambo.

As the horses breasted the summit near Cherhill above the long descent to Avebury, Leander banished the afternoon's damp chill by snuggling deeper into her heavy cloak and began to anticipate the welcome she could expect from Steven.

Now that his right arm was fully recovered, he was proving wonderfully passionate.

CHAPTER 11

1886

'. . . time we had it on a proper footing'

1886 was the year when Giles finally became convinced that the Big Book was a necessity, not a luxury or, as he had sometimes feared, a self-indulgent affectation on his part. He began to feel that he was recording events which would prove important to posterity as well as to himself.

The year's racing was dominated by the first Duke of Westminster's splendid bay colt, Ormonde. He was brilliantly trained by John Porter at Kingsclere, near Newbury, to win the coveted Triple Crown of Two Thousand Guineas, Derby and St Leger. Ridden by George Barrett in the Guineas, Ormonde was then partnered by Fred Archer, who recorded his twenty-first Classic winner at Doncaster. A few weeks later, Archer shot himself at a nadir in the depression that had blighted his life. He was only twenty-nine years of age and had ridden the winners of no less than 2,748 races in his seventeen seasons. There was never any doubt that he would become an immortal legend.

For Steven, it was the year in which he enjoyed his first great success with a horse. Horatio's filly, Precision, a daughter of Bellerophon, had been the apple of Steven's eye ever since she came into the yard as a pretty, high-spirited yearling with a rather overdeveloped sense of fun.

Devoting most of her time and energy to looking after her two sons, Leander did very little around the stable and left the filly to Steven. He, Abraham Merriweather and Michael Pilgrim struck up a deeply felt and rewarding rapport with her, and she demonstrated early promise by winning all her three races as a two-year-old. Then, in 1886, she won the two Classics for which the great Ormonde was not eligible, the One Thousand Guineas and the Oaks.

These two major victories were achieved with Michael Pilgrim, who had begun deputising for Peter Izzard as the Latimer's Barn jockey in 1884, in the saddle. Michael rather than Peter rode Precision in her two Classic races because only he could make her go.

Horatio made sure that Giles understood the full significance of Precision's achievements.

"Trained by Steven, ridden by young Pilgrim. We're starting to get what you might call second-generation successes, Giles."

The point had not gone unnoticed. Giles was glad to see evidence that there were forces at work to back up Leander's indomitable will: his greatest wish was that he would be able to found a stable that would last for generations. These were powerful signs that he was succeeding. He noted the fact in the Big Book.

Michael Pilgrim complemented his racecourse feats by marrying Caroline Stanton, daughter of Lawrence and Daphne. Michael and Caroline had been devoted to each other since the time he spent at Oak Cottage to recover from the outrages of Rowland Fandine-Browne, who, with his life made a misery by the other inmates of Dorchester Prison, had hanged himself in 1884.

When Jim Goakes married Bella Foxton, youngest of the girls at The George, the builders were busy again. This time it was Harry Irons, a son of Jim and grandson of the original Harry, who took charge of building houses in Church Marks for the two pairs of newly-weds.

The year 1886 also saw what many, including Leander, regarded as Giles's finest master-stroke as a trainer. On 23 July, Sandown Park, the beautifully situated course at Esher in Surrey that had opened in 1875, staged the Eclipse Stakes, named after the phenomenal colt of the 1760s who was never beaten in eighteen races. The inaugural running was worth a staggering £10,000 to the winner, more than twice as much as Ormonde had won in the Derby. The race, over a mile and a quarter for horses of all ages, attracted a field of supreme quality.

Giles ran Parallelogram, a four-year-old colt belonging to the Duke of Laverstoke. Parallelogram had looked very useful as a two-year-old, but lost the whole of his second season because of a variety of stomach disorders and strained muscles. Prior to the Eclipse, he had won a minor event at Salisbury, but no one expected him to make any showing in this hotly contested race at Sandown.

For years, Giles had been nursing the theory that it was possible to train a horse to reach peak condition on the day of a race, preferably at about the time he went into the paddock. His persistent claims to have come within an hour or two of achieving this were the source of much merriment in the yard; but no one at Cannings Ambo ever joked about 23 July 1886. One and a half furlongs from home, when the race might have belonged to any of the nine runners, Peter Izzard gave Parallelogram his head and the Duke's colt set about winning the first Eclipse Stakes in the most stylish and convincing manner. He gave a massive boost to the reputation of Latimer's Barn and was granted a fulsome entry in the Big Book.

But the incident that did most to make the year a very happy one for Giles and many others was William's marriage to Ruth Burgoyne. The day of the wedding brought a great surprise and a glimpse of an exciting new prospect for the future. Giles was so impressed that, a few weeks later, he took a decisive step in assuring the future of Latimer's Barn and Cannings Ambo.

William and Ruth had taken their time over the courtship.

They were meant for each other. No one ever doubted it, least of all themselves, yet they went along at their own pace, often causing affectionate irritation.

"What *are* they playing at?" Steven asked early in 1885. "Why doesn't William get on with it?"

"He knows what he's doing," Leander replied.

"What?"

"I haven't the faintest idea, but you may take it from me that he has everything worked out."

Steven was not voicing criticism of William, and Leander knew it. Nevertheless, her tone was a reminder that there were no circumstances in which she was prepared to tolerate even the hint of disparagement of her brother.

Rose House seemed to be the major cause for delay: Leander felt that William and Ruth might have married sooner were it not for the restoration work.

The new roof finally occupied William and Jim for a year as a spare-time activity when they were not doing other jobs around the village. William extended the amount of work required by settling for a mansard shape, which presented endless complications in the construction of the timber framework. He also decided to have the outside walls of the first floor covered with a tile cladding. When finished, the result was very handsome indeed.

"We shall have to pull our socks up," Horatio told Giles. "That boy of yours intends to put our miserable hovels in the shade."

"He's shot his bolt on that roof," Giles said. "We shall have some peace and quiet now."

It was the only time Giles ever underestimated his son.

Egged on by Jim Goakes, William eventually found an excuse for replacing every single piece of timber in the house. And, of course, while they were making such a thoroughgoing mess, it was inevitable that they should decide to start knocking walls down and moving the staircase. By the time John Shepherd began publishing the banns for William and Ruth, Rose House had been virtually rebuilt.

Leander was the first to see it, on the very day that the last bits of decorating were completed. It was impossible to recognise it as the same place in which she and William had played hide-and-seek as children. On one side of the ground floor, the removal of walls had created a room that extended fully from front to rear of the house, about forty-five feet. There were new French windows half-way along the main outside wall to give access to a lawn and shrubbery that the Wesleys had helped create out of a wilderness of brambles and nettles. Everywhere, the workmanship was of exceptional quality.

"What will this be?" Leander asked, her voice echoing oddly in the vast, empty space.

"Dining-room and sitting-room combined, I think," William replied.

She smiled at the novel concept. In his quiet way and in his own time, William was a radical, too.

"I think it's all perfectly lovely, William," she said. "You and Jim have done wonders. This house is a credit to the village."

He nodded and thought about it. "I like beauty," he said. "But it doesn't come naturally to human beings, does it? I mean, look at your horses – they couldn't be ugly or second-rate to save their lives. People are different. They have to try quite hard to produce something nice."

Startled by this unexpectedly profound observation, Leander was momentarily off-balance until, looking out of a window, she noticed the old stable and store. That also was equipped with a new roof.

"What's happening there?" she asked.

"Workshop," William replied.

Leander gave him a searching look. He was fobbing her off, being evasive.

"What's going on?" she demanded.

"Nothing."

"William!"

He toyed with the idea of trying to bluff it out. "It's a secret," he muttered, well on the way to capitulation.

"Who from?"

"Well . . . everybody, I suppose."

"Except me!"

She saw that this must be something terribly serious as William considered whether even their shared twenty-five years was a good enough guarantee that she would respect the confidence.

"All right, come on," he said.

What Leander found in the workshop left her speechless for the longest period that William could remember. Eyes wide, she walked round for over ten minutes, touching and marvelling.

"Oh, William," she whispered when she finally stood back to admire it all. "That is truly marvellous. Have you made all that yourself?"

"Jim and me," he said, basking in her reaction which was the greatest praise he could have wished for.

"How long has all this taken?"

"Fifteen months. Mind you, we had a lot of learning to do."

"And you've been fitting this in with building and decorating and that job at the Rectory?"

"That's right."

"Whatever made you do it?"

"I didn't like the awful stuff in the shops. Neither did Jim. We thought we could do better ourselves and make something that would be of a piece with the house."

"You were right!"

"Don't breathe a word about this to anyone, Lea."

"I won't. I promise." As usual, she sealed the bargain with a kiss and a hug. "When *are* you going to let the cat out of the bag?"

"When I bring Ruth back here after we're married."

"Goodness, she *will* be pleased!"

William's surprise was sensationally well received, not only by Ruth, but by the scores of people who flocked back to Rose House after the wedding. They lined the drive to watch William carry his bride over the threshold, then, no sooner had the guests started to go indoors than the chorus of delight began.

Browsing through Marlborough's second-hand bookshop, William and Jim had found a third edition of Thomas Sheraton's *The Cabinet-Maker's and Upholsterer's Drawing-Book*, first published in 1794. It was an amazing volume with diagrams and full details of much of the furniture made by Sheraton. Working with yellow Scandinavian deal and mahogany veneers, exactly as prescribed by the master, William and Jim had fashioned much of the furniture that now adorned Rose House with consummately graceful elegance.

The small tables and chairs in the entrance hall generated a stir; what was in the big room created an uproar of excitement. Apart from the small, occasional pieces, there were six arm-chairs, a sideboard and, the *pièce de résistance*, a dining-table nearly fourteen feet long with twelve magnificent chairs.

Giles was dumbfounded. "Good Lord, William, have you *really* made all this yourself?" he asked.

"Yes, with Jim," William replied, pointing to his friend and best man who was surrounded by people at the other end of the room.

The hubbub was tremendous as everyone expressed their amazement and pleasure. Only Ruth, the very new Mrs Flamsteed, had nothing to say, but her shining eyes were ample reward for all the frustrating trial and error and hard work that had gone into creating the splendid spectacle. At last she said, "You're extremely gifted, William, my love," to trigger off a burst of applause.

Gradually, bit by bit, as people related and compared their experiences, a comical aspect of the great project emerged.

Horatio had known what was afoot because he was consulted about tools. Some of the special equipment needed, including a machine for turning chair- and table-legs, had come from Beresford Engineering.

Steven was implicated, giving advice on the more difficult carpentry techniques and the tricky business of fixing the veneer.

And while Ellie Goakes and Lucy Miller were spending a week helping William get Rose House ready for occupation, right down to the last teaspoon, they had become very familiar with the beautiful furniture.

All had been sworn to secrecy, and, each believing that they were the only person who knew, respected the vow.

"Why didn't you tell me, you toad?" Leander asked Steven.

"I promised William and Jim not to tell a living soul," he replied, grinning broadly. "You never said you'd seen the finished product."

Leander glowered comically at him.

It was several hours before any of the guests thought of leaving: William and Ruth, making an unhurried start to their honeymoon the following day, were delighted to have their friends around them for as long as possible.

When it was time for the party to end, Ruth's father shook William's hand warmly and said, "Good luck, lad. I must say, this place is wonderful. Ruth's a lucky girl." He hesitated and went on rather diffidently. "Tell you what, we're fair smitten with this furniture of yours. Eileen and me are hoping you'll make some for us."

"You'll have to wait your turn, Harry," Giles told him good-naturedly. "I'm first in the queue."

"Don't build up any hopes," William warned, looking anxiously at

187

several others, certain that they were hovering with similar requests. "It isn't easy, you know. I'm not sure Jim and I want to tackle anything like that again."

"I'm convinced you're wrong," Leander said to William when all except she and Steven had left Rose House. "You'll be making more of that furniture – a great deal more unless I'm very much mistaken."

William gazed at her dubiously.

Steven drove William and Ruth to Savernake railway station at the start of their honeymoon journey. Leander sat between them, issuing a flood of last-minute advice about Torquay: William and Ruth were going to the Imperial Hotel.

"And don't forget the steamer trips," Leander called after William as he waved from the window of the departing train. "The one to Dartmouth is lovely!"

"Don't you wish we were going with them?" Steven asked as they walked back to the carriage.

"They wouldn't thank us for that!" Leander laughed. "In any case, sweetheart, I'm perfectly happy as I am. I've got you and Latimer's Barn. What more is there?"

Two porters smiled indulgently as Leander gave vent to her feelings by flinging her arms round Steven and kissing him with tremendous fervour.

She was absolutely right, Steven reflected as he drove them back to Cannings Ambo. They were very lucky indeed. Their life together was good; they never tired of each other's company; they lived and worked in idyllic surroundings; and they had two wonderful sons.

Named after their grandfathers, the boys were George, now aged three, and Giles, born in 1885 and approaching eighteen months.

They were quite different.

George had the dark colouring of Steven's mother, and, Leander suspected, of her own. He was obviously intelligent, quick both to learn and lose his temper, and frightened of horses. Leander sometimes thought it likely that he might grow up to be too clever for his own good.

Giles was blue-eyed and blond, permanently in a state of relaxed amiability, apparently content to appear somewhat stupid. Leander loved them both, successfully concealing her great preference for Giles.

That day, as on every day except Sundays, Leander had lunch with the children in their nursery while Steven ate in the kitchen with Giles, mulling over stable business. As usual, Ellie Goakes was with them: her absence was the only thing capable of disturbing young Giles's monumental equanimity.

Ellie had come to The House as Leander's maid soon after the honeymoon and the setting up of a new routine in the autumn of 1881. Like their brothers, William and Jim, Leander and Ellie had always been close; as her dressmaker, Ellie often enjoyed Leander's closest confidences.

"What are you planning to do with yourself, Ellie?" Leander asked one day as they were trying to make their minds up about a new dress pattern.

"Well, I haven't come across anyone I want to marry, if that's what you mean," was Ellie's frank reply. She was three years older than Leander, handsome rather than pretty, lion-hearted and most definitely not given to flights of fancy.

"What about Alfred?" Leander said.

"Pooh!" With a toss of the head and a wave of a hand, Ellie dismissed the Marlborough bank clerk who repeatedly tried to make an impression on Ellie. "He's daft!"

"Come and be my maid!" Leander urged on an impulse.

Ellie accepted on the spot and the arrangement was a success from the start.

Bertha Bradley, now formally elevated to housekeeper and cook, and Brigid O'Malley, the general maid, gave Ellie the warmest of welcomes; they never resented her position of privilege with Leander and were glad of her aid. Ellie was an avid helper, with no self-important ideas as to the boundaries of her duties, and a wealth of practical know-how. Irritating odd jobs could now be tackled at once instead of having to wait for a man to tear himself away from the supposedly more important affairs of the stable.

There was no limit to Ellie's talents: she performed prodigies with a paint-brush, knew a great deal about plumbing and was adept at unblocking the sophisticated but sometimes impractical drains that Harry Irons had installed for Lord Francis Rashleigh. When George was born, she was superb and he quickly came to respect Ellie, a favour he bestowed only sparingly on his parents. Young Giles, who adored everyone, had a special corner in his heart for Ellie and was lost without her.

After the boys had gone with Ellie for their post-lunch nap, Leander went in search of Steven whom she found in earnest discussion of a new feed with Abraham Merriweather.

"It's a gorgeous day," she said quietly.

Steven smiled and nodded.

Returning from The House a few minutes later, Leander was carrying an old canvas bag which contained two towels from their splendid, Torquay-inspired bathroom. Steven took a last look round the yard, and, as the afternoon quiet descended on it, they set off for Powell's Pool.

In good weather, they liked to swim at least three times a week: it had become an unashamedly sybaritic ritual in their own private world.

Once within the ring of trees, they stripped off their clothes and Steven found himself studying Leander with even keener appreciation than usual. Bearing two strong, healthy sons had made not the slightest difference to her body. On the contrary, he would have sworn that she looked even better than the day six years ago when she had first demonstrated her prowess as a swimmer. There was something else: since then, every enchanting promise between them had been made miraculously good.

"What is it?" she asked, interpreting his look correctly.

"I'm admiring you," he replied.

She chuckled, placing her arms round his neck as he picked her up. "I think there's a good deal of lust as well as admiration," she said.

"Very much the same thing at times like this," Steven said. Still carrying her, he waded into the water.

Not all their swimming expeditions were followed by love-making, but it was ordained that afternoon. Even in the pool, they were never far apart, coming together frequently in languidly voluptuous embraces.

Afterwards, with the towels spread on their favourite grassy bank, they indulged in a vigorous bout that satisfied their immediate desires while laying the foundation for a much deeper hunger.

They began again almost at once, this time with a slow, sensual concern for every erotic signal and nuance. By holding him very tightly and drawing him searingly deep into her, Leander forced Steven to enjoy a few moments of exquisite stillness: she did this several times before allowing him to continue the dash towards ecstasy.

In the fading moments of her own lucidity, Leander saw that Steven was surprised by the intensity of his climax, as though he had suddenly stumbled across it by accident.

She was certain that his blend of tenderness and power made him the best lover she could ever wish for, and that what passed between them at these blissful times was boosting his confidence towards the day when he would be required to run Latimer's Barn.

And as she felt his strength finally begin to ebb within her, Leander was certain of something else: she had just conceived their daughter, Amelia.

A week after a glowing Ruth and William returned from honeymoon, they were summoned to dinner at The House.

There were six of them round the table, Giles, Leander, Steven, Ruth, William and Horatio. Until the main part of the meal was over, the conversation proceeded along predictably normal lines: Ruth and William were expected to give a report on Torquay; Steven told Horatio about his expectations for Precision, who was to be prepared for an autumn campaign; Giles reminded William about furniture and William promptly looked evasive.

However, when Leander, deputising for Brigid O'Malley who had been given the evening off, cleared the table and brought in fruit and cheese, Giles's manner altered. After an exchange of looks with Horatio, he cleared his throat and said, "There's some business that needs attending to." Despite himself, he sounded rather portentous.

William instinctively sat up straight.

"It concerns you four," Giles went on. "You and your children are the future of Cannings Ambo, and it's high time we started thinking about it."

Horatio nodded, very statesmanlike. Heavens! Ruth thought, this *does* sound serious!

"The future . . ." Giles said again, then paused. "It's time we had it on a proper footing." He collected his thoughts. "I own this estate. I bought it off my father in 1859. What's the worst thing that could happen to it?" He looked round, inviting answers and comment.

"Well . . . I suppose if we lost it," William ventured.

"We aren't going to," Leander said firmly. "I think the worst thing would be if it got split up into bits and pieces."

"Exactly!" Giles smiled at her. "This estate is either a whole or it's nothing. The minute you get people putting boundary fences up, it's finished. Now, I know you wouldn't want to do that, but we've no idea how my grandchildren will see things."

"Some of them aren't even born yet," Horatio said. To Leander's astonishment, he smiled at her, rather than Ruth and William.

"There's another point we must consider," Giles went on. "We don't know what sort of a world your children will have to contend with."

"It won't be that different, surely?" Ruth said.

"Horatio has convinced me that it probably will be," Giles said, turning to his friend with an invitation to say his piece.

"Think seventy years ahead, Ruth," Horatio urged. "That's where your children are going to end up. Nineteen fifty-six. Call it 1960." He allowed time for this to sink in. "You can say that things haven't changed all that much in these parts in the *last* seventy years, and you'd be right. But the towns and cities have altered a devil of a lot in that time, and I don't reckon it's going to be all that long before it starts affecting us."

All except Leander viewed the prospect with dismay.

Giles continued. "As well as the estate, there is the matter of over seventy thousand pounds to my name in the bank."

This time, even Leander was taken aback: Ruth looked positively faint. It was a huge fortune.

"A great deal of that is down to Bellerophon," Giles explained. "He's earned the best part of forty thousand pounds at stud on top of the ten thousand I got from him while he was racing. Let's just remind ourselves that Horatio *gave* me that horse."

"Leander trained him," Horatio growled.

"True. And who was it set me up here?" Giles asked with the benign Flamsteed smile.

"You did it yourself!" Horatio said, betraying impatience. "Get on with the plan."

"I might say that the idea I am about to put to you started with Horatio," Giles said. "He's been badgering me to do it for some years. I've taken a great deal of advice, including His Grace the Duke of Laverstoke's and his lawyers. All that I've been waiting for is William and Ruth." He smiled fondly at them. "And it's required a great deal of patience."

There was a slight pause before he unleashed the plan.

"I propose making you all joint owners, with me, of the estate and the money."

William and Steven gaped at each other; Ruth said, "Oh!" in a small voice and clapped a hand over her mouth; only Leander remained unmoved.

In the amazed silence, Giles saw that his daughter-in-law was puzzling dreadfully hard over something. "Yes, Ruth, what's bothering you?" he asked gently.

"None of us would actually *own* the estate or all that money, would we?" she asked diffidently.

"That's right. We'd all own everything *together*, and you'd work together to make sure it's looked after." Ruth looked immeasurably relieved. "Quite frankly," Giles continued, "there is one thing above all others that commends this idea to me. I shan't have to bother with a will. I wouldn't have had the faintest idea how to write the damned thing!"

"What about death duties?" Leander asked. "Will this scheme help us if the Government brings them in?"

Horatio smiled to himself: trust her to be on to that one!

For more than ten years, rumblings had been coming out of Westminster concerning the possibility of taxing the money a person left at death. Political life in 1886 had been dominated by the drama of the Irish Home Rule question to the exclusion of all else. Now, following the comprehensive defeat of Gladstone's third government at a General Election, it was widely believed that the Marquess of Salisbury's Conservative administration would introduce the tax within two or three years.

"As far as we can tell, this would make us immune," Horatio said. "At the very worst we should have to pay tax on whatever fraction of the whole could be deemed to have belonged to the deceased."

Leander looked pleased. Firmly of the opinion that Cannings Ambo paid quite enough taxes to be going on with, she regarded the concept of robbery from the grave as utterly iniquitous.

She had another point.

"We shall need very strict rules," she said.

"What do you mean?" Giles asked.

"Well, for one thing, access to the money will have to be controlled." Seeing that Steven did not understand the point at which she was hinting, she made it plain. "What if I decide to make off with the seventy thousand the minute I get the chance?"

Steven thought it was funny. "You wouldn't do that, darling."

"*I* wouldn't," Leander replied. "What guarantee can you provide for, say, George, or his children?"

Steven had it in mind to object to such an outrageous suggestion until he saw that Horatio was nodding approvingly.

"Yes, there will have to be rules," Giles agreed. "You must all help me draw them up. Once we've done this, the future will be in your hands as much as mine – more, in fact, because there are four of you and only one of me! I suggest that we call ourselves Trustees. Does that seem like a good idea?"

No one disagreed.

"You will appoint new Trustees as and when you see fit," Giles said. "I'd say that was the most important thing you'll ever have to do. You won't have any trouble with anyone breaking the rules if you pick the right people."

"What about Aunt Elisabeth and Uncle John?" William asked. "Shouldn't they be in?"

"I'd like them to be," Giles replied. "Unfortunately, I think John sees a conflict between his calling and getting mixed up with money and property."

"Be a damned good thing if all churchmen were the same!" Horatio muttered.

"Elisabeth won't join without John, of course," Giles said. "But if anything were to happen to me, you will continue to make sure that they want for nothing. I warn you, though, it's hard work getting them to accept anything."

Leander knew that Giles was paying for her cousin, young John, to be educated at Winchester. "You will be one of us, Horatio?" she said, obviously expecting immediate agreement.

"Oh, no! You don't want to be saddled with an old fogey like me."

"I did try," Giles said to Leander. "He's adamant."

"So am I!" she retorted. "Either you join us, Horatio, or the scheme doesn't start."

"That sounds right to me," William said.

"Do you see? I warned you," Giles said to Horatio.

"Leander, I'm seventy-six years of age," Horatio protested. "I could pop off at any time."

"Don't be ridiculous!" Leander said with cheerful determination. "A man of your experience has a vast amount to offer us. You'll join!"

As Giles pulled a face of mock-resignation at Horatio, Ruth and Steven looked bemused. They still had some way to go before becoming fully used to the Flamsteed way of doing things.

Horatio surrendered.

Ten days later, it was signed, sealed and settled. The sheer volume of the legal documents with their yards of pink tape made Horatio grumble about lawyers, and he made no attempt to understand it all. Leander, however, worked through every syllable of the fearsome pile of jargon and produced a summary for Giles to copy into the Big Book.

"And I've given you some capital letters," she joked.

The six Trustees, constituting a Partnership, were Giles, Leander, Steven, Ruth, William and Horatio. They owned the estate jointly: by virtue of the Married Women's Property Act of 1881, Leander and Ruth had full rights. Clauses were added to the estate deeds to ensure that it could only be disposed of as a whole, which catastrophic event would require the unanimous approval of all the Trustees in office at the time.

Giles's money became 'the Fund', with provision for payments of salaries or allowances to Trustees and wages to staff. Withdrawal of any other sum of money was possible only on the signatures of a majority of the Trustees.

At Leander's insistence, there were conditions under which a Trustee might be expelled from the Partnership. Anyone absenting themselves from Cannings Ambo for more than a month without good reason was likely to be stripped of authority, as were those involved in matrimonial difficulties.

Ruth was still frightened by it all, clinging to the belief that life was going to go on as she and her parents had always known it.

"I doubt it, my dear," Leander told her with gentle firmness. "It's all quite straightforward, and think of this: how many women are there who have a vote in something as important as Cannings Ambo?"

Sooner or later, racing men always came round to Latimer's Barn in their conversations. Alongside the richly deserved victories of the great Ormonde, who was building an unbeaten career to stand in the record books with that of Eclipse, Precision, Parallelogram and a steady stream of other good horses kept Giles firmly in the public eye.

"Just a minute, what might Flamsteed have up his sleeve for this one?" was a question invariably asked when the form of a race was being assessed.

And as well as success on the racecourse, the family of Cannings Ambo was always achieving good things and growing.

Far away in Edinburgh, Charles Stanton, following precisely in his father's footsteps, obtained brilliant results in his intermediate examinations at the University Medical School. After five years of anxiety, Sally Daly presented Conn with another daughter, and confirmation of Leander's third pregnancy was greeted with great joy. Everyone wanted a girl and never doubted her categoric assurances on the matter.

At one stage around mid-summer, there was even talk of a girl in Marlborough who was supposed to be turning Carrot O'Grady's thoughts towards matrimony; sadly, she fell by the wayside of Carrot's appalling, albeit charming, irresponsibility in everything not connected with horses.

But it was also the year in which Giles began to show signs of a tiredness that he could never quite conquer.

Attuned to his every mood and gesture, Leander soon spotted

what he managed to conceal from others. Eventually, she nagged him into consulting Lawrence Stanton: the resultant assortment of pills and tonics was impressive, and, in conjunction with more rest, seemed to do some good.

Another ominous sign was hidden from Leander.

It was the first year since her husband's suicide in 1877 that Alexandra and Giles did not talk about the possibility of their marriage. The discussions, sporadic affairs spread over several weeks, always came to the same conclusion: they were far too set in their ways, master and mistress of their respective domains, and well satisfied with their existing relationship, to consider upheaval.

Nevertheless, they had always debated the issue with keen relish. In 1886, however, they did not.

CHAPTER 12

1891–92

'Let me turn you into a gentleman'

"There's one thing for certain. Those poplars have done well."

Giles was right. Thirty-two years after he planted them, the trees had reached a height of forty feet, transforming the drive into an impressive landmark that was visible from Cannings St John to the south and the main London road to the north.

He was very weak, his breathing was dreadful and Leander had a sickening premonition that those were the last words he would ever utter.

They were.

Giles Flamsteed died later that night, 12 November 1891. He was fifty-seven years old.

It was only in the last two days that Leander appreciated that this second attack of pneumonia was grievous. Before that, it had seemed almost trivial compared to the one that prostrated him during the previous winter, coming close to making him a permanent invalid. What had started as a chill following a thorough drenching at Newmarket on a day when racing was eventually abandoned, proved fatal, especially after Giles had seemed to lose his resolve.

Leander and William were with him at the end. Once they were sure he was gone, there was a long silence as they sat and stared at him. When William finally looked up, he saw that Leander was weeping. Somehow, the fact that her action was serene, completely devoid of effort or blatant emotion, made it all the more arresting.

"I had no idea he was so worn out," she said sadly.

"This place must have been far more of a strain than he ever admitted," William said.

Leander nodded. "Now it's our turn," she said thoughtfully. "I tell you what I think would be nice. Will you make a coffin for him, William?"

"Yes, of course. There was Horatio as well, Lea. Father never seemed to get over him dying."

Horatio had succumbed to a heart attack almost exactly two years ago. Curiously, Giles had taken the initial shock very well; it was not until six months later that a hopeless lethargy began to envelop him.

Leander spent the whole of the following day in the library working on the entry for the Big Book. First, she compiled the simple statistics of Giles's thirty-two racing seasons. He had produced the winners of 821 races and earned prize-money of £256,000. Very noticeably, the year-by-year tally of winners was increasing; in 1890 and 1891 they had won more races than there were horses in the yard, a performance of the highest distinction, achieved by only the very best trainers. It was an astonishing record for a one-time wine merchant, who, on his own admission, had entered racing on impulse, armed only with complete ignorance.

Leander then searched through the Big Book to remind herself of her father's attainments with the village. It was difficult to resist the temptation to draw up a list that went on and on, but she knew it must be done: Giles would have disapproved very strongly of anything that smacked of verbosity or fulsomeness. She worked on, going without lunch, knowing that Ellie Goakes would understand and take care of the children.

At four o'clock, when it was time to light the lamps, Ellie brought some tea into the library and Leander waved her to a seat. She wrote a few more lines, then read through the draft that would make about a page when it was copied into the Big Book.

"What do you think of that, Ellie?" Leander asked, passing the loose sheets across the desk.

Ellie studied it carefully. "Yes, it's all right," she said at last.

"What's wrong with it?" Leander asked with a little smile of resignation. She knew Ellie too well not to detect her dissatisfaction.

"Well . . ." For once, Ellie looked slightly uncomfortable. "I'd like to have seen some mention of what he did for Mother and Father. I can remember the day we came here from that awful place at Lynchetts. It was a miracle. That was about a month before you were born."

Leander sighed and fiddled with her pen. "The trouble is, Ellie, half the people in the village would want me to say something like that about him. If I put it all down, it would ramble on for ever and he wouldn't have liked that."

Ellie nodded. "I see what you mean. Anyway, you know what we Goakeses think."

"Yes, Ellie, and it's very kind of you. What I've put at the end will have to do for everyone."

Ellie read it aloud. "'Because of his efforts to reconstruct the village and his very great kindness, Giles Flamsteed was much loved and will be sorely missed by all.'" After a moment's thought Ellie said, "Yes, you can't say fairer than that. You won't ever write truer words."

People had to stand at the back of the church and in the side aisles for the funeral service. All but two of the entire population of Cannings Ambo were present, the exceptions being Abraham's eldest son, Albert, and Carrot who had, regretfully, stayed in the yard to keep an eye on the horses. Half of Marlborough came and the world of racing was well represented: influential men from London and Newmarket had come down to Wiltshire, some of them having to spend a night in an hotel.

There were nine in the family pew. Steven and Leander had George, Giles and Amelia with them. Amelia, four years old and a perfect miniature copy of Leander, held her mother's hand throughout the service and stared with sad, unblinking solemnity at the coffin; she had worshipped her grandfather. Ruth and William were accompanied by their children Maude and Gerald, aged three years and eighteen months respectively.

At the end of the service, Seamus and Dan Goakes, symbolic of the foundation of the stable, and four other lads bore the coffin out to the churchyard where a grave had been dug at a spot picked out by Leander. Steven, William and John Shepherd who had accompanied her on the mission, had shuffled around uneasily, thinking that she would never make up her mind.

"This isn't easy," she said, reading their thoughts. "I'm not simply looking for the best place to put Father, I'm trying to find a family plot." Seeing that they still failed to grasp her full meaning, she asked, "How many of us will there be in a hundred years?"

Steven was shaken. He knew all about Leander's dedication to the idea of continuity, but realised that he paid only lip-service to it. Her question changed that.

"I take your point, my dear," John Shepherd said. "But oughtn't we to be considering putting your father with or near your mother?"

"No, Uncle John, we should not," she said curtly and the issue was closed, slammed shut and bolted. William, a good deal shaken by her reaction, wondered if Leander had found anything in Giles's private papers to justify this attitude towards the mother they had never known and scarcely ever mentioned.

In her own good time, Leander found what she wanted in the south-east corner of the churchyard. It was alongside the chancel of the church and screened from the Rectory by a line of ancient yews. She indicated a patch of smooth turf, about an acre in extent, and said, "That's the place. Nice and peaceful. Plenty of room."

And that was where Seamus, Dan and the others took him. There were a few simple prayers, Leander and William threw down their handfuls of earth and it was all over. Turning suddenly from the grave, her emotions clamped down, Leander saw George and Maude watching from the path that ran round the church. Her first reaction was irritation: they should never have wandered so far and must have worked deviously hard to escape Ellie's supervision. Then she was struck by the strong likeness between the two cousins, surprised that she had never noticed it before.

A second, closer look revealed the real resemblance to be no more than superficial; the suggestion of similarity had been created by their identical expressions of sulky ill-disposition emphasised by the slovenly way they were standing. They smartened themselves up when they became aware of Leander's hard look. Rejoining the annoyed Ellie, George Hawksworth and Maude Flamsteed were completely unaware of the impression they had created: Leander never forgot it.

There was, of course, a gathering at The House.

It had been in progress more than an hour before Leander encountered Ralph Flamsteed. She had felt honour bound to let him know of Giles's death, and had noticed him in the midst of the congregation in church, but had not gone out of her way to greet him and made no secret of her distaste at finding him still hanging around.

He was in the kitchen where Leander had gone to find out if Bertha and Brigid needed help. The bottle of wine he was guzzling was almost certainly his second and the two women were radiating distressed disapproval.

"It was good of you to come, Uncle Ralph," Leander said. "But I expect you will be wanting to start back. It isn't an easy journey."

Ralph stared at her vacuously. "A sad day," he muttered. "Poor Giles! No age at all." He stared morosely into his glass for a few moments, then he was transformed, suddenly alert and unnaturally bright. "I'm in no hurry, dear niece," he said in a voice that glittered with malice. "I thought I might stay for the reading of the will."

"Come with me," Leander said quietly.

"Eh?"

"I said, come with me! At once, if you please."

She took him to the library.

"There isn't a will," she said.

"What?" It was some time before a possible implication broke through the fuddled state of his mind. "Ah! I see. All a bit sudden . . . went intestate . . . we'll all get a portion."

"Father did not leave a will because there was no need to."

"What do you mean, no need? Look here, my girl, don't get fanciful with me. It won't wash. You can save your high and mighty tricks for the local peasantry."

He was turning unpleasant. Unmoved, Leander told him of the Partnership and the Fund.

He tried raving.

"Monstrous! Absolutely monstrous! I shall sue, of course, you may depend upon it. I'll see the lot of you in hell first before I surrender my share."

"What share?" Leander asked calmly.

"My part of my brother's estate."

"You have no entitlement. However, I'm sure the lawyers will be pleased to hear from you. It might even improve your health if you gave your money to them instead of drinking it!"

He tried pleading.

"Leander, my dear, I have to confess that I *need* money. My business is hounded by bad luck . . . and there is the question of the loan I made to your father."

"Indeed?" Leander regarded him icily.

"Yes. Twelve thousand pounds," Ralph Flamsteed wailed.

"Twelve thousand! Goodness me! It goes up and up, doesn't it? Where will it end?"

Leander's facetiousness succeeded where anger had failed. Ralph was defeated and dumb.

"You will leave now," she told him. "Since this is the last time you will be visiting Latimer's Barn, I will make a concession. A carriage will take you to Calne. You can travel on by train from there."

Warned by Ellie of the trouble that poor Mr Flamsteed's odious brother might cause, Dan and Jim Goakes were glad to have the chance of helping him on his way and set off cheerfully on the trip that might take four hours through an afternoon and evening that threatened rain.

Leander returned to the library after they had gone. Ralph worried her. At best, he seemed destined to be a nuisance: at worst, he was a potential menace and she was not at all sure that it was safe to ignore him. She was considering what she might do about him when a nervous knock came at the door. It was Alexandra.

"I must go now," she said. "Thank you for inviting me . . . and everything."

She had borne herself very well, but grief at Giles's death was now getting the better of her. Leander took her arm and led her to a chair.

"Has that awful Ralph Flamsteed been causing trouble?" Alexandra asked.

"He had it in mind." Leander smiled grimly.

"I told them you'd cope," Alexandra said. "One or two people were getting worried. He was quite rude to Lucy and Daphne Stanton when we came out of church."

Alexandra sat awkwardly, twisting a handkerchief round her fingers. "I shall miss your father," she said. "Very much."

"I know," Leander replied quietly.

There was a pause during which Alexandra seemed to be suffering agonies of indecision. Finally, it came out in a rush.

"I'm sorry to be so miserable, Leander, but the fact is that Giles . . . your father . . . and I were lovers for many years."

Leander gave her the soft gentle smile normally reserved for Amelia. "Since I was eight, I think," she said.

"You knew?" Alexandra looked horrified.

"Yes, of course I did."

"Didn't you mind?"

"Mind? Why on earth should I? I always thought you were good for each other. You certainly made my father happy and you were very *loyal* to him. The Flamsteeds value that highly."

"What about the Hawksworths?" Alexandra asked.

"Even more so," Leander smiled.

Alexandra shook her head in wonderment. "Fancy you knowing all this time," she said.

"Tell me, Alexandra, are you happy and comfortable living in Marlborough?" Leander asked. "Surely that house has some awful memories?"

"Yes, you're right, it does. I imagined it might be all right, and it was at first. But these last two or three years . . ." She waved a hand in a gesture of hopelessness.

"What would you think to living at The Hall?"

Alexandra sat bolt upright. "That's a marvellous idea!" she said. "I'd be well hidden in Cannings Ambo, wouldn't I?"

"That place must have some very pleasant associations," Leander said, a hint of mischief showing that she really did know everything.

"Oh, it does," Alexandra said. "Wait a minute, though. Is The Hall free?"

"There's Lucy, of course. I don't think she's happy all on her own. She hardly goes into most of the rooms these days."

"What about Peveril Beresford? Haven't I heard that he's involved somehow?"

"Not with The Hall," Leander assured her.

Horatio had left Beresford Engineering and a great deal more to Peveril. Half his personal fortune, a sum of about £25,000 was bequeathed to Giles, and hence to the Fund, as was his share in the stud. The Hall, in accordance with the terms of Jasper's wishes, had reverted to the Cannings Ambo estate.

"I thought Peveril had some links with the village," Alexandra said.

"He keeps horses here," Leander replied. "He only does it in memory of Horatio. He never takes the blindest bit of notice of them. I was hoping he'd be here today so that we could talk about it."

"He must be a very busy man," Alexandra pointed out.

"Be that as it may, I don't care for owners like that," Leander said. "But, no, my dear, rest assured that I want you in Cannings Ambo."

"Why, Leander?"

"Your advice will be most welcome. With Father and Horatio gone I shall need all the help and experience I can get."

"You shall have it!"

"Good. Now, I'm going to give you some advice, Alexandra. When you get home, put that awful black dress on the kitchen fire! Father wouldn't have expected it and he certainly wouldn't have *liked* it."

For the first time since Giles became seriously ill, Alexandra laughed.

While Leander was dealing with her uncle and talking to Alexandra, William bowed to the inevitable.

Inveigled by Leander, he and Jim had made more furniture and a great deal of it was in The House. The main dining-room, in which most of the guests gathered, was furnished entirely with fine pieces from the workshop behind Rose House. Not only was the effect extremely pleasing, it was also a superb showroom.

The Duke of Laverstoke chose his moment carefully, moving towards William with natural ease.

"My very deepest condolences, Mr Flamsteed," he said. "Your father was a splendid man. It was an honour to know him."

"Thank you, Your Grace," William said.

"I say . . ." the Duke lowered his voice and edged closer ". . . I

203

hope it's not inappropriate at a time like this, but I've been admiring all this furniture you made. Remarkable stuff!"

"It's good of you to say so, Your Grace."

"My wife is very taken with it, too. Tell me, how much do you suppose you'd want for making a table like that . . . fifty pounds, do you think?"

No one had ever asked the question before, and William was thrown off-balance by it. "I'm sure we could do better than that, Your Grace," he said. "At a guess, I'd say it would be more like forty."

"Steady on, don't cut your throat," the Duke cautioned. "You must bear in mind that I'd want it delivered."

"I think forty-five pounds might be fair," William said after several frantic calculations.

The Duke smiled. "So, you'll make me one, Mr Flamsteed?"

"Yes, Your Grace," William replied with a rueful grin, realising how he had been trapped.

"Good! Now we've got that established, I'd like you to come to Eaton Mandeville and have a look round to see what else you might do for us. The fact is, Mr Flamsteed, I've got a pretty big house and my forebears have neglected certain aspects of it. We need rather a lot of furniture."

And while William was beginning to understand what he had let himself in for, the Duke of Laverstoke went to find his Duchess before William had a chance to change his mind.

The months immediately after the death of Giles were among the most difficult in Leander's life.

The multitude of things she *had* to do presented no problem whatsoever; the difficulties arose from what she knew she must *not* do.

Steven needed to be left alone to look after the yard in his own way.

Although there was no racing to worry about, December saw what was, in many ways, the most crucial event of the annual cycle at Latimer's Barn. The new yearlings arrived, carrying many of the hopes for the next two seasons. This year there were twenty-three of them and they came in twos and threes during the weeks before Christmas. First they had to be settled and made to feel at home, then schooled. One mistake and a horse could be ruined.

There were times when Leander, almost frantic to be in the thick of things and check that everything was being done properly, had to force herself to sit still.

"You bide there," Ellie said, fully aware of her mistress's torment. "He's got to do it without you at him every five minutes."

"I know, Ellie, I know!" Leander wailed. "But that doesn't make it any easier to bear."

"You've no cause to fret."

"You sound very sure," Leander said sharply, sensing fact rather than mere speculation.

"I am. It all seemed nicely in order when I had a look this morning."

"You watched?"

"I did."

"What are the yearlings like?" Leander asked eagerly.

"Well, I'm no judge, of course, but Conn Daly told me that they're a very good bunch. One thing's for sure – your husband is loving them to death."

Leander was in a state to be alarmed at anything. "He's not making them soft and useless, is he?"

"He's doing all right, so hold your trouble!"

That was certainly the impression that Leander gained from her chats with Steven in the evenings, so she had to be content. There was also Ellie's promise to keep an unobtrusive eye on things and the reassuring knowledge that Steven had spent ten years working with Giles.

Steven's greatest triumph was concealing the fact that he, too, was a bag of nerves. The morning after Giles died, he walked into the yard to find all the lads and horses looking at him in a new way, and the sudden weight of responsibility made him feel ill for several days. He knew all the agonies Leander was suffering on his behalf and loved her all the more.

He soon found that failure was unthinkable, utterly out of the question. The best possible tribute to Giles and what he had built was the way the ranks closed round Steven to support him. Two of the lads, unsettled by the change of command, went off to look for work at Newmarket. Before Steven had time to worry, Abraham Merriweather produced a queue of suitable replacements.

"It's amazing," Steven told Leander as they enjoyed their quiet two hours together after the children had gone to bed. "I've no idea where Abraham got them from. They just appeared out of thin air."

"This place has always been like that," Leander told him. "It's as though a secret telepathic message goes out and they all come hurrying."

"Long may it last," Steven said.

"It will – if we carry on getting it right." Leander allowed a slight pause before asking, "How are the yearlings? Do you see any really good ones?"

"They're coming along nicely," Steven replied, smiling at her attempt to appear only partially interested. "And, yes, there are one or two very nice ones. Mrs Fandine-Browne has a filly that we all think might amount to something useful."

"I'd like Alexandra to win a top-class race," Leander said, making it sound inconsequential. Steven knew nothing of the relationship between Alexandra and his late father-in-law, and Leander had no intention of telling him. She loathed gossip: she also thought Steven might disapprove.

On a still, mild day at the end of January 1892, William drove Leander to Calne. As they passed the crossroads at Beckhampton and the horses began the two-mile ascent to Cherhill, William said, "It won't be long before we shall be able to come up here at fifteen or twenty miles an hour, Lea."

"What, in one of those wretched horseless carriages?" She was scandalised.

"Motor car is a better name," William said mildly.

"Monstrosities! People will never take them seriously."

"There are three in Marlborough now. Guy Mallender's getting one next week. He's promised to let me have a go at driving it."

"Don't expect me to come with you, William. Apart from anything else, the very idea of having to creep along behind a man with a red flag!"

"There's talk of Parliament abolishing that soon and setting a more sensible speed limit."

"Pah!"

"Say what you like, Lea, if I had a motor car, we should be up this hill in a trice *and* I could take you all the way."

"I'm perfectly happy with things the way they are," Leander said stiffly.

"You sound like an old dowager of ninety," William chuckled, making her smile.

He took her to the railway station, put her on a train to Chippenham and withdrew to the Lansdowne Arms to wait for her. Rather than worry over the mission that Leander had not explained to him, William made himself comfortable with a pot of coffee and contemplated the strangeness of his sister's mind. She was devoted to the latest gadgets; the Zeiss camera he had bought her for Christmas was her current favourite. But he had a strong feeling that she would never take to the motor car. That unfortunate name 'horseless carriage' was to blame; Leander could not possibly be expected to approve of anything *horseless*.

Leander found a coach for hire outside the station at Chippenham and the driver was as good as his word; twenty minutes later, she was studying the front door of Broadleaze Farm.

"Wait for me," she said to the driver, who, having recognised her, would have done anything she asked. "I shall not be long."

It was Sir Arnold Hastings himself who opened the door.

"Good morning, Sir Arnold," she said. "I am Leander Hawksworth. My father used to train horses for your father. I am sorry to call on you like this, but there is something I wish you to know. I shall not take much of your time."

"Er . . . please come in, Mrs Hawksworth." He was very taken aback and awkward.

Augusta Hastings was reading an illustrated paper in her favourite drawing-room, the one that had no view of the farm. She bristled with anger when her husband introduced Leander.

"I cannot imagine what brings you here, Mrs Hawksworth," Lady Hastings said with acid ill-humour. "You are most unwelcome!"

"Why?" Leander asked calmly.

"Your father ruined my poor father-in-law."

"Augusta, please!" Arnold Hastings said vainly.

"And how did he do that?" Leander asked.

"He encouraged him to gamble!"

"Lady Hastings, my father disapproved of gambling very strongly indeed. He never placed a bet in his life and he encouraged everyone to follow his example. That is the truth. No doubt you will take it or leave it as you see fit. This is also the truth!"

From a pocket inside her cape, Leander produced a document which she unfolded and slapped on the table.

"This is a witnessed copy of an agreement made on the twenty-fifth of May, 1859, between my father and his brother, Ralph Flamsteed," Leander announced. She was given the satisfaction of seeing Augusta Hastings stiffen with interest. "By its terms, Ralph gave my father five thousand pounds and my father surrendered all claim to the family wine business to which he was the heir. Look!"

Leander stabbed a finger on the relevant paragraph, and Arnold Hastings accepted her invitation to examine it. His wife feigned indifference.

"Flamsteed and Sons was a long-established company enjoying a substantial reputation," Leander went on. "I have ascertained that in 1860, the turnover was fifty-five thousand pounds. As a businessman yourself, Sir Arnold, I'm sure you can guess at the likely profit. Following the death of my father's father, Ralph Flamsteed used sharp practice and incompetence until the business was virtually worthless."

"This means that Ralph effectively bought Flamsteed's for five thousand pounds?" Arnold Hastings said.

"That is correct. No other sum of money *ever* passed between him and my father. There were no loans of ten or twenty thousand pounds or whatever the figure is nowadays. My uncle is a liar and a cheat."

"I see. Yes." Arnold Hastings was pensive. "Do forgive my manners, Mrs Flamsteed; won't you please sit down?"

"No thank you, Sir Arnold, I must go. I merely wished to have it understood that my father was an honest, honourable man. Frankly, I see no reason why you and I should ever meet again."

She folded the document and returned it to the cape pocket. With a less than friendly look at Augusta Hastings, she seemed to be going until she paused at the door with a faraway look on her face.

"I'm looking for a man called Sixsmith, Sir Arnold," she said quietly. "Can you help me?"

"No, Mrs Hawksworth, I only heard talk of him, I never met him."

Leander nodded acceptance of this. "He is the son of a man who attempted to organise the burning down of Latimer's Barn thirty years ago," Leander said. "*This* Sixsmith, using money provided by my uncle, tried to abduct Bellerophon, our Derby winner. But I fancy you know about that, Sir Arnold. Goodbye."

As Leander skipped nimbly back into the carriage, Sir Arnold and Lady Hastings were staring at each other in grimly speculative silence.

"Do you suppose we ought to tell Ralph to warn Sixsmith?" Augusta Hastings asked.

"No, we damned well should not!" Sir Arnold roared. "Things are going to be different here, Augusta. That man Flamsteed will not be coming again, do you hear me?"

Lady Hastings nodded meekly.

"Well?" William asked an hour later when Leander strode jauntily into the Lansdowne Arms.

"Perfectly, thank you," she replied. "I'm absolutely ravenous and I want a glass of sherry."

"What have you been up to?" William asked, returning with her drink and a luncheon menu.

"I've been fouling Uncle Ralph's nest," she replied happily. "Your very good health, William!"

Throughout the latter half of April and the first week of May, against the backdrop of the most beautiful spring for ten years, Steven proved that he had the two ingredients essential for a racehorse trainer. Leander had always known that he was talented and possessed an immense capacity for taking pains. Now, he showed that he had the other vital attribute: luck. Five horses went out to race during the three weeks and they all came back winners. At the age of forty-seven, Peter Izzard declared his intention of retiring from race-riding at the end of the season, and, with the full-blooded support of everybody in the yard, intended to finish with a flourish.

Now that no one could possibly believe that she was worrying or interfering, Leander began to show more interest in the work of the stable. Two or three mornings a week, she went out on Cannings Down to see the horses at work. Because she took the children with her, they had to watch the first lot at seven o'clock so that there was no interference with school.

George made no bones about hating it. His current posture was to pretend that the horses and all the falderal associated with them were beneath his contempt. Leander was undeceived: her eldest son was terrified of horses and was bone idle to boot. But for the tiresome necessity to go through this charade, he might have enjoyed another hour in bed.

Giles and Amelia, on the other hand, thought these occasions a vast treat. Giles, nearly seven and looking more like his grand-paternal namesake every day, was a natural horseman and was constantly demanding to be allowed to ride a 'proper' horse. Amelia was plucky rather than talented; she trundled round on her fat, grey pony with a steadfast lack of anything remotely like style. Charmingly, when people laughed at her, Amelia laughed back.

While Giles and Amelia went to school with the other village children, George dragged himself off to the Rectory for private tuition with his great-uncle, John Shepherd. Steven was determined that the next generation would be educated to the highest possible level. Having been impressed by the gentlemanly erudition of John Shepherd junior, now at Oxford, Steven saw no reason why George should not follow him to Winchester. Accordingly, George was made to grapple with Latin verbs and other arcane topics.

What Leander saw on the gallop convinced her that Steven's early successes were not a flash in the pan; barring unforeseeable disasters, there were good days ahead. Free of worry about the stable, she turned her attention to Peveril Beresford.

For a while, Leander thought that she might have to go to Birmingham to see him. Eventually, however, in response to a letter that was, to all intents and purposes, a command, he paid a three-hour visit to Cannings Ambo in June.

At sixty, Peveril remained a reasonably fine figure of a man. His boyish good looks were still in evidence and he had taken care of himself to the extent that he was slightly underweight. Overall, he gave Leander a sense of aesthetic near-saintliness.

Once he and Leander were settled over lunch together, he came straight to the point.

"Mrs Hawksworth, please accept my apologies for keeping you waiting. The fact is, I have been very busy with momentous affairs."

"Oh?" Leander waited.

"I am selling Beresford Engineering," Peveril announced.

"Really?" Leander controlled her surprise. "I expect you have good reasons."

"The truth is, Mrs Hawksworth, I believe that this country has lost its soul and direction. We have become fiendishly dedicated to Mammon to the exclusion of all the real values. I am acquiring a large country house as a refuge for artists, poets and musicians. A lady is helping me and she has found exactly what we want near Droitwich in Worcestershire. I have had this in mind for some years."

Good God! Leander thought.

"I shall be sad to see the end of Beresford Engineering," she said, showing nothing of her feelings. "That company went a long way towards making Latimer's Barn what it is. Our very first winner was The Beresford Lathe, you know."

"Yes. Uncle Horatio was very proud of that."

"And I take it your change of direction means that you wish to give up your racing interests?" Leander prompted.

"I am afraid so, Mrs Hawksworth."

"Would you like me to dispose of your horses?"

"What do you mean by 'dispose'?" Peveril asked nervously.

"Sell them, of course, Mr Beresford. Don't worry! They will come to no harm. In Cannings Ambo the horses are treated at least as well as the human beings."

"Ah!" He was relieved. "Do you suppose that you will have any difficulty selling them?"

"No, I don't. They're all good, honest animals. They would be ideal for someone wishing to make a start in the Sport. I will send you a cheque when the business is done."

The following day, without having bothered Steven with the news that eight of their horses might be leaving, Leander went into Marlborough and sold them to a man who would have to keep them at Latimer's Barn.

All her instincts told her that the Timberlakes were the answer to the immediate problem and that, properly handled, they might provide long-term support.

Godfrey Timberlake was uproariously glad to see her.

"Now then, Leander, you're looking better than ever," he shouted. "Is that husband of yours seeing to you all right?"

"Yes, thank you, Godfrey," she laughed.

"Promise me you'll let me know if he loses his grip."

"Wouldn't one of your sons be more up to that game?" Leander asked, content to play along with him.

"Don't be so bloody silly! James has got himself shackled to a frightful tartar and Rupert never was any good, was he? Damn it, he let you go when he had the chance."

"So, I'll have to make do with you, you old rogue!"

"Watch your lip, my girl. I'm only sixty-seven and I feel forty. I'll give you a serving you won't forget in a hurry any time you like."

"Thank you, Godfrey, I shall bear that in mind," Leander said solemnly.

"Make sure you do. Now, to what do I owe the pleasure, eh?" His eyes sparkled. "What do you want?"

"As a matter of fact, I came to see if there was something I could do for you." She was very earnest.

"Tell me about it."

"How are people treating you?" she asked. "Is it the same?"

Godfrey Timberlake's face darkened. "You mean do they still think we're dirt or carrying the plague?" he asked. "No, it hasn't changed. There are one or two exceptions. That grocer, Mallender, is a decent chap and your friend Mrs Fandine-Browne is always pleasant, but most of them keep their snobbish noses in the air."

"That's bad!"

"It is. It's water off a duck's back to me, but Rupert gets bloody annoyed about it. He wants to be something in the county, not just this one-eyed place."

"It's your money," Leander told him. "They don't like all that wealth from trade."

"What am I supposed to do, give it away?"

"No, that wouldn't help. You'd be common and poor instead of common and rich. Even worse!"

211

Godfrey smiled sardonically at her bluntness. "So what do you suggest?" he asked.

"Let me turn you into a gentleman."

He roared with laughter. "And here I am trying to make a dishonest woman of *you*." Just as suddenly, he was serious again. "How will you manage that, Leander?"

"Quite simply: let me train some horses for you."

He nodded thoughtfully. They had discussed it before.

"Last time we talked about this, you hadn't got any vacancies at that high-falutin livery stable."

"Well, we have now," Leander said. "But I shall need your help. You'll have to keep your mouth shut."

"Why?" Godfrey Timberlake had the feeling that he was going to approve of this scheme.

"Steven doesn't know about it yet. If he knew we'd got eight spare boxes, he'd almost certainly want to offer them to the Duke of Laverstoke. I thought that you should have first refusal."

Godfrey Timberlake winked conspiratorially. "Rely on me, my dear. Not a word!"

"We can say you just happened to hear," Leander said, and went on to explain about Peveril Beresford's decision to give up racing.

"H'm, I'm not surprised," Godfrey said. "I heard he'd got himself mixed up with a damned peculiar woman."

"He mentioned a lady," Leander said innocently.

"Lady!" Godfrey roared. "Well . . . yes . . . she's got a title."

"Do you know about her?"

"Lady Beatrice Wolstenholme. She's a shocker, Leander!"

"Peveril seemed rather smitten. I thought she must have plenty of soul."

"Soul?" Godfrey shook with rumbling laughter. "Soul! She's a raving nymphomaniac who goes on blind about the meaning of life – no knickers, back to nature and let's all be kind to plants! She's the widow of Lord Douglas Wolstenholme, the man who made a fortune out of potted shrimps."

"How long has she been with Peveril?" Leander asked.

"Oh . . . it must be three years now. They were cavorting round Wales together last summer. Made a terrible nuisance of themselves."

"Tell me, Godfrey, how do you know?" Leander asked.

"I make it my business to know things," he growled. "It pays to! It was Cuthbert who told me about her benighted ladyship. Seems she was creating merry hell over the stink coming out of one of our factories."

"Ah, yes." With an effort, Leander recalled Godfrey's elder brother, the irascible inhabitant of the house at the far side of Savernake Forest.

"Anyway, Beresford must fend for himself," Godfrey said briskly. "Are these horses any good?"

"Yes, they are. There's nothing in the Ascot or Goodwood class, but they'll be a good beginning for you. You must come and have a look at them."

"When?"

"Why not do it now?" Leander suggested. "My carriage is outside and Steven has taken a horse to Bath."

"How do I get back?" Godfrey wanted to know.

"Latimer's Barn always gives its owners every possible assistance and courtesy," Leander told him.

"And what if I decide I'm not going to be one of your precious owners?"

"You can walk!" she said and meant it.

Godfrey Timberlake slapped his substantial thighs in sheer joy. "Damn me, Leander, you really are a woman after my own heart!" he laughed.

Steven made Leander tell him the story again as they lay in bed that night.

"And old Timberlake bought the horses?" he asked, still in a state of amused disbelief.

"On the spot! He sent the money back with Conn. I shall go and see him tomorrow about registration and racing colours."

"And I never knew we had a problem!"

"You have enough to worry about in the yard, sweetheart. You must let me do things to help."

"I wouldn't dream of trying to stop you."

"The beauty of it is, I think Godfrey Timberlake and his clan will be very useful to us," Leander said.

"How?"

"They know a lot. Horatio was like that. He was our extra eyes and ears, and I've been wondering how to replace him. There seem to be Timberlakes all over the place and I don't think they miss much."

Steven thought about it, drawing her closer. "Might they even find Sixsmith for you?" he asked.

"Sixsmith?" Leander put up a good display of absent-minded unconcern. "Sixsmith? Oh, you mean the man who planned that raid on the stud?"

"Yes, darling," Steven said patiently.

213

"I hadn't thought about him for such a long time." Leander smiled sweetly. "Why are you looking like that?"

"What was it the Duke of Wellington said?" Steven asked, as if thinking aloud. "Oh yes – 'If you believe that, you will believe anything'!"

Leander frowned beautifully. "I have no idea what you're talking about," she said.

"And fancy old Peveril going off the rails like that," Steven said. "I wonder what will become of him."

"Something awful, I expect," Leander murmured. She was kissing Steven's chest and one of her hands had started to roam provocatively. "And guess what, sweetheart! Godfrey Timberlake swears that this Lady Beatrice Wolstenholme is a dangerous nymphomaniac."

"My God! The poor devil's in a similar mess to me," Steven said in mock-horror.

The September meeting of the Trustees took place at Rose House so that Ruth could keep an eye on her second son, the four-week-old Matthew who already seemed set to become another replica of his grandfather Giles.

For the first few minutes, Alexandra, now settled in The Hall, sat nervously outside the big room while her nomination as a Trustee was debated. Leander had promised that it would not take long and she was as good as her word.

"Carried unanimously," she said with a broad grin as she opened the door and extended a welcoming arm.

Seated round the first table that William and Jim ever made, the major subject of debate was the furniture that was now coming out of the workshop in increasing quantities. Demand was such that they were now providing full-time employment for two young men who had completed an apprenticeship at the Hawksworth boat-yard, only to find that there was no work for them.

"We've been run off our feet since we started obliging the Duke of Laverstoke," William reported.

"How much have you made?" Alexandra asked.

"Over two thousand pounds-worth," William replied.

Steven whistled admiringly.

"And what about the orders outstanding at the moment?" Leander wanted to know.

"Nearly three thousand."

"I think it's time we made up our minds about this furniture," Leander said. "It seems to me that it's starting to look very serious and businesslike."

214

"It is," William admitted.

"Are you going to carry on with it?"

"We don't seem to have any choice," William said. "The orders are coming in every week. And to tell you the truth, Jim and me have started to enjoy it."

"All right." Leander fiddled with her pencil. "We need to decide whether you need better facilities. Ought we to build a bigger workshop?"

"We ought to expand," Ruth said firmly. "There's a big future for that furniture."

It always pleased Leander to see how Ruth was blossoming into the role of Trustee as her confidence grew. Steven and Alexandra nodded agreement, William remained unconvinced.

"Let's leave it another year," he said.

"Very well," Leander said. "We look at it again in exactly twelve months." She made a note. "If the business is still growing, we build a proper workshop. Now, Ruth, you want to suggest that we do something about that dreadful road surface in Church Marks, don't you?"

In mid-October, Leander went with Steven to Newmarket for the Dewhurst Plate. It was her first visit to a racecourse for over four years and she knew that she was going to enjoy herself enormously.

The horse was Hypotenuse, the latest of the Duke of Laverstoke's geometrically named animals, and one of Steven's first batch of carefully nurtured two-year-olds. Hypotenuse was a big, strongly muscled colt by Bellerophon out of one of the Duke's own mares from Eaton Mandeville. He was self-opinionated, inclined to be fractious before a race, but, in his two appearances so far, had annihilated admittedly modest fields at Bath and Salisbury.

Steven himself led Hypotenuse round the paddock since only he could keep the colt anything like calm. Leander stood with the Duke of Laverstoke among the other owners and trainers, keeping an ear open to the buzz of conversation around her.

"Look at the size of that Hypotenuse!"

"He's far too big! Might make a good steeplechaser in three or four years."

"They say he got round Bath all right."

"And he's got tremendous condition."

"Oh, yes. He's a Latimer's Barn horse and no mistake. You can always spot them."

The Duke smiled. "Will that do you, Mrs Hawksworth?" he asked quietly.

She nodded, her face expressionless but for the eyes.

Steven gave Peter Izzard a leg-up for the last important race in which he would ever ride: as if sensible of the occasion, Hypotenuse behaved well and went down to the start like a lamb.

It was a very different matter coming back. Given time to collect his thoughts afterwards, Peter swore that something at the start had upset Hypotenuse and he had bolted in a foul temper. Certainly, it was only during the last two of the seven furlongs that Peter appeared to have any real control over the colt's sensational progress. He was pulling Hypotenuse up towards the end, but the winning margin was still five lengths.

Sir Dugdale Brodie, Senior Steward of the Jockey Club and an ardent admirer of Latimer's Barn, came to join the group in the winner's enclosure.

"An outstanding animal, Mrs Hawksworth," he said. "He's a credit to you. It's good to see that your husband has picked up the knack of turning them out so well."

Steven heard the compliment, but was far too preoccupied with trying to discover the reason for Hypotenuse's dramatic run.

He was none the wiser the following day as he and Leander made themselves comfortable on the train from Paddington that would take them back to Wiltshire. They talked about the Duke's colt for ten inconclusive minutes until, quite suddenly, Steven switched to an unconnected and rather surprising topic.

"Have you noticed how bright Amelia is?" he asked.

"She certainly seems to pick things up very quickly," Leander agreed.

"No, darling, there's more to it than that. Have you seen her playing around with arithmetic?"

"Oh, yes, I have. It's astonishing."

"I think she's very talented indeed. She invents new ways of doing sums, you know. We must make sure she gets the right attention so that she doesn't get frustrated and let it run to waste."

As the train picked up speed, settling into a gentle rocking motion, Leander rested her head on Steven's shoulder and thought, yet again, what an extraordinary man he was. With all the worries of his first season in charge of Latimer's Barn, he could have been excused for failing to observe Amelia's facility with figures.

Unfortunately, he appeared to maintain something of a blind spot over George.

CHAPTER 13
1894

'Protecting you from your enemies'

After Hypotenuse had won the Two Thousand Guineas and Derby of 1893, both Steven who had trained him and Michael Pilgrim who rode him felt a great deal more confident. Brilliant as he was, Hypotenuse could be a beast of a horse to work with; his first appearance of his three-year-old season in Newmarket's Craven Stakes was a dreadful fiasco in which he became insane on the way to the start, jumped the rails, and carted Michael across the Heath and two miles down the Devil's Ditch to the remote village of Reach.

Even after the ultimate victory of the Derby and the prestige that went with it, Steven and Michael were inclined to turn pale when they thought of some of their hair-raising experiences on the way to turning Hypotenuse into a champion.

"Never mind, sweetheart," an exultant Leander told Steven. "You've done it, you've won the Derby. That's the one that counts and you'll never have to handle anything that bad again."

Steven laughed hollowly. "Haven't you seen the evil creature Godfrey Timberlake's given me to train?" he protested.

She had. The bay colt by New Invention, who had been put down in 1892 at the good age of twenty-seven, was quite the most foul-tempered animal she had ever seen. There was clearly talent if only it could be channelled in the right direction rather than into the demolition of stable doors, or the terrorising of other horses. Steven knew he had to do his best, if only because the colt had come from the stud at Cannings St John.

"The Fund got one thousand four hundred guineas for that beauty," Leander told Steven. "Now make the devil run!"

By the middle of 1894, the Fund was also receiving handsome deposits from William's furniture-making.

217

The new workshop behind Rose House, completed by Harry Irons and his men in December 1892 according to Leander's plan, was soon full of work. Four new hands were taken on: after one look at Cannings Ambo, they all wanted to make it their home, so Harry Irons came back to build houses. At the same time, one of the older cottages on Church Green was converted into a grocery store which was run by Guy Mallender's daughter, Ann, eighteen, very pretty and formidably good at dealing with the suggestions of the Latimer's Barn lads. Ann also acted as postmistress, following the Post Office's recognition of Cannings Ambo as a worthwhile entity deserving its own services.

One afternoon in July, Leander was in the library, checking over the stable accounts, when Ellie poked her head round the door. "Mr Timberlake's here and wonders if you'd see him."

"Of course!" Leander closed the ledger. "By the way, Ellie, *which* Mr Timberlake?"

"That Rupert," Ellie replied sourly. She harboured the delusion that he entertained improper thoughts about Leander.

"Show him in, Ellie!"

"You know, she really loathes me," Rupert said as he came into the library and gave Leander's hand a gentle squeeze, his usual greeting.

"She thinks you're after me," Leander chuckled. "Actually, I sometimes think she'd like a go at you herself."

"Ellie? Me?" Rupert's eyebrows shot up. "She's a very handsome woman, of course, but . . ."

"She'd make mincemeat of you inside a week," Leander said. "Before I forget, Rupert, tell your father we're going to try running that monster of his at Salisbury next Wednesday."

"What do you think will happen?"

"I haven't the faintest idea. It wouldn't surprise me in the least if he gets us all warned off Newmarket Heath and locked up. On the other hand, he's good enough to win. Now, what did you come to tell me?"

"We've found your Mr Sixsmith." Rupert looked quite pleased with himself.

"*Have* you indeed!" Leander sat back in her chair and bestowed a smile of gratitude on him. "Where is he?"

"In Bristol. Here."

He passed a piece of paper across with an address on it.

"I don't know the place, so it means nothing to me," Leander said.

"It's a pretty bad area alongside the railway sidings at Pylle Hill," Rupert told her.

"Are you sure this is the right one?" Leander asked after a few moments of thought.

"I think so." Rupert produced a small leather notebook. "Edgar Sixsmith," he said. "A seedy individual, aged about forty-five as nearly as we can tell. Works as a bookmaker's runner, among other things. He's rumoured to have lived in Bath until a couple of years ago and he sometimes shoots his mouth off about the racehorses his father used to own."

"Yes, that will be him," Leander said. She was curious. "Tell me, Rupert, how did you find him?"

"If it's all the same to you, Leander, I'd rather not say."

"Why?"

"Well now, one hardly comes across scum like Sixsmith in the normal course of running a reputable business, does one?" He was self-mocking.

"Rupert, my dear! Are you telling me that what they've always said about the Timberlakes is true?"

"I'm not telling you anything, Leander – except that we know where Sixsmith is."

"Yes, of course. I understand." She smiled sweetly.

"Why are you interested in him?" Rupert asked.

"He once paid a gang to steal Bellerophon from the stud. He damned nearly got away with it, too. We had a tremendous piece of luck. Steven and William had been to a party in Pewsey and they were coming back on their bicycles. It was very late – early in the morning, really – and they saw something suspicious as they came through Cannings St John."

"Ah! Was this shortly before you married Steven?"

"It was."

"Hence the broken arm?"

"Correct."

Rupert looked pleased to have that little mystery solved at last. "So, our Mr Sixsmith is something of a villain?"

"He is indeed. His father caused us an awful lot of trouble."

"Do you want anything done about him?"

Leander looked long and hard at Rupert. She decided that she was not misinterpreting his meaning: the signs were perfectly clear. If she wished, arrangements could be made for something very nasty indeed to befall Edgar Sixsmith.

"No," she said at last. "No, I don't think so."

Rupert Timberlake noticed that it had taken her an appreciable time to reach her verdict and that she seemed less than completely certain about it. He wondered if Steven realised the full extent of her ruthlessness.

"The fact is, I worry about Sixsmith," Leander said. "You never know when a man like that is going to try again."

"According to our observations, he isn't in any position to," Rupert said. "He doesn't appear to make much of a living so he couldn't afford to hire ruffians."

"He was virtually penniless the last time," Leander said angrily. "My uncle solved that minor inconvenience by giving him two hundred pounds!"

"What, Ralph Flamsteed?"

"Yes!"

While Rupert mulled over this astonishing piece of information, Leander thought again. The reports from Charlotte Hastings via Alexandra's daughter indicated that Ralph Flamsteed was completely *persona non grata* at Broadleaze Farm where attitudes were very different these days. With that avenue closed to him, her uncle was probably a spent force.

"I take it that you can continue to keep an eye on this man?" Leander asked.

"Yes, for as long as you like. We have operations in the area that will last for at least five years."

"Good. Thank you, Rupert, I'm very grateful to you."

After he had gone, Leander studied the piece of paper with Sixsmith's address on it. She considered writing a note to him. No. That would make him run and they would have to go to the trouble of finding him again. It was best if Mr Sixsmith remained innocently in his Pylle Hill tenement and was watched.

A few days later, Leander was chatting to Vicky Foxton in The George when Cyril Osgood appeared. Surprised at finding the place deserted save for two ladies drinking tea, he pulled himself together, ordered a pint of ale and proceeded to slake his considerable thirst.

Cyril Osgood had walked from Devizes. Or rather, he had limped the twelve miles. Two months ago he had been invalided out of the Army, being of no further use to them after an ammunition explosion at Dorchester barracks. Rather than being critical of the botched job that the regimental surgeon had made of his left leg, Cyril was grateful for the gift of life. Three of his mates had not been so lucky. He was twenty-four years old, had a pension of two shillings and eightpence a week and was looking for a billet.

Having downed three-quarters of his pint and made appreciative noises, Cyril beamed at Vicky and said, "I'm told this might be a good place to find work, ma'am."

"You're in luck," Vicky told him. "This is the very lady you want to talk to. Mrs Hawksworth."

Cyril Osgood turned to look at the woman who was almost at his elbow and his presence of mind disintegrated. Her beauty was utterly overwhelming: the bone structure, and that complexion! This was Miss Flamsteed as was, of course. All the stories were true, by God they were! Then he became aware of the disconcertingly steady gaze from the blue eyes and realised that he still had his cap on.

"Cyril Osgood, ma'am . . . er . . . at your service," he managed to say.

Leander initially found it difficult to remain serious. When he snatched his cap off, his luxuriant, light-brown hair became hopelessly tousled and looked a scream. However, she liked the look of him: he was tall, brawny, appeared as strong as an ox, and had a face that spoke of honesty and fortitude.

"What can you do, Mr Osgood?" she asked.

He grinned. "Well, they trained me to fight, ma'am, but I'll have a go at anything." Fortuitously, he forgot to mention that he could drive a motor car.

"Where have you come from?"

"Devizes."

"And that's it, is it?" Leander nodded at the old kitbag he had dumped against the bar foot-rail.

"It is, ma'am. Just it and me. There's nothing nor nobody else."

Seeing that she was weighing him up, Cyril decided that he might as well finish his beer while she got on with it.

"Do you want another drink, Mr Osgood?" Leander asked. "You look very hot and thirsty."

"No thank you, ma'am, I'll do to be going on with."

"Come along then, let's see what we can do with you."

After giving Vicky a significant look, something along the lines of, "Here we go again," Leander led the way. Cyril Osgood snatched up his kitbag and followed her, leaving Vicky certain that Leander had gathered another lifelong disciple.

As they went up the drive to The House, with Cyril admiring the poplars that helped to give the place its distinctive air of elegant well-being, Leander became aware of his limp.

"What's wrong with your leg?" she asked.

"I was in that explosion at Dorchester, ma'am."

"Were you! You're a very lucky man."

"I know." He was suddenly worried. "This doesn't make any difference, does it?" he asked.

"No. If you can walk from Devizes, you'll do for me."

"That's very good of Your Ladyship."

This time, Leander did feel entitled to laugh. "Cyril, I'm not a 'ladyship' and never will be," she said.

Cyril Osgood looked disappointed.

"What are you going to do with him?" Steven asked after the ex-soldier had settled in and received the accolade of a line in the Big Book.

"Oh, all sorts of things," Leander said airily. "There are dozens of odd jobs he can do for us and William. That should keep him busy for a while."

"And then?" Steven asked, sensing something else.

"I thought he might look after the gallop when Nat Thomas retires."

"Do you know, darling, I'd completely forgotten about that. I suppose you'd want him to be night-watchman as well?"

"He seems ideal," Leander said briskly.

"You think we still need one?"

"Oh, yes, Steven, we most definitely need one. People don't get any better behaved and we have some valuable animals in that yard."

She could see that he was sceptical and was on the verge of telling him about those who might have a grudge against their success, but thought better of it. Steven's innocence was one of the things about him that she especially loved: if possible, it was worth preserving.

In September, George became the first member of the family ever to go away from Cannings Ambo for any length of time and to make a temporary home elsewhere. Although it felt somehow wrong to Leander, she knew that there was no point in trying to change Steven's mind, and, truth to tell, she was not altogether sorry to see the back of her eldest son for a while.

Accompanied by Steven, George set out for Winchester a day early: they were spending the night at an hotel in the ancient Saxon capital before George became a new boy at William of Wykeham's College of St Mary. It was Steven who behaved like the excited schoolboy, unable to stop talking about the prospect of seeing the great cathedral, whereas George took it all in his stride. Secretly, he was glad that Steven was going with him this first time, but made sure not to betray any sign of that.

Of one thing Leander was certain, and it came across unequivocally as George stood before her to say, "Goodbye, Mother. I shall look forward to seeing you at Christmas." The self-opinionated little beast was actually longing for an experience that most boys found desperately upsetting. The truth was, George was glad to be rid of Latimer's Barn; there might be horrors in store at Winchester, but escaping from the constant presence of horses would be ample compensation.

After the early-morning departure of Steven and George, Leander took Amelia out to watch the first lot at work. Giles was riding a young colt belonging to Alexandra.

"Giles is very good, isn't he?" Amelia said after watching for several minutes.

"Yes, very good indeed," Leander agreed proudly.

"I could never ride like that."

"You're good at other things, darling."

"Is Giles as good as you were when you were a little girl?"

"Oh, he's much better."

Amelia looked doubtful. "Great-Aunt Elisabeth told me that you were riding a Two Thousand Guineas winner when you were eight, and that you were the only one who could do anything with him."

"Well, if you want to know a secret, I think there's every chance that horse Giles is riding now will win next year's Guineas."

For a moment or two, Amelia looked impressed. Then her mind went to work. "There you are, then! Giles will be ten by the time that horse wins, so he isn't as good as you!"

That night, when Leander and Ellie were getting the children to bed, Giles suddenly said, "George was very brave when he went off, wasn't he, Mother?"

As Leander was agreeing with him, she caught sight of Amelia who was standing outside the door of Giles's bedroom. Her face was eloquent: Amelia did not believe a word of it.

Ellie saw it, too. "Amelia thinks the same of George as you do," she said to Leander when they were alone together afterwards.

"My God, I hope not!" Leander laughed, trying to make a joke of it.

"The trouble is, his father sees no fault in him," Ellie muttered, more to herself than Leander.

"That's only natural, Ellie. And a lot of things will change, you know. These are very early days."

At Leander's suggestion, she and Steven repeated their 1892 visit to the Newmarket mid-October meeting. She soon recognised it as one of the worst decisions she ever made.

The colt with whom Giles had done such excellent work during the summer was entered for the Dewhurst Plate, a race that Leander was starting to believe almost belonged to Latimer's Barn. He ran badly, however, finishing last but one, and looking most miserable

223

about it. The moment the winner was past the post, Steven rushed off to the unsaddling area.

When Leander caught up with him, she found him crouching alongside the colt's nearside foreleg, looking very worried.

"What's wrong?" she asked anxiously.

"I'm not sure. What do you think?"

It was a long time since she had run her hand over a horse's leg, but the old skill remained. There *was* something wrong, and the colt confirmed her opinion by shifting and flinching at her touch.

"Well?" Steven demanded, impatient for her diagnosis.

"I don't know. It could be a chipped bone – probably the cannon."

Peter Izzard, now in charge of taking horses to the races, insisted that the colt be got into a box and examined by a good vet. Steven became concerned about Alexandra, the colt's owner, who had come to see what the trouble was.

"Look, this is going to take some time," he said to Leander. "You two don't want to hang around here, it isn't a very nice afternoon. Let me get you a carriage back to the hotel."

Unusually for her, Leander did feel tired; nevertheless, the only reason she agreed to Steven's suggestion was to get Alexandra out of the way. Leander was half afraid that the colt would have to be put down, there and then, without even returning to Wiltshire. Alexandra possibly had an inkling of this, because when they arrived at the White Hart, she slipped away, saying that she was going to take something for a headache and lie down for two hours before dinner.

Leander wandered aimlessly into the hotel's deserted lounge, ordered a pot of tea and began turning idly through the pages of *The Illustrated London News*. She had just found an article that looked interesting when someone said, "Ah! Mrs Hawksworth."

Raising her eyes, she saw Walter Rothwell advancing towards her and groaned inwardly. Rothwell, a recently appointed Steward of the Jockey Club, was a most annoying man, but despite his comparative youth he was already an influential voice in Racing's governing body. He was, in fact, two years Leander's junior and had developed irritating ways of masking his inexperience, the most notorious of which was incessant know-all condescension.

"Good evening, Mr Rothwell," Leander said, making a supreme effort to be pleasant.

"All alone?" he said. "I shall join you, if I may."

Without waiting for approval, he deposited himself on the sofa alongside Leander.

224

"I must say, Mrs Hawksworth, your horse ran extraordinarily badly in the Dewhurst," he said.

"He damaged himself, Mr Rothwell. We are hoping that it is only a chipped cannon-bone." Leander spoke with a calm that anyone less self-centred than Rothwell would have recognised as strained.

"I thought it must be something like that," he said. "I told my colleagues so."

"Was that necessary, Mr Rothwell?"

"Oh, I'm sure you know how these things are, Mrs Hawksworth. There is always someone who wants to believe that a horse may not have been trying."

"What, even a Latimer's Barn horse?"

Rothwell smiled. Although he was fairly good-looking, this particular smile was not a pleasant sight. "*Especially* a Latimer's Barn horse, Mrs Hawksworth. Success often breeds jealousy and suspicion."

"So I have noticed, Mr Rothwell. But I am at a loss to understand what motive might be laid at our door for running a horse in a race like the Dewhurst and making sure he was held up *not* to win. Goodness, we shall be doing it in the Derby next!"

"My dear Mrs Hawksworth, who can tell how these minds work?" Rothwell spread his hands in a gesture of incomprehension. "Anyway, I felt bound to nip the story in the bud."

"Perhaps our honesty will be beyond question if we have to destroy the colt," Leander said acidly.

"Dear me, is it that bad?" For a moment or two, Rothwell appeared genuinely dismayed.

"I don't know yet, Mr Rothwell. My husband is still at the racecourse, seeing to it."

"Oh dear!"

Rothwell looked round the lounge. Instinctively, Leander knew that he was checking that the large room, with all its nooks and crannies, was empty. He moved closer.

"I would be pleased to be of assistance to you, Mrs Hawksworth," he said, lowering his voice.

"In what way, Mr Rothwell?"

"Protecting you from your enemies."

"Do I have many?"

"Enough, Mrs Hawksworth, enough."

"That seems kind of you, Mr Rothwell, but even assuming that it is necessary, I cannot see why you would wish to do it."

"I would view it as part of a mutually beneficial arrangement."

She stared at him in disbelief. Mistaking her expression, Rothwell explained.

"Come, Mrs Hawksworth, you are intelligent enough, you know the answer." Rothwell moved even closer, trying to look roguish. "You are a most attractive woman. To be perfectly honest with you, I have been an admirer of yours for quite some time."

Leander sat absolutely still. For the first time in her life, she averted her eyes from someone with whom she was in conversation. This man was dangerous and time slid back thirty years, so that she was a little girl again, listening to Aunt Elisabeth's: "Careful, Leander. Be very careful!"

"I have a husband, Mr Rothwell," she said tonelessly.

"And I have a wife, but I have no intention of allowing her to stand in the way of my pleasure. There is a very nice place in Surrey where we could be quite safe and alone – it belongs to a friend of mine who is the soul of discretion."

"I am afraid that I must decline your offer, Mr Rothwell." Leander curbed the desire to say more.

"Oh, come now, you haven't given yourself a chance to think about it." Cajoling, Rothwell became offensively familiar. "Consider carefully before depriving yourself of a great treat, Mrs Hawksworth. Let me assure you that I am an expert in the ways of love – much more so than your husband, I'll wager."

Very nearly blind with anger, Leander realised that she must say nothing; her refusal of Rothwell's odious proposition would inevitably cause him offence, there was no point in adding to it by giving full vent to her feelings. White as a sheet and trembling, she got to her feet, hurried from the lounge and somehow achieved the safety of her bedroom.

Steven was so late returning that they barely had time to order dinner before the kitchen closed for the night. On one hand, Leander was glad of the long delay; it had given her time to calm down. On the other, she dreaded the news about Alexandra's colt.

But Steven was cheerful. "He's going to be all right," he said, crossing his fingers and touching wood. "Three vets have had a good look at him, and they all think he can cope with that bone."

Both Leander and Alexandra turned bright smiles of relief on him. Leander went a long way towards forgetting Rothwell.

"There's no question of him racing again, of course," Steven said. "Even a steady canter is probably too much for him. And there's the worry of how to stop him hurting himself when he's loose in a paddock."

The salvation of her colt from the knacker's yard had given

Alexandra a look of such wistful beauty that Leander knew she must do all she could to help. "We'll fix something up," she said reassuringly.

"Could I breed from him?" Alexandra asked.

"Well . . ." Steven scratched his head and considered it.

Named Long Barrow after the ancient burial mounds all over the Downs between Marlborough and Calne, the colt was wonderfully bred, being by Bellerophon out of an Ormonde mare. Given a successful racing career, his stud earnings potential might have been huge. "I don't see any reason why you shouldn't try it," Steven concluded. "But there'd be no price at all for his progeny."

"That doesn't matter," Alexandra said. "He's such a lovely animal that I'm sure he'll produce something wonderful if we can find the right mare for him."

Still doubtful, Steven detected Leander's slight nod and gave his blessing. "All right, Alexandra, we'll do what we can."

Whatever the attraction that caused her absence, Leander was invariably glad to be back at Latimer's Barn. Her return from that appalling few days in Newmarket produced feelings close to rapture.

"What *is* the matter, darling?" an amused Steven asked. "You're skipping around like a two-year-old."

"You know I always adore coming home," she told him.

It was a well-known fact that she did, and Steven was content to let the matter rest, blithely unaware that she was hoping her beloved Wiltshire would wash away the sensation of contamination left by the encounter with Rothwell.

Curiously, and much to her own surprise, Leander told Rupert Timberlake about the incident when he shared a pot of coffee with her in the library after his weekly look at his father's horses.

"Difficult for you," he mused quietly. "Steven doesn't know, of course?"

"No!" Leander said passionately. "And he never must!"

"Trust me," he said. "I suppose this Rothwell could cause you a deal of trouble if he put his mind to it?"

"Indeed he could!" Leander pulled a sour face at the prospect. "What a disgusting individual!"

Rupert was surprised: he saw that Leander's sense of outrage was exacerbated by a naïve chink in her armour. "Men in positions of power frequently attempt to put it to such uses," he said mildly. While she was bristling at the lesson, he went on: "Would you like me to do anything about him?"

"You?" She looked baffled. "What could you do?"

"I could arrange for him to be dealt with in such a way that he never troubles a lady again." He spoke very calmly and quietly. There was a silence as she stared at him, assimilating his meaning. "It's often the only way with such people," he added in a matter-of-fact tone.

"These are your 'men', I take it," Leander said carefully.

"Yes."

"You really are an astonishing person, Rupert," she said without any trace of censure.

"Oh?"

"Butter wouldn't melt in your mouth and you genuinely are the nicest of men, yet you seem to have ready access to ruffians."

"I'm afraid so, my dear," he said with a wry smile. "I'm not at all keen on the idea, but bitter experience has taught us that it's necessary sometimes."

She nodded. "Yes, I'm afraid you may be right. Look at our experiences with this place over the years!" She sighed reflectively. "No, Rupert, I think we'll leave Rothwell in one piece. But thank you."

"Fair enough. Bear in mind what we have at our disposal, though, won't you? You may need our special services one day."

There was nothing on the agenda for the November meeting of Trustees, and half an hour went by on the discussion of minor matters like the need to redecorate the bar of The George and the deteriorating state of the Rectory guttering. Leander was about to suggest they all went away and got on with something useful when William cleared his throat and smiled nervously.

"Well, I've done it," he said as everyone looked at him.

"Done what?" Leander asked.

For answer, William pulled a piece of quarto-size paper from the large notebook he always brought to their meetings. Casually, he pushed it into the centre of the table. It was blank. While Steven and Alexandra stared at it in mystification, Leander reached out to grab it. Turning it over, she gurgled with delight at what she found. It was a printed letter-heading:

W^M FLAMSTEE D

& SONS
Makers of Fine Furniture

Rose House, Cannings Ambo, Wiltshire

"Good!" Steven said, looking over Leander's shoulder. "And about time, too."

228

"I decided I'd better get on with it once Leander stopped nagging me," William said, and she burst out laughing, trying to kick him under the table. "I had these printed some time ago, but the loose ends didn't get tied up until the other day. William Flamsteed and Sons is a limited liability company set up under the provisions of the 1890 Partnerships Act. At the moment, only Ruth and I are partners, but I think we should change the rules of the estate so that this can be incorporated into it and the company becomes part of the Cannings Ambo Partnership."

"What about Jim Goakes?" Steven asked.

"Yes, I've been wondering about him," William admitted.

"He's played a very important part," Steven said.

"We wouldn't have got very far without him." Ruth was quite forceful about it.

"Don't you think we should have him as a Trustee?" Steven asked.

"I came to the conclusion that it might be best to wait a year or two," William replied.

"Oh, William!" Leander burst out in exasperation. "Do you think he might run off with the spoons or the small change? Look at what Jim and his father have done for us! Dan rode our first winner the day I was born and they've been doing us proud ever since!"

Ruth and Alexandra, who did not know very much about the early days of Latimer's Barn, were impressed by this information.

"Leander's quite right," Steven said. "I propose that we make Jim a Trustee."

"And I second it," Leander said. "Anyone against?"

"Right, let Jim know, William, and we'll arrange for him to sign all the necessary papers," Steven said.

"While we're about it, I think Abraham Merriweather ought to be a Trustee, too," Leander announced.

Again, Steven was the seconder and there were no objections.

William was watching Leander having another look at his letter-head and smiling to herself.

"What's tickling you, Lea?" he asked.

"It's this 'fine'," she replied. "'William Flamsteed and Sons – Makers of *Fine* Furniture.' I like that!"

William shifted uncomfortably. "That was Ruth's idea," he said. "I'm not too sure about it."

"Poppycock!" Leander snorted. "Your furniture *is* fine – and so it needs to be to match our horses. Everything about Cannings Ambo is 'fine'!"

Alexandra gazed at Leander admiringly: dear Giles would have been so proud of her. But, of course, he always had been.

A few days later, when it was all settled, Ellie Goakes told Leander of the reaction to Jim becoming a Trustee.

"It's left him wondering whether he's coming or going."

"Jim isn't embarrassed, or anything silly, is he?" Leander asked.

"Oh, no, bless you! He's over the moon," Ellie smiled. "And he's doing his best to be ever so modest about it. Mother and Father seem far more excited than he is. Mother got quite upset, you know, very emotional."

"Well, I hope she'll feel better soon," Leander said. "And you tell her from me that it's no more than the Goakes family deserve."

The happiness surrounding Jim's appointment and that of Abraham, who did his dignified best to take it in his stride, cheered Leander after a difficult time with Amelia, who was devastated by the abrupt and premature end to Long Barrow's racing career.

"Do you *really* think he would have been ever so good, Mother?" Amelia asked after she had digested the bad news.

"Yes, darling, I do."

"Oh, dear." Amelia started to cry.

"What is it?" Leander asked. "Long Barrow is going to be all right. Seamus and Paul will make sure he's looked after."

"I know, but he won't win the Guineas, will he? That means Giles won't be able to say that he's *nearly* as good as you."

Despite Leander's best efforts, Amelia remained inconsolable, at least for a few days. In the end, it was Giles who put her right. At the age of nine, he proved that he already had a deep understanding of the sometimes tragic switchback of fate that played such an inescapably important part in the life of a racing stable.

"It is very sad about Long Barrow," Leander overheard him telling Amelia when they thought they were alone, "but there'll be plenty of others, just you see."

"I wanted you to be as good as Mother," Amelia protested.

"Don't be silly, no one's as good as Mother," Giles said. "It isn't possible!"

"How do you know?" Amelia was starting to sound much more like her old self.

"Father told me."

And they say eavesdroppers never hear well of themselves, Leander thought as she crept away.

Three weeks later, the arrival of two people who had a substantial contribution to make to the life of the village bucked Leander up again.

230

After completing his medical studies in Edinburgh and working in a hospital there for three years, Charles Stanton decided to return to Cannings Ambo. He was thirty-one years old, and gave up what seemed to be a promising career as a surgeon to return to the village he loved.

His decision was supported by his Edinburgh-born wife. Flora Mackenzie, as she had been, was proud of her native city without being blind to the charms of other places. Three visits to Cannings Ambo caused her to fall in love with it: its beauty made an impact on her and she liked the way the Partnership was committed to preserving it and treating everyone with decency.

She also adored horses, and was enchanted by the prospect of being surrounded by the finest thoroughbreds. Naturally this guaranteed her a place in Leander's affections, but there was more to it than that. Leander was full of admiration for any woman who would uproot herself and move more than four hundred miles into what was virtually a foreign country to support her husband.

And when the younger Stantons first dined at Latimer's Barn, it soon emerged that Flora had been a schoolmistress at Corstorphine on the outskirts of Edinburgh.

Steven smiled at Leander's reaction to the discovery. He knew that Flora Stanton was about to be given a job.

"Do you want to carry on teaching, Flora?" Leander asked.

"Well . . . yes . . . I'd love to. Mind you, it would have to be convenient for Charles."

Leander approved of the sentiment. "It couldn't be more so, my dear. Only a few yards from Oak Cottage."

Flora's eyes opened wide. "You mean your village school?"

"Yes!"

"But what about . . .?"

Leander stepped in to save her embarrassment. "What about my Aunt Elisabeth and your mother-in-law? Like us all, they aren't getting any younger. They'll welcome your help and by this time next year they'll be letting you do most of it – if your circumstances permit, of course." Flora was not the sort of girl to indulge in discomfort at the suggestion of pregnancy. "In any case," Leander went on, "you're a qualified teacher. It's time we had one. I shall arrange it."

Flora understood perfectly that it was as good as done.

"That's one of your favourite occupations, isn't it?" Steven said later, as they prepared for bed.

"What is?" Leander asked.

"Organising continuity."

"Sweetheart, if we don't organise it, it probably won't happen, and everything we've worked for will be in danger."

"That was a pretty good effort, even for you," Steven said. "We'd already got a doctor to replace Lawrence when he retires, now you've found a teacher."

"Health and education *are* rather important," Leander told him with the Flamsteed earnestness that occasionally assumed others were incapable of seeing such truths.

Not since he was a toddler had George made Leander want to laugh. He achieved the feat within seconds of arriving home for the Christmas holidays.

Jim Goakes, keen to pick up two packages of hinges and screws for Wm Flamsteed & Sons, collected George from Marlborough railway station.

Exuding complacency rather than genuine excitement at being home, George strode into The House with a patronising smile and said, "Here I am, Pater!"

It was the look on Steven's face that came dangerously close to causing Leander to giggle.

Steven Hawksworth was thirty-eight and at the peak of a life he had never imagined in his wildest dreams until comparatively recently. He had the love and confidence of the most beautiful and exciting woman for miles around. A whole community respected and trusted him. He had trained a Derby winner and was besieged by would-be owners.

Now, after one term at Winchester, this arrogant young puppy swaggered into Latimer's Barn and called him 'Pater'.

CHAPTER 14

1897

'What's the twentieth century going to be like?'

In 1897, Her Majesty Queen Victoria, Empress of India and Defender of the Faith, celebrated her Diamond Jubilee. Or, as an unimpressed Leander saw it, the powers that be fabricated an occasion to encourage pomp and junketing.

Mindful of Horatio's prophecy of change, Leander was alerted by the rising passion for imperialist conquest to take a greater interest in current affairs. Busy as she was with a hundred other things, she now made time to study at least two newspapers each day, and it was not long before she passed harsh judgement.

"This is no good, you know," Leander told Steven one evening in April. "The country isn't being run properly."

Her poor opinion of government was not new. Unfortunately, it had started in a way that allowed people to question Leander's objectivity, and Steven was deceived into believing that she was still grinding the same old axe.

In March 1894, midway through his fourth term as Prime Minister, Gladstone resigned. His decision was based on sheer old age; he was eighty-three and had been in Parliament for sixty-two years. His place was taken by Archibald Philip Primrose, fifth Earl of Rosebery, destined to be Prime Minister for a mere fifteen months.

Lord Rosebery was a keen supporter of the Turf and owned a string of very good horses. Whatever else he did during his brief period of office, he won the Derby twice, with Ladas in 1894 and Sir Visto the following year. As if to add insult to injury, both the Prime Minister's victories were achieved at the expense of Latimer's Barn colts.

Leander's strictures on Rosebery's Government were taken with a pinch of salt since people suspected that envy was the root of her disapproval.

But the Marquess of Salisbury's administration fared no better, and it was not long before Leander's views were gaining support, particularly after a spectacular international incident.

Throughout the century, the colonisation of Africa had been proceeding at a break-neck pace as European countries competed to grab their place in the sun. Nearly two hundred years before, the earliest settlers were the Dutch farmers who populated the Cape, later being joined by Huguenots escaping from persecution in France. The resultant people became known as *Boers*, from the Dutch word for farmer.

In 1814 the British annexed the Cape and began putting pressure on the Boers to give ground. Peace-loving, simple and obstinate, the Boers retreated piecemeal until, in 1836, they began the 'Great Trek' to escape from British rule. Under the command of Hendrik Potgieter, the Boers drove the Zulu tribes of Moselekatse across the Limpopo, using another great river, the Vaal, to mark the southern boundary of their new state, Transvaal.

The simple life-style of the Boers was short-lived. Within fifty years their world was turned upside-down by the discovery of gold in quite unbelievable quantities on the Witwatersrand. Foreigners, a high proportion of them British, flooded into the Transvaal to exploit it.

From the start, the attitude of the Transvaal authorities was uncompromising towards the newcomers, or *Uitlanders*. Paul Kruger, the President, gave them no rights, no votes and penal taxation. "I may not be able to stop you raping our land," he seemed to be saying, "but, by God, we will take most of your profits." The Uitlanders, agog with avarice, accepted Kruger's harsh terms.

Others were not so happy. To Cecil Rhodes, dreaming of painting the whole of the map of Africa red, Kruger's Transvaal was a damned nuisance that needed to be taught a swift lesson. His instrument was a man called Jameson, a British doctor who had long since given up the practice of medicine in favour of high adventure motivated by delusions of imperial grandeur.

On 29 December 1895, Jameson led a force of 470 mounted men with eight machine guns and three artillery pieces on a raid from Mafeking on the Transvaal border. His intention was to reach Johannesburg, nearly two hundred miles away, and incite an Uitlander rising.

On their fourth day into the escapade the raiders were confronted by the Boers at Krugersdorp and the game was up. The subsequent frenzy of diplomatic activity proved that the British Government had no idea what was going on, that it disapproved of Jameson's action, but had no stomach to control those whose sentiments had sent him off on the crazy venture.

Amid all the telegrams that flew around there was one to Kruger from Kaiser Wilhelm II of Germany, congratulating him on repelling the raid without appealing for help.

Steven was baffled. "What's the Kaiser playing at?" he asked Leander.

"The wretch can't wait to get his foot in the door of Africa," she replied. "Even so, sweetheart, you can't blame Willie for trying to make capital out of a mess like this. That man Jameson must be a criminal idiot!"

Worse soon followed.

The Boers handed Jameson over to the British authorities and he was brought to London for trial. It was then that his full name became emblazoned across a press very much prejudiced in his favour. It was Leander Starr Jameson.

Most people kept well clear of Latimer's Barn and Mrs Hawksworth for several days after that.

Jameson's trial was a sham. Given only fifteen months' imprisonment for a desperate act of international piracy, he was released after only four months to popular jubilation.

"It's absolutely ridiculous!" Leander fumed. "Doesn't the Government realise where condoning that sort of thing is going to get them?"

"And another thing!" Leander stared round the dinner table challengingly. "What's all this nonsense with the Navy?"

It was a large gathering and all except Guy Mallender looked startled or uncomfortable.

"I agree," Guy said. "I don't like it."

"I'm afraid I don't understand," John Shepherd said with his customary bashful smile. "Could one of you explain, please?"

"Go on, Guy," Leander said after they had exchanged questioning looks. "This is man's work."

"The Royal Navy always used to believe that a ship of the line – what we call a battleship now – has a useful life of sixty years," Guy began. "For example, Nelson's *Victory* was forty-five years old at the time of Trafalgar. All that has changed in the last ten years. Gunnery has been revolutionised and warships are now armoured. Better armour means someone has to design a better gun, and that's a vicious circle. We seem to have reached the stage where there's no question of a battleship having an effective life of more than five years. The *Royal Sovereign*, which is only four years old, is reckoned to be utterly useless

235

against the latest German vessels, and she cost over a million pounds. The building estimates for this year are twenty-two million."

"How long has this been going on?" Alexandra asked.

"As Guy said, ten years," Leander replied.

"It's a wonder the Exchequer can stand it," William said.

"It can't!" Leander told him. "They're going to be after much more income tax soon."

"There is talk of yet another new type of battleship," Guy added. "They really do seem determined to find one that can't be outclassed while it's still on the stocks."

"Who else is doing this?" Ruth wanted to know.

"Everybody!" Leander said. "Germany, France, Russia – even Japan. The Germans seem to be making the best job of it. They are building twelve new capital ships at the moment."

"How do you know all this?" Steven asked.

"I suppose we must read the right newspapers and periodicals," Guy Mallender said.

"And use our brains!" Leander sounded quite sharp about it.

Eventually, it was John Shepherd who broke the thoughtful silence that fell round the table. "Where do you suppose all this is leading, Leander?"

"I haven't the faintest idea, Uncle John, what's more I don't think the governments responsible know either. One thing *is* certain: the world is becoming less safe by the day."

"And you think that public feeling is being inflamed by the Jubilee?" John Shepherd asked.

"Yes, I do. The popular press is quite dreadful. According to them, might is right and we should not hesitate to use it whenever anyone disagrees with us."

"And you fear Africa is a trouble-spot?"

"It looks likely, doesn't it? It seems to me that when a government supports men like Jameson, anything is possible."

Everyone fell silent once more, beginning to understand some of Leander's misgivings.

"Well, I'm going to try and get something useful out of this Jubilee," William said.

"How?" his Aunt Elisabeth asked.

"I've decided to take some furniture to one of the exhibitions," William replied. "Lea's been badgering me to do it."

"Which one?" Leander asked.

"Birmingham."

She smiled, thinking that Horatio would have approved of the choice.

236

"Is this the start of an expansion scheme, William?" Lawrence Stanton asked.

"It might be. We'll see." William was cautious.

Wm Flamsteed & Sons was at a crossroads. Their furniture was gracing houses in Wiltshire, Berkshire, Gloucestershire and Dorset, and the recommendations of the satisfied owners produced a steady stream of new business. In 1896 sales exceeded £10,000 for the first time and all the signs were that this could be maintained into the foreseeable future without a great deal of effort.

William and Jim were in a quandary about what to do next. In theory, they knew that there was a huge market waiting for them, but were uncertain whether they wanted it. William feared that the costs of advertising and distribution could easily get out of hand.

They went to Birmingham in May in search of answers.

The exhibition, held in a new hall near the centre of the city, was concerned with the home and all the things that might make it more comfortable and elegant, or save work and money. After William and Jim finished setting up their stand on the evening before the opening, they strolled round to look at the other exhibits.

"One thing's for certain," Jim said as they went to their hotel, "nobody's got any furniture like ours."

The grand inauguration took place at ten o'clock the following morning. The Lord Mayor made a bombastic sort of speech to a group of about two hundred worthies who took a quick look round and disappeared, presumably to attend to what they thought were more important matters.

Nothing happened for over an hour, then groups of businessmen and well-heeled members of the public began to appear. The young man was one of the first to pay the rather expensive entry fee of two shillings.

William noticed him at once. He was smartly turned out in a dark blue suit and shoes that gleamed. Having darted into the exhibition area, he paused to take stock of his surroundings. As he did so, he was perfectly still, but poised on the balls of his feet like a fighter about to unleash a punch: the impression was of tightly coiled energy seeking an outlet. When he set off, he was moving systematically from stand to stand, away from William and Jim.

It took him over an hour to move full circle. During that time, several people paused to admire the furniture, but there was no question of anything remotely like a sale, and William was beginning to experience discomfiture.

Then the young man came back.

He walked round the display three times, scrutinising the table, sideboard and chest of drawers with a close attention to detail that made William and Jim uneasy. Their sign, announcing that they were from Cannings Ambo in Wiltshire, seemed to puzzle him. Twice he was on the verge of saying something; twice he changed his mind. After crouching to peer under the table, he darted away, disappearing through the main exit.

"This is how animals in a zoo must feel," Jim muttered, and William nodded ruefully.

Lunch-time came and went: there was a flurry of visitors then everything quietened down again.

"Perhaps when folk start leaving work," Jim suggested hopefully.

William was not so sure. From what he had seen of Birmingham, it was not a place to loiter in once the need to earn a living was satisfied.

An hour passed.

Suddenly, Jim gripped William's arm. "He's back again!"

The young man came into the exhibition hall, and, without a moment's hesitation, was heading straight towards them. Purpose was stamped all over him.

"Are either of you two gents Mr Flamsteed?" he asked.

William was quite taken aback by his first encounter with a real Birmingham accent: the last part of his name – 'steed' – received a most peculiar treatment.

"Yes, I'm William Flamsteed," he said.

The young man's face lit up in a friendly grin. "My name's Fred Cartwright, Mr Flamsteed. I'm very pleased to meet you."

Trance-like, William shook the hand that was thrust at him. It was uncannily like meeting an old friend.

"I'm sorry I dashed off before," Fred Cartwright said. "I thought I'd better go and see Uncle Sid first."

"Uncle Sid?" William was baffled.

"He works for the *Birmingham Post*, and what he don't know he can soon find out. My trouble is that I don't take any notice of racing, otherwise I'd have known about this Cannings Ambo place, wouldn't I?"

Some light dawned on William.

"Now then, Mr Flamsteed, this furniture of yours: it's very nice. Real classy. We don't usually get to see stuff this good in Brummagem."

"Thank you," William said.

"According to Uncle Sid, you've been doing this for a few years in a small sort of way," Fred Cartwright went on. "Are you looking to expand the business?"

"We don't know," William replied and felt a bit of a fool. There was no earthly reason why he should say such stupid things to a nosy stranger.

"What are you doing here, then? This jaunt must be costing a bob or two."

It was very nearly impertinence, yet William found himself reacting favourably to Fred Cartwright's directness.

"Yes, we are thinking about expansion," he admitted.

"Right! Very sensible of you, Mr Flamsteed. Your gear will go like hot cakes providing you *sell* it right."

"And how do I do that?" William asked.

"Me!" Fred Cartwright stuck his chest out and made it plain that he was in deadly earnest. "I'm a bank clerk, Mr Flamsteed. A very good one, as a matter of fact, but I don't like it. I'm twenty-three and I'm not spending another forty years toadying so's I can end up a fat old fogey with a gold watch on a chain."

William found it impossible to believe that Fred Cartwright, lean and sinewy with nervous energy, would ever run to fat.

"I heard about this exhibition," Fred continued, "and I thought, 'That's it, there's bound to be one or two there as could give me a chance', so I asked for three days' holiday and here I am!"

This, William thought, was enterprise. "And have you seen anything that takes your fancy, Mr Cartwright?" he asked.

"There's something over there that might turn out all right." Fred Cartwright made a vague gesture. "But it don't look as if they really know what they're doing. You're the best – stands out a mile. There's too many here trying to sell trumpery and gew-gaws."

"That's very kind of you, Mr Cartwright, but nobody's taken all that much notice of us yet."

"That's because you haven't got me," Fred Cartwright said with complete confidence. "How about it, Mr Flamsteed, will you give me a job?"

"Well . . ." William exchanged looks with Jim. "I'm prepared to think about it."

"Fair enough. Think about this as well – take me on for six months, and if I haven't earned my keep and expenses ten times over, get rid of me."

"Very well, Mr Cartwright, my partner and I will consider it."

"Right! I'll be back!"

"Well, what do you make of that?" William asked after Fred Cartwright had marched off as though half of Birmingham was clamouring for his attention.

"Blessed if I know," Jim said. "He isn't short of push."

"He isn't! I wonder if he could be of use to us?"

They talked about it for the rest of the uneventful afternoon and over dinner in the hotel. They were, of course, totally in the dark.

Fred Cartwright showed himself capable of throwing brilliant light on to the problem.

He reappeared the minute the exhibition opened on the second day. This time he was accompanied by a distinguished and shrewd-looking man in his mid-thirties.

"Mr Flamsteed, this is Mr Henry Fletcher," Fred said. "He owns the big department store in Corporation Street."

William, who had read about Harrods in London and was thus familiar with the idea of the shop that sold everything, eyed Henry Fletcher keenly.

"How do you do, Mr Flamsteed?" Fletcher said. "Young Fred insisted that I needed to come and look at your merchandise. He virtually dragged me here."

Behind Henry Fletcher's back, Fred winked at William.

"So this is your furniture?" Henry Fletcher asked, looking round the stand.

"It is."

"My word!" The department-store owner seemed entranced by what he saw. "Yes, indeed, that *is* nice. Beautiful workmanship, Mr Flamsteed . . . yes . . . let's have a good look at that sideboard, eh? Mmmm . . . yes. I must say, Fred . . ." Turning in search of him, Henry Fletcher found that Fred Cartwright had disappeared. Neither William nor Jim had seen him go.

"What an extraordinary thing!" Henry Fletcher went on. "I know that young man from my visits to the bank where he works. Yesterday afternoon, he came into the shop and demanded to see me. Said he wouldn't shift until I'd given him five minutes. He told me that I'd never forgive myself if I didn't come to see your furniture, and he was right, by Jove!"

Henry Fletcher spent ten minutes admiring the Cannings Ambo workmanship, making copious notes in his pocket-book.

"Gentlemen, I must be off," he said. "I have an important meeting in fifteen minutes. Look here, will you have supper with me this evening?"

"With pleasure," William replied.

"Good. Let's say eight o'clock at the Grand Hotel – they know how to look after a man's stomach."

The remainder of the long day was rather tedious. People strolled past William and Jim, stopped, stared, nodded approvingly and passed on. The Lord Lieutenant of Warwickshire, an incredibly bad-tempered old General, made a swift visit, dragging a harassed bunch of petty officials in his wake, charging round the exhibition as though it were a parade-ground.

But there was no sign of Fred Cartwright.

Knowing Leander's interest in all new gadgets except the motor car, William filled in a little time by visiting the electric light and telephone displays, collecting leaflets extolling the virtues of the two technical wonders.

Henry Fletcher wasted no time once they were seated in a quiet corner of the Grand Hotel's magnificent dining-room that evening.

"I want to sell your furniture in my shop," he said, almost causing William and Jim to fall off their chairs. "But there is a difficulty we have to solve. At least for the first few years, I want to be the sole outlet in Birmingham. That's very important to me, Mr Flamsteed. Exclusivity carries a lot of weight round here, and I fancy we could both do very well out of it."

William nodded, pretending great sagacity; in reality, not daring to say a word.

"Now young Cartwright has given me a tip-off." Henry Fletcher lowered his voice and checked that no one was listening to them. "I understand that you've had that scoundrel Pearson sniffing round. Believe me, Mr Flamsteed, letting him have any of your furniture will end only in disaster. That man hasn't the first idea how to present quality goods and he'd end up getting us all a bad name."

William took a deep breath and did his best to ignore the look on Jim's face. "Well, I . . ." he began, only to be cut short by Henry Fletcher.

"Mr Flamsteed, I understand your position. We're both men of the world trying to turn an honest penny, and if I want a favour from you, I must demonstrate my good faith."

"That's very generous of you, Mr Fletcher," William said solemnly.

"If I want sole rights to sell your furniture in Birmingham, I must make it worth your while with an order that shows I mean business."

"What sort of quantities were you thinking of?"

"A hundred of each of the items you have on show."

When Jim Goakes spoke about Wm Flamsteed & Sons in the years ahead, he always selected this moment for special mention. "I damned nearly keeled over," he would say. "But, do you know, William didn't turn a hair!"

"I think we can give you sole distribution rights for an order like that, Mr Fletcher," William said.

"Splendid! If my judgement is anything to go by, there'll be plenty more orders. And permit me to tell you that my judgement is never wrong, Mr Flamsteed. *Never!*"

William was forcing himself to be calm by thinking of practicalities. "You won't want them all the same size, will you? That table we've put on the stand seats twelve. You could do with some sixes and eights, I imagine."

They worked out the precise details of the order over the meal, using blank menu cards supplied by a waiter who clearly knew Henry Fletcher and his generosity. Shortly before they parted, it was all settled: for the three hundred pieces of furniture, sent by railway to Snow Hill station in batches of thirty at three-weekly intervals, the agreed price was a little over £12,000.

"We shall need to take on extra staff," William said to Jim as they walked back to their hotel, heads still reeling.

"Aye," Jim agreed. "And one of 'em had better be that young fellow Cartwright."

Fred arrived at the exhibition early the next morning, affecting a look of innocence.

"'Morning, Mr Flamsteed, and to you, too, Mr Goakes. Er . . . how did you get on with Mr Fletcher?"

"Very well indeed," William said. "He gave us a good order . . . well, actually, it's a huge order. We shall have to set more hands on in the workshop."

"That's good, ain't it?" Fred beamed.

"It is, and we're very grateful to you for making Mr Fletcher come and see us," William replied.

"That's all right. Any time!"

"There was one thing that puzzled us when we were talking things over with Mr Fletcher last evening," William said.

"Oh, what's that?"

"He seemed to have a dreadful bee in his bonnet about a chap called Pearson."

Fred chuckled. "That's Joe Pearson. He's got an 'orrible shop down the bottom end of New Street on the backside of the Bull Ring."

"Mr Fletcher thought that I was going to let Pearson have some furniture," William said tentatively.

"That's right. *I* told him."

For a few moments, William and Fred Cartwright looked at each other with dreadfully straight faces, then they burst out laughing.

"Can I offer you a job, Mr Cartwright?" William asked.

"You can indeed, Mr Flamsteed, and I accept!"

242

"When will you be able to start?"

"Where will you want me? In this Cannings Ambo of yours?"

"Yes."

"Right. Give me two months. I want to get Mam and me sister fixed up with a better place to live before I clear off."

They shook hands on it.

Determined to cut a dash, Leander attended every day of the Diamond Jubilee Royal Ascot, and, with Ellie's dressmaking skills at the peak of their form, turned quite a few heads.

There was much to annoy Leander. She had always been acutely conscious that the occasion was little more than a show-place for people who knew next to nothing about horses and racing, but this year it seemed to have turned into a veritable playground, an upper-class beargarden.

The Prince of Wales was there, of course, as popular as ever despite, or possibly because of, the scandals that continued to surround him. He was going to be fifty-seven in November and Leander thought he looked pretty fed-up and tired with it all. Was he ever going to be King? "I don't mind praying to the eternal Father," he was supposed to have said, "but it's the very devil having an eternal Mother!"

However, notwithstanding the underlying currents of patriotic bombast, Leander enjoyed herself hugely. A good race meeting, one of her natural habitats, and the pleasure of watching high-class horses do their best, were supplemented by Latimer's Barn successes. On each of the four days, Steven took a horse into the winner's enclosure and Leander amused herself by listening to the comments of the spectators.

"My word, doesn't that filly look well?"

"That race has hardly winded her."

"Say what you like, they know how to turn horses out from that Cannings Ambo place. Where *is* it, by the way?"

Say what you like!

The British really were an incredible bunch, Leander decided, now realising that they frequently became uneasy when confronted with excellence. In fact, they probably regarded its wholehearted pursuit as not entirely the done thing. In cricket they had this ridiculous division of Gentlemen and Players: well, they would have to accept that this strange Cannings Ambo was full of Players!

Leander committed her thoughts to the Big Book when she got home. "We shall be as polite and self-effacing about it as we can, but we intend winning whenever and wherever possible," she wrote.

Sitting and looking at the words, she found it strange that it had taken the best part of forty years to put them down.

The Sunday following Royal Ascot, 20 June, was the exact sixtieth anniversary of Queen Victoria's accession to the throne, and Jubilee services were held at eleven o'clock in every place of worship in the land. From the chancel steps of his beloved church of St Luke and St John, John Shepherd happily surveyed a congregation almost as large as that which had assembled sixteen years ago for the wedding of Steven and Leander.

There was a bonfire the following night on the ridge of Cannings Down. It was one of two thousand five hundred over the whole length and breadth of Queen Victoria's realm, nearly four times as many as there had been at the Golden Jubilee. Steven, Leander and Amelia joined the gathering around it, and as the flames soared upwards, Amelia suddenly asked, "What's the twentieth century going to be like, Father?"

Steven laughed. "I've no idea, my dear. Ask your mother. She knows about things like that!"

Leander gazed into Amelia's eyes and struggled with the question in them.

"Much the same as this, darling," she replied in a voice that Steven knew lacked conviction.

"We shan't have a queen," Amelia said.

"No, we shall have a king. And you will become a mathematical genius and we shall win lots and lots of good races!"

Steven felt cheerful again: that sounded much more like it.

Leander thought long and hard about it and came to the conclusion that she was damned if she was going to beat about the bush: as the train drew into Marlborough station with Giles looking anxiously out of a window, she knew she was right.

There was a moment when they stood on the platform, thirty yards apart and quite still. It passed and they were running towards each other. In the last few strides, Giles dropped his bags and leapt into her arms, almost knocking her flat.

The ordeal of his first year at Winchester was over; the purest joy swept worry and sadness away. Eight glorious weeks of holiday lay ahead.

"Mother!"

"Giles! How are you, my darling?"

"I'm very well, thank you."

"Has it been awful?"

"No, not really. How is that filly progressing?"

"Wait and see! You shall ride her tomorrow."

As Leander let Giles slip so that his feet touched the ground once more, she was aware of George glowering at them, his thoughts written all over his face.

Leander stared back defiantly. "No!" was the message she transmitted. "I don't come to meet *you*, or ever behave like this with you, do I? You'd very likely spit in my eye if I did!"

Forced to drop his eyes, George came to the conclusion that he must carry his own bags to the carriage; Cyril Osgood, acting under strict instructions, was having nothing to do with them.

That particular summer holiday was one of the worst times of George's life. He made half-hearted attempts to be friends with his contemporaries in the village. The sons of the older stable-lads and the men who worked for William treated him with a mixture of awe and contempt. His birth and parentage may not have set George Hawksworth apart, but the way he was reacting to his education most certainly did. The village boys were inevitably influenced by what they had heard their fathers say: "The guv'nor's got his work cut out with that useless, stuck-up so-and-so," was typical.

The consequence was isolation from all except routine family groupings at meal-times, and then the dominant conversational topic of horses, horses and still more horses left no time for anything else. Even Amelia seemed to be turning into an expert, though nothing like the sanctified Giles, of course!

Sometimes, sheer loneliness forced George to accept the company of his cousin Maude, who was desperately eager to worship him. She had the disadvantages of being a girl and only nine; nevertheless, there were times when he was prepared to put up with her, if only because she was a very good audience. They did reach agreement on one thing that summer: Cannings Ambo was the most dreadful place imaginable. Much as George disapproved of horses, Maude was disgusted by the factory at the back of her house.

The results of Fred Cartwright's endeavours were already in evidence. Wm Flamsteed & Sons had taken on three more men and houses were being built for them, using most of the profit from Henry Fletcher's first order.

"I'm sure this is the way to do it," William said at the meeting of Trustees that approved the expenditure. "If we make sound investment in people and their conditions, we shouldn't go far wrong."

"It's exactly what Father and Jasper would have wanted," Leander said and the proposal went through on the nod.

In those first hectic weeks, as a cottage industry was transformed into a professional undertaking, everyone helped out. Alexandra and Lucy Miller rounded up the village women to polish the furniture before it was sent off to Birmingham. Somehow, the delivery dates were met, each one being a little less hectic than the last, and Henry Fletcher wrote to express his satisfaction.

Then, in the middle of July, Fred Cartwright arrived, lugging two bulging suitcases made secure by string.

William was able to laugh about it afterwards, but at the time it was happening, watching Fred's chirpy self-confidence evaporate was a most alarming business.

The trouble was Cannings Ambo: Fred had never seen anything like it. Once, he had gone on a half-day Sunday-school trip to the Lickey Hills; apart from that brief excursion into the country, the memory of which was dim, Birmingham had been his entire life. The discovery of peaceful lanes that were almost a tunnel through luxuriant trees, friendly people who lived in pretty houses, freedom from mindless noise and a powerful sense of community spirit hit him like a sledge-hammer.

"Here, this is nice," he said in a strange, hushed voice and shut up, staring around with wide eyes as if expecting the whole thing to disappear if he said any more.

"I'm going to get you a house of your own built as soon as I can," William said. "In the meantime, Mrs Fandine-Browne and Lucy Miller are going to look after you at The Hall."

To Fred's immense relief, William stayed with him to guide him through the meeting with Alexandra and the first sight of his temporary quarters, a newly refurbished bedroom, a small sitting-room with a view of Latimer's Barn and Cannings Down and a bathroom, fettled to Leander's exacting standards.

"Will this suit you to be going on with, Fred?" William asked anxiously.

Fred nodded. "I'm gob-struck, Mr Flamsteed," he said.

Alexandra smiled and gave a bewildered William a translation. "He is speechless with admiration," she said.

"Oh, good." William laughed with relief. "You're to come and have dinner with us at Rose House tonight, Fred. Mrs Fandine-Browne will bring you along when it's time. Now then . . ." he pulled his wallet out, ". . . while I think about it, here's your first commission on sales."

He gave Fred twenty crisp five-pound notes.

"I haven't done anything yet, Mr Flamsteed," Fred protested.

"What about Henry Fletcher?"

"That was a free sample. You know, like passing a test to get the job."

"Your 'free sample' is keeping us going day and night, Fred. Go on, take it, you deserve it."

"Thank you very much, Mr Flamsteed," Fred said when he was finally sure. "I'll send most of this to me mam."

"See Ann Mallender at the shop," William instructed. "She runs the post office as well, and she'll be able to tell you how to send it safely."

A few hours later, having unpacked and taken a bath, some of Fred's composure was starting to return as he sauntered along the village street with Alexandra. Pausing to gaze admiringly at the area around Church Green, he said, "It makes you think it'll all be exactly the same in a hundred years, don't it?"

"The way things are run round here, there'll be all hell to pay if it isn't," Alexandra told him.

It was only a small dinner party, but not as small as Fred had hoped for: Leander and Steven were also present. Fred's Uncle Sid, of the *Birmingham Post*, had provided an accurate biography of Leander that was more than enough to be going on with, but faced with her startling beauty and individuality, Fred felt that he was in the presence of royalty and very nearly lapsed into overawed silence.

William had saved up the story of how Fred had initiated the first big sale for Wm Flamsteed & Sons on the open market, and Leander listened to it with obvious relish.

"Where did you learn tricks like that, Fred?" she asked. "Not in a bank, surely?"

"Oh, no, Mrs Hawksworth! You wouldn't find out how to knock the skin off a rice pudding in a place like that. No, I made it up. Seemed sensible to me."

"I agree. But what happens when Mr Fletcher and Mr Pearson get together? Won't Mr Fletcher be annoyed when he finds out that Mr Pearson was never interested in our furniture?"

"It won't happen! Mr Fletcher don't talk to Joe Pearson. Wouldn't be seen dead doing it."

"Why?"

"Joe's a low-class crook from the gutter. Henry Fletcher knows all about that because that's how *his* dad started out. But he's forgotten all that now, see? In any case, he's been on his best behaviour for a couple of years, since he married a classy young woman nearly half his age from London and got himself a big house in Barnt Green. No, you won't catch posh Henry within a mile of grubby Joe!"

Leander's eyes gleamed with approval. "I can see that you're going to be very good for Cannings Ambo, Fred," she smiled. "Tell me, are you new to the country life?"

"Yes, Mrs Hawksworth, I am. It looks smashing to me, but it ain't half going to take some getting used to."

"I can't imagine I'd be much use if I was suddenly dumped in the middle of Birmingham," Leander told him reassuringly. "You'll soon get used to it. You'd better start off by having a look round the stable."

"My sister is very proud of Latimer's Barn," William told Fred. "It *is* the most important place for miles around."

Fred noticed that Leander made no attempt to deny the statement or water it down with simpering modesty. "Ten o'clock tomorrow morning," she said. "Come round to the back door and ask for me."

"Oughtn't I to be doing something for Mr Flamsteed?" Fred asked, shooting a worried look at William.

"There's plenty of time for that, Fred," Leander told him. "Let them catch up with what you've sold already!"

In the event, Fred satisfied his conscience by turning up at Rose House at half past seven the following morning, and spending over two hours looking round the workshop with Jim Goakes before setting off to obey Leander's summons.

Outside The George, he came across a girl who stopped him dead in his tracks. She was rather slight but very pretty, with dark hair and eyes that showed a spirit very similar to his own. She proved the point at once.

"Hello, you must be Fred Cartwright," she said boldly.

"I am. And who might you be?"

"Tish Merriweather. My father is the head lad of Latimer's Barn." She was, Fred thought, tremendously proud of the fact. "My name's really Letitia. Everyone calls me Tish, of course."

"I'm on my way to the stable now," Fred told her.

"I know. Mrs Hawksworth told me. Come on, I'll walk with you."

"How long have you been here?" Fred asked as they set off.

"Always. I was born in the village."

She sounded pretty pleased about *that* as well, Fred decided. Trying to sneak another look at her as they walked, he found her staring back at him, frankly, trying to weigh him up.

"What's Birmingham like?" she asked.

"Well . . ." Fred struggled and gave up. "Different," he said. "Very different."

248

"I've heard it's awful!" Tish said bluntly.

"None too clean and pretty," he admitted.

"Never mind, you're all right now. This is the best place on earth. Look, that's where we live."

They had reached the Devizes Lane, and Tish was pointing towards the house at the foot of the Latimer's Barn drive.

"Very nice." Fred was impressed. It was the sort of place the manager of a big bank in Birmingham might aspire to. He began to realise that a head lad was important.

"Mr Flamsteed built it for us the year after we got here," Tish said. Seeing that Fred was looking confused, she hurried to explain. "That was the *first* Mr Flamsteed. He was Miss Leander and Mr William's father. I can see you need educating."

"Will you do it?" Fred asked boldly.

"If you like. Do you want me to come up to The House with you?"

Looking up the poplar-lined drive that seemed to go on for an awfully long way, Fred was suddenly less sure of himself.

"Er . . . yes, if you wouldn't mind. To tell you the truth, Tish, this is all a bit much for me."

She laughed. "You'll soon get used to it."

"Everybody keeps telling me that," Fred replied. "I hope they're right!"

"Oh, they are!" Tish said firmly. "People round here always know what they're talking about. That's why we're so good! Mr William must have a fair idea what he's doing with you, even though you are so young."

"I'm twenty-three!" Fred said hotly, as if claiming the wisdom and experience of a Methuselah.

"Very old!" Tish said mockingly, then hastened to soothe his injured pride. "It's all right, Fred, I'm only nineteen, so we're both babies." She saw movement through the screen of poplars and broke into an urgent trot. "Come on, they're bringing the second lot out, you mustn't miss that!"

"What's 'the second lot'?" Fred asked as he broke into a run to keep up with her.

Leander told Steven about it as they put their feet up and enjoyed a pot of tea before he went out for evening stables at six o'clock.

"The poor boy's going round in a trance, of course. Cannings Ambo is a bit too much for him."

"Oh dear! Is he going to fit in?"

"Steven!" Leander laughed. "Have you forgotten what it was like the first time you looked round this place?"

His smile conceded the point. "I seem to remember being rather preoccupied with you, as well," he said.

"And I think Fred was in a similar predicament. He was with Tish when he arrived."

"Ah! Was he . . .?" Steven waved a hand vaguely.

"Utterly! I'm sure he wasn't paying any attention to what I was telling him. He kept on looking round for her."

"She was bound to break a heart sooner or later," Steven said. "I hope this won't make things awkward for William."

"I don't think Tish has any intention of allowing that," Leander said.

Ten days later, Tish and Fred began walking out together. During the intervening period, Fred had been to Norwich and sold furniture to another department store.

Constable Wilcox bicycled from Marlborough to Cannings Ambo on a sultry August afternoon that threatened thunder. He considered himself to be the bearer of bad news.

"I'm very much afraid that we've heard from our colleagues in Chippenham that your uncle has been found dead, Mrs Hawksworth," he reported with due gravity. "In his shop, it was. This morning."

"I see. Were there any suspicious circumstances?" a perfectly calm Leander asked.

"Not that I know of, ma'am. It was heart failure apparently. Am I right in saying that you are his nearest living relative?"

"Yes. Mrs Shepherd at the Rectory is his sister, but I can deal with it. What has become of the body?"

"It's in the mortuary at the cottage hospital, ma'am."

"Very well. I shall attend to it tomorrow. Thank you for your trouble, Mr Wilcox. I'm sure you can persuade one of the maids to give you a cup of tea before you go back."

While the constable was returning to tell his sergeant that Mrs Hawksworth was a tough one and no mistake, Leander went to Rose House to collect William and they both walked to the Rectory.

"William and I will go to Chippenham first thing tomorrow morning and arrange for a decent funeral," Leander told Elisabeth. "What do you think we ought to do about the shop and house?"

"They aren't any good to us, are they?" Elisabeth asked.

"Not really." An idea came to Leander. "You wouldn't want that property, would you, William?"

"Good gracious, no! We're working flat out to keep up with Fred, without opening a shop."

"We'll put it in the hands of an agent," Leander said briskly, eager to be done with the business.

The following day, William stood by, trying to look useful while Leander dealt with her late uncle's affairs and funeral arrangements. To ensure no stain on the family name, she gave her word that all Ralph Flamsteed's outstanding bills would be paid.

It all took her precisely one hour and thirty-one minutes, including a delay of twelve minutes caused by a dilatory solicitor's clerk who was acquainted with the error of his ways.

At the end of the summer holidays, both Leander and Steven took George and Giles to the railway station in Marlborough. As they walked back to the carriage after the train had gone, Steven kicked at a stone and shook his head. It was such an uncharacteristic gesture that Leander stopped and looked at him in surprise.

"What's the matter, sweetheart?" she asked.

"I was hoping that school might do George some good," Steven muttered gloomily.

"When? When did you think that?"

"Oh, right from the start, when we sent him away."

So, he *had* known all along. Leander put an arm round him.

CHAPTER 15

1900

'My God, George, what *have* you got there?'

The second of June, 1900, was cool and showery with only fitful patches of weak sunshine. No one would have given a farthing for its chances of becoming a day to remember and look back on.

It was the day after Leander's fortieth birthday.

She had never felt better in her life. At the previous evening's celebration, she had been inundated with compliments on her youthful appearance; only William teased her, and that was done quietly, in private.

"You're turning into a proper old tyrant," he said, referring to her insistence that the party should finish at ten o'clock in order to permit the work of Latimer's Barn to start again at six the following morning. "I must say, though," he added admiringly, "you're looking damned well on it."

She still worried: forty was a watershed, and, if one believed some of the rubbish that was put around, it was all downhill to the grave from here.

So, in the middle of the morning after, when The House was disturbed only by the noise of clocks, she went upstairs to the bedroom, flung off all her clothes and had a good look at herself in the long cheval-mirror.

After striking several poses so as to carry out the inspection from as many different angles as possible, Leander came to the conclusion that she was in much better trim than most women of her age. Three children and seventeen years of marriage had left her unscathed and clean-limbed. Her muscles needed tuning up, of course, and she knew the answer to that.

Leander rummaged furiously through drawers in search of riding breeches. When she found them, they looked dreadfully small, and sure enough, the first pair she tried on were impossibly tight. But

252

the next two pairs, badly creased and reeking of mothballs, fitted perfectly.

There were a few moments of hesitation; she laughed at the sight of herself in the mirror, bare-breasted and clutching at the behind of the breeches to pull the creases out. Then her mind was made up. The most demanding years of motherhood were over, it was time to return to her first love.

Eager for immediate action, Leander was out of the bedroom and marching along the corridor.

"Ellie!" she bawled from the top of the landing. "Ellie!"

Emerging from the kitchen, Ellie looked up, apparently unsurprised by Leander's nakedness and the two pairs of breeches that flew down towards her.

"Can you run an iron over those, please," Leander said. "And get a message to Conn Daly in the yard. He's to come back after lunch. We're going riding."

"Riding?"

"Yes, Ellie, riding! On a horse."

After that, the only thing that caused comment was that Leander and Conn went out on hacks: Steven half expected her to take one of the best horses in the yard.

"Don't be so silly, sweetheart," she said. "I need to practise first. I tell you what, though, we'll have the stirrups shorter. I rather like the look of the way that American rides."

"What, Tod Sloan?" Steven was horrified. "He's a shocking man, darling. The Jockey Club have refused him a licence and told him to clear off home."

"That was because of his gambling, not his riding! I had a word with Morny Cannon at Kempton Park the other day and he swore that all jockeys would be riding short in five years at the most."

Very unwillingly, Steven agreed that the opinion of the Duke of Westminster's six-times champion jockey might be of value.

When Conn finally got home to Sally and their two daughters after evening stables, he was a happy man. He had always cherished the memory of the work Leander and he used to do together on Cannings Down and hoped that those days might return.

"By gum, I'll bet Mrs Hawksworth will ache tomorrow morning," he chuckled to Sally. "But you should see her ride. I'd swear she'd never stopped. And these short stirrups are going to catch on."

Two weeks later, when Michael Pilgrim produced a winner for Alexandra at Royal Ascot, he caused a stir by riding with his stirrup leathers shortened in the American style.

*

Behind the face that she presented to the world, Leander frequently worried, although she usually succeeded in doing so constructively, without losing sleep. At forty, and with the new century six months old, she felt that she was beginning to get the measure of life's ebb and flow at Cannings Ambo. Sometimes, she had the fanciful notion that she and her father's poplar trees understood it all.

They had been sighing dolefully in a chill wind the night she hurried down the drive to go to Dan Goakes at Church Green. The new century was barely three weeks away, but Dan was perfectly content not to see it. He went peacefully at three o'clock in the morning in his eighty-first year, delighted that Leander was with him and justly proud of what he had done with the second half of his life.

Dan's Jennie, vigorous as ever at sixty-five, had spent Christmas with Jim, Bella and her four grandchildren at Lea Bank, Jim's splendid new house between Rose House and the church. After the holiday, there seemed little point in her returning to Church Green, so the cottage in which she and Dan had spent almost forty happy years was taken over by a new man who had come to work for Wm Flamsteed & Sons.

Godfrey Timberlake, who agreed with Leander about the twentieth century's endless possibilities for mischief, actually declared that he would cut his throat rather than have anything to do with it. There was no need for such a drastic measure: both he and his brother, Cuthbert, died during 1898.

Godfrey was never sure whether owning horses at Latimer's Barn had made any difference to his social standing in Marlborough, nor did he give a damn; he found that he enjoyed racing, and that was enough for him. After his death, Rupert took his horses on, and was eager to raise standards.

For a reason that was unclear to Leander, but which she never questioned, Rupert became undisputed head of the Timberlake clan. Although his cousins Basil and Nigel were older, they seemed content to defer to Rupert as he began to wield the authority handed down from Godfrey. And, in his quiet way, Rupert wanted expansion and increased power: during September 1898, when the Fashoda incident blew up, he was in the North of England, acquiring another company.

Fashoda, a hitherto insignificant village and fort on the White Nile, some 450 miles south of Khartoum, had been declared French territory by a Captain Marchand after a 2,800-mile march across Africa with a small detachment of Senegalese troops. No, said the urbanely courteous Sir Henry Kitchener, arriving on the scene ten weeks later, there must be some mistake, Fashoda was definitely

British. While the two soldiers flew the Union Flag and Tricolour side by side and behaved with impeccable dignity, the Government dithered and the popular press bayed for war.

On his return from Bradford, Rupert listened to Leander's fulminations on the subject.

"They're mad, Rupert, stark-raving mad! The press actually *want* war."

"So do a lot of the public," he replied. "I saw a demonstration on my way through London yesterday."

"What *is* to be done?" she demanded.

"Nothing, my dear. It will all blow over. Kitchener's a good man. He won't allow it to get out of hand."

"But there is going to be serious trouble, you know."

"Yes. And in Africa."

They were right. Intransigence from Kruger in the Transvaal pitted against the by-products of British imperialism was bound to produce conflict, and a fearful shambles it turned out to be.

The Boer War was well on the way to changing the face of British politics before it even began. Then came the shock of the military disasters of Kimberley, Mafeking and Ladysmith, proving that the much-vaunted British Army was nothing more than an ill-prepared load of hot air.

By 1900, it seemed a safely established fact that Cannings Ambo was capable of regenerating itself.

The great Bellerophon, twenty-seven years of age and suffering from a heart disease, had to be put down at Easter. The £100,000 he had earned for the Fund was almost nothing compared to the sixteenth birthday present he had given Leander on Epsom Downs. When the time came, she went to the stud, and paid the old hero the honour of doing the job herself, swiftly and cleanly. Then, taut-faced, she rode back to Latimer's Barn on one of his grandsons and made a laconic single-line entry in the Big Book.

Bellerophon's sons and daughters were being used for breeding all over the world; at Cannings St John, his line was carried on by Hypotenuse and Alexandra's Long Barrow, a most unlikely stallion. After his almost non-existent racing career, not even his adoring owner expected him to be popular at stud, but when his first limited crop of two-year-olds began winning good races in 1898, demand for his services mounted swiftly.

Four of the lads who had come to Latimer's Barn when the new yard opened in 1874 now had sons working in the stable, and if new blood was necessary, Cannings Ambo brought it in.

Tish Merriweather and Fred Cartwright wasted no time once their minds were made up. They married early in 1898 and moved into a restored house almost opposite Oak Cottage. Fred, now thoroughly familiar with the village's history and fascinated by the part played in it by Horatio, insisted on naming the house 'Alma Cottage'.

"We must be grateful for small mercies," Leander told Elisabeth and Alexandra. "Fred was dead set on calling it 'Alma Works' until Tish put her foot down!" Secretly, she was delighted at the commemoration of Horatio, his factory and the horse her father had used to ruin the Association.

The marriage of Tish and Fred was pure enchantment. When it came to selling furniture, Fred tore round the country like a tiger: William suspected that it was best to remain in ignorance of some of the techniques that yielded such spectacular success. But when Fred returned to Cannings Ambo, he devoted himself to treating Tish as though she were the greatest lady in the land. She, for her part, teased him mercilessly on minor matters while deferring to him on all the things that were important: wickedly witty on the subject of the strong Birmingham accent that defied Fred's attempts to refine it, she was fiercely proud of his achievements as a salesman. And during the first March of the new century, Tish presented an ecstatic Fred with a daughter whom they called Adelaide.

She was christened by John Shepherd junior, who had taken over the duties of Vicar of Cannings Ambo that very week.

The Good Shepherd was sixty-seven and had been ill for some months. Charles Stanton, already as popular as his father, made no bones about his diagnosis: it was stomach cancer, and, apart from a difficult operation with a questionable chance of success, there was nothing to be done.

The diocesan authorities were notified and sent a replacement, a pompous individual of about sixty who set about antagonising folk the minute he set foot in the village. Leander's hackles rose when he began addressing her as though she were a particularly dim-witted public meeting, and the miserable man's fate was sealed once he exhibited impatience to have the Shepherds out of the Rectory.

"It's time you used your influence," Leander told Steven.

"What influence?"

"You're the squire. The living is in your gift. We ought to have thought of this before we let them foist this awful Tompkins on us."

"And how am I supposed to start playing the squire?" Steven asked, vaguely amused by it all in spite of Leander's serious mood.

"Write them a letter."

In the end, Steven signed what Leander had written with help from Alexandra, Vicky Foxton and Margaret Wesley, all of whom had taken strong exception to Tompkins.

The authorities resisted. Losing patience, Leander descended on the Dean in his close at Salisbury: it was not an interview that he was ever able to recall with any pleasure. When Leander had tea with Steven's sister, Henrietta, who was now headmistress of a small school in the city, she was gleefully aware that enough feathers had been ruffled to secure her purpose.

Leander not only demanded the removal of the lamentably unsuitable Tompkins, she wanted him replaced by her cousin, John Shepherd junior, ordained a clerk in Holy Orders in 1897 and sent to languish as a curate in Sheffield.

"Being stuck in a place like that may be good for John's soul," Leander told the Dean of Salisbury, "but I can't see him *achieving* anything, whereas he will be fully appreciated in Cannings Ambo."

"Madam, I cannot tell the Bishop of Sheffield what to do with his clergy," the Dean protested.

"You will if you don't want Cannings Ambo to become a heathen outpost!" Leander snapped before sitting back and treating him to a particularly hard look. "I am right in saying, am I not, that our contributions to your funds have always been adequate, if not generous?"

The Dean understood perfectly: this strong-willed and, he had to confess, fearfully attractive woman, would stop the flow of very useful finance without compunction.

The younger John Shepherd's joy at being transferred to his home village was matched by the warmth of the welcome he received. All would have been perfect were it not for the state of his father's health; there were days when the Good Shepherd suffered a great deal of agonisingly debilitating pain, causing Charles Stanton to become angry.

"I don't know what God thinks He's playing at," he fumed to Flora one evening. "What *can* be the point of making poor old John suffer like this? I had to give him morphine again today."

Charles did, however, have successes, the most highly acclaimed of which was Cyril Osgood's leg.

Always irritated by the sight of such a fine specimen limping, Charles waylaid Cyril one day as he came out of The George after a mid-morning thirst-quencher.

"I'm going to fix that leg of yours," Charles declared as though the job was as good as done.

"How's that, then, sir?" Cyril grinned amiably and prepared to humour Charles.

"Look here, Cyril, they've got an X-ray machine at the big hospital in Swindon. It can take pictures of what's *inside* your leg. Will you come with me and give it a try?"

Curious to see the new apparatus, but not believing a word of it, Cyril agreed.

The machine was big, noisy and every bit as temperamental as a Latimer's Barn thoroughbred. To Cyril's great amusement, one of the men in white coats was a mechanic, not a doctor, and his stock-in-trade was a tool-bag instead of a stethoscope. By turn the contrivance hummed, made violent spitting noises, then fell completely silent: it was all to do with electricity.

At last, after three hours, with much clanking and banging, they got a picture and Charles was jubilant when he saw it.

"There you are, Cyril, look at that. Plain as a pikestaff."

They peered at the plate as Charles held it up to the light from a window. Cyril blinked; the bone structure was exactly like the drawings he had seen in books, but there were three jagged objects about the size of a silver threepenny piece that had no right to be there.

"Shrapnel," Charles said. "Bound to be. Look at that brute!" He pointed to one near the ankle bone. "That's what's causing your trouble, Cyril."

"Well I'll be blowed!" Cyril seemed happy enough now that he knew.

"They'll have to come out," Charles said. "We can't have you walking about with scrap-metal inside you."

This was different. Cyril rubbed his chin, had another look at the X-ray plate, stared at the floor and finally gazed earnestly at Charles.

"Would you do it, sir?" he asked.

"I'm a bit out of touch with a scalpel, Cyril," Charles said doubtfully.

"I want you to do it," Cyril replied doggedly.

The operation was carried out in Oak Cottage. Charles might have preferred taking Cyril into hospital to do the job, but, just as he wanted someone he knew and trusted to wield the knife, Cyril insisted on having it done at Cannings Ambo.

Within a week, it was apparent that Charles had succeeded and that Cyril would soon be walking normally again.

"These new scientific things are marvellous," Leander enthused to Steven. "I wonder if we could use one of those X-ray devices on the horses?"

He smiled indulgently. Leander could hardly wait to get electricity and the telephone into the village; now she was thinking of something that seemed outrageous. Yet despite her innovative flair, she still remained implacably opposed to the motor car. Steven suspected that William was putting off getting one because of her strictures.

But about three weeks after Leander took up riding and working in the yard again, a Daimler spluttered up the drive to Latimer's Barn. Steven kept a straight face. The ducal coronets on the vehicle's doors guaranteed the owner immunity from Leander's wrath.

Until the death of his father the previous year, Hubert Charles Prideaux had been Marquess of Glastonbury; now, he was the seventh Duke of Laverstoke. Four years younger than Leander and with an ample measure of his family's languid good looks, he had been slightly infatuated with the mistress of Latimer's Barn ever since he started keeping a few horses of his own there in 1889. He flirted with her shamelessly, even in the presence of his recently acquired wife who took not the blindest bit of notice of his caperings. Clementine, Duchess of Laverstoke, a famous beauty and herself the daughter of a duke, was only twenty-three, but regally sure of herself.

"Good God, Hubert!" Leander exploded after marching up to the car. "Have you gone completely off your head? What do you want one of these contraptions for?"

"Oh, they're all the rage, my dear," he replied. "And I'm expected to put on a show, you know. Old Beaufort's got half a dozen of the things up at Badminton and I've got chaps at Eaton Mandeville pulling long faces at getting left behind." He extricated himself from the car and kissed her hand ardently. "In any case, Clem insisted on having one."

"Pah! Why do men always blame their wives when they want to behave idiotically?" Leander demanded. She peered closely at the chauffeur, who, in his goggles and gauntlets, already felt enough of a fool.

"It seems a very nice piece of work to me, Your Grace," Steven said, eyeing the motor enviously. Whether it was a need to preserve proprieties, or because he still felt occasionally unsure of himself, he always treated his noble patron with due respect.

"Thank you, Mr Hawksworth! I imagine it's about time you thought of getting one."

"We're rather afraid of the effect it might have on the horses," Steven replied, looking at Leander for approval.

The Duke laughed. "Horses are a damned sight more sensible

than we are," he said. "They've always put up with a fair amount in cities and war."

"Not horses like ours!" Leander said firmly.

"Oh, come off it, Leander. Even your pampered creatures are quite sensible when you get down to it. Tell you what, why don't I have my man drive round the yard a few times? We'll soon know if they're likely to be difficult."

"Hubert!" Leander said menacingly.

"All right, all right, I'll behave. Now, what's all this I hear about you?"

"What's that?"

"You've started riding again."

"I have. Who told you?"

"That's a secret! I'm not having you getting at my trusty spy. Are any of my nags getting the benefit?"

"Of course, Hubert! I'm rather pleased with Equilateral." The new Duke was keeping up his father's tradition of geometric names.

"Really? I thought she wasn't all that clever."

"She wasn't last year, but she's come on a lot. I think we should give her a run at Goodwood."

"Does she have any chance?"

"No, not really. She'll probably get tailed off last." For a moment, the Duke was deceived by Leander's mock-hopelessness and was off guard when she delivered her salvo. "Honestly, you do ask some silly questions, Hubert! Our horses *always* have a chance. We don't send them racing just for a change of scenery, you know."

Steven lay on his back, stared at the bedroom ceiling and luxuriated in the after-glow of brilliantly well-spent passion.

"Isn't this getting awfully decadent?" he said at last.

"Why?"

"We seem to be spending every afternoon in bed."

"Nonsense!" Leander made herself sound dismissively severe. "It's only Mondays, Wednesdays and Fridays – except when you go racing."

"It's still a lot."

Propping herself up on an elbow, she stared at him with an intentness he mistook for seriousness. "Are you complaining?" she asked.

He shook his head and a strange look clouded his face. She knew what he was thinking: Steven Hawksworth, the boy from the boat-yard who had never thought all that highly of himself, still had difficulty in believing what had become of him. His wonderment had increased again since the invigorating effects of fresh air and exercise caused her to take a determined lead in rescuing their love-making from the rather mundane rut into which it had lapsed.

Hating him to feel beholden to her, Leander made him think of other things. "Did you see George's letter?" she asked.

"Not yet. What's he got to say for himself? Usual stuff, I suppose."

"No, it isn't. He's been invited to spend most of the summer holidays with the parents of Blayne-Singer – you know, that boy he's always crowing about. His father owns a merchant bank or something."

"Is he going?"

"He's asking for permission."

Steven smiled mockingly. "That's a turn-up! Where do the Blayne-Singers live?"

"All over the place! They're spending some of the time on their estate in Norfolk, then they might go to Nice for a week or two on their yacht."

"Nice! On a yacht?" Steven was amused.

"I imagine that this 'yacht' is a steamship weighing several hundred tons, sweetheart."

"Oh, I see." Far from seeming impressed, Steven was derisive.

"Do we let George go?" Leander asked.

"Can you think of a good reason for stopping him?"

"No."

"Neither can I and nor do I want to." Steven was deeply thoughtful for a few moments before asking, "What *is* going to become of George?"

"I don't think you need to worry about that," Leander replied. "I believe he's made his mind up, but he doesn't want to tell you yet."

"Why not?"

"He's worried about hurting your feelings."

"I suppose there has to be a first time for everything," Steven said. "What's his plan?"

"He seems to have set his mind on Oxford. After that, I expect he'll want to work for Blayne-Singer's. From what I can gather, it seems a way of earning a good deal of money without too much effort."

"Good luck to all of them!" Steven said with a wealth of meaning. "So, with George out of the way, you'll have Giles to yourself all summer."

"Yes. Isn't that lovely!"

As if captivated by the idea, Leander began to swarm enticingly over Steven.

"Oh, no!" he groaned.

"Don't be silly!" she whispered. "There's plenty of time before evening stables."

He had no choice in the matter. After twenty years, the witchery in her eyes was, if anything, even more powerful.

Given the gift of marvellous weather, Goodwood, in its magnificent setting on the Duke of Richmond's estate, really *was* glorious. Leander and Giles spent a whole week there, staying with the Duke and Duchess of Laverstoke at the house they had taken on the outskirts of Chichester.

The Sussex Stakes, the main attraction of the third day, provided resounding proof that Leander had lost none of her intuitive genius for spotting a brilliant horse and giving it the best possible preparation for a race. Equilateral, with Michael Pilgrim riding exactly as specified by Leander, waited half a length behind the leaders until the furlong marker before cruising so effortlessly into the lead that all the other jockeys were convinced they had a chance of getting back on terms with her. They were wrong. The further they went, the more Equilateral stretched them and her lead.

"My word, Leander, you *do* know about these things, don't you?" the Duke of Laverstoke said.

"I have an idea or two, Hubert!"

"Father used to go on about you. I see what he meant."

Leander's afternoon was dimmed by a voice behind her saying, "Congratulations, Mrs Hawksworth."

Turning, she found Walter Rothwell smiling at her in what he no doubt imagined was an attractive manner.

"Thank you, Mr Rothwell. I *am* rather pleased with that filly, as a matter of fact."

"Yes, indeed! I see Pilgrim is persisting with the short stirrups."

"We're finding it very effective – as you saw!"

There was an awkward pause with Leander half afraid that Rothwell was about to make another attempt at propositioning her. However, he thought better of it in the presence of her fifteen-year-old son and walked away with a curt nod.

Giles was immensely glad to be back in Cannings Ambo for the long summer holiday and Leander adored him for it. His love of the place was every bit as great as hers and his grandfather's, and she suspected that he suffered untold agonies while away from it.

An opportunity presented itself the following afternoon as they rode out on hacks, purely for the joy of being on a horse.

"How is Winchester?" Leander asked casually.

"Very nice," Giles replied. He was always convincing: he appeared to regard it as a duty to be so. For once, he added to the platitude. "I don't much care for being 'Hawksworth Minor' – but it's all right apart from that."

"Oh, yes, of course, George is 'Hawksworth Major'." Leander laughed. "Do you see much of George when you're at school?"

"No, not really. He's a bit of a swell now he's in the sixth form."

"So he sticks to people like Blayne-Singer?"

"Blayne-Singer is *very* important," Giles said earnestly. "He goes to tea with the headmaster every Thursday. He gives some of the fags the most tremendous beatings."

"Does he, now?" Leander sounded disinterested. "What about George? Does he thrash the smaller boys?"

"Not as much as Blayne-Singer."

"But he does it?"

"I think it's more or less expected of chaps in their position."

"Will you ever be in that position, Giles?"

"I hope not! I think I shall be all right, because I'm not all that clever and I don't belong to enough societies and clubs." He grinned. "I'm pretty insignificant, really, Mother."

Leander gave him one of her most radiant smiles. "You aren't insignificant here, darling," she told him. "Far from it! You do realise, don't you, that you'll be taking over Latimer's Barn one day?"

Giles nodded thoughtfully. "George doesn't seem very interested," he said.

Leander declined to point out that what George thought was not relevant. "I presume you're happy with that?" she said.

"Oh, yes!" Giles's eyes shone.

Not wanting to say any more for the moment, Leander urged her horse into a gallop. Giles hung back. The greatest pleasure of this holiday was watching his mother ride; Conn Daly and dear old Seamus at the stud had told him how marvellous she was on a horse. Now, at last, he was able to see how right they were.

Runcton Hall near Thetford in Norfolk was very much to George's taste. Sir Reginald Blayne-Singer, head of the family merchant bank and several other enterprises, was a youthful forty-five-year-old who did not allow the demands of business to interfere with his enjoyment of life. The vast house with its thirty bedrooms, billiards room, indoor swimming pool and goodness knows what else, was opulently furnished to give an atmosphere of luxurious abandon.

Quite without meaning to, Sir Reginald set his young guest back on his heels the moment they were introduced.

"Very pleased to meet you, my boy. Alec has told me all about you. Now, look here, I wonder if you could do me a favour."

George smiled eagerly, overwhelmed at being in such a fortunate position so soon. "I shall do my best, sir."

"Splendid! The fact is, I keep a few racehorses at Newmarket. They cost me the earth, but they never seem to do any good. Do you suppose we could persuade your father to take them on?"

"I could certainly talk to him, sir," George replied, masking his dismay at the topic.

"Good man! This Latimer's Barn place of yours is *awfully* well thought of. People keep telling me that I couldn't do better than send my animals there. Mind you, isn't it your mother who has all the know-how?"

"She is very good, sir," George replied with an attempt at filial pride.

"Well, see what you can do," Sir Reginald urged.

"I told you, George," Alec Blayne-Singer said when they were alone a few minutes later. "You might think the place stinks, but all the nibs are full of Latimer's Barn."

George was surprised: the very last thing he had expected to find was that his parents, and particularly his mother, were famous. Initially, he felt quite put out, annoyed at the disruption of his prejudices, but life at Runcton Hall was far too pleasant to allow his mood to last for long.

As well as Sir Reginald's immediate family, there were a dozen guests, all very wealthy indeed and unashamed of the fact. When he came to think about it, George had no recollection of money ever being mentioned at home. He decided that this meant that training horses was, after all, not a very lucrative business. If you had money, why not boast about it? His new-found friends did and George approved.

There was another heady, albeit unidentifiable ingredient in the atmosphere.

Alec laughed when George asked him about it. "That's the night-time revels, my boy," he said with a smirk and a huge wink.

"Night-time revels?" George looked and sounded baffled.

Alec Blayne-Singer lowered his voice. "Who ends up in bed with whom is anybody's guess," he said. "You could run a book on it. It's like musical chairs and they're all at it!"

"What, everybody?" George asked, aghast with a mixture of shock and excitement.

"Everybody!" Alec replied firmly.

"Even your mother and father?"

"*Especially* the parents! Dash it, they started it all off. That Miss Jessop — you've noticed her, I suppose?"

"Yes."

"She's meant to be the governor's secretary. Very occasionally she gives him a letter to sign or makes an appointment, but that's about all. What she *does* do is spend most of the night in my parents' bedroom."

"With both of them?"

"Yes. Why not? Mother has catholic tastes."

"And you?" George asked tentatively.

Alec looked smug. "You don't imagine I'd miss out on a thing like this, do you?"

George was dazed. Tall, well-built and looking older than his seventeen years, he was at the point where sexual curiosity had long since turned to urgency. The picture sketched out by Alec plunged him into a fearful state that worsened as he watched his fellow-guests with hawk-like vigilance and began to discover evidence that Alec had not lied to him.

At the end of the first week, a new group arrived to stay, and Ursula was among them.

She was some sort of cousin to Alec, eighteen or nineteen, with an unremarkable face but a wondrous figure. She had colossal self-assurance: taking in the scene in the crowded room where tea was being served soon after her arrival, she nodded to those she knew, kissed a few aunts and uncles, and strode over to George who was alone in a corner.

"Hello, I'm Ursula," she said. "Who are you?"

They became inseparable, walking in the extensive grounds, boating on the lake, playing tennis and visiting Thetford to have lunch at an inn.

"I think Ursula's pretty keen on you, George," Alec said after five days. "If I were you, I'd grab her."

"Really? Do you think I have a chance?"

"There's no doubt about it, my boy. And I'm sure Ursula is experienced, so you won't have any of the virginal nonsense."

Ursula herself suggested that they should go to the summer-house the following afternoon, and she it was who instigated their first kiss.

"Come along, George," she instructed after he had made several

blundering attempts to improve matters. "We must get this right . . .
you stay there . . . like that . . . now!"

Made dizzy by her expertise, George began mauling her breasts,
receiving little more than an impression of whalebone. To his surprise,
Ursula moaned with pleasure, yet no sooner had she done so than she
was pulling his hand away.

"No, George," she said. "Not here."

"No one can see us," he complained.

"I know that. This place simply isn't *comfortable*. We can't do it
properly."

"What, then?" George asked desperately.

She smiled reassuringly. "Calm down, my dear. I shall come to
your room tonight."

The rest of the day was interminable and George's nerves played
him false. After Ursula had gone to be dutifully polite to Lady
Blayne-Singer, he searched high and low for Alec, frantic for advice.
After an hour he discovered that his friend had gone into Norwich
with one of the female guests and was not expected back until lunch
the following day.

On three separate occasions over dinner, Sir Reginald looked
solicitously at George and asked, "Are you *sure* you're all right, my
boy? Not going down with anything, are you?"

While George thought of excuses for his nerves, Ursula sat impas-
sively at the other end of the table, exchanging polite conversation
with Algie Jenkinson, a young man with a bright future on the Baltic
Exchange.

After the meal, there was still anything up to three hours to go.
Ursula became involved in a game of whist and George roamed the
grounds until twilight drove him indoors where he passed time by
having a bath.

It was almost midnight when she slipped noiselessly into his room,
going first to the windows to draw back the curtains, admitting the
light of a full moon.

"Romantic!" she sighed and let her robe fall.

As she sat on the edge of his bed, George reached out to touch
her breasts. He was gentle now and soon discovered the prominence
of her nipples.

"You haven't got any clothes on, have you?" she asked, sinking
down contentedly on top of the counterpane.

"No," he assured her, and she began kissing him passionately,
revelling in his excited exploration of her body. She allowed it to go
on for ten minutes or so, until she, too, was trembling with greedy
anticipation. Scrambling under the sheet with him, she knew that

266

she would have to show him the way, and while he attempted to dominate her with a kiss of Herculean power, Ursula grasped his almost painfully erect penis.

He felt the fire go from her as though doused by cold water. She was rigidly still, and when she spoke, her voice was icy.

"My God, George, what *have* you got there?" she asked.

He stared at her in the pale, silver light, with no idea what had stopped her dead in her lusty tracks.

"That is absolutely *enormous*," Ursula said in a hushed, unnatural voice. "Let me have a look."

Pulling back the bedclothes, she turned up the lamp on the table. George had often wondered whether he ought to be proud of his penis and began to feel quite lordly at what he took to be confirmation of his conjecture.

There was no real indication that Ursula was discomposed to any great extent; she continued to stroke it as she spoke. "I've *never* seen anything like that, George. Tommy Westbrook and Bertie Hawkins are well endowed, but *that* is gigantic!"

"And I suppose it might get a bit bigger yet," George said complacently.

"You may well be right," Ursula said. Standing up, she reached for her robe and put it on.

"What's the matter?" George demanded.

"My dear George, I couldn't possibly accommodate a thing that size," Ursula said. "It would split me in two!"

She was politely matter-of-fact about it and gave him an affectionate peck on the cheek before leaving to find out if her friend Algie Jenkinson had company for the night.

George was mortified.

For two weeks, he was tortured by the thought that he was some kind of dangerous freak. The small mercy, for which he was pathetically grateful, was that Ursula appeared to maintain a discreet silence and Alec made no attempt to discover why the affair had not come to fruition.

At the end of this time, George went unwillingly to Nice, purely because he had to escape from Runcton Hall and could not bear the thought of going home.

Phyllida Warburton, wife of Sir Reginald Blayne-Singer's general manager, was already aboard the yacht *Maid of Orleans*, and George was aware of her predatory interest as he walked up the gangplank on his arrival.

"Watch her," Alec advised from the side of his mouth. "She's a man-eater!"

"What about her husband?" George asked.

"Good God, old Warburton isn't allowed out on sprees like this! He gets seasick while we're still tied up. Besides, somebody's got to look after the shop while we're enjoying ourselves!"

Mrs Warburton commandeered George to sit next to her at dinner. He found her enchanting. He had no idea how old she was, since once people were obviously past thirty they became lost to him in a uniform haze of middle-age. But, unlike any other adult he had ever met, she made him feel at ease to the extent that their age difference vanished. When the meal was over, he complied at once with her request for 'a turn round the deck'.

After only two circuits, they adjourned to her cabin. Whatever her age, Mrs Warburton proved to have a phenomenally attractive and lissome body which she used with voracious skill as George's erstwhile embarrassment was transformed into his pride and joy. Mrs Warburton's eyes glittered with excited longing when she saw it.

"Oh, George, that is *magnificent*," she breathed. "*Stupendous!* I only hope I can do justice to it!"

She did. For two whole weeks, she did little else.

When George returned to England, it was with a very different perspective on life and his part in it. Phyllida Warburton had done much more than show him that he was not a freak; he was well on the way to believing that he was the answer to every woman's prayer.

Leander had spent nearly a year finding a school that would suit Amelia's abilities. Her final choice was the Godolphin School at Salisbury, founded by Elizabeth Godolphin in 1726 and now undergoing a renaissance under the aegis of a truly remarkable woman.

Mary Alice Douglas, the headmistress, was six months younger than Leander and they established a warm rapport from the very start of their first meeting.

There was never any doubt that Miss Douglas was the ideal person to guide Amelia and that Miss Jones, who taught the all-important subject of mathematics, was fully up to the task. Above all else, Amelia would *enjoy* herself at the Godolphin School, a precious gift that had been denied to Giles.

"This may be an appropriate school for Amelia in very many ways," Miss Douglas said when all the arrangements had been finalised. "I believe members of our founder's family were prominent in horse-racing."

"Yes, indeed. The second Earl imported a horse that became

known as the Godolphin Arabian," Leander said. "He was one of the three stallions from whom all our modern thoroughbreds are supposed to be descended."

Miss Douglas looked suitably impressed.

"And," said Leander, bringing out her trump card, "the first race that Latimer's Barn ever won was called the Godolphin Stakes. It was the day I was born!"

"Then we have no choice in the matter, do we, Mrs Hawksworth?" Miss Douglas laughed. "We shall make Amelia very happy here, I promise you."

But Amelia herself was given the final say in the matter. Leander took her to Salisbury in May to meet Miss Douglas, who told her to look round the school and decide whether she thought she would like it.

It was love at first sight.

"She really is a delightful girl, Mrs Hawksworth," Miss Douglas said. "I'm sure she'll be a credit to us. And my goodness, doesn't she look like you!"

Leander laughed. "In a few years' time, Miss Douglas, I am hoping that no one will be able to tell us apart. That rather depends on me, of course!"

When it was time for Amelia to set off in early September, the future held no terrors, and once she had gone there was not the same feeling of empty dread that had hung over poor Giles's first sortie to Winchester. Instead, Leander was left pondering the discovery she had made during her last serious talk with Amelia. It emerged that she was worried about her cousin Gerald, William and Ruth's eldest son.

"Why?" Leander asked.

"He has an awful time with Maude," Amelia announced in the direct, Flamsteed-like way that was becoming one of her strongest characteristics. "She bullies him and makes fun of him."

"Why on earth does she do that, darling?"

Amelia thought about it.

"Well, Maude is quite a nasty person," she said with devastatingly cool objectivity. "I think she's cruel. Also, she believes we're all fools."

"Why ever does she think that?" Leander asked.

"It's because we don't want more excitement."

"Excitement?" Leander was bemused.

"She thinks we lead very dull lives," Amelia explained. "She goes on a great deal about 'the world' and silly things like that."

"And what about Gerald?" Leander asked.

"Gerald can't wait to start work with Uncle William. He says that Maude's a pig."

"So she's horrible to him?"

"Yes. Mind you, Matthew stands up to her. He clouted her with a saucepan the other day."

Leander almost laughed at the thought of the extrovert and brave Matthew defending Gerald against the outrages of the spiteful Maude, but the underlying seriousness of the problem worried her. She toyed with the idea of saying something to William: no, he *must* be aware of Maude's attitude.

In any case, George gave her more than enough to think about.

George passed through Latimer's Barn briefly on his way from Nice to Winchester.

Initially, his marvellous sun-tan and apparently relaxed air caused Leander to think that the long holiday had done him a great deal of good.

Then she discovered that behind the façade, her eldest son had, in the space of a few short weeks, turned into the most overweening pain in the neck she had ever had the misfortune to encounter. Although she was blissfully ignorant of the fact, Leander was witnessing the delusions of grandeur induced by the sexually over-active Mrs Warburton.

And within an hour of George's arrival, he and Steven ran into their first serious trouble.

"By the way, Father, I told Sir Reginald Blayne-Singer that you'd train some horses for him," George declared loftily.

"Oh, did you?" Steven gazed at him mildly. "That was rather silly of you."

"Why?"

"I don't have room for any more horses." Steven pulled out the leather-bound notebook that he had inherited from Leander's father. "It's going to be at least two years before I have any space in the yard," he said after consulting his plans and commitments for the future.

"Well, really!" George exploded. "The first time I want anything from that bloody stable, and you can't do it. So much for the great Latimer's Barn!"

Steven's face remained impassive, but the anger in his voice made George wilt. "If you *ever* speak like that in front of your mother again, George, I will fetch a whip from that stable you so despise and thrash you! Do you understand me?"

"Yes," George replied sullenly, adding, "sir!" with a fair imitation of sincerity. He turned to Leander. "I'm sorry, Mother. I mustn't allow myself to get so angry."

"That's quite all right, my dear," Leander said stiffly.

"Look here, George," Steven said, "how would it be if I wrote to Sir Reginald and explained the position? I can make sure that you are absolved from all blame so that he doesn't think badly of you."

"Thank you, Father, that's very decent of you," George said.

Although the crisis had been negotiated, the atmosphere remained strained, and Leander heaved a great sigh of relief when George set out early the following morning to begin his last year at Winchester.

The incident left George out of sorts, somehow unnerved. Despite his ineptitude at showing it, he was very fond of Steven. Leander was a different matter: George was never able to decide whether he loved or loathed her. The flow of adoration between her, Giles and Amelia, baffled and enraged him by turn. Why, he had always asked himself, was his mother unable to show *him* such effortlessly bounteous affection?

George worried about it for the first two weeks of the new term until Alec Blayne-Singer drove all thoughts of Cannings Ambo from his mind.

"What are you doing for Christmas?" Alec asked, coming into George's study with a letter in his hand.

"Going home, I suppose," George replied with marked lack of enthusiasm.

"I think you should come to Runcton," Alec said. "I've had a letter from the governor – he's all right about those horses, by the way. Doesn't blame you at all. Mrs Warburton will be spending the festive season with us and has specifically requested your presence. Actually, it sounds more like an order to me."

"Well, we'd better not disappoint her then," George grinned.

Before receiving this exciting piece of news, George had been giving consideration to ways in which he might improve his standing with his parents, particularly his mother. The prospect of Phyllida Warburton stopped the process.

It never started again.

CHAPTER 16

1903

'For God's sake, do your best and be sensible'

Neither Queen Victoria nor the Good Shepherd lived to see the end of the Boer War. Her Majesty died on 22 January 1901 and was succeeded by the Prince of Wales as King Edward VII; John Shepherd finally gained release from his suffering four months later, in May, a year before the war ended in 1902.

What little inclination Cannings Ambo had to celebrate the defeat of the Boers was destroyed by a tragedy that occurred on the very day that peace was announced.

Particularly when the breeding season was over, the stallions at Cannings St John required as much exercise as a racehorse. Paul Izzard always looked forward to his spins on Hypotenuse. "It's the only way I'll ever get to ride a Derby winner," he repeatedly joked.

On the whole, Hypotenuse was much better behaved at the stud than ever he was in training at Latimer's Barn, and a number of ribald explanations of his pleasantness went the rounds. But on the morning of 30 May 1902, something terrible got into him. Without warning or provocation, he lashed out with both his back legs at Paul. A witness was certain that the horse's violent action was quite deliberate. The impact of the two hoofs landing squarely in his chest hurled Paul backwards like a rag doll.

Charles Stanton came to the conclusion that death was almost instantaneous: Paul suffered a massive heart attack brought on by shock. Leander's grief at the sudden loss of a lifelong friend was reflected by the whole village, but for her, it had to be a time of action.

"Amazing, isn't it?" Steven said to William afterwards.

"She's always been like that," William replied proudly. "She dives straight in. You're afraid that she can't possibly know what she's doing, yet it all comes out absolutely right."

272

Leander dealt first with the problems of Paul's widow.

Polly Izzard, not yet fifty, was full of life and took Paul's shocking death with great fortitude: but what was to become of her? Leander rolled it into another problem and solved the pair at a stroke.

Bertha Bradley was sixty-seven and starting to find it difficult to cope with the demands of being the housekeeper at Latimer's Barn. After Leander, Bertha and Polly had discussed the matter for a few minutes, the answer was obvious: Bertha retired and Polly took her place.

Then there were Seamus and Lizzie O'Malley, the first to realise that Paul was dead. They were badly unnerved by the catastrophe and, suddenly, Seamus looked his age.

"I'd no idea he was seventy-six!" Steven said to Leander as they rode back home at the end of an afternoon at the stud spent talking things over with Seamus and Lizzie.

"I must confess, I'd forgotten he was *that* old," Leander said. "I'm not surprised he's had enough."

"He told me he wouldn't mind retiring tomorrow," Steven said.

Not even Leander was able to organise it that quickly, largely because it took her four days to persuade Steven to part with the two lads she wanted.

"Come along, sweetheart," she said at last. "It's easy enough for you to find new staff for the yard, but we *must* have people we know and can trust at the stud."

So, Sam Ruddock and Ephraim Wilkins went to Cannings St John. Both were aged about forty and had been at Latimer's Barn for ten years. Sam was married, but had no children; Eph, who was to be his assistant, was single and widely regarded as conscientious albeit a bit simple.

Leander had one other difficulty. The Duke of Laverstoke, who had inherited Hypotenuse from his father, wanted the animal put down.

"Don't be ridiculous, Hubert," Leander told him forthrightly. "What good will that do?"

"Damn it, Leander, the beast's a killer! I've had nightmares about that poor chap Izzard."

"Hypotenuse didn't do it deliberately!"

"Josh Taverner swears he did!"

"Josh is very well-meaning, Hubert, but he doesn't have the vaguest idea what he's talking about."

"It could happen again, you know."

Leander knew that he was right and made no attempt to deny the suggestion. "Sam Ruddock and Eph Wilkins will be on their guard," she said.

"Even so . . ."

"Hubert, you are not going to have that animal put down, and that's an end of it. We're running a stud-farm, not a slaughterhouse!"

She was right. It was the end of it.

The Boer War was hardly mentioned at Latimer's Barn until the spring of 1903 when it had been over for nearly a year. The Duke of Laverstoke's brother, Lord Randolph Prideaux, a professional soldier, had served in the conflict as a lieutenant-colonel in the Royal Horse Artillery, and Leander encouraged him to talk about his experiences one evening when he was a guest for dinner at The House.

"Most of it wasn't anything like a proper fight," Lord Randolph said. "At least, it wasn't anything like the Army *thought* a proper fight should be."

"The Boers used guerilla tactics," Leander said.

"Exactly. Mount a set-piece against that and you end up looking a complete fool."

"Which we did for the first six months."

"Rather longer than that actually."

"Still, we got there in the end," Steven said, trying to inject a note of optimism into the conversation.

"Yes, we did." Lord Randolph sounded a good deal less than enthusiastic.

"Come on, Randolph, what's bothering you?" Leander said.

"It was the cavalry that finally did for Kruger and his boys. The only answer, really, with that terrain and Boer tactics. So, the mounted brigades have come out of it pretty well and they're even more full of their own importance than ever. Over the next few years, I can see them getting their senior chaps promoted to the point where they're running the whole Army."

"And this isn't a good thing?" Leander asked.

"Most cavalry officers are blood, thunder and glory merchants," Lord Randolph said. He tapped his forehead. "They aren't all that good at thinking. There's something else, too. We lost less than six thousand men out of four hundred and fifty thousand. It was quite a freak, of course, but I understand that certain senior idiots are already starting to bank on that sort of ratio in a European war."

While Leander looked disapproving, Steven said, "Surely there isn't going to be a war in Europe. Leander always said the balloon would go up in Africa. It has done and everything will be all right now."

Lord Randolph looked grave. "I'm afraid I couldn't advise you to bet on that, Steven," he said.

"Who on earth would we be fighting?" Steven asked, clearly believing that the whole concept was ludicrous. "We don't have any enemies."

"Nor do we have any friends," Leander told him. "As things stand at the moment, *anybody* could trump up half a dozen good reasons for picking a quarrel with us."

The talk of the Boer War went on all evening, avoiding one topic: there was no mention of the concentration camps in which over twenty thousand Boer women and children had died of typhoid and dysentery. Well over a year after the dreadful facts had come to light, Leander continued to be disgusted that the British Army could stoop so low as to make use of such an odious practice. Little wonder that the Government had tied itself in knots of denial and embarrassment.

Although Latimer's Barn had no aspirant to the highest honours that year, all the horses that went out to race performed remarkably well. At one stage in June, twenty-three winners had come from thirty-one runners.

When Leander went to the Godolphin School at the end of the summer term, one of two or three visits she liked to make every year, Miss Douglas mentioned it at once.

"One can scarcely open a newspaper these days without seeing Latimer's Barn," she said. "It's quite exciting!"

"Really, Miss Douglas," Leander laughed. "What would your governors say if they knew you were studying the racing pages?"

"It's all part of the broad base of knowledge I need to equip my girls for modern life," Miss Douglas replied in a mock-serious tone. "You do seem to be doing amazingly well."

"Yes, it is a good year in one way, but I like winning the big, important races," Leander said. "Unfortunately we don't seem to have anything good enough at the moment. Now, tell me about Amelia."

Leander liked to supplement the written report on Amelia's work with a chat.

"She has made brilliant progress this year, Mrs Hawksworth." Miss Douglas sat back and thought, smiling as she did so. "I think that Amelia is very like you. She's only interested in the very best. Fortunately she only has to rely on her own ability and hard work, rather than the horses she is given to train! Between you and me, Miss Jones is fully stretched to keep ahead of Amelia at mathematics."

"Is she still enjoying herself and being kind to the other girls?" Leander asked, rather more anxious about that than Amelia's academic prowess.

"Of course! She's the mainstay of the cricket team."

"I always want to laugh at that," Leander said. "It's such a complicated and manly game."

"Not the way Amelia plays it!" Miss Douglas laughed. "The other thing we've discovered this year is that she has quite a flair for languages, especially German."

"Is this the time when we ought to be thinking about her future?" Leander asked. Amelia was sixteen. "She appears to be capable of making a career for herself."

"Oh, she's capable enough," Miss Douglas replied. "What we must do is to find out what Amelia *wants*. We mustn't force her into anything."

It was the last day of term, and Leander discussed it with Amelia as they travelled home together.

"Do you think there's anything I could do in the village?" was the first question Amelia asked after Leander had set the scene.

"There are probably dozens of things, darling," Leander told her. "But it seems to me that you have a much wider choice of opportunities and we need to think carefully."

"Giles is coming home to stay, isn't he?"

"The day after tomorrow!" Leander said happily. Giles had very nearly completed the ordeal of Winchester and had his mother's wholehearted support for his wish never to leave Latimer's Barn again.

"And George?" Amelia asked. "What's he going to do?"

"We expect that he's going to find a job in London when he leaves Oxford," Leander said. "To be honest, there never has been any question of him working in the stable."

Amelia nodded. "I think I'd like to go to university," she said. "Miss Douglas and Miss Jones want me to have a go at Cambridge."

"Goodness!" Leander glowed at the prospect. "For mathematics, of course."

"Yes."

"Fancy us producing someone that clever!"

"We shall have to wait and see," Amelia said cautiously. "The competition is incredibly fierce, so I might not get a place. In any case, Father may not like the idea."

Leander shook her head vehemently. "Darling, your father will be even prouder of you than I am. He's the one you get your brains from!"

Any doubts Amelia might have harboured about Steven's reaction were swept away within minutes of arriving at Latimer's Barn.

"Definitely!" he said when Leander had explained things to him. "That's a marvellous idea. It's what you want, is it, my dear?"

"Yes, please, Father."

"Then you shall have my full support!" Steven beamed at Leander. "There can't be many girls go to Cambridge to study mathematics," he said. "You see, we're up there with the leaders again!"

After hugging Steven, Amelia ran off to Rose House. It was always the first thing she did when she came home on holiday; before attending to anything else, she had to reassure herself that Gerald was all right.

Because Maude had come to the conclusion that she was destined to be an artist, she now gave herself airs and graces that ensured a quieter life for Gerald. She did have some talent, and Ruth was encouraging it by paying for lessons with a lady in Marlborough who occasionally had pictures hung at the Royal Academy. Maude often set up her easel on Cannings Down to execute paintings of the horses at work and some people were impressed by the results. Leander had serious reservations: she felt that Maude was simply playing games with a smattering of technical competence and that her pictures were wooden, lacking spirit and life.

Leander made the event of Giles's home-coming very special indeed.

She went to the railway station to meet him on her own, dispensing with the services of a coachman.

And to hasten the reunion, she drove to the main line at Savernake, rather than wait another twenty minutes while Giles caught the connection to Marlborough.

When he got off the train, they stood for a long time, simply smiling at one another. He seemed very grown-up and every inch *the* grandson of Giles Flamsteed.

The long embrace which they eventually allowed themselves was a vow that they would never part again.

Something very unusual happened during the second week in August: George came home and gave the impression that he intended staying for a week or more. After two years at Oxford University, the sum total of his holiday visits amounted to eight days. Now, he appeared to be trying to settle in Cannings Ambo for a few weeks.

Leander was immediately suspicious, especially when she saw that George was doing his best to be alone with Steven, even to the extent of loitering round the yard, something he had vigorously avoided all his life.

There was indeed an urgent purpose behind George's visit, a matter so serious that he had unwillingly torn himself away from

277

Runcton Hall and the unquenchable fire of Phyllida Warburton's sexuality to deal with it.

Steven proved impossible to isolate. George was unsure whether this was deliberate or not: he knew very little about his father's working routine. The only time when George could hope to catch him on his own was when he was walking between The House and the yard, and, as often as not, Abraham Merriweather was with him. Inside The House, Steven was always with Leander or Giles, inevitably engaged in earnest discussion of stable business.

On the fourth day of his stay, George found himself having lunch with Steven and Leander. Giles was in the yard, attending to a horse with a strained tendon, Amelia had been driven into Marlborough by Cyril Osgood to meet two horse-mad school-friends who were coming to spend part of their holiday at Latimer's Barn.

While the meal was in progress, Steven and Leander discussed a strongly worded directive sent out by the Jockey Club to all owners and trainers. After several years of controversy, the practice of administering artificial stimulants to horses was being outlawed.

"You think all this doping is the American influence?" Leander asked Steven.

"Almost certainly," he replied. "Apparently they do it all the time over there. Everyone believes that Wishard is permanently as guilty as sin." Enoch Wishard was an American trainer operating from stables near Newmarket under the auspices of two millionaire fellow countrymen. "It's spreading, too," Steven went on. "English trainers are doing it. Both Harold Weston's horses at Royal Ascot were doped up to the eyeballs."

Leander nodded: she remembered the bewildered outrage when the two animals, with not a shred of form between them, had won prestige races.

"I presume these drugs can be detected?" she asked.

"Oh, yes. It all comes out in a blood test. I've no idea how they're going to do it. Personally, I'd like to see every winner tested on the spot, but there's no indication that they intend going that far."

"What will they do if they find drugs in a horse?"

"Fine the trainer a few pounds, I suppose," Steven said.

"That doesn't sound too frightening."

"It isn't." Steven paused to clear his plate. "There's hope of better things to come, though. Last time I was at Newmarket, all the talk was of licences for trainers. Everyone reckoned that it's coming soon."

"Ah!" Leander looked pleased. "That's very overdue."

278

"It is. You know what your father used to say: they should have done it twenty-five years ago when they licensed jockeys."

"Then they can make doping a serious offence?"

"*If* the Jockey Club is prepared to revoke licences, we shall be on the way to getting the business cleaned up."

George listened, taking it all in without being very interested. Even if his mind were not full of his own troubles, it would never have occurred to him to consider how far his father, the young man from the boat-yard, had progressed: Steven Hawksworth was at the peak of his profession, a much-respected trainer, demanding the outlawing of malpractice, yet sceptical of the governing body's resolve.

It came as a shock to George to discover that Steven, having said his piece, was staring at him with a look of mild speculation on his face.

"Well, George," Steven said, "we might as well have it out. What's the trouble?"

"Trouble? Er . . . I don't know what you mean, Father."

"You want something, George. That's the only reason you're here. Tell us, then you can stop hanging around and making the lads feel uncomfortable."

Although Steven's voice remained calm, his manner was incisive: there was to be no nonsense.

George betrayed himself by shooting an apprehensive glance at Leander.

"Your mother needs to know, as well, George," Steven said.

George hesitated, faced the fact that he had no choice and took a deep breath. "Well, the fact is . . . you see, I've got myself into a bit of a hole."

Steven and Leander both stared at him with expressionless faces. There was neither word nor gesture to make it easier for him.

"I owe some money and the fellows concerned are getting impatient. Actually, they're threatening to make things very difficult."

"How much?" Steven asked.

"I'm afraid it's rather a great deal, sir."

"How much?"

"One thousand eight hundred pounds."

"Is this some kind of joke, George?" There was an edge on Steven's voice.

"No, sir. I wish to God it was!"

Leander saw that George was genuinely distressed, but her face remained fixed.

"How have you acquired this debt?" Steven's calmness was becoming ominous.

279

George lowered his eyes. "Gambling," he said in a voice that was barely audible.

"Gambling!" Leander had not meant to speak; the word seemed to have shot from her by the force of its own will. She looked at Steven, saw that he was displeased and blushed, inclining her head apologetically. George was startled: were some of his assumptions wrong? Was his father master of Latimer's Barn after all?

"Tell me about this gambling," Steven said.

"It was cards, sir."

"Cards?"

"Yes. Baccarat."

Steven smiled ironically. "I might have known it wouldn't be horses," he said. "Who are the people to whom you are in debt? Are they undergraduates?"

"Yes, sir. One of them is Lord Truro's son."

Steven took his time thinking about it and his eventual question surprised George.

"Have you decided what you will be doing after Oxford?"

"Yes. I'm going to work for Blayne-Singer's."

"That's settled, is it?"

"It is, sir."

"Providing Lord Truro's son doesn't queer your pitch?"

"That is a big worry," George agreed.

"We mustn't have that," Steven said. "If you let me have the addresses of the two gentlemen, I will see that they are paid."

"Can't I have the money and settle it?" George asked. To Leander's astonishment, he had the gall to sound petulant.

"No, George, you cannot!" Steven replied and showed no inclination to offer an explanation.

"Very well, sir. Er . . . thank you."

"That's quite all right, George. I'm sure you'll pardon me for asking, but are you at all sorry for this mess?" Steven looked and sounded faintly bewildered by it all.

"Well, yes . . . in a sense, I suppose I am."

"In a sense! What the devil does that mean, eh? You grace us with your presence to tell us that you've lost nearly as much playing cards as your grandfather paid for this whole estate, and the best you can do is say you're sorry – 'in a sense'!"

George was not alone in recoiling from the outburst: Leander had never for a moment imagined that Steven was capable of such anger.

George opened his mouth to speak, then thought better of it. Steven was on his feet, walking towards a window. He stood looking across the lawn towards the stable-blocks for a long time. When he turned back to George, he was in control of himself again.

"I have no idea what Sir Reginald Blayne-Singer is going to do with you," he said. "On the evidence of this miserable business, I think the man's a complete and utter fool if he lets you anywhere near money. However, that's up to him."

Steven walked back to the table to stand behind the chair in which he had been sitting. "You'll be twenty-one next year, George," he went on. "That's the time to think about making you an estate Trustee. To save you worrying about it, I'll tell you here and now that you will *not* be receiving an invitation to join the Partnership. If any of the others suggest it, I shall block it. You are not fit to be involved in running Cannings Ambo and *that* is final."

George looked stunned: it had simply not occurred to him that he would be denied Trusteeship.

"I take it that you will be leaving now you've got what you came for," Steven said to George. "Be sure to leave those addresses. And understand this, George. If you land yourself in trouble again, don't expect me to bale you out. Is that perfectly clear?"

"Yes, sir."

There was silence after Steven had gone.

"My word," Leander said eventually. "I have *never* seen your father so angry, George."

She went to the window. As Steven left The House, the way he walked and the set of his shoulders showed that he was still in a very bad mood. But half-way to the yard he met Giles; they exchanged a few words at which Steven burst out laughing while Giles assumed the rather comical expression that came over him when he had made a profound discovery about a horse.

Turning towards George, Leander knew there was something she had to say. Taking a seat opposite him, she clasped her hands together on the table and stared at him steadily.

"I must be honest with you, George," she said. "What your father just said about not making you a Trustee came as a great surprise to me. But . . ." she held up a hand to stop him interrupting, ". . . but, he's saved me a job I wasn't particularly looking forward to. You see, *I* intended voting against you when the time came."

George nodded. "Well, thank you for telling me, Mother," he said. "It's what I was expecting." He smiled, rather sadly, Leander thought. "I wouldn't have misused the Fund, you know."

"I never thought you would, but there's much more to it than that, George. It's a very great responsibility as well as an honour to be a Trustee of this place, and, quite bluntly, I know you're not up to it. For one thing, you don't care enough about the village, do you?"

"No, Mother, I'm afraid I don't."

"I could never trust you to say and do the right thing," Leander said. "You wouldn't want to milk the Fund, but you might well develop some rather unpleasant ideas as to what should happen to this estate in twenty or thirty years' time. I'm not allowing that! I'm not even prepared to risk it."

"I understand, Mother."

"I'm very much afraid that you don't, George, otherwise we should not be having this conversation. Now, look, I'm sure you'll make a go of banking. Will you try?"

"Yes."

"Make sure you do. For God's sake do your best and be sensible. Choose your company carefully from now on."

"I will."

They stood up. It was all over.

"I shall see that your allowance is maintained for as long as you need it," Leander said. "I might even try to get an increase so that you can be more comfortable."

"That's kind of you."

Two hours later, George was in a London-bound train from Savernake. At Newbury, he looked at his watch and shook himself out of the depressed state of mind that had haunted him since Freddie Truro had turned nasty over the money. He would be in London in time for dinner with Alec, after which, they might go to a show. A couple of days of that would be an excellent preparation for the wanton exertions that awaited him at Runcton Hall.

Steven stayed away from The House until half past six when evening stables were finished.

"Has George gone?" he asked Leander as he bathed before dinner.

"He has. Almost straight away."

"You didn't go soft on him?"

"No, sweetheart, I did not! I told him that if you hadn't stopped him being a Trustee, I would have done."

Steven was reflective as Leander scrubbed his back. "I'll tell you something that's bound to surprise you," he said.

"What's that?"

"I'm pretty sure you and I made up our minds about George at exactly the same time."

"And when might that have been?"

"The day of your father's funeral. Do you remember, when he and Maude were skulking round like a pair of mischief-makers?"

"You're right. I am surprised," Leander said.

"There you are, you see, I'm not as green as I'm cabbage-looking! By the way, I think we should go for a swim tomorrow if this weather holds."

"I thought you were taking a horse to Bath."

"Giles has asked to go. Insisted on it!"

"Will he be all right?" Leander asked uncertainly.

"He'll have Peter Izzard and Conn with him," Steven replied. "Don't you think he's up to it?"

It was a deliberately teasing remark to which Leander responded by climbing into the bath.

To avoid misunderstanding, Steven made the announcement at the earliest opportunity, the September meeting of the Trustees.

"There is something quite important," he said when they reached the stage of considering any other business. "George comes of age next year, and I assume we might have been thinking of giving him a seat round this table. However, I have to tell you that I shall not be putting his name forward. In my view, it would be quite inappropriate to do so."

"I agree with that," Leander added firmly.

Jim Goakes looked very surprised, Alexandra, who was hosting the meeting at The Hall, less so. William and Ruth had already been warned. Abraham Merriweather did his best not to look relieved.

"You will want Giles to be a Trustee, Steven?" Alexandra asked.

"Of course. And Amelia when the time comes."

William fell into step beside Leander as they walked back towards Rose House along the village street.

"It's still a bad business once it finally happens, isn't it?" William said.

"I'm afraid so, my dear." Leander was unusually tense: she had not enjoyed a process that was tantamount to disowning her eldest son.

"There's one thing, though," William said. "I suppose it's created a precedent, and I shan't have to be the first."

"Maude?" Leander asked quietly.

"Yes." William took a few paces in unhappy silence. "Things might improve. Ruth keeps telling me that Maude's at a difficult age."

"Any age is difficult," Leander said, attempting to lighten the gloom.

"It certainly seems so with Maude," William replied. "I don't think

283

she is going to grow out of it, Lea. As a matter of fact, I think she's a complete wrong 'un."

Distressing though the news was, Leander felt grateful for it: at least William knew.

Abraham Merriweather was wondering when he should retire. He was only sixty-four, and as sound in wind and limb as the day he had come to Latimer's Barn twenty-six years ago. Nevertheless, after fifty years of hard work which he had loved so much that he had hardly ever taken a day off, Alice was saying it was time he put his feet up to watch the world go by.

The heir-apparent was firmly in place. In 1901, Abraham's eldest son, Albert, startled everyone by marrying at the ripe old age of twenty-eight. No one had the vaguest idea how Albert could possibly have met and wooed his wife, a delightful girl called Grace Thomson who came from West Lavington, all of fifteen miles away on the other side of Devizes. Within the year, Albert and Grace had a son whom they called Alfred, and they were living in a new house at the end of the drive, opposite Abraham and Alice.

A week after Alfred Merriweather was born, Fred Cartwright and Tish presented Abraham with a second grandson, Ernest. The two babies shared a christening with Leander as godmother to them both.

"Let's pray for one thing," she said afterwards as she stood in the front parlour of Abraham's house, a sleeping baby cradled in each arm. "If the Lord is good to us, we have a head lad and a furniture salesman here to take us well past our first hundred years."

Abraham drank to it, realising that he must not leave it too long before he stood aside to give Albert a chance to show what he could do, so paving the way for the three-week-old Alfred.

Steven never raised the subject: he was far too used to the idea of Abraham being in the prime of life and completely in control of a difficult job. It came as a surprise to him when Abraham said one day, "If it's all right with you, sir, I'd like to retire in two years."

It was a hazy afternoon in the middle of October: Steven and Abraham were leaning on the fence of the paddock at the stud, inspecting six yearlings shortly to enter training.

"Are you sure, Abraham?" Steven asked. "I reckon you've got a good few years left in you."

"And Alice says I ought to spend 'em in the garden," Abraham said. "Albert will see you right."

"Oh, I know he will," Steven said. "Leander keeps telling me how lucky I am to have him – not that I need any telling, mind."

"So, is that all right?" Abraham said tentatively.

"If that's what you want, that's what we'll do," Steven replied. After a thoughtful pause, he asked, "Why two years?"

Abraham smiled. "Because I want to handle that fellow." He pointed to a handsome chestnut colt who was regarding them with great interest.

"Ah, Mrs Fandine-Browne's beauty," Steven said.

"That's right, sir."

The chestnut was by Alexandra's much-loved Long Barrow out of her own mare, Saxon Princess. His name, The Atheling, was the title always given to the eldest son of the ancient Saxon royal house, the equivalent of the Prince of Wales.

"You think he's going to be good?" Steven asked.

Abraham nodded, staring into space as though he were forming his opinion all over again from scratch. "It wouldn't surprise me if he didn't turn out to be the best horse you've ever had," he said at last.

CHAPTER 17

1905

'. . . cross her and by God you'll pay for it'

All trainers were required to apply for licences in January. A week after the closing date, the sporting press reported that the first of the coveted licences were being sent out. They were, it was said, for the well-established trainers of repute, men beyond reproach, about whom questions were unnecessary. Nothing came to Latimer's Barn.

At the end of February, Leander insisted that Steven write to the Jockey Club to ask what had become of his licence. The precious document came by return of post with an apology for the administrative oversight apparently responsible for the delay. Leander continued to worry. She found herself obsessed by the idea that Rothwell, now *Sir* Walter Rothwell and well up the ladder of Newmarket influence, had attempted to block their application. The looks that Rothwell gave her whenever their paths crossed on a racecourse indicated that he had not forgotten her rejection of him: the thought of an unseen enemy seeking spiteful revenge sometimes made Leander's flesh creep.

But The Atheling was a great diversion.

The public thought he was invincible after his two-year-old campaign of 1904. Undefeated in five appearances, including the Coventry Stakes at Royal Ascot, he rounded off the season to Leander's great satisfaction with a runaway victory in the Dewhurst Plate that left the opposition looking worse than ordinary.

While the 'experts' spent the winter predicting that the Triple Crown of 1905 already belonged to Latimer's Barn, Leander walked the colt every day and worried.

The transition from precocious juvenile to champion three-year-old was the most notoriously difficult journey in the whole of racing. The annals were littered with thousands of horses who had failed to make it, often for reasons that remained a complete mystery to their trainers: Latimer's Barn had known more than thirty cases of bitter disappointment. All that Leander could do was watch The Atheling like a hawk, hope and worry.

On a day in early March, Leander took a deep breath, closed her eyes and prayed. For two weeks, the colt had been cantering a few furlongs every other day and adjusting to a working diet. Now the time had come to let him down and gallop him.

Steven and Abraham Merriweather, watching through binoculars, knew at once that everything was going to be all right. Within a few strides, long before The Atheling had worked up to anything like top speed, they saw a happy grin spread across Leander's face as she got the feel of him.

"We've done it," Steven said. "He looks wonderful!"

Abraham waited until the colt had covered two furlongs before passing his judgement. "I reckon his action's improved. He's more compact."

As a two-year-old, The Atheling had galloped in an extravagant fashion, tending to carry his head high and throw his forelegs about in a spectacular but wasteful display of exuberance. All that was gone; he had grown up and decided to use himself more sensibly.

Working with him was absolute joy that drove all thoughts of Rothwell from Leander's mind: as spring advanced, the weeks sped by in a fever of excitement and expectation.

At the end of April, Alexandra, seventy-five and a little tired, but otherwise showing little sign of her age, went to Newmarket with Steven and Leander to see her colt race in the Two Thousand Guineas. With Michael Pilgrim providing no more than occasional guidance, The Atheling never gave them a moment's anxiety. He fairly flew along the Rowley Mile, was never headed, and had the opposition off the bridle in desperation by the time he passed the Bushes, two furlongs from home. His new record time carried his owner into the history books with him. Sadly, Leander thought, the crowd of *aficionados* at Newmarket, still steeped in nineteenth-century tradition, gave only modest recognition to the fact that Mrs Alexandra Fandine-Browne became the first woman to own the winner of a Classic race.

In the winner's enclosure afterwards, Leander saw that Alexandra was close to tears and knew that she was thinking of that awful day when it seemed that Long Barrow might have to be put down: eleven years later, his son was being hailed as the best Guineas winner since the brilliant New Invention in 1868.

Sir Dugdale Brodie, the Senior Steward, was among the first to offer his congratulations.

"You see, there is justice in life," he said.

"What *do* you mean, Sir Dugdale?"

"My dear Leander, I've been saying it for years – if a lady ever were to win a Classic, there was only one stable the animal could come from!"

Next day, Steven smiled at the way Leander looked as they neared the end of their train journey back to Marlborough.

"I know what you'll be doing the minute we get in," he said.

"What?"

"The Big Book!"

She feigned surprise. "Oh, yes! I suppose I ought to put something in it!"

There was another entry for the Big Book two weeks later.

After three years of planning and preparation, Newbury racecourse opened. Half a mile east of the town, it was intended to be a major attraction, and the Great Western Railway built a station to serve it. It was barely twenty miles from Latimer's Barn, so, on the inaugural day's racing, Steven and Leander went with three horses.

On a sparkling May afternoon, a large part of the crowd felt that it would be perfectly right and proper for the very first winner to come from the stables of the great John Porter of Kingsclere who had been the driving force behind the development of the new course. Now sixty-seven, Porter had announced his intention of retiring at the end of the season, terminating one of the most distinguished careers that the Turf had ever seen. He had trained the winners of twenty-three Classics, including an incredible seven Derby heroes, the jewel of whom was the legendary Ormonde.

No, it was not asking too much of Fortune that she should give John Porter that first ever winner on 'his' course.

With the race at the two-furlong marker, the stage seemed set for the dream to come true: John Porter's horse moved into an effortless lead and it seemed all over bar the shouting. But against the background of the happy buzz from the crowd, Steven muttered, "Oh dear!"

Leander squeezed his hand and grinned impishly. She, too, was aware of the relentless progress being made by Tangent, carrying the Duke of Laverstoke's azure and gold silks. Michael Pilgrim, instructed to see what he could do with a horse who was something of an unknown quantity because of his aversion to exerting himself at home, had his own ideas on how the race should be run.

Once Tangent was on terms, the last furlong developed into a ding-dong battle that set the crowd on a knife edge until Tangent gained the upper hand in the last few strides.

"It's no good looking like that," Leander told Steven. "We always run our horses to win, remember."

"H'm. It would have been nice if Mr Porter's horse had won it, though," Steven said, affected by the uncontrolled disappointment from the packed grandstand.

"Stuff and nonsense!" Leander retorted. "It doesn't matter what that lot think, *he* doesn't mind. Look!"

As the horses were led in from the course, John Porter raised his hat to Leander and gave an almost imperceptible nod of approval. Although his taciturn, humourless approach to life was a byword, he was a thoroughgoing sportsman and gentleman.

There was still no motor vehicle in Cannings Ambo, so Steven and Leander had travelled to Newbury by carriage and train, the journey taking what Steven thought was a rather tiresome two hours. After Tangent's success, another of the Latimer's Barn horses won the third race, putting Leander in such good humour that she accepted the Duke of Laverstoke's offer of a lift home in his new car.

"I can see a bright future for us here," she said as they set out. "This is going to be our lucky course." After a mile or so, having noticed the quiet smoothness of the ride, she said, "I have to confess that this new machine of yours doesn't seem too bad, Hubert. What is it?"

"It's made in Manchester by a chap called Henry Royce," the Duke replied. "I believe he used to work for some railway company or other, so you should feel safe, Leander."

"It seems to be going along quite nicely."

"Oh, it does. I wouldn't be surprised if we didn't get you home in less than an hour."

His Grace was quite right: having left Newbury at five, they reached Latimer's Barn at a few minutes to six, just as Giles was going to the yard for the evening stables inspection. Steven noticed Leander look at her watch and pull a face to herself, but was careful to say nothing.

She broached the subject when they had their feet up with a cup of tea.

"You know, sweetheart, that journey up to Newbury this morning was an awful waste of time, don't you think?" she said.

"A little boring," he said non-committally.

"I mean, that course is virtually on our doorstep, yet it took us two hours to get there."

"Easier coming back," Steven pointed out in the most neutral voice he could muster.

"Yes. Do you think we could get more done if we had one of those motors?"

"Yes, I imagine we could. I suppose we do have better things to do than be waiting for trains all the time."

"Most definitely! I think you ought to look into this, sweetheart. We must move with the times, you know!"

Steven smiled to himself, not in the least put out by the suggestion that he had somehow been impeding progress: he also had the treat of telling William that the motor car was no longer banned in Cannings Ambo.

"It seems to me that it's a hell of a shame you don't get on with your people, George," Alec Blayne-Singer said.

"Why?"

"We'd get some awfully good tips for the gee-gees. That second winner at Newbury the other day strolled in at ten to one, if you please."

It was Saturday afternoon. Their work in Sir Reginald's bank was finished for the week and they were lounging in their Kensington flat.

"I believe they don't always know when horses are going to win," George said. "I would imagine that pair at Newbury were a bit of a surprise." Nearly two years on from earning Steven's wrath, George's views on Latimer's Barn had mellowed considerably, albeit mostly as a consequence of his very satisfactory life-style.

"I can handle surprises like that," Alec replied wistfully. "Tell me, why don't you go down there and suck up to them? The place must be awash with money."

George shook his head. "No good, Alec. The old man might swallow it, but Mother wouldn't – not in a thousand years."

"Your mother's a pretty tough egg, isn't she?"

"Yes, I suppose you could say that." George's rueful smile was tinged with admiration.

"But she writes regularly and sends you a good allowance."

"That's only to make sure I never go near the place," George said facetiously, trying to make light of it.

"It's a rum do," Alec said, baffled. "You've always hated it, haven't you? I remember when we were kids at Winchester, you went on blind about the place."

"It's the horses, Alec. They put the fear of God into me. I can't stand the brutes. I shall be glad when they get them off the streets."

"There's a good few years to wait for that, my boy. Motoring's damned expensive. The governor nearly split a gusset when he found out what the cars at Runcton are costing. And we can do without the stink of the things – especially on a day like this."

London was wickedly hot. While George stared idly at his newspaper, Alec was unfastening his tie and stiff collar.

"Tell you what, let's get out of it," Alec said brightly. "Why don't we run down to Farnborough and tantalise those two girls we met at Archie's party?"

"Sorry, old man, I'm spoken for. I shall have to be making a move soon."

"Oh!" Alec looked crestfallen. "Celia again?"

"That's right."

"Is her husband *never* at home?"

"I keep telling you, Alec, he's a very busy man."

"God! Some people have all the luck."

George laughed and went to his bedroom.

Half an hour later he reappeared dressed as the country gentleman and carrying an overnight bag. Alec, now surrounded by rumpled newspapers, looked at him morosely.

"Not back until tomorrow evening?" he asked.

"Correct!" George looked insufferably well pleased with himself: whatever regrets he might have been experiencing about his parents and Cannings Ambo were gone.

"By the way," Alec said, "all these papers think there's nothing to stop The Atheling winning the Derby."

"They're probably right," George replied. "Mother spoke very highly of him in her last letter. But don't expect to get decent odds on him, Alec. He's likely to be the hottest favourite for years."

George took a cab to Paddington and boarded a train to Maidenhead where he would change for Marlow. He spared a last thought for his friend, spending a weekend alone in London in sweltering weather.

And George derived considerable satisfaction from the fact that Alec could not possibly suspect one-thousandth part of what went on at Marlow. A lady called Celia *was* indeed the focal point of his activities, but to believe that he was entertaining another bored wife was a gross over-simplification of what went on at Hartford House, the gracious residence whose gardens sloped down to the River Thames.

Celia's husband was always busy and if, as everyone expected, he became Home Secretary after the next election, he would be busier still.

Leander's preparation of The Atheling for the Derby was unaffected by an incident that could well have been a major cause of disruption. Even people well used to her methods were surprised by what she took in her stride in less than twenty-four hours.

It began one afternoon over tea with Rupert Timberlake. Rupert was paying his regular weekly visit to Latimer's Barn to look at his horses and, on this particular occasion, Leander was especially pleased to see him since Steven and Giles were away at Newmarket for a few days.

They talked first about the latest developments in the naval arms race, the building of HMS *Dreadnought*.

"What's this one supposed to be able to do, Rupert?" Leander asked wearily.

"Blow everything else out of the water at a range of ten miles," he replied.

"And will it?"

Rupert spent several minutes explaining that *Dreadnought* was a turbine-powered floating gun-carriage, equipped with the most formidable guns in rotating turrets. "So it sounds as though it might do the job," he concluded.

"Until Germany starts building them?"

"Correct!"

"Pah!"

Rupert lapsed into silence after Leander's expression of annoyance: he looked fixedly at his hands for a few moments, then gave her the suggestive look she knew so well.

"Come on, Rupert, spit it out!" she ordered.

"I've been hearing funny stories," he said.

"What about?"

"A friend of mine up in Yorkshire breeds horses – nothing too grand, just half a dozen brood mares. He does it as a hobby more than anything else. There's another fellow near Peterborough who's a little more serious about it. Takes yearlings to various sales."

"Go on, Rupert!" Leander was irritated by his hesitant way of embarking upon an important subject.

"In the last few weeks, both my friends have been approached by a man offering the services of good stallions at greatly reduced fees – fifty guineas instead of two hundred."

"Which stallions?" Leander asked.

"Several. Hypotenuse and Long Barrow were among them."

"I see." Leander gazed thoughtfully out of a window, impressing him with her calmness.

"What would be the point of such a stunt?" Rupert asked. "If someone's slipping mares into the stud like that, they could hardly claim that the foal was sired by Hypotenuse or Long Barrow, could they?"

"No." Leander had to work it out as she went. "Let me see . . . they would most likely forge a certificate naming a very moderate stallion as the sire . . . preferably an animal hardly anyone knows." She nodded to herself. "There is every chance that the foal will turn out to be much better than his breeding suggests. After a couple of races to demonstrate how mediocre he is, they could then win something with him *at long odds*. I think it's a betting job, Rupert." She raised a hand for silence while she carried on thinking. "It's probably immensely complicated to operate. As well as a supply of decent mares, I think they'd need a trainer who was none too straight."

"And a great deal of patience," Rupert said.

"Oh, yes, the people who are looking after the foal will have to wait two or three years," Leander said. "I'm not bothered about them. I want the man who is organising it." Sensing what was coming, Rupert felt uncomfortable. "When did you last check on my friend Mr Sixsmith?" Leander asked.

"Not for eighteen months, I'm afraid."

"It may be time you had another look at him." It sounded no more than a suggestion.

"Of course, straight away!" Rupert hesitated before asking, "How is your man at the stud getting away with this?"

"What, Ruddock? I'm afraid we've been trusting him, Rupert. To be honest with you, I've forgotten when Steven or I last went down there."

"What about his assistant?"

"Eph Wilkins is rather simple. He'd do whatever Ruddock told him without question."

"Do you want to know about the other stallions that appear to be involved?" Rupert asked.

"No, I don't think so," Leander said thoughtfully. "Let's not even think of starting a scandal. If I can nip this in the bud, the odds are that the business will cave in."

No one would have guessed that Leander's mind was furiously occupied with another, pressing, topic as she deputised for Steven and Giles at evening stables. Several lads received a ticking-off for poor grooming of their charges and two were hauled over the coals for sloppiness in their own personal appearance.

At the end of her tour, when she nodded to indicate that they were free to go to their homes or the hostel, only Abraham Merriweather saw Leander beckon to Conn Daly with her eyes.

"Will you spare me a few minutes, Conn?" she said quietly as he moved unobtrusively to her side.

When Conn left fifteen minutes later, he was under strict instructions not to breathe a word to a living soul, not even to Sally, who would have welcomed some warning of her imminent move to a bigger house.

Later, when she knew that he would have finished his meal, Leander went down the drive to talk to Abraham.

Cyril Osgood thought that six o'clock on a fine May morning was just about the best time to be alive: his night watch on the yard was finished, and he had twenty minutes to himself before Abraham turned up to set the day's routine in motion. He went to his cubby-hole in the old coach-house, where the kettle had been singing for an hour or more, and made a pot of tea.

No sooner had he sat down than he was on his feet again, startled.

"Mrs Hawksworth, ma'am!" Her approach had been swift and silent.

"It's all right, Cyril, don't upset yourself," she said. "Is there a cup for me?"

He watched her as she took the first eager sips. She wore breeches and boots, a plain cotton blouse and the old canvas jacket they said she'd had since she was a slip of a girl.

"There's a job I have to do," she said. "I want you to come with me, Cyril."

"Of course, ma'am."

She said no more until the tea was finished and he was looking at her expectantly.

"We're going to the stud," she said. "We'll walk."

Rather than go down the drive to the Devizes Lane, Leander took the shorter direct route across the gallop. It took Cyril Osgood the best part of three furlongs to pluck up the courage to ask a question that had been bothering him for days.

"Beg pardon, ma'am, but is it true that The Atheling is going to win the Derby?"

Leander laughed. "If only I knew, Cyril, if only I knew! He's certainly good enough and I want him to do well for Mrs Fandine-Browne's sake. He certainly won't disgrace us."

"I think I might venture a little flutter," Cyril said, convinced that he had Leander's personal guarantee of success.

"Be quick about it, then. I believe the best odds you can get now are six to four. That price is bound to shorten."

"I'll bear that in mind, ma'am."

Ten minutes later, they breasted the rise that gave them a view of the stud. Leander stopped, frowning at the wide-open main gates.

"I have reason to believe that there may be something badly wrong here, Cyril," she said. "I am going to do my best to put it right. It may be whimsical of me, but I suppose there is a possibility I may be attacked."

Cyril Osgood bristled angrily and drew himself up to his massive full height. "That'll be over my dead body, ma'am," he growled.

Leander nodded. "Thank you, Cyril. Come on, let's get cracking."

It was exactly a quarter to seven when Leander strode in through the gates. At first, everything seemed quiet; then she heard sounds of mucking out and caught a glimpse of Eph Wilkins in Long Barrow's box. Turning quickly, she caught the guilty twitch of a curtain in the house occupied by Sam Ruddock and his wife, Ethel.

As Leander moved towards the house, the front door opened and Ruddock appeared in breeches and shirt, his face half-covered in lather, the razor still in his hand.

"Mrs Hawksworth, this *is* a surprise," he said. Whatever his feelings, he was gushingly pleasant.

"Good morning, Sam," Leander replied. "I thought it was high time I paid you a visit. I'm afraid we've neglected you shamefully. Look, don't let me keep you from getting ready: I can amuse myself until you've finished."

Ruddock had to accept what she said, but his eyes dwelt suspiciously on Cyril Osgood. "Very well, ma'am, I'll be as quick as I can," he said and scuttled back indoors.

Cyril had to break into a trot to keep up with Leander as she made towards the boxes where the mares were kept, as far as possible from the stallions and well screened by trees.

"Right!" she muttered to herself after she had opened all the doors and counted the still-drowsy occupants: all but one of the twelve boxes were occupied. They had four mares of their own, the other seven were visitors.

Arriving with his face red from exertion, Sam Ruddock made the mistake that precipitated the confrontation. "Mrs Hawksworth," he blustered, trying to use attack as defence, "what are you doing *here*?"

Leander was in no hurry to answer him. Instead, she gave him a look which Cyril Osgood described in The George that night as, "Fit to shrivel the balls off him."

Eventually, Leander gave Sam Ruddock his answer. "I own the place," she said. "Or had you forgotten that?"

The lash of her remark left him trailing behind her as she set off at top speed, straight towards his house and in through the door.

"There are seven visiting mares out there," she snapped. "I want them accounted for. Get the book!"

"There's no need for that, Sam, you'll only look a bigger fool!" Ethel Ruddock, a sour-looking woman at the best of times, glared venomously at Leander.

"Ethel . . . please!" Ruddock pleaded.

"Don't be so damned silly!" his wife spat at him. "She knows, don't you Mrs-clever-clogs-high-and-bloody-mighty-Hawksworth?"

Cyril Osgood, who was feeling badly out of place in the confines of the entrance hall, winced at the resounding crack of Leander's hand across Ethel Ruddock's face. The woman staggered back, dazed and frightened.

"How many?" Leander demanded. "How many of those mares are your fifty-guinea specials?"

"Five," Ruddock muttered.

"Have they had service?"

"No, ma'am, not yet."

"Has anyone paid anything for them?"

"No. The money was collected afterwards."

"And how long has this been going on?"

"It's the second year."

Leander looked at each of the Ruddocks in turn: they both averted their eyes. Even Cyril Osgood felt scared of her.

"Tell me," Leander said, quiet now, "how much do we pay you?"

"Five pounds a week, Mrs Hawksworth," Ruddock mumbled.

"And the house," his desperate wife added.

Leander turned towards the door. "Come along, Cyril," she said. "We'll wait outside."

She flung herself down on the lawn, drawing her knees up under her chin.

"What the devil are we supposed to make of folks like that, Cyril?" she asked. "Five pounds a week, a good house and they rob us blind."

"It's very bad," an awestruck Cyril replied.

Leander looked up at him and smiled. "Never mind, we've stopped it. Make yourself comfortable."

"What are we waiting for?" he asked when he was seated beside her.

"Conn," she said, leaving him none the wiser.

Cyril decided to turn round so that he was facing the house, glaring at the Ruddocks who were peering from a window with fear and bewilderment. It did not take them long to creep away, and for the next half-hour, nothing happened. Eph Wilkins left the stallion boxes and set off towards the mares. If he noticed Leander and Cyril sitting on the Ruddocks' lawn, he gave no sign of it.

When they heard the rumble of cart wheels announcing the arrival of Conn, Cyril asked, "How do you reckon he was getting those mares here without us knowing? You'd think we'd have seen 'em coming through the village and wondered what was going on."

"No, Cyril, they'd come that way," Leander told him, pointing south, away from Cannings Ambo. "There's the railway at Devizes, you see."

Conn was driving a flat cart. He was accompanied by three of the lads on hacks and the Marlborough Black Maria driven by the formidable Sergeant Hopkins with two constables in attendance. Now that he saw the extent of Leander's planning, Cyril gaped.

Leander sprang to her feet and called out to the police van.

"They did it all right, Sergeant. They've admitted it."

"So you want them locking up, Mrs Hawksworth?"

"Yes, please. I'll come to the station as soon as possible to prefer charges."

The Ruddocks were stupefied. They had reached the conclusion that they were to be sent packing and had already gathered the most important of their belongings. The possibility of arrest, trial and imprisonment had simply not occurred to them.

As the Black Maria went away, Ethel Ruddock screamed abuse from the back window: Leander turned her back on it and addressed herself to Conn, Cyril and the three lads.

"Take all the furniture out of this house," she ordered. "I suppose you'd better put it somewhere under cover for the time being . . . find a shed. Conn, I want you and Sally moved in by tonight. Cyril, you'll be here for two weeks. Sooner or later, people are going to come for those mares and there might be trouble. You have my permission to deal with it!"

"Yes, ma'am!" Cyril was delighted.

"Eph Wilkins can stay here, Conn. I don't think he's the faintest idea what the Ruddocks were up to and he certainly wasn't part of it. Would someone fetch Eph so that I can tell him what's going on?"

Half an hour later, Leander took one of the hacks and rode back to Latimer's Barn. In the pocket of her canvas jacket, she carried Sam Ruddock's bank book, found by Cyril in the mattress of an unused bedroom. The deposits recorded in it were enough to convict ten men.

"There's only one thing to be thankful for, Conn," she said as he gave her a leg-up on to the hack.

297

"What's that?"

"The Atheling wasn't due to work today. We'd never have managed *that* as well as this rumpus!"

They grinned at each other and she was gone.

Cyril Osgood got all his beer paid for in The George that night as the village gathered to hear the tale that needed no embellishment.

Martin Foxton senior, sixty-nine years old and looking a sprightly fifty, stood behind the bar, listening to it all in impassive silence.

"I always had it in mind that Sam Ruddock was a fool," he said when Cyril had finished.

"How's that then, Martin?" someone asked.

"Well, fancy him not being able to weigh Mrs Hawksworth up! Treat her right and she's the best friend a man could ever want, but cross her and by God you'll pay for it!"

"What I want to know is how she found out."

"Ah!" Martin looked knowing. "Mrs Hawksworth gets to hear of everything," he said. "And it's generally a damned sight quicker than this, I don't mind telling you. Why, the bugger had been at it for two years!"

The following day, Leander welcomed Steven and Giles back home and listened patiently to their hard-luck stories. Both their horses had been beaten by the narrowest of margins, and, as Leander had already learned from *The Sporting Life*, one of the decisions was highly dubious.

"Still, it's no use crying over spilt milk," Steven said at last. "We must grin and bear it and try again. I suppose everything has been quiet here, my dear?"

Leander looked at him with a perfectly straight face. "More or less," she said. "There was one thing I had to deal with."

They goggled at her, saucer-eyed, as she recounted the events at Cannings St John.

"And you've had the Ruddocks charged?" Steven asked.

"Yes, with stealing two thousand five hundred guineas from us," Leander said. "Poor old Hypotenuse and Long Barrow have had to serve an extra fifty mares in the last two breeding seasons."

"I don't suppose they minded," Steven said flippantly, causing Giles to smile.

Leander gave them a pained look. "The police have opposed bail because the Ruddocks will obviously disappear if they're given half a chance."

"So, they're locked up?"

"Yes. They'll be tried at the assizes."

"And I've lost Conn?"

"I'm afraid so, sweetheart."

"What does Sally think about it all?" asked Steven, unable to imagine how even a dyed-in-the-wool Cannings Ambo-ite like Conn's wife had coped with the upheaval.

"I suppose it was all a bit sudden," Leander conceded. "But the house is much nicer, of course, and she'll soon be straight. Alexandra is organising a sewing party to make curtains for her."

"And Conn?"

"I don't think he minds too much. He looks on it as a great honour and I'm giving him six pounds a week."

Steven nodded his approval of the princely wage and said, "We must make sure we go down there to see him as often as possible."

"We must, indeed," Leander agreed. "Conn won't rob us, but he'd welcome the support."

How, everybody asked, would The Atheling win the Derby?

There were no 'ifs' or 'buts' about it, just *how*, in what manner would he accomplish it? His penchant for front-running, for jumping into an immediate lead and running the rest ragged while he dictated the terms of the race, was well known. Was that how it was to be at Epsom, or would a brilliant new tactic be devised to help him through the supreme test?

In all the thousands of speculative words written and spoken about him, no one mentioned the nerve-wracking trait that he had only ever displayed once, during his debut a year previously. The Atheling was capable of becoming so interested in his surroundings that he forgot to take the race seriously.

Not many people had seen him do it at Salisbury; there were half a million to watch his repeat performance on Epsom Downs.

"Oh dear," Steven muttered as the ten runners began the great swinging turn of Tattenham Corner. "Oh dear, oh dear!"

"Where is he?" Leander asked, momentarily unable to see.

"Last but one and going very wide. He would choose today, wouldn't he?"

"There are an awful lot of interesting things out there," Leander said, as if she were making excuses for a wayward yet much-loved child.

Steven ground his teeth and glared through the binoculars.

"What's happening now?" Alexandra asked, her anxiety mounting.

"He's just the same . . . Jardy has finished the turn now and his jockey's shaking him up . . he's going clear . . . two lengths already, I'd say."

"Oh dear!" Alexandra moaned, catching Steven's gloom.

"No! Look!" Leander cried. "Michael's getting him going."

Michael Pilgrim subsequently swore a solemn oath that he did no such thing: what happened, he said, was that The Atheling suddenly realised that he was in a rather important race, that he was making a mess of it and that it was about time he did something to improve matters.

"What's he doing?" Alexandra asked, responding to the crowd's first murmur of excitement.

"He's in the straight now," Steven said.

Leander climbed on to a seat. "He's passing the others," she said. "There's three done for . . . and Lord Rosebery's horse . . ." The satisfaction in her voice at *that* was tangible. "He's only got two in front of him now."

"Jardy still hasn't finished," Steven said, his knuckles white on the binoculars as the leading group passed the furlong marker.

For five seconds, the vast crowd fell silent until, with half a furlong to run, The Atheling got his nose in front. Then they cheered him every inch of the way as he turned it into a procession that ended with him four lengths clear of his nearest, badly tired, rival.

It was the first and only time that Steven ever saw Leander overcome by tension and agitation: she and Alexandra collapsed into each other's arms, laughing and sobbing.

"My dear, you've won the Derby," Alexandra said.

"My dear, so have *you*," Leander replied.

"Come along, you two," Steven said gently. "Let's go and lead him in."

Epsom, without the starchy, ingrained reserve of Newmarket, afforded Alexandra thunderous congratulations on being the first woman to own a Derby winner. Glued to her side in support, Leander found herself dangerously close to tears as she thought of her father.

Giles Flamsteed would have enjoyed this. He would, of course, have been exactly like the modest hero of the hour: The Atheling, at a loss to understand what all the fuss was about, was interested only in the possibility of finding sugar lumps in Alexandra's handbag.

Sadly, after five wonderfully happy years, Amelia left the Godolphin School in July. She did so amid a welter of promises to keep in touch with all her friends, most especially Miss Douglas and Miss Jones, both of whom were immensely proud of her. "She's a true daughter of Cannings Ambo," Miss Douglas told Leander at their farewell.

"Why do you say that?"

"She's our first girl to win an open scholarship to one of the universities. I rather gained the impression that you liked being first with things, Mrs Hawksworth."

"I do, Miss Douglas," Leander smiled. "I do, indeed."

What a summer it was! The award granted to Amelia by Girton College at Cambridge was regarded by many, including Leander, as more important than The Atheling's achievements.

"We shall win lots more Derbys," Leander told Steven after he had expressed surprise at her entry in the Big Book, "but I can't see us getting another open scholarship for a long time!"

For the first week of her holiday, Amelia was with Gerald in the workshop behind Rose House every day, coming home at seven o'clock with wood-shavings and sawdust in her hair.

"I hope Amelia isn't being a nuisance," Leander said when she met William and Jim Goakes as she was on her way to call on Ruth one morning.

"Nuisance!" William said, staring at her in amazement while Jim chuckled. "Amelia a nuisance? Lea, that girl's a genius! She saved us over fifty pounds the first day she was here."

"Good Lord! How?"

"We're doing another big contract for Henry Fletcher," Jim explained. "There's hundreds and hundreds of pieces to be cut out. Amelia took one look at the way we were doing it and told us we were wasting too much. 'All right,' I said, 'show us how.' So she gets cracking with a pencil and paper and inside the hour, she's done it!"

"Tell you what, though," William said. "I made the mistake of asking her how she'd worked it out."

"And?" Leander asked.

"We couldn't understand a word she said," Jim laughed. "She's up here somewhere." He held a hand high above his head.

Maude had gone to Cornwall for the summer; she was staying with a titled family to whom William had sold furniture. The lady of the house was much taken by Maude's painting, and insisted that Cornish light would bring her on in leaps and bounds. Maude lived for eight weeks as a pampered member of a family that spared itself no luxury, basking in the admiration her work attracted. Following her seventeenth birthday, she was moved to make a present of her virginity to the estate's eldest son and heir.

After making her improvements at the workshop and satisfied that

301

Gerald was happy, Amelia devoted most of her time to Giles. Now that the school-days that had forced them apart were past, they slipped back easily into the devoted closeness they had shared as children. Utterly incapable of assuming the merest vestige of style when she sat on a horse, Amelia nevertheless rode everywhere with Giles, loving every minute of it. Not once, in all their wide-ranging conversations, did they ever mention George.

As the September days shortened and the time for Cambridge drew near, Amelia approached Leander with uncharacteristic timidity.

"Mother, can I ask you a big favour?"

"Ask away, darling."

"Do you think you could possibly spare the time to come up to Cambridge with me? Just for a few days until I get used to the place."

"You don't mean to tell me you're nervous?"

"Yes, I am." Amelia looked as if she were expecting the roof to fall in on her.

"Of course I'll come with you!" Leander hugged her. "To tell you the truth, I'm dying to see it. I didn't like to ask in case you thought I was interfering."

"It's very beautiful, but a little bit intimidating," Amelia said. She had spent three days there, taking the scholarship examination and being interviewed by a battery of formidable women.

Leander agreed with her on both counts within an hour of arriving in the city. They took rooms in the Blue Boar in Trinity Street and spent two days sightseeing, during which they walked miles and gave themselves sore feet. Leander loved every minute of it.

"It's wonderful," she told Amelia. "I'm certain that I can feel the atmosphere."

"I'm very lucky," Amelia said.

"You're very clever! That's why you're here, young lady. Luck has nothing to do with it."

"What if I hadn't had a chance to be clever?" Amelia asked. "What if I'd been a grubby little wretch in the back-streets of somewhere like Birmingham or Manchester?"

Leander eyed her suspiciously. "You aren't getting strange ideas, are you, Amelia? Have you been reading Socialist and Fabian tracts?"

"No, Mother!" Amelia bubbled with laughter. "All that I'm saying is that I consider myself extremely lucky to have been born your child. Giles thinks exactly the same, by the way."

"Oh!" Leander sagged against the backrest of the bench and stared across The Backs towards King's College and its glorious chapel. "I don't know what to say to that," she said in a rather small voice.

"Say nothing!" Amelia advised with a mock-serious face. "Always the best." Then she burst out laughing at the look on Leander's face and flung her arms round her. "You're the best mother in the world!"

They looked up to see an old gentleman smiling at them with quite the pinkest face either of them had ever seen.

"Please forgive me, ladies," he said, removing his hat and bowing slightly. He addressed Amelia. "Until I overheard what you just said, young lady, I was convinced that you were sisters."

"Thank you, sir!" Leander said, and the old man basked for a moment or two in the most radiant of her smiles.

"There!" Amelia whispered as he pottered on his way. "That's another ambition you've achieved. You've always wanted to be taken for my sister, haven't you?"

"How long have you known that?" Leander asked.

"Ages and ages! I'm clever, remember, you said so!"

On the afternoon of Leander's third and last full day in Cambridge, Amelia had to go to Girton College to begin the formalities of enrolment. After a late lunch, Leander wandered down to Magdalene Bridge where she watched two pairs of swans glide downstream and wait, with regal patience, for someone to feed them. She also saw scores of young men wearing undergraduate gowns, many of them riding bicycles. Some looked carefree, others earnest, and one or two looked as if they had already shouldered the cares of the world.

Would any of them take a fancy to Amelia, and would she return the feeling? Leander picked out three that might do, then, smiling at such capricious notions, she retraced her steps to the Blue Boar in search of tea.

She had settled into a corner and given her order to a waitress when she heard a well-known, thoroughly detested voice in the reception hall beyond the lounge.

"It's been good to see you again, Claude. I'll talk to my committee and let you know. As I say, I don't envisage any problems."

Sir Walter Rothwell!

"Are you all right, madam?" the waitress asked, concerned at Leander's sudden flush of panic.

"Yes, yes, thank you," she whispered, trying to make sure that her voice did not carry into the hall.

But it was to no avail: attracted by the chink of teacups, Sir Walter entered the lounge. His face registered amazement, followed by what could easily have passed for genuine pleasure.

"Mrs Hawksworth! What a surprise." He sat down at her table and gestured to the waitress. "What are you doing here?"

"I'm with my daughter, Sir Walter. She has come up to the university."

"*Has* she indeed? My word, she must be a very bright young lady."

"She is," Leander replied. "And you, Sir Walter: may I ask why you are here?"

"I live here, dear lady. At Cherry Hinton. It's very handy. I can be in Newmarket in fifteen minutes in my motor car and, of course, Cambridge has an excellent train service to London."

Leander inclined her head politely, and, as if sensing her discomfort, Rothwell launched into a soothing flow of small-talk. Had she seen Lord Rosebery's new colt? It was a very impressive animal and had worked quite remarkably over the Limekilns the other day. What a shame that John Porter was retiring: a *great* loss to the Sport. What about The Atheling: was he to be kept in training as a four-year-old?

Constantly on her guard, Leander maintained her end of the conversation. She was well aware of the rumours: Sir Dugdale Brodie was talking of retirement and those in the know were tipping Rothwell to take his place as Senior Steward of the Jockey Club.

Rothwell was charming, however. He took a second cup of tea, looked at his watch and smiled apologetically. "Forgive me, Mrs Hawksworth," he said. "I must go . . . an important meeting, you know." On the point of departure, he leaned across the table. "The years are being exceptionally kind to you," he said in a quiet but firm tone. "I really do believe that you will go on being astonishingly attractive for ever."

As Rothwell left the lounge, Leander's control was superb: the waitress thought that the beautiful blonde lady looked very much better for her nice chat with the distinguished-looking gentleman.

Fortunately, Amelia provided a distraction by coming back from Girton in a turmoil at her first insight into what the next three years had in store.

"I'm going to have to work like stink, Mother. They throw you out if you aren't any good."

"I can't see that applying to you, darling."

Amelia looked doubtful. "Miss Forbes – she's my tutor – is a tremendous dragon."

"Didn't Miss Douglas warn you about her?"

"Yes – but I've got the awful feeling that Miss Forbes's bite may be even worse than her bark!"

On Cambridge railway station the following morning, Leander wavered, her courage almost deserting her. "You will take good care of yourself, won't you, darling?" she said very earnestly.

"I will," Amelia promised.

"And try not to change too much."

"I won't change at all, Mother."

Leander knew that she could rely on it.

Leander arrived home to find Steven and Giles with long faces.

The Atheling had been unable to take part in the St Leger because of a pulled muscle. There was still hope that he might win another good race, and, while Leander had been away in Cambridge, Giles had ridden the colt out for his first serious piece of work for over a month. After less than a hundred yards, he had damaged the muscle again.

Leander shrugged it off. "It doesn't matter all that much," she said. "The important thing now is to get him to the stud in one piece."

"I thought you liked winning, Mother," Giles said. "I'm absolutely certain he could have got us another."

"Giles, my dear," Leander said, as though speaking to a harmless idiot, "he won the *Derby*. That will do. You can't ask much more of a horse than that."

Secretly, she was disappointed: until his mishap, The Atheling had seemed to have the St Leger at his mercy and would thus have claimed the Triple Crown, an honour that had so far eluded Latimer's Barn. Concealing her feelings, Leander did not have long to wait for a boost to her spirits. When Rupert Timberlake turned up the following day, he wasted no time with preliminaries.

"I've found Sixsmith," he said. "He's in Bath, been there for nearly a year and living in some style. Ruddock has given a full description of the man who planned the operation and took twenty per cent, and I've spoken to my friends in Yorkshire and Peterborough about the man who approached them. It was Sixsmith."

"You're sure, Rupert?"

"No doubt about it!"

"Thank you." Leander held out her hand. "The address, please, Rupert."

She slept on it, then asked William to drive her to the police station in Marlborough.

"And if it can be arranged, Sergeant Hopkins," she said as she was leaving, "I'd very much like to speak to him when you've got him."

A minor problem over swearing a warrant delayed matters for five days, but at last Sergeant Hopkins sent word.

Leander, escorted by Cyril Osgood, walked calmly into the cell and stared with cool hostility at the unprepossessing individual hunched on the edge of the miserable bed. Looking up, Edgar Sixsmith recognised her at once: incredulity made him look almost comical.

"I want you to know how you came here," Leander told him. "You have been under observation since your attempt, in cahoots with my late uncle, to steal Bellerophon." Sixsmith looked aghast. "I am surprised at your stupidity. You saw what happened to your hirelings, yet you try again. Why didn't you stay in Pylle Hill? I was quite happy to leave you there in peace. You shall pay this time, Sixsmith. I will *not* have scum like you defiling Cannings Ambo or my horses!"

The next time Edgar Sixsmith saw Leander Hawksworth, he was in the dock and certain that her evidence would seal his fate once and for all.

CHAPTER 18

1906

'What are we supposed to do . . . sell picture postcards?'

Without any slackening of his efforts, George looked round at the audience. The turnout was below par; on a Saturday at the height of the London season, some were probably resting. There were only nine this afternoon. At least twice that number was normal.

The four women and five men on the semicircle of sofas only a few feet away were, like George and his partner, all naked.

George's attention settled first on Sadie Drummond, wife of a Lancashire mill owner and, by all accounts, both a pillar of society and an utter tyrant in her native Blackburn. As ever at Hertford House, she was playing an enthusiastic part in the proceedings, encouraging the two men on either side of her to fondle and kiss every part of her voluptuously statuesque body.

There was something very interesting indeed to the left of Sadie Drummond's group. It was the first time George had seen the beautiful young woman with copper-coloured hair and the body of his dreams. Unlike other newcomers who turned up from time to time, she was not in the least shy or embarrassed; while appearing to enjoy the none too expert attentions of a Coldstream Guards subaltern, she was watching the performance on the pile of cushions with breathless fascination. When George looked directly at her, she smiled and there was no mistaking her meaning.

Beneath him, Celia's sighs became louder and more demanding as she approached another climax. Sadie Drummond gave George a completely unnecessary reminder of his function.

"Come on, lad, give it to her! Let's see her squirm."

In the epicurean world of Hertford House, George was worshipped by women, envied and respected by most men and had become the complete showman. He stepped up his efforts to bring both himself and Celia to orgasm, making it look even more spectacular than it was, so that everyone, including the blasé Sadie Drummond, moaned with feverishly excited approval.

George recovered quickly, fully aware of the ferment of activity he had unleashed around him. All four of the women were now engaged in intercourse: there had been a struggle over Sadie, and while the victor was lunging frantically between her thighs, the other man eagerly awaited his turn. The lovely girl with copper-coloured hair was pretending to be content with the subaltern, but as George detached himself from Celia and walked from the room, her eyes followed him.

After the heat of the morning-room, the comparative chill of the corridor was a relief to George as he padded down it to the extension added to Hertford House by an enterprising hedonist around 1850. It was a marble hall with a huge, sunken bath, already filled with water, and George sank into it with a gasp of pleasure.

The outrageous world of Celia's sexual fantasies translated into stunning reality, and his colossal good fortune in being part of it never ceased to astound and delight him.

It seemed to have been going on for about five years: loath to look a gift-horse in the mouth and conscious of the need for discretion, George had asked no questions and was content to accumulate the occasional snippet.

Celia – Lady Celia Blennerhasset – and Sadie Drummond had been the founders. How on earth had two such disparate women come to be such close friends in the first place? Clothed and involved in life's normal routine, the over-refined Celia and exceptionally down-to-earth Sadie seemed the most unlikely partners. About the only thing they had in common was that they were attractive, rapacious women of around thirty-five with much older husbands whose energies were devoted to other things. Sir Compton Blennerhasset was a politician with ambitions that exceeded his talents; Herbert Drummond made money, carried out good works with maximum ostentation and enjoyed himself once a week with a mill-girl.

But, somehow, they had done it; somehow they had conceived and implemented the idea of a shrine to erotic pleasure based mainly on exhibitionism. George suspected that its prime purpose was for the gratification of women but, like all the other men invited to take part, he did not complain. He never ceased to bless Mrs Warburton for bringing him to Marlow as a parting gift when illness forced her to relinquish her membership of what Celia called 'The Temple of Venus'.

Dear Celia! She loved investing things with a sense of mystery, turning them into a sort of secret society. And there was no doubt about it, this caper had to be kept secret; all hell would break loose if ever it became known what went on twice or three times a month at the country home of a senior Cabinet Minister.

Reaching for the soap, George found that he was no longer alone. The girl with copper-coloured hair had arrived on noiselessly bare feet and was looking down at him, affording him a splendid view of, among other delights, her lovely legs.

"Hello," she said. "I'm Jane Anstruther."

"How do you do?" George replied with mock-formality. "I'm George Hawksworth."

"I know." She slipped into the bath beside him as though it were a perfectly ordinary thing that she did every day.

"Is this your first time?" George asked.

"Yes."

"How are you finding it?"

"Well . . ." She hesitated. "A little disappointing so far. My man came off much too quickly."

George nodded sympathetically. "Teddie is always like that, I'm afraid. Celia's trying to think of a way to get rid of him."

"He wasn't the only one. Both Mrs Drummond's men were the same. She was livid."

"It's her own silly fault – she gets them too worked up first. But you mustn't worry, you've plenty of time. Are you staying the night?"

"Yes. My husband is away in Paris."

"Really? I know it's supposed to have a lot to recommend it," George said, "but I'd think several times before I left you."

Jane Anstruther smiled. "He's quite old. In any case, it's his job. He's with the Foreign Office."

"Not another politician?" George said, simulating horror.

"No, he's a diplomat. I think he's gone to prepare the ground for Sir Edward Grey."

"Brushing up the *Entente Cordiale*, eh?"

"Something like that. You're part of the Hawksworths who train racehorses, aren't you?"

"I am indeed." George put an arm round her and she moved closer to him. "I'm the eldest and least favoured son."

"Celia told me they'd thrown you out."

"That's putting it a bit strongly. Let's say they're always glad not to see me."

"So you have to earn your own living?"

"Yes, I'm with Blayne-Singer's." Her face showed that she was

309

impressed. "And what about you, Jane? What on earth are you doing married to a dried-up old stick in the Foreign Office?"

She pulled a face. "Henry is a friend of my father's," she replied. "His first wife died a few years ago and he decided he'd like an ornament for a second. Father was all in favour – he said it would keep me out of trouble."

George chuckled. "It doesn't seem to be working very well."

Jane noticed the reaction that the proximity of her body was causing between George's legs and slid a hand down his stomach to expedite his erection.

"No," she said. "It isn't working at all. I say, George, you were really thrilling just now. Everyone said how marvellous you were."

"That's why they put up with me," George said, stretching out luxuriously. "I usually manage to stir them up."

"Oh, you did, and you've got the most gorgeously enormous thing. I was watching you with Celia."

"I could see you were."

"I nearly came just by looking at it."

"Well, it's all yours now, Jane, my sweet, but don't rub it like that or you'll have me in the same state as poor old Teddie. Get on top of me . . . like this, look."

Jane Anstruther gurgled delightedly as George lifted her astride his thighs.

There were times during the next few days when George came close to imagining himself in love. While Sir Henry Anstruther remained embroiled in European affairs of state, George and Jane spent every available minute in bed.

"Are you trying to kill yourself?" Alec asked peevishly.

"Here, steady on, Alec," George laughed. "You're starting to turn green with jealousy."

On Friday morning, Celia telephoned him at his office.

"Celia, I wish you wouldn't," George muttered into the instrument. "You know how busy I am." Most of the trouble was caused by George's dislike of the telephone: he was still a long way from feeling comfortable with it.

"All you have to do is say 'yes', George, and you can get back to counting money. I want you to come down on Saturday afternoon. There'll be just the two of us."

"Er . . . I don't think I can manage that," George said furtively.

"Of course you can, George. Don't be so silly!" There was anger as well as pleading in her voice. Curiously enough, George had been feeling guilty about the way his discovery of Jane had caused him to neglect Celia throughout Saturday evening and Sunday. And he was always afraid that if she became too upset, she might ban him from her Temple of Venus. He thought quickly. Yes: he could go down to Marlow, then spend Sunday with Jane.

"Very well, I'll come," he said.

"You will indeed!" Celia replied with a wealth of innuendo. George smiled. He much preferred her when she abandoned her aesthetic airs and graces.

On an afternoon that was sultry with the threat of thunder, Celia wanted to make love in the garden. They had done it before, relishing the possible danger of being seen by the passengers of pleasure craft on the river. Today, however, George insisted on the cool of the marble bathroom.

To make amends for his cavalier treatment of her the previous weekend, George took the trouble to linger over Celia's preparation, ardently deploying all the skills that Phyllida Warburton had so enjoyably taught him.

"My God!" she gasped when he finally penetrated her, lancing forcefully into her vulva. Celia liked him to disregard the gentleness that many other women found essential; with her, he plunged in savagely, taking brutal possession of her so that she experienced the sensation of violation.

"Quickly, George! Do it to me quickly!" she panted, writhing her hips, drawing him deeper and deeper into her.

Oh, it's one of those days, George thought. Right, my lady, you shall have it.

He was young, fit and strong, yet not even the blind onslaught of lust he unleashed on her was enough.

"Harder, damn you! Faster!" she cried, panting, bucking and raking her finger-nails down his back. "I'll show you I'm as good as Jane Anstruther!"

"So that's it, you bitch!" George said savagely, plunging at her salaciously educated loins with a barbarity that made her shriek at the prospect of an orgasmic experience to surpass all others.

The resonant acoustics of the marble chamber amplified the noises they made in their wild struggle for gratification, rendering them deaf to anything else. It was only when the uproar in the corridor was on top of them that they heard it. A fraction of a second later, Celia's face drained chalk-white and she screamed. The paroxysm of terror that convulsed her was enough to fling George from her at precisely the instant he started to climax; he landed on his back,

311

momentarily senseless as erupting semen spattered his chest and stomach.

"What in God's name do you think you are doing, madam?"

The marble made it sound like the roar of ten enraged bulls.

"Compton! I thought you were making a speech in Newcastle," Celia wailed.

"Get away from that man! Out of my sight, woman. Out!" The voice dropped ominously as Celia scrambled dementedly to obey him. "I will deal with you later."

George opened his eyes in time to see Celia, attempting to cover herself with a towel that was too small, disappear into the corridor where at least two maids were having hysterics. Then he was aware of Sir Compton Blennerhasset towering over him. There was nothing George could do except lie there and be proud of his huge penis; a look of astounded resentment on the politician's face was some compensation for his mortifying predicament.

The press were right, George thought: whatever his shortcomings, and they were alleged to be legion, Sir Compton at least *looked* the part of the distinguished statesman.

"Unfortunately, sir, I believe my position precludes me from having you horse-whipped," the Home Secretary snarled. "However, when you have dressed yourself, I will interview you."

After an horrific twenty minutes with Sir Compton, George fled back to London and Jane. Fortunately, he had not attempted to deceive her about where and how he was spending the afternoon; confident that he would return to her, she had, in fact, been rather amused by Celia Blennerhasset's desperate need for George.

There was not a vestige of amusement when he told his story. She was appalled.

"What do you think old Blennerhasset will do?" she asked.

"I don't know. He didn't say. He struck me as a pretty spiteful blighter."

"Celia's going to cop it," Jane said. "We can wave goodbye to the fun and games at Hertford House. Never mind, we've got each other."

Returning to the flat in Kensington on Sunday evening, George was in the blackest of moods. The shock of Blennerhasset's devastatingly sudden appearance and worry over the repercussions had caused him to become impotent, even in Jane's skilled hands. Frantic to learn what Alec might have to say about the business, he was confronted instead with a chirpy note to tell him that his friend was staying with a lady in Wimbledon.

For the first time in his life, George passed a sleepless night.

Sir Reginald Blayne-Singer wasted no time. George was summoned to his magnificent office at nine o'clock on Monday morning.

"Well, my boy," Sir Reginald said in a kindly way. "You've really been and done it, haven't you?"

George nodded miserably.

"I have been told that if I do not dismiss you, the bank will never handle Government business again. It seems that Blennerhasset has friends in the City, too. There are a couple of insurance companies breathing down my neck."

"I quite understand, sir." George said. "I'll leave at once."

"That's very decent of you. Can't tell you how sorry I am."

"No, sir, I'm the one that should be sorry for putting you in such an invidious position."

Sir Reginald waved a gently dismissive hand. "Would you take my advice to save yourself a damned tricky scene?"

"Of course, sir."

"Don't go near your club. I gather you've been expelled. Expect they'll be writing to you. Oh, yes, I'm afraid he means business, George. This is only the beginning."

"Have you actually seen Sir Compton, sir?"

"Yes, damn it! The bounder got through to me on the telephone yesterday morning and summoned me to the Home Office. I was intending to stay in Norfolk for a few days. He was in a dashed ugly mood, George."

They stared at each other glumly for a long time, then Sir Reginald leaned forward with a slightly raffish air about him.

"Tell me, was she worth it?"

George shook his head firmly. "*No* woman is worth the loss of an excellent job, sir."

"No. No, I suppose not. But she was good, eh?"

"Oh yes, sir, very good indeed. As a matter of fact, she was quite superb. A man couldn't want for a better mistress."

Sir Reginald smiled happily. "I've always imagined Celia as a bit of a goer. And there's been talk, you know. You're not the first by any means."

"No, I don't suppose I was." George stood up. "Goodbye, sir. I've enjoyed working for you."

Sir Reginald shook his hand. "Goodbye, my boy. Let Alec know if there's anything I can do to help you."

When Alec came home that evening, he brought news from Sir Reginald. First, however, he was compelled to comment on the story that had been revealed to him during the day.

313

"Christ Almighty, George, aren't you the lad! Caught in the act of banging it up a Cabinet Minister's wife in . . . where was it? . . . a marble bathroom."

"It was the coolest place," George said with a tolerable attempt at insouciance. "You know how hot it was on Saturday afternoon."

"Not nearly as hot as it's going to be. Now, listen, a message from the governor. He advises you to go home. At once."

"Why?"

"I don't know for sure. I think Father suspects that Blennerhasset is going to drag your parents into it."

George felt sick.

Unfortunately, the letter came before George's telegram.

Leander, who was not riding out that morning, read it while Steven was busy with the first lot. It was from a solicitor in Henley-on-Thames:

Dear Mr Hawksworth,
The Home Secretary, Sir Compton Blennerhasset, has instructed me to act for him in a matter of the utmost delicacy concerning your son, George. Since it is necessary to resolve this lamentable matter with the greatest speed, I propose calling upon you at noon on 29 June.
Yours etc.
W. Scrivenor

Mystified, but in no doubt as to the seriousness of the matter, it was some time before Leander realised the significance of the date. "It's tomorrow," she said to herself. "He's coming tomorrow!"

As was the custom, Steven, Giles, Albert Merriweather and Peter Izzard came in for breakfast between the first and second lots. Leander quietly persuaded Steven into the library and showed him the letter. While he was reflecting Leander's bafflement and worry, the telegram was delivered:

ARRIVING MARLBOROUGH ON 11.46 TRAIN.
GEORGE

"Well?" Leander asked.

"I have no idea," Steven replied, doing his best to be calm. "It's clearly very serious, but speculating won't help us. We must wait." He looked at his watch. "Not long, only an hour and a half."

Back in the kitchen, Steven finished his breakfast, kept warm for

314

him by Polly Goakes, and said to Giles, "Look after the second lot. There's something I must attend to."

Giles was far too pleased with the responsibility to waste time asking questions about what had caused the sudden change of plan.

Steven left at eleven o'clock, driving the carriage himself and gently deflecting Leander's requests to go with him. "No, my dear, I have an idea that this is one of those man-to-man affairs," he said. "I'm thinking of taking George to lunch somewhere to give him a fair chance of telling me. Be patient."

George looked haggard after another sleepless night. Apart from welcoming him warmly and sensing that it was much appreciated, Steven said nothing until they were seated in a private room at the Ailesbury Arms and had ordered lunch.

"We've had a letter from a solicitor this morning, George," he announced evenly. "He alleges that there is some trouble between you and the Home Secretary – of all people! Is this true?"

"Yes, Father."

"This solicitor is coming to see us tomorrow, so you must tell me all about it."

Slowly and painfully, George began. There was a slight improvement in his confidence as he went on, but it never ceased to be an ordeal for him, with frequent pauses to fight embarrassment or to choose the most euphemistic words. He decided to tell his father everything, including the goings-on in 'The Temple of Venus'. His account took up the whole of the meal. Although sometimes irritated by George's hesitant delivery, Steven never interrupted: he sat and listened with the most expressionless face he could muster.

"Is that it?" Steven finally asked when an abnormally long silence seemed to indicate the end.

"Yes, sir." George's eyes were glued to his empty coffee-cup.

Steven stared at him in silence.

"Words fail me," he said at last. "Perhaps your mother will think of something."

"You aren't going to tell her?" George was aghast.

"I shall have to. After that letter, she wants to know what all this is about and I can't fob her off. Once I've told her, she will think of something. She always does."

Back at Latimer's Barn, George took refuge in the orchard as Steven, looking far from sure of himself, went to talk to Leander. Wandering around among the luxuriant foliage of apple and pear trees, George almost fell over Amelia who was sitting with her back against one of the trees, poring over a textbook.

"Hello, Amy," he said. "How's Cambridge?"

315

"Very nice. Hard work, though."

"Oxford wasn't."

"Ah, but I want a decent degree."

George grimaced at the textbook as he flopped down beside her. "What on earth's that grim-looking stuff?" he asked.

"Partial differential equations. Is there trouble?"

"Sort of."

"I thought so."

"Why?"

"Mother's in a very funny mood, Father dashes off unexpectedly, and now you turn up. What's it about?"

For an insane moment or two, George considered telling her, but he put the idea away quickly. As well as looking like their mother, George had always suspected that Amelia used similar thought processes to arrive at identical conclusions.

"It's all a bit difficult and messy," he complained, seeking to give the impression that it was nothing whatsoever to do with him. "I think it's going to get sorted out tomorrow."

"Oh, what a shame, I shall miss it. I'm going to the races with Giles."

"How's he getting on?"

"Brilliantly!"

George wasn't really in the mood to listen to an hour-long recital of his brother's virtues: there was, however, no alternative.

Leander was normal and composed over dinner. George had half-expected to be cut dead, with the conversation steered adroitly round him as though he did not exist. Instead, Leander made a point of seeking his opinion on several issues, especially about when he thought the motor car might become a viable, practical proposition for everyday use. Either, George thought, it was her best performance yet, or his father had funked it and given her a much watered-down version.

After the meal, Leander took him briefly to one side.

"I'm in exactly the same boat as your father, George," she told him. "I simply do not know what to say. We must wait and see what this Mr Scrivenor wants."

"Yes, Mother."

"It seems that you have been dismissed from Blayne-Singer's."

"Yes."

"So, at the very least, we must find you another job."

"But not here, presumably?"

"No, George, definitely not here."

316

There was nothing to indicate that when Steven had finished battling through George's incredible story, Leander had laughed until tears rolled down her cheeks.

"What on earth is so funny?" an astounded Steven asked.

"Oh, sweetheart, I'm sorry, I can't help it. I never imagined that George was that much of an idiot – and you realise what all this means, don't you? We've found something he must be *very* good at! At last!"

Watching the truth dawn on Steven, she laughed again.

Upon his prompt arrival, Mr Scrivenor was shown into the small sitting-room and was immediately unhappy with the arrangements.

"Forgive me, Mrs Hawksworth, I wonder if this conversation will be *quite* suitable for a lady," he said.

"Our son has told us all about it, Mr Scrivenor," Leander said. "Please have no fears on my account."

"Yes. I see. H'm." Mr Scrivenor shifted uncomfortably in his seat, looked at George, then Steven. "Do you think it might be best if we had this discussion *without* your son's presence, Mr Hawksworth?"

"I doubt it," Steven said affably.

"You wish your son to be present?"

"Of course."

Mr Scrivenor took a sheaf of papers from his bag and arranged them neatly on the table.

"May I take it, Mr Hawksworth, that your son has given you an account of the circumstances in which Sir Compton Blennerhasset found him and Lady Blennerhasset last Saturday afternoon?" Leander saw that he had decided to solve the problem of her presence by ignoring it.

"Yes, he has," Steven replied. "My son and Lady Blennerhasset were indulging in sexual intercourse."

Mr Scrivenor swallowed hard and demonstrated a determination not to be put off. "You will understand that Sir Compton is displeased."

"So I should think with a wife like that."

Mr Scrivenor frowned. "He is *extremely* displeased with your son, Mr Hawksworth."

"I gathered that from the fact that Sir Compton has already caused my son to be dismissed from his employment and expelled from his club."

George looked up sharply: there was a strong tone of disapproval in Steven's voice.

"Yes . . . quite so." Mr Scrivenor fiddled with his papers. "Not unnaturally, Sir Compton wishes to be assured that the deplorable events of Saturday will never be repeated."

"I can understand that," Steven said. "George!"

"Yes, definitely. You have my assurance, sir," George said.

"I regret to say that Sir Compton is not disposed to accept such bland and . . . er . . . unenforceable promises."

"Oh!" Steven leaned forward, causing Mr Scrivenor to shuffle. "So what do you suggest? And bear this in mind, sir, unless my understanding of the situation is very much awry, Lady Blennerhasset was a far from unwilling partner in this fiasco."

"I do not wish to concede that point, Mr Hawksworth. However, I am at liberty to reveal that Lady Blennerhasset is currently staying with her sister-in-law in Scotland and is expected to remain there for some considerable time."

"So what is expected of us?"

"Your son must leave England, Mr Hawksworth. Sir Compton suggests that he avails himself of one of the many opportunities in the colonies."

"*Must?*" Steven said.

"Yes, Mr Hawksworth."

There was silence. Stared at hard by Steven, Mr Scrivenor fiddled with his papers again.

"Actually, that's probably not a bad idea, Father," George said. "I'm certainly never going to find a decent job in this country until God knows when."

"Shut up, George!" Steven showed the first signs of anger. "No, Mr Scrivenor, I don't like that at all. I think your client has thrown enough of his weight around already without dictating where my son should live."

Leander gripped the arms of her chair as Steven's intense dislike of all politicians began to emerge.

"I have to tell you that sanctions will be applied if you do not agree to Sir Compton's proposal," Mr Scrivenor said.

"Really?" Steven sounded threatening.

Leander, with a fair idea of what was coming, grudgingly admitted that Scrivenor made a fair job of grasping the nettle. "My understanding is that if you do not accede to Sir Compton's wishes, you will experience difficulties in renewing your licence to train next year." There was a pause for Steven to absorb this. "Nor would a licence be granted to any member of your family to carry on the business of training at Latimer's Barn."

"You mean we could go somewhere else and do it?" Steven asked. Leander's stomach turned over.

"That information is beyond my sphere of knowledge and competence," Scrivenor replied, taking refuge in pomposity.

"Tell me," Steven asked. "What about 'The Temple of Venus'?"

"I'm sorry, Mr Hawksworth, to what are you referring?" Mr Scrivenor looked genuinely puzzled.

"I am referring to the sexual orgies organised by Lady Blennerhasset."

"Mr Hawksworth, that is a monstrous suggestion!"

"Is it? You think it a slur on the name of a lady who has an absolutely unimpeachable reputation? Ah, I see you do not. The blunt fact of the matter is that blackmail is not the sole prerogative of Cabinet Ministers, Mr Scrivenor. Two can play that game."

"Steven!"

Leander was on her feet, her face taut.

"Would you excuse us for a few minutes, please, Mr Scrivenor?" she said, already moving towards the door. "Please help yourself to refreshments."

Steven went with her automatically, George because he could not face being alone with Scrivenor.

Leander did not sit down once they were inside the library; Steven and George watched as she paced round and round the room. When she finally came to rest, she weighed her words before she spoke.

"I know what you're thinking, sweetheart. Yes, we could make a devil of a stink over this 'Temple of Venus' nonsense. We could give the popular press a scandal that would keep it going for a year . . . we might even ruin Blennerhasset. *But* . . ." she spoke slowly and with forceful emphasis ". . . at the end of it all, we would *not* have a licence. We would not be training horses."

"I'm sure there's a way out of it, my dear," Steven replied.

"Oh? And what might it be?"

Although Steven was blind to the fact, George had never seen his mother looking so dangerous.

"I need time to think about it. I will not kow-tow to the likes of Blennerhasset."

"Very, very commendable!" The sneer in Leander's voice pulled Steven up short.

"There are principles at stake here," he said hotly. "In any case, how can we be sure that the Jockey Club would yield to pressure?"

Leander looked at him sadly: for all his success, Steven could still be shatteringly naïve. Of course the Jockey Club would give in, even without the malign influence of Sir Walter Rothwell.

"We may take it that they will," she said quietly.

"I don't accept that," Steven argued. "We should think about this very carefully."

It was the last straw. Leander exploded.

"I have been thinking about it all my life, Steven! What are we supposed to do if we can't train horses here? Take up farming? Sell picture postcards of Bellerophon and The Atheling? Or perhaps you think we should retire and grow roses in Bournemouth? Well, do you?"

Steven was sullenly silent.

"My father killed himself to lay the foundations of a *permanent* establishment here and I will not have it endangered because that over-sexed half-wit is unable to control his tom-catting!"

George took a pace backwards as Leander pointed an accusing finger at him: it was like a savage slap in the face.

"Well, what's it to be?" Leander demanded. "That man in the sitting-room wants an answer. Do you agree with me, or do I have to call an emergency meeting of the Trustees *now*?"

"Giles isn't here," Steven said weakly.

"*I* will vote for Giles," Leander snapped.

Steven capitulated. "Very well," he said. Suddenly he felt like the upstart from the boat-yard.

"Right, I shall tell Scrivenor!"

After she had gone, Steven and George exchanged anguished looks.

"She's right, Father," George said. "Thanks for trying, though. It really will be better all round if I'm out of it."

"Yes." Steven reconsidered what had happened. "It's funny, isn't it? I've always known she cared deeply for this place, but I'd no idea she felt like *that*."

They remained deep in thought until Leander came back ten minutes later.

"We have three months to make all the necessary arrangements," she said. "George, you will leave this country no later than the thirtieth of September."

The tension in The House was unbearable. Giles and Amelia felt it the instant they returned from Newbury.

"You could cut the atmosphere with a knife," Giles said after they had bolted a meal and escaped outside. "Even poor Ellie looks grim. What's going on?"

"George has done something totally awful," Amelia replied.

"What?"

"You mustn't say a word."

320

"I promise."

"It's something to do with the wife of a Cabinet Minister. Mother told me this morning. She's furious."

Giles looked horrified.

In their room, Steven and Leander lay with formal rigidity on their respective halves of the bed. She was studying *The Racing Calendar*, Steven was pretending to understand an article on a new method of treating colic. When it was time to put the lamps out, they mumbled their goodnights and turned their backs on each other.

Leander told Rupert Timberlake all about George's escapades.

"Frankly, I'm inclined to laugh," he said.

"I *did* – at first. Then we found out Blennerhasset's terms. George is to be banished to the colonies or we lose our licence."

"Rather heavy-handed."

"Possibly, but Blennerhasset has a lot at stake. This 'Temple of Venus' business could be poison to a man in his position. George swears – and I believe him – that two marchionesses and a duke's daughter were regularly mixed up in it."

Rupert nodded. "I believe it, too. There's been a fair bit of talk about Celia Blennerhasset over the years – not that that helps you, of course. Are you unhappy about George having to go?"

Leander took a deep breath. "No, Rupert, I am not! George has rarely been anything other than a pain in the neck and it will be a relief to see the back of him."

"You can't say fairer than that. Where's he going?"

"I don't know. The only thing certain is that he has to be gone by the end of September."

"And you've no ideas?"

"None at all."

"Can I help?"

"Would you?"

"I'll do my best. Give me a week."

He was eight days and began with a complaint.

"When are you going to get the telephone, Leander? It saves an awful lot of time."

"Soon," she promised. "Have you got anything for me?"

"I think so. South Africa is the place for George. I actually believe he might do very well for himself out there. Standards and attitudes are completely different to England and the opportunities seem limitless."

"Is it safe?" Leander asked doubtfully.

"Yes. Things have straightened themselves out nicely since the war

321

and everyone seems determined to get the Union working smoothly. I think I can get George a job in insurance in Johannesburg."

"That's wonderful!"

"There's a fellow in London would like to see him for a fairly informal interview, but unless George makes a complete hash of it he should be home and dry."

"I shall make sure he understands that," Leander said in a way that caused Rupert to feel a twinge of pity for George. "So, your network of contacts is international."

"We cover one or two countries," was the cautious reply.

Leander laughed. "Don't worry, Rupert, I'm not going to pry."

George was agreeably surprised. Fully expecting to be put under house arrest, he mooched disconsolately around Latimer's Barn for several days before plucking up the courage to ask Steven if he might go to London.

"Have you got something you could be doing quietly and inconspicuously?" Steven asked.

George, sensing sympathy, smiled. "Yes, Father, I have."

"Be damned careful," Steven urged.

"I will. Mind you, it doesn't much matter now, does it?"

Unhappily, Steven agreed.

George stayed at the flat with Alec. Jane Anstruther was beside herself at his reappearance. Her husband had returned from Paris, but this did not impair their enjoyment of each other; while Alec was working at his father's bank, they spent most days at the flat, making love with furious intensity.

The only thing that threatened to spoil their pleasure was Jane's reaction to George's imminent departure: to his surprise, she was very upset by it.

"Bloody hell, it's not fair," she stormed. "The minute I find a man who knows what he's doing in bed, he gets banished to South Africa!"

George did his considerable best to give her every consolation in the time available to him.

He also attended an interview with the London representative of Brandt and De Kuyper. It was a great success.

Vincent De Kuyper was one of the co-founder's sons. He was tall, strongly built, wore an almost white suit and radiated the freshness of radical new horizons. When George shook his hand and said, "I'm very pleased to meet you, sir," he roared with laughter.

"You're going to have to forget all about that 'sir' bullshit in South

Africa, George," he said. "We don't have any call for arse-holing like that."

They got on famously, discovering close affinities in almost everything, particularly their attitudes to life's greatest sport, women. And the salary was over twice what Blayne-Singer's had been paying him.

George left England on 14 September.

William drove him and Steven to Southampton in his motor car the day before. After a night in an hotel, George boarded the Union Castle liner at eleven o'clock. Steven and William went with him to look round the ship, then waved from the quayside when she sailed on the tide at one.

Steven showed no sign of wanting to move. Eventually, William had to take his arm to draw him away. "Let's go home, Steven," he said.

They stopped in Andover for a pot of tea and exchanged the only conversation of the whole journey.

"We're probably going to have something like this with Maude," William said grimly.

"Not such a mess, though," Steven replied.

"I hope not." William was thoughtful before adding, "Leander's been *very* upset by all this, Steven."

"Yes. I only realised that these last few days. Before that, I thought she was taking it all in her stride."

"No, she's had a terrible time. Be nice to her."

Steven needed no telling: he had, of course, never been *nasty* to her. But, in the year of their twenty-fifth wedding anniversary, the full extent of Leander's determination to keep Latimer's Barn going as a racing stable had taken him by surprise. One of the consequences was that he had persuaded himself that he had never really been in charge of the place at all, that he was an outsider, there on sufferance. How ridiculous!

"Come on, William, let's see how fast this rattle-trap of yours will go," he said.

He found Leander in the kitchen. She was preparing vegetables and a mouth-watering smell of roasting beef came from the oven. "I've given everyone the evening off," she said after she had kissed him. "Giles and Amelia are in Marlborough having dinner with the Timberlakes."

"We're all alone?" he asked.

"We are indeed. Why don't you have a bath before dinner?"

Steven had missed two days' work and evening stables and Leander had the answers to all the questions he wanted to ask. By unspoken mutual consent, that was their topic of conversation over dinner. Not until they had taken a pot of coffee into the small sitting-room did Leander put the inevitable question, and she made sure that she was close to Steven with his arm round her when she did so.

"He went all right?"

"Yes. He seemed pretty cheerful about it all."

"Much more so than you?" Leander asked gently.

"Good gracious, yes! He's looking forward to it. He told me last night that South Africa seems to be his sort of place."

"Did you give him some money?"

"Yes."

Leander did not ask how much: she knew that Steven would have been generous. They were silent, her head on his shoulder. When she moved slightly and looked up at him, he was worrying, far away.

"George will manage," she said. "This will be the making of him."

"Yes, I think you're probably right. But it's not much thanks to us, is it?"

"Do you think we failed him?"

"I don't know. One thing's for sure – he was never part of this place. He never looked as though he belonged."

"I suppose we might have done more, although it's difficult to see what," Leander said. "Still, look on the bright side – Giles and Amelia are wonderful. Two out of three isn't bad."

Steven smiled as he thought about it. "We'd be all right if we could do that at Epsom."

"Ah! That reminds me." Leander sprang away from him impetuously as she spoke.

"What?"

"Wait there!"

He sat bemused as she rushed from the room. She was back almost immediately, staggering slightly under the weight of the Big Book.

"Look!" she said, opening it at a place already marked by a finger. "Before you get all miserable and grumpy, remember what a *good* year it's been."

Steven smiled ruefully when he saw the entry at which she was pointing:

Broadside won the Derby. (This is our fourth.) The colt is owned by Mr Rupert Timberlake.

"Do you know, my dear, I'd almost forgotten about that," he confessed.

"Oh Steven! He won it by half a street. How could you forget that?"

"Wasn't it more like two lengths?"

"Yes, if you insist on being prosaic! He still made a good job of winning it."

"Tell me, my dear, have you forgiven Lord Rosebery now that *we've* won it two years running?"

"No!"

Laughing, he turned the pages of the book and saw that there was no mention of George.

"Are you going to put anything in about this South African business?" he asked.

"Just a line with the bare facts," Leander said in rather an off-hand manner. "This sort of thing is far more important."

She indicated the notes recording the deaths of Lucy Miller at the age of seventy-two and dear old Seamus at eighty.

"They gave us most of their lives," Leander said. "Seamus was here nearly twenty years before Father. Lord Francis Rashleigh threw him out when he broke a leg."

Steven nodded at the reminder of the stable's less than illustrious beginning.

"And there's the other side of the coin," he said. It was a wedding:

John Shepherd, our vicar and son of the 'Good Shepherd', married Mary, eldest daughter of Conn and Sally Daly.

"There are always compensations with this place," Leander said. "Now then, Steven Hawksworth, what do you say to an early night before the children come home?"

CHAPTER 19

1908

'We have to go that way . . .'

Steven was probably no more difficult than any other man would have been, Leander thought, but because he was hers and she loved him, he seemed impossible.

When he finally agreed to consult Charles Stanton in January 1908, he had been feeling unwell for over six months. Leander could see for herself that he was almost permanently tired; Steven managed to disguise the strange headaches that plagued him every day from the middle of the afternoon onwards.

Charles spent an hour over the examination, using his stethoscope and sphygmomanometer with punctilious care.

"I don't like your blood pressure, Steven," he said as he finally put the instruments away.

"Is it very bad?"

"No, not *very* bad, but it's a good deal higher than I like to see in someone of your age."

"Can we do anything about it?"

"Oh, good Lord, yes!"

Charles moved to the medicine cupboard where he selected a huge glass jar of pills. "These will help. You must take two a day." He counted out a month's supply into a pillbox. "That's *one* of the things you must do," he said, placing the box in front of Steven.

"What else?"

"Eat less meat and avoid anything that's been in a frying-pan. Always remember, Steven, the frying-pan has killed more men than the bayonet."

"All right." Steven nodded solemnly. Secretly amused by Charles's vehemence, he was on the point of making his escape.

"One more thing," Charles said.

"Yes?" Steven asked suspiciously.

"You must arrange to do a damned sight less."

"Don't be silly, Charles, I can't." Steven's reaction was automatic and Charles was ready for it.

"I suppose you're going to tell me that your job is unique and that there isn't another living soul who could help you?"

"Well . . . no . . . it isn't *quite* that bad," Steven admitted.

"Come along, Steven, that stable of yours is bursting with talent," Charles said briskly. "Giles must be very nearly capable of running the place."

"Yes, he is."

"I suggest you let him do as much as possible. The experience will be very useful to him."

"Why?" Steven was suspicious again.

"Because I'm going to keep a very close eye on you, Steven, and in two or three years I shall very likely insist that you retire."

Steven thought it over, his disappointment plain. "I suppose I'd better do as I'm told," he said.

"I would," Charles advised. "Save a lot of trouble."

"Very well, I'll do my best." Steven shuffled awkwardly. "Tell me, Charles, is there any reason why Leander and I shouldn't . . ." he groped for words ". . . carry on leading a normal . . . er, married life?"

Charles grinned. "None whatsoever. Some experts say that it's highly therapeutic."

"Is it really?" Steven asked eagerly.

"You won't find me arguing with it!"

They soon reached what appeared to be the ideal solution: Giles looked after the two-year-olds, Steven did the rest. It gave a very nearly equal division of work, and, since Giles insisted on exercising his string as first lot, meant that Steven was able to indulge in the luxury of staying in bed until half past seven each morning.

The two-year-olds were soon the principal topic of conversation wherever they ran.

"There goes another of the beauties," the Duke of Laverstoke said to Leander as they watched one of his own fillies win effortlessly at Bath. "Giles has got the youngsters performing remarkably well."

"He's having the luck, Hubert," Leander replied. "This year's intake is the most gifted bunch we've seen for some time."

The Duke gave her a hard look. "You're not trying to deprive the boy of his due, are you?" he asked. "You can be a deuced hard woman to please, Leander."

"Giles is doing very well," she replied forcefully. "And so is Albert

327

Merriweather. But they're still learning and finding their feet, so let's give them time before we start praising them to the skies."

"All I was saying . . ."

She cut him short with a smile. "I know, Hubert, and Giles *is* good. Don't forget that the older horses are doing well, too. Steven still has a remarkable way with a horse."

That spring was beautiful and successful. Leander supervised Steven's careful new life-style with loving firmness, went out with Giles on the gallop to teach him all she knew and enjoyed the steady stream of winners produced by her husband and son in friendly competition. She relaxed to the extent that her interest in current affairs diminished; she even stopped worrying about battleship building.

On an evening during the Easter holiday, a few weeks before her final examinations, Amelia had a question for Steven as they sat down to dinner.

"Would you like to come to Cambridge to see me get my degree, Father?"

He looked at her with a dreadfully straight face. "Are you going to get one?" he asked.

"Oh yes." Amelia's assurance was rock-solid. "Actually, Miss Forbes thinks I might be given a pretty decent one."

"I see." Steven rubbed his chin. "Well, if the dragon thinks that, I suppose we'd better make the effort. What do you think, my dear?"

"Steven, don't be dreadful!" Leander said. "Thank you for asking us, darling. Of course we shall come."

"The only problem is finding you somewhere to stay," Amelia said. "The hotels are hopelessly full if we leave it too late."

"We shall be all right," Steven said inconsequentially.

"How do you know?" Leander asked.

"I've already booked rooms."

Leander and Amelia gaped at him in astonishment. "When did you do that?" Leander asked.

"Oh, ages ago."

"When?"

Steven smiled. "Last September, actually."

"Oh, Father!" Amelia left her chair to hug and kiss him.

"Here, what about me?" Giles asked. "Don't I get an invitation to this beanfeast?"

"Don't be silly, Giles," Amelia told him. "You'll be here, working. Someone has to look after the horses."

To Leander's delight, Steven agreed to spend five days in Cambridge: it was almost a holiday. And Amelia met them at the railway station

328

with the news that she had gained a first-class honours degree, one of only seven awarded by the university for the Mathematical Tripos that year.

On their first day, Steven allowed himself to be taken on the conducted tour and was enchanted, wandering through college courtyards and quadrangles in a trance.

After lunch, a carriage took them across Magdalene Bridge, up Castle Street and a mile and a half along the Huntingdon Road to Girton College, where a tea-party was given in Amelia's honour.

Bemused at being surrounded by what he thought of as frighteningly clever young women, Steven was content to be an inconspicuous adjunct to the occasion, smiling to himself as Leander became the centre of attraction. Six of Amelia's friends, all of whom were now graduates of one of the most famous universities in the world, quite literally sat at Leander's feet and bombarded her with questions ranging from fashions to the issue of votes for women and what careers they should pursue.

Perched on the arm of Steven's chair, Amelia detected his small, private smile. "What's the matter?" she asked.

"Wouldn't you have thought that your mother might have been just the tiniest bit out of her depth here?" he asked quietly.

"No. Would you?" Amelia replied and they both smiled.

The following afternoon, while Steven rested at the hotel, Leander and Amelia walked along the river until a cricket match on Jesus Green commanded their attention.

"Still no young man, darling?" Leander asked after they had been chatting of this, that and the other for ten minutes.

"No." Amelia thought about it with the same brief frown of fierce concentration that she brought to bear on mathematical problems. "Plenty of offers, but they all seemed so immature. Do you know what I mean?"

"Oh, yes! Men take much longer to grow up and come to hand than us superior beings!" Leander replied.

Amelia smiled at the equine terminology. "Giles isn't like that, though," she said.

"That's because he takes after your father. He was very mature as a young man."

"You know, I sometimes think that Father will hate it if I marry," Amelia said.

"Yes, in some ways you're still his little girl. But for heaven's sake don't let that put you off when you find the right man. Your father will understand."

Forty-eight hours later, Steven experienced one of the proudest moments of his life. One of hundreds on the lawn outside the Senate House, he and Leander posed for their photograph with Amelia, attired in gown, hood and cap, standing between them. He had found much of the ceremonial to be pure mumbo-jumbo, apparently performed for the benefit of the professors, Fellows and other permanent denizens of the university, each and every one of them arrayed in amazing finery. But, at the moment when his Amelia mounted the platform to receive her degree scroll, there were tears pricking at his eyes.

"That proves it," he said, confident that he had an arm round the two most beautiful and talented women in Cambridge, if not the world.

"Proves what?" Leander asked.

"We're not only good with horses and furniture in Cannings Ambo, we can do anything!"

As they were walking away from the crowds, Leander caught a glimpse of an astonishingly attractive young man whom she had noticed earlier at the degree ceremony. Now, he was the centre of a large, admiring group.

"Amelia, who's that?" she whispered.

Something very akin to disapproval registered on Amelia's face as she followed her mother's gaze and picked him out.

"That's Rupert Brooke," she said. "Rugby and King's College."

"He's *very* good-looking," Leander said.

"Do you think so?" Amelia remained as unimpressed as she had been for the past three years. "Mr Brooke wants to travel and put the world to rights."

"That should keep him pretty busy," Steven said.

"I believe he writes poetry," Amelia said.

"He looks as though he might!" Leander was enthusiastic.

"And there are stories about nude bathing," Amelia said, her disapproval now obvious. "Freda Stothert from Newnham swears they're true."

To Amelia's utter astonishment, her parents pulled po-faces at each other and burst into gales of laughter.

"You see, we managed it after all."

Steven was sure they were going to miss the three-fifteen from Paddington and had become strangely flustered about it. They arrived twenty minutes late at Liverpool Street from Cambridge, then the cab got stuck in a jam behind a motor waggon with a broken axle outside Madame Tussaud's Waxworks Exhibition in the Marylebone Road.

The three-fifteen was Steven's favourite train. It ran to Plymouth over the newly opened direct route through Westbury and Castle Cary, calling at Savernake on the way. He hated missing it and waiting for the four-thirty.

Leander had come close to sharing Steven's agitated misgivings, but once clear of the traffic obstruction, the cab driver performed miracles and there was ample time to find their compartment and settle down before the train pulled out.

"Are you comfortable there, sweetheart?" Leander asked.

"Yes, thank you, my dear." He sank into his corner seat and was asleep within seconds.

Quietly, as though discussing a matter of immense confidentiality, Leander and Amelia talked of the forthcoming Royal meeting at Ascot and the dresses that Ellie had made for Amelia. As the train left Newbury, a little over an hour after its departure from Paddington, Leander woke Steven, gently, by rubbing her cheek against his.

Stretching and yawning, he seemed to be experiencing great difficulty in waking up and adjusting to his surroundings. Leander was concerned for him until he brightened up after catching his first glimpse of Savernake Forest as the train rounded the curve at Bedwyn. He smiled and nodded as she read his thoughts.

"Yes, it has been a lovely time," he said, squeezing her hand, "but I shall be glad to be home."

Fred Partridge, the porter at Savernake, was looking out for them. Having helped with their hand-luggage, he trotted back to the guard's van with Amelia to unload her two cabin trunks. It was done smartly, the guard waved his flag and the train began to move.

It was at that instant that Leander, looking round for Giles who was supposed to be meeting them, turned sharply back to Steven, alarmed by his gasp.

"What is it?" she asked.

"Pain. I've got a pain."

"Where?"

He did not answer her. He turned his face up to the sky; then, as his chin sank back on to his chest, Leander saw that he looked lost and bewildered. He said, "Oh dear!" in a matter-of-fact sort of way, gasped again and clasped his arms across his chest.

"Steven!"

Leander's cry arrested Amelia's attention. She saw her father sink to his knees, remain there for a few moments as if in prayer, then pitch forward to lie face-down on the platform.

Giles, much later than he had intended because of a filly who had broken loose in the yard and injured herself, had just arrived on the

331

other side of the station in the new Rolls-Royce motor car. When he turned the engine off, he could hear Amelia above the noise of the accelerating locomotive.

"Mother! What's happened? Father! Father!"

Sick with apprehension, Giles was out of the car and on to the platform. He saw nothing until the last few coaches of the long train had moved out of the way.

Leander and Amelia were kneeling at Steven's side, looks of stunned disbelief on their faces; Fred Partridge was horror-stricken. No one else had got off the train, the platform was deserted. A sudden flurry of breeze caught Amelia's hat, which had fallen by her luggage, and sent it cart-wheeling towards the signal-box.

Giles jumped down and walked across the tracks, his awkward steps across the ballast the only sound. Reaching the edge of the platform, he found that his eyes were almost level with his mother's; in that terrible instant, he saw deep into her soul.

A few days past her forty-eighth birthday, Leander was a widow.

"No, Charles, you are not to blame yourself. I don't see how you could have spotted it. And in any case, what if you had? What would you have done? Put Steven in cotton wool?"

Surely, Charles Stanton thought, this was ridiculous: the day after Steven's funeral, and here was Leander comforting *him*. He had plucked up courage to go to The House to apologise for what must have been an incomplete diagnosis. If Steven had been susceptible to such a massive heart attack, why had he not seen the danger signs?

"For goodness' sake, sit down, Charles," Leander said. "You'll upset me if you carry on like this."

He did as he was told, having no wish to be the one who broke her iron control. But for her, Cannings Ambo might have fallen apart in the last six days.

There was no question of sending horses racing yet: apart from a period of mourning, Latimer's Barn had no right to do so until Giles had obtained a licence. But, on Leander's tight-lipped insistence, not a single day's work had been lost. Dismayed though the lads were by Steven's shockingly sudden death, the horses still needed attention.

"Well, what *could* you have done?" Leander asked.

Charles spread his hands helplessly. "Told him to take greater care of himself," he said lamely.

Leander smiled sadly. "He *was* taking care of himself, Charles," she said. "He simply would not have done any less."

"Possibly the trip to Cambridge?" Charles suggested.

"He wouldn't have missed that for the world."

"It *was* Cambridge that caused it, Mother," Amelia said urgently. "I don't think I should go back there. In any case, you need looking after."

Charles felt extremely out of place as he feared that grief was about to spill over into a quarrel.

"Amelia, please don't be silly." Leander's voice was tender. "What on earth gives you the idea that I need 'looking after'? Do you think I need wheeling round in a Bath chair?"

"No, of course not, but . . ."

"Listen, darling, hush!" Leander held up a hand for obedient silence. "You have been given a research scholarship. This is a great honour. It means that there are people at Cambridge who think you will have something important to say. It is also a responsibility and you will accept it. Is that understood?"

"Yes, Mother."

"Listen – both of you," Leander said. "There must be no regrets, no reproaches, no getting silly and maudlin. We can't live our lives like that . . . at least not here, in Cannings Ambo. We have to go that way . . ." she pointed ". . . the way our noses are pointing. If we don't, we may as well sell up and retire. Is that perfectly clear?"

Both Amelia and Charles Stanton nodded.

By the time William came to see her that evening, Leander felt much less sure of herself. She had spent the afternoon wracked with grief in the bedroom that she and Steven had shared for twenty-seven years and was haggard, weary and lonely. If anything, William looked even worse.

"What is it?" she asked.

"Maude. There's been an awful row and she's decided to go to London."

"What, out of the blue?"

"So she wants us to believe," William said. "I fancy she's been hatching it up for some time."

"And what brought this on?"

"She says it was the funeral."

"The funeral?" Leander frowned. "How odd."

William sat down beside her and clasped her hands in his. What could he say?

"I can't stand this any longer," Maude had stormed. "It's too ridiculous for words! I know Uncle Steven's death was upsetting, but there was no need for that performance at his funeral. Really! He only trained racehorses, Father – anyone would think someone important, like Renoir, had died!"

333

Ruth's reaction had been natural but unhelpful. "How dare you speak like that," she cried and slapped Maude's face.

"Exactly what I'd expect!" was the sneering response. "All this village ever thinks about is itself and God help anybody who doesn't agree with that. Look at poor George. He got damned short shrift, didn't he?"

It went on for nearly an hour and had brought William to the brink of hitting his daughter. Now, he had to find something to tell Leander.

"I'm afraid Maude thinks we're far too wrapped up with ourselves in Cannings Ambo," he said.

"She wants the world?"

"Something like that."

"When is she going?"

"Tomorrow."

"Oh!" Leander was surprised. "Where is she going to live?"

"With friends," William replied tersely, obviously not liking the implications.

"And what will she do in London?"

"Paint. She says she'll be able to get some 'proper' lessons and encouragement."

"What does Ruth think?"

"She's very annoyed, of course," William said quietly. "But she believes it's good riddance to bad rubbish." He paused reflectively. "It's a shame. I'd hoped we could make use of Maude's flair in some way."

"I think you'll find Ruth is right," Leander said.

"You've never thought Maude is all that talented, have you?" William asked.

"Not really, William," Leander said sadly. "And her attitude is awful – just like George's. Sometimes I wonder if that's our mother showing in them."

"Was she like that?"

"I don't know, William, but I've always had the idea that she was a bit of a wrong 'un."

William looked startled. The topic had never arisen before. "Did Father ever say anything to you about her?"

"No, but Aunt Elisabeth very nearly did on more than one occasion. I'm *sure* there was badness there. Don't worry, my dear, Gerald and Matthew are fine boys. You couldn't wish for better. And look at Giles and Amelia."

"Yes, but . . ." William's voice trailed off as he struggled to form his thoughts into some sort of order. "I suppose I must have failed her."

Leander shook her head vigorously. "Of course you didn't! The only mistake you might have made is giving her too much of her own way. Nine times out of ten she's been ungrateful and behaved badly. Look at this latest performance, for God's sake! Why did she have to choose today of all days? Did she think we hadn't got enough to worry about?"

Knowing that she was right made it no easier. William turned away, still in turmoil.

They stared into space for a long time; then, as their eyes met again, William saw that Leander had changed completely. All her strength and defences were gone.

"Oh, William," she whispered, "whatever am I going to do without Steven?"

The dam burst, and she was weeping. William put his arms round her, felt her tears on his face and hugged her in an attempt to share the grief that wracked her.

"You'll do what you've always done, Lea," he said. "You'll manage."

She did.

There were good things that helped and bad things that threatened to push her into the abyss, but she managed.

The village was wonderful. Cyril Osgood, known to be especially close to Leander, was elected spokesman.

"They're all very upset, ma'am," he said. "Mr Hawksworth was a fine gentleman and you must be grieving something terrible. Folk aren't going to make a nuisance of theirselves, but if you want anything doing, just give me the word and it'll be fixed."

For a few days, she considered asking for help to move furniture: she had the idea that it might be best to use another bedroom. In the end, she decided to stay put, with the bathroom and her memories of Steven.

Someone at the Jockey Club moved quickly, and two weeks after Steven's death, Giles received his licence. Eight days after that, he sent his first runner to Newbury, and, as if to emphasise the way Latimer's Barn evolved and regenerated itself, the jockey was Michael Pilgrim's son, Mark. The following morning, Giles, a mere twenty-three years of age, had the satisfaction of seeing the words: 'Winner trained by G. Hawksworth – Cannings Ambo, Wiltshire', at the end of the results and description of the race in *The Sporting Life*.

Her son's first winner sent Leander to the Big Book, and, as she lifted it on to the library table, she faced the necessity to record Steven's death. As with her father, the unhappy task took most of the day. At the end of it, Leander was left uncomfortably aware that Steven had died even younger than her father – fifty-two instead of fifty-seven. Surely, she told herself, it was sheer stupidity to imagine that the pattern would go on repeating: it was nothing more than a tragic coincidence.

The weeks crept past and a letter came from George, replying to news of his father's death. Leander, keeping away from the yard until she had recovered from her initial shock and giving Giles a chance to establish his authority, sat in her lonely bedroom to read and re-read the letter.

Since arriving in South Africa, George had written at intervals of roughly one month. He always began with news of his progress at Brandt and De Kuyper, usually couched in fairly bombastic terms in order to emphasise his princely salary and the esteem in which he was held. Then his social life received similar treatment. These tales invariably came close to amusing Leander: not for one moment did she doubt George's ability to be a centre of attraction and enjoy himself, but the numbers of attractive women who allegedly flung themselves at his feet were surely grossly overstated. Finally, as often as not, there would be complaints, some very bitter, about his banishment. These seemed almost convincing until one realised an important omission. Not once did George ask about the village, the stable, or the people who worked so hard to make them what they were.

Things were different this time, however. A comparatively short letter was devoted solely to Steven's death. George's expressions of sadness were obviously sincere, but were followed by a passage that Leander felt sure was specifically designed to hurt her.

I suppose Father must be reckoned to have been a wealthy man, yet, against all established custom, things are organised in such a way that the eldest son is completely disinherited. Never mind, Mother dear, I shall console myself with the thought of you, utterly triumphant as queen bee! Giles has always been so biddable, so I expect you will have even less trouble running things your way than when poor old Dad was trying to pretend that he was in charge. Long live Cannings Ambo and its self-appointed Duchess!

After a great deal of heart-ache, Leander wrote a reply that ignored this jibe. She also resisted the urge to stop paying George's allowance through a bank in Johannesburg. He had, she reminded herself, been fond of Steven. But she took careful note of the depth of rancour displayed by her wayward son.

*

In August, Amelia was elected to the Partnership and attended her first meeting as a Trustee. That same week, Giles asked for Leander's help and advice in the yard. Life was returning to normal.

When Leander came in for breakfast on her third day back at work, Ellie Goakes thought how much like her old self she was looking: the colour was in her face again and she was arguing furiously, but good-naturedly, with Giles and Albert Merriweather about the best way to deal with a fractious young colt.

Ellie waited until Leander had finished eating and holding forth before beckoning her out of the kitchen and into the small sitting-room.

"What is it, Ellie?" The expression on her dear friend's face made Leander urgent.

"Mary Shepherd came up from the Rectory just after you'd gone out," Ellie said.

"It's Aunt Elisabeth, isn't it?" Leander sagged resignedly.

"Yes."

Leander sat down; her colour was going. "During the night?" she asked, and Ellie nodded.

Elisabeth had been in the cottage hospital at Savernake for nearly four months, so ill that she had not even been told of Steven's death.

"I suppose we must look on it as a happy release," Leander said. She was trying to convince herself of this when she noticed Ellie's demeanour: it should have been relaxed now that she had delivered the bad news. Instead she looked more tense.

"Yes, Ellie?" Leander's voice sounded harsh.

"When Ann Mallender took Mrs Fandine-Browne's breakfast up to her, she found her dead."

Leander's face was bleached white, her hands shaking. "Dear God!" she muttered. "Was she in bed?"

"No. Next best thing, though. She was sitting in an armchair in her room."

"Both together!" Leander was dazed into disbelief.

"Don't you dare let go," Ellie told her sternly. "You're needed round here."

"I won't, Ellie," Leander promised. "But it isn't easy."

Ellie looked at her quizzically. "Is it supposed to be?" she asked. "I don't ever remember hearing that!"

Leaving Giles to look after the second lot, Leander went straight to The Hall. She met Charles Stanton on the way. They surveyed each other grimly.

"This is turning out to be a dreadful year, Charles," she said.

337

He nodded agreement. "I think Alexandra went quickly," he told her. "It was a cerebral thrombosis."

"I suppose that's a consolation," Leander said and hurried on to The Hall.

Ann Mallender had come to live at The Hall after the death of Lucy Miller. The arrangement served two purposes: it meant that Alexandra, good for her age, but undeniably seventy-seven, had capable help on hand. It also rid Ann of the daily bicycle rides to and from Marlborough in pursuit of her duties at the Cannings Ambo post office and general store. Leander was already thinking of Ann's future as she walked up the drive of The Hall.

Charles Stanton, assisted by Flora and Ann, had laid Alexandra out in her bed in the blue room where she and Giles Flamsteed had shared the delight of each other. Death had removed all signs of age in her face so that she was beautiful once more. Leander stood at the bedside for a long time before bending to kiss the cold forehead.

"You were very fond of her, weren't you?" Ann said as they walked downstairs together.

"Very, very," Leander replied. "She was a wonderful woman. Finding her must have been an awful shock for you, Ann."

"No, it wasn't. Not really. I must have spent nearly a minute looking at her and thinking how peaceful she looked."

Leander allowed a pause before asking, "Will you carry on living here, Ann?"

"I don't know. I haven't had time to think about it."

"No, I'm asking you to. The place needs living in and looking after."

"Isn't there anyone else you want to put in?" Ann asked.

"No."

Ann made up her mind. "All right! It's big, but I'm getting used to it. Thank you."

After visiting the Rectory to offer John and Mary her condolences for Elisabeth's death, Leander headed towards Rose House.

"Terrible!" William said, welcoming her with a pot of freshly made tea. "Two together. Unbelievable." He gestured towards the workshop. "Gerald and Matthew are making the coffins now – they asked to."

"That's nice." Leander suddenly found herself close to tears. "Well, William, that's both our mothers gone."

"Eh?" William was mystified.

"Aunt Elisabeth brought us up." As William nodded, Leander took a deep breath. "Father and Alexandra were lovers for years and I think she always regarded us as her children."

William gaped at her. "Father and Alexandra?" he asked.

"Yes."

"Are you sure?"

"Of course I am! Alexandra told me when Father died, but I'd known about it for years and years. Remember when he used to go to The Hall to see Jasper and Horatio and how he was always very late coming back?"

Slowly, understanding dawned on William and he began to remember things. There was the awful Mrs Dallow who had tried to stir up trouble in Marlborough: what was it Leander had said at the time? "Mrs Fandine-Browne will take care of that. She thinks highly of Father." That was thirty-three years ago, when Leander was fifteen.

"Well I'm blessed!" William said. "Why didn't you tell me this before?"

"I thought that you would have disapproved," she replied.

"Yes, I think I might have done at the time. Not now, of course."

"Quite! They deserved their happiness. They both had enough problems without people disapproving."

Elisabeth and Alexandra shared a funeral and burial; Elisabeth was placed in John Shepherd senior's grave, Alexandra was laid to rest between Giles Flamsteed and Steven.

That same afternoon, the Trustees gathered at Rose House to hear Alexandra's will read. Leonard Cockayne, the personable young solicitor from Marlborough who handled all the estate's business, took less than a minute over it.

"Put simply, Mrs Fandine-Browne left everything she had to the Partnership," Cockayne said. "The major items of bequest are the sum of forty-five thousand pounds in cash and the two stallions, Long Barrow and The Atheling."

Leander and William exchanged glances across the table. Their adopted 'mother' had remained true to the end and done them proud.

Alexandra's death brought a clamour from those who realised that Latimer's Barn was now able to take on more owners. Giles was content to leave the decisions to Leander, who, for the first time, could indulge in the luxury of turning people away because she considered them unsuitable. Those who were admitted were two gentlemen strongly recommended by the Duke of Laverstoke and Guy Mallender.

Guy, now the owner of grocery shops in Chippenham and Swindon as well as Marlborough, turned up one afternoon with an affable stranger whom he introduced as Harry Giffard.

"Harry's by way of being something of a colleague of mine, Mrs Hawksworth," Guy explained. "He has shops in Cirencester, Stroud and Tewkesbury and we club together to buy."

"We can get better prices when we purchase in bulk," Harry Giffard added.

Leander, who had taken an instant liking to him, smiled and said, "What a good idea. How did you meet in the first place to think it up?"

"My boy Jocelyn is married to Harry's daughter," Guy replied. "We got to talking about business one night and next thing you know, we'd hatched this scheme."

"And the beauty of it is, we can pass better prices down to our customers," Harry Giffard was at pains to point out.

"That's very clever." Leander was deeply impressed. "Do you have any plans for full partnership?"

"Yes!" Guy rubbed his hands enthusiastically. "We're hoping to open a shop in Cheltenham next year and it's going to be called 'Giffard and Mallender'."

Harry Giffard grunted and scratched his nose. "Say what you like, Guy, that don't sound right to me. 'Mallender and Giffard' is best. What would you say, Mrs Hawksworth?"

"You must decide for yourselves!" Leander laughed.

"Yes, quite right, shut up, Harry!" Guy said. "The thing is, Mrs Hawksworth, we thought we'd like to try owning a horse. We reckon we could afford it if we went halves. What do you say to that? Could you help us out?"

Leander thought rapidly. In many ways it might be a nuisance, but she looked on Guy Mallender, the man who had taken the photographs of her wedding, as an old and valued friend and wanted to oblige him. She also had a strong premonition that Mallender and Giffard, or whatever they decided to call themselves, were going to amount to something and last a long time.

"Yes, of course we can," she said. "But . . ." smiling, she held up a hand to restrain their exuberance ". . . we shall have to decide which one of you will be the registered owner. The Jockey Club and Weatherby's will insist on there being only one name."

"Oh dear!" Guy Mallender and Harry Giffard exchanged looks of dismay, rather like two schoolboys who knew they were about to be denied a treat.

"What shall we do, Harry?"

"Toss a coin?"

"Aye, that'll fix it."

340

It landed in favour of Guy Mallender, who duly became the registered owner of a horse that had belonged to Alexandra.

Before leaving Cannings Ambo that afternoon, the two grocers called in at Rose House and spoke to William about the possibility of Wm Flamsteed & Sons fitting out their new shop in Cheltenham.

Leander nodded appreciatively when the news came back to her. "We've had a few doors slammed in our faces this year," she said. "Now the new ones are beginning to open. That's progress. It's what we must have. Standing still won't get us anywhere except up Queer Street."

She looked and sounded supremely confident; people marvelled at her. Only the ever-watchful Ellie knew the truth. Without her beloved Steven, it was going to be a long time before Leander Hawksworth was able to enjoy a night's sleep or appear without red-rimmed eyes each morning.

CHAPTER 20

1909

'In circumstances like this, *I* decide the law'

Between taking over Latimer's Barn in June 1908 and the end of the season, four months later, Giles Hawksworth conjured nineteen winners out of twenty-seven runners. The racing world held its breath and suspended judgement: in all probability it was nothing more than beginner's luck based on what his father had left behind.

In April and May 1909, only one of the eleven horses sent out from Cannings Ambo failed to win and the verdict was unanimous. Giles Hawksworth was hailed as a genius with a golden touch.

Leander remained calmly unsurprised by it all.

"It's what I would expect," she told Giles. "You're our first proper born-and-bred trainer." She smiled. "So far we've had to make do with a wine-merchant and a boat-builder."

Then, early in June, something very curious happened. The Epsom stewards made a dope test on one of Giles's horses that had finished third in the race before the Oaks.

The test was negative, but the incident disturbed Leander profoundly. When she asked why the test had been carried out, she received the standard reply about the policy of selecting animals for test at random. However, the man who made the statement was unable to look Leander in the eye. Something dire was afoot.

A week later, Mark Pilgrim was desperately worried as he rode into the winner's enclosure at Sandown Park.

"This horse isn't right, sir," he told Giles.

"What's the matter?"

"That wasn't natural. I've never known a horse gallop like that. It felt all wrong."

Looking closely at the colt, Giles saw signs of distress and sent for a vet. At the same instant, the stewards ordered a dope test.

Like their colleagues at Epsom, they had received an anonymous letter.

This time, the test was positive: the colt had been given a massive dose of a stimulant. Scandalised whispers flashed round the course. What on earth was Giles Hawksworth playing at? Did this explain his phenomenal string of successes?

Leander and Giles had travelled up to Sandown in the Rolls-Royce. She was deep in thought during the journey home until, at nearly eight o'clock, she realised they were cruising down Savernake Hill into Marlborough.

"I want to call on Rupert Timberlake," she said. "We need help with this."

Rupert listened very carefully: apart from his desire to be of service to Leander, he was the owner of the doped horse.

"What will the authorities do?" was his first question.

"Giles will have to appear before the Jockey Club to give an account of himself," Leander replied.

"And what's the likely outcome of that?"

"I stand to lose my licence," Giles replied. "This is a *very* serious business."

"So we need to get to the bottom of it," Rupert said. It was a statement, not a question. "Any theories?"

"Yes!" Giles was absolutely certain. "It must have happened while the horse was in the racecourse stables last night."

"Aren't they well guarded?" Rupert asked.

"They're supposed to be!" Giles sounded very bitter.

"We used to look after them ourselves until a few years ago," Leander explained. "We only stopped because we thought it had all become very law-abiding." She smiled ironically.

Rupert mulled it over.

"Isn't this a damned funny way of carrying on?" he asked. "Wouldn't a villain normally fix a horse to *stop* it winning?"

"I believe that's usual," Giles said. "It's the gambling fraternity in action."

"So, what's going on here?"

"The Sandown Park stewards had received a letter saying that we had doped Sarsen Stone to win," Leander said. "Jimmy Watkinson showed me the letter. The funny thing is, I'd swear it was written by a woman."

"Someone's trying to ruin you," Rupert said.

"Yes, and it's quite a good way of doing it." Leander sounded almost as though she admired the enterprise. "It's far less trouble and risk than trying to burn Latimer's Barn down. All you need is a bent stable-lad and they must be two-a-penny."

"Is this one of Sixsmith's cronies, or someone connected with the Ruddocks?" Rupert asked.

"I don't know," Leander said. "Whoever it is, I want them found. *Quickly!*" She paused slightly. "This seems to be a job for those men of yours, Rupert, the ones you sometimes hint at."

He nodded. "I'll give it to Silas," he said. "I think he'll enjoy it."

Although Leander had never heard the name before, she did not react: her faith in Rupert was complete.

"There's one other thing," she said. "What are you doing tomorrow, Rupert?"

"Nothing much. I promised to look in on Basil, then I thought I might put my feet up. Why?"

"I want to go to Sandown Park. They're racing again."

"What time shall I come and collect you?" Rupert asked.

"Eleven o'clock will be early enough."

Giles waited until they were home before asking, "Why are you going to Sandown tomorrow, Mother?"

She took her time and spoke with great deliberation. "There are two reasons, my dear. I want to show people that we have nothing to be ashamed of and I'm going to do my best to buy us some time while Rupert and his men get cracking."

"How will you do that?"

"I don't know yet, but I'm sure I'll think of something."

Leander promised herself that she would never lie to Giles again.

Most of the crowd at Sandown Park were stunned when Leander appeared ten minutes before the first race. She was on Rupert's arm and seemed quite unconcerned.

No one had any excuse for ignorance; the doping and disqualification of Sarsen Stone was in all the newspapers. Some, hoping for a long-running sensation with a stream of shocking revelations, had put it on the front page.

Leander was amused by the reactions to her presence; most ignored her without going quite so far as to cut her dead; a few smiled weakly and passed on their way. Only one man had the guts to walk up to her and ask her what was going on.

The Honourable Oliver Derwent, fourth son of an earl, trained at Saxon Court near Compton Norris on the Berkshire Downs. Leander regarded Saxon Court as one of the few stables in England fit to hold a candle to Latimer's Barn. Derwent had a faraway, ethereal look about him and affected the manner of a dilettante. His down-to-earth approach gave the lie to his appearance.

"Now then, Leander, what the hell's all this about, eh?" he demanded.

"Somebody got at our horse while he was here the other night. It's the only possible explanation."

"That's what I thought. You want to nail the scoundrel, fast! There are some thoroughly bad hats about."

"Don't worry," Leander assured him. "We're giving it our best attention."

"Need any help?"

"No, thank you, Ollie. It's in good hands."

"Don't forget to shout if there's anything I can do."

"What an amazing fellow," Rupert said, after Oliver Derwent had gone to get a horse ready for the next race.

"He's one of the best," Leander replied. "I'll tell you something else, as well, my dear. He's a damned good trainer."

"Good Lord!" Rupert was astounded. "You don't say that about many of them."

"If I remember correctly, Rupert, I've *never* said it about *anyone* before," Leander said.

By the time the third race was being run, Leander was disturbed; there was no sign of the man she had come to see. She was on the point of giving up and asking Rupert to take her home when he appeared, strolling nonchalantly along the paddock rail.

"Who's that?" Rupert whispered. "He looks as if he owns the place."

"He does, in a manner of speaking. That, Rupert, is Sir Walter Rothwell, the new Senior Steward of the Jockey Club."

"Is it, by God!" Rupert looked long and hard at the man he knew had propositioned Leander.

"I want to talk to him," Leander said. "Stay here."

Leander's seemingly aimless wandering was perfectly judged: their meeting looked entirely accidental.

"Good afternoon, Sir Walter," Leander said.

"How do you do, Mrs Hawksworth?" He raised his hat. "I must have misread my racecard – I don't recall seeing that you had a runner today."

"I haven't. I came here to be seen."

"That's very brave of you."

"It is, isn't it?"

She watched his mind working as he resisted the temptation to look round to discover who was observing them.

"I think you and I have matters to discuss, Mrs Hawksworth," Rothwell said carefully. "The starter's office will be empty. Will you come there in ten minutes?"

"Yes, I will."

He raised his hat and walked away. Leander exchanged a joke with a passing acquaintance, spoke to Rupert, then went to the offices at the side of the grandstand by a circuitous route.

Rothwell was perched on the edge of a desk: Leander sat down on a conveniently placed chair and gazed at him.

"That was a serious business yesterday," Rothwell began. "Your son is likely to forfeit his licence over it." Leander inclined her head to show that she understood. "Tell me, Mrs Hawksworth, what is your view of the matter?"

"The horse was got at in the stables here."

"I understand that possibility is being investigated. However, I am told that the man who looks after the stables is very reliable." He paused. "It seems a long time since I told you that you would need a friend. You rejected the idea."

"I had a husband then," Leander said quietly.

As Rothwell stared at her, the atmosphere between them became tense.

"Are you telling me that things have changed?" he asked.

"My husband has been dead for nearly a year."

"And you are prepared to accept my offer?"

"Yes." Leander's reply was barely audible.

"I think you are very wise, Mrs Hawksworth," Rothwell said in a voice as near expressionless as he could make it. "May I suggest that we need to bring our arrangement to . . ." he groped for a word ". . . fruition . . . as soon as possible?"

"I agree," Leander replied boldly.

Relaxing visibly, he pulled out a slim pocket-book. "I thought I might look in at Lingfield next week," he said. "One of my own horses is likely to run. I usually stay with a friend whose discretion can be relied upon absolutely."

Leander nodded. "Very well, I shall look forward to it," she said. There was nothing to indicate anything but sincerity.

As they made the arrangements, Leander was astonished by Rothwell's grasp of the railway timetable, which he recited from memory. When she saw that he was inordinately proud of his expertise, she had to contain an unexpected surge of amusement.

There was comment round the paddock afterwards about Sir Walter Rothwell's exceptionally benign manner.

"What's he up to?" one owner asked another.

"He's probably found a new way to nail some poor devil."

The truth was already ten miles away: having achieved her objective, Leander asked Rupert to take her home.

At six o'clock, when both the day's racing and the three-day meeting were over, Arthur Elliot went home for his tea. Until the next racing in four weeks, he had very little to do, but would keep himself busy for the sake of appearances. At thirty-five, he was very lucky to have landed such a comfortable billet with a reasonable wage and a good house, beautifully situated in open country on the edge of Sandown Park. It came close to making up for the twenty thankless years in a Newmarket stable run by a deranged tyrant. Elliot had only one complaint: he wanted more money. However, things might be looking up: that fifty pounds the other night simply to go home for an hour could be the first of many such payments.

He knew at once that something was wrong. Bustling in through the back door, he found the kitchen empty and unusually tidy. No attempt had been made to get his meal ready and the house was deathly quiet.

"May?" he called uncertainly.

"In here." Her reply, from the parlour, was strained.

Elliot found his wife sitting bolt upright in the armchair by the empty fireplace. Elsie, their six-year-old daughter, was clinging to her skirts. Mother and child were petrified by the four men who occupied all the small room's available chairs and space.

Three of them were well-dressed ruffians, made presentable for a special occasion. None of them had uttered a word since forcing their way into the house an hour ago. Because they preferred action to being cooped up like this, they were bored and dangerous. But the elegant young man in the armchair facing May Elliot and her daughter was completely at ease. Every line of his strong, lithe body was in repose, yet the air of menace about him was all-powerful.

If Rupert Timberlake's cousin, Martha, had married Silas's father, the boy would have carried a noble name, but Martha Timberlake insisted on retiring to Savernake Forest to rear her by-blow alone. Now twenty-five, Silas was Rupert's most trusted lieutenant for unconventional or dangerous jobs.

"You let someone into your stables the other night, Elliot," Silas said. "I want to know where I can find that man."

"I did no such thing!" Elliot blustered. "What a scandalous thing to say. Get out of my house!"

"Oh dear!" Silas sounded sorrowful. Very slowly, as though the effort was too much for him, he stood up, walked to the window, and spent a long time studying the view.

"This is a very pleasant spot," he said inconsequentially. Turning to face Elliot, his face remained expressionless as he went on: "Unfortunately for you, it seems somewhat isolated – we must be at least a mile from anywhere." His manner changed abruptly. "I am a very busy man looking into a serious business, Elliot. I have no time for silly games. Tell me what you know or I will have it beaten out of you."

May Elliot believed him. "Do as he says, Arthur," she urged.

"Be quiet!" Elliot snapped at her. He glared defiantly at Silas. "I've told you, I know nothing."

Wearily, Silas Timberlake nodded to his men. Two of them sprang to their feet and May Elliot wailed with fear as they dragged her husband outside to the shed.

"I regret this, Mrs Elliot," Silas said. "But we really are determined to get at the truth."

Joe Symes was taken from his seedy lodgings in Reading at nine o'clock. He arrived at Latimer's Barn two hours later, after his first ride in a motor car, a nightmarish journey that he would never forget. Thanks to the telephone, Leander and Giles were waiting up, expecting him.

Symes was forty. Until two years ago, he had worked in the same Newmarket training establishment as Arthur Elliot; unlike Elliot, he had been unable to find regular work since. On the way down from Reading, Silas Timberlake had made him brutally aware of the seriousness of his crime: not that there was any need for the frightening lecture. Joe Symes loved horses and was disgusted with himself for sticking a needle in one: he'd starve rather than do it again.

The House was bright and cheerful, lit by electricity from the generator that Cyril Osgood had recently installed in a shed next to the old coach-house. Frog-marched into the small sitting-room, Joe Symes had time only for fleeting impressions of fine décor and spaciousness.

Like everyone else in racing, and a good few outside it, he knew Leander by sight; he had first seen her at Newmarket nearly twenty years ago on a Two Thousand Guineas day. It might have been a trick of the new-fangled lighting, but she looked lovelier than ever and she must have been well into her forties. The very handsome young man standing behind her chair was obviously the one they called Giles the Second, the man whose licence was in grave danger.

348

"Why did you dope our horse, Mr Symes?" Leander asked in a way that sounded like everyday conversation.

"A gentleman paid me, Mrs Hawksworth, ma'am. I was in a bad way and needed the money, but I wish I hadn't. It was wrong."

Leander considered this and his obvious distress for a moment or two before she asked, "Who was this man?"

"I don't know, ma'am."

"Have you met him?"

"Oh, yes, ma'am. Captain Beamish introduced us."

"Captain Beamish?"

"Life Guards . . . regular gentleman, ma'am." Joe Symes paused to reconsider this statement. "Well, perhaps he isn't."

"Do we know this Beamish?" Leander asked Silas.

"No, Mrs Hawksworth."

Leander turned to Joe Symes again. "Where did you meet the man who gave you your instructions and paid you?"

"At a pub in Reading, ma'am. Captain Beamish fixed it up."

"And he was quite clear what he wanted you to do?"

"He was, ma'am. I thought it was a bit funny and made him tell me all over again. I mean to say, gentlemen of his sort usually want a horse *stopping*."

"How many times have you met him?"

"Three. I was supposed to do one for him last week, but I couldn't manage it."

"That was at Epsom?" Leander said.

"Yes, ma'am. I couldn't find a way into *those* stables. I'm meant to be seeing him next Friday to fix something for Ascot. I'd made up my mind not to go – not that it matters now."

"Why doesn't it matter?" Leander asked.

Joe Symes did his best to look brave. "Got no choice, have I, ma'am. No magistrate is going to let *me* out on bail."

Leander looked at him thoughtfully. "I want this man, Mr Symes," she said. "If we don't proceed against you, will you help us catch him?"

He blinked in disbelief. "You won't turn me in?"

"No."

He considered it, but not for long. The story was that her word was good. "Yes, I'll do it," he said.

"Silas?" Leander raised an eyebrow that posed a wide range of questions.

"Yes, Mrs Hawksworth, we can handle it."

"Mr Symes, please tell this gentleman exactly where and when your meeting is," Leander said. "You will keep the appointment.

Other than that, there is no need for you to do anything. We shall handle it."

"Yes, ma'am. Anything you say. I won't let you down."

Suspecting that Joe Symes might be about to indulge in an embarrassing display of gratitude, Leander moved to pre-empt it. "What does this man look like?" she asked.

"Well . . . he's tallish . . . darkish hair . . . good-looking sort of chap . . ."

"How old is he?" Leander asked impatiently, eager for some definite information.

"Oh, young. No more than twenty-five I'd say."

"Right. Is it possible to take Mr Symes back home tonight, Silas?" Leander wanted to know.

"Yes."

"Now, you do understand the position, don't you?" Leander said to Joe. "Play fair with us and what you did to Sarsen Stone will be overlooked. If you don't do the right thing, your life will not be worth living. Is that perfectly clear?"

Joe could have sworn that her gorgeous blue eyes had turned frosty-grey. "Yes, Mrs Hawksworth," he said earnestly.

There was a long silence in the small sitting-room after they had gone.

"You're going to have this man brought here?" Giles asked eventually.

"Yes."

"Then what?"

"I shall find out why he's trying to ruin us and take the appropriate action!"

It was a chilling statement to which Giles's failure to reply gave tacit approval. On the whole, Leander was glad of that, even though she had every intention of doing what was necessary with or without her son's blessing.

Leander was forced to suppress a giggle: the whole thing was too theatrically comical for words. The train drew into the remote station on the border of Surrey and Sussex, and, as she alighted from a carriage at the rear, Sir Walter Rothwell emerged from the front. With only Lord James Hartley's chauffeur as a credulous witness, they enacted the pantomime.

"Mrs Hawksworth!"

"Sir Walter!"

"My dear lady, I had no idea you were on the train."

"How did we miss each other at Victoria Station?"

Comfortable in the motor car, they set off on the two-mile drive to Reedswood House. What little conversation passed between them left Leander's mind free for the final collection of her thoughts.

Her unprecedented absence from Latimer's Barn had made Giles extremely nervous.

"Will you really be away for two or three days, Mother?" he asked repeatedly.

"Yes, my dear. I have things that must be attended to."

"Giving us time?"

"Something like that, yes."

Unsure, but knowing that he must trust her, Giles had forced himself to shut up.

Throughout the journey to London, then into this strangely secluded corner of England, Leander had found that she was perfectly calm. Once her mind was made up on the way to save Latimer's Barn from disgrace and ruin, she saw no point in worrying. Almost the reverse in fact: she looked at Rothwell speculatively, causing him to smile self-consciously as he came very close to comprehending her thoughts. For a very long time, his blatant avowal of lust for her had been distressing; but now, it would not be long before he was forced to show what he could do with her.

Reedswood House was two hundred years old and set in a lush park of about fifty acres. Leander knew that Lord James Hartley, widely suspected of being a ravenous lecher, had substantial interests in banking and insurance; she assumed that this pleasant rural retreat enabled him to set money-grubbing to one side while he concentrated on serious sport.

The butler met them with the news that their host was out for the day.

"Good afternoon, Sir Walter, Mrs Hawksworth. Lord James and Mrs Armytage-Hanson have gone to the coast. They will be back in time for dinner."

Leander kept her face straight: Lily Armytage-Hanson was an ex-actress who had married extremely well, but not well enough, it seemed, to render her faithful.

When they were shown up to their rooms, the thoroughness of the arrangements was immediately apparent. Leander and Rothwell had adjoining bedrooms at the end of a corridor tucked into a discreet corner of the house; she found that there was a connecting door with the lock on her side.

After their cases were brought up and an efficient maid had unpacked for her, Leander unlocked the door and went briskly into

351

Sir Walter's room. He seemed surprised and a little awkward to be caught with his jacket off and waistcoat unbuttoned.

"Ah . . . Mrs Hawksworth . . . I was wondering if you would care to walk in the park before tea," he said.

Leander thought quickly. She had already decided that the only way to handle what lay ahead was on her own terms: and there was no time like the present.

"Could we not stay here and have tea brought up in an hour or so?" she asked.

"Yes . . . er . . . yes, by all means, if you wish to rest."

Leander smiled at him. "No, I don't want to rest," she said. "Far from it! I see that my bathroom has a shower. I've always wanted to try one. Come to me afterwards. Fifteen minutes."

She closed the door before he had time to speak.

Sixteen minutes later, Rothwell tapped on the door and appeared, clad in a long bathrobe, to find Leander brushing her hair at the dressing-table. She wore a loose-fitting silk wrap.

"Did you enjoy the shower-bath?" he asked, doing his best to appear in command of the situation.

"Yes, thank you. It was very stimulating." She smiled, giving emphasis to the word, seemed satisfied with her hair and moved towards the bed, which she had already turned down.

"Well, Walter," she said when she was stretched out comfortably and he was perched somewhat diffidently on the edge of the bed, "here we are!"

"Indeed."

The confidence that Rothwell wore in public life had gone, leaving him hesitant and vulnerable. Perhaps, Leander thought, he had expected to take her in his own way, with brisk, uncomplicated mastery. Deprived of the scope to do that, he was in a quandary that threatened to become humiliating unless she acted swiftly.

Sitting up, she laid her cheek against his, slipped an arm round his shoulders and guided one of his hands to her breasts. Once she had soothed the initial clumsiness of his kiss, they found themselves moving into a more comfortable position. Nerving herself, Leander took the final step and pulled at the waist-belt of her wrap. As the garment fell apart, Rothwell's reaction was most gratifying.

"Oh, Leander!" he gasped. "You are magnificent!" Clearly entranced, he smoothed the palm of a hand over her taut stomach and down between her thighs. "I don't believe it! How old are you?"

"No, Walter," she chuckled. "That's one thing you shan't have."

Reverently, he lowered his face to her perfect breasts and began teasing the nipples with his tongue. Relaxed and diverted by his attentions, Leander lost track of time and was unaware of his mounting urgency until he reared up, struggling to enter her.

As she accepted him, she had a clear perception of what was about to happen. After no more than a dozen stabbing lunges, he was convulsed by his climax. She lay completely still, holding him tightly in a comforting embrace.

"I'm so sorry," he muttered into her shoulder. "I got myself over-excited."

"Hush! Perhaps it was my fault."

"Oh, no, Leander, it was mine!"

She smiled secretly. Never had she dared imagine that things would turn out this well. "Never mind," she said. "Everything will be all right next time."

It was, and very soon. Enthusiastically using tricks that she had not been aware she possessed, Leander roused Walter Rothwell to intense lust in no more than ten minutes.

She did not see the birthmark until they were back in her room after dinner with Lord James and Mrs Armytage-Hanson.

Following another bout of carnal exercise that Leander had found far less unpleasant than she had feared, Walter Rothwell declared himself capable of carrying on all night once he was fortified by a glass of brandy and went, naked, to his room to get it.

Watching him through half-closed eyes, Leander spotted the distinctive mark on his left buttock. It was an almost perfect equal-sided triangle with sides of about two inches.

She stifled the urge to comment; there was every chance that he might be upset by mention of such a personal thing. And there was a strong intuitive feeling that it would be better if she pretended not to have seen it.

The two full days that Leander spent at Reedswood House proved to be an unexpectedly peaceful interlude. For much of the time she was thrown into the company of Lily Armytage-Hanson as Rothwell and Lord James Hartley attended the races at Lingfield Park.

During one of their walks in the park, Lily gave Leander a piece of good news.

"Are you here for something special, Leander?" she asked.

"Yes. Can you keep a secret?"

Lily grinned. "Got to, haven't I? I wouldn't last five minutes if I couldn't keep my mouth shut."

Leander saw the truth in this. "It's to do with that doping business at Sandown Park."

"Oh, yes, that was one of your horses, wasn't it?" Lily nodded knowingly. "Walter will do the right thing by you."

"Will he?" Leander asked, anxious for reassurance.

"Yes, he will. I know he's a swine to most people, but James says he can be very grateful."

On their last night, Leander made a special effort to ensure that Walter Rothwell enjoyed himself: she was rewarded by having him fall into blissfully deep sleep in her bed after she had ensured that he experienced two highly satisfactory orgasms.

They parted on the deserted railway station the following morning. Before he walked to the other end of the platform so that they could travel to London separately, Rothwell thanked Leander profusely for their time together.

"I must keep my side of the bargain now," he told her. "I will do everything I can to help you."

"This particular individual won't be doping any more of our horses," Leander assured him.

"You sound very confident."

"I am!"

He studied her quizzically. "Are you going to tell me who it was?" he asked.

"No."

"One of your 'friends' from the Association?" he prompted.

She laughed. "Dear me! I always thought that was a secret feud. No, they were done for years ago – apart from Sixsmith's son, and he's safely under lock and key."

He pursued it no further. Kissing her on the cheek he said, "I would like us to meet like this again."

Leander smiled enigmatically. Rothwell's attempt to mask his insincerity was half-hearted. He had achieved his ambition, enjoyed himself in the process and would discharge the obligations of their pact. But he knew there was no basis for friendship between them. Out of the bedroom, what little time he had spent with Leander had been largely a struggle to generate conversation that was tolerably rather than embarrassingly banal. They had nothing in common and he would return to a younger, more impressionable woman who could be relied upon to be abidingly grateful for his patronage.

There was no sign of him at Victoria and Leander took a cab to Paddington Station, where a suitable train was leaving in twenty minutes. After finding a first-class, ladies-only compartment, she removed her hat and set her hair to rights with the aid of the mirror above the seats. "Well, my girl, here's a thing," she muttered to her reflection. "Forty-eight years of age and you start whoring!" She grimaced. "Never mind, it was in the best possible cause."

Suddenly, without warning, she was shaking, utterly at a loss to know how she had managed to go through with it. Sinking to a seat, she reached for her handbag and the flask of brandy held in reserve throughout the escapade. After drinking avidly, she found herself opening the window and wafting her broad-brimmed hat about in a vain attempt to dispel the fumes.

She need not have worried: no one disturbed her peace and the train was soon under way. Safe from prying eyes, she drank again.

The soothing effect of the strong spirit, allied to the motion of the train heading for her precious Wiltshire, gave Leander a new perspective on the distasteful episode. Pathetically inadequate though he was, Walter Rothwell had actually sharpened her memory of Steven. For several days afterwards, Leander felt his loss more keenly than ever, and, for the first time, her bereavement was distressingly physical.

George was enjoying his holiday in England.

Only Jane Anstruther, with whom he had corresponded frequently, knew of his arrival and met him at Southampton. Once they were safely inside her house at Maidenhead, it was two days before they re-emerged after satisfying their immediate need of one another.

Now twenty-nine, Jane was a rich widow. Sir Henry Anstruther had died a year after George went to South Africa, leaving Jane with more than enough money to finance the most extravagant of life-styles. She was, however, content to sell the London house and use the proceeds to acquire a property on the Thames at Maidenhead where she lived fairly quietly. Her letters to George made no secret of her experiments with several lovers and their abysmal failure to reach anything like his standard of performance.

After their first two days, when George and Jane needed a respite and began to take stock of their situation, there was serious talk of marriage. The only obstacle was Jane's reluctance to go to South Africa.

"There's no earthly reason why we shouldn't stay here, George," she said. "That old fool Blennerhasset is finished and I'm sure Blayne-Singer's would give you a job again. Alec virtually said as much a couple of months ago."

"My God, have you been to bed with *him* as well?" George laughed, before becoming very earnest. "No, my love, England is no place to be. As sure as I'm sitting here, there's going to be a war."

Jane's face clouded. "A lot of people think that."

"They're damned well right," George replied.

"Surely we'd be all right with my money?" Jane suggested.

"Not if I had to fight! If you want to put money to good use, South Africa's the place. We could start our own business."

After several days of discussion, Jane was beginning to agree with him. George's intended campaign against his mother was an irritation that distracted them from their plans, rather than anything she was prepared to take seriously. Nevertheless, she made frequent protests about it.

"Are you sure you want to do this?" she asked.

"Yes, I am!" George was suddenly livid with hatred. "She treated me abominably and I want to pay her back. The poor old governor's safely out of the way so I can do for her and that prig Giles."

"But isn't what you're doing rather terrible? Couldn't it ruin the stable and the village?"

"I'm hoping so," was the grim reply.

Still unaware that lust for revenge was the prime reason for George's presence in England, and rather struck by the idea of marrying him, Jane enlisted the help of her brother.

Howard Beamish, a captain in the Life Guards, knew an astonishing number of unsavoury characters. He unearthed Joe Symes and made the introduction to George inside a week. Jane worried when George insisted on conducting the negotiations himself, without the use of a go-between.

"Don't be silly, darling, nothing can possibly go wrong," George assured her with easy confidence. "Doing it this way is essential to ensure my instructions are carried out precisely, and in any case, I'm meeting him at a public house in Reading where no one can possibly know me from Adam. Now, there's something you can do to help."

Leander had been right: the anonymous letters to the Stewards were written by a woman.

There was the false start at Epsom, then the success at Sandown Park, the newspaper coverage of which caused George to gloat.

"One more should fix them for good," he said. "And if I can arrange it for Royal Ascot, all hell will be let loose." He looked wickedly gleeful. "Imagine the great Leander Hawksworth being made to look a shyster in front of the cream of English society!"

"George, do you *really* want to carry on with this vendetta?" Jane asked anxiously, repeating a question she had put to him at least ten times already.

"Of course. Now stop fretting, my darling." George was dressing, getting ready to travel to Reading for his meeting with Joe Symes. Jane was lying on the rumpled bed from which he had just prised himself. Seeing her disquiet, George decided that it was time for the present he had brought from South Africa: she watched in wonder as he took the two ten-carat diamonds from their tissue paper, placing one in her navel and the other in the midst of her fascinating pubic hair. Kissing her on the nose, he left while she was still distracted.

The weather put George in a bad mood and possibly impaired his powers of observation. All that concerned him as he hurried from Reading railway station to the inn a few streets away, his umbrella braced against the driving rain, was the need to point out the climatic advantages of South Africa to Jane.

Joe Symes was waiting in a corner of the dingy bar. George gave the room a cursory glance and settled to business.

Silas Timberlake, who had never seen George before and had no idea who he was, was taking no chances: eight of his men were sitting in pairs in various parts of the room. As soon as they were sure that they would recognise George once he was outside in the foul evening, they drifted away at random intervals to guard the four alleys, one of which George must use when he had finished with Joe Symes.

Silas remained alone at his table, waiting for the signal that the conference was nearing its end.

Distaste for his surroundings made George impatient to be done. He attributed Joe's very tense attitude to nervousness and congratulated himself on having come prepared to anticipate it.

"Look here," he said, "I appreciate that there may be extra difficulties for you at Ascot, so I'm prepared to give you a hundred pounds. For that, I want *two* of Hawksworth's horses seen to. I understand he'll be sending six to the meeting, so you've a good choice."

As instructed by Silas, Joe proved difficult to convince, finally giving in when Silas lit a cigarette to indicate that his men would now all be in position. As the linen bag containing one hundred sovereigns was pushed across the table, Silas left.

His was the most difficult task, to have the motor car in a position such that George did not have to be dragged far before he was bundled in. In the event, it was easy: coming out of the public house and glowering at the weather, George made straight for the most obvious of the alleys. Silas had a comparatively easy dash round a block of about twenty terrace-houses to get to the other end where his men were lurking.

Because he held the umbrella in front of his face, George never saw them. By waiting until he was very nearly at the end of the narrow passage, the Timberlake men had to propel him only three paces into the expertly positioned car. As it drove off, the blinds were pulled down and Silas tooted a signal on the horn so that the six who had not been needed could fade away to make their own way back home.

Initially taken completely by surprise, George's subsequent struggles were fierce but vain. His captors were strong and brutal; the car had barely travelled half a mile before he was bound hand and foot and gagged.

Joe Symes stood in the rain looking down the alley at George's umbrella, left behind in the fray. He decided to collect it to avoid arousing the curiosity of a patrolling policeman. As he did so, he recalled Silas Timberlake's final instruction.

"Mrs Hawksworth wants to see you tomorrow at Latimer's Barn. If you've got any worthwhile belongings, I'd take them with you."

By the time George was escorted into The House at a few minutes to eleven, Leander and Giles had received a telephone call from Rupert to prepare them for the shock. When Silas had stopped in Marlborough to collect an extra car and more men, Rupert had, of course, recognised their captive.

Leander staged the confrontation in the rarely used large sitting-room. As George faced her, he was fully aware of what this meant: it was the equivalent of an assize court. Rupert and Silas Timberlake flanked him, three of Silas's men stood behind him. Giles was at Leander's right, their arms linked.

George glared defiantly at his mother, waiting for her to speak. She took her time.

"When did you return to England, George?" Leander asked calmly.

"Mind your own damned business!"

She gave no sign that his virulent hostility had touched her. When, after a pause, she spoke again, her voice was level. "What has this been in aid of? Are you trying to ruin us?"

"Yes!"

"Why?"

"You ruined me."

Leander stared steadily at her eldest son, quite content to let the silence build up between them.

"Well?" George demanded angrily. "Haven't you anything to say to that?"

"No. I refuse to bandy words with you."

"Wonderful!" George sneered. "I suppose I have that rat Symes to thank for this. By God, I'll see he gets his come-uppance!"

Leander appeared startled, finding George's idea almost laughable. "Whatever gives you the idea that you will be at liberty to do so?" she asked.

"Why shouldn't I be?" George asked. "Or are you going to persuade the police to take me in?"

Ignoring him, Leander addressed Rupert. "My Steven had only one fault: he never gave this specimen the damned good hiding he so richly deserved. Would you attend to that, please, Rupert? Then lock him up for a few days to cool his heels."

"You can't do that!" George yelled, fear taking a hold on him. "That's wrongful detention. It's against the law!"

Leander gave him a look of implacable loathing. "In circumstances like this, *I* make the law," she said. "You have been responsible for a disgusting crime – not against me, or your brother, but against an innocent animal. Horses who are given stimulants can become seriously ill, or even die after over-exerting themselves in a race. Did you know that, George? And if you knew, did you care? Get him out of my sight, Rupert!"

When they were alone, Leander turned to Giles and saw that he was white-faced with distress. "You will not breathe a word of this to anyone," she said. "Anyone at all! Do you understand?"

He nodded.

"And first thing tomorrow morning," Leander went on, "you and Albert Merriweather will take that yard by the scruff of the neck and carry on as though nothing had happened."

Fifty miles away in Maidenhead, Jane Anstruther was beside herself with worry.

Joe Symes reached Marlborough at one o'clock the following day and set out to walk to Cannings Ambo. Although mystified by it, he had followed Silas Timberlake's advice and brought a bag containing all that he wanted to salvage from his lodgings.

He was overawed by what he found. He knew that it was bound to be a bit out of the ordinary, but was unprepared for such beauty and the aura of well-being.

Abraham Merriweather, pottering in his garden, eyed Joe suspiciously as he hesitated at the foot of the drive.

"Yes? What do you want?" he demanded.

Joe resisted the urge to run away and said, "Mrs Hawksworth wants to see me," as boldly as he could.

Not believing him, Abraham escorted him up the drive and round to the back door of The House.

"He says the mistress sent for him," Abraham told Ellie Goakes, implying that the idea was ridiculous.

"Are you Joe Symes?" Ellie asked.

"Yes, ma'am."

"Come in! Have you had anything to eat?" Ellie produced a special smile for a baffled-looking Abraham and ushered Joe to a chair.

Summoned by a maid, Leander came at once.

"Thank you for your efforts yesterday evening," she said. "We have the man."

"He gave me a hundred sovereigns," Joe said. "What shall I do with them?"

"Put them in a safe place for your old age," Leander said.

"What's happening to him?"

"He is being dealt with," Leander replied in a tone that indicated the topic was not to be discussed. "Now, what about you, Joe? What's going to become of you? Can you find work?"

"I expect so, ma'am. I shall be all right."

"No you won't," she said bluntly. "You were prey to the first villain that came along and you will be again. You strike me as a man who has worked in a stable."

"Yes, ma'am, I was with Major Blenkinsop."

"That lunatic! What was it like?"

"Mostly very bad. He had some lovely horses and ruined them. He should have been put away."

"I want you to work for us," Leander said.

Joe was flabbergasted. "What, here? At Latimer's Barn?"

"Yes."

"What would I do?"

"You can help out with general work in the yard and go to the races with Peter Izzard, our travelling head lad. Your main job will be to keep your eyes and ears open for trouble. I want to know if people are trying to do us down."

"I'll do that, ma'am."

"Good! Don't ever make me regret this decision, Joe."

"No fear! I reckon you'd have the hide off my back."

"You're right, I would! Let's find you somewhere to live."

Leander did not attend the first day of Royal Ascot. Instead, Rupert drove her to the isolated lodge in Savernake Forest that was the home of Silas and temporary prison for George.

When her son was brought in from the outhouse in which he was locked for most of the time, Leander stared at him without a trace of emotion. A week after the beating, the cuts and bruises on his face were healing, but he still looked a mess with his black eye and badly split lip.

"I want to send a letter to someone," he said sullenly.

"You can't!" Leander snapped. "Sit down."

"I only want her to know I'm still alive! She'll be worried. We're going to get married."

"Sit down," Leander repeated. "Is this lady in South Africa?"

"No, here, in England."

"Then you won't be marrying her," Leander said. "Oh, yes, George, you're going back. But first, you will sign this." She pulled two sheets of paper covered with typewriting from her bag. "This is a confession. If you ever set foot in this country again, I shall use it."

George took the paper from her and scanned the first paragraph with weary cynicism. It struck him as being an excessively long-winded statement that he had caused the colt Sarsen Stone to be drugged with a view to ensuring that it won at Sandown Park. Bored, he was about to skip to the end when a sentence from the much shorter second paragraph leapt off the page at him.

"What the hell is this?" he demanded. "It says here that I threatened Joe Symes with blackmail and violence if he didn't do what I wanted."

"That's right," Leander said evenly. "I advise you to look closely at the second page."

As he did so, incredulity, anger and hysterical amusement spread across George's face. "May I ask who Doris Parker is?" he said, making much of the effort to keep calm.

"She's one of our maids."

"According to this, I raped her."

"Correct!"

George ran his hands through his hair, then stabbed a nervous finger at the paper. "The story is that after you taxed me with doping your precious horse, I ran amok and raped a maid." As he stared at Leander in quiet desperation, Rupert Timberlake shifted uneasily. "Mother, have you gone completely insane?" George pleaded.

"No." Several moments passed before Leander saw the necessity to amplify her stark reply. "There is the evidence of the girl, of course. We also have a medical opinion."

"You can't have!"

"Yes we can."

"The penalty for rape is life imprisonment," George shouted in a sudden distraught frenzy.

"I'm glad you realise that," Leander said.

Mother and son stared at each other: thinking that George was on the verge of manic and violent action, Rupert became alarmed, shooting an anxious glance at the unresponsive, imperturbable Silas. Slowly, the fury drained out of George. For a second or two he looked defeated, then, with a flash of contempt, he flung the paper across the table into Leander's lap.

"Ridiculous!" he said.

"I shall call again in a week," Leander said, returning the confession to her bag. "It seems to me that he wants some more sense knocking into him, Rupert."

When they were in his car, ready to leave, Rupert turned to gaze sombrely at her. "Look here, Leander," he said, "are you sure about this? Those men of Silas's are damned rough."

"Yes, Rupert, I am sure," she said wearily. "I know what you're trying to tell me and I appreciate your concern. But that was an appalling thing George did and I want to be *absolutely* certain that he will never bother us again."

Rupert braced himself. "This is an awful thing *you're* doing," he said. "Quite apart from the ethics of it, there could be the most fearful repercussions."

"Do you suppose I don't know that, you stupid man!" Rupert had never believed her capable of such incandescent anger. "Do you think I'm doing this for *fun*? What else *can* I do? Pay George whatever he wants out of the Fund and let him stay in England? Wait in fear and dread for the rest of my life for him to think of another trick? Throw the whole mess open and have the police *and* the newspapers deal with it? Well?" Her eyes glittered like diamonds as she glared at him for a few moments. When she continued, her voice was lower, but trembling. "That scoundrel is still my son, Rupert, so don't you *dare* assume that this isn't crucifying me!"

The silence between them was painful. Eventually, Rupert plucked up courage to speak.

"You can't possibly have a medical opinion about Doris," he said. When she failed to answer, doubt set in and he asked, "Can you?"

"In these circumstances, Rupert, I might," she told him. "And just remember this about George: I believe Steven's death had something to do with the worry and trouble he caused over that awful Blennerhasset business."

Rupert started the engine and they set off.

*

362

That afternoon, the first two races at Royal Ascot were won by Latimer's Barn horses owned by the Duke of Laverstoke. The crowd was soon buzzing with the news that, at the insistence of Giles Hawksworth, both horses had been given drug tests and were clean.

Clementine, Duchess of Laverstoke, deputising for the Duke who had dislocated something in his back while messing about in the kitchen garden at Eaton Mandeville, gave Giles's action her wholehearted approval.

"That's the ticket," she said gleefully. "That's made the buggers sit up and take notice. Look! They're all smiling at you now."

In a euphoric state of mind, Giles went back home as fast as the Rolls-Royce would take him, only to find that his good news would have to wait because Amelia had returned from Cambridge several days earlier than expected.

"You'll have to show your sister much more respect now," Leander told Giles as he and Amelia hugged each other.

"Why?"

"That's *Doctor* Hawksworth you've got there, my lad!"

"Amelia! I say, are you a real nibs?" Giles asked.

"Yes, I'm afraid so." Amelia blushed with pride.

"Doctor of Philosophy, eh? What will you do now?" Giles asked.

"They want me to take up a lectureship at Cambridge, and I've been invited to go to the University of Nuremberg for two terms."

"Imagine that!" Leander said. "Giving mathematics lectures in *German!*"

"Blimey!" Giles gaped at his beloved sister in mock-awe.

"It's quite easy," Amelia said with modest inaccuracy.

They were half-way through a delayed dinner before Leander asked what had happened at Ascot. Giles was gratified by the way her eyes widened as he recounted his afternoon.

"And *you* insisted on having them tested?" Leander asked.

"I did!"

"My word! I'll bet that went down well."

"I think it raised a bit of a stir," Giles said happily. "Her Grace seemed pretty bucked by it."

"Oh, Clem would love it! That was brilliant, darling."

"So, is this doping affair finished and done with?" Amelia asked. She had seen the press reports and been very worried.

"Oh, yes," Leander said with firm confidence. "The man responsible has been nailed. Giles still has to appear before the Disciplinary Committee, but that ought to be a formality."

"Who was it?" Amelia wanted to know. "Someone with a grudge?"

"Something like that, darling," Leander replied airily, and, to Giles's immense relief, Amelia was satisfied.

The following day's newspapers were full of Giles's success at Ascot and the way he had dealt with it. Jane Anstruther scanned the reports avidly without knowing what to make of it all. Why, she asked herself repeatedly, had Giles Hawksworth been so confident that his horses were not doped? Had George made his peace with his family?

One thing was certain: George was not coming back to her. Now that the initial shock of his disappearance was fading, Jane was coming to the angry conclusion that he had never intended to, despite the gift of diamonds, which now seemed very baffling. There was nothing else for it, she decided, the persistent and devoted Alec Blayne-Singer would have to do: he did, after all, have the most excellent prospects. If she worked hard, she might improve his performance as a lover.

Eight days after her first visit to Silas's forest lodge, Leander went to see George again. Although not broken, his spirits were low and he was losing weight. She placed the confession on the table and silently stared him into a submissive dropping of his eyes.

"You really do intend to keep me here for ever, don't you?" George said in a dead, empty voice.

"If need be."

He nodded, jerkily and repeatedly, as though finally convincing himself of her ruthless resolve. "And you'll let me go if I sign this?"

"Not immediately – you have to be got fit to travel. But you will be allowed more pleasant conditions."

George picked up the pen and signed.

"Witness it, please, Rupert," Leander commanded.

When it was done, Leander put the document away and looked at George more in exasperation than anger. "I will never understand you if I live to be a hundred," she said.

"I think it's easy enough," George replied. "I've always been in dread of you."

"That is pure bunkum, George," Leander said crushingly. "You may invent whatever cock-and-bull yarns that take your fancy, but the blunt truth of the matter is that you've always regarded Cannings Ambo as beneath your dignity. Not once have you ever looked like shouldering the responsibilities of an elder son."

"You might be right." He paused to think. "I thought I had a fair idea what you felt about your precious Latimer's Barn, but I was wrong! I never imagined you'd go to *these* lengths."

She laughed bitterly as she stood up. "Believe me, George, you will never know the half of it. I shall come to Southampton with you when you are ready."

"To wave a fond farewell?"

Leander ignored him. "If you attempt to leave here before the proper time, I shall go straight to the police with your confession."

Ten minutes later, as Rupert drove slowly out of the forest, Leander turned to him and asked, "Could I spend a few hours at your house before I go home, Rupert?"

"Of course, my dear. Why?"

"So that I can be thoroughly upset in private!"

The following week, Giles appeared before the Jockey Club's Disciplinary Committee and was exonerated of all blame after a hearing lasting less than five minutes. Sir Walter Rothwell himself took the chair, having made it plain to his colleagues beforehand that he was in possession of confidential information that proved there was no case to answer. Such was his influence that his committee members, many of them content to be ciphers, accepted his ruling without demur. In the interests of good order and discipline on the Turf, the authorities at Sandown Park were given a severely worded directive to improve the security arrangements in their stables and the matter was closed.

Not until the middle of August, after a recuperation period of seven weeks, was George fit to travel. Sensing that Silas, unyieldingly hostile, might have welcomed an excuse to kill him, he remained constantly on his best behaviour.

Rupert and Leander took him to Southampton in Rupert's car. All that George possessed was a first-class single ticket to Cape Town and a trunk of clothes bought by Silas to see him through the voyage. They arrived at ten o'clock, one hour before the ship sailed.

"I don't suppose a living soul apart from you two and Silas knows about all this," George said as they left his stateroom with bells clamouring to order visitors ashore.

"That's right," Leander said. "Giles is the only one who knows what you did. Joe Symes never found out who you were."

"And what does Giles think became of me?"

"That you were sent back to South Africa with a very large flea in your ear."

George smiled. "That's about right," he said, then did something that Rupert thought rather bizarre. He shook Leander's hand, firmly, as though she were a business associate. "Don't worry, Mother, I won't ever tangle with you again," he vowed.

As she watched the liner move away from the dock, Leander shook her head.

"What is it?" Rupert asked, sensing that she was annoyed.

"He *still* never said he was sorry. He didn't the first time, you know."

They drove down to Lymington to watch George's ship clear the Solent, after which they found an hotel where lunch was available. At the end of the meal, they took coffee in a lounge with French windows that were wide open on to a huge, beautifully kept garden through which a trout stream hurried.

"I'm very grateful to you," Leander said once they were comfortable. "George would have got away with that stunt but for you, Rupert. You've been wonderful." She smiled ruefully. "There are times when a man is necessary."

"Have you ever considered getting married again?" Rupert asked.

"No, I don't think so. Why, were you thinking of it?"

"Not really." He chuckled. "I'd have to change *my* name to Hawksworth, I suppose."

"Or even Flamsteed," Leander laughed.

They were wrapped in companionable silence for a time until Leander gave Rupert a look of almost innocent conjecture that completely belied the momentous decision she had just reached.

"Mind you, there's nothing to stop us becoming lovers," she said. "What's the matter? Have I said something awful? Doesn't that idea appeal to you?"

Rupert Timberlake was looking utterly flabbergasted. It was a long time before he was capable of speech. "Do you want me to be absolutely honest with you, Leander?" he asked.

"It's rather silly if you aren't."

"I've wanted to take you to bed for nearly thirty years. Ever since I first saw you in Marlborough High Street."

"And you still do?"

"Yes."

"Good!" She stood up.

"Where are you going?"

"Shan't be long."

She was ten minutes.

"Well?" he asked impatiently when she came back. She was looking very pleased with herself, but was in no hurry to let him into the secret.

"They have some very nice rooms here. I've booked one. And the manager let me use his telephone. I spoke to Amelia."

"What did you tell her?"

"Rupert, are you sure you're going to be all right? Don't you dare get ill on me! Amelia? Oh, I told her that I was in a very nice place, that I'd decided I needed a rest and that I'd see her in a few days. Is there anyone you need to talk to? How about your housekeeper?"

"Yes. Mrs Green would worry about me."

"By the way, Rupert, it's just occurred to me that you will have to become a Trustee. What do you think of that?"

"Whatever you say, my dear. Shall we go and have a look at this bedroom?"

"It's very nice, I promise you. I shall expect you to do a very good job in it!"

"What, even a stupid man like me?"

"After thirty years, Rupert, you are required to be *especially* good!" She put an arm round him. "I'm sorry I said that to you. I didn't mean it."

"I know." He made their embrace more total. "It was a bad time."

"A terrible, *terrible* time." As so often during the past weeks, her face clouded. "But it's done with! Come along, my dear, let us ascend."

On the verge of laughing at her mock-formal tone, Rupert Timberlake found himself the recipient of the witchery in her eyes. Thirty years suddenly seemed quite a short time.

CHAPTER 21

1912

'They don't know what they're doing'

About a month after her fiftieth birthday in June 1910, Leander became convinced that Giles had met the girl who was to be his wife. The Duchess of Laverstoke, also a witness to the encounter, was in complete agreement. Their subsequent attempts at match-making caused widespread mirth; Giles and his beloved went about things at their own careful pace, and did not marry until the end of the 1912 racing season.

It all began on a perfect mid-summer afternoon at Newbury when Giles went into the paddock to watch the horses parade before a good-class race for two-year-olds. With him went Leander and Clementine Prideaux, now an owner in her own right, whose runner, Valpariso, a son of Hypotenuse, had already won his début race in convincing fashion.

Giles was enjoying a magnificent year: with the 1909 doping scandal well and truly buried, he could do no wrong. "If Hawksworth runs a three-legged donkey, back it!" was the watchword. He had failed by half a length to win the Derby, but the Two Thousand and One Thousand Guineas had fallen to him, as had the Oaks and five plum races at Royal Ascot, a very muted affair that year because of the death of King Edward VII. Barring unimaginable disaster or bad luck, he was, at the age of twenty-five, well on the way to becoming champion trainer for the first of what must surely be many times.

Never ceasing to surprise and delight Leander with a maturity well beyond his years, Giles took it all in his stride. Totally without illusions of self-importance, he seemed bewildered by his success. The myth sprang up that his results were achieved by hours spent talking to his horses: certainly he did chat to them a great deal, but this was only one small component of the meticulous work that went into preparing an animal for a race. When the story escaped from Latimer's Barn to be spread round racecourse grapevines by Peter Izzard and Joe Symes, Giles was amused and began playing up to it.

He had a quick word with Valpariso in the paddock that day at Newbury, then walked towards Oliver Derwent to congratulate him on winning the previous race with a horse that had been widely regarded as a dead loss. Leander and the Duchess of Laverstoke were thirty yards away, talking to Lady Angela Dalrymple, the mother of a bright young trainer at Newmarket.

"Aha! I thought she might make him sit up and take notice," the Duchess said as Oliver Derwent introduced Giles to the lovely girl accompanying him. Giles's enchantment was indeed very plain to see.

"That's Ollie's daughter?" Leander asked.

"Yes, that's Emma," Angela Dalrymple replied. "Isn't she a sweetie?"

Emma Derwent was twenty and looked a picture. Almost as tall as Leander and Amelia, she had the same ramrod straight bearing allied to a captivating gracefulness of movement and gesture. Her long, light-brown hair was collected in a bow, and, as Giles was discovering, she had eyes in which a man might cheerfully drown.

"I say, Clem," Leander whispered, "Giles looks as though he's going to keel over."

"No, I think he's just about got a grip on himself," the Duchess replied. "It's mutual, look. Ollie's gel seems pretty impressed with your boy."

"Emma's one of the very best," Angela Dalrymple told them. "Her mother died when she was born and she's more or less looked after Ollie since she was old enough. Rides damned well, too."

"Does she have any brothers or sisters?" Leander asked.

"No. Ollie and Clara had only been married about twelve months," Lady Dalrymple replied. "It was a shocking business. I believe there was some talk of the doctors making a mess of it."

"And Ollie's never remarried?"

"Hasn't looked at another woman, by all accounts. Betsy Fairbanks set her cap at him."

"*She* would," the Duchess remarked sourly.

"Didn't do her a scrap of good, though."

Leander had a fascinated half-smile on her face as she continued to watch Giles and Emma Derwent. "I do believe he's fallen in love," she said. "What do you think Clem?"

"H'm. It wouldn't surprise me." The Duchess sounded very much as if she were commenting on a highly desirable *fait accompli*.

Valpariso duly won the race, but Leander paid far more attention to the fact that Giles had no sooner finished with the formalities in the winner's enclosure than he found an excuse to engage Emma Derwent in conversation.

"Yes, definitely!" the Duchess pronounced.

"This has been a lucky course for us since the day it opened," Leander said, well content with what she had seen.

She was careful not to appear too eager to broach the subject with Giles and left it until they had been back home for over two hours.

"Miss Derwent seemed very pleasant," she said briskly, making the remark part of their discussion of plans for Valpariso's future.

"Who?"

Unable to decide whether Giles's vagueness was genuine or assumed, Leander forced herself to be patient. "Ollie's daughter, my dear. Emma. You talked to her."

"Oh, yes, of course! She's very nice," Giles said. "She's extremely knowledgeable."

"What about?" Leander asked.

"Horses," Giles replied, looking at her as though she was losing her grip on essentials.

Leander decided to shut up.

Staying shut up as weeks passed and nothing happened was very difficult. When, as a result of Giles's inactivity it became downright impossible, Leander took action. She spoke to Oliver Derwent on the telephone.

"I know what you're up to, Leander," he said conspiratorially. "It seems like a damned good idea. Yes, I'll drive over to have lunch with you on Sunday and Emma shall come with me."

When the day came, Giles and Emma played their parts with due solemnity, giving the impression that they were completely innocent of any ulterior motive for the meeting. Counting the day to have produced a favourable outcome after Giles and Emma had spent over an hour in the yard together, Leander decided to organise the next move.

Accordingly, she and Giles visited Oliver Derwent's Saxon Court three Sundays later where the procedure was enacted all over again. Giles and Emma returned from their walk betraying no sign of the conversation that had passed between them.

"Miss Derwent, may I ask you a personal question?" Giles said, when they had finished looking at the horses and were admiring the view across the gallops.

"Certainly, Mr Hawksworth." Her head was held slightly to one side in amused anticipation.

"Do you approve of what your father and my mother are doing?"

"Do you, Mr Hawksworth?"

"Yes, I do," Giles replied without the slightest hesitation.

"So do I!"

They smiled happily and a little shyly at each other.

"The only snag is that they may be expecting an outcome far too soon," Emma said. "Father should know better."

"What is the trouble?" Giles asked.

"I look after Father," Emma replied. "He would never admit it, but he's totally dependent on me. It's quite out of the question for me to leave here until I've made other arrangements for him."

"I quite understand," Giles said.

"It may take some time," Emma said anxiously.

"Don't worry." Giles took her hand and squeezed it reassuringly. "We don't have to be in a hurry. We have all the time in the world."

"Will you really wait for me, Giles?"

"Of course I will! In any case, we're going to get lots of opportunities to be together. The Duchess of Laverstoke is about to start joining in the fun. We shall be receiving an invitation to one of her weekend house-parties at Eaton Mandeville soon."

"How lovely!"

"That's a secret, Emma, so you must pretend to be surprised."

"I will."

At that point, they permitted themselves the luxury of their first kiss before sauntering back to irritate Leander with the impression of a complete lack of progress.

As 1910 became 1911 and that year ran its course, there were times when Leander felt moved to box Giles's ears. All that stopped her laying hands on the son she loved so dearly was the gradually increasing frequency of his meetings with Emma. After the spring, when Valpariso won the Two Thousand Guineas, they began making their own arrangements to meet, rather than relying on the efforts of others.

Yet no matter how many times Giles and Emma saw each other, nothing definite ever seemed to come of it and Leander fulminated to her three closest friends, William, Rupert Timberlake and the Duchess of Laverstoke.

"So help me, William," Leander said one day, staying behind at Rose House after a Trustees' meeting. "If he doesn't do something soon, I'll get the poor girl to pop the question to *him*!"

"This is getting to be like a royal household must be," William said gently.

"What do you mean?" Leander asked.

"Honestly, Lea, poor Giles is still finding out how to do the job and you want to secure the succession. You're after a grandson!"

Her smile was almost that of a child caught out in naughtiness. "There's more to it than that, William – Giles and Emma are absolutely meant for each other. But, yes, you're right, I am looking ahead. We've got through the first fifty years. My grandson will secure the next fifty."

"Just be patient," William advised. "You remember they came to us for tea last time Emma was here?" Leander nodded. "Well, Ruth and I were very smitten with them. They're a lovely couple: they're also very sensible. I reckon they know what they're doing." William hesitated, weighing up the pros and cons of saying more. "As a matter of fact, they joked about it."

"Joked about what?" Leander asked suspiciously.

"You lot who can't wait! Emma does a very good imitation of Clem Prideaux with the bit between her teeth."

"Does she, indeed?" In spite of herself, Leander smiled. She had half suspected that, for all her demure appearance, Emma had a mischievous sense of humour. "We're doing our best to keep calm, William, but it's been dragging on for over a year now."

"Just be patient," William advised. "There's a fair way to go yet."

Long afterwards, Leander was cross with herself for missing something vital: she should have realised that Giles and Emma had confided fully in William.

In February 1912, Oliver Derwent's younger sister, Winifred, came back to England with her twelve-year-old twin sons. She had fled from Ceylon and a marriage that had gone disastrously wrong.

Having married into a noble family, Winifred was somewhat surprised in 1899 when her husband announced his intention of going to live on the tea plantation in the hills above Trincomalee left to him by an uncle who, for nearly forty years, had provided enough scandal for several families.

From the day she arrived in Ceylon with teeth gritted to make a go of it, Winifred recognised the possibility of failure and established her own secret bank account into which every spare shilling was siphoned. After putting up with so much, she was actually surprised when her husband's drinking and relentless pursuit of native women finally disgusted her beyond redemption. With the stalwart assistance of her sons, she packed and set out for England, confident that all would be well once they had survived the three-day train journey to Colombo.

Winifred went first to her eldest brother, the Earl, at the family seat in Somerset. Cedric, nearly twenty years older than her, and a legendary misogynist, made no bones about her being a confounded nuisance. As soon as Oliver Derwent discovered that his favourite relative was back in the country and in difficulty, he invited her to live with him at Saxon Court and all Emma's problems were over. She and Giles announced their engagement in June, with the wedding fixed for mid-October.

Leander, who had been utterly dismayed by the loss of the *Titanic* six weeks previously, set her depression behind her and rejoiced. But, no sooner had the society papers begun to build the forthcoming marriage into one of the social events of the year, than the long-expected final upset with Maude took place.

She arrived without warning and caused trouble at once.

Two railway company motor vans were standing in the forecourt of Rose House, waiting to back down to the workshop to load a consignment of tables for Henry Fletcher in Birmingham. Fred Cartwright, ever watchful over the needs of his oldest client, was preparing to supervise the operation and received the sharp edge of Maude's tongue when the cab that she and her companion had used from the station was unable to make a grand, sweeping approach to the front door.

Out of respect for William, Fred said nothing, thinking it likely that Lady Muck, as he always called Maude in private, was putting on a show for the man. The Lord alone might know why she wanted to bother: Fred thought him quite the most unprepossessing individual seen in Cannings Ambo for a very long time.

Once inside Rose House, Maude gave an astonished Ruth a fusillade of facts in place of a greeting.

"This is Donald Emerson, Mother. He's a *very* talented painter whom I'm lucky to have as a friend . . . he's given me an *immense* amount of help and encouragement. We have decided that this country is hopelessly and irredeemably philistine, so we're going to Paris. It is the *only* place for artists when all is said and done."

Emerson attempted to soften the blow by shaking hands rather clammily with Ruth and saying, "I'm delighted to make your acquaintance, Mrs Flamsteed. Maude has told me so many wonderful things about you," in a voice that, unhappily, matched his appearance.

Ruth looked at him in horror. Donald Emerson was a decrepit bohemian of thirty-eight who looked sixty. He might, Ruth thought, be talented, but he was most certainly not even remotely successful. He was also a bare-faced liar: Ruth doubted whether Maude was capable of saying anything complimentary about her, let alone 'wonderful'.

When William, alerted by Fred, came into the house ten minutes later, a blazing row was in progress between Ruth and Maude, with Emerson a helplessly embarrassed spectator.

Maude's expectations of life in Paris specifically excluded all romantic notions of near-starvation in poor living conditions: life with Donald Emerson had already given her an uncomfortably close view of deprivation. Her mind was set upon extracting a substantial sum of money from William, and, recognising that this was unlikely to be easy, she planned to spend a few days at Rose House.

"That will be nice," Ruth said, doing her best to get on terms with the situation and seeing a chance to talk Maude out of the insanity of Paris. "We always keep your old room ready . . . let me think where I can put Mr Emerson."

"We need a room together," Maude declared arrogantly.

"Not in my house, you don't!" Ruth retorted and the row was under way.

"Will someone be so kind as to tell me what this is all about, please?" William asked in his customary mild manner when he broke in on the scene.

Much to the admiration of Donald Emerson, who was completely ignored, William sat down and looked perfectly at ease as Ruth and Maude launched into simultaneous explanations. The first thing that William did when he understood what all the fuss was about, was to look Emerson up and down in disgusted disbelief: moral issues aside, he could not understand why any woman would want to share a bedroom with such a specimen.

"You will respect your mother's wishes, Maude," William said firmly. "Mine, too," he added for good measure. Then he pierced her resentful silence with a question. "Why have you come here?"

"To say goodbye to you," Maude replied. "It may be some time before I see you again."

William's face hardened as he looked her disconcertingly straight in the eye and said, "Nonsense!"

Maude was shocked. She had spent the whole of her life under the illusion that William and her fearsome Aunt Leander were so different that it was impossible to think of them as brother and sister. Suddenly, she discovered her mistake.

"Father, what *do* you mean?" Maude's rapid descent from high-handedness to crafty innocence served only to confirm William's suspicions.

374

"You haven't been near us for goodness knows how long," William pointed out, "and it's at least three months since we had a letter from you. Now, you turn up out of the blue to stay for a few days. Why, Maude? What do you want? Come along, spit it out and perhaps we can save ourselves a great deal of time and trouble."

"Well . . ." Maude stopped, looked at Emerson for support, only to find his eyes firmly averted, and plunged on. "Donald and I will need some money to tide us over. Since I don't intend ever coming back here, I thought you might give me at least part of my share of the Fund."

"Maude, you don't have a share," William said equably. "*No one* has a 'share' of the Fund, even when they are Trustees – which you are not."

"I've never been good enough, have I?" Maude flared, realising that her plan was doomed.

William took his time replying. "I think your attitude shows how very right we were not to make you a Trustee," he said. "If you were a member of the Partnership, we should now have the distasteful job of expelling you."

"Why?"

"Because Trustees are supposed to live and work in Cannings Ambo. Amelia is the only exception, and she has good reason to be away. She also does her best to come here as often as she can and takes a great interest in the place. Trustees do not go gallivanting off to London and Paris when they feel like it, and they most certainly do *not* take estate money with them."

"So I don't get anything?" Maude said.

William pulled out his pocket-book and placed the money it contained on the table. There were seventeen five-pound notes. "Eighty-five pounds," he said, pushing it towards Maude.

"And that's it, is it?" she said, picking it up.

"It is."

"Is that all I'm worth?"

"Maude, if you had ever wanted to be part of us and all the good things we have here, things would have been very different. As it is, I'm inclined to think that eighty-five pounds is far too much."

"My God," Maude seethed, "you're as hard as that queen bitch at Latimer's Barn!"

"You seem surprised," William said. "Did you imagine that I was a soft touch?" Fleetingly, he seemed amused. "Dear me, you have misunderstood things, haven't you? Your aunt and I have always shared exactly the same aims for Cannings Ambo, and you must be the only person who's never appreciated that. Now, let me save you the trouble of getting a cab. I will drive you back to the station. I'm sure there are better things we can all be doing than wasting time like this."

Her brothers set the seal on Maude's departure: they were coming in for lunch as she and Emerson left. Both Gerald and Matthew stared at her without any sign of recognition.

"So that looks like it, then," Leander said that afternoon as she and William discussed the morning's events in the library of The House.

"Yes!" William was pleased to be rid of a problem that had worried him for some time.

"Do you think she'll come back?"

"I told her not to when I took her to the station."

"And it's to be Paris, is it?"

"Yes, although I can't see it lasting long." After a few moments of reflective silence, William became strangely animated. "Do you know what hurt the most, Lea?"

"What?"

"The *creature* she was with. You should have seen him! It might have been quite funny seeing what you made of him. She's a lovely girl, despite the life she's been leading. She could take her pick of the best men, yet she ends up with a revolting thing like that."

"She's a rebel, like George," Leander said. "Every other family gets them, so shall we."

"And we must grin and bear it."

"I don't see what alternative there is, William. As a matter of fact, the way we do things, we might get more than our fair share of people who want to kick over the traces. We must be thankful that Father set the Partnership up as he did."

"I suppose George and Maude might have ruined this place if they'd had half a chance," William said.

"It's happening all the time, my dear. Clem was telling me about the Davenport-Billson shambles yesterday: that was all caused by a feckless son."

Ten days later, on the day that Amelia returned to Cannings Ambo for the summer, Ruth and William received a short note from Maude to inform them that she and Emerson had arrived in Paris. No address was given and it was the last anyone in Cannings Ambo ever heard of her during her lifetime.

Since Christmas, Amelia had been lecturing and collaborating in research at the University of Nuremberg. Her postcards and letters had given a vivid picture of the quaint, idyllic existence within the ancient city, but they had deliberately omitted a very important part of Amelia's life which Leander detected at a glance.

"Tell me about him," she said the moment they were alone.

Amelia blushed. "Oh dear, is it that obvious?" she asked.

"Yes, darling, it is. He's made a complete woman of you."

"His name is Ludwig Lehmann and he's an assistant professor. He's thirty-one."

"He must be very clever."

"He's brilliant, Mother, quite brilliant!"

"And what does he look like?"

"Oh, he's tall and strong and very good-looking."

"Fair or dark?"

"Fair."

Leander smiled. "He sounds very Germanic."

"Yes, he is," Amelia said.

"And are you in love with him, darling?"

"I rather think I am, Mother."

"In that case, you should have brought him with you so that we could all have a look at him!"

Amelia's face clouded. "I suggested that, because I knew you would like to meet him, but he wasn't able to come. He's spending all his summer holiday doing reserve training in the Army."

"Good gracious, do they take it that seriously? I'd have expected a professor to be exempt from games like that."

"Ludwig is immensely keen. He's an officer in an artillery regiment. It isn't quite compulsory, but I believe it's very much frowned upon not to go. They're expecting war, you see. There seem to be a great many people in Germany who *want* it."

"Why, for heaven's sake?"

"It's something to do with proving their superiority. The Kaiser says that Germans are better than everyone else."

"Surely no one believes that clap-trap?"

"I'm afraid they do, Mother, and that includes an awful lot of intellectuals who really should know better."

"Who is this war going to be against?" Leander asked.

"France, of course," Amelia replied. "That's the main objective. After that, we seem to be the most disliked."

"Why?"

"Agadir is the latest excuse."

"Ah, yes." Leander looked dispirited.

In April the previous year, French troops had occupied Fez, the principal town of Morocco, with the avowed aim of protecting the Sultan against an insurrection. Treating this as an infringement of her interests in the area, Germany had sent a warship to seize the port of Agadir. The consequent crisis had reached its height in July, when David Lloyd George, Asquith's Chancellor of the Exchequer, made a speech at the Mansion House in which he stated that peace at any price was something that Britain could not tolerate. This, coming from a man widely regarded as a pro-German pacifist, sent shock-waves through the chancelleries of Europe and appeared to have paved the way for the German climb-down.

"They lost that one without fighting," Amelia said. "That won't be allowed to happen again. And the trouble is, I think all these silly alliances are a nightmare."

"I thought they were supposed to make Europe safe!" Leander protested.

"I know they are, but in reality, the alliances give virtually everybody an excuse to go to war with everybody else if someone so much as sneezes in the wrong way!"

Leander was frightened, wishing that she felt able to ignore Amelia's opinion. That was, of course, impossible: only an idiot could disregard the views of such an intelligent, well-informed person. Nevertheless, Leander wanted the unpleasant truth pushed into the background for the time being. "What about Giles and Emma Derwent?" she asked.

Amelia clapped her hands delightedly. "That's marvellous! Why did it take so long?"

"Someone had to be found to look after Ollie," Leander replied. "If a long-lost sister of his hadn't turned up, God knows how long it might have gone on."

"Where will they live after the wedding?"

"Here! Where else? There's plenty of room. The builders are coming next week to make them a nice suite. One of these days, we might realise the full potential of this place."

"It really is a barn, isn't it?" Amelia laughed. "I've often wondered what that man Rashleigh had in mind."

"Sheer stupidity and ideas above his station," Leander said dismissively. "But don't you dare go criticising it. I've lived here all my life and I adore it."

"So do I," Amelia said. "I miss it terribly when I'm away."

"Where will you be going next?"

"Back to Cambridge in October."

"And when do you expect to see your good-looking assistant professor again?" Leander asked gently.

"I don't know. There has been talk of him coming to Cambridge for a year next autumn. We shall have to wait and see."

The marriage of Giles Hawksworth and Emma Derwent was solemnised in the church of St Matthew and All Saints, Compton Norris, on 19 October 1912 before a congregation of over four hundred. At least half of Cannings Ambo had contrived to get itself to Emma's parish church, half a mile from Oliver Derwent's Saxon Court stables and about thirty miles from Cannings Ambo.

A week before the great day, Giles had turned out yet another Dewhurst Plate winner and was already sure to be champion trainer for the second time. Among those present in Compton Norris on a golden autumn day were scores of journalists, anxious to tell their readers all about the most exciting wedding in Racing for many years.

None of this meant anything to the main players. Once Emma had joined Giles at the altar rail, they were oblivious of everything except one another and their ceremony. Only after they had signed the register in the vestry and were walking back down the aisle, Emma with her veil now off her face, did they become aware of the immense wealth of good wishes surrounding them.

They came out of the church to find themselves beneath a ceremonial arch of riding whips held aloft by lads from the two stables, twelve from Saxon Court, twelve from Latimer's Barn. Then there were the photographs.

The gentlemen of the press had more than half a mind to make a disruptive nuisance of themselves until Leander, the Duchess of Laverstoke and Oliver Derwent's sister bore down on them in battle formation. After that, Guy Mallender, with a much more convenient and reliable camera than at Leander's wedding thirty-one years ago, took a fine set of pictures, including a magnificent one that was destined to become the foundation of the Latimer's Barn portrait gallery. It showed Giles and Emma looking at each other with total serenity, while two of Racing's most distinguished practitioners and servants, Leander Hawksworth and the Honourable Oliver Derwent, the proudest parents on earth, flanked them.

Slowly, the crowd moved away from the church, across the village green and into the Fortescue Arms, Compton Norris's inn-cum-hotel, where the wedding breakfast was to be held. The main dining-room had been laid out to accommodate seventy people; the rest of the guests spilled into adjoining rooms and bars, falling silent when it was time to try to listen to the speeches from the dining-room.

379

Once the formal part of the proceedings was over, and Giles and Emma had disappeared to change into their going-away clothes, Leander moved round the rabbit-warren of rooms, speaking to as many people as possible. A group of Saxon Court stable-lads were struck dumb until they thought she had passed safely out of ear-shot.

"Blimey, she's like royalty, ain't she?"

"I reckon old Ollie should have fixed himself up with her while he was sorting this lot out."

"Ollie didn't do no sorting. It was Mrs Hawksworth and the Duchess of Laverstoke – her over there, look."

The others looked across the room to where Her Grace was laughing at something Oliver Derwent had said. "'Strewth, she's another one! They don't half go in for some smashing women at Latimer's Barn."

"And have you seen the groom's sister?"

"She's a corker. Supposed to be a Cambridge professor an' all."

"Mind you, our Emma is as good as any of 'em."

It was perfectly true: Leander, who *had* heard the conversation, very nearly went back to tell them how much she agreed with the sentiment.

Jammed in a passageway leading to the kitchens, William was being instructed to make furniture by another Duchess, wife of one of Oliver Derwent's owners, while Fred Cartwright was telling the owner of the Fortescue Arms that Wm Flamsteed & Sons could brighten the place up no end. And in the yard at the back of the inn, at least one romance between a Saxon Court lad and a girl from Cannings Ambo was taking root.

When Giles and Emma set out on their honeymoon journey, it seemed entirely appropriate that they should be driven away in the very latest model of Rolls-Royce motor car, with ducal coronets on the doors. They also had a duke for a chauffeur, Hubert Prideaux looking ludicrously pleased with himself, especially since the cap he had borrowed from his man, Barlow, was far too big for him. On arrival at Reading station, the station-master presented Emma with a bouquet of flowers and showed them to their reserved compartment on the train to Torquay.

That night, they began their lives together in the same suite of rooms occupied by Leander and Steven, as well as Ruth and William, on their honeymoons. Giles and Emma Hawksworth consummated their love as they had conducted their long courtship, with an almost studious respect for each other.

Afterwards, they lay in each other's arms, lost in the wonder of the miraculous blend of sensations they had conjured up.

"I didn't know it was going to be like *that*," Emma said at last.

"Good?"

"Oh, yes!"

Giles smiled, suddenly looking shy. "Mother said it ought to be if we got it right."

"She talked to you about it?"

"Yes, of course!"

"Father wouldn't dare do a thing like that and Aunt Winifred was very off-putting when I asked her."

"From what we've heard about your Uncle Archie, he sounds like the sort of chap to put anyone off," Giles said.

"Yes, I suppose so." Emma was thoughtful. "Your mother really is remarkable."

"Very remarkable indeed!" Giles smiled. "I sometimes feel very sorry for the people who don't realise that."

After the three-day sojourn in the New Forest that finally brought them to the peak of their relationship, Leander and Rupert spent an amusingly jumbled six months before finding a satisfactory venue for their love-making. Even Leander had to admit that Latimer's Barn would not do.

"Giles and Emma would be offended," she grumbled, leaving Rupert with the problem of placating his housekeeper and maid.

At last, after a period of scheming and jiggery-pokery that more often than not left Leander helpless with laughter rather than sexually satisfied, a day came when Rupert drove her into Savernake Forest. Half a mile beyond Silas's lodge, they came to a tiny cottage completely hemmed in by trees. Even in March it was difficult to pick it out; in summer it would be invisible.

Despite its neglected external appearance, the place had been put to rights inside, with new carpets and furniture. The stove in the kitchen was alight and there was a huge supply of freshly cut logs for the fires in the sitting-room and bedroom.

Leander was enchanted. "Rupert, you've found us a love-nest!" she cried, rewarding him with the best thanks of all, that special sparkle in her eyes.

They went to the cottage every Tuesday afternoon, arriving at half past one, never leaving until six. Everything was always spotless: the feather bed was made up with clean linen, there was milk and tea, sandwiches and cake between two dinner-plates wrapped in a moist towel, fires lit when necessary and vases of fresh flowers. They never saw another living soul.

"I suppose this is all part of the Timberlake way of doing things, is it?" Leander asked one day and Rupert replied, yes, it was.

On the Tuesday after the wedding of Giles and Emma, Leander woke from a shallow sleep as Rupert placed a tea-tray at the side of the bed and stirred the fire into greater life. The mist shrouding the forest was adding to the gloom of autumnal dusk and he decided to light the lamp. Blinking, Leander smiled, pushing her hair from her face. Lately, Rupert had noticed one or two grey streaks in her luxuriant mane, but for the most part, it was still the glorious gold of thirty years ago.

"What are you goggling at?" she asked, smiling drowsily.

"Your arms," he replied. "A man would be very hard put to say that they didn't belong to a young girl."

"H'm." She studied her arms critically. "My legs are probably better," she said, and stuck one out of bed for his inspection and acclaim.

"Marvellous!" Rupert enthused. "Is that what riding does for you?"

"It helps, I suppose. Personally, I'm convinced it's more to do with mental attitudes."

She drank the tea he had poured for her and was fully awake.

"I say, you'll *never* guess what happened this morning," she said, quite the capricious young girl.

"You're right, I won't," he smiled.

"I had a letter from George."

"Well I'll be damned!" Rupert stared at her in amazement. "What did he say?"

"See for yourself, it's in my handbag."

Rupert reached across, found the envelope easily enough and extracted the two large, well-filled sheets of paper from it. When, at the end of reading the first page, his incredulity got the better of him, he looked up to find Leander smiling and nodding.

"That's what I thought," she said.

"It's beyond belief," Rupert spluttered. "He's chatting away, giving you all the news, as though you and he had never exchanged a single cross word."

"The next page is even better," Leander said.

"Good God, he's married! How do you pronounce this name – Gertrude van der Viljoen?" He turned the 'j' into an 'h'.

"Something like that, I expect." Leander was disinterested.

"He says she's from a good family."

"Whatever that may mean in South Africa," she said contemptuously. "Probably money and the fact that her parents supported that dreadful man Kruger."

"Now, now, Leander," Rupert chided. "I expect she's a very nice girl."

She looked at him in a way that half-threatened an outspoken piece of her mind, then softened. "Yes, of course. Anyway, I've written back to congratulate them and wish them luck."

Rupert read the letter again before returning it to its envelope and the handbag. The look on Leander's face told him that the subject was closed: she had informed him, now George could slip back into the past. Recalling the events of three years ago, he looked pained as an unpleasant thought occurred to him.

"What is it?" Leander asked.

"Has that man Rothwell ever been in touch with you again?"

"No." She took his hand, seeing the effort the difficult question had cost him. It had seemed natural to take him into her confidence over her visit to Reedswood House with Rothwell; only afterwards did Leander begin to discover that in his quiet way, Rupert was desperately jealous.

"He's never pestered you for a repeat performance?" Rupert asked.

"No. He found himself a nice *young* woman almost immediately. Kate Sinclair has been the apple of his eye for the last two years."

"Bill Sinclair's wife?" Rupert asked, naming a young Newmarket trainer who always seemed to be struggling.

"Yes. Kate and my friend Sir Walter have been seen together in some very strange places."

"So he'll leave you alone?"

Leander laughed. "He's finished with my body, if that's what you mean, but as far as Latimer's Barn is concerned, I wouldn't trust him any further than I could throw your new motor car."

Rupert nodded thoughtfully. "By the way, how do you know about Kate Sinclair?" he asked. "This isn't Timberlake information, is it?"

"No, my dear, it isn't. Joe Symes keeps an eye open for me."

"Aha! I wondered why we'd been getting less requests for snooping," Rupert smiled.

"Your time will surely come again," Leander told him. "Joe can't be everywhere, whereas your lot seem to manage it very easily. And Silas's merry little band might be needed any day if we hit serious trouble."

"Silas is looking forward to it. He thinks it's a great honour to serve you. By the way, he has a very high regard for Amelia. As a matter of fact, I think he's carrying a torch for her."

"Poor Silas," Leander said. "I think he's awfully nice."

"Hopeless, is it?" Rupert asked.

"At the moment. Amelia's extremely fond of a German she met in Nuremberg. She went to see him in August, and he's supposed to be coming to England for a year next autumn."

"It sounds serious," Rupert said, making up his mind not to tell Silas.

"It is. The trouble is, she gets so depressed about it."

"That doesn't sound right."

"It's all to do with Germany, not Ludwig. Amelia has become convinced that they're spoiling for a war."

"Hush! I'm certain that everything will be all right. No one could possibly be such a lunatic as to start a war."

Gently, he pushed her back against the pillows and began to stroke her breasts, an action that always brought her close to purring. For several minutes, they drifted away from the world's problems, Leander wrapped in soothing pleasure, Rupert marvelling at the beautifully satisfying relationship he now enjoyed with the woman he had desired and idolised for so long.

But the spell faded. Leander opened her eyes and was troubled. "It's all very well saying nobody could be lunatic enough, Rupert, but they don't know what they're doing. They're playing with things they can't control. Look at the *Titanic*! That ship was supposed to be unsinkable, and what happened?"

"It didn't even complete one crossing," he replied.

"It was travelling too fast and there weren't enough lifeboats. One thousand five hundred people killed – you can't imagine it, can you?"

"Not really," he said.

"And now they're saying that there was another ship so close it could have saved them all. Why didn't it? Why should people sit around like stuffed dummies and let a thing like that happen right under their noses?"

There was nothing he could say.

"They don't know what they're doing," she said again. "Doesn't it make you wonder what sort of world Giles and Emma will have to cope with?"

CHAPTER 22

1914

'We can't have a war, there's enough trouble already!'

The Black Prince, a wonderful bay colt by The Atheling, won the Derby two days after Leander had celebrated her fifty-fourth birthday. This, following his Two Thousand Guineas victory, was universally hailed as signalling the end of Giles Hawksworth's apprenticeship.

As they left Epsom, Leander whispered, "I want you to take me to the cottage tomorrow, Rupert."

"But it's a Thursday!" he protested, laughing.

"I'm not waiting until next Tuesday," she hissed.

During the next three weeks, they visited the cottage ten times and Rupert began to wonder how much longer he could keep up with Leander's demands.

"I'll get you a tonic," she said. "I'm not having you going useless on me just as we're starting to enjoy ourselves properly. This is lovely!"

Then, on 28 June, Gavril Princip stepped off a pavement in the Serbian town of Sarajevo and fired the shots that killed the Archduke Franz Ferdinand, heir to the Hapsburg throne, and the partner in his morganatic marriage, Princess Sophie von Hohenburg.

Franz Joseph, the eighty-four-year-old Emperor, might possibly have grieved for his nephew and his unsuitable wife, but no one else of any importance in Vienna gave them a second thought. The *true* heir had been the Archduke Rudolph, Franz Joseph's only son by the ill-starred Elizabeth of Bavaria. Franz Ferdinand became heir only as a result of Rudolph's suicide in 1889 in the scandalous hunting lodge at Mayerling, and in that sweltering June of 1914 there were those in Vienna who were thoroughly glad to see the back of him.

But Franz Ferdinand and his much-ridiculed wife were to be used to ignite the immense powder-keg that had been thirty years in the making.

Amelia woke early on 29 June. It was Monday and Ludwig was returning to Germany on Friday. She studied him, fast asleep beside her. At times like this, it was impossible to believe that this vigorous lion of a man was a professor of mathematics. Easing herself out of bed, she pulled on a wrap and padded downstairs to find the sun already streaming into the kitchen to herald yet another scorching day in the hottest summer that most people could remember.

At the end of the academic year, they had taken the cottage for a month. It had been mostly holiday, but the books and papers on the kitchen table attested to the fact that last evening they had become absorbed in their work. Noticing her stockings across the back of one of the chairs, Amelia smiled: after nearly two hours of thrashing out a new approach to diophantine equations, other passions had come into play. Still barefoot and munching at an apple, she went into the garden.

The cottage was near, but hidden from, the village of Waterbeach, about five miles north of Cambridge. Standing at the confluence of the River Cam and Bottisham Lode, it had water on two sides of it. However unbearably hot some of the days had been, the evenings and mornings were always cool and tranquil. Amelia shrugged off her wrap and waded into the shallows.

She laughed now at her priggishness over Rupert Brooke and his nude bathing: Ludwig had long since banished such inhibitions.

Almost immediately, she heard the whistle of a train and trod water to watch it pass, less than a hundred yards away. It was the breakfast-car express from King's Lynn to London, a few minutes late this morning. At first, Amelia had imagined that the driver always whistled to draw the world's attention to the naked woman swimming in the hallowed River Cam. The discovery that the eldritch shriek was nothing more than a device to ensure the wakefulness of a notorious signalman was a disappointment.

She swam strongly for half an hour, then returned to the cottage to make tea on a spirit stove. Later, she would brew a pot of very strong coffee for Ludwig, but not until he was awake, at least another hour yet.

Taking her tea into the front parlour, Amelia sat in the window and gazed down the river towards Cambridge. Inevitably, she thought about the future and was sad. She and Ludwig had finished their work and the manuscript of a book had gone to the University

386

Press. It only remained to correct the proofs: that was Amelia's job. Ludwig's visiting professorship at Cologne would allow him no time for such trivia.

At Easter, they had talked about marriage. The discussion had lasted all of ten minutes. Yes, Ludwig was all in favour of it: with her command of the language, Amelia would be welcome at any German university. They could be together at the weekends in Nuremberg or Cologne: Ludwig did not deem it necessary to consider any other way of spending their lives together.

After that, it was only their work that kept them together, with Ludwig blithely unaware that Amelia was unhappy. Matters were made worse on the day that she admitted to herself that she preferred not to be without his accomplished love-making. She smiled ruefully. What a state of affairs! Doctor Amelia Hawksworth, one of the jewels of English mathematics, was a cat's-paw to the sexual prowess of a hulking German.

Suddenly, something caught her attention. Shielding her eyes against the glare of sun on the water, Amelia picked out the figure of a bicyclist coming along the towpath. She glanced at her watch: not yet eight o'clock. This was unusual.

Another ten seconds and she was able to recognise Josie Prior, a promising young graduate of Newnham College whose doctoral thesis she was supervising. Josie was pedalling like fury, even to the extent of neglecting her safety on the difficult path. As Amelia hurried out to meet her, Josie took the newspaper from the basket on the handlebars and waved it.

"Josie, whatever is it?" Amelia cried.

Allowing her machine to fall to the ground, the girl thrust *The Times* at Amelia. "The Austrian Archduke," she gasped. "Assassinated yesterday. At Sarajevo in Bosnia."

"Where's Bosnia?" Amelia asked, unable to take in the news.

"It's part of Serbia," Josie gasped, trying to get her breath after the long, hard ride. "That's the country Austro-Hungary cobbled together from various bits they've annexed."

"This Archduke was the heir-apparent?" Amelia asked, struggling to absorb the newspaper report.

"Yes."

Amelia was baffled. "It's awful, of course," she said. "But what does it amount to?"

"Professor Willington was talking to some people on King's Parade and telling them that it meant war," Josie said.

"What means war?" Ludwig's gentle voice, almost without a trace of accent after all his rather pedantically hard work to master English, came from above them.

Amelia and Josie looked up to find him leaning out of the bedroom window: Josie blushed at the sight of his broad chest and shoulders.

"The Archduke Franz Ferdinand has been murdered," Amelia said.

"Where?" Ludwig's manner changed completely. Now, he was alert and eager.

"Sarajevo," Amelia told him.

"Wait! I come down."

In no time at all he had pulled on a shirt and trousers and hurried out to them. "Please!" he said, virtually snatching the paper from Amelia.

He read quickly, occasionally muttering to himself in German. Although Josie Prior did not understand a word, his meaning was all too plain.

"Thank you," he said, returning the paper to Amelia. "I must prepare. There is no time to waste."

"Prepare?" Amelia was off-balance. "What for?"

"To go home. To Germany! There will be war and I am needed."

"War over this?" Amelia was incredulous. "Between whom?"

"Austria and Serbia. Those Serbs – pah! They have been wanting a lesson."

"What has that got to do with Germany?" Amelia asked.

"We are Austria's friend," Ludwig replied. Amelia very nearly laughed at the way he drew himself up and threw his chest out. "There will be war in three, maybe six weeks."

"Why wait that long?" Amelia demanded.

"There are good reasons," Ludwig told her officiously.

"Then you can stay until Friday," Amelia said.

"*Nein!*" He turned to Josie. "You are going back to Cambridge, *Fräulein* Prior?"

"Er . . . yes . . . I suppose so." Josie looked doubtfully at Amelia, in search of guidance, but Ludwig did not allow the luxury.

"You will be so kind as to send a taxi, *Ja?*" he said. "There!" He pointed to the road on the opposite side of the river.

"Ludwig, are you sure you must go?" Amelia asked with a hint of desperation in her voice.

"They will lock me up if I stay. I will be an enemy alien, *Liebchen.*"

Amelia looked at Josie helplessly. "Yes, please," she said. "You'd better send a cab."

He caught the midday train to London.

By now, he was in the grip of a terrible excitement that had

388

possessed him and mounted as they packed. The thought of one last act of love never occurred to him and when they rowed across the river to the taxi, Amelia felt a stranger.

She looked back for a last glimpse of the cottage as the motor car rounded the bend into the village and felt that the summer of her life had gone. They halted briefly outside the inn at Waterbeach where she left the keys of the cottage with a spur-of-the-moment explanation for their early departure.

There was one perfunctory kiss as he leaned out of the carriage window, not concealing his impatience to be away. When the train pulled out, Amelia waved like an automaton, the film of tears blinding her to the fact that he had closed the window and taken his seat.

She knew that she would never see Ludwig Lehmann again.

Half an hour later, Amelia arrived at the house of a friend in St John's Street and asked to be allowed to use the telephone.

Daphne Stanton died in the early hours of that day, 29 June. The secret of the wild life she had led before her long and very happy marriage to Charles went to the grave with her. Apart from her husband, only one man, Giles Flamsteed, had known about her madcap escapades and he had never breathed a word to anyone, not even to Leander. Daphne, seventy-four years old and rightly regarded as a mainstay of Cannings Ambo, was a sad loss.

As a consequence of Daphne's death, Leander's morning routine had been abandoned; she had not yet looked at the newspapers when Amelia's telephone call came through: she knew nothing of the assassination, nor was she prepared to believe that it meant war. For twelve months or more, the prospect of a European conflict had been pushed into the background by troubles in England and Leander refused to accept that the murder of the man she called 'a tin-pot nonentity' was going to alter things. Nevertheless, she was quick to recognise Amelia's distress at Ludwig's precipitate departure and told her that she must come home at once.

When Amelia reached Latimer's Barn at seven o'clock, she went straight up to the nursery to see her ten-month-old nephew, Giles's and Emma's son. Born in September 1913, he had, at Emma's insistence, been christened Steven, preserving the 'wrong' spelling of his grandfather's name. As ever, he showed immense pleasure at seeing Amelia, then went straight back to sleep again.

"Still no trouble, I see," Amelia said to Emma.

"Never a moment!" Emma's attitude changed abruptly. "Mother says you think there will be war."

Leander derived great pleasure from the warmth of Emma's adoption of her as the mother she had never known.

"Well, it's Ludwig, really," Amelia said. "He went dashing back to Germany as soon as he heard about the Archduke."

"How awful! Will you see him again?"

"I don't think so," Amelia said dully. "To be honest, Emma, it doesn't need a war to break us up."

"Oh dear, what a shame. I'm terribly sorry. By the way, Giles thinks that Ludwig is probably right."

"God! Does he?" Amelia was dismayed.

Emma grinned bravely. "Mother's told him not to be silly!"

She did it again over dinner. "Giles, we can't have a war, there's enough trouble already!" Leander said sharply.

It was all too true. Following a three-year period of steadily deteriorating relations between employers and trades unions, the summer had seen the persistent threat of a general strike, with a mounting tide of serious disorder, particularly in the northern cities. The possibility of civil war in Ireland over the question of Home Rule and the separation of Ulster was strong; there was even talk of such an insurrection infecting mainland Britain. Throughout these and many other problems, the Prime Minister, Herbert Asquith, did little more than follow his notorious dictum of 'wait and see'.

And then there was the Women's Suffrage Movement, something that had annoyed Leander since its foundation by Mrs Pankhurst in 1903. Never remotely likely to look kindly on their activities, Leander was moved to write a letter of resounding condemnation to *The Times* after the deplorable incident that had marred the previous year's Derby. As the horses were rounding Tattenham Corner, Emily Wilding Davison threw herself in front of them, bringing down Anmer, the King's entrant.

Above the gasps of the crowd, Leander's comment was memorably audible over a wide range. "My God, I hope that horse is all right! Oh, yes, he's getting up!"

Emily Davison was never mentioned, even when her death from the injuries she sustained was reported three days later.

Ironically, Leander, who had expected trouble for so long, was convinced that war simply was not possible.

During the next two weeks, events, or rather the lack of them, seemed to be proving her right. Over the weekend of 17–19 July, the Duke and Duchess of Laverstoke, godparents to young Steven, stayed at Latimer's Barn. Hubert Prideaux, who always took his duties as a member of the House of Lords seriously, and had been attending the Chamber every day since the murder at Sarajevo, gave Leander massive reassurances.

"No, definitely not, my dear. You can take it from me that the Government does not expect war," he said.

"They haven't *expected* all sorts of things," Leander replied acidly.

He took the point. "No, they've really got their eye on the ball over this one, I promise you."

England turned its full attention to the continuing fine weather and Giles, admitting to Emma that he had been far too pessimistic, put the finishing touches to the five horses he was sending to Goodwood.

Then, on 23 July, twenty-five days after Franz Ferdinand's assassination, Austria presented Serbia with an ultimatum.

It was couched in terms that were calculated to make its rejection certain, yet, within the forty-eight hours allowed for reply, Serbia accepted all but two of the fourteen points: these, it was suggested, might be referred to international arbitration.

"A triumph!" the Kaiser declared. "Every cause for war has disappeared."

Austria was having no part of it: rejecting the abject Serbian reply, she declared war on 28 July. Within hours, Belgrade was under artillery fire.

The next week was unreal; for much of the time, it seemed that a gaggle of overwrought children were playing a frenzied game to outbid each other and have the last word. There was the illusion that their appalling antics could not possibly touch Cannings Ambo.

The news, stark facts without any indication of the frenzied diplomatic activity behind them, came by special editions of the newspapers and Fred Partridge, the porter at Savernake station, who got it from the drivers of West-of-England expresses eighty minutes after they left London.

Russia ordered general mobilisation on 30 July as a protective act for its Slav brothers in Serbia; Germany followed suit a day later. On 1 August, Germany declared war against Russia, then against France on 3 August. The Kaiser and his High Command were so stupendously confident that they embarked upon a war on two fronts.

Also on 3 August, Germany delivered an ultimatum to Belgium. To gain easy access to Paris, the German armies needed to pass through Belgium: the Belgians would be so kind as to allow this. By a treaty of 1839, Great Britain was honour-bound to defend Belgium's neutrality and declared war on Germany on 4 August.

The British Expeditionary Force was rushed across the Channel to France. It was, the newspapers claimed, the best prepared British Army ever to go to war. No one knew that its commander had no better idea in his head than to join up with Joffre and the French Army and offer some sort of help. The sixty thousand Englishmen, who included John Merriweather, Abraham's youngest son, were supposed to stop at least ten times as many Germans: they were, the Kaiser said, a contemptible little army.

On the evening of Sunday 30 August, Leander sat with Giles, Emma and Amelia after returning from church. No one spoke. Then young Steven, who was lying on a folded blanket beside Leander, stirred in his sleep. She rubbed his hand with a forefinger which he grasped, gurgled happily and fell asleep again.

"He will never believe this," Leander said, placing a protective arm round him. "When he grows up and reads about this, he'll think the world went mad."

Paris was in turmoil. Despite the confident patriotism of some of its inhabitants, others were convinced that the city would fall to the Germans within a week: the optimists gave it a fortnight.

In the middle of the afternoon of 8 August, Donald Emerson told Maude that he needed to slip out for cigarettes. Once outside their lodgings in an obscure side-street off the Rue St Vincent near Sacré-Coeur, he turned away from the shops and hurried towards the Boulevard de Magenta. Five minutes later he was at the Gare du Nord where he bought a single ticket to Calais. His luck was in; despite the chaos caused by troop and equipment movement, he found a train that left in half an hour. At the Channel port, there was a wait of nearly twelve hours for a place on one of the overcrowded ferries to Dover: Emerson was patient, never suffering a moment's regret about the decision to abandon Maude and save his neck.

It took Maude less than an hour to realise what had happened; Emerson had made half-hearted suggestions that they should return to England three times in as many days. She had rejected the idea out of hand; not only did she like France, the idea of crawling back was anathema. That he should abandon her was totally in keeping with what she now knew of his character.

Left alone in a foreign and potentially dangerous city, Maude Flamsteed knew exactly what she must do.

Along with the discovery of Emerson's unsatisfactory character, she had come to take a more realistic view of her own painting talent. Although she had sold some pictures, the money involved was modest, and she knew there was little hope of improvement. She was, however, much in demand as a model.

The morning after Emerson's flight, she kept an appointment to pose nude for Pierre Guillaume in his studio on the Rue de Trois-Frères. Guillaume was a young Breton whose paintings were immensely popular and always fetched high prices. Maude liked him; he had a sparkling sense of humour and his countryman's good looks were reinforced by simmering, omni-present virility.

As usual, the sight of Maude's body prompted him to make risqué suggestions. Anticipating her customary barricade of polite rebuffs, he laughed at himself and carried on with his work. Slow on the uptake, it was some time before Pierre Guillaume realised that, this time, Maude was encouraging his advances.

She moved into his comfortable apartment that evening.

The war wasted no time in touching Cannings Ambo. On 2 September, a telegram arrived to say that John Merriweather had been killed at Le Cateau.

Leander and Tish sat with Alice all day and John's brother, Albert, joined them during the stable's quiet period in the afternoon. Tish got out the atlas she had used as a child and they tried to find the place where one of their number had fallen. They could not; the scale of the maps was too small. The pointless exercise simply added to the sense of shock and bewilderment.

"Still, there's one thing," Alice said with stoic calm as Leander was eventually leaving to go back to The House. "Abraham didn't live to see this and I'm glad. There! Fancy having to say that!"

Leander kissed her and went sadly up the drive. Abraham Merriweather, the man who had ploughed colossal efforts into the success of Latimer's Barn, had died nearly twelve months ago; now she was going to record the loss of his son in the Big Book. And as she did so, the fear that John Merriweather would be the first of many laid an icy grip on her.

The Defence of the Realm Act was rushed on to the statute book during the first month of the war: the Duke of Laverstoke was uneasy.

"To put none too fine a point on it, it's a ban on free speech," he told a dismayed Leander and William. "The Government aren't allowing war correspondents anywhere near the action, so the papers have got to print what they're given, and to cap it all, the Commons have turned into lap-dogs and agreed not to ask awkward questions."

Deprived of fact, the newspapers printed myth and rumour to flesh out the official communiqués. There were the Angels of Mons who had fought alongside the British riflemen and the million Russians who landed at Aberdeen one evening and passed through England to France. Rumour bred hysteria: the newly laid tennis court behind Harry Giffard's house on the outskirts of Cheltenham was suspected of being a site for a German gun emplacement. People with German-sounding names were pilloried unless, like the King or Prince Louis of Battenberg, they were able to change to an acceptable alternative.

There were obvious contradictions. Hand-in-hand with the widely stated belief that it would all be over by Christmas, the recruiting drive began. When Leander saw one of Kitchener's posters outside the Town Hall in Marlborough, she was shocked. The accusing finger and baleful stare above the command 'Your Country Needs YOU' made even her feel uncomfortable. What, she wondered, would have been her reaction if she were a young man? By the end of September, 750,000 of them had enlisted, the greatest volunteer force ever raised in the history of the world.

On 5 September, the French Army under Generals Joffre and Gallieni halted the German advance on Paris. For twelve hours, the vast German forces were in mortal danger with a flank turned and exposed across the River Marne, but the Allies lacked the strength to press home their advantage.

Their position on the Marne was untenable; the German Army fell back across the River Aisne and started digging the first of the trenches.

Giles, like Steven before him, regarded the Dewhurst Plate in mid-October as the end of the season. Racing carried on for another month, but no one at Latimer's barn was ever able to see the point of working and racing horses in worsening weather for the poor prize-money on offer at that time of year.

"The war doesn't seem to be having any effect on the racing programme so far," Giles said to Leander when they relaxed for a few days before starting the winter routine of the yard and preparing for a new batch of yearlings.

"I don't think it's going to be allowed to," she replied, basing her opinion on the stream of tit-bits that Joe Symes brought back from racecourses and the talk in Newmarket bars.

This was confirmed by Oliver Derwent when he came to Cannings Ambo for a few days at the end of October. One of his owners was a Member of Parliament and had been able to provide him with the nearest thing to official information that existed.

"It's definitely going to be business as usual," he said. "Unless something utterly unforeseen crops up, they're going to run a normal programme of racing for the duration. There's one funny thing, though: the Derby and Oaks will be shifted to Newmarket. And the Leger."

"How strange," Giles said. "What's the idea behind that?"

"No idea," Oliver replied. "Seems damned silly to me."

"No, it isn't," Leander said. "At least, not if you're the Government. What happens if they run them at Newmarket?"

"I should think hardly anyone will go and watch them," Giles replied.

"Exactly! Would you want half a million people trooping off to Epsom and two hundred thousand to Doncaster if you were trying to run the country under present conditions?"

Oliver Derwent looked at her through half-closed eyes before nodding. "Yes, see what you mean," he said.

"There are the transport problems," Leander told the still unconvinced Giles. "And who knows what sort of seditious stories might start going round in a big crowd. You know what Epsom's like at the best of times. Now . . ." she clapped her hands for a complete change ". . . I believe Emma has some *good* news for us. Come along, darling, you went to see Charles Stanton this morning. What did he say?"

Emma blushed slightly, looked at Giles, and, in response to his smile, turned to Leander and Oliver. "You're going to have another grandchild," she said.

Leander, who had suspected as much for a month, and known at least a week before Charles Stanton confirmed Emma's pregnancy, put on a convincing show of surprise. Oliver, to whom the welcome news really did come as a revelation, made his feelings very plain.

"I say, that's wonderful!" he said, holding out his arms to Emma, who promptly moved to sit on his lap. "Give me a girl this time? You've got your son to carry this place on, so have a thought for me."

"I'll do my best, Father," Emma laughed.

"I'm sure you will, my sweet. Hey, this calls for a celebration. Have you got any champagne, Leander? Let's wet the baby's head!"

"It's usual to wait until after it's born, Ollie," Leander said, already on her way to find Polly Izzard or one of the maids. As she moved towards the door, she saw Emma glance anxiously at Giles: for a moment, she looked quite frightened. Giles, laughing and joking with his father-in-law, did not appear to notice.

Leander wondered what else, apart from the baby, Giles and Emma might have been discussing.

Secretly, Ruth had been rather pleased when Gerald began taking an interest in Penelope Meadowes. Almost certainly as a result of his experiences of Maude, Gerald displayed considerable unease in the company of girls: he seemed to regard them as dangerously unstable chemical compounds that were likely to explode in his face. With the exception of Amelia, to whom he remained devoted, Gerald gave most young women a very wide berth.

Penelope, eldest daughter of a family who had moved to Marlborough in 1904, changed his mind. They met in May 1914 when Gerald visited the Meadowes' house to supervise the fitting of bookshelves in a room that was, purely for affectation Gerald suspected, about to become a library.

Penelope was twenty-one and a quite astonishing beauty. She flirted shamelessly with Gerald and came close to turning his head. Amelia met her and took an instant dislike to her: the best that could be said about Miss Meadowes, she decided, was that her mother was putting her up to it: there were very many worse fates in life than marriage to a Cannings Ambo Trustee.

On the first Saturday of November, Gerald received an invitation to dinner from Mrs Meadowes herself. Matthew, ever the cheerful and sometimes irreverent extrovert, poked immediate fun at the painstakingly written letter, but changed his tune when Gerald told him that he, too, was invited.

"You're to be paired up with Pauline, Matt," Gerald said.

"Really!"

"Well, it doesn't say so, of course, but that must be what Mrs Meadowes has in mind."

"Blimey! Pauline is a tasty bit of all right!"

Pauline, nearly two years younger than Penelope, was indeed very pretty and intelligent enough to have earned Amelia's praise. She was, however, very serious-minded, and probably no sort of match for Matthew.

The dinner-party passed off well enough, apart from the usual display of insufferable airs and graces from Mrs Meadowes: her taciturn husband seemed to have made a great deal of money by being 'something' in Swindon, and she was determined to build a social position from it.

At the end of the meal, it was Benjamin Meadowes who ushered his daughters into the drawing-room with Gerald and Matthew. "Perhaps you might care for a few rubbers of whist without the interference of us old fogeys," he declared with a forced attempt at joviality, and the shrewd Matthew realised that their host was anxious to have his daughters safely married.

Pauline set up the card table, Matthew arranged the chairs, Gerald began the serious business of shuffling the cards and Penelope watched. Matthew did not like the way she did it: there was a mixture of indecision and devilment about her. No sooner had she taken her seat at the table than she was on her feet again, walking towards the sideboard. Watching her closely, Matthew became certain that his suspicions were correct, she *had* drunk too much wine with her dinner.

No one saw what she took from the drawer – she had her back to the room all the while – and she carried the object to the card table in cupped hands as if it were a butterfly.

"A present for you, Gerald, dear," she said in an unnaturally bright voice. Opening her hands, she let the white feather flutter into his lap.

While Gerald was staring at the thing in stupefaction and Matthew was flushing with anger, Pauline was the first to react.

"Penelope! What do you think you are doing?"

Penelope was unrepentant in the face of her sister's considerable wrath. "I'm telling Gerald that he ought to be fighting for King and Country, not idling around in the lap of luxury. It's the only way to be worthy of me."

"Worthy of you?" Matthew exploded. "Why on earth should a good man want to be worthy of a woman who does a thing like that?"

Gerald held up a restraining hand. He was deathly white, but in perfect control of himself. "I was talking about enlistment with someone only the other day," he said quietly.

Matthew looked at him sharply. This was no idle boast; Gerald always told the truth, even to appalling creatures like Penelope Meadowes.

It cut no ice with her. "It's no good *talking* about it, Gerald, you must *do* something."

"Really, Penelope, this is altogether wrong of you," Pauline said angrily. "We're supposed to be having a pleasant evening together, not talking about dreadful things like the war."

"We aren't doing anything any more," Matthew said. He was on his feet. "Come on, Gerald, we're going home."

"Oh, please don't, Matthew," Pauline cried. "I'm sure Penelope didn't mean to be so rude. She'll apologise."

"I will not! Why should I say I'm sorry to a coward."

Matthew had thought that he might have to drag Gerald from the house, but Penelope had now gone too far.

Meadowes and his twittering wife hurried into the entrance-hall, drawn by the confused babble of angry voices.

"What on earth is the matter?" Mrs Meadowes asked.

"My brother and I are going home," Gerald replied calmly. "Why?"

No one made any attempt to answer her. However, Matthew, seething with rage, marched up to the sullen-looking head of the household. "Mr Meadowes, your daughter is a bitch," he said. "She needs a damned good hiding." Turning on his heel, he followed Gerald out of the front door. As they got into the car that they owned jointly, they could hear the beginnings of what promised to be a prolonged shouting match.

With Gerald driving, they covered the short distance back to Cannings Ambo in silence. There was a great deal that Matthew wanted to say, but he kept his mouth shut out of respect for Gerald's feelings.

When the car was in the garage at the back of Rose House and Gerald had turned off the engine, neither of them made a move to get out and the silence continued.

"You must never say a word about that to anyone," Gerald said. "Promise me."

"Isn't she a bitch!" Matthew seethed.

"Promise me!"

"Damn it, Gerald, she's worse than Maude!"

"Matthew, will you please promise me never to breathe a word about that to anyone?"

"Yes, all right, if it's important."

"It is."

There was a pause before Matthew asked, "Who did you talk to about enlisting?"

"Giles," Gerald replied. "And it's a secret at the moment, so keep that under your hat, as well!"

Matthew whistled softly. "Aunt Leander will throw ten fits," he muttered.

Two days later, one of the worst weeks in Leander's life began. Although Giles did his best to introduce it in the most casual manner, she knew at once that something desperate was afoot.

They were in the yard, watching the yearlings being put back in their boxes after a morning of schooling.

"You know, this place almost runs itself," Giles said.

"It does at this time of year," Leander replied, masking her apprehension. "The season is a very different matter."

"Oh, yes, but you and Albert could handle that."

"I could do it on my own," Leander said firmly. "But who would hold the licence if you weren't here? It's absolutely essential that we keep going, Giles."

"I know, that's why I mentioned Albert. He could take out a licence – or a permit if you felt that was going too far."

"And what if Albert wants to volunteer?" Leander asked, showing that she knew where Giles was steering the conversation.

"He's too old," Giles said triumphantly. "They're not keen on men over forty *and* he's got something wrong with his left ear-drum. He'd never get past the medical. In any case, he doesn't want to go."

"And you do?"

"I think I see it as my duty and I'd much rather volunteer than be conscripted."

"Don't be silly, darling, there's no question of conscription being introduced."

"Not for a year or so," Giles replied grimly.

Looking round the yard, Leander saw five faces among the lads that were, as yet, unfamiliar to her. They were men of between fifty and sixty, who, despite their wealth of experience, would normally have been lucky to find a job: Giles had set them on instantly to replace the young men who had gone to France. Yesterday she had learned from Rupert that Silas was leaving at the end of the month.

"Have you spoken to Emma about this?" Leander asked.

"Yes, Mother. It worries her, of course, but she wouldn't try to stop me."

Oh, yes, it worries her all right, Leander thought, it worries her sick. "Do you *really* think it's your duty, darling?" she asked.

"Yes, Mother, I do."

She nodded, trying to take it all in. "I don't want you to go, but I know that's a very selfish reaction," she said. "You must do your duty."

After lunch, she went to Rose House to see William, only to discover that Gerald and Matthew had raised the same topic with him during the morning.

"*Both* of them?" she said.

"Yes. Matthew won't let Gerald go on his own – he says he's not fit to be let out without someone to keep an eye on him." Although William did his best to make light of it, Leander could see that he was profoundly uneasy.

"What does Ruth think?" she asked.

"She's upset," William replied tersely.

Questioning William, Leander discovered that purely from the business point of view, the absence of Gerald and Matthew would make no difference unless the war went on for a very long time. William, Jim Goakes and Fred Cartwright could cope with an order book that was expected to run down in 1915. If William noticed now closely Leander quizzed him on the amount of spare time he expected to have, he attached no significance to it.

For two days it seemed to hang in the balance. Giles, Gerald and Matthew met several times, giving Ruth, at any rate, the impression that the idea was losing its attraction for them. While Leander was on tenterhooks, Amelia made one of her regular telephone calls from Cambridge and was horrified to learn what was being considered.

"Mother, you must stop them, you simply *must*," she said frantically.

"I only wish I could, darling," Leander said wearily.

"You can! If you forbid Giles to go, I'm sure that will put Gerald and Matthew off."

"I'm not sure that I want to forbid Giles to do anything."

"For God's sake do it! This isn't *our* war, Mother."

"Oh? Whose is it then?"

"The politicians and armaments manufacturers."

"Is that the official Cambridge view?" Leander, intensely patriotic, asked sharply.

"What if it is?" Amelia said defiantly. "It seems perfectly sensible to me."

The conversation left them both feeling wretched for hours afterwards. All that Amelia could do was pour out her misgivings in a letter to Miss Douglas at the Godolphin School with whom she corresponded regularly, especially in search of guidance.

Throughout three more days, there was a succession of conflicting signs as first Giles, then Gerald, seemed to have turned against enlistment. Although they concealed it even from themselves, these vacillations were caused by fear and a desire to carry on living the comfortable, preordained pattern of their lives. Later, much later, Leander discovered that there was every reason for them to draw back until the very last minute. If, for example, the pleasantly bumbling old major who presided over their attestation, after virtually promising them commissions, had made it clear that they were very unlikely to be serving in the same regiment, Gerald would have pulled out, taking Giles and Matthew with him.

But all the checks and balances failed, just as they had in the greater European context. On 25 November, Giles Hawksworth, Gerald Flamsteed and Matthew Flamsteed drove to a recruiting office in Salisbury and committed themselves to serving their country. Two weeks later, they were called to a hurriedly constructed training and transit camp on Salisbury Plain.

*

400

Leander went to Rose House knowing exactly what she wanted, but unsure of how to set about it. After ten minutes of idle talk, it was Ruth who gave her the opening.

"How will you manage at the stable without Giles?" she asked Leander.

"Albert and I will be all right. Our only difficulty is that we need someone to hold the licence. They won't give it to me, of course. Women aren't supposed to know about such matters!"

"What about Albert?" William asked. "He'd do splendidly, wouldn't he?"

"Probably." Leander paused. "But I don't want that. Even though it's only a temporary emergency measure, we must keep it in the family. Father would have wanted it that way."

William nodded sagely, appreciating the rightness of Leander's thinking: meanwhile, she watched, slightly amused by his failure to make the simple deduction.

"That means you, William," she said quietly after allowing him more than enough time to think it over.

"Me!" William reacted as though he had been stung by something extremely unpleasant.

"There isn't anyone else," Leander said, doing her best not to laugh at the look on her brother's face.

"But I don't know a thing about horses," William protested.

"You don't need to. All I want is someone to hold the licence and look the part while Albert and I get on with the training."

"Is that allowed?" William asked, hoping for help from the rules of Racing.

"I haven't the faintest idea," Leander said airily. "If it isn't, I shall find a way round it."

"Leander's right, William" Ruth said. "Latimer's Barn must keep going and it's got to stay in the family."

William looked helplessly at them, clearly engaged in the search for a good excuse.

His pathetic cry of: "But I'm fifty-three, Lea," gave her the excuse to burst out laughing.

"I'm fifty-four, you ninny, and I'm going to be doing most of the work," she said. "Fifty-four and a grandmother, my dear, and I intend riding out every day. Don't you think you might manage to stand in the wings and pretend to be in charge?"

William grinned sheepishly and it was as though twenty-five years had slipped away from him. Ruth was glad; this might help him to forget the problems that beset them. Much as Gerald and Matthew occupied his thoughts, she knew that he still worried about Maude, even though it now seemed certain that the Germans would not be able to overrun Paris.

"All right, Lea, I'll do what you want," William said, adding, "As usual!" with a special type of smile that went back to their growing up together.

After the Ruddock fiasco, Leander always visited the stud at Cannings St John once a week without fail. With Conn Daly in charge, this was not a precaution, but a means of keeping the two halves of an increasingly important enterprise in touch with each other.

She went for lunch on Wednesdays, riding across Cannings Down on a hack. On 23 December, as well as Christmas presents to deliver, there was important news.

"The Jockey Club have transferred the licence to my brother," Leander was able to tell Conn and Sally after a sympathetically fast piece of work by the authorities at Newmarket. "Albert and I will be doing the training, of course."

"That's nice," Sally said. "It's going to be like old times with a Flamsteed in charge."

Conn nodded agreement, but he wanted to know something else. "Albert not mind?" he asked succinctly.

After thirty-seven years of working closely with Leander, he felt entitled to ask such a question and she answered it frankly.

"No, he doesn't. Actually, he's very relieved not to have the responsibility." Conn was satisfied. "Now then, it's nothing but bad news wherever you go these days, and I've got some for you."

"You want me to carry on here until the war's over," Conn said, making a statement rather than asking a question. He was sixty-five and there had been some talk of his retirement just before Sarajevo and what followed it.

"Yes, please."

"That's good news, not bad," Conn said.

"He doesn't want to retire, Mrs Hawksworth," Sally said. "He's been dreading it."

"Well, thank God *somebody's* pleased at the way things are turning out," Leander said with great feeling.

"This war's turning everything upside down," Conn said. "We've often wished we could have had a son, but now . . ."

Leander took his point: what a pass things had come to when a couple could be glad they did not have sons to worry about. Briskly, she turned to a discussion of plans for the 1915 breeding season. They agreed that it was time to retire Hypotenuse, now twenty-four and suffering from blood-pressure problems.

"Broadside and The Atheling will keep us going for a few years yet," Conn said.

"And we've got The Black Prince to think of," Leander said. "We haven't yet decided whether to race him for another season. And I want another Derby winner within the next three years!" Her face was resolute with determination. "War or no war, I'm going to win that race again before I'm very much older!"

"Oh, Mrs Hawksworth . . ." Sally rummaged through a pile of newspapers and magazines ". . . look. Yesterday's newspaper called it the 'Great War.'"

She held up the front page for Leander to see the new name embodied in a glaring headline.

"The Great War," Leander repeated tonelessly.

And that was what everyone always called it after the Christmas by which it was to have been over.

CHAPTER 23
1916

'Where the devil is Beaumont Hamel?'

It was, Leander thought, some compensation for what they were enduring.

On a magnificent late-May morning, she was riding a first-rate horse along the gallop. The colt, called Thermopylae, was a son of Broadside, and had already won the Two Thousand Guineas: this was his last piece of serious work before the Derby.

With a fraction over a furlong to go, Leander gave Thermopylae his head and revelled in the surge of power as he left his three galloping companions behind. It would soon be fifty years since she had first experienced the vivid acceleration of a truly outstanding horse, yet the sensation was always thrillingly fresh.

She looked ahead to the group of spectators surrounding William and smiled. After a desperately self-conscious few months when he had hardly known where to put himself, William really was entering into the spirit of the thing: he looked like a trainer, he was starting to sound like one, and he went to race meetings with relish. He had even discovered that he was no longer frightened of horses and earned considerable respect from the hawk-eyed sceptics in the yard.

"Dammit, Leander, that boy of yours might have to find another job when the War's over," the Duke of Laverstoke had said. "I do believe that William's starting to get delusions of grandeur!"

The Duke was one of the men with William, the others being Rupert Timberlake and the proud owners of Thermopylae, Guy Mallender and Harry Giffard. Giving them a Classic winner had meant a lot to Leander and she was looking for a repeat in a few days' time.

The War had reached a state of totality that affected everyone. The measure of its influence on civilians was in the rapidly emerging concept that something called 'The State' could intervene in everything. The idea was born from the necessity to co-ordinate and maximise the production of the vast quantities of armaments needed for the Western Front. The Ministry of Munitions, headed by Lloyd George, acquired sweeping powers to interfere with and direct private industry.

The shortage of able-bodied men brought another change that was clearly destined to have far-reaching implications: women had to do men's jobs. Half a million of them took over the clerical work in offices; eight hundred thousand worked in engineering workshops where they found shorter skirts necessary to avoid sweeping dirty factory floors. Women acted as conductors on buses and trams; and two hundred thousand of them swelled the ranks of the Civil Service, spreading the influence of the State.

But perhaps most significant of all, January 1916 saw the introduction of military conscription for all unmarried men between the ages of eighteen and forty-one. Leander was both relieved and proud to find that the Act did not touch Cannings Ambo: all those who would have been liable had long since gone as volunteers.

There was something profoundly awful about the State placing its citizens under compulsion to kill and be killed, and Leander saw that it was bound to bring social change, particularly when married men had to be included and the question of their widows and children arose.

She always remembered Horatio's predictions of change and feared that events in France would achieve, in a very few years, what he had envisaged taking a century to come about.

The progress of the War remained a sketchily reported mystery.

In 1915, the Second Battle of Ypres took place, bringing the introduction of poison gas into the ghastly equation of the Western Front. Despite the German use of chlorine, the engagement was indecisive, as was a subsequent battle centred on Loos, near Arras. The stalemate was dreadfully plain to see.

Leander found the Gallipoli campaign quite beyond belief and suspected that the statements on its progress were even more deliberately misleading than those covering the other theatres of war. She was at a loss to understand what the operation was meant to accomplish: surely, only an idiot could imagine that the Dardanelles, the straits swum each night by her mythical namesake, were a back door to Berlin.

And in the midst of all the gloom and confusion, the question of Home Rule for Ireland finally boiled over with the 1916

Easter Rising in Dublin. Torn between the belief that it was a treacherous stab in the back and her sympathy for the Irish, those softly-spoken geniuses with horses, Leander was sure of only one thing: the British handling of the rebellion was catastrophically inept.

The war news on the day after Thermopylae won the Derby seemed very much like the last straw.

There was no denying that a Derby run at Newmarket carried far less prestige than the genuine article at Epsom, and at £2,900, the prize-money was substantially below pre-war levels. Nevertheless, Thermopylae and Mark Pilgrim made a thorough job of winning an exciting race, and the colt's delighted owners found no difficulty in convincing themselves that he would have done exactly the same over Epsom's more demanding mile and a half.

Thermopylae's Derby was given scant coverage in the following day's newspapers because of the spaces devoted to what soon became known as the Battle of Jutland. Very nearly two years after the War began, the mighty battle fleets, whose construction had done so much to heighten international tension, actually came together and fought an action.

Not surprisingly, the newspapers claimed it as a famous victory, but Leander was not so sure. Giles and Matthew, by happy chance home on leave together, worked through the papers with her and agreed.

"They're telling lies," Leander asserted.

"Perhaps . . . but it's more likely that no one has the faintest idea what went on," Matthew said. Most of his happy attitude to life was still miraculously intact, although his opinions tended to be more cautious these days.

"I'd give ten pounds to see a German newspaper," Giles said. "I'll lay odds they think *they* won it." He spoke with a confidence that, for him, was strangely forceful.

"And the news from Verdun doesn't seem to improve," Leander said after glancing at the two paragraphs reporting progress on the huge battle that had been raging for over three months. "Why are the Germans making such an issue out of Verdun? It seems such an unimportant place."

"It's on the way to Paris, Aunt Leander. Look." Matthew showed her in the battered old atlas that she always kept handy these days. "Perhaps they think they would have an easy run through Chalon if they can break Verdun."

But Giles was shaking his head. "They've picked on Verdun

406

because the French regard it as very special," he said. "Pétain has declared Verdun to be the very soul of France and it must be defended to the last man."

"And what does that achieve?" Leander asked.

"A hell of a lot of dead Frenchmen! Hundreds of thousands. That might weaken the front further north, say around Cambrai, and let the Germans through. That's the quickest way to Paris."

Again, the confidence that Leander found so surprising. Her greatest worry when Giles enlisted was not that he would get killed, but that his rather retiring nature would take a beating; that whatever it was that was going on in those trenches might break him.

Nothing remotely like that had happened. From the moment he donned his uniform and was given the King's commission, Giles had gained in confidence and stature. Against all the odds and expectations, he even *looked* more of a soldier than Gerald, or the extrovert, slightly swaggering Matthew.

And whatever he might already have endured in France, he seemed unscarred mentally and spiritually.

"Is Giles *really* all right?" Leander had asked Emma after his last leave. "Does he talk about the War?"

"Only a little," Emma replied. "He tells me about his men . . . they're all very good . . . and the other officers. He thinks some of them aren't so good."

"Does he ever seem frightened?"

"Never! He says he thinks of me and the children and prays each night and he's sure everything will be all right."

And there was no doubting it. Giles's delight in Emma was just as it had always been, calm and deep, with not a hint of desperation at the precious time they snatched together. As well as Steven, now approaching his third birthday, they had the year-old Rachel, born on 24 May 1915, the last day of the Second Battle of Ypres in which Giles had been heavily involved.

Rachel, named to commemorate Emma's mother, was as pretty as a picture and the apple of Giles's eye. Much as he loved the placid and well-behaved Steven, Rachel, full of impetuous mischief, commanded a special place in Giles's heart. Both children had the combined good looks of Flamsteeds, Hawksworths and Derwents, yet whereas Steven's manner acted as a disguise, Rachel already seemed to be flaunting her beauty.

Giles never showed strain. The previous day he had been at Newmarket to watch the Derby, behaving like a country gentleman, quietly enjoying himself without a care in the world. Solemnly, and to the great amusement of the onlookers, he had congratulated William on training Thermopylae, the colt he himself had earmarked for possible greatness as a yearling.

Definitely, Leander thought, her Giles was an amazingly brave man. This was confirmed by two of his comrades-in-arms at The Hall.

The use of The Hall as a convalescent home for officers stemmed from a suggestion put forward by Victoria Fandine-Browne. Early in 1915, at the age of sixty-two, she had retired from St Thomas' Hospital and taken a small house in Marlborough. She wasted no time in cadging a lift to Cannings Ambo with Rupert Timberlake.

"They're crying out for places where the wounded can recuperate after they've been put right in hospital," Victoria told Leander. "The Hall would be perfect. What about it?"

"That's a marvellous idea!" was the immediate response. "I've been wondering what we could do to help."

After thinking it over for half an hour, Leander telephoned the Duke of Laverstoke.

"Hubert, I want you to cut some red tape and pull strings for me."

"Certainly, my dear," he replied, chortling at the mixed metaphor. "What's the problem?"

"I want to turn The Hall into a recuperation home for soldiers, but Vic Fandine-Browne tells me it might take ages. I don't want to be up to my waist in forms and pox-doctors' clerks, so can you do anything?"

"I should think so. One of Lloyd George's understrappers owes me a favour. Leave it with me for a couple of weeks."

"Good God, Hubert, what do you want to do, set up one of your infernal sub-committees? I'll give you a week!"

Four days later, an official arrived to inspect The Hall. As a result of the Duke's efforts, the man was senior enough to give approval on the spot: the scheme could go ahead. In one respect, however, Leander was thwarted.

"Definitely not, Mrs Hawksworth," the man from the Ministry said with tight-lipped primness. "You may not run a home for all ranks. It must be officers only."

"Why?" Leander demanded truculently.

"One cannot have officers and other ranks mixed in what is essentially a social environment. That is prejudicial to good order and discipline."

"What utter poppycock!" Leander snorted.

"In any case . . ." the man became smug as he played his trump card ". . . we do not provide such facilities for other ranks."

Leander caught Victoria's eye and understood the message: argument was pointless and might wreck the whole scheme. She gave in with bad grace and fumed about it for weeks afterwards.

But she won every other argument. The Army was to provide only one man to help run the home, a cook. Apart from that, they delivered thirty beds and a vast quantity of blankets and linen, made provision for paying for the patients' food and left Cannings Ambo to get on with it.

The men's physical well-being was to be in the capable hands of Victoria Fandine-Browne, who would live in The Hall as matron. Charles Stanton was to receive an honorarium to act as medical officer, while Ann Mallender would continue to live at The Hall and provide whatever help she could while continuing to look after the post office and shop.

A week before the first batch of men arrived, a senior army doctor came to see Leander and Victoria to tell them what to expect. He was a kindly old colonel to whom Leander took an instant liking.

"It's damned good of you to put such a fine billet at our disposal, Mrs Hawksworth," he said. "Some of these poor chaps need a place like this very badly."

"What can we do to help them?" Leander asked.

"Peace and quiet, plenty of good food and someone to talk to when they feel the need of it . . . mother and sister sort of touch. Quite a few of them will be suffering from shell-shock on top of their wounds."

"Shell-shock?" The phrase was new to Leander. "What's that?"

"Each major attack by either side starts with a heavy artillery bombardment to soften up the enemy positions. These bombardments can last several days."

"Days?" Leander gaped at him.

"Yes, ma'am."

"Day and night?" Leander whispered.

"Absolutely non-stop."

"The noise must be awful!" Leander said.

"It is. And if you're on the receiving end . . ." The colonel saw no need to finish the sentence.

"I think I see what shell-shock is," Leander said grimly.

"Well, it's not quite that simple, Mrs Hawksworth." The old colonel looked sad. "A lot of these chaps are badly unhinged . . . to be honest with you, some of them are well on the way to being certifiable." He paused to tug at his moustache. "Trouble is, not everyone is affected – some fellows hardly seem to mind it. So some people have decided that shell-shock is a malingerer's complaint, a form of cowardice, if you get my meaning. Even the chap's family think that sometimes."

Leander bristled. "I wonder if they might be the same charming folk who gave their boys white feathers," she said.

"I wouldn't be at all surprised," the colonel replied. "You see the difficulty we have?"

"Yes, you've got some badly frightened young men in need of understanding and love. They shall have it! Ours will be the best home in the country."

Appreciating the extent to which she meant it, the colonel went back happy to the military hospital near Swindon. He never knew it, but Leander's vehemence was caused by the opportunity for killing two birds with one stone. Amelia had been talking repeatedly of going to France with the Voluntary Aid Detachment and Josie Prior, whose doctoral thesis was hopelessly in the doldrums, wanted to go with her.

"They can come here and work in my convalescent home," Leander told William. "We've sent more than enough people to get involved in that War!"

A week later, fifteen officers arrived to stay at The Hall and Cannings Ambo began to discover what was really happening on the Western Front.

On their very first night, Leander sat with a twenty-one-year-old second lieutenant who, after seeming perfectly normal at dinner, joking about the leg wound that had brought him back to England, broke down and cried himself to sleep.

A moment or two before he went, he opened his eyes to look at her with a simplicity that was almost frightening. "Mrs Hawksworth, I'm the luckiest man alive," he said. "Your son is my section commander, and if it weren't for him, I wouldn't be here now. He's a very brave and good man."

Six months later, a nineteen-year-old who had gone straight to France from Eton, told her the same thing.

On 6 June, two days before the end of Giles's leave, the newspapers announced that Lord Kitchener, Secretary of State for War, was missing, presumed dead. The previous day, he had sailed from Scapa Flow on HMS *Hampshire*, heading for Russia on a secret mission. Barely two hours out, *Hampshire* hit a mine and went down with virtually all hands in a matter of minutes.

"Well, isn't this a pretty kettle of fish!" Leander fumed. "Five days after our great naval victory at Jutland, and it isn't even safe to venture out in our own back-yard. Rule, Britannia! And when is someone going to do something about these German U-boats?"

"Look on the bright side, Mother," Giles said. "With old Kitchener out of the way, we might be lucky and get someone in charge who knows how to conduct this war."

Leander was scandalised at this dismissal of the hero that England so badly needed, but said nothing. Perhaps Giles's bitterness was an understandable sign of war-weariness. Yet, when she went to The Hall after lunch, she found precisely the same sentiments among the officers there.

"I believe the old fool was a liability, ma'am," a Royal Artillery major told her. "A complete and utter liability."

"Hang on, Bertie," said a Grenadier, struggling to master a wooden leg. "I'm no admirer of the man, but I'm told on good authority that Asquith had him pretty trussed up. There isn't much you can do once the politicians start meddling."

"And Lord Kitchener did build us a splendid army," Leander said. "The greatest there has ever been. We owe him gratitude for that."

"You're quite right, Mrs Hawksworth," the gunner admitted, setting off a chorus of agreement.

None of them could possibly have imagined that in little more than a month, Kitchener's Army would be following its creator to an unknown grave.

Maude and Pierre Guillaume left Paris at the end of 1914. They did so not out of fear, but boredom. Paris might, for the moment at any rate, be safe: it was, however, a city of shortages from which much of the sparkle had gone. They went instead to Pierre's father at his farm on Belle Ile, the island off the Breton coast at the entrance to Quiberon Bay.

The farm was situated on high cliffs above the village of Port Donnant on the western side of the island. On the morning after they arrived, a south-westerly gale sprang up and by nightfall it was battering the high tide against the cliffs with an elemental, earth-shaking fury. Maude thought it was the most awe-inspiring place and made up her mind on the spot that she wanted to spend the rest of her life there.

One glance at Achille Guillaume was enough to show where Pierre's looks and physique had come from. Although at least sixty, Achille was a magnificent specimen of manhood: clearly he entranced the two servant-girls who looked after him and the massive, white-washed house that had stood four-square against the Atlantic winds for at least two centuries. Maude sensed that Achille, a widower, regularly took one, or even both of them, to his bed.

Pierre made up his mind to paint landscapes, something he had not attempted before, and set about it with ruthless single-mindedness. He was, he said, going to found a new school. Achille humoured him and kept Maude company during Pierre's three- and four-day absences in search of suitable subjects.

On a drowsy afternoon in June while Pierre was on a longer visit to the mainland, Maude and Achille became lovers, and a vastly satisfying experience they both found it, although Maude returned her favours to Pierre when he came back from a week's ramble round Ushant. That was how it continued and Achille thought it vastly entertaining.

The handful of local people shrugged their shoulders and accepted the wilful, attractive Englishwoman. Achille's two sons by his second marriage, Jacques and Michel, both younger than Pierre and the men destined to carry on the farm, came home on leave to treat Maude with cautious and bewildered respect.

There was no respect for anyone from the officials who came looking for Pierre every two or three months. Unlike England, France had no qualms over conscription, first used for the Napoleonic armies and now employed with great rigour to satisfy the demands of the conflict with the hated Germans.

If Pierre was at home when they came, he raced off to hide in the barn or the fields: there was plenty of time because the car could be seen for miles, spluttering up the road from Le Palais, and someone always gave the warning. Achille, apparently unconcerned by his eldest son's wish to avoid military service, spun a virtuoso web of lies, smiling disarmingly the whole time.

The cat-and-mouse game took a whole year to play out before coming to an abrupt end in March 1916. Three men from the *Préfecture* in Quiberon came on a Sunday: approaching from a new direction, they caught Pierre as he sat at his easel on the road to Sauzon. They gave him his call-up papers and made him sign for them. He was to report in one week.

Achille and Maude offered sympathy without disturbing themselves too much. They both knew what Pierre would do. The following day, he set off at first light with a few clean shirts and his pockets stuffed with money: the question of Maude going with him was never mentioned.

He wrote a brief note from Bayonne, saying that he intended to cross into Spain and take a ship to Martinique.

"Well, *chérie*, what now?" Achille asked.

"I want to stay here," Maude said.

"*Mais oui* – providing I make an honest woman of you!"

"Get married?" Maude was pleasantly surprised.

"It is the least you can do," Achille said, with his persuasive smile that carried the hint of depravity. "I must have an attractive young wife to make people forget that my son is a coward!"

They were married at a civil ceremony as soon as a licence could be obtained. A week later, Maude's pregnancy was confirmed and Achille laughed until tears streamed down his cheeks.

"What will it be?" he asked, helpless with mirth. "What are you carrying, *chérie*? My son, or my grandson?"

The plan was widely believed to be invincible. Only one or two brigade commanders grumbled that the 'Staff Johnnies' responsible for it had not bothered to see the terrain for themselves; due to immense pressure of work, there had been no time to leave their headquarters, fifty miles to the rear.

No matter. 'The Big Push', as it was universally known, would do the trick: trench deadlock was to be broken by a tremendous military feat.

An hour before dawn on 24 June, over one thousand five hundred British field guns opened fire simultaneously over an eighteen-mile stretch of Picardy between the towns of Albert and Combles. The Germans, against whom the hail of demoralisation was directed, knew that a major attack was coming.

The barrage lasted for over eight days, until seven o'clock on the morning of 1 July. Half an hour later, thirteen British divisions – over two hundred thousand men – clambered out of their trenches. They grouped up in no-man's-land into curiously old-fashioned formations, and advanced with fixed bayonets gleaming in the bright sunshine that followed two days of continuous rain.

The tactics, worked out by Douglas Haig, were perfectly simple: the infantry was to take the surviving Germans prisoner, clear up the wreckage of the bombardment and then stand aside while the cavalry, Haig's pride and joy, swept through into the open country behind the enemy lines to start the rout.

During the inexplicable delay between the lifting of the barrage and the appearance of the British infantry, the Germans emerged from the dug-outs they had spent eight months perfecting, moved into their forward trenches and set up machine guns. An amazing spectacle presented itself in their sights: Kitchener's Army was coming towards them in serried formation at a ponderously measured pace. Each man had a sixty-six-pound pack on his back and held his rifle

413

at the regulation angle across his body. The sun was in their eyes. Strung out across the front of the mass of infantry was a thin line of junior officers. They carried revolvers and some of them had swords.

The machine-gunners of the 3rd Brandenburg Infantry, impregnably entrenched in front of a village called Beaumont Hamel, opened fire at twenty-one minutes to eight.

When the attack was abandoned for the day, British casualties amounted to 19,000 killed and 57,000 wounded, the greatest loss ever suffered in a single day by the British Army and a hideous record that was to stand for the rest of the Great War.

Among the first to die, cut down by the Brandenburgs at Beaumont Hamel, was Captain Gerald Flamsteed of the 4th Battalion of the Wiltshire Regiment.

By a cruel irony, Gerald had been feeling almost at home that morning. With its rolling chalk downs and escarpments, the terrain over which the Battle of the Somme was fought was very evocative of his native county.

Telegrams had long since been abandoned as pointless. Nowadays, the dead man's commanding officer had to write a letter when he could find the time.

Gerald's CO was himself killed leading a night attack on 2 July. During the next chaotic forty-eight hours of advance, counter-attack and carnage, the replacement CO was badly wounded and the second substitute did not reach the line until 5 July. It was another three days before he was able to sit down to write letters.

On the morning of 14 July, William, not needed at Latimer's Barn that day, Jim Goakes and Fred Cartwright were discussing business plans in the office of Rose House when Ruth came in with the letter that Ann Mallender had just brought. It was addressed to both of them, but she had not opened it.

"It's Gerald," she said. "I know it." She looked ghastly.

William's hands were shaking as he took the buff-coloured War Office envelope from her. "I expect he's only wounded," he said in an unreal voice, not bothering to question her premonition. He put the letter on the table and sat staring at it.

After a while, Jim Goakes realised that William was not going to open it. Jim, whose eldest son, Dan, was still recovering from the gas at Ypres and whose second son, Jeffrey, had died at Gallipoli, felt that he must do so and reached for the envelope. He was conscious of Fred's eyes on him as he read the letter: William and Ruth were gazing at each other in dread.

"Yes, I'm afraid it's Gerald," Jim said quietly.

"Dead?" Ruth whispered.

"Yes."

"When?" William asked, wondering why he should think it mattered.

"The first of July. First day of the Somme offensive."

"Two weeks ago!"

With a sighing sob that sounded strangely genteel, Ruth fell to her knees beside William's chair and buried her face in his lap. Jim saw rather than heard her weeping; she remained silent while her shoulders moved convulsively.

Fred took the letter from Jim, read it, but made no comment. "Do you think somebody ought to let Mrs Hawksworth know?" he asked.

"Yes, it's probably best," Jim said, answering for the dumbly grief-stricken William.

Fred jumped into his car and drove up to Latimer's Barn without realising that he was still clutching the letter. Finding Leander at the back of The House with Albert Merriweather, he merely thrust the crumpled piece of paper at her. Although Fred's attitude and the look on his face had prepared her for something dreadful, it came as a shock.

"God!" she said softly. Her face lost most of its colour and she put a hand on Albert's shoulder for support.

"Ma'am?" Albert Merriweather, who adored Leander even more than his father had done, braced himself to support her.

"I'm all right, Albert," she said shakily. "I'm very much afraid that Mister Gerald has been killed in action."

Albert remained silent, deeply upset.

Leander glanced at the letter again.

"Where the devil is Beaumont Hamel?" she asked.

"No idea, ma'am," Fred replied.

"I'll look in my atlas later. It won't be there, though. These dreadful places never are."

"I don't suppose it was a dreadful place before all this lot happened," Fred said. "I'll bet it was a lovely little village, just like ours."

"You're quite right, Fred," Leander said. She shivered at the thought of a line of trenches through Cannings Ambo, with artillery shells raining down on it: that's what was happening to Flanders and Picardy. "Ought I to go to Rose House?" she asked.

"That's why I came," Fred told her.

They arrived, Fred suspected, in the nick of time. Jim was standing outside on the gravel drive, looking helpless. Leander was out of the car in a flash and ran in through the front door, closing it behind her.

"Are they taking it badly?" Fred asked Jim.

"Very." Jim thought for a few moments. "What's starting to grieve them more than anything is that they won't be able to give him a decent funeral."

"Oh, bloody hell, yes!" Fred's voice was hushed. "Your Jeffrey's buried in foreign parts, ain't he?"

"And John Merriweather," Jim said. "That's if they bothered burying them."

"I wonder what it's like out there?" Fred was thinking aloud, not asking a serious question.

"We shall never know, thank God!"

After Leander had done all she could to comfort Ruth and William, she went to The Hall: it was one of the days on which Amelia was working a fourteen-hour stint.

She was in the kitchen, helping Sam Briggs, the army cook, prepare to dish up lunch. Josie Prior and Carrie Goakes were waiting to serve: there were forty men now, with pressure every week for more places. Already a wall had been knocked down to enlarge the dining-room.

Even though Leander broke the news as gently as she knew how, Amelia's reaction was far worse than anyone could have foreseen. At first, it seemed that she was paralysed into silent immobility: but then she started to scream.

"No! That can't be true, it can't! Not Gerald! Never!" It went on and on. Leander saw that she was becoming hysterical.

"Darling, be quiet! That won't do any good," Leander said sternly. She grasped Amelia's shoulders and shook her: to no effect. Glancing quickly at the others in the kitchen and seeing what Amelia's screaming was doing to them, Leander gave her daughter a resounding slap across the face.

It shut her up. It also brought the tears. A few seconds later, her face turned grey and she swayed.

"'Ere, watch 'er! She's gonna faint," Sam Briggs called urgently. He was a big strong Cockney of about fifty, in good condition apart from difficulty in one leg from a wound sustained at Mafeking. Despite the leg, he still crossed the kitchen in time to catch Amelia as she fell, lowering her gently to the floor. No sooner had Josie rushed to her side than the door from the dining-room opened.

"I say, heard a bit of a flap, is there anything I can do to help?" The young man, none too steady yet on his crutches, his left leg amputated above the knee, looked down at Amelia in distress.

Leander hurried to him. "It's perfectly all right, thank you, Captain Singleton. My daughter has had a very nasty shock."

"Oh . . . I see . . . is it someone dead?"

"I'm afraid so. My nephew, Amelia's cousin. She was very fond of him."

"I'm terribly sorry, Mrs Hawksworth."

"Thank you, Captain Singleton."

"Where did it happen?"

"At a place called Beaumont Hamel."

"Ah! I see. This business on the Somme. The chaps are keeping a close watch on that . . . trying to sort out the truth from the twaddle in the papers, you know."

"And what's the verdict?" Leander was guiding him back to the dining-room.

"It's a shambles," he said. "What's worse, it isn't going to achieve anything. We're a pretty keen bunch as you probably realise, but we're all glad to be here not out there."

"Even you, Captain Singleton?" Leander looked pointedly at what remained of his left leg.

"Yes, Mrs Hawksworth, even me!"

Ann Mallender and Sam Briggs always had a pot of tea together in the quiet period of the early evening when Ann had finished at the post office and Sam was waiting to start cooking dinner.

To the few people who shared their secret, Ann and Sam were two of the few bright spots in the unrelenting gloom and tragedy of 1915 and 1916. The seemingly dedicated spinster and hardened bachelor had taken a shine to each other from the moment of Sam's first appearance and were confidently expected to marry once the War was finished and Sam was discharged from the Army.

"I knew it was something terrible when I saw that letter," Ann said. "William and Ruth Flamsteed must feel awful."

"Miss Amelia passed out when she 'eard," Sam replied. "Straight out like a light, poor lamb."

"I'm not surprised. She was always very fond of Gerald – used to look after him when they were children, and he needed it sometimes. He had a sister who was a right madam."

"She the one that buggered off to France?"

"That's right. Maude. She'll come to a bad end, I should think. Is Amelia better now?"

"I hope so, love. Doctor Stanton came down and gave her something, then Mrs Aitch took her back up The 'Ouse."

"Oh dear, that reminds me," Ann said miserably. "Old Doctor Stanton died this afternoon."

"Blimey, never rains but what it don't bleedin' well pour down, does it? Minjew, 'e was a good age."

"Eighty last May."

"And 'e died in 'is own bed. There's a lot don't get a chance to do that these days."

Cannings Ambo made a special point of turning out in force for the funeral of Lawrence Stanton and his burial alongside Daphne. There was, of course, a good deal of respect for Lawrence himself, but another powerful motive was at work. For many, it was a relief to be able to go to a real funeral: in doing so, they were paying their respects to Gerald Flamsteed, John Merriweather, Jeffrey Goakes and the three Latimer's Barn lads now known to have died on the Somme within days of Gerald. Everyone realised that their graves were likely to remain lost and unmarked, so that homage to Lawrence Stanton was the nearest they would ever get to being able to do the right thing by their war-dead.

When it was all over, Fred Cartwright found himself walking towards Rose House between Leander and William. He sensed that this was no chance occurrence and began to feel positively apprehensive when they steered him into William's office.

"Don't look so worried, Fred," Leander said. "We aren't going to tear you limb from limb."

Reassured by her smile, Fred was immediately thrown into disarray by William's question.

"You are happy here, aren't you, Fred?"

"You know I am, Mr Flamsteed. I'm as happy as a pig in . . ." Fred stopped abruptly as he remembered Leander's presence.

"Have you ever wanted to leave and chance your arm somewhere else?"

"Bless you, no! If I even thought of such a thing, Tish would have my guts for garters. Why?" Fred was suddenly very ill at ease. "You don't think I should go, do you?"

"Don't be so silly, Fred!" Leander said. "We thought we'd better ask these questions because we'd like you to become a Trustee."

"A Trustee!" Fred was dumbfounded.

"I don't see why not," Leander said. "How long have you been with us? Nineteen years, isn't it?"

"Yes, but it's a very great honour, Mrs Hawksworth."

"It is," William agreed. "And you've earned it. I take it you know how much business you've brought in over the years?"

"Er . . . no . . . not *exactly*."

William was surprised: the efficient Fred, with his photographic memory, usually had a massive array of facts and figures at his fingertips. "Over three hundred and fifty thousand pounds," he said. "I checked last night."

"'Strewth! That's not bad!" Fred smiled self-consciously, impressed at his own performance.

"So you'll be a Trustee?" Leander asked.

"Yes . . . and thank you very much."

"Apart from the fact that you deserve it," William said, "we're doing this for the future. We have to make sure there is one."

"How do you mean?" Fred asked.

William glanced at Leander: it was her sort of question.

"People are getting killed," she said with a bogus brutality that very nearly concealed her sick fear. "You and your boy Ernest are safely out of it. If the worst were to happen, the day might come when we're looking to you to run William Flamsteed and Sons."

"Ernest could be in it," Fred said.

Ernest Cartwright was fourteen and about to leave school to start an apprenticeship in the workshop.

"If this war goes on long enough to bring Ernest to call-up age, Fred, there are going to be even worse problems than keeping Cannings Ambo afloat," Leander said ominously.

Two weeks later, Fred was formally elected a Trustee.

The Somme offensive eventually petered out on 16 November. Although the Allies had gained some ground, the stalemate persisted and the slaughter was unimaginably terrible. Over a million men had died, 400,000 of them British: untold numbers had been wounded, many of them marked or maimed for what was left of their lives. Now it was certain, Leander thought: no matter what happened next, England and Europe could never be the same again.

A new Army had to be raised and a new Government was needed to direct its use. Asquith, the fastidious Liberal with feet of clay, was discredited and had to go. Somehow, a way had to be found of prosecuting the conduct of the War more successfully. Lloyd George stood at the head of a social revolt and rode it to power. The Midlands and the North were sick of London's self-assumed political pre-eminence. They were providing most of the war-effort in terms of men and munitions and they wanted Lloyd George. The machinations and air of crisis lasted for nearly four weeks until, on the evening of 7 December 1916, David Lloyd George went to Buckingham Palace to kiss King George's hand upon his appointment as Prime Minister and First Lord of the Treasury.

CHAPTER 24
1917

'We know things can't get any worse'

The first eleven months of 1917 were gruelling, dreary and worrying for everyone at Cannings Ambo. In terms of the number of winners sent out, Latimer's Barn had its best season ever, with sixty-two, but no one derived much pleasure from it. Nineteen-seventeen was the year in which the full grinding futility of the War spread to every corner of England, bringing the dread that the conflict would go on and on until exhaustion, not victory, dictated an outcome.

For much of the country, shortage of basic items of food became a problem, although, thanks to superhuman efforts on the Wesley smallholding in Church Marks, the village was well provided for. David and Dora Wesley had lost their eldest son, Clifford, on the Somme and Gordon was serving with the Royal Navy, but Daisy, only seventeen and very much in the Tish Merriweather mould, always found plenty of labour for her grandiose schemes by bullying the inmates of the bar at The George.

Leander slept badly and was weary.

"Do you know, this is almost too much trouble," she said to William as they drove back from Newbury one afternoon in September.

"Doesn't four winners in six races strike you as all that good, then?" he asked, doing his best to be facetious, surprised that she was so depressed after such a startling performance.

"We were racing against rubbish!" she scoffed. "I sometimes think we're the only people bothering to get horses right and I'm starting to wonder why we do it. It certainly isn't for the miserable prize-money."

"You don't mean that, Lea," William said, his mild tone of reproof pulling her up short. "Carrying on as best we can is the least we can do for the lads at the Front."

She knew that he was referring to every member of the Army, not just the twenty-six from Cannings Ambo: she also knew that the most fearful battle yet was in progress.

"You're quite right, William," she said. "I'm sorry!"

She never moaned again.

The newspapers were full of the latest offensive which appeared to be producing some success. The scale of the operation had been in no doubt since Giles, Matthew and Silas came home on leave together for three weeks in May and June. Giles, now a major and Silas, a sergeant with the Military Medal, were not only in the same battalion of the Rifle Brigade, they were the commanding officer and senior NCO of the same company.

"They're an amazing pair," the ever-cheerful Matthew told Ruth and William. "They get themselves talked about all the way up and down the line. I've been fifteen miles away from them all winter and spring, yet it's nothing but Hawksworth and Timberlake."

"Why, what do they do?" William asked.

"Look after their men better than anybody else," Matthew replied warmly. "Some of the stories are unbelievable. I watched them march through Miraumont in January and you've never seen anything like it! You wouldn't find cleaner or better-fed men at Royal Ascot. Everyone calls them 'Hawksworth's Rifles' – even the top brass."

Leander soon noticed the special bond between Giles and Silas. There was no suggestion that they were inseparable or locked in a private world away from the War, but they made a point of meeting every day and always had a great deal to discuss.

"From what little Giles has said, I think they've saved each other's lives several times," Emma told Leander. "That would account for it, don't you think?"

"It would indeed," Leander replied, struggling to imagine what it must be like to *need* a friend like that at every twist and turn.

Naturally, Silas was invited to the dinner that Leander gave in honour of Giles and Matthew at the end of their first week of leave, and he showed his worth almost at once.

Once the initial flow of social chatter had worn itself out, Leander asked Matthew what he thought would happen next in France.

"No idea, Aunt Leander," he said in the carefree style she so admired. "Better ask the expert." He nodded at Giles.

"Well, Silas?" Giles smiled. "Where's it to be?"

"We're all going back to Flanders," Silas said calmly. "Haig wants the high ground beyond Ypres. He sees it as a big morale-booster if we could get that. The politicians would like it, too."

"Not Wipers *again*!" Matthew groaned. "I've lost count of the number of times I've been through that place. Are you sure about this, Silas?"

"Oh yes! I met Tom Jackman and Billy Humberstone on the train from Amiens to Boulogne and they said the Sixteenth and Twenty-seventh Engineers have been digging new trenches since February. There's three thousand tons of ammunition a day going up . . . I know that's true because we got stuck in a siding outside Abbeville for six hours while the perishing stuff went past."

"And did your two cronies know whether this one was going to work?" Matthew asked.

"I don't know." Silas was thoughtful for a few moments. "I think they might be trying to kick off with a bit of a surprise. Tom told me there was talk of fun and games on the Messines Ridge."

The three soldiers then became wrapped in an argument on the merits of various strategies that might have bored the other five people round the table, were it not for one thing: they sounded for all the world as though they were discussing something of merely academic interest. There was nothing to suggest that this was fire and slaughter in which *they* were to be involved.

Only Giles appeared to strike a serious note.

"I hope to God we can do without a bombardment. That terrain won't stand it."

"Why not?" Matthew asked.

"It's a potential swamp. The locals have struggled for over three hundred years to turn it into useful land. If Haig and his fellow genuises insist on pumping shells into it, we could be up to our armpits."

The other thing that Leander remembered was the look she saw Silas give Amelia shortly before he went back to his lodge in the forest. It was an expression of such love and yearning that Leander almost gasped. Amelia, deep in conversation with Emma and Giles, was unaware of it.

The offensive began in a devastating fashion with the biggest explosion yet created by man.

For nearly two years, both sides had been attempting to burrow under the other's lines: little had been achieved in the subterranean network of tunnels except grisly death for the Sappers, many of whom were miners from all over the world including South Wales. At Messines, however, the tunnels did not cave in, nor were they detected by the enemy, and four hundred tons of explosives were placed in eighteen chambers directly below the German trenches.

At ten minutes past three on the morning of 7 June, all eighteen mines were detonated simultaneously. The explosion caused panic in Lille, fifteen miles away, and was audible in London. General Plumer's Second Army, made up mostly of Anzac troops, swept forward to dispose of the stupefied German survivors.

Mysteriously, the main offensive to the north, around Ypres, did not begin until 22 July when three thousand British guns fired the first of four million shells at the German positions. On 31 July, as the barrage was lifted and the infantry attack got under way, what was to become seventy-two hours of continuous torrential rain was beginning.

There was no doubt about it, Leander thought, *this* time there did appear to be gains, although following the course of the action was not easy.

"These names get worse," she said to William and Ruth as they pored over the map in a newspaper one evening. "We can't even pronounce this lot!"

She had given up the struggle with Steenstrat, Bixschoote, Wieltje and Verlorenhoek and was frankly baffled by Hill 60 and Polygon Wood.

There was mud everywhere: newspaper reports followed the line put out by Sir Douglas Haig's Staff and blamed the heavy rain. Giles made whimsical reference to it in his first letter.

The state of the going is really rather dreadful, he wrote. *We spend an awful lot of time stuck in it. Now that the drainage system has been destroyed by shelling, it will probably never dry up.* Then, in the next paragraph, the complete switch to more pleasant topics. *If it rains for York, that filly of Rupert's ought to have a fair chance over ten furlongs. It slipped my mind completely when I was on leave, but I think she will do very much better on soft ground.*

A consequence of the mud seemed, for once, to have annoyed the imperturbable Matthew.

It's a fair old nuisance, he wrote to Ruth and William. *Everything gets bogged down. The other day we spent seven hours dragging an ammunition cart out. The men get tired and frustrated, but I do wish they wouldn't use that awful four-letter word all the time. It's really catching on! Although it might ease their feelings, it does become so dreadfully boring and meaningless.*

Boring and meaningless, Leander thought, when William showed her the letter: was that some sort of portent for the future?

Silas proved that he was a good deal less phlegmatic than some had supposed by writing to Amelia, asking if they could correspond as pen-friends.

"Definitely!" Leander said when Amelia consulted her. "It must be ten times worse out there without anyone to write to. And Silas won't have done that lightly, you know: he'll have spoken to Giles first to get his blessing."

It was from Silas that Amelia heard of the new German tactics.

We are discovering the hard way that Gerry has learned new tricks, he wrote. *His front line is held quite weakly, hence our gains so far. But after that, it is a very different story. They have built concrete shelters which we call 'pillboxes' and they are the very devil to deal with! However, we are coping. Giles has perfected a way to dispose of them.*

Towards the end of September there was a ripple of amused annoyance from Leander when she discovered that Giles and Silas had been to Paris for the weekend.

"Here's a thing!" she said. "They're gadding about enjoying themselves while we've got our backs to the wall!"

Emma, who had the facts in a letter from Giles, posted before he went back to the Front, laughed.

"Their battalion was taken out of the line to rest for five days, Mother," she explained. "They were told not to leave the rest-camp, but they thought they might as well have a go at seeing Paris. With all the difficulties of travelling, they only had thirty-six hours there."

"What did they think of it?" Leander asked, making it clear that she had been joking.

"As a matter of fact, they seem to have spent the whole time wandering round Longchamp racecourse," Emma replied. "Giles says it's very beautiful – nicer than Ascot, even – and he thinks we ought to consider sending horses there when the War's over."

"Does he?" Leander considered it. "You know, my dear, that might not be a bad idea."

After that, the autumn was uneventful. The Third Battle of Ypres rolled on, Giles, Matthew and Silas wrote every week with news of their continuing survival, laced with dry touches of humour, and the racing season ended with Leander in dangerously high dudgeon. A colt belonging to Guy Mallender and Harry Giffard was beaten by the shortest of short heads in the Dewhurst Plate and Leander swore that the judge was either blind or drunk: only with the greatest difficulty did William restrain her from giving what would have been a catastrophically lurid interview to a writer for the gutter press.

It was the nearest she had ever come to an error of judgement that would have endangered Latimer's Barn and William took it as an indication of the strain she was feeling.

Leander followed his advice: she put her feet up and hoped for better things in 1918. Six weeks passed and she persuaded everyone that the turning of the year would see something new and hopeful.

Then, on the last day of November, after eleven months of drudgery, it seemed that the world had come to a terrible end.

Cannings Ambo reacted to the news of Giles Hawksworth's death in a way that everyone subsequently regarded as strange.

It started with Emma and Leander who were stunned into immobility by the letter from the War Office.

"I really believed he was lucky," Leander said at last.

"He's been out there for three years," Emma said. "He must have survived some terrible things."

The present tense, as though Giles were still alive: and that was the way the village saw it for the first two days. The loss was too enormous to comprehend. Then, prompted by an informed whisper that Giles had been recommended for a posthumous Victoria Cross, the newspapers took the story up and the bubble burst.

The most gifted trainer of his generation was gone, killed near the end of a battle already seen as the greatest piece of folly and bloodshed in the entire history of mankind. Lloyd George and Haig were rumoured to be at daggers drawn over it, or would have been, were they in the habit of communicating. One editor wrote a leading article in which he cited Giles, a scintillatingly talented and very brave man, as the epitome of the senseless sterility of Haig's strategy.

That evening, the wreaths began arriving at The House. It was astounding that such beautiful flowers should be obtainable at that time of year, but they came from far and wide. No one called: the tributes were left in the porch outside the little-used front door. By morning, when Albert Merriweather told Leander, there were over a hundred. Tight-lipped and near the end of her tether, Leander issued the order that the front door must *never* again be opened.

As an antidote to her crushing grief, Leander had Emma's courage. In the privacy of her bedroom, Emma spent hours crying herself into a shallow, worthless sleep each night. For the rest of the time, however, she maintained a fortitude that made Leander feel ashamed of her own emotions.

Emma produced the very best of her indomitable efforts for the children. When Steven and Rachel were told of Giles's death, Rachel, though hardly comprehending what had happened, raged uncontrollably. It was Steven, four years old and almost frighteningly serious-minded beyond his years, who eventually calmed her down by means of a careful blend of love and firmness.

"Was Daddy *very* brave?" he asked Emma.

"Yes, my darling, he was. Some people are saying that the King wants us to have a very important medal for him."

426

Steven considered this, his arm tightly round Rachel. "We must be brave as well," he said.

Two evenings later, when Emma was tucking the children in bed, she found Steven gazing up at her with a most sorrowful expression on his face.

"What's the matter?" she whispered anxiously.

"I'm worried about you," Steven replied. "It's bad for you without Daddy."

Emma remembered that searing insight for as long as she lived. She always said that Steven became the best son a mother ever had on that stormy December night in 1917 when it seemed that everything lay in ruins in the relentless path of a war that would never end.

The battle finally ground to a halt on 7 December. Five days later, Colonel Harold Alexander halted his car at the foot of the Latimer's Barn drive and told Albert Merriweather that he was looking for Mrs Hawksworth.

Albert studied him: he knew a thing or two about the Army from his late brother, John, and recognised the badges of rank on Alexander's uniform. The medal ribbons were also impressive, but even the lingering signs of battle-weariness could not conceal the officer's youth. Harold Alexander was only twenty-six, but had already been in command of a battalion for two years.

"Which Mrs Hawksworth were you looking for, sir?" Albert asked deferentially.

"Both of them," Alexander replied with a sad smile.

"It's about Mr Giles, is it?"

"That's right."

Albert rode with him up the drive to guide him round to the back of The House, where Leander and Emma were at the door with William. At the sight of the uniform, they froze in expectation of still more terrible news as Alexander climbed from the car and walked towards them.

Taking off his cap and tucking it under his arm, Alexander addressed himself to Leander.

"Mrs Hawksworth, my name is Harold Alexander. I was your son's Commanding Officer. I've just got back to England on leave and I felt I must come and see you."

"That is most kind of you, Mr Alexander," Leander said, light-headed with relief. "This is Emma, Giles's wife."

"My very deepest sympathies to you, Mrs Hawksworth," Alexander murmured gravely.

427

"And may I introduce my brother, William Flamsteed," Leander said.

Alexander looked keenly at William as they shook hands. "Is your boy Matthew with the Fifth Wiltshires?" he asked.

"Yes, he is." William was torn between eagerness and desperation.

"He's been wounded," Alexander said. "Don't worry, he's going to be all right. It's a leg, but no cause for alarm. I understand that there isn't any question of amputation and he's on his way home."

"Oh, thank you," William gasped and looked pleadingly at Leander.

"Yes, William," she smiled. "Go and tell Ruth. Please come inside, Mr Alexander. Have you come far?"

"From London, ma'am."

"Did you have lunch?"

"I'm afraid I didn't."

"We must see to that!"

Steven and Rachel insisted on coming into the small sitting-room, where Steven climbed on to Alexander's knee as he attempted to eat the sandwiches that had been spirited up in next to no time.

"Did you know my father?" Steven asked solemnly.

"I did, Steven, very well indeed. He was a brave man."

Steven mulled this over for a while, then became fascinated by the red tabs on the lapels of Alexander's jacket. "What are they?" he asked. "Daddy didn't have them on his uniform."

"I'm a colonel," Alexander replied.

"Oh!" Steven pondered. "You seem awfully young. I thought colonels were old dodderers with white moustaches."

"Steven!" Emma exclaimed in horror, only to see that Alexander was smiling.

"Please don't worry, Mrs Hawksworth," he said. "I'm used to it. And Steven is quite right! Most of them are like that."

Eventually, Steven was satisfied, thanked Alexander for coming to see him, and took Rachel back to the nursery.

"Amazing!" Alexander said wonderingly. "He's just the sort of son I would have expected Giles to have."

"Where did Giles die, Colonel?" Emma asked.

"Near a village called Passchendaele." Alexander paused carefully. "It might help you to know, Mrs Hawksworth, that he died instantly. There was a German sniper in a shell-hole and he made a very clean job of it. We recovered his body and he was looked after very decently."

"Thank you," Emma said, white-faced but in control of herself and grateful for the information.

"I believe there has been some press speculation about Giles getting a Victoria Cross," Alexander said. "I don't know how they got hold of the story, but it's true enough. I saw General Gough in Amiens on the way out and he told me that he's approved the recommendation that went up from Brigade."

"Which you presumably instigated, Colonel?" Leander asked.

"Er . . . yes . . . I did, as a matter of fact."

It was, thought Leander, probably one of the very few occasions on which Colonel Alexander would show discomfort.

"Now . . ." He fished a piece of paper out of his pocket. "Sergeant Timberlake is a friend of yours, I believe."

"Very much so!" Leander declared. "My word, Colonel, you have been doing your homework!"

"He was badly wounded in the same spot of bother. Stomach, I'm afraid."

"Oh dear!" Leander was pale.

"Well, I'm hoping he's going to pull through. We got him back to hospital at Armentières pretty smartly and a first-class surgeon fixed him up. He isn't in very good shape, but the medics say the signs are good. He's on his way back, too, and I imagine that he's seen the end of the War."

"Thank God for that," Leander said quietly.

The winter dusk closed in quickly, bringing wind and rain; Alexander, on his way to visit friends in Exeter, was easily persuaded to stay the night at Latimer's Barn and make a fresh start in daylight after a good night's sleep.

As he and Leander went outside in the uncertain light of the following day's dawn, Alexander looked round appreciatively.

"Giles loved this place," he said. "He was always talking about it, but I can see that he didn't do it justice. It must be wonderful in summer."

"It is," Leander replied. "It was very good of you to come, Colonel. We appreciate it. I shall pray that you remain safe. One day you will make a marvellous general, but I hope to God we never need you!"

And to Harold Alexander's utter astonishment, she kissed him on the cheek.

She wandered aimlessly down the drive after his car and suddenly found herself very near to tears as she remembered the day Giles had come home from Winchester at the end of his last term. They had vowed then that they would never be parted again: the incredible mess that man was making of the twentieth century had ruined that dream.

Matthew Flamsteed and Silas Timberlake came home on the same day, discharged from military hospital, but both in need of care and attention while they convalesced. Matthew was as cheerful as ever, despite the pain from his left leg: Silas was in such a terrible state that Leander almost averted her eyes from him.

Although possessed of tremendous physical and moral strength, the aristocratic features of his unacknowledged father and his porcelain-like complexion had sometimes given him an air of weakness. Now, with his spare frame nearly two stones lighter and the shadow of the bullet and massive surgery still hanging over him, he looked frightful.

"There isn't anyone to take care of you, is there?" Leander asked him.

"Well, I suppose Rupert will fix something up," he replied, the effort of speaking costing him dear.

"It's already done! You're staying at Latimer's Barn, my lad."

"That's very kind of you, Mrs Hawksworth, but . . ."

"But nothing! You're one of us!"

As well as following the dictates of common decency and the debt she owed him, Leander inadvertently helped two other people by bringing Silas to The House.

Amelia and Ellie Goakes, both laid flat by Giles's death, were showing no sign of being able to pick themselves up. Sympathetic to them, Leander nevertheless felt like shaking them several times a day, so worn down was she by their helpless grief. Silas was the miracle they needed: the chance to care for the man who had been within inches of Giles when he died, lifted them back to near-normality within an hour of his arrival.

And two days later there was confirmation of what Harold Alexander had suggested. The dear old colonel came from his military hospital near Swindon to see Silas. Accompanied by Charles Stanton, he studied the case notes and X-ray plates, then gave Silas a thorough examination.

"I hear you're getting a bar for your Military Medal, my boy," he said as he poked around with his stethoscope. Silas nodded and smiled weakly. "Good show . . . yes . . . turn over . . . deep breath . . . and again . . . that hurt at all?" It went on for five minutes until the colonel finally let out a grunt of satisfaction. "Yes, you'll do. It's going to take a few months, but you'll make it. You couldn't be in a better place. One thing I can tell you here and now. You're finished with the Army."

"Really, sir?" Silas asked.

"Absolutely!"

"Oh." Silas's face remained grey and expressionless.

Two hours later, the colonel decided to recommend that Matthew was also invalided out of the Army. Leander went to Rose House the moment she heard the news.

"We've got a fair idea of what's in store for us now," she told Ruth and William. "We know things can't get any worse."

They both knew what she meant. With Matthew freed from the appalling mathematics of the Western Front, they must start planning.

"Well, there's one thing I've already managed to work out for myself," William said.

"What's that?" Leander asked.

"It's going to be at least seventeen years before Steven can apply for the licence."

Leander nodded. "Nineteen thirty-four if they let him start when he's twenty-one. I think 'thirty-five is the year to aim for."

"I shall be seventy-three by then," William remarked absently, obviously without any expectation that Leander would take any notice of him.

"You must put Matthew in charge of things here as soon as he's back on his feet," she said.

"Of course. I suppose you'll want me as a full-time trainer?" William asked.

"Yes. You've been getting the hang of it wonderfully."

"What will you do if anything happens to me?" William sounded curious rather than anxious.

The reply came like an arrow. "I shall have the licence transferred to one of the Prideaux family until Steven is old enough. It's about time Hubert's brother got off his backside and did something useful."

"Have you spoken to them about it?"

"Of course not! They will be told if and when the need arises – which it won't!"

"And what do I do if anything happens to you?" William had to ask.

"There's no need to worry about that, William," she assured him forcefully. "I have no intention of allowing anything to 'happen' to me until I know that Latimer's Barn is safe for all time!"

Shortly after Leander had left Rose House, Ruth came out of a period of deep thought and said, "I believe her."

"Oh, so do I!" William agreed. "Until she's done what she's got to, death would never stand a chance!"

Even so, Jim Goakes and Fred Cartwright, who saw Leander go, thought how tired and ill she looked.

Leander arrived back at The House to find Emma in the small sitting-room while Steven and Rachel played with Ellie Goakes in the nursery. Clutching a letter, Emma seemed to be struggling with some new sadness.

"My dear, what's the matter?" Leander asked, hurrying anxiously to her side.

"Oh . . . nothing really . . . I suppose." Emma made an effort to compose herself. "I've had a letter from Father. He says he's giving up Saxon Court next year."

"Why?" Leander was unpleasantly surprised by the news.

"His doctor has told him to." Emma waved the letter.

Leander said nothing: the last time she had seen Oliver Derwent, some three months ago, he *had* looked rather ill.

"It isn't only what the doctor says," Emma went on. "I think he's lost the heart for it. It's this damned war again!"

Leander knew that Ollie had made himself sick with worry after hearing first-hand reports of the horrors of the fighting from the son of an owner. There was one aspect of it that had particularly upset him.

"It's the horses, Leander!" he told her one day when they were strolling round his yard. "Fancy dragging those poor creatures into a mess like that! They're getting maimed and blown up as well, you know. What a mess!"

Leander had agreed with him: it *was* an unbearable thought.

Taking the letter from Emma, she read it. After an opening in which Ollie sent his obviously heart-broken sympathy for Giles, there was the doctor's diagnosis of the stomach ulcer that could only get worse unless a regime of complete rest and relaxation was introduced. The surprise was that Saxon Court was already sold. Joshua Fielding, a man of about thirty who had built a sound reputation with a small yard in Newmarket, was taking over within a few months.

"They say that Mr Fielding is one of the coming men in Racing," Emma said.

"He's certainly made a good showing these last two seasons," Leander replied. "If I remember rightly, he was only in the Army a matter of months."

"How on earth did he manage that?" Emma demanded angrily.

Leander took hold of her hand. "My dear, he lost his right arm at Mons," she said gently. "The First Battle of Ypres – or whatever they call it."

"Oh dear, I never knew that!" Emma was trembling. "Father never mentioned it."

"It's much kinder not to. In any case, I read somewhere that Fielding reckoned it wouldn't make all that much difference to him.

He's left-handed, you see! What are your father and Winifred going to do?"

"Grow roses in Devon."

"How lovely! But you'll miss Saxon Court, of course?"

Emma nodded unhappily.

Leander paused before asking: "Do you want to go and live with them?"

"No!" Emma's reaction was almost violent. "My place is here. You don't think I should, do you?"

"Certainly not, my darling." Leander embraced her. "I simply felt that I should ask. You might have wanted to be with your father."

"No, with you," Emma stated simply. "In any case, Steven would be *tremendously* upset if I took him away from here. He's your grandson, Mother, as well as my son. He asked me this morning when he would be able to take over the yard."

"Really? What did you say?"

"Well, he thought he'd be able to manage it when he was ten or eleven. I told him that might be too soon, but I promised we'd look after it very carefully until he was ready."

"I've just been talking to William about that," Leander said.

"And he agreed to carry on?"

"Naturally." Leander smiled self-mockingly. "He knew I wouldn't give him any choice in the matter!"

"I could help, too," Emma suggested hesitantly.

"I know, my dear, and so you shall!"

After ensuring that Emma was back to what had to pass for normal these days, Leander decided that it was time to ask for her assistance in one of the most difficult tasks she had ever had to face. The Big Book still awaited the entry for Giles.

Emma's courage came to the fore again, and with little or no disagreement as to what should be written, the job was finished in two hours, a long time, but still nothing like what Leander had feared. After Emma had gone to prepare tea for the children, Leander sat for some time wondering what the world was coming to when the death of someone as vital and talented as Giles had to be taken more or less as a matter of course. She realised that the answer had been self-evident since the late-summer's day over three long years ago on which John Merriweather had died at Le Cateau.

Obeying an impulse, Leander stayed in the library and wrote to George. It was a long letter, giving an account of how the last two years had affected Cannings Ambo. When she read it through before sealing it in the envelope, she noticed no expression of regret at George's absence during the cataclysmic period. Deep within her,

Leander knew that George would have been no comfort; she was also convinced that he would have added to the strain by going to any lengths to avoid becoming involved in the War.

Leaving the library with a silent prayer that she would soon have good news for the Big Book, Leander found Emma and Ellie in a half-hearted discussion about Christmas.

"That's what we must do!" Leander said. "I know it's difficult, but we ought to make a bit of a show. I'll telephone Rupert and get him to find us a tree."

Ellie agreed. "It might cheer us up a bit. We could do with it, God knows!"

"Especially Amelia," Emma added. "She seems rather bad-tempered at the moment."

Josie Prior was hopelessly in love. Two days ago, she had announced her engagement to be married. Amelia thought the marriage was doomed before it started: she was also jealous. Shown that happiness could spring from the all-pervading grimness, she detested not being a part of the miracle of renewal.

Jeremy Dundas had arrived at The Hall in May. He had long since recovered from a couple of minor wounds but was, Charles Stanton spotted at once, a very sick man. He was suffering from chronic shell-shock.

For the first month of his stay, Amelia and Josie gave him the same attention as their other charges and he seemed to make some sort of progress. Then he received a visit from two self-important, obviously well-to-do men and an attractive but slightly sour-looking young woman. They were his father, his prospective father-in-law and fiancée, and they insisted on taking Jeremy for a walk. As they set out, Amelia heard one of the men say, "Now look here, old chap, this won't do at all, you know. People are starting to talk. You must pull yourself together and get back into action. We can't have folk saying that a Dundas is a malingerer."

When they came back an hour later, Amelia watched from a window as the three visitors, all angry, got into their car and drove off, leaving Jeremy standing. He was still there five minutes later when Amelia, bustling about making beds, glanced out of another window. Hurrying out to fetch him indoors, she found him dazed and uncommunicative.

Three days later, Jeremy Dundas received two letters. Once he had read them, he degenerated into a pitiful state, cringing in corners, flinching at the slightest noise and making Charles Stanton believe that he might have to be removed to a mental institution.

After four days, he showed Josie the letters. He did so in a trance-like condition, barely conscious of what he was doing, yet the simple act was his first step on the road to salvation.

One letter was from his father, a managing partner in a St Albans law firm. Every syllable of the verbose missive testified to the writer's immensely high opinion of himself. But it was the last sentence that beggared belief. *I have to tell you that in view of this terrible defect in your character, I can no longer regard you as a son of mine.*

The second letter was from someone who signed herself Edith Bradshawe in an over-elaborate hand. In four cruel lines, it terminated her engagement to Jeremy Dundas.

Amelia wept when Josie told her. "Are such people worth fighting for?" she asked.

"I doubt it," Josie replied. "What are we going to do about Jeremy?"

"Well . . ." Amelia struggled to find words. "We must do our best to look after him . . . somehow." She feared that the task was beyond them.

However, when Josie spent the whole of the following day with Jeremy, talking to him, making sure that he ate and simply sitting in silence when that was what he wanted, a bond sprang up between them that every day grew stronger.

After two weeks, when it was commonplace to see them constantly together, and, more often than not, hand in hand, Amelia felt constrained to give Josie a warning.

"Be careful. He's getting awfully fond of you."

"That's perfectly all right," Josie replied. "I'm getting fond of him!"

Every two weeks, the old colonel from the military hospital came to see Jeremy: at the end of August, he brought a specialist from London with him. They were closeted with Jeremy for over three hours and when they re-emerged the colonel took Leander to one side.

"This is a bad business about young Dundas, Mrs Hawksworth," he said. "A very bad business indeed."

"Why?" Leander inquired with bland innocence.

"We're going to have to discharge him as unfit. As a matter of fact, that fellah from London thinks he's completely unsound – not that I go along with that, you understand."

"It's a great shame for the poor boy," Leander said. "What is *your* problem?"

"There's nowhere for him to go. It seems that his family have disowned him and he'll never get a job in his condition. If he's left wandering around, he'll be locked up inside a week."

435

"Don't worry, Colonel, Jeremy won't be wandering around."

"Eh? What will he be doing?"

"I don't know, but he'll be here, in the village. There are half a dozen families prepared to take him in."

"By Jove, Mrs Hawksworth, that's splendid!"

"Not at all, it's just another part of the Cannings Ambo service!"

Jeremy went to live at Oak Cottage with Charles and Flora Stanton who treated him as a substitute for their eldest son, David, killed early on in the latest great battle at Ypres. Once there, visited constantly by Josie, his improvement was measurable by the day. As the fourth Christmas of the War approached, although still some way from full recovery, he had gained the confidence to propose to Josie. Her unhesitating acceptance was, Charles Stanton swore, worth a hundred times more to Jeremy than all the medicines ever invented.

Amelia protested at the intended marriage.

"That's all very well, Josie, but what are you going to live on? You know that Jeremy will have difficulty finding a job."

"*I* shall work until he's able to."

"What about Cambridge? You have a thesis to complete."

"No, I haven't, Amelia. Times have changed. There are far more important things than doctorates to think about now."

"You ought to consider this very carefully, Josie. I think you may be making a big mistake."

But in her heart of hearts, Amelia admitted that she was motivated by envy. During one of the worst years in the history of England, her thirtieth birthday had passed and it suddenly seemed that she had nothing to look forward to apart from the unexciting prospect of a return to Cambridge.

She sat with Silas every evening. Although they found a sort of solace in each other's company, it was a curiously quiet relationship with minimal conversation. Silas was unwilling to talk about his experiences at the Front, and refused categorically to discuss the dreadful morning when Giles was killed and he received his near-mortal wound.

Virtually the only topic on which he seemed prepared to bother stringing sentences together was the short visit to Paris with Giles. And even when he spoke of this, there was much that he held back. During those few days away from the abomination of Flanders, Silas had told Giles of his love for Amelia; Giles, much taken with the idea, had promised to find a way to put in a good word for him.

Only Silas knew the savage pointlessness of Giles's death; the German sniper was himself badly wounded and abandoned with rotting corpses in his stinking shell-hole. By shooting Giles Hawksworth, he sacrificed his last slim chance of life.

As Amelia struggled to make conversation with him, Silas Timberlake also knew that he had been right all along: she *was* too good for him. And while he was thinking it, she found him very remote and unrewarding.

As the year ended, no one had any idea what lay in store.

Something like the full story of the Ypres offensive was leaking out. The casualty lists produced simmering outrage in a population that thought itself inured by the losses on the Somme, especially since nothing appeared to have been achieved beyond a few square miles of slime that gorged on tens of thousands of rotting corpses in its oozing depths.

Now Russia had collapsed.

For over three years, Germany had fought a war on two fronts. From the theoretical point of view it was an impossible state of affairs that should have led to her defeat within months: in practice, the German Army had never seemed in the slightest danger of losing its grip.

Russia began the War in the worst possible shape, riven by long-festering social unrest and the permanent menace of revolution. The repeated slaughter of ill-equipped peasant armies pushed affairs to the point where, in March 1917, the Tsar was forced to abdicate. A provisional government under Alexander Kerensky proposed carrying on the War as best it could.

Not for long. In April, some evil genius in the German High Command conceived the plan of releasing Vladimir Ilyich Ulyanov Lenin from detention in Switzerland and sending him to Petrograd on board a sealed train. Immediately after the consequent Revolution, Leon Trotsky opened peace negotiations with Germany. In the spring of 1918, Germany was, for the first time since August 1914, to have superiority of numbers on the Western Front by virtue of the men released from the east.

Then, as Leander gathered her family and many friends round her on the afternoon of New Year's Eve, notification arrived that Giles had indeed been awarded the Victoria Cross. The Duke of Laverstoke arrived with a copy of the *London Gazette* in which the full citation was printed.

For over an hour, The House fell silent while everyone took turns to read it and pride mingled with sorrow as they discovered what he had done.

And Giles was to have a memorial that would last for all time, for as long as men struggled with the human condition and sought ways to improve it.

Officially, those four hideous months in what had once been the poppy-strewn fields of Flanders were known as the Third Battle of Ypres, but press and public were having none of this.

For them, one word was enough to encapsulate what had happened. An entire generation was to think of it as a symbol of futility with only the faintest glimmer of hope enshrined in men like Giles Hawksworth.

The word was Passchendaele.

CHAPTER 25
1918–19

'It could almost be like old times'

1918 was a terrifying year.

Even as the incredible switchback was running its berserk course, Leander perceived what it meant. The twentieth century had come of age: from now on, there would be an ever-increasing stream of problems that would defy the attempts of governments and peoples to find a solution. And change – often for its own sake – was going to be unstoppable.

In a world apparently hell-bent on destroying itself with change if attempts to do so by all other means failed, there were times when only one thing seemed constant: the horses. Accordingly, in March of 1918, Leander set about organising the work programme with particular zest and purpose.

She and Alfred Merriweather were convinced that the horses they had in the yard gave them one of their strongest hands for many years, an idea enthusiastically supported by Michael and Mark Pilgrim.

Michael had taken over the duties of travelling head lad from Peter Izzard, now enjoying retirement. Mark was exempt from call-up as part of the Government's undeclared policy of keeping Racing as normal as possible. He suffered a conflict of emotions over this, swinging between guilt and relief; his younger brother, Philip, a volunteer since October 1914, had been wounded twice.

The only possible way forward, he found, was to bear in mind Leander's dictum. "The village has done more than it's fair share in this damned war. Let's concentrate on the horses. They're most likely our only hope of keeping sane."

And the new season provided powerfully emotive support for the idea.

Emma began riding out on the gallops. She had been brought up to it at Saxon Court, but had ridden a docile hack only occasionally since coming to Latimer's Barn. Now, after two weeks of secret practice with Mark Pilgrim during February, she was out with the first lot each morning.

"Mrs Hawksworth's pretty good," one of the lads said in the hostel after her first appearance. "But not as good as Mrs Hawksworth."

It was the first good laugh for a long time. After that, they called Emma 'Mrs Giles', a mark of the greatest respect and affection.

The trouble was, Leander realised afterwards when it was safely over, they had become used to the idea of a static war of attrition fought from trenches. Anything else was a shock. What happened in 1918 was very likely a close approximation to what everyone had expected in 1914.

But no one was able to see it like that while it was all taking place.

The German Army had its reinforcements from the Eastern Front while the British were below strength: it was being said that Lloyd George had absolutely refused to let Haig have any more men until he could think of a better plan than getting them slaughtered.

The offensive launched by the Germans on 21 March was shatteringly successful. On the first day, forty miles of British front line between Arras and St Quentin were breached and overrun: a week later, the Germans had advanced forty miles to threaten the outskirts of Amiens. There, for a reason that was not clear, the devastating thrust ran out of steam, but it seemed a mercy too small to warrant even token gratitude.

On 9 April, a further twenty-four miles of front line were wiped out between Hollebeke and Givenchy. Three days later, the British Army and public were staggered by Haig's Order of the Day: *There is no other course open to us but to fight it out. Every position must be held to the last man. With our backs to the wall and believing in the justice of our cause, each one of us must fight on to the end.*

It went down especially badly in view of a story that was going the rounds and gaining credence. Towards the very end of the action at Passchendaele, one of Haig's senior staff officers had condescended to climb off his backside at GHQ in order to pay a visit to the scene of the battle. Upon reaching the lethal quagmire, the general, unnerved to the point of being near tears, was reputed to have said: "My God! Did we really send men to fight in this?" Leander remembered Randolph Prideaux's misgivings about the cavalrymen who had made their reputation in the Boer War: Haig was one of them.

At Easter, as if oblivious of the mounting air of crisis, Jeremy Dundas and Josie Prior were married on a day that was as happy as the village could make it. For the moment, they had to carry on living at Oak Cottage with the Stantons, but Leander made it plain that they would not have to wait long for a house of their own.

"I don't give a damn what happens in this war," she told them. "We're going to start building soon."

Jeremy set to helping Daisy on the smallholding. "Are you sure you don't mind?" David Wesley asked. "It's back-breaking."

"It's exactly what I need," Jeremy replied, glad that his career as a solicitor was over and delighted to be doing something to repay the village's kindness to him. "My only worry is that I shan't be with you next year. Mrs Hawksworth says she'll have a job for me."

"So I hear," David smiled. "Don't fret about that, Jeremy. I'll be grateful for whatever you can do."

Josie carried on at The Hall although she could easily have become a teacher. In one of her letters, Miss Douglas of the Godolphin School asked for Amelia's help in filling a vacancy and a headmistress in Marlborough was desperate for someone to look after mathematics. For the time being, Josie was content with what she saw as her duty to look after the convalescing officers and provide support for Jeremy.

The flood of disastrous news from France kept pouring in. On 27 May, thirty miles of the Allied trenches between Reims and Soissons were breached; by 1 July the Germans had fought their way back to the Marne and, two weeks later, Paris itself seemed in real danger once more with the establishment of strong German positions at Château Thierry and Epernay.

The splendid performance of Latimer's Barn horses seemed only to heighten the garish unreality. Until Royal Ascot, precisely half the runners that went out in William's name came home as winners. At the Royal meeting itself, four Latimer's Barn horses out of six won their races, but all thoughts of celebration were stillborn in view of the fear that the meeting might not even take place in 1919.

"We're well on the way to losing this war," Rupert said to Leander one Tuesday afternoon while they were in their forest cottage.

"And what would that mean?" she asked after a pause to consider the enormity of what he had said.

There was silence as Rupert's face registered a variety of expressions, all of them showing degrees of puzzlement.

"I have no idea," he said at last. "We'd probably have to pay out a lot of money in reparations."

"But we wouldn't have Germans all over the place?"

"I can't see why they would want to bother." He fell silent, wracking his brains again. "I'll tell you something else, my love. I don't know what it will mean if we win. Isn't that interesting?"

Leander gazed at him wide-eyed as the dismal truth dawned on her. "What on earth are we fighting for?" she asked.

Rupert made no attempt to answer.

In a curious way that most people were unable to appreciate, the spectacular advance of the German Army sowed the seeds of its own destruction. Supply and communication lines were·extended to the point where they became inefficient or broke down. And there was another factor: the arithmetic was changing, swinging inexorably against Germany with the arrival in Europe of a quarter of a million American soldiers each month.

The opening blow of the Allied counter-attack, meticulously planned by a group that excluded Haig, was executed with a flair hitherto completely lacking. Subsequently described by an unnerved General Ludendorff as the blackest day of the German Army, the events of 8 August were a decisive prelude to victory. As the advance eastwards gathered momentum, a new pattern to the fighting emerged: the number of Germans who allowed themselves to be taken prisoner, instead of risking death, increased by the day.

Once the tide had turned, the flow of good news became a torrent. Truth to tell, there was too much of it. Leander suspected that very little of what was crammed into the newspapers could be trusted completely and even if it were accepted, forming a complete picture of the turmoil now destroying centuries-old institutions and customs in Europe was impossible. Because she was disinclined to believe the speculation about the German Government's alleged demoralisation and secret peace overtures to America, the end seemed to come suddenly.

On 9 November, the Kaiser was forced to abdicate: if the victorious Allies were going to have their way and arraign him before the bar of world opinion, what was left of the Government wanted rid of him.

Two days later, at the eleventh hour of the eleventh day of the eleventh month, the shooting stopped. Sitting in the library as the clock struck, Leander tried to envisage the eerie silence descending over the hundreds of miles of trenches, the eyesore that had been the most bloody killing ground in all history.

Then, at five minutes past, she wrote a letter to Joe and Tom Irons in Calne.

"What's this about?" Amelia asked when she offered to walk down to the post office with it.

"I've no idea what Lloyd George can or will do," Leander replied. "But I intend building a village fit for heroes."

Amelia had never seen her mother looking so determined.

*

442

Cannings Ambo celebrated Armistice Night in its own way.

Although it was a Monday and the previous day's two church services had been well attended, everyone went to the impromptu Evensong put on by John Shepherd at five o'clock. When it was over, they all gravitated to The George, which had never seen such a large but subdued gathering. There was no laughter or raised voices: instead, it was a time to think of the fourteen dead, from John Merriweather when the Great War was only a few days old, to Jack Izzard, killed at St Quentin ten days before the end.

Leander sat in a group that included Jim Goakes and Jack Izzard's grandfather, Peter, now seventy-three, yet every inch the man who had ridden Bellerophon to fame in 1876, forty-two years and a different world ago. As she sipped at half a pint of bitter beer, it was understood what she was thinking: grievous though the loss of Giles might be, she did not consider that she had suffered any more than those around her.

A remark of Rupert's to Martin Foxton at the bar caused a worried silence to steal through the gathering.

". . . so that's the thing. We've won the War – or Germany's lost it – now we have to see what we can do about winning the peace."

"Is that going to be hard, sir?" Mark Pilgrim asked.

"I'm blessed if I know, Mark," Rupert replied. "It doesn't look too easy to me. My word, there are some problems! Forget about all the obvious ones, what does anybody do about Bolshevism?"

Leander felt all eyes on her. "I'm afraid that Mr Timberlake may be right," she said. "However, we shall solve the problems that concern us and find a way round the others!"

There was not a particle of doubt in the nods and murmurs of assent that greeted the statement. But afterwards, as Rupert was getting into his motor to drive back to Marlborough, he caught a flash of concern on Leander's face.

"There's got to be an election soon, hasn't there?" she asked him in response to his raised eyebrows.

"Very soon," he replied. "This Parliament is three years over its statutory limit. In any case, Lloyd George will want a mandate for the Peace Conference."

"I'm dreading it," Leander whispered hollowly.

"Why?"

"Can you imagine what might happen when all those women start voting?"

Unable to decide whether her apprehension was genuine or mock, Rupert found himself admitting that she might have a point. In June, with no further excuse for procrastination after the sterling work done by women in the war-effort, Parliament had passed a Bill granting the franchise to all females over the age of thirty.

"You'd be torn limb from limb if they heard you preaching such heresy," Rupert chided.

"Stuff and nonsense! Try talking to the women in this village and see what they think about it." Leander lowered her voice. "To tell you the truth, Rupert, there's only Amelia and me who have any idea what it's about and I sometimes worry about Amelia!" She chuckled and gave him an affectionate kiss in full view of an astonished group of stable-lads. "Let's go home and see what we can make of this peace business!"

Before she went to bed, Leander wrote to George, undeterred by the fact that she had received no reply to her previous letter telling him of Giles's death. George had no cause to think fondly of her; but that would not necessarily stop him being glad of first-hand news of England and the village.

In the days that followed 11 November, Cannings Ambo learned about the riotous nature of the Armistice celebrations in the big cities and towns, and shook its head in amazement. The newspapers reported what was tantamount to a three-day orgy in Trafalgar Square that left the plinth of Nelson's column scarred and blackened from the huge bonfire that had raged against it. Drunkenness had reigned supreme, there was looting of shops and, astoundingly, total strangers had copulated to the cheers of those around them.

Sifting through the papers with William, Leander was outraged.

"What on earth were the police thinking of?" she demanded. "Why did they let this lot go on for three days and nights?"

"My guess would be that they thought it too dangerous to intervene," William said.

"How utterly ridiculous! I . . ." Leander stopped when she saw that William was shaking his head, gently and sorrowfully.

"They would be terrified of starting a riot that might lead to revolution," he said. "It's the same all over Europe. You've been telling us for long enough that we were heading for a different sort of world. Well, Lea, it seems to have arrived."

Tom and Joe Irons, great-grandsons of Harry who had built Latimer's Barn for Lord Francis Rashleigh, were in no doubt about being able to cope with what was wanted, drastic though it was. The past twenty years had seen a remarkable expansion of their firm, and they were more than a match for Leander's ambitions.

William, Treasurer of the Fund, told the December meeting of Trustees that the account now stood at a little over half a million pounds, having sustained a growth of nine per cent a year since 1908. It was, he reported, an astonishing achievement, largely brought about from the activities of the stud, furniture-making and, of course, bank interest payments: during the War the stable had barely paid its way, actually showing a small loss in 1917. No one doubted Leander's ability to put things back to normal in 1919 and her construction plans were unanimously approved. Twenty-five thousand pounds was voted to pay for the work.

Flying round the village even faster than normal, the news gave a tremendous boost to morale.

"By gum, Mrs Hawksworth don't half mean business!" one of the carpenters from Wm Flamsteed & Sons said in The George once the full scale of the work was known.

"I never doubted she did," Martin Foxton replied. "My dad told me she's been like that since she was old enough to get on a horse. Mind you, we're due for a fair bit of upheaval. I believe we're having new drains and plumbing for everybody and there's a good few houses to be fettled as well as all this new building."

Martin was right; the first job was to dig up the village street for an improved mains water-pipe and sewer. At the same time, new roads were being laid out: Church Marks was extended to the south with the foundations for six houses alongside it, and the Back Stretch and Roadway came into existence.

Having had a good tarmac surface laid on the drive from the Devizes Lane to a point well past the orchard, Leander sat down with Joe Irons to sketch out a plan that would determine the future expansion of Latimer's Barn. Once the road rectangle around The House, lawn, orchard, lads' hostel and the 1840 yard had been drawn in and named, Leander marked two crosses on the sketch.

"What are they for?" Joe Irons asked.

"Two more forty-box yards," Leander told him, then smiled at the look on his face. "Don't worry, Joe, that's for the future, but I like to know where I'm going. I tell you what we do need now . . ." she drew a rectangle to the east of the Back Stretch ". . . it's high time we had a paddock. Will you put a nice fence round that for me? And I want a Village Hall. That can go there." She marked the junction of Church Marks and the village street. "And I'm going to have a War Memorial. Do you know of a good mason?"

"You won't do better than old Hezekiah Dangerfield down at Compton Bassett."

"Will you speak to him for me, please, Joe?"

"Aye. I'd best do that straight away afore he gets busy."

*

The moment Christmas and the New Year were out of the way, Leander mounted an all-out assault on the difficulties surrounding her. Everything was to return to normal as quickly as possible and she went at a breakneck pace. —

Amelia, who had been receiving monthly pleas from her professor to return to work, was packed off to Cambridge at the end of the first week in January. Silas Timberlake, now almost his old self again after twelve months of painfully slow recovery, was in Cannings Ambo that day doing a job for William from which he took half an hour to drive her to Savernake railway station for a London train. They said very little to each other during the fifteen-minute journey and it never occurred to either of them that they were starting a pattern that would prove to be of immense importance.

A week later, on the day after Sam Briggs was demobbed from the Army, he and Ann Mallender were married.

"This is all on condition that you agree to live at The Hall," Leander told them. "I have no idea what I'm going to do with the place now, but it needs living in."

"That's 'andsome of you, Mrs 'Awksworth," Sam said. "We'll look after it as if it was our own."

Leander had no doubt of it: Sam's sense of responsibility, allied to his delight in Ann, his freedom from the Army and the job he was about to start with Mallender and Giffard, made him the ideal tenant.

When she was not involved in planning and inspecting the building work, Leander was busy in the yard. As well as the annual schooling of yearlings, there was the question of the staff to be resolved. The twenty-four lads, a mixture of old hands and new starters, had to be welded into a cohesive team with the spirit to do all that was required of them. And there were three men who had come back from the War with disabilities that prevented them riding to the required standard.

Leander was horrified to discover that they were all expecting to be sacked.

"Good God, don't you know me better than that?" she stormed at them, furious that they should think her capable of such a despicable act.

"I'm very sorry, ma'am," one of them said shamefacedly. "It seems to be the way things are these days."

"Where?" Leander snapped.

"Everywhere."

"Well, this is Cannings Ambo and it's different!" She calmed down: stories of the shabby treatment being meted out to war veterans

446

were distressingly common. "There's absolutely no need for you to worry," she assured them. "You'll be found proper jobs once we get everything straight again. In the meantime, make yourselves useful in the yard. And you can paint that fence that Joe Irons is putting up for the paddock."

They grinned. The paddock was on the grand scale, with over five hundred yards of post and rail fence that would surely keep them busy until she thought of something else.

For nearly three months, Leander's only periods of relaxation were the Tuesday afternoons with Rupert: for the rest, her life was so hectic that she even gave up reading the newspapers. Having discovered that most of the news was both complex and depressing, it was a sacrifice she made willingly.

As a result, she had no idea of the progress of the great conference in Paris that was supposed to be setting the world to rights, or of the terrible state of affairs in Germany. Rupert, well aware of the defeat of Woodrow Wilson's lofty idealism and the shifty bargains being struck, decided not to add to her worries and kept quiet.

Amelia heard about Ludwig Lehmann two days after returning to a Cambridge that seemed, by pre-war standards, to be rather subdued and dull.

It came from the University Press, who had been trying to contact him since Christmas 1914 over difficulties with the book that he and Amelia had written. After more than three years of delay, someone at Nuremberg University had forsaken belligerent national pride to write back with the information that *Herr* Professor Lehmann had died at Verdun in 1915.

It was over four and a half years since Amelia had seen him; she knew they were done for that day when his haste to get back to Germany had been unseemly. Yet a flicker of hope, nourished by the memory of their love-making, had continued to burn deep within her.

The desiccated old pedant who gave her the news was oblivious of the desolation that enveloped Amelia.

"It has been extremely difficult for us, Doctor Hawksworth," he said. "I can't remember ever having had such trouble with a book. What are we to do with it?"

"Oh . . . I don't see any point in publishing it after all this time," Amelia said. "I would think that someone else must have done the same work by now."

"Yes, indeed, so I believe." There was a flash of waspish animation. "I'm told Godfrey and Wallace have produced a similar work. Oxford, you know!"

447

For the whole of that term, the only thing that stopped Amelia running back to Cannings Ambo was the prospect of Leander's wrath.

At the end of January, an event occurred that brought a smile to the faces of everyone in the village. What made it particularly exciting was that it came out of the blue, a complete surprise. One of the consequences was that Leander and Joe Irons had to modify their building programme.

Henry Fletcher, the man persuaded by Fred Cartwright to place the first big order for William's furniture, took up a long-standing invitation to visit Cannings Ambo for a few days. With him came his twenty-year-old daughter, Louise, a pretty girl with an hour-glass figure, rich auburn hair and an uncontrollable sense of fun. Inside forty-eight hours, an astounded Henry Fletcher was being asked to give his consent to her engagement to Matthew Flamsteed.

Matthew was fully recovered from his Western Front experiences and with only a slight limp to show for his leg wound: he and Louise first clapped eyes on each other at six o'clock on a murky January evening and were laughing together within minutes. They were destined never to stop.

After breakfast the following morning, Matthew said, "I wonder if I might show you something of our countryside, Miss Fletcher?"

"What a good idea, Mr Flamsteed!" was the instant and enthusiastic response. "It will give our fathers a chance to talk business in peace."

When they returned in mid-afternoon after a drive to Devizes, then Chippenham for lunch, they both looked extraordinarily happy, alerting Ruth to what lay in store. William and Henry were too preoccupied with working out their business plans for the difficult post-war times ahead to take any notice.

Matthew proposed – and was accepted – over lunch on the second day, this time at the Ailesbury Arms in Marlborough. Henry Fletcher was told at three o'clock, soon after Louise and Matthew arrived back at Rose House. He was flabbergasted and delighted.

"Are you two sure about this?" he asked.

"We are utterly adamant, Father," Louise told him. "If you don't agree, I shall elope with Matthew and forbid him to let you have any more furniture!"

William looked anxious. At sixty, Henry Fletcher had a fairly young family, the product of his marriage to a girl many years his junior. Sadly, his wife had died, leaving him two sons to take over the running of the big shop in Birmingham and the smaller one in Coventry, and two daughters to look after his home: William inevitably wondered if Henry might resent the loss of Louise, supposedly his favourite.

But there was no need to worry. In response to Louise's trenchant statement of her intentions, Henry laughed and raised his hands in surrender.

"I wouldn't dream of objecting," he said. "I still have to ask if you two know what you're doing."

"Yes, sir, I can appreciate that." Matthew moved to Louise's side and placed an arm round her waist. "It *is* very sudden, I know, but we've been over it carefully and we're certain."

"We're going to be very happy," Louise said firmly. "And there isn't any point in beating about the bush. We want to get on with it."

"What do you think about this, William?" Henry asked.

"Well..." William was at a loss for words. "I'm sure Ruth will agree with me that Louise is the best daughter-in-law we could ever have wished for." He paused to rub his nose, then grinned boyishly. "Mind you, I think Matthew's got a bit of a nerve grabbing at her like this."

"I encouraged him," Louise declared stoutly and the matter was settled.

That evening, Matthew took Louise to dinner at Latimer's Barn. Introduced to Louise and told of the engagement in the same breath, Leander did no more than look mildly curious.

"She's a wonderful girl," she said to Matthew when they had a few quiet minutes together. "I suppose your father was very surprised by this?"

Matthew chuckled. "I'm afraid so, Aunt Leander. In all fairness, we did rather spring it on him."

"And yourselves, I imagine."

"That's true enough! Dash it all, a chap hardly expects to walk slap-bang into a girl like Louise, does he?"

"If you know what you want, there's no point in spinning it out," Leander said, adding as a quiet afterthought, "especially after what you've been through."

"You mean the War?"

"Yes."

It was not the first time that Matthew had been impressed by his aunt's penetrating insight.

Later, she showed the practical, forward-looking side of her nature when she asked, "Where are you two going to live?"

"Oh Lor'!" Matthew slumped back in his chair, looking poleaxed. "I hadn't even thought of that."

"There seem to be some very nice houses in Marlborough," Louise volunteered. "I'm sure we could find one to suit us."

She saw at once that she had made her first mistake: Leander frowned slightly, Matthew gazed at her in horror.

"Oh, no, darling," he said. "The Flamsteeds and Hawksworths have *always* lived here, in the village."

Smiling at his enthusiastic over-statement, Leander hastened to clarify the issue. "We've been here for sixty years, my dear. As a matter of fact, you're our Diamond Anniversary present." Louise bloomed at the compliment. "It would be best if you lived here. With all this work going on it will be very easy to build you a nice house with all the features you want."

"Where would you put it?" Matthew asked.

"How about the Back Stretch? To be honest with you, I'm longing to build something on it now that I've invented it!"

Leander showed them the latest version of her plan and they went to inspect the lie of the land the following morning. Louise was convinced at once, choosing a spot roughly midway between the drive and the Roadway: before the day was out, Joe Irons had pegged out the site for a spacious house that would face the orchard with rear views towards the Down and Powell's Pool.

Throughout February and March, Louise divided her time between Birmingham and Cannings Ambo. She watched progress on her new house, took a very active interest in Wm Flamsteed & Sons, where William was in the process of handing over full control to Matthew, and spent a great deal of time in and around Latimer's Barn, falling hopelessly in love with horses.

She also went to Buckingham Palace.

According to the letters that Matthew and Emma had received, it was at the insistence of the King himself that they should attend the same investiture, Emma to receive Giles's Victoria Cross, Matthew for the Military Cross won in an action that he resolutely refused to discuss with anyone, not even Louise. Another letter from the Lord Chamberlain's office stated that, since the Queen wished to meet as many as possible of Giles's relatives, the restrictions normally applied to the number of guests would be eased.

At first, Emma was quite panic-stricken at the prospect of going before His Majesty.

"Wouldn't you like to receive Giles's medal from the King?" she asked Leander. "I'm sure you would make a far better job of it than me. I shall be so nervous!"

"No, my dear, you must do it. I'm sure that's what Giles would have wanted. When the time comes, you won't be in the least nervous."

Emma worried dreadfully, finally getting herself into a state in which she felt positively ill on the early-morning train up to London. The moment they were inside the palace, however, her composure returned: by the time they were ushered into the magnificent ballroom where the investiture was to take place, she felt almost confident. In the ante-room, Emma had befriended a girl who was scared witless.

The occasion was devoted to high military honours, and Rhona Anderson, the only other woman present apart from the Cannings Ambo contingent, was Emma's natural companion. She had come all the way from Uachdar on the Hebridean island of Benbecula for another posthumous Victoria Cross, one that had been awarded to her brother.

Whatever her state of mind, Rhona Anderson had a moral strength and dignity that protected her from the worst excesses of her nerves: she was also greatly helped by Emma, who held her hand tightly as they sat next to one another during the ceremonial preliminaries.

The proceedings were conducted in alphabetical order according to the seniority of the award and Rhona was the first of the hundred-odd recipients to be called. The King kept her for a full minute, his voice lowered so that no one could hear what he said, no matter how hard they tried. When she returned to her seat, Rhona Anderson was flushed with pride and had tears standing in her eyes.

It was the same with Emma.

"Your husband was a very brave man, Mrs Hawksworth," King George said to her. "I'm so very sorry you lost him. Tell me, how are you managing at the stable?"

Their conversation became so interesting that an equerry had to signal to His Majesty that he should terminate the interview. For the next hour, Emma and Rhona held hands and were lost in their secret thoughts as the investiture went on its way. They both operated the spring-release catch on the beautifully tooled leather cases the King had given them and stared at the gun-metal cross with its crimson ribbon starkly emphasised by the white silk lining of the case.

Queen Mary had asked to see Emma, Matthew and all their friends afterwards, so Leander, William, Ruth, Louise and Amelia also filed into a small, intimately furnished apartment where they were given coffee and spent half an hour chatting to Her Majesty.

Leander and the Queen, seated side by side on an opulent sofa, got on famously, especially after Queen Mary had demonstrated that she was phenomenally well informed about her guests.

"Mrs Hawksworth, I understand that you once met His late Majesty, my father-in-law, at the Derby?"

"Yes, ma'am, in eighteen seventy-six. His Majesty was still Prince of Wales at the time, of course."

The Queen smiled sadly. "That was a *very* different world, Mrs Hawksworth. I am afraid that we shall see nothing like it again." For a moment or two she was sombre, suddenly brightening up as she realised that they had a stranger in their midst.

Emma, not letting go of Rhona Anderson's hand, had dragged her into the audience, too. "Come here, my dear," the Queen said, patting the vacant cushion alongside her. "Aren't you the young lady who has come all the way from the Hebrides? Tell me about yourself."

Rhona, still clutching her dead brother's Victoria Cross, found herself chatting to the Queen as naturally as if she had been Mrs Logan in the village stores back home.

All too soon it had to finish: a lady-in-waiting came in to remind Her Majesty that there were other people waiting. As they walked along corridors and down elegantly shallow staircases, Rhona, wrapped in the middle of the Cannings Ambo group like one of the family, noticed that everyone they passed either smiled or inclined their heads courteously according to their rank.

Outside, Emma asked Rhona, "Are you going back home now?"

"Yes. I'll get as far as Glasgow tonight and stay with my Uncle Hamish."

"Then what?" Emma asked.

"I'll be at Mallaig tomorrow night to wait for MacBrayne's boat on Friday. Goodbye, Mrs Hawksworth. Thank you for helping me. It was very good of you."

"I was glad to, Rhona, and helping you helped me, if you see what I mean. You will write to me, won't you?" They had exchanged addresses.

And Rhona Anderson strode off, ignoring the line of waiting taxis. Realising that she intended walking to Euston, Emma very nearly ran after her with the money for a cab. Having taken the first few steps, she stopped, abashed by the idea of offending Rhona's serene, Gaelic propriety.

On the west-bound express from Paddington, Matthew and Louise slipped away from the others for a pot of tea in the buffet car.

"Are you all right, darling?" Matthew asked when they were settled. "You're not feeling ill, are you?"

"No, not at all." Louise smiled, dispelling the rather grave expression that had been worrying him since they left the Palace. "Today has shown me what I'm marrying into. Father has always said you were a remarkable bunch, and he was right!"

Matthew grinned. "I've always thought we were pretty ordinary."

Heads turned at Louise's boisterous laugh. "If you lot are ordinary,

Matthew Flamsteed, God knows what the rest of the world is!" Suddenly she was serious. "I say, wasn't Emma marvellous? I'm sure I couldn't have carried it off like that."

"Emma's wonderful," Matthew replied. "She always keeps her chin up. Remember, though, she's been one of us for seven years, so she'll have had time to pick up a few tricks from Aunt Leander."

"Your aunt!" Louise gurgled with partly-suppressed laughter. "Did you see how she put the Queen at her ease?"

Matthew nodded. "Always follow Leander and you won't go far wrong," he said. "I remember hearing Father tell Mother that when I was little, and it's the best advice you could have."

Even more than her visit to Buckingham Palace, it was the Duke of Laverstoke's beautiful chestnut filly, Honeysuckle, who taught Louise what life at Cannings Ambo would be like.

She first saw the animal when William took her out on the gallop one morning to watch the filly work.

"Look at Honeysuckle," William urged excitedly. "Isn't she a corker?"

The four horses coming up fast were half a mile from where Louise and William were standing.

"Is that the one Emma's riding?" Louise asked, still more at home recognising people than horses.

"No, it's Leander's."

Louise saw it all, the gracefully fluent action, the carefully controlled power and the filly's obvious relish for the job in hand. When Leander let her down, she was clear of her galloping companions in three strides; thereafter, she was being gently restrained. The point had been proved and it made no sense to stretch Honeysuckle more than was strictly necessary.

"Yes, she's very nice," Louise said. "But I must say, Leander is amazing. I mean, she's not exactly *young*, is she?"

"Fifty-nine this year," William replied, his everlasting pride in his sister making him smug. "She's been riding on this gallop for over fifty years."

Shaking her head in disbelief, Louise asked, "Is that filly going to be good?"

"She is already," William said. "We're getting her ready for the One Thousand Guineas."

"That's quite a big and important race, isn't it?"

William laughed gently. "It's a *very* important race, my dear. It's a Classic and Leander likes winning them." Taking her by the arm he led her back towards The House. "I can see that I shall have to teach you the rudiments of this game," he said. "If I tell you everything I know – which should take all of ten minutes – you might be able to avoid putting your foot in it!"

Louise did not believe a word of William's self-deprecation: her shrewd observations of Cannings Ambo told her that everyone respected William's abilities at the difficult profession he had taken up as an emergency measure. She soon discovered, for example, that it was William, not Leander, who had first spotted Honeysuckle's outstanding potential. And when Matthew took Louise to Newmarket to watch the One Thousand Guineas, she noticed that other trainers tended to seek William's opinion.

Honeysuckle won it more or less as she pleased. With a furlong to go, most of the spectators thought that either of the two Irish contenders might lift the prize; however, Mark Pilgrim had given Honeysuckle a very tender run to that point and she responded instantly when he shook her up. At the line, she was three lengths clear and looking very much as though she was ready to gallop on for ever.

"Well, what do you think of that, m'dear?" the Duke of Laverstoke asked Louise after they had finished in the winner's enclosure. "Pretty impressive, what?"

"Oh, yes, very much so, Your Grace," Louise replied.

"I say, we can't have this 'Your Grace' twaddle," the Duke said in a confidential tone. "You're going to be one of the family, so you'd better get used to calling me Hubert."

So, on her very first visit to a racecourse, Louise Fletcher saw 'her' horse win a Classic and found herself on Christian-name terms with a peer of the realm.

On the train back to Wiltshire, however, Matthew began to look alarmed as he listened to Leander and William coming to the conclusion that Honeysuckle *would* get a mile and a half.

"What's the matter?" Louise whispered.

"They're going to run her in the Oaks," Matthew replied.

"What's wrong with that?"

"It's being run on the Saturday of Whitsuntide."

"Oh dear!" Leander was looking at them apologetically. "That's the day you were thinking of getting married, isn't it?"

"Yes!" Matthew looked dismayed.

"We can change the date, darling," Louise said, completely unconcerned.

"What to?"

"The week after, of course!" Louise grinned. "I don't want to miss that race for anything!"

After that, Leander's opinion of Louise was inestimable.

The house on the Back Stretch was finished four weeks later, on the day Honeysuckle did her last piece of hard work before the Epsom Classic. At Matthew's insistence, it was named 'Louise House', a felicitous capping of Joe Irons's superb creation which was much admired by the volunteers who worked each evening to make gardens around it. The final touch was the special range of furniture designed by William and Jim Goakes; Louise's eyes opened saucer-wide when she saw it all in place.

"You'll need your order book when Father sees this lot," she told Matthew.

"It isn't bad, is it?" he replied, affecting nonchalance. "Fred Cartwright's been going on blind about it, but I'm not sure that we want to sell stuff like this to the hoi-polloi in Birmingham!"

"You'll jolly well do as you're told after we're married, my lad!" Louise said with mock-severity.

"I expect you're absolutely right, darling," Matthew replied, more than happy at the prospect.

Honeysuckle went to Epsom as favourite for the Oaks and gave her supporters a worry-free run from start to finish. While the race was in progress, it seemed to be no more than an easy-paced amble, but her four lengths victory was accomplished in one of the fastest times ever recorded for the race and none of her opponents ever looked likely to get on terms with her.

But much as the beautiful filly was the focus of attention for ten minutes or so, there was no doubt that the day belonged to Leander.

"Look at her!" Louise said after it was all over and Leander was engulfed by a crowd of newspaper reporters. "How old does she think she is?"

Matthew studied his aunt admiringly. "I'd say she feels as old as she looks, which is about thirty," he said.

Louise looked again. Ignoring the fashion for shorter skirts, Leander was wearing one of the dresses that Ellie had made for Royal Ascot in 1890; no alterations had been necessary. It was rumoured that the honey-coloured straw hat with the huge brim was even older.

"No, in all fairness, I'd say she looked thirty-five," Louise said.

"All right," Matthew agreed. "But if Leander is only thirty-five, the War never happened, and that's exactly the idea she's trying to put across."

"I have to say it, my dear, you look like a cat that's found the way into the creamery," Rupert Timberlake whispered.

"I feel entitled to," Leander replied. "We've won a Classic and had a lovely wedding all in one week. It could almost be like old times."

They were among the crowd milling around outside Rose House where Louise and Matthew, now married, had just emerged to begin their honeymoon journey in Matthew's new motor car. Louise had paid Cannings Ambo the great compliment of asking to have her wedding in the church of St Luke and St John rather than at her old home in Birmingham and had been a wonderful bride. A nervous-looking Matthew had nearly tripped himself up as he joined her at the chancel steps for the start of the ceremony; thereafter, it all went like a dream.

Now, young Mr and Mrs Flamsteed posed for a last set of photographs and as they did so, there was a moment when they looked at each other with unashamed physical longing. Smiling to herself, Leander laid private odds on them disappearing into a field at the earliest opportunity, unable to wait until they reached Torquay.

An instant later, Leander noticed Amelia. She, too, had seen what passed between the newly-weds and responded with a look of such envious desolation that Leander felt pierced by it.

In Belle Ile, Maude became thoroughly bored with 1919. Most of the year was so tedious that, against all her natural inclinations, she was driven to become a reasonably good mother.

The cause of her apathy was the great Peace Conference, in which the French people, unlike the majority of English, took an intense interest. In the main, this was due to fear of Germany with whom they had to live cheek by jowl without the protection of the English Channel; there was also worship of their current idol, Georges Clemenceau, 'The Tiger'.

Clemenceau, one-time physician and leader of the extreme left was now, at the age of seventy-eight, Premier for the second time and leader of the French delegation at the conference. Clemenceau it was who had set himself vigorously at the head of the movement sworn to make Germany pay for every Frenchman killed and every cubic centimetre of France despoiled, and his countrymen adored him for it. Bankrupting Germany was also seen as a way of ensuring that she was powerless to mount another war.

Every move in the drama was followed and debated avidly, even in such remote places as the Guillaume farm, and, for the first time in her life, Maude found herself yearning for the peace and quiet of Cannings Ambo. After Germany had been forced to sign the Treaty on 28 June 1919, the fifth anniversary of the day in Sarajevo that had sparked

456

it all off, Maude expected a return to normal, only to find bitter disappointment. Conversation became dominated by the most effective way to extort the reparations payments from the detested foe.

Maude's son, Henri, now two years old, and with looks that suggested his father was Achille rather than Pierre, was her only source of comfort. Although lacking in maternal instincts and abilities, Maude became devoted to him, and he to her. The happiest times were when they wandered along the cliff-tops, enjoying the sea in all its moods, Maude sometimes promising herself that she would soon start to paint again.

When not arguing about Germany with his sons and neighbours, Achille was a good, affectionate husband and although he was now sixty-five, his virility was as fiery as ever.

Clothilde was the menace: she was the one whom Maude feared might make life unbearable.

Both Achille's sons had returned from the War without a mark on them. Michel, the younger, threw himself into working the farm and enjoying the quietest possible life. Jacques, on the other hand, was roaring drunk for almost the whole of his first month back and seemed surprised to find, when he finally sobered up, that he had married a young widow from a neighbouring village.

Clothilde Dumas, as she was before her husband was killed at Epernay, came from sound peasant stock with the complete range of associated virtues and vices. She was a stupendous worker and intensely loyal to those whom she thought worthy. Her appetites were prodigious: she ate like a labourer and most nights her orgasmic cries rang through the vast, rambling length of the old farmhouse, causing Achille to chuckle and become aroused.

But she was also passionately suspicious of strangers, and made it plain that she considered Maude an interloper. Clothilde was civil enough when she knew that others, especially Achille, were watching: when they were alone, however, she treated her step-mother-in-law with sly, calculated contempt.

The great building programme was complete in September and Leander was able to make the last of her changes. Conn finally retired: he and Sally went to a comfortable new house on the Latimer's Barn drive, directly opposite the two Merriweather houses.

"You'll be able to watch things from here, Conn," Leander told her old friend and workmate. "Make sure the youngsters are keeping up to the mark."

Conn's place at the stud was taken by Jeremy Dundas, a choice that surprised a great many people, including Jeremy himself.

"But, Mrs Hawksworth, ma'am, I don't believe I can cope with the job," he protested. "I don't know the first thing about horses. I suppose you could say I am a bit of a misfit."

Leander laughed. "Jeremy, I'll let you into a secret," she said. "When my father was getting this place going, sixty years ago, he was accused of hiring misfits to do the job." It was the first time she had ever mentioned an item from Giles Flamsteed's private notebook. "They didn't do badly, did they?"

"Indeed they didn't!" Jeremy replied warmly. "Who said that to him?"

"Someone who should have known a great deal better," Leander said dismissively. "Will you do this job for me?"

"I'll have to talk to Josie about it."

"Of course – although I can tell you here and now what her answer will be!"

Leander was right: thrilled at the idea of having her own house and the responsibility being offered to Jeremy, Josie persuaded him to accept within minutes.

"I can stop teaching and we'll have a family," she said, setting the seal on Jeremy's rehabilitation and happiness.

When Jeremy and Josie moved to Cannings St John, they found that their staff were to be the three lads whose war disabilities prevented them from riding properly.

Even Leander never imagined that she had set the stud on a course of cheerful efficiency that was to last for over thirty years.

On Tuesday, 11 November, every man, woman and child in the village, together with thirty friends from Marlborough, gathered for the dedication of the War Memorial and Village Hall.

The Memorial, finally placed in position by Joe Irons and three of his men the previous afternoon, was a wonderful piece of work that was to earn Hezekiah Dangerfield a bonus and Leander's special thanks. It was a slab of Portland stone some ten feet high, surmounted by a dais upon which the statue of a soldier lay, covered by his greatcoat. The letters, carved in capital serif, were inlaid with gold. High up was the inscription:

IN LOVING MEMORY OF THE MEN
OF CANNINGS AMBO
WHO FELL IN THE GREAT WAR
1914–1918

THEIR NAMES WILL LIVE FOREVER

Then came the list of names, fourteen in alphabetic order, without military rank, so that GILES HAWKSWORTH VC came just over half-way down.

John Shepherd conducted a short service which finished precisely as the church clock struck eleven. Then, after everyone had bowed their heads to observe a two-minute silence, Leander stepped forward to lay the first wreath: it was made up of blood-red roses, lovingly nurtured by David Wesley in a greenhouse.

When it was done, Leander took Emma's arm to walk back to The House. Rupert Timberlake watched her go, stiff with resolution, aware of how she intended spending the rest of the day. For weeks, all the photographs ever taken of life at Latimer's Barn had been examined by Leander, William, Amelia and Emma: twenty-two had been selected, from Giles Flamsteed with Bellerophon to the wedding of Louise and Matthew. All had been framed identically and were now to be arranged on the wall of the corridor that ran the length of The House's ground floor.

Among them, in its oak and glass case, would be Giles's Victoria Cross.

CHAPTER 26

1920

'. . . we shall be a great deal better for that'

England was experiencing a multitude of problems, both economic and social, all supposed to be a consequence of the War. At the April meeting of the Trustees, Leander commented on the phenomenon of violence that was afflicting many racecourses.

It had begun the previous year as what seemed like aimless fights between rival gangs. Usually the fists flew after racing was over and in most cases the reason seemed to be gambling disputes. Now, however, there was a growing tendency to intimidate stable-lads, jockeys and even officials.

"Have we suffered at all?" Jim Goakes asked anxiously.

"No. Nor are we likely to," Leander replied with an authority that was at once comforting and thought-provoking.

"Why's that?" Fred Cartwright wanted to know.

"Silas Timberlake looks after our interests," Leander said. "He's very efficient and determined."

"He has some good men at his disposal," Rupert added by way of explanation.

Matthew and Louise looked at William, whose face was blandly innocent, then at each other.

"That sounds a rough business!" Louise signalled on their private telegraph.

"Doesn't it just!" Matthew responded. "Better ignore it, Lou. Auntie knows best."

The meeting shared this view and allowed Leander to move on to the next item on the agenda.

Smoothing the path for Latimer's Barn horses to race without encountering difficulty or violence made Silas a busy man, but on the second Wednesday and Thursday of each month, he kept himself available for a special task.

At half past eight on those precious Wednesday evenings, he drove to Savernake station to meet Amelia off a train from London. The following day, after a buffet lunch that was the customary end to a Trustees' meeting, he took her back for the ten minutes past two train. Apparently, if all went well, she was in her rooms at Cambridge by six-thirty.

No one ever questioned Silas's self-imposed and jealously guarded task which had begun in January 1919, when Amelia first returned to Cambridge: they were glad to have Amelia safely spirited to and from Cannings Ambo for the conferences she took so seriously and to which she always made such useful contributions.

Sometimes, Silas had to make elaborate plans and drive long distances to keep the monthly appointments, always with the reward outweighing any difficulties. Once every four or five weeks, he was alone for two infinitely precious fifteen-minute periods with the woman he worshipped.

When she climbed into his motor on 13 May, he felt the tension at once. Normally, Amelia was eager to tell him about the meeting: today she was tight-lipped and distant. There was something in her demeanour that Silas found forbidding and they were drawing into the station yard before he spoke.

"Did something go wrong this morning?"

"No!" It sounded so like a mind-your-own-business rebuff that Silas gave up any hope of salvaging the conversation. Next month might be different, he thought, stopping the car somewhat abruptly.

He always got out, walked round the bonnet and opened the passenger door for her. Eager to enact the ritual as a means of being rid of her and the tension, Silas found her hand on his arm, restraining him.

"No, Silas, wait," Amelia said.

Startled, he saw that she was examining every detail of the scene before them: Savernake station, deep in its wooded cutting, the place where her father had died, was completely deserted. Fred Partridge was presumably on duty as usual, but he was keeping well out of the rain, driven on a cold wind.

"Do you have a telephone in your lodge?" Amelia asked, still scanning.

"Yes, I do."

She nodded and smiled wryly. "Business, I suppose?"

"I couldn't manage without it. I'm in touch with your mother or Albert Merriweather all the time."

Suddenly, her mind made up, she turned to look at him with a

461

look of such power that disbelief was his only possible reaction. He must be mistaken: he was imagining the hunger in her eyes.

"Take me to your lodge, Silas," she said. She had to repeat the instruction, quietly and with burning emphasis before he nodded, started the engine and set them on their way.

No one saw them: Silas made sure of that by using the narrow forest tracks. Amelia laughed as they bumped over ruts and pot-holes, light-headed now that the die was cast.

While Amelia used the telephone, Silas busied himself with lighting the sitting-room fire. Although the calendar said May, the day was more like November: he was also glad of something to occupy himself during what seemed an interminable wait.

"It's settled," she said when she came into the sitting-room. "I shall go back to Cambridge tomorrow evening – I have to give a tutorial on Saturday morning, otherwise . . ." She did not finish.

Silas, kneeling in front of the fire and not daring to speak, watched as she studied the room, evidently giving it her approval: he remained incredulous of what was happening and half-frightened of the immediate future. But when she knelt down beside him, he was seized by a reckless confidence and as his arms went round her and their lips came together, all thoughts of his unworthiness were obliterated.

From the instant of its birth, the kiss was an unbridled expression of passionate longing and their hands were already exploring each other's bodies, surveying the delights ahead. Once that first rush of excitement had been assuaged, they were gazing at each other with a mixture of wonder and impatience.

Silas was never able to recall which of them pulled the curtains to shut out the miserable afternoon, or grabbed the cushions from the chairs to pile on the floor; and which of them began undressing first. The dream-like sequence of events culminated in his shudder of delight as they flung themselves together again, this time without a stitch of clothing between them.

They were both ready, but Amelia's impatience was the greater; Silas's erection, even harder than the rest of his spare, lithe body, quickened her desire and she drew him into her with an urgent sensual strength.

It was over too quickly. They both knew that and were unconcerned. There was time.

Her hands never stopped roaming over him until she said, "You're beautifully *firm* and strong, Silas. I imagined you would be!"

He seemed shocked. "You thought of me like that?"

"Yes! I was confused and ashamed at first. Then I decided it didn't matter."

"And when did you reach that conclusion?"

"About an hour ago, outside the station! And what about you? You've thought about me, haven't you? Am I what you expected?"

"No, you're even better," he said simply, and she knew he was telling her the truth.

One of her hands brushed lightly across his stomach and she was aware of the scar. "Let me look," she said, easing into a sitting position. "Oh! That's not too bad, is it?" she said. "At least . . ." she looked closely ". . . I suppose it could have been a lot worse."

"I was very lucky," he smiled. "I got a good surgeon."

"Silas, please tell me what happened," Amelia said. "How did you get that wound?"

"No, it's over and done with," he said. "Come here!"

His embrace dispelled her curiosity in a matter of seconds and her delight as she felt him rising up hard again was infinite. When he drove into her, she smiled luminously and wrapped her long, elegant legs tightly round him.

"Make a good job of it this time, Silas," she said.

At first, he was still a little deferential.

Then she found the key. "Silas, think of all those awful wasted years," she whispered. "All the times you wanted me . . . well, here I am!"

A vision of Giles, looking mildly surprised before he pitched forward into that filthy mud, came to Silas; he saw himself grabbing Jacko's rifle and lunging the bayonet towards the German who looked like something out of a rotting hell; he remembered the appalling pain that tore his guts apart as the poor devil who turned out to be Wolfgang Schorr of the 3rd City of Leipzig Infantry fired his last round.

And he remembered a glimpse of Amelia long ago in the orchard, while the world still thought it was in its right mind.

Systematically, with only a tenuous thread holding him back, Silas went mad. Groaning at the sharp onset of unparalleled pleasure, Amelia shifted and bucked, pushing and pulling at him to drive him even harder. Magically, with the frenzy purging the anger from him, he became calmer and more assured the further they went until at the end, with them both flung headlong into the maelstrom of ultimate gratification, Amelia Hawksworth and Silas Timberlake were the only two people in a world where the bad was stripped of significance and all that mattered was the good.

For five minutes, they lay in a close embrace, hearts pounding, their breathing gradually returning to normal. Amelia let out a huge sigh of contentment and smiled. "I imagine that we shall be a great deal better for that," she said.

Silas nodded slowly. "I think so," he agreed and was lost in deep thought. "Well, that's the past done with. Shall we start on the future?"

"Yes, and I can tell you all about that!" For the first time, Silas saw the serene confidence of her mother in her. "I don't intend to marry, but you shall be my best friend and only lover for as long as you wish. How does that seem?"

"Perfect!" Very gently, he rolled away slightly and was immediately lost in admiration, a hand sliding over her silken thighs. "Tell me, do all lady mathematicians have legs like yours?" he asked, absolutely serious.

"I don't think so," she replied, equally straight-faced. "It's probably got a lot to do with having the right breeding. Rather like horses!"

Amelia knew that she would tell her mother about Silas when she thought the time was right: meanwhile, it seemed best to keep their relationship a secret. So, with them both enjoying the air of mystery, he drove her to Newbury the following afternoon for the London train at half past four. No one saw them.

As they waited on the platform, Silas stroked a hand across her cheek and said, "You look better already, Amelia. Passion suits you."

She grinned wickedly. "*You* suit me," she corrected. "Can you wait a whole month?"

Grimacing, he shrugged his shoulders in a gesture of resignation. "If I have to."

"Well, you don't!" she said. "I don't often have to do Saturday tutorials. I'm free from about three o'clock most Friday afternoons."

"Oh!" Silas looked ludicrously pleased.

An hour later, the emptiness of the lodge depressed Silas until he forced himself to the telephone to make arrangements to look after two horses who were going to Kempton Park the following day. He found that a tip-off of trouble gave him something to look forward to: dealing with ruffians would be an ideal antidote to his feeling of loss.

On Monday morning, however, Silas Timberlake's world changed permanently with the arrival of the post. As soon as she was back in Cambridge, Amelia had written him a letter of such tenderness and erotic potency that he dashed outside to bellow his joy into the cathedral-like vault of the forest's trees.

Joe Symes, carrying out his duties to perfection, was the first to hear the whisper. He picked it up on the rails of the Silver Ring at Kempton Park.

Five days later, the Duke of Laverstoke invited himself to lunch at Latimer's Barn and confirmed the story. A fellow peer, whose brother was a member of the Jockey Club, had given him the wink in the smoking-room of the House of Lords.

Leander sent for Rupert that evening.

"Can we go over the main points again?" Rupert said, looking slightly ruffled with the effort of trying to understand what was going on. "You're saying that Rothwell is getting his knife into you again?"

"Most definitely!"

"He's saying that your horses aren't being ridden to win?"

"Yes."

"Do trainers do that?"

"Frequently!"

"Why?"

"Betting usually." As ever when she was forced to mention gambling, Leander was contemptuous.

"So it's a pretty serious business?" Rupert asked.

"Very. If dirt like that sticks, William could find himself in front of the Disciplinary Committee quicker than you could say 'Jack Robinson'. Mark Pilgrim would be in trouble, too."

"But surely, Leander, no one is going to believe a story like that?"

"Normally, it would get laughed at. Not this year, though."

"Why?"

"Oh, Rupert, really!" Leander was exasperated. "Haven't you been taking *any* notice of our results?"

"I'm ashamed to say that I haven't, my dear. I've been up to my neck in all sorts of nasty things."

Leander knew this to be true: the Timberlake businesses had needed a great deal of attention in an increasingly uncertain economic climate. Looking slightly abashed, she explained. "So far this season, we've sent out forty-two runners. Only two of them have won, which is terrible by any standards, let alone ours. Ten of them got nowhere and the other *thirty* finished second or third. Now do you see?"

"Yes, I do. What's been the trouble?"

Leander threw her hands up in despair. "Everything! First we couldn't get them fit because of a virus, then we had a load of bad feed that made half of them sick. They've been coughing and we've had damnable luck in several races where Mark got boxed in and couldn't get a run at it. Father had a year like it once – 'seventy-nine. It was awful!"

Rupert mulled it over. "So, Rothwell starts a whispering campaign and eventually people come to him suggesting that Latimer's Barn is investigated?"

"That would be a possibility."

465

"What's his motive?"

"God knows!" For once, Leander shook her head hopelessly.

"Does William know about this?" Rupert asked.

"No, nor Mark Pilgrim, and you're not going to tell them."

"Quite right," Rupert smiled now that he had the full measure of her mood. "What's to be done?"

"The wretch has to be stopped, of course!"

"How?"

"I don't know." She looked and sounded thoroughly irritated by her lack of ideas.

Rupert was thoughtful for a while. "What you need is a good scandal," he said finally. "Something that will cause him grave embarrassment or, better still, ruin him."

"Even if I had something, how could I spread it?" Leander asked, half convinced that the suggestion was useless.

"One of the popular newspapers might help you out."

"Don't be silly, Rupert, they wouldn't take any notice of me."

"*The Clarion* would."

Leander stared at him very hard. "Rupert, you sound awfully sure about that," she said accusingly.

"Do I?"

"Yes! Why?"

"Because I have a substantial interest in it," he said and did his best to look brave.

"You've got shares in *The Clarion*?" Leander was appalled.

"Yes – rather a lot actually."

"What on earth possessed you to invest in that *thing*? It's a cesspit!"

"Now Leander . . ." Rupert raised a mollifying hand ". . . we have an understanding, right? You ask me no questions about my business interests, especially when they can be useful to you." She nodded with truculent lack of grace or conviction. "For ruining someone, you couldn't have a better instrument than *The Clarion*. You find the dirt on Rothwell and I'll make sure it's printed."

By the time Rupert went back to Marlborough two hours later, Leander had moved towards grudging, partial acceptance of his idea. The following day, after William had been called before the Stewards at Newbury to explain the running of a Latimer's Barn horse, her mind was made up and she thought of a way the plan might be made to work.

The job was both tedious and difficult, but Joe Symes did it brilliantly.

Early on a mid-June Friday morning, he left Cannings Ambo with Silas who drove him to Savernake station for the first train of the day to London. Joe had a well-laden pack on his back, precise written instructions from Leander, and, as well as money in his pockets for train tickets and incidentals, there was thirty pounds for emergencies in the lining of his jacket.

In London, he went to Victoria Station and caught a stopping train to the south coast, alighting at a tiny halt on the North Downs where a five-mile hike lay ahead of him. By eleven o'clock, Joe was scouting round a copse on high ground above a weald village. Finding a good, concealed vantage point, he unslung his pack, pulled out a telescope and settled down to survey Hordens Green and its environs.

He found the house almost at once, looking exactly as Leander had described it. Reedswood House, home of Lord James Hartley, was half-way down the shallow valley, about a mile from the village and half a mile from where Joe was crouching. Although Joe did not know it, this was where Leander had spent two days with Rothwell eleven years ago.

The view was good: with the aid of the telescope, Joe found that the two men working in the gardens of Reedswood House were discernible. He would recognise them if he passed them in the street.

Joe Symes made himself comfortable.

At one o'clock he ate some of his bread and cheese and made a brew of tea by boiling half a pint of the gallon of water he had brought with him.

Absolutely nothing happened for over five hours: unusually for a large country house, there was not the slightest sign of activity. Even the gardeners had disappeared.

Patiently, Joe remained alert, amusing himself by scrutinising the occasional flurry of activity in the village. A little before half past six, two large motor cars emerged from the rear of Reedswood House and set off towards the railway station.

They returned fifteen minutes later, setting down two men and four women at the front door where they were greeted by four men from the house. All the men were middle-aged, the women seemed to be about thirty and acted, Joe thought, like whores.

There were no more arrivals that day. As darkness fell, Joe took his groundsheet and a blanket from the pack and spread them under a bush. After more bread and cheese and the luxury of two mugs of tea, he waited until nearly midnight when the last lights went out in the house, then settled down to sleep.

Surprisingly, three of the men left shortly after seven the following morning, heading south towards the coast, and the car did not return.

Joe never once allowed boredom to get the better of him during the next twelve hours. As always when his circumstances were tiresome, he reflected that, but for Leander, he would either be in prison, or eking out a miserable existence on charity.

At nine minutes past seven, after thirty-two hours, what she had been hoping for happened and Joe chuckled gleefully. The car returned with only one passenger and there was no mistaking his identity. Sir Walter Rothwell, acting as though he owned the place, was pounced on by two of the women the moment he set foot on the gravelled forecourt of Reedswood House.

There was no point in trying to get back to Cannings Ambo that night, so Joe slept contentedly under the bush again and set off soon after dawn, a last inspection of Reedswood House having revealed nothing but curtained windows. He was in the kitchen of Latimer's Barn by one o'clock.

Leander sat at his side and listened to the story he told between mouthfuls of roast leg of lamb with four different sorts of vegetables.

"You're sure it was Rothwell, Joe?" she asked.

"As certain as you're sitting there, Mrs Hawksworth!"

"And these women?"

"Pooh!" Joe looked disgusted. "Harlots if ever I see'd 'em. Trollops on the game!"

"All right. Wait while I make a telephone call."

She was in the library for ten minutes, returning from her conversation with Rupert to find Joe tucking into apple pie.

"It's going to be tomorrow afternoon before I know what's happening next," she said. "Can you be here at tea-time?"

He nodded and made as if to get up from the table, but Leander pushed him back. "Eat your fill, Joe," she smiled. "I think you've earned it."

Sidney Pickering and Joe Symes were not much to each other's taste and could easily have been daunted by the prospect of spending a good many hours on a hillside together. Joe was happy to do it for Leander; Sidney Pickering never placed limits on his efforts to enhance his inglorious reputation as *The Clarion*'s premier muck-raker.

They had the support of one of Pickering's lackeys who was able to bring them food and drive his master to a comfortable bed when darkness fell and there was no chance of seeing anything else.

This time, Friday was an exceptionally busy day at Reedswood

House. Using a pair of German binoculars which he claimed to have captured, but had bought from an Army Surplus store, Pickering watched the comings and goings avidly.

"There's half the merchant bankers in London trooping in and out of that place," he muttered. "What *is* that clever bastard Hartley up to?"

Joe Symes neither knew nor cared.

After the procession finally stopped at four o'clock in the afternoon, the rest of the day was uneventful and Sidney Pickering grumbled until he was taken away to dinner and a bed at nightfall, leaving Joe to his groundsheet and blanket.

Saturday was a disaster. Not a living soul went anywhere near Reedswood House all day.

By the middle of Sunday afternoon, when a repetition of Saturday seemed entirely possible, Joe was so fed up that he accepted some of *The Clarion*'s cold chicken together with a bottle of stout.

No sooner had he done so, than a gleaming Rolls-Royce motor car, the very latest model, appeared in the village street. Joe trained the telescope on it with hands that trembled as he willed the vehicle to turn into the long drive of Reedswood House, rather than passing by.

"This had better be good," Pickering said grimly. What little affinity he felt for the countryside had been wiped out by Saturday.

As the car emptied at the front door, Joe very nearly shouted with joy: this was definitely it.

"That's Rothwell, all right," Pickering said, viewing the scene through his binoculars. "Looking pretty damned pleased with himself, too. Look at that – *three* lovely ladies with him. What have we got here, eh? Ah, yes, our dear friend Barbara Humphreys, so-called actress, widely believed to do anything if the money's right."

"Which one's she?" Joe asked.

"The pale blue. Bloody hell! Now *that* is something."

"What's up?" Joe asked.

"Her in the pink and white with the gorgeous tits . . . that is none other than Charmian, Lady Lapworth . . . well, well, well! Ted Baxter has always sworn that she's a tart, but this is the first time anybody's ever caught her at it."

"What about the other one?"

"I don't know her. I'd guess she's a novice, she looks out of her depth to me. Christ, will you look at the gear they've brought with them!"

Two cabin trunks and several large suitcases were being lifted from the back of the Rolls-Royce by a flustered gaggle of servants.

"Good!" Pickering said, rubbing his hands enthusiastically. "Let's get out of this hell-hole!"

Joe insisted on spending another night out in the open to ensure that Rothwell and the women remained at Reedswood House. They did.

In accordance with his editor's strict instructions, Sidney Pickering travelled to Marlborough to see Rupert Timberlake before writing the story.

"And be on your best behaviour," the editor snarled. "Mr Timberlake owns at least half of this rag!"

Pickering was in Marlborough only long enough for Rupert to explain what was going to happen.

"I'm taking you to Cannings Ambo to see Mrs Hawksworth. She has some information you will find interesting."

"*The* Mrs Hawksworth?" Pickering asked. "Leander?"

"That's right. She's a good friend of mine."

Since Leander and Rupert knew nothing of Pickering's normal standards, they were unaware of how much he was on his best behaviour for their meeting: afterwards, Leander went so far as to express pleasant surprise at the representative of the detested gutter press. Not only did he have his editor's warning; Pickering, like so many before him, was struck dumb by Latimer's Barn.

"You may care to know an extremely personal detail about Sir Walter Rothwell," Leander said, not wasting a moment on preliminaries. "He has a very prominent and unusual birthmark on his left buttock."

Taken completely by surprise, Pickering gaped at her and asked, "Are you sure? How do you know?"

"I am *totally* sure, Mr Pickering, and the source of my knowledge is none of your business. I hope you will consider this item interesting enough to include, but you will not mention my name."

"No, of course not, Mrs Hawksworth!"

"Forget that, Pickering, and your job won't be worth a row of beans," Rupert said in a voice that Leander had never heard before.

"You might also care to know that the mark is in the form of a triangle," Leander continued and watched benignly as Pickering went through the motions of making a note.

"Er . . . what colour might it be, Mrs Hawksworth?"

"Dark brown," she replied unhesitatingly. "When do you think this article – or whatever – might appear, Mr Pickering?"

"Well, it's not a matter of urgent topical interest, so I shall have to wait for space. I believe we aim to print it within the week."

"You do," Rupert said with authority.

"I shall look forward to it," Leander said sweetly.

During the next three days, Leander wondered whether she ought to contact Rupert and have Pickering stopped. With the perversity that only luck knows, circumstances moved rapidly to deprive Rothwell of a chance of harming Latimer's Barn.

The day after her brief meeting with Pickering, Michael Pilgrim took two horses to Newbury: they both won. Within forty-eight hours there were three more winners, this time at Newmarket.

She decided against a last-minute intervention to reprieve Rothwell. If he really was determined to drag them down, he would find other opportunities, so it was best to destroy him and have done with it.

On the morning that *The Clarion* published the scurrilous piece, Lady Rothwell was presiding over a Conservative and Unionist Party coffee morning at Newmarket. Knowing that she would not have seen the rag, several friends queued up to show it to her, all protesting a degree of innocence.

"I don't actually read the thing, of course, Honoria. My husband's valet told Cook about it!"

Sidney Pickering had done a thorough job.

Sir Walter Rothwell, the energetic and popular Senior Steward of the Jockey Club, arrived at the Sussex home of Lord James Hartley last Sunday afternoon for a well-earned rest from his onerous duties.

Accompanying Sir Walter were the exciting Lady Lapworth, Miss Barbara Humphreys and a young lady unfortunately not known to your correspondent. Readers will not need to be reminded that Miss Humphreys, once the constant companion of Marmaduke Hunter, the war-profiteer, had an inauspicious six-month career as an actress of sorts a few years ago.

Why, one may well ask, were the three ladies so obviously enthused by the occasion? Reedswood House has much to recommend it, yet a little bird tells us that even greater excitements were on offer. Lady Lapworth, Miss Humphreys and Miss X, like so many ladies before them, have almost certainly developed a liking for the astonishing birthmark on Sir Walter's left buttock.

There was a great deal more.

Lady Rothwell read it through twice, then, white with anger, strode across the High Street to the Jockey Club where she knew her husband was spending a day in his office.

Inside the hallowed building, none of the servants or clerks dared to

471

get in her way; they had all read the newspaper she was clutching and knew that Sir Walter himself had sent out for a copy an hour ago.

Barging into his office, Lady Rothwell's opening gambit of: "Walter, you're a bloody idiot!" was delivered over the heads of the two officials seated in front of his desk. While Rothwell was doing his best to look annoyed at the invasion of his privacy, the dismayed men faded away.

"What the hell is all this about?" Lady Rothwell demanded, slamming *The Clarion* in front of her husband.

"Lies, Honoria, all lies. I intend to sue!"

Lady Rothwell, a young and vigorous fifty, and daughter of a family who had waged successful war on East Anglian farming conditions for over three centuries, gazed at him with contempt.

"Where were you on Sunday, Monday and Tuesday?" she asked.

"I told you at the time – with Gregory Willard at Arundel."

"You're a liar, Walter," Lady Rothwell said in a matter-of-fact tone. "Did my ears deceive me, or did you say you were going to sue?"

"Of course I shall take action!"

"I see. And what do you propose doing about that birthmark? Will you get one of your doxies to paint it out so that you can wave your arse at the court with impunity?"

Rothwell looked trapped.

"That was an amazingly accurate description of your affliction, my sweet," Honoria Rothwell said acidly. "And I have a feeling that Pickering did not get his information from one of your more recent playfellows. Some lady has been saving this up, Walter, my dear. I know, dreadful, isn't it? Who could it have been? Cynthia Carlyle? Daphne Hartigan?" Rothwell gazed at her in horror as she named two of his past favourites, both closely-kept secrets in their time. "Now, let me tell you what you are going to do. This afternoon, you and I are leaving for a *long* holiday abroad. When we return, you will plead ill-health and withdraw from public life. Is that clear?"

"Perfectly, my love." Rothwell sounded as if he were swallowing broken glass. "Yes, what is it?" he snapped at a worried-looking clerk who came into the office.

"Sir Walter, I do beg your pardon, but Lord Lapworth is on the telephone. He insists on speaking to you."

"Oh dear!" Honoria Rothwell sighed, smiling happily. "Poor Charmian is due for *such* a basting. You know what Jimmy Lapworth is like when he's roused."

On a Sunday afternoon at the beginning of August, Amelia and Silas rattled up the drive to Latimer's Barn with their hearts in their mouths. To go any further without telling Leander was, Amelia felt, tantamount to deceit; nevertheless, she was dreading it.

They were lucky and got a good start. Leander was alone in the kitchen studying the racing papers that were spread all over the table.

"Amelia! This is nice," she said. "Have you just come back from Cambridge?"

"No, Mother, I've been here since Wednesday . . . that is, I've been with Silas."

"I see." If Leander was surprised, she gave no sign of it. "Hello, Silas. Sit down, the pair of you. Why are you both looking so furtive?"

"Silas and I are in love, Mother. I thought it was time you knew."

"I do know – and you're looking very much better."

Amelia was stunned. "How do you know?"

"I saw the two of you mooning around on Newbury station four weeks ago."

"You couldn't have done!"

"I did!"

"Where were you?"

Leander smiled. "On a train coming home from London. You never bothered hiding from *them*, did you?"

Silas smiled sheepishly while Amelia gathered herself together. "The thing is, you see, Mother, we aren't intending to get married . . . that's my fault, by the way."

"It's more or less what I would have expected," Leander said calmly. "What do you think about that, Silas?"

"Well . . . I . . . er . . ."

"You're happy to do whatever the wretched woman wants?" Leander said.

"That's about the size of it, ma'am."

"Good. If you're both satisfied, that's all that matters."

Amelia was puzzled. "Don't you disapprove, Mother?"

"Why should I?"

"We shall be living in sin!" Amelia blurted out. "Well, for some of the time, at any rate."

Leander burst out laughing. "Oh, Amelia, you're so funny sometimes! Did you really think I might bite your head off?"

"No, not really." Amelia sounded less than convinced.

"I've been responsible for some pretty startling views in my time," Leander said. She paused, looking at Amelia and Silas in turn, assessing their moods. "Did I ever tell you, darling, that you were conceived up by Powell's Pool?"

"No, Mother, you did not!"

Silas suppressed the urge to laugh at Amelia's state of shock.

"Yes, you were," Leander continued, unconcerned by her daughter's gaping mouth. "Steven and I used to go swimming there in the afternoons. It was quite lovely – I thoroughly recommend it." Silas was careful not to look at Amelia. Leander's manner became briskly organising. "You'll stay to dinner, of course. William and Ruth and a few others are coming for a little celebration."

"What's the occasion?" Silas asked.

"You know that filly who won at Goodwood the other day?" Silas nodded: he had been on the course with two of his men. "She was the three-thousandth winner we've sent out."

"Really?" Amelia was back to normal again and her face was animated by excitement.

"Yes. William thought we had another twenty to go, but he'd added the figures up wrong."

"That's wonderful, Mrs Hawksworth," Silas said. "And the first on the very day you were born."

There was a very distant expression in Leander's eyes as she looked back over her sixty years. Something special caught her fancy: the sparkle in her eyes was quite bewitching. "My God," Silas found himself thinking, "you're still a corker. Forty years ago, you must have been a holy terror!"

With Amelia and Silas, there were twelve people at dinner, including Guy Mallender and Harry Giffard, the owners of the filly who had created the milestone of three thousand winners. Silas was comfortably aware of their acceptance of his position: far from earning disapproval, it seemed that he had been granted membership of the family.

At the end of the meal, as they were all moving into the small sitting-room, Leander excused herself for a few minutes. "I'm on duty this evening," she said, "so I must take a look round the yard." Correctly interpreting the look she gave him, Silas went with her.

Nothing was said until they were inside the quadrangle of boxes and Leander's acute senses told her that all was well; the horses were peacefully settled.

"There's the question of George," she said, looking at Silas with a slightly worried expression.

He understood her at once. "I take it that Amelia doesn't know about him coming back to cause all that trouble?"

"No, she doesn't," Leander replied. "And she has no idea of what I did to him."

474

"You had no choice in the matter," Silas said. "Don't worry, Amelia shall hear nothing from me."

"Thank you, Silas." Leander looked relieved. "I'm not at all sure that Amelia would approve."

"She never mentions George."

"What about Giles?"

"She's starting to. I think she's reaching the stage where she can think about him without getting upset. Do you ever hear from George?"

"No. I write occasionally, but he never replies. I don't much mind. It's Maude that's the problem. We haven't the faintest idea what's become of her and William worries a great deal."

Silas knew of the difficulties Maude had created and found it impossible to be sympathetic. He changed the subject instead.

"May I ask you something, Mrs Hawksworth?"

"You may."

"This business in *The Clarion*."

"Which business?"

"Walter Rothwell."

"Oh, yes. What about it?"

"Did you have anything to do with it?"

"Me?" Leander's eyes became very blue saucers of purest innocence. "Whatever makes you think that, Silas?"

"I heard that Rothwell was doing his best to make things awkward for you. And Rupert has a big say in *The Clarion*."

"Pure conjecture based on circumstantial evidence, Silas!"

"I'm aware of that, Mrs Hawksworth."

She took his arm as they began to walk out of the yard. "You simply would not believe what a poor old widow has to do in order to keep her head above water," she said with mock sorrow.

Emma was in a quandary.

If she rode out with both lots every morning, Steven, now seven, and Rachel, five, were inevitably neglected. Ellie Goakes would have loved to look after them, but rheumatism was slowing her down and she found Rachel far too much of a handful. Distressingly, the ever-exuberant Rachel had taken against Ellie to the extent that she would torment her, often without mercy. Not even Steven's stabilising influence was able to solve this problem.

Emma gave up riding out for a couple of weeks and was wretched: apart from her enjoyment of the work, she felt she owed it to the memory of Giles to play a part in running Latimer's Barn.

"We shall have to get someone to look after that pair," Leander said. "A strong-minded sort of person!" This was the nearest she ever got to criticism of Rachel for whom she had a very soft spot.

"Yes, but who?" Emma asked. "There isn't anyone suitable in the village and I'll be damned if I'll let some old school ma'am terrorise them."

The answer was Rhona Anderson, the lovely Hebridean girl they had met at Buckingham Palace.

She and Emma had conducted a prolific correspondence from which it did not take Emma long to deduce that post-war life in Benbecula was very hard indeed. The Western Isles were one of the areas with no reserves or protection against the economic difficulties that came with the peace. Whereas Leander occasionally grumbled about the falling levels of prize-money in some races, Emma realised that food was not always in plentiful supply for Rhona, her mother and father, and younger brother.

Not that Rhona ever made direct reference to hardship: she was far too brave and proud for that, devoting much of her writing to describing the beauty of the islands, a response to all the photographs of Cannings Ambo that Emma enclosed in her letters.

The first indication of trouble came in February, when Rhona doubted the ability of the croft to support four people for very much longer. Two weeks later, she left to live with her uncle in Glasgow where she was hoping to find work.

But something, Emma never discovered what, went wrong, and Rhona began to talk of chancing her arm in London.

"That's awful," Emma told Leander. "She'll shrivel up and die in that place."

"You're probably right. What do you want to do about it?"

"I'm sure she'd be a wonderful asset to us if I could get her to come here."

After three dispiriting days in London, where she failed to find a job, Rhona travelled to Cannings Ambo for a weekend, fell in love with it on first sight and agreed to take on Rachel and Steven.

She took up her duties at the end of September, living in The House. At their first meeting, Rachel had smiled at Rhona in rather a forlorn way and behaved like an angel. Steven, who thought Rhona was a gift from the gods, knew exactly what his sister was thinking: "Oh dear, Miss Anderson, you're very nice, but you aren't going to stand for any nonsense, are you?"

So it proved. After a week, Rachel experimented with a bout of naughtiness and received a fearful dressing-down, all the more telling since the exposition of her misdemeanours and promises of retribution if they were repeated was carried out in a low, sweet voice, with Rhona showing not a trace of anger.

Louise was not long in enlisting Rhona's help with her son William, born at the end of 1919, and something of a weakling who cried far more often than was good for him, or anyone within earshot. Once Rhona had removed all the patent baby foods and medicines from Louise House and started treating little William like a baby Hebridean, his weight and temper improved by leaps and bounds.

More than pleased with the turn of events, Emma cheerfully kept her side of the bargain she had struck with Rhona. Every month, a five-pound note was sent by registered post to Mr and Mrs Anderson in Benbecula while Rhona lived in the lap of luxury on five shillings a week.

"The only problem is the men," Louise said to Emma one day when they were extolling Rhona's virtues. "They simply flock round her."

"They aren't a nuisance, are they?" Emma asked.

"No, but one of them may marry her and then where shall we be?"

"There's no need to worry," Emma said. Rhona's unusual beauty had indeed caused a near-sensation among the village's single men, many of whom had laid siege to her, but Emma was armed with Leander's searching observations on the matter. "Rhona's made her mind up, but it's going to be some time before anything happens. He doesn't know yet and he's awfully shy."

"Who's the lucky man?" Louise asked eagerly.

"Mark Pilgrim."

"Oh!" Louise seemed disappointed. "He's much older than her."

"He's only thirty-two."

"And he's a confirmed bachelor."

"Let's see how long he can keep that up once Rhona gets going!"

As the year neared its end, the motive for Rothwell's attempt to discredit Latimer's Barn finally emerged. Leander told Rupert in their forest cottage on a December afternoon when the windows rattled and the trees groaned in the teeth of a savage south-westerly gale.

"You know Cross Gates Farm down at West Kennet?" Leander asked. "Rothwell was trying to buy that during the spring."

"What for?"

"To turn it into a stable for his nephew."

"But it's a fearful old ruin of a place!" Rupert protested.

"Joe Irons could have fixed that up in a couple of months and there's plenty of room for a decent gallop."

Realisation came to Rupert. "I see, so he was trying to put the local opposition in its place before his blasted nephew even started?"

"Something like that."

"The man's an idiot! By the way, what's he doing with himself these days?"

In accordance with his wife's plans, Sir Walter Rothwell had resigned all his Jockey Club positions on his return from Cannes at the end of August. After the predictable expressions of regret, the establishment moved swiftly to plug the gaps and seemed to be managing perfectly well without him.

"He's devoting himself to good works," Leander said. "Unfortunately, he doesn't seem able to get himself on any worthwhile committees."

"Why?"

"Clem Prideaux runs them all!" Leander chuckled. She snuggled closer to him in the sumptuously comfortable feather bed and they fell into a companionable silence.

"What sort of job are we making of doing what you said, winning the peace?" she asked after a few minutes. She was tentative, half dreading the answer.

"Cannings Ambo is doing *very* well."

"That isn't what I meant, Rupert."

He sighed. "No, I know it wasn't. It doesn't look too good. We have some nasty economic problems, but the man in the street isn't in a sympathetic mood. He wants the jam Lloyd George promised him."

"What about Europe?"

"Well, Germany's in a shocking state," Rupert replied. "There's no telling where they'll end up. The terms of that iniquitous Peace Treaty can only make things ten times worse."

Leander felt a twinge of guilt at her resolute unwillingness to take notice of the newspapers.

"As far as I can see, the whole of Europe is in uproar," Rupert went on. "No one has the faintest idea what to do about Russia, of course."

The threat of Communism, creeping plague-like across the whole continent, was something Leander did not want to understand. She shivered and burrowed deeper into Rupert's embrace.

CHAPTER 27

1929

'They play games, make a lot of noise . . .'

Leander did not need the benefit of hindsight to see the decade from 1920 to 1929 as one of the most difficult in England's history. Six governments – under Lloyd George, Bonar Law, Stanley Baldwin and Ramsay MacDonald – struggled with a mountain of problems, achieving varying degrees of failure.

For many, the creation of a Ministry of Health and Pensions in 1919 made life more pleasant, and a few enjoyed a luxury previously undreamed of. The advent of the wireless provided the opportunity for a better-informed nation and there were queues outside the picture palaces every night of the week except Sunday. But whatever good was accomplished, the abiding memories were of the General Strike.

In the Budget speech of 1925, Winston Churchill announced the return to the Gold Standard, abandoned as an emergency measure in 1919, but this was soon found to be an empty gesture. The sovereign did not return to circulation and international trade remained sluggish: in 1927, the best year for exports, the figure was only eighty per cent of the pre-war high of 1913.

Cannings Ambo came through more or less unscathed. Wm Flamsteed & Sons, inspiringly led by Matthew, and with Fred Cartwright inventing new tricks of salesmanship, expanded. Four more skilled men were taken on and Matthew invested heavily in an apprenticeship scheme to secure the future. Under Jeremy Dundas, who became a Trustee in 1925, the stud prospered, with The Atheling a very popular stallion. Two of his progeny won the Derbys of 1923 and 1926, and although this pleased Leander, she was annoyed that neither of them was trained at Latimer's Barn.

The 1920s were, in fact, the stable's leanest period since the early days. In the eight racing seasons of 1921–28, 476 winners went out: a good enough total, but although the success was there, prestige was lacking. There were no Classic victories and only a handful of wins at Royal Ascot and Goodwood.

But, by the start of 1929, the Fund stood only a few thousand pounds short of one million. For twenty years, Leander had been saying that this was the figure that would make her believe that Cannings Ambo was becoming safely insulated from the vagaries of the world: now, she thought that two million might be a better goal.

There had been loss and sadness along the way. Conn Daly died only two years after his belated retirement and Sally followed him two years later. Peter Izzard, the man who rode New Invention and Bellerophon, died in 1923, Guy Mallender the following year and Harry Giffard in 1926.

Among the compensations, William now had two grandsons, his namesake who was in the workshop as soon as he could walk, and John, born in 1921.

An important decision was made about Steven when it was time to think of a fuller education than the village school was able to provide. Emma asked Leander for her opinion.

"I don't think you should send him away, darling," was the immediate response. "Giles hated it and I'm sure it never did him a scrap of good."

"That's what Steven wants," Emma replied. "He's been dreading going away. He's set his heart on the Grammar School in Marlborough so that he can be with his friends."

"Much the best!" Leander agreed. "To be perfectly honest, after the effect it had on George, I wouldn't have wanted Steven to go anywhere near Winchester."

Emma knew that this was an unjust slur on a great school, but was content with the outcome: Steven stayed at home and was thus able to spend at least two hours a day with the horses.

Things were different with Rachel, however. At her own insistence, she was packed off to become a boarder at the Godolphin School in Salisbury.

"She thinks she's following in Amelia's footsteps," Emma said to Leander.

"That would be nice."

"It would be a miracle!" Emma laughed. "If that little tearaway ever does well in exams, I'll start eating all your Ascot hats."

Leander, the confidante of both her grandchildren, knew that Rachel's academic aspirations were minimal.

"I don't expect I shall be a nibs like Aunt Amelia," Rachel said, "but I want to be as happy as she says she was."

That, Leander thought, was a very good reason for choosing a school.

Her responsibilities for Rachel now at an end, Rhona Anderson moved to Louise House to look after William and John Flamsteed. She also took a delighted and comically bemused Mark Pilgrim as her husband on a day that the village celebrated with tremendous gusto.

The truth of the matter was that it was a dull and nervous decade: although Cannings Ambo was making progress, the pre-war sense of excitement was missing. Mark Pilgrim was horrified when he discovered the intention to turn his wedding day into a major occasion, and was not particularly comforted by Leander's explanation.

"I'm afraid everything has been pretty dreary since the War, Mark. This is their big chance to have a knees-up, so you'll have to grin and bear it."

Then, at long last, there *was* something to excite people and keep them on their toes again. At Royal Ascot in 1928, the Duchess of Laverstoke's colt, Agamemnon, made his début in the Coventry Stakes and Cannings Ambo knew it had another champion.

By the time he retired to stud at the end of the 1929 season, Agamemnon had won over £50,000 in prize-money, a new record. In 1929, he made Clementine Prideaux the leading owner and William champion trainer, and those who had started looking on Latimer's Barn as simply another competent, workmanlike stable were given a series of spectacular shocks.

Leander and a few others were able to draw even greater comfort from the colt's racecourse performances because of what they had seen on the gallop at home. It was Agamemnon who showed that the fifteen-year-old Steven was to be a trainer of great talent.

When Agamemnon, a good-looking son of The Atheling, had arrived as a yearling, everyone thought he was destined for great things, but his schooling and subsequent attempts to train him produced long faces. Whatever his attributes as a natural athlete, Agamemnon was far too self-consciously awkward to realise anything like his potential.

"I'm very sorry, Clem," Leander finally said to the Duchess as they walked alongside the gallop one Saturday morning. "We thought that colt of yours was going to be brilliant, but we can't do a damned thing with him."

"Good God, what an admission! I thought you could train *anything*. Hubert swears you could get a giraffe into the winner's enclosure."

"As a matter of fact, that's what I thought," Leander confessed.

"This one's got us beat, though. None of us has any idea what's wrong with him. It's not badness, he's thoroughly decent."

"H'm." The Duchess squinted down the gallop, to which Leander had her back. "Have you tried Steven on him?" she asked.

"No, we haven't."

"He rides a bit, doesn't he?"

"He's very good indeed. I suppose there's a chance that he *might* do the trick."

"Would you bet on it?"

"No!" Leander laughed. "That's a mug's game at the best of times, let alone with a perverse creature like your colt."

"What a pity," the Duchess said wistfully. "I could have got myself a new dress out of that without bringing one of Hubert's funny spells on."

Puzzled, Leander frowned, then turned to look down the gallop for the source of Her Grace's amusement. What she saw flabbergasted her before lighting up her face in a triumphant smile.

Four horses due to race within the next few days were doing a sharp piece of work over seven furlongs. With Mark Pilgrim setting the pace they were moving at a good clip. About fifty yards behind them was Agamemnon with Steven on him, his slightly ungainly riding-style immediately apparent.

Leander knew at once what must have happened. Having persuaded Albert Merriweather to let him ride the colt, Steven had been gripped by a unique surge of devilment and set off in pursuit of the four being worked. It was extremely naughty and startlingly effective.

"You told me that animal wouldn't go," the Duchess said accusingly, enjoying Leander's discomfort.

"He never has."

"There doesn't appear to be much wrong with him now. I think he's going to catch the others."

"No, he isn't," Leander said, relieved to see that Steven's rush of blood was over and that he was pulling Agamemnon up to avoid straining him.

"I don't know much about these things, of course," the Duchess lied, "but he seemed to be going pretty well to me."

"He was going very well indeed," Leander replied. "Let's hope we've found the answer."

After making a strict point of not interfering with the roasting that Steven's irresponsibility earned from Albert Merriweather, Leander arranged to repeat the process five days later.

This time, Steven was instructed to take Agamemnon over six furlongs against two older horses whose considerable ability was a well-proven fact: between them, they had won nine races. Agamemnon beat them easily without coming off the bit.

"That's all very well, Lea," an impressed William said. "What do we do now? How do we make him do that in a race with Mark Pilgrim riding him?"

"Patience and guile," Leander replied confidently. "We've been doing it for sixty years. Remember New Invention?"

"He was Horatio's first good horse."

"At first, he would only go for me, so we had to make him run for Peter Izzard."

As well as persuading him that anything was possible, the memories that came flooding back to William were startling. When New Invention gave them that first Classic success, Leander was a precocious little girl of eight: sixty years later, she seemed defiantly incapable of showing any sign of age beyond a well-preserved fifty.

"Why are you staring at me like that, William?" she asked.

"Oh . . . nothing," he replied, returning to the present with a jolt. "Nothing at all. I'm looking forward to seeing you sort this one out."

The job was, of course, done brilliantly well. With two furlongs to run in the Coventry Stakes, the question of the second place was the sole issue in doubt.

Because of Leander's conviction that Agamemnon was a horse of the very highest class, he raced only twice more as a two-year-old to minimise the risk of injury or strain. In August he went to York for the Gimcrack Stakes and in October to Newmarket for the Dewhurst. Two overwhelming successes left him as a clear ante-post favourite for both the Two Thousand Guineas and the Derby of 1929.

After an uneventful winter, mercifully free of alarms, Agamemnon's 1929 campaign began with the Craven Stakes at Newmarket in mid-April. Mark Pilgrim's sole contribution to the race was to ensure that his mount did no more than was necessary to win.

A fortnight later, things were very different in the Two Thousand Guineas.

"Let him go, Mark," was Leander's instruction in the paddock. "It's ten years since we won a Classic and I'm fed up with waiting!"

Agamemnon made all the running to win by six lengths.

For William, the five weeks to Derby Day were the most nerve-wracking of his life. Each day that passed without Agamemnon going lame, pulling a muscle or developing a stomach complaint was counted as a miracle. Even when the colt had completed his final gallop five days before the great race, William was still looking for disaster round every corner.

"If you don't pull yourself together, I won't let you come to Epsom," Leander told him. "We shall have enough on our plate without carting a bag of nerves around."

By contrast, Mark's wife *had* to go.

Rhona had never been to a race meeting. This was not due to lack of interest: she adored the horses and watched them at work whenever the chance arose. But she was always too busy to take a day or more off from looking after children, first Emma's and Louise's, then her own two, Michael and Morag. For this Derby, however, Leander would not countenance a refusal.

"No, my dear, there are dozens of perfectly competent women to look after your children for the day, so you are coming with us and we'll have no more argument, if you please."

It was a day that Rhona never forgot.

As a much-loved and honoured guest, she travelled in the same car as Leander and Emma with Cyril Osgood as their chauffeur. From the moment they encountered the first of the crowds, Rhona felt like royalty.

With the car hood down to take advantage of glorious weather, they were spotted at once.

"Look 'Arry, there's Leander!"

"Blimey, yes! Cor, don't she look a picture!"

"How're you doing, darling; all right, are we?" someone shouted, receiving a dazzling smile and wave in return.

There was speculation about Rhona's identity, finally resolved when she joined Mark, who had travelled up from Wiltshire the previous afternoon as part of Agamemnon's entourage. After that, Rhona found that she was receiving respectful greetings from total strangers.

It was when she struggled into the packed ranks of the bookmakers to place a bet with the five pounds that Leander had given her that Rhona discovered the full extent of the public's faith in her Mark, Agamemnon and Latimer's Barn. Scarcely a penny was being wagered on any other horse, and when Agamemnon went to post as the five-to-four favourite, he was carrying well over a million pounds of punters' hopes. With the bookmakers standing to receive an historic drubbing, the atmosphere was electric.

For the first mile of the race, Mark kept Agamemnon covered up and out of trouble at the rear of the field while lesser animals fought a scrappy duel for the worthless privilege of being in the lead for fifty or a hundred yards. The disjointed nervousness of

484

it all was a sign that the other jockeys felt that the result was inevitable.

Mark made them wait. Not until they were down the hill and safely round the worst of Tattenham Corner did he ease Agamemnon away from the mêlée and let him go.

The vast crowd came to noisy life at once: it was an age for the adoration of heroes. By far the most popular was the kindly, unassuming Steve Donaghue and the great roar of, "Come on Steve!" frequently echoed across every racecourse in the country. But today, Steve was on a horse without the glimmer of a hope, and as Agamemnon took flight down the centre of the track, the shout was, "Good old Leander!"

William, doing his best to keep calm, went forward to help the Duchess lead in the sixth Derby winner with which Leander had been associated, the first, fifty-three years ago when he and Jim Goakes had waited for the erratic Lucifer to bring news of Bellerophon.

"What's up, William?" the Duchess asked, seeing his abstraction.

"I don't think any of us ever imagined that it would turn out like this," he replied.

Clementine Prideaux understood him. "I'll lay you a thousand pounds to a pinch of horse muck that *she* did."

William looked round to see Leander following them, grinning hugely and dragging an overawed Rhona to greet her triumphant husband: the Duchess was almost certainly right, he thought.

On the day after Agamemnon won the Derby, there was a General Election. An electorate made up of everyone over the age of twenty-one was to choose the sixth government of the decade. For the first time, Cannings Ambo had its own polling station, situated in a corner of the Village Hall.

Leander had attempted to follow the campaign on the wireless, a gadget that had received her enthusiastic support since its arrival in 1922. These days, however, her interest in affairs beyond the village and racing was much diminished. Amelia, noticing the decline, put it down to the traumatic effects of the Great War: after that, it seemed, nothing was worth worrying about.

The election was a desperately dull affair, devoid of real issues because none of the would-be leaders had the courage to raise them. Lloyd George had hatched up a few radical policies, yet no one trusted him very much these days, his private life was a disgrace and wireless exposed him as a pretty awful communicator. Despite Stanley Baldwin's mastery of the new medium, people were tired of his avuncular assurances that it was not really necessary to do anything. Although they had no grasp of the difficulties facing the country, the public felt that someone should be taking action.

It was the hope and promise of a new idealism that elected James Ramsay MacDonald and a minority Labour Government. When Leander discovered that the Prime Minister would be relying on the support of a motley bunch of fifty-nine Liberals, most of whom were united only by detestation of Lloyd George, she looked disgusted.

"Don't you think much of this, then?" Rupert asked, trying to introduce a note of levity.

"No, Rupert, I don't," she replied. "I've nothing against MacDonald and his men, it's just that they're not up to the job. They're heavy on ideals and light on experience. It's very worrying."

"Never mind, what about Agamemnon? What are your plans for him?"

"The Eclipse and the St Leger," Leander replied without a moment's hesitation. "Wouldn't it be nice if running the country was as easy?"

"Don't worry, *chérie*, you are provided for and that Clothilde will not be able to harm you!"

Those were Achille Guillaume's last words to Maude, an hour before he died in November 1926. He had never before said a word against his daughter-in-law; at the end, however, he showed that he had her measure.

He was barely in his grave before Clothilde was screaming at Jacques, her brow-beaten husband, to contest the will that had left everything in three equal shares to Maude, Jacques and Michel.

Jacques began going through the motions for the sake of peace and quiet, but it did not take long to discover that Achille had anticipated trouble and gone to great lengths to frustrate it. Not only was his will completely watertight, three doctors had sworn an affidavit that he was of perfectly sound mind when he made it.

And Maude had the answer to the poisonously anti-social campaign that was unleashed against her.

"Unless you learn to keep a civil tongue in your head, dear Clothilde, I will sell my share of the farm to René Raimond," she announced sweetly.

The prospect of their hated neighbour owning a third of her livelihood cowed even the virulent Clothilde, who soon found herself confronted with another, more serious threat. Michel, quiet, hard-working and nearly as handsome as his father, had never married and had come to admire Maude greatly. The suggestion that he should, after a decent interval, marry his bereaved step-mother, much approved of by young Henri, was an idea that struck terror into Clothilde: if that should happen, Michel would effectively own two-thirds of the farm.

Maude did nothing to encourage Michel, but neither did she discourage him. Since he was easily pleased, the merest word or gesture was enough to keep his hopes alive, subduing Clothilde into a passable semblance of good behaviour.

Her position secure, Maude lived her own life, painting and ignoring the work of the farm. Her painting expeditions took her to the mainland and to the estuary of the River Loire near St-Nazaire where she was found by Gaston Ferraud.

Ferraud was a writer of considerable repute; Maude had read and enjoyed three of his novels and was naturally flattered by his interest in her work.

In the spring of 1927, Maude was thirty-nine with her looks holding up well, and Ferraud was thirty-two and unmarried. When they became lovers, the difference in their ages was immaterial; secretly, Ferraud was delighted by the expertise that Maude brought to his bed and assumed that this came from a wealth of past involvement. They soon settled into a routine in which Maude spent two four-day periods each month at Ferraud's villa above the estuary.

Ferraud was in the habit of shutting the villa and spending December, January and February in Paris. In 1929, it was the end of April before he returned and Maude threw herself so whole-heartedly into a tumultuous welcome that it never occurred to her to question his extended absence, or to detect the slight edge of unease about him.

At the end of June, she noticed a two-week-old English newspaper set carefully to one side on the verandah of the villa.

"Dupont left that here last week," Ferraud explained. "I saved it for you. They have been having an election. Apparently they are in the same sort of mess as us."

Maude took the paper out to the terrace while Ferraud settled down to answer letters. After half an hour, she gave up trying to make sense of what was happening in England. Inasmuch as anything could be deduced from the mass of report and comment on the General Election result, it was that the country was groping round in a fog, completely unsure of the way ahead. It was the same as in France and Germany.

Idly turning the pages, she came to the sports section and smiled cynically at the news that a South African cricket team was touring England. Was George lending them support, she wondered. Not if his infernal mother had anything to do with it!

Progressing to the next page, Maude received one of the worst shocks of her life. Two pages were devoted to racing and from one of them a photograph of William and Leander stared at her; it was at the head of a long article on Latimer's Barn inspired by Agamemnon's Derby win.

Maude studied the picture, annoyed to see that Leander had hardly changed, pleased that William was carrying his years so well.

Then came the revelation that her father was a racehorse trainer. Incredulous, she settled down to read. Everything was explained. She learned of the death of Giles and her brother, Gerald, of Matthew's marriage and the fact that he was now running Wm Flamsteed & Sons while William looked after the stable until Leander's grandson, Steven, was old enough to take over. Steven, the article made abundantly clear, had worked the magic with Agamemnon and was expected to be another brilliant addition to the Latimer's Barn galaxy when his time came.

Maude said nothing to Ferraud about what she had discovered, but took the newspaper back to the Guillaume farm when they parted, he to spend two more mysterious weeks in Paris, she to indulge in another bout of the melancholy that had dogged her throughout the long winter.

She thought seriously of selling her share of the farm and having done with it. René Raimond's latest offer stood at two million francs, something like £12,000 in what she still thought of as 'real' money. With a sum like that at her disposal, she could take Henri back to England; there might even be a welcome for her in Cannings Ambo.

After five days of agonising she finally decided that the idea was ridiculous. During this time, her son watched her closely. Now twelve, Henri loved his mother dearly, even though they had moved apart since Achille's death: he was prepared to forgive her anything, and constantly did his best to be only mildly disappointed at her failure to marry Michel.

On the sixth day, Maude glanced at *Le Figaro* as usual and stumbled across the announcement of Gaston Ferraud's engagement to Gilda Gabrielli, an Italian actress. To judge by the photograph, Signorina Gabrielli was sensationally beautiful: she was also twenty-two, little more than half Maude's age.

The weather had been dreadful for two days, with a series of deep depressions dashing across the Bay of Biscay. That evening, as the wind built up to near hurricane force, Maude slipped away from the farmhouse after supper and set off along her favourite cliff-top walk.

After a mile, she found the spot that seemed to be ideal. Immediately after she had jumped, there was a moment of hysterical wonderment as she thought the fearsome wind was going to blow her back. The first crazy somersault of free fall was a blessed relief.

It was two days before the fishermen found her battered body in the next bay. After fixing a verdict of death by misadventure, Maître Fenélon divested himself of a completely unnecessary ten-minute homily on the dangers of walking along the cliffs in extremes of weather.

Deeply upset by Maude's death and far from convinced that it was an accident, Henri made a point of beating Clothilde to the systematic search of his mother's room.

First he found her birth certificate, then the prayer book given to Maude on her confirmation in 1896. Her name and address were written on the fly-leaf and there were snapshot photographs between the pages. They gave clues to the carefully folded page from an English newspaper which the bi-lingual Henri studied with great care.

Surprised and saddened by what he had learned, Henri put it all in a safe hiding-place and settled down to wait for the row that must surely erupt over the division of his mother's share of the farm.

Two weeks before Agamemnon won the St Leger and became the first Latimer's Barn horse to win the coveted Triple Crown, the Duchess of Laverstoke watched him work. She was accompanied by her eldest son, who was paying his first visit to Cannings Ambo.

Charles Prideaux, Marquess of Glastonbury and heir to the dukedom, was twenty-four and amply endowed with the family good looks. He was also an extraordinarily nice person.

"It's a miracle," the Duchess confided to Leander. "I mean, Eton and Oxford turn most chaps into the most appalling ticks, but he's a charmer. Don't you dare tell him I said so!"

That day, Agamemnon, who had won the Eclipse Stakes and York's Great Voltigeur Stakes since the Derby, did a mile at three-quarters pace. He was ridden by Steven, working alongside a huge chestnut gelding belonging to Rupert who was also a spectator. To Rupert's astonished delight, Rachel was on his horse.

"How long has she been doing that?" he asked Leander.

"Nearly a year. Not bad, is she?"

"She's marvellous. What a family!"

"We need to be," Leander reminded him. "Mind you, Amelia's old school is doing wonders for Rachel. It's ages since Emma had any trouble with her."

When the gallop was over, however, and Rachel was introduced to Charles, she demonstrated that growing up had its problems, too.

"Oh, gosh!" she said, blushing in confusion. "How do you do, sir . . . er, Your Grace . . . no, it's my lord, isn't it?"

"Please call me Charles," he said, shaking her hand gravely.

"I'm afraid I've got to put this horse away," Rachel said, as though speaking of the greatest tragedy of her life. "Would you like to come with me and look at the yard, Charles?"

"I'd love to, Rachel."

After they had gone off together, Emma clenched her fists, raised her eyes to the sky in a show of mock-horror and looked pleadingly at Leander. "Unless I'm very much mistaken, that's schoolgirl pash at first sight," she said.

"No doubt about it," the Duchess said. "And it's mutual. Charles looked pretty smitten by her."

Leander, vastly entertained by what she had seen, made the effort to be serious. "You'd better have a word with him, Clem. Rachel might look seventeen, but she's only fourteen."

"Leave it to me, my dear, I know exactly how to deal with that sort of thing!"

There was a look of such fiendish glee on the Duchess's face that Leander chuckled as she took Rupert's arm and steered him towards The House.

"It's George," she said, after they had walked in silence for a while.

"You've heard from him?"

"No, but my last letter has been returned marked 'Not known – gone away'. You know the sort of thing."

"Perhaps if you tried his company?"

"I did. I sent them a cablegram. George left them nearly a year ago to set up some sort of business on his own."

"And they don't know where he went?"

"They say not."

"Do you want me to find out if he's in England?"

"If you would, please, Rupert. I'm inclined to doubt it, but I suppose it's better to be safe than sorry."

He could see that she was worrying.

Later, they had something to laugh about.

"I have the official verdict on Charles Prideaux," Emma announced over lunch; the Duchess and her son had gone back to Eaton Mandeville. "He is 'scrumptious'!"

Doing their best to keep straight faces, Leander and Rupert turned to Rachel who was glaring at her mother with infinite loathing.

490

It was Steven who made Leander split her sides when he looked up from his plate and said, "Actually, he struck me as a jolly decent sort," as though passing judgement on a horse.

With the approach of another autumn, Leander braced herself for what she imagined might be one of the worst crises the village had ever had to face.

There were no two ways about it, they were getting a lady doctor.

Charles Stanton was sixty-six and due for retirement. The assumption was that a new man from outside would have to be persuaded to take over the practice since David and John, the two handsome sons that Flora had borne Charles, had joined the Army before going to Medical School, David as a volunteer, Ian as a conscript. Hezekiah Dangerfield had carved both their names on the War Memorial.

If they ever knew in the first place, most people lost sight of the fact that there was a third Stanton and that *she* had qualified as a doctor.

Kathleen, sent away to the Godolphin School in accordance with the growing Cannings Ambo belief that girls should receive the best possible education, won a scholarship to Edinburgh University in 1916. Only her proud parents and Leander, who noted the fact in the Big Book, took any notice of what was, in all honesty, a fairly insignificant event in that appalling year of the Somme.

After graduating, Kathleen worked in a Glasgow hospital for three years before moving to a general practice in Newcastle-upon-Tyne. Mindful of the fact that she would have to persuade Kathleen to come and work in Cannings Ambo one day, Leander always spent time with her when she came to Oak Cottage for a holiday.

Their conversations rapidly assumed an unexpected rapport and intensity, for it was from Kathleen Stanton that Leander obtained a new insight into the War.

On her first day in Glasgow as a working doctor, Kathleen had seen thirty-five patients. Twenty-eight of them were ex-soldiers, suffering from the effects of the Somme, Passchendaele, or some other bloody fiasco. That was how it carried on.

"To be honest, I hoped it might improve when I went to Newcastle," Kathleen admitted. She smiled sadly. "Then I found what was left of the Tyneside Scottish Battalions."

The men soon came to trust her and had told her stories they had kept from their loved ones or mates. Some had been unnaturally calm about it, others broke down and cried: almost without exception, they were agonising over what had happened to their friends, not to themselves. As she listened, Leander gathered more pieces in the jig-saw of what Giles, Gerald, Matthew and all the others had endured.

By the time that the question of a replacement for Charles was starting to assume urgency, Leander was half afraid that Kathleen, dedicated to her loyal Geordies, would not wish to return to Cannings Ambo, and until the summer of 1929, this was the case. Then something happened to produce a dramatic change overnight: with her customary unerring intuition, Leander suspected that a long-standing love-affair had come to an abrupt, messy end.

For whatever reason, a new plate appeared outside Oak Cottage in September. At the age of thirty-one, Doctor Kathleen Stanton was coming home; the arrangement was that she would work as her father's assistant for about a year, taking over completely when they both felt the time was right.

The younger women took to Kathleen immediately and began to spread persuasive propaganda among the older members of their sex, but apart from a few young wags from the yard who fancied a bit of sport at the expense of the lady doctor, none of the men would go near her. Aware of this, Charles and Kathleen played games. At least once a week, Flora would go into the waiting-room, smile sweetly and say: "I'm afraid my husband has been called out to an urgent case. Not to worry, my daughter will attend to you."

After that, they would peer through the keyhole to watch the men's anguish as they concocted excuses or sudden miracle cures that would enable them to slip away without too much loss of face.

It was entertaining while it lasted, but the time came when Leander decided that it must stop. Arriving at The House on a morning in November, Rupert Timberlake found Cyril Osgood and Sam Briggs at the back door. They were receiving a fearful dressing-down.

"You've had that pain in your shoulder for two months to my certain knowledge, Cyril, and as for you, Sam Briggs, your bowels are a disgrace! Go and see the doctor – Doctor *Kathleen*. She won't bite you. Right?"

"Yes, Mrs Aitch," Sam said, eager to end the ordeal. Cyril nodded, touched his forelock and they shuffled away, cringing visibly at Leander's final shot.

"And don't try any old-soldier tricks! I shall check up."

"That's telling them," Rupert chuckled.

"Well!" Leander's eyes flashed and she looked as though she was about to stamp a foot in exasperation. "I'm surrounded by idiots!"

"Yes, my dear. You have to carry this place single-handed. But by God, you look well on it!"

Reaching out, he ran a caressing finger down her cheek, dwelling under her still-firm, perfectly shaped chin: he had been an admirer of that bone structure for the best part of fifty years, confident that it would never fade.

Flustered, she bundled him into the kitchen. "Really, Rupert, what *will* people think?" she asked, feigning annoyance.

"Nothing like the truth, that's for sure."

"H'm!" She was unconvinced. "Anyway, what are you doing here at this time of day? We're busy!"

"I'm on my way to Bath, so I thought I'd look in to tell you we haven't found any sign of George."

"You've looked thoroughly?"

"We haven't scoured the East End of London," Rupert admitted with a touch of irony. "But all the likely spots have had a going-over. We're carrying on."

"Very well." Leander was slightly uneasy, anxious for reassurance while preserving her innocence of Timberlake activities.

"I've got Claude working on it," Rupert said. "You know, my nephew, James's and Abigail's boy."

"Is he all right?" Leander asked dubiously.

Rupert laughed. "He's good enough to be taking over a great deal of my work. Yes, Leander, I'm thinking about the future, too. I'm older than you and not nearly so damned indestructible!"

On the afternoon of the same day, Amelia had a frightening experience. She never forgot it.

Since 1923, work with brilliant and stimulating post-graduate students, aided by the contentment generated in her relationship with Silas, had brought her back into the forefront of research. Inundated with pleas to speak about her studies, Amelia always felt guilty when she rejected Otto Edelson's invitations to conduct a symposium.

Edelson, once a close colleague of Ludwig Lehmann, was now Professor of Mathematics at the University of Munich, and wrote to Amelia three times a year, always at the beginning of each term. Longing to see how the country she had loved so much was faring, she accepted the request waiting for her on the first day of the Michaelmas Term.

Something akin to relief came over her on the express train that ran all the way from the Hook of Holland to Munich: the views from the carriage window suggested that life was returning to normal. As yet, the only sign of the new Europe was the passport that Amelia carried; on her last visit, sixteen years ago, such documents did not exist.

Otto, white-haired, fatter, but exactly his old self, was waiting at the ticket barrier. Grinning hugely, he crushed her in a warm hug.

"Amelia! As beautiful as ever!"

"You, too, Otto! Oh, it's lovely to see you again!"

"Come!" He was collecting her bags. "We take a taxi. My Elsa and the children are longing to meet you. Do you know, Hans and little Otto have demanded to sleep in the loft so that you can have their room?"

The happiness lasted four minutes. That was the time it took the taxi to turn out of the station square and become embroiled in the most frightful uproar Amelia had ever seen at such close quarters.

She knew that Bavaria, never a comfortable or compliant member of Bismarck's unified Germany, had suffered terrible agonies after the War. The brutal repression of a Communist uprising by several detachments of *Freikorps*, the irregular bands of soldiers upon which the infant Weimar Government had been forced to rely, had added to the ferment of South German ideas and individuality. To an extent, Amelia was forewarned: but not for anything like this.

An immense Mercedes motor car was almost blocking the narrow street. It was a convertible with the hood down. Standing in the back, a youngish man, made old by the skull-like appearance of his head, was haranguing a crowd of about a hundred through a megaphone. He wore an immaculate lounge suit, but the ten thugs surrounding and protecting the car were dressed in brown shirts, breeches and riding boots.

"Oh dear, not again!" Otto Edelson laughed.

It was a few moments before Amelia spoke; unable to decipher what the man in the car was bawling, she was, nevertheless, acutely conscious of evil. "What is this, Otto?" she asked, her voice strained.

"The National Socialists. They're one of our jokes! And you see that fellow in the car? He's the biggest joke of all. Joseph Goebbels, what a buffoon!"

"What about the others?" Amelia asked. "Why are they dressed like that? What are those armbands?"

"They are *Sturm Abteilung*." Edelson was mocking.

"Why does a political party need Storm Troopers?" Amelia asked.

"They play games, make a lot of noise because they cannot get votes. It is nothing, believe me."

By mounting the pavement, the taxi-driver had found a way round the Mercedes and they were on their way again. Looking back, Amelia saw three of the Storm Troopers moving menacingly towards a group of hecklers.

"As a matter of fact, those Nazis have someone even funnier, now

494

I come to think of it," Otto said as they were drawing up outside his house in a pleasant rural suburb of the city. "The leader calls himself Hitler, but I think his real name is Schickelgruber. Imagine that! They tell me he was a corporal."

Amelia felt ill. After looking into the eyes of Joseph Goebbels, she had no desire to see Otto's idea of an even bigger joke.

CHAPTER 28

1933

'We don't know any people like that . . .'

The economic collapse that began on Wall Street in October 1929, and soon engulfed Europe, was known from the start as 'the Great Depression' and universally regarded as an inevitable, almost natural, catastrophe. Leander, William and the other Trustees believed that was a myth to deceive the public: the hard fact was that Cannings Ambo continued to prosper and it was all due to a quality of management sadly lacking in Government.

When Ramsay MacDonald was forced to drag Stanley Baldwin and his cronies into a National Government in August 1931, Leander allowed herself a brief burst of I-told-you-so satisfaction before tackling the problem of demand for increased capacity in the yard.

The first pressures came from Jocelyn Mallender and Joe Giffard, who were making a strong fist of running Mallender and Giffard which now had fourteen shops in Wiltshire and Gloucestershire. Whereas their fathers had been content to be joint owners of a couple of horses, Jocelyn and Joe wanted three each. Then Claude Timberlake, now in almost complete control of the Timberlake empire, and newly married to a beautiful young woman from London, acquired four horses and was constantly wanting more. By pressing the six boxes at The Hall into use once again, Leander was able to cope with most of their demands.

However, no sooner did she have a grip on the situation, than Ernest Cartwright set about making life impossible for her.

Ernest, now twenty-eight, was part of the new generation at Wm Flamsteed & Sons; he did all the selling while Fred looked after the Fletcher account and helped Matthew in the office. At the same time, young Jim Goakes was taking over from his father on production.

After an eight-year apprenticeship alongside Fred, it was a foregone

496

conclusion that Ernest would bring in the business, even though his style was so very different from that of his father. Every bit as confident as Fred, Ernest cultivated the manner of a pre-war landed gentleman and it worked splendidly, especially with the new breed of hard-nosed, self-made businessmen in the Midlands and North.

Ernest generated a completely new type of order. He kept domestic furniture moving along nicely, but encouraged engineers, scrap-merchants and textile barons to introduce elegance into their offices and boardrooms.

"To tell you the truth, love, I've no idea how he does it," Fred said to Tish as they sat over supper at Alma Cottage on a day that had seen the arrival of a spectacular order from an ironworks in Rotherham.

"Don't you?" Tish looked mildly surprised. "You trained him."

"I know, but I never thought he'd be *this* good."

Tish cocked her head on one side like an inquisitive sparrow and her dark eyes sparkled. "I think it's the women," she said.

"What women?" Fred looked at her as though she was talking double-Dutch.

"Most of these Lord Mucks that Ernest is selling to have wives and I reckon Ernest gets *them* interested first. I think he's very friendly with some of those ladies . . . very friendly indeed!" Tish's eyes sparkled with impish innuendo.

"I've never heard such rubbish!" Still sounding very Brummie, Fred used horror to conceal the fact that the same thought had been going through his mind.

"I was with him last year, remember."

Fred nodded. In 1932, smitten with a desire to see her parents' native Yorkshire, Tish had spent ten days in the North with Ernest, combining sightseeing with sales follow-up calls.

"I was in the way sometimes," she said, smiling at the memory. "Most of the women are quite refined, you know. They can take to a young gent who treats them nicely."

Astounded by Tish's ready acceptance of their son's techniques, Fred returned to his study of a newspaper.

Some of Ernest's new customers had social aspirations that went beyond the commercial cliques of Birmingham, Manchester and Sheffield. Horse racing was a magic world to them and they had the money to try cutting a dash in it. Ernest, known for his links with Latimer's Barn, was soon being called upon to give advice on how to become an owner.

In blaming Ernest for her increased problems, Leander was, of course, far from serious.

"It's all our own fault," she said to Emma, William and Steven during one of their frequent discussions. "Success seems to come so easily these days."

She had been afraid that after the exploits of Agamemnon they were bound to suffer a few seasons of anti-climax. Certainly there was no horse yet to match the brilliance of their Triple Crown hero, now earning huge stud fees at Cannings St John, but there had been a steady stream of good winners, including the One Thousand Guineas and Oaks of 1930, the Two Thousand Guineas of 1931 and the Oaks of 1932.

Hidden away behind the success, as yet hardly known to the outside world, but constantly living up to his early promise, was Steven. Two years ago, when he was eighteen, he had started full-time work in the yard the day after he left school and was already treated as though he held the licence.

"So what are you going to do?" William asked. "It hurts me to see us turning customers away."

"It's obvious," Steven said. "We must build another yard. You agree, don't you, Leander?"

She had always hated the thought of being called 'Grandmother' so that both Steven and Rachel had always been encouraged to use her name.

"You know I do," she replied.

"Where shall we put it?" William asked.

"Show him!" Steven urged Leander and she took them to the library, where, pressed flat in the Big Book, was the sketch-map used to plan the building programme of 1919.

"There and there," Steven said, pointing out the crosses that Leander had pencilled in alongside the Roadway, one to the south of the 1874 yard, the other facing the 1840 block of ten boxes.

"We'll build there first," Leander said, indicating the location nearest the present yard, opposite the hostel.

"When?" Steven asked eagerly.

"There's a Trustees' meeting next week," Leander replied. "I fancy we shall have Joe Irons here to size it up two or three days after that."

The scheme to build a replica of the 1874 yard, thus turning Latimer's Barn into one of the biggest training establishments in the country with ninety boxes, got under way in March, and for nearly three months normal stable work had to go on alongside a building site. As well as the new quadrangle, further hostel accommodation for twenty extra lads was constructed; the place chosen was adjacent to the new yard on an east–west line that would dictate the pattern of future expansion.

It was a time of excitement, though not for William. At first he seemed merely absent-minded; by the end of April he was clearly wracked with worry.

"What on earth is it, William?" Leander finally asked.

It was one of those very rare occasions when he considered trying to avoid the question; in the end, the instincts of seventy years were far too strong.

"It's Ruth," he replied. "She's been a bit off colour for some time."

"What's the trouble?"

"She says it's nothing."

"She hasn't consulted Kathleen?"

"No."

Only two days ago, Leander had noticed that Ruth was pale, apparently losing weight, and that the customary sparkle was missing.

After a visit from Leander, Kathleen Stanton called at Rose House that evening on the pretext of talking about a bring-and-buy sale that she and Ruth had promised to organise for church funds. William, banished to his study while Ruth and Kathleen discussed 'important women's business', had no idea what passed between them; he was simply grateful when Ruth went across to see Kathleen in her surgery at Oak Cottage the following morning.

Kathleen was fearful from the outset; however, she concealed her suspicions until Ruth had spent a morning at a big hospital in Swindon for X-rays and tests and there had been a chance to discuss the findings with a consultant.

When she could put it off no longer, Kathleen found that it was even worse than anything she had experienced while looking after ex-soldiers in the North.

Ruth, on the other hand, was perfectly calm. "It's bad, isn't it?" she said.

"Yes, I'm very much afraid it is." Kathleen fiddled with the file of papers on her desk.

"Cancer?"

"Yes."

"Whereabouts?"

"We think the pancreas is very badly affected. It doesn't seem that surgery would be useful."

Ruth nodded. "How long?" she asked. "Come on, Kathleen, spit it out. Don't be shy. You've known me long enough."

That, thought Kathleen, was half the trouble.

"It's difficult to say. The pancreas controls the insulin supply to the blood, so all sorts of things start going wrong." She took a deep breath. "Somewhere between two and six months is the best estimate."

After staring out of the window at one of the oak trees that was just coming into leaf, Ruth said, "Poor William." It was the only time she ever expressed sadness.

"I was wondering if you might be more . . . er . . . comfortable in the cottage hospital," Kathleen suggested.

"Good gracious, no!" Suddenly the Ruth of old danced into life. "I belong here. In any case, could you see Leander allowing that?"

Kathleen managed to return the smile. "It's worth thinking about," she insisted gently.

"Will I be a nuisance?" Ruth asked. "People have got more than enough to do without bothering about an old crock."

Kathleen conceded defeat. "I think you might be better off here," she said. "If the Government wants to see how to run a proper welfare system, it ought to come and have a look at Cannings Ambo."

Having helped with nursing the terminally ill often enough, Ruth took the point. "Will the pain get worse?" she asked, betraying slight fear for the first and what was to prove only time.

"Don't worry about that. I'll see that you get the right tablets."

"Thank you, Kathleen – and do cheer up."

Declining the offer of a cup of tea, Ruth went back to face the most difficult task of her life, telling William.

Twelve weeks and four days later, at lunch-time on the first Wednesday of June, Ruth Flamsteed died.

Earlier that morning, she had seemed very much better when William took tea and toast up to her.

"I dreamed about Maude," she told him.

"Oh. How peculiar."

"She's dead, you know. I believe it was all rather dreadful."

Astounded by the matter-of-fact way she said it, William took no notice of the statement. Instead, he persuaded her to eat a little toast, attributing her state of mind to pain-killing drugs.

That afternoon, William used the tools of his trade for the first time in nearly twenty years. Helped by the semi-retired Jim Goakes, he set about making Ruth's coffin.

While they were doing it, the Derby was run. Latimer's Barn was without a runner that year, and, already busy with funeral arrangements, Leander did not listen to the commentary on the wireless: she was, in any case, far too upset.

Hyperion, the diminutive horse who was so small and sickly that they very nearly put him down shortly after he was foaled, won it for Lord Derby. Joe Symes, as vigilant as ever on Leander's behalf, was there to see what was to go into history as one of the greatest performances of all time.

Later, in a public bar between Guildford and Farnborough, when Joe had given up all hope of finding a lift back to Wiltshire that night, he eavesdropped on an intriguing conversation at the next table. A fortune-teller on Epsom Downs had predicted Hyperion's victory and gone on to say that he would be a prepotent sire of fillies.

Not much in that, Joe thought, until the confused babble threw out a staggering fact. Gipsy Ruby O'Grady had made the prophecy at the *previous* year's Derby. Three men swore to it.

Joe finally reached Cannings Ambo to find the village in mourning and it was nearly a week before he was able to report this to Leander. She was strangely impressed by the story of the gipsy's forecast and made a brief note of it in the Big Book after she completed the entry on Ruth's death and funeral.

First William, then Matthew, followed by her grandsons, William and John, threw their handfuls of earth on to Ruth's coffin and it was all over. Cyril Osgood, acting today in his capacity as parish sexton, set to with his spade and the large crowd, that included Fletchers from Birmingham, began to move away from the grave. It was in the special family plot that Leander had chosen over forty years ago, the plot where the graves of her father and husband were already well established.

Amelia, down from Cambridge for the occasion with Silas at her side, watched her mother closely. Ruth's death had produced an unexpected effect on the normally resilient Leander. She had faltered visibly as if momentarily dazed, making Amelia realise how close the two sisters-in-law were in their undemonstrative way.

Silas felt Amelia go tense in the expectation that help might be needed, but Leander was more than equal to the situation. Moving with imperceptibly swift purpose to William's side, she gently displaced the ill-at-ease Matthew and took her brother by the arm.

One of the old carriages was waiting for them at the lychgate. As they set off towards Latimer's Barn together, Amelia was aware that Leander and William were, in many respects, back where they had started. Until young Steven Hawksworth rode along the Devizes Lane on that famous bicycle all those years ago, Leander and William had been closer than most lovers.

Now they went back to Latimer's Barn, the place where they were born, in the transport of their youth, to resume that old relationship.

The new yard and hostel were ready for the end of June and were soon filling up with horses and lads. As in the past, the word that staff were wanted in Cannings Ambo had produced a stream of applicants from all over the country without the need to place an advertisement. For the moment there were to be only seventy horses, but when the yearlings arrived at the end of the year, all ninety boxes were expected to be full.

For Leander, Steven, Emma and Albert Merriweather, the extra horses and a bunch of lads in need of indoctrination presented a challenge that seemed, at first, to defy solution. There were always lads or horses in the wrong place; tack got mixed up or lost; feed-times were chaotic.

"My God, this is worse than 1874," Leander complained at the end of the second week of going backwards. "And that was a much bigger step up than this one. What's wrong with us?"

But things soon started to come right and, as they did so, Leander noticed that William was doing his best to help, and enjoying it. An idea occurred to her.

"William, I know Steven will be old enough to take over the licence next year, but why don't you carry on for a bit longer? I think it would be good for you."

He accepted the point. His work with the stable, especially taking horses to the races, to some extent kept his mind away from the loss of Ruth.

"What about Steven?" William asked. "Won't he be disappointed?"

"Leave him to me," Leander replied.

William went through the motions of mulling it over for a couple of days.

"Mind you, Lea, I don't want Steven upset about this," he said. "If he doesn't like it, I'll bow out gracefully."

"Steven thinks it's a splendid idea," Leander told him. "He says you can take as long as you like."

"You've spoken to him already?"

"I saw no point in messing about!"

"All right," William said. "While you're in that sort of mood, there's something else we must attend to. I think I should come and live with you all the time so that Matthew, Louise and the boys can have Rose House."

William had hardly spent any time at Rose House since Ruth's death, but Leander was upset. "Oh, William, what a shame!" It was the impulsive reaction of a very much younger Leander who hated the thought of him leaving the house that he and Jim Goakes had rebuilt. A few moments' consideration showed that he was right, however.

"And what shall we do with Louise House?" she asked.

"Oh, I don't know," William said, waving a carefree hand. "I expect you'll think of something. You always do, Lea."

She soon did. Taking over the lovely house on the Back Stretch, which she had admired since it was built, appealed instantly to Amelia.

"Have Silas there if you want," Leander said. "But be discreet about it. And I shall probably want to use it for bed and breakfast when people like Clem and Hubert come to stay. When you're not at Cambridge, I shall expect you to be the perfect hostess."

"As long as you don't start foisting any old Tom, Dick or Harry on me," Amelia said.

With a look that the Duchess of Laverstoke at her most imperious might have envied, Leander said, "We don't know any people like that, my dear child!"

Eric Hargreaves, who regarded himself as a man of the times, put paid to that illusion.

He was one of the four new owners captured by Ernest Cartwright, all self-made men in search of a social cachet. Whereas three of them approached Latimer's Barn with suitable diffidence and respect, Eric Hargreaves barged in like a bull in a china shop, spraying over-familiarity, nauseating bonhomie and sheer ignorance everywhere.

"Now, Mother," Amelia whispered as Leander's face became a picture after Hargreaves's opening display, "don't be a snob. Times are changing. We have to be much more democratic nowadays."

Leander's struggle to avoid laying violent hands on Amelia was not helped by the fact that her daughter was nearly choking with bottled-up laughter.

Not that Hargreaves noticed: he was far too engrossed in talking to William, rather as if he were addressing a group of mentally defective shareholders.

"I'm going to be straight with you, Mr Flamsteed — I'm always straight with folks and I daresay you'll soon get used to it. Now, look here, if you can prove to me that you know what you're doing with these six ponies of mine, I'll consider getting another half-dozen. I

503

can't say fairer than that, can I?" Taking another look round, he gave a sniff that might have been appreciative. "And I must say, this isn't a bad little place you've got here – bit too soft and pretty-pretty for my taste, but none the worse for that."

Like Amelia, William was able to appreciate the funny side of it. To Hargreaves, money was God: ten minutes after arriving in Cannings Ambo, he boasted of being able to lay his hands on one hundred thousand pounds if pushed. William curbed a strong urge to tell him that, a few days ago, the Fund had passed the one and a half million pound mark.

Eric Hargreaves seemed to be aged about forty-five and was the overweeningly proud owner of a small but expanding engineering works to the north of Manchester. He had started in scrap after the War, a conflict in which he had played no part due to a minor medical defect: his repeated lamentations on the subject were among the worst of his many awful characteristics.

Utter insensitivity to atmosphere was another. After reducing one Sunday to a shambles with an unannounced visit, he repeated the performance the following week, turning up with his wife.

"The good lady and I drove down yesterday afternoon," Hargreaves insisted on telling William. "We put up at an hotel in Chippenham. Between you and me, Mr Flamsteed, Mrs Hargreaves prefers the city to this country caper. I'm hoping to convert her."

One look at the sour-faced, overweight woman, who was even more conscious of the Hargreaves money than her husband, caused William to doubt whether she could be converted to anything. In this case, Tish Cartwright's theory must surely fall flat: whatever else might have induced Eric Hargreaves to become a racehorse owner, it was hardly Ernest's beguiling influence on this self-centred battleaxe.

"So help me," Leander fumed when peace and quiet returned. "If that awful man does that again, I'll swing for him!"

The following Sunday, Hargreaves appeared yet again, this time finding his own way into the newest of the yards without being spotted from The House or hostel.

Not quite everyone had their feet up or was out enjoying the fine weather. Hearing footsteps, Steven emerged from the box of a filly whose off foreleg was causing great concern and advanced on the unwelcome visitor. They had not met before, but Steven knew both the identity and character of the bombastic individual who was beginning to think that he owned part of Cannings Ambo.

Something about Steven made Hargreaves uneasy: if this was a hired hand, he seemed to have a damned high opinion of himself, and Steven's, "Good afternoon, may I help you?" was altogether too cocky.

"Hargreaves. I've come to look at my horses," was delivered in a manner calculated to take the wind out of upstart sails. Instead, the conversation careered off in a direction that left Hargreaves hopelessly wrong-footed.

"Oh, forgive me." Steven's manner changed from supercilious caution to friendly acceptance. "How do you do, Sir Eric? I'm Steven Hawksworth. I shall be taking over in a year or two when Great-Uncle William decides to retire."

Bemused, Hargreaves submitted to Steven's firm handshake and found that his attempt to speak was defeated.

"Your horses are a nice bunch," Steven said warmly. "There's one in particular that I fancy might do rather well. If you'll come this way, please, Sir Eric."

Hargreaves was left with no option; he had to follow Steven at a fast pace across the cobbles to a box on the other side of the quadrangle.

"You've got it wrong, lad . . . er, Steven," he managed to say when they arrived. "I'm not *Sir* Eric. It's just plain Mister."

"Oh!" Steven stepped back in surprise. "I say, I'm awfully sorry. I'm afraid I assumed . . ." After appearing to think about it, he was pleased. "I think it's a good thing . . . sign of the times and all that."

"How do you mean?" Hargreaves asked.

"Well . . ." Steven looked round furtively to make sure they were alone. "Don't breathe a word of this, Mr Hargreaves, but it's Grandmother, you see. She really is tremendously class-conscious."

"What, old Mrs Hawksworth? What's she got to do with it?"

"Oh, she runs Latimer's Barn! Didn't you realise that?"

The look on Hargreaves's face was eloquent of his conviction that women should keep in their place and not be allowed to run anything. "Isn't she a bit old to be interfering in things she doesn't understand?" he asked.

"Oh no!" Steven remained perfectly serious. "She's only seventy-three and she knows an immense amount about the business. She did her first Derby winner when she was sixteen – and there have been five more since, of course. No, her only problem is this awful class thing. She's never let anyone less than a baronet be an owner here."

The lie, delivered with conviction, put Hargreaves back where he had started, grappling with the awful feeling that he was out of his depth.

"I can't tell you how pleased I am that she's decided to let ordinary fellows like you in," Steven continued. "It's going to make a big difference. I've nothing against our old-established owners, but they can be a pain in the backside . . . still, you'll find out about that soon enough. Let me tell you about this colt. We're sending him to Salisbury next week and I can't see him disgracing us. He worked well the other day. We let him down at the distance and he came away very nicely."

They visited all six of Hargreaves's horses. No one came near the yard, and for over an hour Steven talked total rubbish, wrapping it all up in every piece of racing mumbo-jumbo he could think of. Not once did Eric Hargreaves have the courage to ask for an explanation of what was spouted at him: he simply prayed for it to end.

When they finally left the yard and walked along the Roadway, Steven halted as they passed the gable-end of the 1840 stable and indicated the lawn.

"Don't *ever* walk across that," he whispered. "It is *absolutely* forbidden. I did it once when I was little and got skinned alive. It's a thing that goes back to Great-Grandfather's time." While Hargreaves was absorbing this, Steven added a juicy morsel. "Great-Grandfather came here in 1859, by the way. You'll be expected to know things like that. Ah, there's Hubert and Clementine."

Like all friends and honoured guests, they had left their car at the front of The House and were strolling round to the back door.

"Who are they?" Hargreaves asked, made suspicious by the cut of their clothes and their bearing.

"The Duke and Duchess of Laverstoke," Steven replied, returning the Duke's cheerful wave. "Come in and have tea with them."

"No, thank you, Steven." Hargreaves looked at his watch with ostentatious vigour. "I must think about making tracks . . . there's a bloke at Macclesfield I want to see on the way back." He was hurrying now, very nearly breaking into an ungainly trot. "Thank you, Steven, that was very interesting. I must come again some time."

"Remember, don't breathe a word about me marking your card," Steven said.

"You can rely on me, Steven," Hargreaves promised and dived for his car.

He managed to escape just before Leander appeared, as it was inevitable that she would. Steven smiled as he pictured what the Duchess must have said. "I say, Leander, there's a most *extraordinary* person out there with young Steven. Is everything all right, do you suppose?"

Glaring at the back of the car disappearing into the cool, dark

506

shade of the poplars, Leander seethed. "Was that Hargreaves?" she demanded.

"It was."

"That man is the limit. The very next time he sets foot here . . ."

"Leander! Shush!" Steven said. "I think I've fixed him."

"Really? How?"

As he explained, she smiled, chuckled and finally laughed so much that Steven had to support her.

"Oh, my dear," she gasped, wiping tears away, "that is gorgeous! Did you think he'd come today?"

"I had a feeling."

"Aha!" She nodded happily. "I was wondering why you'd stayed in. That was good of you. Come on, let's tell Clem. She'll enjoy this!"

Steven worked at least sixty hours a week at Latimer's Barn with a calmly studious dedication that won great admiration. Unlike any of his predecessors, however, his education in Marlborough had left him with a close circle of friends who were nothing to do with racing.

Clive Redmayne's father, an architect, had a passion for sailing which he indulged by keeping an eighty-ton schooner, *Merry Dance*, at Lymington on the Solent. Steven had fallen in love with the beautifully restored old vessel when he was thirteen and had shamelessly scrounged a day out aboard her at every opportunity. Norman Redmayne, hampered by the war-legacy of an artificial leg, was constantly grateful for offers of help and encouraged Steven. At eighteen, Steven acquired his own car, an Austin Seven, and left Cannings Ambo no later than five o'clock on Sunday mornings, returning after midnight. When there was no racing, he sometimes went on Saturday afternoons to spend the night afloat.

His companions on the journeys to the coast were usually Jack Langton, another school-friend, now building a promising career for himself with Mallender and Giffard, and his sister Molly, a year younger than Steven. Molly was a plain, robust girl who achieved a measure of attractiveness by virtue of a cheerful and kindly disposition. Very fond of horses, Molly visited Latimer's Barn from time to time and the assumption gradually grew that she and Steven had some sort of 'understanding'. Certainly Rachel thought so and teased her brother incessantly over 'good old Molly'.

Steven was content to allow the myth to drift on: during the summer of 1933, he sheltered behind it, concealing the fact that he had been knocked off-balance by a new member of the schooner's crew.

Norman Redmayne's daughter, Ann, was seventeen. Steven's long-standing relationship with Clive had naturally made him aware of a little sister, but because she was a confounded nuisance, she was ignored or avoided. It was a relief when she was sent away to a boarding-school in Kent: Steven never saw her for six years.

Then, quite out of the blue, she turned up at Lymington one weekend, a vision of perfect loveliness. Incapable of treating her with anything other than tongue-tied awe, Steven actually did his best to avoid her, a far from easy thing in the confines of the *Merry Dance*. The basis for his action was the belief that half the eligible young men in Wiltshire would be queuing for her favours so that his pathetic efforts could only be greeted with disdain. Ann Redmayne, prepared to be impressed by the heir to Latimer's Barn, thought him a very odd fish.

Steven's ineptitude with Ann stemmed largely from the fact that he felt none of the average young man's desperate need for the approval and love of a woman outside his family. For the time being, the three very special women in his life, Emma, Amelia and Leander, gave him everything he wanted.

Despite her widowhood, Emma often thought that she was one of the luckiest women alive. Steven had always shown her the greatest love and respect; she felt that he was constantly doing his best to make up for Giles's dreadfully untimely death. At least once a week, he brought her flowers or some other small gift, almost as though he was trying to woo her. And always, there was an old-fashioned courtesy: Steven stood up when his mother entered a room, opened doors for her and was invariably on hand when she needed help.

When Steven had a knotty problem, he took it to Amelia, who sometimes found it difficult to live up to the high expectations he had of her intellect. They spent hours on end talking about everything under the sun, with Amelia coming to look on him as a brother rather than a nephew.

Some people did not know what to make of Steven's relationship with Leander. Even Jim Goakes, who had known her all his life and thought he was used to her unorthodox ways, was sometimes dismayed by the apparent lack of respect that Leander tolerated from her grandson. When the occasion demanded, they were capable of behaving according to the rules, but mostly they were like a pair of exuberant children, constantly threatening to become naughty.

"He's keeping her young," Emma said to Amelia one afternoon as they walked over Cannings Down in search of wild flowers, while Leander and Steven trailed along behind, a constant stream of irreverent comment and laughter running between them.

"I'd never thought of that," Amelia said. "I suppose even she needs it."

508

And there was Rachel, eighteen, finished with school and wanting nothing more than to spend the rest of her life in the yard. She understood Steven better than anyone else: one of her favourite pastimes was to shock and outrage that part of him that she considered far too stuffy for his own good. On a sultry August afternoon, she was given the chance of a lifetime.

"Steven! You'll never guess what," she gasped as she burst into the tack-room, breathless and sweating after running all the way.

"You're right, I won't," Steven replied, irritated by the interruption to his experiments with a bridle.

"Aunt Amelia and Silas are having sexual intercourse up by Powell's Pool."

It was indeed the best yet: Steven gaped at her. She could see that he was trying to disbelieve her and not making a very good job of it. "How do you know?" he asked.

"Because I *saw* them! If I'd gone any further I should have fallen over them. They were going at it hammer and tongs."

"What were you doing up there?"

"I was going for a swim. I imagine that's what they'd been doing before they got carried away."

"Rubbish! You're making it up, Rachel. Aunt Amelia's far too old to go in for that sort of thing."

Rachel exploded with laughter. "Steven, you're the world's biggest idiot! And you don't know anything *important*. Aunt Amelia's only forty-six."

"Are you sure?"

"She was born in 1887. It's in the Big Book for goodness' sake! She's no age at all, really – and she's got the most lovely breasts. I wish mine were as good."

That was too much. "Go away, sister!" Steven commanded. "I've got work to do."

During evening stables, conducted that day by Steven, Amelia and Silas sauntered into the new yard to have a look at one of Claude Timberlake's horses, a filly of whom great things were expected. When they went back to Louise House, they were puzzled by the succession of extremely strange looks they had received from Steven.

Only a few days after that incident, Rachel's life took a most dramatic turn.

The Duchess of Laverstoke telephoned Leander.

"Will you warn Emma that my blasted son is coming to see her on 'a matter of some importance'." She used a mock-solemn voice for the last part.

"Who, Charles?" Leander asked.

"He's the only one I've got who's still hanging around, thank God!"

"What does he want, Clem?"

"He's going to ask permission to take your granddaughter out to dinner."

"And press his suit?" There was laughter below the surface of Leander's voice.

"Oh yes, I'm afraid so! He really does seem to be rather taken with her. For what it's worth, I've told him he has my blessing. Rachel's a good gel."

When Charles Prideaux came to Latimer's Barn to speak to Emma, he wasted no time in placing all his cards on the table.

"I've been told that it's high time I gave serious thought to marriage, Mrs Hawksworth," he said and Emma was able to imagine how the Duchess had put the point to him. "The fact of the matter is that I'm very fond of Rachel and she's certainly the most *suitable* girl I've come across. Even my mother thinks so!"

"We must wait and see what Rachel herself thinks about that, Charles," Emma replied, giving no indication of what she thought. "I have no objection to you asking her – at the appropriate time, of course. Don't be in too much of a hurry."

Rachel, who had never forgotten her 'scrumptious' marquess, made no secret of her delight at his dinner invitation and brought a glow to his face with the enthusiasm of her acceptance.

"My word!" Leander said when Emma gave her the details. "This is a bit of a turn-up for the book, isn't it? It looks very much as if our little bundle of joy is going to grow up to be a marchioness."

"And probably a duchess, if that's what she wants – and if she doesn't make a mess of it," Emma replied.

"Charles won't let her do that," Leander said. "He's got a very good head on his shoulders, despite what Clem says about him."

She was right. In one evening, Rachel's dinner with Charles Prideaux gave her maturity and a new sense of purpose that left Emma open-mouthed. Almost immediately, she received a formal invitation from Charles's mother to spend a weekend at Eaton Mandeville.

On the same miserably wet morning at the end of October, both Matthew and Leander received reminders of the War.

Matthew was busy in his office at Rose House when Louise came in with his morning coffee and a message.

"There's a Mrs Brown asking to see you, darling. She's been

510

hanging about for nearly an hour. I told her you were busy with the accounts, but she insists."

"Brown?" Matthew looked blank. "Am I supposed to know her?"

"She says so. Apparently her maiden name was Meadowes."

"Ah . . . Penelope Meadowes!" Matthew hunched forward over his desk, looking grim as the memory of that appalling evening nearly twenty years ago came back to him.

"Is anything wrong?" Louise asked anxiously.

"No, it's all right. Send her in, Lou."

Although he had not seen her for years, Matthew knew most of the story. She had married a man called Leslie Brown, some sort of financier, just after the War and had gone to live in London. Thereafter, she was seen alone in Marlborough far too often for anyone to believe that the marriage was a success. Three years ago, she had returned to Marlborough for good and there was talk of divorce.

Her parents were dead, their house sold to pay debts and her younger sister, Pauline, was said to be doing well in Australia. Matthew presumed that Penelope was having difficulty supporting herself.

When Louise guided her into the office, Penelope's appearance shocked him: most of her beauty was gone, lost in pinched hope-lessness.

"Thank you for seeing me, Matthew," she said and subsided into the chair he indicated. She realised that he was not going to speak so that it was up to her.

"That white feather . . ." she began and faltered.

"Water under the bridge," Matthew said brusquely.

"It was a terrible thing to do. Pauline has never forgiven me. I don't even get a Christmas card from her these days."

"Lots of people did the same thing," Matthew told her. "It was the 'spirit of the times'." There was a sneer in his voice.

"You never told anyone about it, did you?"

"No. Gerald made me promise not to."

"That was good of you, Matthew."

"It was probably better than you deserved," he said. "If my Aunt Leander had ever found out about that, Penelope, you would have had a very unpleasant time, I can assure you. Now, why have you come to see me?"

"I need a job. I heard you were looking for polishers and fin-ishers."

Remembering all that he had learned from his father and sorely missed mother, Matthew crushed the desire to tell her to go to hell.

"Those jobs aren't right for you," he said. "I don't suppose you're used to that sort of work." Before she could protest her willingness to do anything, he went on, "I happen to know that Mallender and Giffard have some vacancies. That would be much more up your street. I can talk to Jocelyn Mallender about it."

"That's very good of you, Matthew. I won't let you down."

"Worry about Mr Mallender, not me," Matthew said and reached for the telephone.

As he arranged an appointment for Penelope to see Jocelyn, Steven was driving Leander into Marlborough for a minor shopping spree.

When she had found what she wanted, Leander hauled Steven into the bookshop in search of the latest Lord Peter Wimsey novel by Dorothy L. Sayers, a writer she enjoyed and felt duty-bound to support after discovering that she was an old girl of the Godolphin School. Having found *Murder Must Advertise*, she carried on browsing while Steven stuck his nose in a book about navigation. Very soon, her eye was caught by a collection of poems by Rupert Brooke. As she took it down from the shelf, her mind flew to the time she had caught a brief glimpse of him, the day that he, Amelia and several hundred other hopefuls had graduated twenty-five years ago. What was it a disapproving Amelia had said? 'He wants to travel, set the world to rights and write poetry.'

He had, Leander discovered, died on his way to Gallipoli in 1915, only seven years after that golden occasion. She looked through his poems until an impatient Steven indicated his desire to be off.

People found multitudes of reasons for avoiding the subject, but Leander knew that the mass slaughter of young men had damaged the country badly. In commerce, industry and public life, the absence of their talents was painfully evident. How many hundreds of thousands had there been like Giles and Gerald, who, now aged between forty and fifty, would be at the height of their powers?

At least it could never happen again, and soon the baleful after-effects of those terrible four years might finally disappear.

CHAPTER 29

1935

'They'd think I was going ga-ga'

Amelia was uneasy from the start. As the train sped down the Rhine gorge between Coblenz and Mainz, beautiful even on a grey March morning, she asked herself over and over again why she had come.

To her shame, she admitted that it was pride that had brought her back to Germany. During the last three years, the research project she was directing had produced findings of such startling significance that she wanted her friend Otto Edelson and his colleagues to be the first to hear about them. So, while the papers for the learned journals were being typeset, she was on her way to Munich, assured of an appreciative audience and warm congratulations. There was even talk of the great Professor Ernst Walther joining them from Dresden.

She was undertaking the trip against the advice of Silas, and, once pride was set aside, her own instincts. In January 1933, Adolf Hitler, the big joke, the man who would never win votes, had become Chancellor of Germany. Joseph Goebbels, whom she had last seen bawling hatred and abuse through a megaphone, was Minister of Public Enlightenment and Propaganda. She feared for the sort of country she was going to find.

Just as he had done in his letters, Otto said all the right-sounding, optimistic things when he met her, but his every word and gesture had an undercurrent of strain. It was the same with Elsa: as they ate the dinner, Amelia saw that she was always listening, alert to the sounds outside the house. Hans, young Otto and the twin girls, Annaliese and Trudi, born since Amelia's previous visit, watched their mother constantly, sharing her nervous restlessness.

"Otto, what is wrong?" Amelia asked him when they were alone for a few minutes. "What are you all waiting for?"

"Nothing, Amelia. We sometimes get very . . . er . . . wound-up by the pace of life in our country these days. That man Hitler is performing wonders, you know."

"He isn't a joke any more?"

"No, oh no! There is an economic miracle and we all have to work very hard."

Completely unconvinced, Amelia let the matter drop.

Much the same atmosphere pervaded the Mathematics Faculty at the university; after three days of expounding her theories to an attentive audience of twelve top-class mathematicians, Amelia was becoming used to it.

When they gathered again on the fourth morning, the questions began. The critical dissection of Amelia's hypothesis was fiercely enthusiastic, but friendly, and, as ever, she thrived on the challenge.

They had been embroiled for an hour or so and Amelia was busy developing an argument on the blackboard when the door burst open and old *Doktor* Kesselmann, one of the university's administrators, almost fell into the small lecture-room. He had been pushed by two thugs in brown shirts; behind them were more men, in dark suits.

"Er . . . Professor Edelson . . ." Poor old Kesselmann hardly knew what he was doing. "These gentlemen wish to interview you."

Otto did his best to brazen it out.

"Really, Kesselmann, we're very busy. Can't you see that? You should have known better than to interrupt us."

At once, one of the dark-suited men stepped forward: Amelia thought it strangely menacing that he should be wearing skin-tight black leather gloves.

"Professor Edelson, you will come with us. At once, if you please." The tone was soft, the intimidation unmistakable, and the brown-shirts were poised.

Grumbling, Otto stood up, went to the door and was gone. Kesselmann hesitated, looked round helplessly, then followed. In the vacuum of embarrassed, speculative silence, the tension mounted until, one by one, Otto's colleagues mumbled excuses and left, all ten of them slinking away with hardly a sound, leaving only Amelia and Ernst Walther.

"Pah! These Nazis interfere in everything!" Walther snapped. "Come, *Doktor* Hawksworth, we carry on with your theory. There are one or two questions I have."

To Amelia's immense relief, Otto was away for less than half an hour; any longer with the punctiliously determined Walther acting as though nothing had happened and she would have screamed.

"What is it?" she asked Otto, who looked dazed, incapable of speech.

"I am dismissed." He smiled sadly. "It is because my grandfather was a Jew." Irrelevantly, he added, "He came from Cracow."

"Otto, there must be some mistake. They can't do that. It's monstrous!" Amelia was outraged.

"Oh yes, they can, dear lady," Walther said. "They act as they please and there is nothing to be done about it. Otto, my friend, I am sorry, very, very sorry." Ernst Walther was suddenly a far more sympathetic man than Amelia had imagined.

Ex-Professor Edelson nodded his thanks. "I have to clear my cupboards out. Tomorrow will do for that. I think we go to Elsa now, Amelia."

Elsa's reaction seemed astonishing. "So, it has happened. Good! We know where we stand. Now you will take that post at Harvard."

"I don't know, my dear," Otto murmured unhappily. "It's a very big step . . . an upheaval."

"So, what do you do instead, eh? You think Schickelgruber's bully boys will let you work somewhere else? No, of course not! How shall we live, Otto?"

"What *is* going on in this country?" Amelia asked.

"The Nazis despise Jews," Elsa said. "The Jews are responsible for everything that has ever gone wrong with Germany, according to our *Führer*. So, the Jews are being removed from all the professions and public office. That is the first step. In a while I think maybe they start shooting us!"

"Elsa! Please!" Otto said. "This is only supposition, wild rumour!"

After they had eaten the scratch lunch that Elsa produced at short notice, Amelia shifted uncomfortably in her chair. "Otto, I'm afraid that Germany is making me feel sick," she said. "I must go home as soon as possible."

"Of course, my dear! There is the sleeping-car train to the Hook of Holland at eight o'clock this evening. I will go now to get you a reservation."

The tension of people pretending to be normal under impossibly difficult circumstances made the afternoon interminable. When Otto drove her to the train, Amelia had Elsa's final words ringing in her ears.

"This man Hitler will not only be bad for Germany, Amelia, he will ruin it for *everybody*. He is building up the Army and telling us that we must have more *Lebensraum*. There will be war!"

"Elsa is overwrought," Otto said as they walked down the platform in search of Amelia's carriage. "She is seeing demons that do not exist."

"Is there really a job for you at Harvard?" Amelia asked.

515

"Yes, there is. Not a professorship, of course, but a good offer all the same. I think I will take it."

"You must, Otto, for Elsa and the children."

"I expect so," he said vaguely.

"Promise me you will! And write to me, Otto, write!"

"I expect so," he said again, looking round in bewilderment. They could hardly hear themselves speak for the noise: propaganda was blaring through the loudspeakers and a group of black-shirted *Schutz Staffeln*, the élite of the Third Reich's thugs, were creating uproar as they dragged two pitiful-looking old men off a train for Switzerland on the adjoining platform.

"Nazi Germany is a very noisy place," Otto remarked wryly as he waved goodbye.

There was frightening mayhem when the train stopped at Augsburg, and two hours later, at Stuttgart, the SS went through every carriage, demanding identification papers.

Amelia spent a frightful night. She lay on the hard berth, fully clothed, clutching her passport to brandish like a talisman at intruders. A little before six in the morning, when the train crossed the Dutch border, she finally fell into a fitful doze.

On a night that seemed terrifyingly dark and stormy, Silas met her at Savernake off the last train from London. She insisted on going to his forest lodge rather than Louise House and told him of her experiences as they banged and rattled their way towards the sanctuary which she craved so desperately.

"It was dreadful, Silas, absolutely dreadful," she concluded. "The atmosphere in Germany is poisonous."

"That's why I wasn't very keen on you going," he said sadly.

"How did you know?"

"It's all there if you read the right newspapers carefully."

Seated in front of a cheerful fire with a mug of tea to which she had allowed Silas to add a little whisky, Amelia remembered Elsa's warning.

"*Frau* Edelson believes that Hitler is hell-bent on war," she said.

"One or two think that," Silas replied. "Claude was talking to a chap the other day who reckons 1942 is the year to look out for. Germany will be very strong by then."

"This can't be true, Silas."

"I don't know." He was thoughtful for a few moments. "Most people seem to have their heads in the sand and don't want to believe it. It is a bit far-fetched, but I've got a nasty feeling that Hitler *does* mean business."

516

"Oh dear! I suppose I'd better warn Mother."

"You can try," Silas smiled. "I don't know how much notice she'll take of you. There's this, you see." He passed the previous day's *Times* to her, open at the Court page and folded so that the paragraph was strikingly prominent.

The engagement is announced between The Most Honourable Charles Prideaux, Marquess of Glastonbury, eldest son of Their Graces the Duke and Duchess of Laverstoke of Eaton Mandeville and Rachel, only daughter of the late Major Giles Hawksworth VC and Mrs Emma Hawksworth of Latimer's Barn, near Marlborough, Wiltshire.

"The wedding is in July," Silas said.

"Oh!" Amelia was taken aback by the news. "I thought this wasn't going to happen until next year when Rachel was twenty-one."

"Rupert says they got fed up of waiting."

Before travelling to Germany, Amelia had spent a month at Cambridge, deeply immersed in her work; the decision had been taken during that period.

"Well!" She considered it. "We shall need some *real* gladrags for the wedding. It's going to be the biggest do we've ever had."

Silas nodded. "And while they're getting ready for it, I don't give much for your chances of persuading them that Hitler is looking for trouble."

Amelia smiled weakly. "That surely can't be right, anyway," she said.

"I hope not. Come along, you're exhausted." Taking her in his arms, he carried her up to bed.

There was excitement at Latimer's Barn and in the village about the forthcoming wedding, but it was all carefully controlled; there was certainly no question of its being allowed to interfere with the work of getting ninety horses ready for a new racing season. Indeed, once the initial surge of pleasure and comment that followed the announcement had died down, there was more interest in the changes taking place in the yard.

Steven was now in charge and only twenty-two, despite the impression he often gave of being much older. As well as being a year younger than his father when he assumed responsibility for the licence, he was going to be the first man for over sixty years to care for the horses without the day-to-day advice of Leander. At seventy-five, though still nimble and with all her senses as powerfully alert as ever, she had decided to retire. Everyone knew that she spent a great deal of time at her bedroom window with binoculars each morning, and she was out on the gallop in a carriage on Wednesdays and Saturdays when Steven organised the most strenuous pieces of work, but she was content to say very little.

To emphasise the change, there was a new head lad. At William's suggestion, Albert Merriweather retired slightly early, thus avoiding an awkward transition later on and the possibility of disagreement with Steven. Albert was the first to admit that after nearly twenty years with William, he was far too accustomed to his own way to be at ease with a young man known to have novel ideas. So, without the slightest ripple, Albert's son, Alfred, became Steven's right-hand man and a Trustee. They had already demonstrated how closely alike they thought and wasted no time in tackling difficult problems.

Logarithm had been controversial from the start.

Many considered it an act of downright disloyalty when Charles Prideaux had bought him at the Newmarket yearling sales. What, they muttered, was wrong with their own 'home grown' produce from the stud? Some extremely funny looks were exchanged when it became known that Steven was with Charles as his adviser on the day of the purchase.

Hardly had the colt set foot inside the yard than Rachel commandeered him, acting on the principle that she was the natural choice to look after her beloved's valuable property, and no one saw fit to argue with her.

Logarithm's two-year-old career was a travesty that made people laugh or come close to tears, depending on their mood and the circumstances. He was, by turn, bone idle and affable, or highly strung and almost dangerously temperamental. One day, Rachel would be unable to get him to canter, the next, he would cart her all the way to Cannings St John to see Josie Dundas, for whom he had developed a soft spot.

He was risked on a racecourse only once, at Newbury in September, two months after the most backward of his contemporaries had made their débuts. It was to prove the only time in all the thousands of rides he had that Mark Pilgrim became thoroughly irritated with a horse. Half-way through the seven furlongs, Mark gave Logarithm an almighty swipe across the rump, so surprising the perverse animal that, for the first time ever, he produced a rousing gallop that gained him nearly twenty lengths to finish a respectable-looking fourth. Mark had no wish to discuss the race afterwards and Logarithm was allowed to go his own way for what was left of the season.

In March 1935, when Rachel was eager to have another go at the wayward colt, Steven shook his head firmly.

"No, Rachel, you'll be leaving to marry Charles in July," he said. "It isn't fair to the horse to swap and change."

"Oh, Steven, don't be a spoilsport! I quite like the wretch, and it isn't as if he's ever going to be any good."

"I'm giving him to Jimmy Farrant," Steven said, trying to make it sound inconsequential.

"Oh! I see!" Rachel was alert, with narrowed eyes.

Jimmy Farrant, barely sixteen and in only his second year at Latimer's Barn, was already something of a lucky charm to Steven and Alfred Merriweather. A native of Chippenham, Jimmy had what Leander swore was quite the most outrageous riding style ever seen on Cannings Down; he also possessed a degree of self-confidence that sometimes seemed alarming to a casual observer. Yet Jimmy had a phenomenal ability to turn a difficult horse into something resembling pure silver if not gold.

"So, what's the plan?" Rachel asked.

"There isn't one at the moment," Steven replied. "I simply want to see what Jimmy can do with him."

Logarithm had wintered well and came into his coat early, giving an impression of condition and vitality. He seemed to think he should have a prize for this; instead, on his first time out with Jimmy Farrant, he learned that acting the fool would no longer be tolerated.

Swept up into arrangements for her wedding, Rachel missed all the subsequent fun and games, and knew nothing about the race at Newbury in mid-April until the day after it was run when she opened a newspaper and found that Logarithm was being spoken of as an exciting prospect for the Two Thousand Guineas.

Rachel was spending a few days at Eaton Mandeville; she, Emma and the Duchess were drawing up detailed plans for the wedding and it was late evening before Rachel was able to telephone Steven.

"What the devil have you been doing to my boy Logarithm?" she demanded.

"Nothing. Jimmy's had a few words with him."

"Was this a good race he won?"

"Not bad." Steven allowed himself the luxury of a slight pause for effect. "One or two chaps seem to have been impressed with the way he clipped a few seconds off the course record."

"Is that why they're saying he looks like a good each-way bet for the Guineas?"

"Who am I to understand how the minds of the 'experts' work?" Steven asked demurely.

"But you are running him?"

"I shall have to talk to Charles, of course, but I think the beast deserves a chance after yesterday. Mark was pleased with him."

"Ought we to go and watch this race?" Rachel asked in an attempt to make Steven commit himself.

"You might kick yourselves if you don't," was the tantalising reply.

Only a handful of fleecy-white clouds disturbed the blue sky above Newmarket Heath on the day the Two Thousand Guineas was run and a much larger gathering than usual turned up to see it. Many treated it as a social occasion to herald the start of the summer that would celebrate the Silver Jubilee of King George and Queen Mary. It was also confidently expected to see the end of the Depression, giving England a chance to rejoice over peace and a measure of prosperity for the first time in over twenty years.

Logarithm received massive home support. Steven was accompanied by Emma and Leander, both of whom regarded the Guineas meeting as one of the highlights of their year; Rachel and Charles were in a party that included the Duke and Duchess, Matthew and Louise, and, as a specially honoured guest, Rhona Pilgrim. There were also the Timberlakes: Rupert had brought Claude and his attractive wife, Lily, for their first visit to Newmarket. Silas, free of his protection duties now that law and order had returned to racecourses, escorted Amelia.

In addition to the usual motley collection of racing journalists, there were several reporters and photographers from society journals. Once they had spotted her, Rachel soon found herself coping with her new status as they pestered her for words of wisdom and pictures of her and Charles looking happy together.

And after the race, the most thrilling Two Thousand Guineas for many years, there were dozens more photographs as Charles led Logarithm into the winner's enclosure, a consequence of the colt's decision to make a proper job of it as the field passed the Bushes, about two furlongs out.

"I thought that horse was supposed to be useless," the Duchess grumbled to Leander, peeved at having missed the generous odds of ten to one. "What's your grandson been doing to him?"

"Jimmy Farrant," Leander replied.

"Oh, him! I see." The Duchess knew of Jimmy's magical properties. "Still . . ." she brightened up ". . . I see Rachel's doing well with those magazine people. We should be able to fill a scrapbook or two with today's handiwork."

She was proved right and Leander had every reason to be doubly proud. While the high-quality magazines extolled the virtues of the future Marchioness of Glastonbury, the national and racing press devoted a great deal of space to Steven's production of a Classic winner at his first attempt, predicting a brilliant future for him and his famous stable.

Secretly, Leander still grieved for Giles. Because of his youth, his death was the greatest loss of her life: but the children he and Emma had produced were the finest possible compensation.

By the time her wedding day arrived, Rachel had opened dozens of fêtes and fairs on the extensive Laverstoke estates, and attended so many balls at which she was the focal point, that her natural talent to grab and enjoy the centre of the stage was honed to perfection. This was just as well, for the ceremony that made her a marchioness was a very grand and daunting affair.

The setting, Bath Abbey, was dictated by a family tradition extending back to 1773.

"To be perfectly honest with you, I wish we could have a nice quiet do at your place," the Duchess had confessed to Leander.

"We haven't got nearly enough room," Leander said, rather looking forward to the splendour of the abbey.

"No, and even if you had, Hubert would put his foot down. He's a stickler for the family whatnot! I'll tell you this, it put the fear of God up me when I had to go through it and Charles is starting to go green at the prospect."

Rachel, however, had no such qualms. She took the rehearsal, an embarrassingly botched affair that left Charles on the brink of a nervous breakdown, in her stride, and sailed up the aisle as the personification of confidence on the day itself. Her self-possession was so great that she was able to steady Matthew who was giving her away: entering by the west door, he took one look at the congregation of over six hundred that included a Royal duke as well as half the House of Lords and felt decidedly sick.

When it was all safely over and they were back in the Great Hall at Eaton Mandeville for the wedding breakfast, the Duke beamed at Leander and said, "We finally did it, my dear. Patience and persistence, you see! Come to think of it, I've half a mind to adopt that as a new family motto."

"What *are* you going on about, Hubert?" Leander asked.

"Have you forgotten that my dear old Uncle Piers once proposed to you?" the Duke asked.

"Oh Lord, yes, so he did!" Leander laughed.

"And you turned him down flat."

"I'm afraid I did, Hubert."

"That caused fearful ructions in the camp, I don't mind telling you," the Duke explained to an avid audience that included an open-mouthed Emma. "I was at Eton, so I missed most of the fun, but it seems that Piers went broody and damned nearly got himself shipped off to Malaya."

"He was rather sweet," Leander said, the memory making her momentarily wistful. "What happened to him?"

"Came to a bad end," the Duke said, causing Rachel and Emma considerable anxiety. "Went into insurance and married Mervyn Maltravers's widow. Terrible woman! He was a broken man within six months. Anyway, the point is this, Leander, we got there in the end, d'you see? A Prideaux has broken into the Cannings Ambo tribe."

Leander saw the point. "And look where patience has got *us*," she replied. "Rachel is already a marchioness, whereas I would only ever have been a 'Lady'!"

"You've always been a lady, my dear," the Duke said gallantly.

After giving their good wishes to the happy couple, Amelia and Silas were among the first to slip away from the revel. Amelia was quietly lost in thought all the way from Eaton Mandeville to Latimer's Barn; perfectly content with the quiet companionship that was such an important feature of their fifteen years as friends and lovers, Silas said nothing until he was making a pot of tea when they were back at Louise House.

"A penny for your thoughts. Or are they worth much more than that?"

Amelia smiled as she came down to earth. "Nothing very much," she replied. "I was thinking about Rachel."

Silas nodded. "She was smashing, wasn't she?" After a careful pause, he decided to say it and have done with it. "Giles would have been very proud of her."

Although she agreed with him, Amelia was suddenly close to tears. "I expect you'll think me very silly," she said. "But I sometimes feel it's awfully callous of us to have managed so well without him."

"He wouldn't have wanted anything else," Silas told her.

"Oh, I know that! At least, I think I do. We always make assumptions about what people might have wanted so that we can be happy or complacent about what we've done."

"Your mother still misses him terribly," Silas said gently. "For a start, she's convinced that the stable would have done much better under Giles."

"Really?"

"She often talks to Rupert about it. She believes that Giles was a genius who could have persuaded any horse to do more or less anything."

"He was. I used to watch him do it."

"So, he's not forgotten, you see."

"I'm glad." Amelia looked happier. "Steven's got the right ideas, though. Look at Logarithm!" She sounded as though she were rushing to the aid of someone under critical attack.

Silas smiled; the crisis was past.

The Marquess and Marchioness of Glastonbury finally left Eaton Mandeville to begin the first part of their honeymoon at four-thirty that afternoon. Scores of estate-workers had gathered outside the massive gates of the beech-lined drive to wave: while a rather frayed Charles concentrated on his driving, Rachel produced her own supply of confetti to throw back at their well-wishers, who enjoyed her antics enormously.

They went first to a house near Lyme Regis, made available to them by one of Charles's uncles. After that, they were going to Switzerland, then setting off on a tour of Italy.

Rachel watched her husband closely and with much concealed amusement. There was absolutely no doubt that Charles was as pleased as Punch at having made her his wife, but the day had been an ordeal for him with all its ceremony and speeches; curiously, now they were rid of it, his nerves appeared to be giving him no respite.

The house at Lyme Regis came complete with a full staff of highly accomplished servants who greeted them like royalty and produced a wide range of light snacks that were an ideal substitute for dinner after such a remarkable day. When they had eaten their fill, Charles cleared his throat portentously and said, "What would you say to a turn along the beach, my dear? It's a beautiful evening."

"I don't think so, Charlie," Rachel replied. "There are much more important things to be getting on with. Let's go to bed!"

"It's only nine o'clock!" Charles protested.

"Good! That gives us plenty of time."

Charles's discomfort became complete when they encountered the butler at the foot of the stairs.

"We are retiring now, Baines," Rachel told him with clarion confidence. "We'd like breakfast at nine o'clock, please."

Once they were safely inside their bedroom, Charles stopped acting like a cat on hot bricks, took Rachel in his arms and came out with the truth. "Look here, old girl, I'm rather looking forward to this," he said. "You'll just have to bear with me while I get the hang of it."

523

Rachel feigned a variety of surprise akin to disappointment. "Are you telling me that I've married a virgin?" she asked.

"Well . . . er . . . yes."

"No wild oats at all?"

"No. I suppose there might have been one or two opportunities, but it always struck me as being a dicey sort of business. Besides, these last few years, I've been rather keen on you."

Rachel, already half-undressed, gave him a warming smile of appreciation. "Never mind," she said. "I've got a fair idea of what we should be getting up to." She laughed. "There's no need to look like that, I'm as pure as the driven snow."

"So how do you know?"

"That's a secret. Now, come on, Charlie, I'm longing to see what it's like, so get your clothes off and let's have a bash at it!"

Twenty minutes later, an astounded Charles was feeling quite pleased with himself.

"That wasn't at all bad," Rachel said happily. "There's room for improvement, but I reckon we'll soon manage that."

"I thought it was wonderful," Charles said, shifting his head slightly to gain a better view of her body. "I really would like to know where you picked up all this hot inside information."

Rachel stared at him speculatively. "Promise you won't tell?" she said.

"Not a word!"

"You mustn't! It would be fearfully blush-making if word got around."

"My lips are sealed, darling," Charles said. "Come on, tell me!"

"Well, Aunt Amelia and Silas quite often make love in that wood around Powell's Pool," Rachel said, spluttering at the look on his face. "It's true, I tell you, they do! I found them at it by accident one afternoon two years ago, and I've kept my eye on them a few times since."

"You watched them?" Charles was at a complete loss to know what to make of it.

"Absolutely! Studying a couple of experts seemed as good a way as any of learning."

"Are you telling me that your Aunt Amelia gets up to the sort of tricks you've just been showing me?"

"Yes . . . and lots more besides, and she's much better at it than I am."

"Well I'm blessed!" Charles had a bemused smile on his face. "I must confess that I've always thought Amelia a bit dull . . . very beautiful and brilliant, but dull, if you know what I mean."

"She jolly well isn't!" Rachel said. "She's an amazing person. Anyway, all the Hawksworths and Flamsteeds are a pretty remarkable bunch, and don't you ever forget it."

"I don't think anyone doubts that, my darling. It's only the privileged few who know *how* remarkable they are."

Squirming over him enthusiastically, Rachel grinned broadly. "Welcome to the club, Charlie," she said. "You've had a rest, so let's try some more tricks!"

Rachel's departure from Latimer's Barn was an opportunity for changes and the arrival of the decorators. When everything was returned to normal, Leander and William were back in the rooms they had occupied as children and the sitting-room in which they had spent so much time together was restored. They were there each evening to listen to the wireless and read.

On an evening in October, Leander, tired, stiff and feeling her age for once, allowed herself to be helped to a chair by William, dumping herself down with a sigh of relief. After insisting on going to Newmarket with Steven, she privately admitted that it might have been too much for her. And there was disappointment adding to her weariness: Claude Timberlake's strongly fancied runner in the Dewhurst, victor of all his previous four races, had run unaccountably badly to finish nowhere.

"What a shame," William said when he had heard the sorry story. "You've always regarded that race as your personal property, haven't you?"

She grinned at the note of mischievous reproof in his voice and promptly looked younger. "We did win the first one, William," she reminded him.

"I know, Lea, and there have been nine more since. But other people deserve a crack at it."

"Why?" she demanded and they both chuckled.

"Don't you think you should be taking things a lot easier now?" William suggested. Undeterred by Leander's look, he went on. "I know you don't do anything in the yard, but all this dashing off to race meetings is taking the stuffing out of you."

For a moment or two, he thought that she was going to throw something at him. Then her face relaxed into a smile. "You're right, William," she said. "I'm seventy-five and it's time I put my feet up. In future I shall only go to Newbury . . . oh, and Ascot, of course. You can't expect me to go without that. And perhaps if I take care of myself, I can go to Newmarket occasionally. I do so love it there."

"Take a leaf out of my book," William advised. "Be the elder statesman and let everyone dote on you. It's great fun!"

Leander had already decided that William was awfully good in the role. Two or three mornings a week, he strolled down to Rose House, had coffee with Louise and Matthew and then looked into the workshops to see what was happening. It was rumoured that William had been known to express disapproval of workmanship or design, but he usually smiled, murmured a few words of praise and went away happy. Everyone, especially the younger apprentices, felt a little uplift at a kind word from the man whose hobby had turned into an ever-growing enterprise that brought them safely through the Depression.

"I couldn't do that, William," Leander said. "It would worry people. They'd think I was going ga-ga."

William saw her point. In his potterings around the village, he never ceased to wonder at the way every little difficulty was greeted with a: "Mrs Hawksworth will soon have that sorted," or an: "Oh dear! Mrs Hawksworth isn't going to like that!" Presumably it had always been the same, it was simply that he had the time to notice it nowadays. If she renounced any of her responsibilities, Cannings Ambo would suffer.

"Do the best you can," he said. "Try not to get mixed up in so many things."

"I will," she promised. "We've earned a rest."

"I think so. We've worked damned hard. Wouldn't it be nice if Father could see what we've done? I think he'd be pleased."

"Yes, he would. And imagine the look on old Rashleigh's face if he could see his stable now!" After a flash of glee that briefly took sixty years off her, Leander was sombre as she added, "I wonder where we might have been if it hadn't been for the War."

William stirred uneasily. "Amelia thinks there's going to be another one, you know."

"Yes." Leander sounded dismissive. "I think she got far too carried away by that business with what's-his-name . . . Edelson, wasn't it? I can see that it must have been very upsetting for her, but Germany can't possibly be in any position to start a war."

"And Italy, too," William said. "Remember what Rachel and Charles said when they came back. The country's in a raving uproar. That Mussolini seems a terrifying individual."

"Pooh!" Leander waved a contemptuous hand. "He's a musical-comedy character, that's all."

"He must have something about him," William said. "They say he made the trains run on time. That's a miracle in Italy."

"It may be, but it doesn't amount to very much, does it? Don't worry, William, there isn't going to be another war."

And William, thinking that his sister was as well informed as she had been a quarter of a century ago, believed her.

Leander and William were aware of and recognised change, but it was the local change that had been part of the ineluctable cycle for seventy years. That November, Jim Goakes, the oldest of their friends, died, making them inclined to dwell on past achievements and increasing their dependency on each other's company.

They were unaware of the fact that, only a few days after Amelia had fled from Germany, Hitler had introduced military conscription, making clear his intention of raising an army of over half a million men. Such a large force was expressly forbidden under the terms of the Versailles Treaty: by now, however, the Treaty was largely held in disrepute, even by those nations who had framed it. Attempts to make Germany maintain the vast reparations payments had long since been abandoned, and every European government was up to its eyes in other problems.

So, when the *Führer* began to raise and arm his divisions, not a single voice was raised in protest.

CHAPTER 30

1937–38

'I really believed that nothing could touch us now'

Leander's semi-retirement lasted for six months. That was the time it took for the memory of 1935 to fade into comfortable oblivion and for 1936 to turn into a startling and demoralising year. All the signs were that something was going awfully wrong: it was as if those precious few old values that had survived the Great War and its confused aftermath were finally being trampled down.

The chain of events that most upset Leander was that which caused 1936 to be the year England had three Kings.

After a short illness, the final severity of which came as a shock, King George V died on 28 January 1936. His eldest son was proclaimed his successor as King Edward VIII and the general feeling was that the immense popularity he had enjoyed as Prince of Wales would continue.

Some, however, were unconvinced: Leander was hostile.

"He's forty-one, rising forty-two, and he isn't married," she said to Emma one day, by way of explanation.

"You'd like a queen and an heir?" Emma asked.

"I'd also like to be sure which bed he's in," Leander replied grimly.

Her misgivings mounted when the Duke of Laverstoke passed on a piece of gossip from the House of Lords grapevine. "Keep this under your hat, my dear, but His Majesty is seeing an awful lot of that Mrs Simpson. One or two chaps are getting the wind up."

The news worsened as the year wore on. The thoroughly unsuitable Mrs Simpson, married and with a previous husband – whom she had divorced – still alive, seemed to be the King's constant companion. At Royal Ascot, Leander came within five yards of her and immediately formed an opinion that was to echo repeatedly round Cannings Ambo.

"I wouldn't mind nearly so much if the wretched woman were in the least bit attractive, but she's the most awful hag! And she's the commonest commoner you'd ever want to meet."

The crisis developed swiftly and with self-destroying purpose. The King took Mrs Simpson on an Adriatic cruise, then to the holy of holies, Balmoral. By the middle of September, the gossip columns of American newspapers and magazines were in a ferment of speculation while the English press maintained a boot-faced silence. They kept that stance until the beginning of December, by which time Mrs Simpson was divorced again and the King was talking of marriage.

Eleven days of pure pantomime followed, with Leander fuming as each new development seemed more bizarre than the last. There was talk of a 'King's Government' and mass demonstrations of support for the King, one of which included a ludicrous alliance between Communists and Fascists. But, whatever romantic hot air was spouted, Stanley Baldwin and Cosmo Lang, the implacable Archbishop of Canterbury, wanted the King to go, and go he duly did.

"Thank goodness that's all over," Leander said after listening to the man who was now Duke of Windsor make his abdication speech on the wireless. "I think the Duke and Duchess of York will do a first-rate job."

She was, Emma and Steven realised, outraged but not particularly surprised by the sorry episode: with standards going down the drain every day, there was nothing especially remarkable about a king who did not know how to behave.

In March, Germany reoccupied the Rhineland. This flagrant breach of not only the worthless Treaty of Versailles, but of the 1925 Treaty of Locarno, into which Germany had entered voluntarily, was a tentative escapade. Because of chronic misgivings on the part of all his generals, Hitler used a minimal force of only three thousand men, little more than might have been deployed on a weekend exercise for reservists. Had France lifted a finger of objection, the whole thing would have fallen flat. Instead, every government in Europe bent over backwards to find reasons for Hitler's move being perfectly right and proper.

Whereas Amelia's repeated misgivings about Germany had fallen on deaf ears, the Rhineland adventure caused Leander to voice concern at the next Trustees' meeting.

"I don't like the look of this," she said. "Hitler is out for trouble."

There were one or two round the table who might have wanted to disbelieve her until Matthew spoke up.

"I was in Birmingham the other day," he said. "Simon Fletcher told me an interesting story over lunch. A chap he plays golf with is production director of the Austin Motor factory at Longbridge. It seems they've had an approach from the Government to find out how quickly they could turn the place over to making tanks or aeroplanes."

While several people stared at Matthew incredulously, Amelia made a telling point.

"We are spending an extra thirty million on armaments this year," she said. "It's being kept very quiet, but Viscount Halifax dined with the Master of Trinity two weeks ago and they talked about it." While this information from the Secretary of State for War himself was being digested, Amelia added, "My professor was with them," by way of explanation for her knowledge of such secret information.

"So, ought we to do anything?" Steven, who was acting as chairman of the meeting, asked.

"I think I ought to have the job of keeping an eye on things," Leander said. "If there is going to be another war, we must prepare for it."

No one argued. Louise suppressed the facetious urge to ask whether Leander intended leading Cannings Ambo into battle in person and listened as Steven charged Amelia with finding out how a future conflict might affect civilians.

"You can probably put your ear to some very interesting doors and discover what the experts are thinking," he said.

But there was not long to wait before they had a demonstration of what to expect. Within weeks, the Civil War that erupted in Spain gave arms manufacturers an opportunity to test their latest products.

Long after it happened, when a trace of normal routine was being restored and people were able to think calmly once more, they realised how lucky it was that Leander made herself so busy. But for her, the terrible night of 25 June 1937 would have been an even greater disaster.

Since it was a Friday, Beryl Walters had the evening off from her duties as a maid at Rose House. As usual, she met Ted Marshall at The George where Ted drank a pint of bitter while she sipped a glass of lemonade. At exactly eight o'clock, they left the bar to hurry through the trees, across the Devizes Lane and Cannings Brook and into the new yard, now almost silent as the horses became drowsy.

There was no danger of them being seen: Cyril Osgood, still a vigorous night-watchman at the age of sixty-seven, did not begin his patrol until ten o'clock. Scuttling into the feed-store, they ascended a ladder to the loft in the roof-space. In summer, they had the benefit of the light from a small window.

Ted and Beryl had been courting for nearly two years, ever since they arrived in the village within a week of each other. Beryl, twenty-three, was a local girl from Swindon, Ted came to Latimer's Barn from a stable in Newmarket. He was twenty-six. For eighteen months, their Friday evening assignations had taken them to the loft where a plentiful supply of straw provided a comfortable place for their love-making.

Having settled themselves, they waited, exchanging whispered confidences while they listened. Ted heard the footsteps first and placed a forefinger on Beryl's lips. She knew that it must be half past eight and that Alfred Merriweather was making his final round; he always left his house on the drive at twenty past and came to the newest yard first.

As usual, they held their breath and smiled at each other. The footsteps crossed to the southern side of the yard and a box door creaked open. Ted nodded. "There's a filly with an abscess on her leg over there," he whispered. "I'd have bet on him looking at her."

Alfred's thoroughness made Beryl nervous. In fact, his inspection that seemed like an eternity took only two minutes: the box door was shut and there was silence for a few moments. Ted pictured Alfred looking round in that apparently casual way that shirkers found so deceptively comforting until they discovered that he could spot sloppiness at ten furlongs. The firm tread that faded into silence as he passed through the arch indicated his departure.

Relaxing, Beryl found herself grabbed in Ted's enthusiastic though not particularly skilful embrace. "Come here," he growled. "I'm ready for this!"

"Ted!" He frowned at the wheedling tone in her voice as she avoided his kiss. "Have you been thinking about what I said?"

"What's that, then?" he asked, knowing only too well what she meant.

"About us getting wed."

"Beryl, how many more times have I got to tell you? We've got a lot of saving up to do." His tone of laboured patience barely concealed his annoyance.

"You did well out of Ascot," Beryl said accusingly.

"Oh no, I didn't! You know how miserable they are."

Beryl, who had learned a great deal about racing from Louise, knew

531

that this was a bare-faced lie. Both the horses that Ted did had won at the Royal meeting, and their owner, the Duke of Laverstoke, was known to be generous. Ted would have pocketed at least seventy-five pounds, enough to set them up and pay for a week at a decent hotel somewhere really nice, like Bournemouth.

"*I've* got enough to get us started," Beryl said resolutely. "And Mrs Hawksworth would soon find us a house."

"Oh no!" It was time for Ted to enact the ritual of wanting to do it all himself and not be beholden to anyone. "I want us to have a nice little place that's all our own in Marlborough, then we can be private, away from all this lot. I've told you before, Beryl, I don't care for this Cannings Ambo morning-noon-and-night caper. A man needs a bit of peace and relaxation away from the bosses. Now, come on, let's stop wasting time, eh?"

As purposefully as he tried to push a hand up Beryl's skirt, she grabbed his wrist to prevent him.

"No, Ted, we can't. It's *that* time of month."

" 'Strewth!" He broke away from her as if she had a contagious disease. "You might have said so, Beryl! I could have stayed in The George and had a session with the lads!"

Humiliated, Beryl bit back tears as Ted stood up to get at his jacket which he had hung on a nail in a roof beam. Snatching a battered packet of cigarettes from a pocket, he lit one, flicking the match over his shoulder.

It was an irritating, childish habit that Beryl hated. Whenever she protested, Ted cockily demonstrated how the spin he imparted with a thumb and finger always put the match out.

But this time, anger made him forget to employ the technique and Beryl's distress was such that she did not watch the match in flight, to check that it was extinguished.

About ten feet behind Ted Marshall there was half a bale of straw that had, over a period of several weeks, disintegrated and been scuffed up into a tangled, well-ventilated mess. The match landed in the middle of it.

"Ted, for God's sake, look out!" Beryl said urgently. "I think that straw's alight."

At that moment, a car stopped in front of The House. Matthew was bringing Leander home from Marlborough Town Hall where she had been attending a lecture and slide-show on the Spanish Civil War. As he drove off, Leander hesitated: she knew that Steven would be busy in the library, poring over race entries and assessing the strength of the opposition. Wanting a breath of air after the stuffiness of the cramped room in the Town Hall, Leander decided to look at the yards.

In the loft, Ted Marshall turned to look at the burning straw: he kicked at it petulantly.

Unbelievably, there was what appeared to be an explosion as the dust and minutely fine chaff disturbed by his stupid action turned into a fireball. Before Beryl's horrified eyes, two full bales of straw were ablaze. She started to scream.

If Ted Marshall's priorities had been different, there might have been a faint chance of saving the situation. Instead of trying to suffocate the fire, however, his sole concern was to stop Beryl screaming.

"Shut up, you silly bitch!" he snarled.

She did not. He grabbed her, clamping a hand over her mouth. "Be quiet, damn you! Come on!" He was hustling her towards the ladder. "We've got to get out. Go on, out!"

Two or three vital seconds were lost as Beryl, her head still twisted awkwardly by his grip, missed her footing and nearly fell, dragging him with her. When Beryl was finally on her way down, Ted Marshall looked round to gauge the progress of the fire and was appalled: three of the struts supporting the roof were alight.

Descending the ladder at a breakneck pace, he grabbed Beryl, bundling her to the feed-store door.

While he waited, straining his ears, Leander walked through the archway into the 1874 yard; Ted Marshall did not hear her and she was unaware of anything amiss.

"Go home!" Ted hissed to Beryl. "Run like buggery and don't let anyone see you. I'll see to this."

After she had fled, Ted dashed across the Roadway into the entrance hall of the hostel. The racket from the games room indicated that, as usual on a Friday evening, at least half a dozen lads were clustered round the snooker table recently installed by Steven.

Tormented by a quandary of indecision, Ted turned and walked back out to the Roadway, almost bumping into Leander as she hurried between the two yards.

"Can you smell burning, Ted?" she demanded.

He made a show of sniffing. "No, Mrs Hawksworth, ma'am, can't say as I do."

"It's coming from the new yard," Leander insisted. She moved towards it, only to stop dead as she saw the smoke curling insolently from one of the ventilators. "Get everyone outside, Ted," she ordered. "And run up to The House for Mr Steven. Come on, jump to it!"

The lads from the snooker table were outside within seconds, those from the new hostel were not far behind. As Leander led them into the yard, the first signs of distress were coming from the horses:

they were coughing and kicking at the doors to their boxes: smoke was starting to seep through the slates along the whole northern arm of the roof. Speculating on the seriousness of it, Leander was briefly abstracted until she realised that twenty-five lads were staring expectantly at her.

"We must have the horses out," she shouted. "Never mind the fire for the moment, get the horses out."

She herself was the first to open a door.

So far, the fire had been struggling to find air in the snugly closed stable. As doors were flung open, a demonic updraught drove the simmering flames into fury; part of the roof above the feed-store collapsed only feet from where Leander was struggling to drag a crazed horse to safety.

Emma and two maids pursued Ted Marshall across the lawn while Steven telephoned for the Marlborough fire engine. After that he rang Alfred Merriweather and Matthew, telling the latter to rouse the village.

Ted Marshall stopped at the corner of the lawn, dimly aware that Emma and the girls ran on past him. Although he could not see into the quadrangle of the yard, he was overwhelmed by horror.

Flames were now leaping upwards through three holes in the roof and there was a dreadful groaning sound as the entire structure teetered towards destruction. While he was watching, a new collapse of slates showed that the fire was moving into the eastern arm of the square.

But what froze his blood and made Ted Marshall feel sick were the noises. Most of the horses were frightened and creating a racket that drowned the shouts of the lads; rising above it all, however, the terrible shrieks of at least two horses indicated something far worse than fear.

Not knowing how he got there, Ted Marshall found himself in the hostel. He was by his bed, feverishly ransacking the lining of the mattress for the three hundred and fifty pounds saved from his shares of prize-money and judicious bets. Then he was stuffing clothes into a canvas hold-all.

Steven and Alfred Merriweather reached the Roadway to be confronted with two horses bolting towards them. Instinctively, without a word, they spread themselves with arms stretched wide. Their luck was in: the horses, wild-eyed, necks and withers lathered, stopped, allowing themselves to be taken by their head-collars.

"This is damned bad," Steven muttered grimly, hanging on to his captive and deducing what was happening. Released from their boxes, the animals had been left to their own devices because those inside the yard could think only of rescue. Unless something were done, it would happen again and again, scattering terrified horses to every corner of the estate and beyond.

Salvation came with the first arrivals from the village. Among them were half a dozen of the most experienced lads who had been playing darts in The George. One of them raced to Steven's side.

"Get everything out of the coach-house, Tom," Steven ordered. "We need somewhere to pen these horses."

The three motor cars presented no problem, but manhandling the old carriage turned into a confused shambles in which a lad broke an arm. At the height of the muddle, and aided by rapidly falling darkness, Ted Marshall slipped past, disappearing into the orchard. All that lay ahead of him was Louise House, dark and empty, and open downland. He intended making a wide sweep to reach the London–Bath Road at a point two or three miles west of the Devizes Lane.

As order was restored outside the coach-house and the first horses taken inside, an ashen-faced Kathleen Stanton was running away from the fire. Having seen the flames and smoke from Oak Cottage she had rushed to help; now she was going to make a call for an ambulance while collecting her doctor's bag.

The first of what was to prove a series of horrific events took place within two minutes of the evacuation beginning. A blazing roof section collapsed on to a horse still trapped in its box. No one had yet fetched the humane killer, so the stricken animal, injured and pinned down by wreckage, burned to death in the conflagration of its own bedding.

The second horse to suffer an almost similar fate was dispatched by Alfred Merriweather, but not before the hapless filly had kicked out at the lad who was trying to help her, sending him senseless into a pile of blazing straw, prey to falling debris.

Steven and Alfred dragged him out, smothering his burning clothes with a blanket and scorching themselves in the process. It was while they were kneeling beside the badly injured lad that another major roof collapse took place into two adjacent boxes, this time in the southern arm of the yard. The fire was now consuming the whole roof, throwing a hellish light on a scene of nightmare havoc.

The latest roof-fall had done fearful damage; looking into one of the affected boxes, Steven felt sick with dismay at the sight of yet another severely injured horse and a lad lying under a massive joist. Then he realised that several people, including Leander, were struggling to get the timber away from the lad. Jumping in to help them, he found that his mind cleared.

As they carried the lad out, water was coming on to the scene. At least thirty people from the village had brought buckets with them and were bringing gallons of the precious stuff from the mercifully close Cannings Brook. The Marlborough fire engine was now in position with two hoses and a powerful new motor pump; within minutes, the fire was under control and Steven was feeling light-headed with relief.

It was bad: there was no denying that. But it could have been very much worse. On the verge of convincing himself that they had pulled off a remarkable feat, Steven thought that Kathleen Stanton was behaving rather foolishly. Kneeling at the side of the first lad to be injured, she gave a shake of the head, set aside her stethoscope and drew the blanket that was covering the lad over his face.

"Come on, Kathleen, don't be silly," Steven chided. "Let him breathe."

When Kathleen stood up, her face was drawn and haggard. "There's no need for that," she said. "He's dead."

It was well past midnight when they paused, crowding round the kitchen door for a mug of tea, or flopping, exhausted, on to the lawn.

No one wanted to speak.

The toll was dreadful. Steven saw it first in Leander's smoke-grimed face and his heart sank. He wondered how he could have felt those few moments of optimism.

Two lads were dead. One more was in the hospital at Savernake, another was on his way to Swindon for emergency surgery.

"Thank God none of them are married," Leander said. It was the nearest they were to get to a crumb of comfort for a long time.

Two broken arms and over a dozen people receiving treatment for burns from Kathleen Stanton and a Marlborough doctor who had come to help seemed an insignificant addition to the casualty list.

Five horses were lost. After the first, forced to suffer a terrible end without assistance, four others had been destroyed. Learning that Leander herself had gone into the flames to deal with two of them, Steven found that he was not, after all, drained of all emotion.

But even as he looked at his grandmother in astounded admiration, Emma brought further bad news.

"Alfred says there are two horses not accounted for."

Steven went to check the count. There was no doubt about it: two had succeeded in bolting.

An hour later, when Steven and Alfred had identified the missing animals, Leander seemed to be on the verge of breaking down. Steven, feeling more helpless by the minute, found himself praying that she would hang on, knowing that if she cracked, everyone else would cave in. He suddenly realised that there must have been similar occasions during her life at Latimer's Barn, but surely none as terrible as this.

Both the missing horses were very high-class two-year-olds, winners at the previous week's Royal Ascot. The Duke of Laverstoke's colt, Tungsten, had won the Coventry Stakes, an odds-on favourite by virtue of his earlier brilliant performances at Newbury and Bath.

But it was the filly that threatened to finish Leander.

Hyperborean was by the already-legendary Hyperion out of a good mare called Borealis. Leander had fought tooth and nail to buy her at the Newmarket yearling sales of 1936, eventually going to 12,800 guineas to secure her against determined bidding. Moved by the gipsy's prophecy a year before Hyperion won the Derby on the day that Ruth died, Leander kept the filly for herself, becoming an owner at the age of seventy-seven. Her action caused a stir in racing circles as well as the village, and no one was in the least surprised when the filly trotted up to win the Queen Mary Stakes at Ascot by an effortless-looking four lengths.

Now she was gone and, better than anyone else, Leander knew that the chances of recovering her unscathed were negligible.

Rupert Timberlake, made to look old and ill by the night's hideous events, persuaded Leander to lie down on a sofa in the upstairs sitting-room.

"Well, this will teach me, won't it?" she said as William sponged the grime from her face.

"What?" both William and Rupert asked.

"I thought we were safe," she said bitterly. "I really believed that nothing could touch us now."

Then, to the surprise of her two companions, she fell asleep. William stayed to watch over her.

No one else rested: by the light of scores of hurricane lamps, lads and villagers set to work to clear the roof debris away from the shell of the yard while Steven and Alfred Merriweather began to move horses from the dangerously claustrophobic confines of the coach-house to the paddock.

As the first tentative signs of the mid-summer dawn appeared in the eastern sky, Jeremy Dundas arrived with more bad news.

"I've just nipped home to let Josie know what's happening," he said. "Tungsten's in our back garden."

Steven, having understood the look on Jeremy's face, waited for him to continue.

"He'd obviously tried to jump the fence, but he made a terrible hash of it. Both his forelegs are broken."

"I'll come down straight away," Alfred Merriweather said.

"There's no need. I've done it." Misinterpreting Steven's reaction, Jeremy added, "Don't worry, I made a decent job of it."

Despite the dejected weariness that was dragging him down, Jeremy displayed a trace of quiet pride at the way he had handled the harrowing task.

Latimer's Barn became very busy as the morning progressed.

Joe Irons and his two senior foremen arrived early to inspect the damaged stable. After a consultation with Steven, they went off quickly in their van and Leander, watching from her bedroom window after a bath that had freshened her up, nodded approval at what she was sure was being planned.

Rachel and Charles, with their four-month-old son, Henry, arrived at ten: the Duchess was not far behind them, explaining that although the Duke was busy on government business in London, he was doing his best to get away. At midday, Silas drove up with Amelia, delayed on her dash from Cambridge by a missed train connection in London.

Kathleen Stanton was, by far, the most welcome arrival because of the news she brought. Poorly though they both were, the two lads in hospital were considered to be out of danger. A weak smile lit Leander's face and she found the strength to talk to the newspapermen.

The editor of the local paper, tipped off by an ambulance driver, had telephoned news of the disaster to an old friend in Fleet Street during the early hours of the morning. The story had spread nearly as fast as the fire itself; now, at least one representative of every major newspaper was hanging around, hoping for a few words to supplement what their eyes told them. Steven was doing his best to cope, but Leander knew that a statement from her was what they really wanted.

After the respectful murmurs that greeted her appearance among them had faded away, the questions began.

"Have you lost any horses, Mrs Hawksworth?"

"I am very sorry to say that two lads are dead as a result of this terrible business," Leander said, crushing the questioner's wrong priority with a reproving look. "There will have to be an inquest, of course. Two more of our staff are quite ill in hospital, but I was told an hour ago that they are going to pull through."

"How did the fire start?"

"We have no idea."

"Was it arson?"

"The police are looking at that possibility."

"Is it true that your dress was burned to tatters while you were rescuing horses, Mrs Hawksworth?"

Leander smiled. "I'm afraid not, Mr Tucker. The hem got rather scorched, that's all."

"I take it you're going to rebuild?" The man asking the question looked round at the scene of smoke-blackened ruin.

"Yes!"

They saw that she had no intention of elaborating.

"What about the horses, Mrs Hawksworth?"

She took a deep breath to steady herself. "We lost six."

"Will you tell us which ones?"

"No, not until we've spoken to the owners."

"And there's one missing?"

"Yes, I'm afraid so." Leander drew herself up. "I can tell you about that one, she's mine."

"What, Hyperborean?"

"That's right. She's been gone for what must be over fourteen hours now, so the outlook is not very good."

They were all scribbling away furiously when the sound of hoofs on the Roadway arrested them: turning rapidly, Leander saw the filly framed in the archway of the burned-out yard. She was at the point where exhaustion had finally conquered terror and was ready to drop, yet when Leander called, her ears pricked and she stumbled forward.

"Oh, sweetheart!" Leander cried and flung her arms round the filly's neck. As Steven bent to examine Hyperborean's legs, Leander was kissing her muzzle.

"She's sound," Steven announced quietly after completing his check. "There's a cut knee, but it's nothing to worry about."

Leander bowed her head against the filly's neck and wept with gratitude. A photographer broke away from the pack and advanced to within four feet of her, camera at the ready.

However, when he saw her tears through his viewfinder, he turned away, abashed.

Kathleen Stanton came back to Latimer's Barn at six o'clock.

"Good gracious, why aren't you sleeping?" Leander asked. "You look ready for it."

Kathleen did indeed look worn out: despite this, there was an intense excitement about her that commanded attention.

539

"I've found out how the fire started," she said, thankfully accepting a cup of tea and slumping into a chair. "Louise called me out this afternoon. Her maid, Beryl Walters, was having hysterics . . . at least, that's what Louise called it. The poor girl is in a bad state of nervous collapse."

Kathleen then proceeded to relate all that a guilt-wracked Beryl had told her, the full story of her unsatisfactory relationship with Ted Marshall and the match casually thrown over his shoulder.

"At least that explains one thing," Leander said when she had finished. "We know why we can't find Ted Marshall anywhere."

"He's disappeared, has he?" Kathleen asked.

"Yes. To be honest, what with one thing and another we didn't realise he was nowhere to be seen until about two hours ago. Then we wondered if . . ." Leander stopped short. "Well, never mind what we thought. It doesn't matter now." She frowned in concentration. "That explains why he was hanging around when I came back from Marlborough."

"What are you going to do about him?" Kathleen asked.

"I shall let the police know. I expect we shall be keeping a look-out for him ourselves, too." Leander sounded almost casual.

"From what I can gather from Beryl, I don't think he did it deliberately," Kathleen said, acutely conscious that the point was irrelevant. "But he doesn't seem to have made any attempt to put it out or get help."

Leander seemed not to have heard. "How's the girl?" she asked.

"Very, very upset. I've given her some pills to calm her."

When Kathleen had returned to Oak Cottage with strict instructions to get some sleep, Leander made a number of telephone calls before going outside in search of Steven and Alfred Merriweather. After telling them about Ted Marshall, she ordered them to bed.

"Go on, get off, the pair of you! I don't want you falling down half-dead."

"What are you going to do about Ted Marshall?" Steven asked.

"I've spoken to the police about him," Leander replied. "Now, do as you're told."

On her way back to The House, she went into the 1874 yard to visit Hyperborean, fast asleep in a box made available by the transfer of its normal occupant to the paddock. For ten minutes, Leander knelt in the straw alongside the filly, stroking her neck and listening to her steady breathing. Before leaving, she offered a prayer of thanks for the safe deliverance of the beautiful creature of whom she expected such great things.

*

It was half past two the following afternoon before Ted Marshall saw a newspaper. Someone had left it on a chair in the saloon of the boat from Fishguard to Rosslare and he picked it up out of sheer boredom.

Seconds later he was feeling faint.

Under the headline:

FIRE TRAGEDY AT LATIMER'S BARN

the story began on the front page and carried on inside.

It took him several minutes to begin comprehending the awful facts: two lads and six horses dead. A dramatic photograph showed the extent of the damage to the yard. Over sixty column-inches of text were devoted to an embellished account of the fight to save the horses from a blazing death-trap. It was, the paper declared resonantly, a tribute to the unstinting bravery of the management and staff that so many horses had been saved.

Gradually, Ted Marshall calmed down. Getting a drink from the bar, he read the piece through for a third time and saw that there was no mention of him; Beryl had not yet told the tale. She would, he thought grimly: not that it made any difference. Once in Ireland, he was beyond their reach.

After taking advice, Leander doubted whether there was anything all that serious with which the police could charge him. Feeling certain that he would make for Ireland, she and Silas had toyed with the idea of intercepting him.

"It's either Holyhead or Fishguard," Silas said. "I reckon we could be there in time by road."

Leander found that she had to reject the idea. "He may already have gone," she said. "In any case, I haven't the faintest idea what to do with him."

"I've a few ideas," Silas said savagely.

"So have I, my dear, but they're all illegal." Silas was struck by the wistful note in her voice. "We shall have to wait until I can think of an appropriate punishment."

"You think you'll be able to find him?" Silas asked.

"I shall rely on the Timberlake bloodhounds," Leander replied grimly.

To guard against the unlikely eventuality of Ted Marshall's action being forgotten, Leander added two damning sentences about him to the account of the fire in the Big Book.

Four owners had lost horses. The Duke of Laverstoke was worst hit with a four-year-old gone as well as the highly talented Tungsten. He

541

was the first to become aware of the compensation that Leander was proposing the Fund should pay and pooh-poohed it out of hand.

"Don't be ridiculous, Leander! It's very good of you to make the offer, but forget it. I'll see what my insurers have to say. I'm dashed if I'm having you out of pocket over a piece of infernal bad luck like that."

Claude Timberlake and Joe Giffard were the same. Joe pleased Leander by striking a bargain. "Tell you what, Mrs Hawksworth, I'll get another horse and you can train him for a year for nothing."

Leander had been offering him well over six thousand pounds; the year's training fees for one horse were equivalent to about four hundred.

Eric Hargreaves was the remaining owner and no one expected anything other than trouble. Steven telephoned him with Leander at his side.

The initial reaction was friendly and sympathetic.

"Here, Steven lad, I've just been reading about this fire you've had. What a terrible business!"

"We're all extremely upset, Mr Hargreaves."

"I should think you are. Dear me! How did it start?"

"We don't know," Steven lied. "The police are looking into it."

"It's like that, is it? Take my advice, lad, you want to find the swine that did that and nail him good and proper. You can't afford to have people like that wandering round."

"Don't worry, Mr Hargreaves, we're doing our best. Now, I'm afraid I have some rather bad news for you. One of your horses was among those poor animals that were killed."

"I see." The change in Hargreaves's voice was ominously dramatic. "Which one?"

"Domino Lady."

"She was the best!"

Steven strangled the urge to point out that the dead filly was no better or worse than the other half-dozen horses that Hargreaves kept at Latimer's Barn. A victory in even the lowest class of race would have been a miracle. "She had promise," he said smoothly, pulling a face at Leander.

"What are you going to do about it?" Hargreaves demanded.

"We're offering owners twice what they paid for their horses. This is to provide some recompense for any prize-money that might have been won."

"So, this means you're accepting full responsibility for what happened?"

"The horses were in our care," Steven replied guardedly.

542

There was a long pause: Steven had the disturbing feeling that he could hear Hargreaves's mind at work. "I shall have to think about this," was the eventual curt response and Steven found himself cut off.

"I might have known it," Leander sighed. "He's going to be unpleasant."

"It won't get him anywhere," Steven muttered angrily.

Leander looked uncertain. Her judgement was that Hargreaves was the type of man who might want to drag the matter into a court of law. The prospect preyed on her mind to such an extent that she talked it over with the Duke of Laverstoke when he popped in on his way to Eaton Mandeville from London that evening.

Because of difficulties with his wife, who suspected his affair with an attractive young woman employee, Eric Hargreaves did have litigation in mind. For once, those stuck-up so-and-so's in Cannings Ambo seemed vulnerable: a legal victory with a public washing of dirty linen would put them in their place and boost his flagging spirits.

Soured by domestic animosity, Hargreaves made a spur-of-the-moment decision to go down to Wiltshire to make a nuisance of himself: it seemed a sporting opportunity far too good to miss.

He arrived in Cannings Ambo to find sombre groups of people blocking the Devizes Lane and the Latimer's Barn drive. His opening exchange with Leander was bad-tempered.

"What the devil's all this about?"

"We've been burying James Munroe and Timothy Daniels."

"Who are they?"

"The two lads we lost in the fire. What are you doing here, Hargreaves?"

"I've come to talk about that horse of mine," he replied, very annoyed by her unvarnished use of his surname.

Without another word, Leander walked away from his car, leaving him trapped by pedestrians and incapable of pursuit.

Fifteen minutes later, what Hargreaves intended to be the first exchange of words took place outside the kitchen door.

"Now, look here, Mrs Hawksworth, twice what that filly cost me is nowhere near enough compensation."

"Why not?" Leander snapped.

"You're taking no account of her stud value. I could have lost tens of thousands on the foals she might have had."

Leander looked disdainful. "Mr Hargreaves, for a horse to have any value at stud, it must win races, *good* races. To be perfectly blunt, I don't think Domino Lady was capable of it."

"And whose fault was that, may I ask?"

"Yours, Mr Hargreaves! Did you know that you are the only owner we have *ever* had who has failed to win a race?" While Hargreaves was looking surprised, Leander pressed on. "Do you know why? It's perfectly simple. You consistently ignore our advice when buying and give us nothing but mediocrities to train."

Hargreaves was livid.

"That's not going to wash! You're going to have to come up with something a damned sight better than that when I get you into court. And while we're about it, we're going to have to decide whether you lot are fit to be in charge of valuable animals. The Jockey Club might be wondering that for themselves."

"If you will excuse me, I have funeral guests needing my attention," Leander said and slammed the door in Hargreaves's face.

Steven and the Duke of Laverstoke were in the kitchen to witness the scene and exchanged worried looks as Leander went off to the large sitting-room where everyone had gathered.

"I don't think she handled that terribly well, you know," Steven whispered.

"Possibly not," the Duke agreed. "Tell you what, Steven, you go and mingle while I have a word or two with our troublesome friend."

Hargreaves was inspecting the gutted yard and was surprised. Only six days after the fire, progress had been very rapid. The smoke-blackened brickwork was scrubbed clean and most of the new roof timbers were in position. Joe Irons and a hand-picked dozen of his men were about to resume work after attending the funeral of James and Timothy.

"Quite impressive, what?" the Duke said. "First-class chap, Joe Irons. I'm Hubert Prideaux, by the way."

"Oh. Hargreaves is the name."

Although the two men had never met formally, Steven and others had pointed out the Duke to Hargreaves on more than one occasion. Preoccupied with his aggrieved self-importance, however, Hargreaves failed to recognise his companion, except as an irritating nuisance.

"You're a fellow-owner, I believe," Hubert Prideaux said.

"Yes. One of my horses was killed."

"Dear me! What a shocking business!" The Duke saw no reason to mention his own loss. "Mind you, this rearmament caper is a funny do! That fellah Hitler seems to be getting everybody into a terrible stew."

"Eh?" Completely baffled by the abrupt change of subject, Hargreaves gaped at the Duke who carried on blithely.

"Still, it's an ill wind and all that. Bit of luck for the chaps who've picked up the job of making all the beastly stuff. What's that contract of yours worth? About a hundred and eighty-seven thousand, isn't it?"

Hargreaves was aghast. "How do you know that?" he asked.

"Leslie Hore-Belisha told me. He's an *awfully* decent fellow. You've met him, I take it?"

"You mean the Minister of War?" Hargreaves asked disbelievingly.

"That's right!" The Duke beamed happily.

"And why should he give *you* confidential information about my contract?"

"I'm on the Defence Procurement Committee," the Duke replied. "As a matter of fact, I'm the chairman."

Hargreaves looked at him with a mixture of fear and respect. "Who did you say you were?" he asked.

"I'm the Duke of Laverstoke. I do a fair bit in the House of Lords." There was a slight change in His Grace's attitude and tone: he was no longer the bumbling old buffer.

While Hargreaves was assimilating this and wondering how he should behave towards an influential member of the aristocracy, the Duke gave him still greater pause for thought.

"I daresay you're hoping that this contract you've got will be the first of many."

"Yes. Well . . . that is . . . I thought if we made a proper job of it . . ." Hargreaves petered out.

"Yes, quite so. Of course, yours isn't a big factory, is it?"

"No." The admission was very grudging. "But I intend expanding soon."

"If you get the chance."

"What do you mean?"

"You may not get any more Government contracts."

"Nobody knows," Hargreaves said. He had no idea where the conversation was leading, but he was apprehensive.

"Oh, I do!" the Duke said brightly. "If you don't make your peace with Mrs Hawksworth on *her* terms, I will give you my personal guarantee that you never get another contract. I'm perfectly sure that we can manage to rearm without your small contribution."

"That's blackmail!" Hargreaves was petulant rather than angry.

"It is indeed!" The Duke gave him a bland half-smile. "Not done in the best circles, I know, but I'm dashed if I can think of any other way of making sure that you don't drag this place through a mire of your own making. I won't have it, Hargreaves, so you'd better get used to the idea."

"I'll lodge a complaint," Hargreaves fumed. "By God, I'll ruin you."

"You won't, you know, so don't be silly." The Duke sounded as though he was talking to a backward child. "Who on earth would believe you? You're a complete outsider and I've never spoken to you. Tell you what, if you don't play ball, I think it's most unlikely that this contract you've got will turn out right! You've no idea how difficult it can be meeting the specification sometimes."

And with that, Hargreaves was left to think it over.

Sitting down on a stack of new roofing laths, he seethed. He needed those army contracts; they were essential. The prospect of a bigger factory and the prestige that went with it was not the main attraction these days: much more important was the chance of a new life with his young woman. For weeks, they had been talking about going to Australia or New Zealand, somewhere well away from the everlasting European ferment.

The Duke had meant what he said; despite the politeness, the steely determination of the Establishment was lurking just beneath the surface. Swallowing his pride, Hargreaves went back to The House and asked if Mrs Hawksworth could spare him a few minutes. He was very polite.

Hargreaves was thirty miles north of Latimer's Barn before Leander was able to persuade the Duke of Laverstoke to tell her what had happened.

"My word, Hubert, that's very impressive," she said. "And the thing is, he believed you."

"Of course he did," the Duke said with a trace of pique. "I damned well meant it."

Leander looked at him dubiously. "Are you *really* that important, Hubert?"

"Yes, dash it, I am!" He puffed himself up and looked quite affronted until he saw Emma and Steven shaking with laughter. "I'm a pretty big wheel actually. I'm not nearly the idiot I look, you know!"

"Oh, Hubert," Leander smiled affectionately. "I've never imagined that you were an idiot. Seriously, my dear, very seriously, I'm grateful to you." She kissed him.

"Ah . . . well . . ." The Duke was embarrassed. "We can't have the Timberlakes doing *all* your dirty work."

Caught off guard by the sly little dig, Leander looked startled, but the moment passed as Emma asked her a question.

"What did you say to Hargreaves?"

"I was absolutely charming to him," Leander replied. "I gave him a cheque for one thousand two hundred pounds, which was twice what he paid for that beautiful but untalented filly, and made him sign a paper to say that he was satisfied."

"It's all settled, then?" Emma sounded relieved.

"It is indeed." A look of the purest contentment stole across Leander's face, dispelling some of the strain of the last few days. "I also told him to get his other horses out of my sight at the first available opportunity."

"How did he react to that?" Steven asked.

"He was as good as gold."

"All we have to do now is get back to normal," Steven said without much relish. Like everyone else, once the momentary elation of dealing with Hargreaves had passed, he looked ill with strain.

Three weeks to the day after the fire, the yard was ready for use again after a phenomenal effort by Joe Irons and his men. Apart from the obvious newness of the roof, there was virtually nothing to suggest that this had been the scene of a fearful disaster.

All the lads understood that the roof spaces of both the main stable blocks were to be kept spotlessly clean and free of everything except essentials. Daily inspection of the lofts became part of the evening stables routine, and woe betide the yard captain, the senior lad responsible for overall cleanliness, if so much as a single stalk of straw was found out of place. The edict that anyone found with cigarettes and matches outside the hostel would be dismissed instantly was applauded. The only thing that the lads grumbled about was the failure of the police to find Ted Marshall. The departure of Beryl Walters to work for Joe Giffard at a new shop in Newbury was noted and approved. Hostel opinion regarded her as "a stupid cow who should have hung on to the sense she was born with".

In addition to all the tangible loss and damage, the fire wiped out the mid-season tempo of the work schedules. For three weeks, the horses in the paddock had done only minimal exercise and Steven was faced with the problem of beginning the year all over again.

The first runners did not go out until the second week in August. In an attempt to make a splash that would act as a morale-booster, Steven sent no less than eleven runners to a three-day meeting at Newbury. They all looked good, they had performed well on the gallop, and it was their 'lucky' course. At the end of it all, they had third place in a four-horse race and nothing else.

"That was terrible," Steven said to Leander when the ordeal was over and he was back in the comforting safety of The House. "I doubt if we've ever had such an awful run. What am I doing wrong, Leander?"

"You aren't, darling," she told him firmly. "You've been born into one of the funniest professions in the world, but you're too young to appreciate that yet."

Steven grinned. "Tell me about it, wise one!"

"You've run out of luck, that's all. It will come back."

"Are you sure?" Steven was a long way from being convinced.

"It always has done."

"When is this miracle going to happen?"

"I've no idea," Leander replied casually. "But since there isn't very much of this season left, I wouldn't worry about it. Keep going, do your best and be patient. Next year will be altogether different."

When he became champion trainer fourteen months later, Steven accepted the wisdom of what Leander had said. Sadly, however, 1938 was memorable for much that was worrying and downright disagreeable.

The first sign of trouble came in March when Germany took over Austria in a move that became known as the *Anschluss*. With the local Nazi Party acting as a Trojan Horse, the entire operation, meticulously planned and ruthlessly executed, took only two days. As it became apparent that not a word was to be uttered in protest, William's reaction was wrathful.

"We're living in a madhouse!" he stormed, astonishing Leander by his anger. "Hitler does as he pleases and no one has the guts to stand up to him."

"Most people seem to think it's a reasonable idea, William," Leander pointed out. "Austria has a right to be part of Germany. I believe they talked about it at the Peace Conference in 1919."

"That's left-wing clap-trap, Lea," William said with a force that made her blink. "Austria also has a right *not* to be part of Germany, but you don't hear anything about that. What country will the *Führer . . .*" he invested the word with a wealth of sarcasm ". . . want next? We shall have to let him have it straight away, of course!"

Six months later, the gravity of the situation, precipitated by Hitler's next land-grab, was apparent to all. Stories flew down from London that gas-masks were being issued and trenches dug in Hyde Park: Claude Timberlake heard a rumour that the Royal Navy was on stand-by.

This time, the German-speaking part of Czechoslovakia, the Sudetenland, was to be annexed. The Prague Government and the majority of the Czech people courageously opposed Hitler's demand and a war in which France was bound by treaty to support Czechoslovakia loomed. With the crisis at boiling point on 15 September, Neville Chamberlain embarked on what was to prove the most remarkable and least defensible mission ever undertaken by a British Prime Minister. He flew to see Hitler at Berchtesgaden, his eyrie in the Bavarian Alps.

For the next nine days, William spent virtually all his waking hours by the wireless, following each step in the drama, growing angrier by the hour.

When Chamberlain finally returned on 1 October after two more meetings with Hitler, it was to wave a piece of paper which meant, he alleged, 'Peace in our time'. While millions seemed delirious with joy, William's indignation knew no bounds. Chamberlain had, he said, been instrumental in forcing the Czech Government to give Hitler what he wanted.

"Do they have racing in Germany?" he asked Leander a few days later, apparently calming down.

"Yes, although I don't think the standard is very good. Why?"

"If Hitler ever asks for the South of England, that's where you'll be sending horses," William declared. "Chamberlain would hand over the lot!"

As the days passed, William lapsed into apathy. Looking back afterwards, Leander realised that it was during the first week of October that William must have started giving up the ghost. For him, the world had become a terrible place and he wanted to remain in ignorance of how it was all going to end.

Throughout that worrying year, Leander shared William's concerns, but did her best to conceal her misgivings. She felt that she owed it to the village to appear optimistic; she was buoyed up by a marvellous racing season that included an event beyond her wildest dreams.

After the fire, Steven took personal charge of the filly, Hyperborean, doing absolutely nothing with her except walk her each day, with a gentle canter twice a week. The first two months were very worrying; she was nervous, off her feed and lost weight.

Then, after a month during which Steven slipped into his father's habit and talked to her incessantly, she began to improve. Her confidence returned, her appetite became healthy and she was filling out.

At the beginning of October, Steven felt able to leave her on Sundays in order to go sailing with Norman Redmayne once more. The disturbingly attractive Ann was nowhere to be seen: after leaving school and spending a year in Canada, she was now away at university.

Not wishing to betray his interest in her, Steven never asked where she was or what she was studying.

Hyperborean came through the winter well and was clearly eager to train on.

"What do you suggest we do with her?" Leander asked after watching the filly's third good gallop in ten days.

"I think she's going to be very good at middle distances," Steven replied. "She might get longer trips as well."

Leander took special note of his unhesitating confidence and decided to go along with it.

At Newbury in mid-April, Hyperborean sauntered away from a moderate field in a mile and a half race and won by six lengths. A month later, she did the same at Lingfield against better-class opposition.

When Leander sat down with Steven to discuss the next phase of the filly's campaign, she received a shock.

"Presumably you think she's worth a crack at the Oaks?" Leander asked.

"I think she should go to Epsom, but not for the Oaks," Steven said, staring hard at her.

His meaning was plain: for a moment or two, Leander was at a loss for words. It was fairly common practice to enter very good fillies for the Derby as well as the Oaks. Six fillies had won the Derby and four of them had achieved the very remarkable feat of winning both races within the space of two or three days.

"I didn't know you had her entered," Leander said.

Steven smiled.

"Do you think she's good enough for the Derby?" Leander asked.

"There's only one way to find out," Steven told her.

She accepted his decision without argument. Emma always said that it was the most important milestone that Steven passed on the way to becoming a great trainer.

For two hours before the race was run, the crowd on Epsom Downs buzzed with excitement at the news that Leander Hawksworth was on the course. While she ate a hearty lunch in the members' dining-room, a constant stream of admirers and well-wishers came to her table.

"Don't mind them, my dears," she whispered to Amelia and Emma as her self-appointed guardians for the day started to look flustered at all the attention. "They have to make the most of it. Remember, at my age, they may not get another chance!" Laughing at the looks on their faces, she added, "Besides, it's awfully nice."

It was indeed, so much so that Steven suspected her head was turned by it all. In the paddock, Leander seemed like a little girl experiencing the atmosphere of Derby Day for the first time, and nearly a mile of the race had been run before she paid any attention to what was happening.

As the field completed the long turn of Tattenham Corner, Mark Pilgrim let Hyperborean down and she took flight: not one of the ten colts had a snowball's chance in hell of catching her; the huge crowd knew it and cheered her every inch of the way to the winning post.

Leander was visibly overcome by the warmth of the tremendous ovation she received when she led Hyperborean into the winner's enclosure. As the following day's newspapers and cinema newsreels pointed out, the eighth winner of the Derby to come from Latimer's Barn was the most popular in living memory.

Highly charged and unforgettable though the occasion was, Steven's most treasured memory of the year came three months later at Doncaster.

Sixty-two years after she and Bellerophon had won the hearts of Yorkshire, Leander made the long journey north to watch her filly compete in the St Leger. Her victory, even more convincing than at Epsom, confirmed Steven as champion trainer and drove the crowd to ecstatic heights. When someone shouted, "Three cheers for the grandest filly of them all!" Leander laughed, realising that she, not Hyperborean, was the object of their admiration.

As Steven stood with her and the filly, posing for photographs, Leander said, "By the way, do you know what her name means?"

"I didn't think it meant anything," Steven said. "Didn't you get it from Hyperion and Borealis?"

"I did. Then Silas told me that it had a meaning. In ancient Greek legend, the Hyperboreans were a people who lived in sunshine and plenty beyond the north wind. Don't you think that's nice?"

Steven never forgot the way her face lit up at this beautifully fitting description of the filly who had come through fire to give his grandmother the two sweetest racing triumphs of her life.

That radiant glimpse of the Leander Flamsteed of sixty years ago became etched indelibly on the retina of his mind to act as a beacon in the dark years ahead.

CHAPTER 31
1939

'It isn't a scrap of use sitting around like that'

Leander took special care over Joe Symes's funeral.

The one-time scoundrel had served her well and faithfully for thirty years and his death was a sad loss. He was duly afforded the final courtesy of a well-attended burial.

Looking into the grave, Leander expressed silent gratitude for the secrets that Joe had taken with him and turned away with a sigh that caused Amelia and Emma to exchange an anxious glance.

A month ago, a Christmas meant to be a brave attempt to dispel the blackness of the international situation had been darkened by Rupert Timberlake's heart attack. Kathleen Stanton, by merciful chance a guest at the same dinner, had saved his life. But Leander knew only too well that her staunchest and oldest friend, the man whose love had contributed enormously to her battle against old age, was now living a perilous existence on borrowed time. At her insistence, Rupert had given his home in Marlborough over to Claude and Lily and moved to Louise House.

"I want you where I can keep an eye on you," he was told. "And please *don't* argue, Rupert, it will only aggravate your condition."

On top of that, there was William.

For three weeks, the pneumonia had encountered not a scrap of resistance.

"I'm afraid that he seems to be surrendering to it," Kathleen told Leander.

"Yes." Leander nodded weary acceptance. As if by way of explanation, she said, "He is seventy-seven."

It would be quite remarkable, Amelia and Emma thought as they walked away from Joe Symes's grave, if Leander were *not* deeply preoccupied with thoughts of her own mortality.

The Duke of Laverstoke's interpretation of affairs in Europe was

552

uncompromisingly bad. "There's going to be a show-down with Hitler. It's got to the stage where the world isn't big enough for him and anyone else. They say that even Chamberlain believes it will happen."

The Duke was one of the few people with a good word for the Prime Minister. "I don't know how committed he really is to this appeasement game, but it's given us a bit of breathing space to build up our strength. Winston's going on blind about it, of course, whereas I'm not so sure that we shouldn't be handing poor old Neville a bit of credit."

Whatever the merits or otherwise of Chamberlain's dealings with Hitler, Leander was fully convinced that bad times lay ahead.

Henri Guillaume knew that the country he loved was in deadly peril.

After Maude's death, he had put up with life at the farm until he was sixteen. Then, disgusted by the antics of Clothilde, Jacques who had become a drunkard, and Michel whose new-found predilection for very young girls caused scandal and uproar at frequent intervals, he vanished. He gave no warning, left no note: at four o'clock on a June morning in 1933, he climbed out of his bedroom window and set off for Paris. He neither knew nor cared what would happen to the share of the farm that he had inherited from his mother.

A strong, good-looking boy, he soon found employment in a café near to the Opéra: as well as an adequate wage, a clean, comfortable room went with the job. Before long he had graduated from washing dishes to waiting, at which a natural flair made him very popular with the customers.

And what customers they were! Café Rostand was popular with opera-goers and some of the performers. One evening in 1934, the great Conchita Supervia had dinner after singing what was, by all accounts, a stunning *Carmen*. Waiting on her as she scintillated and enthralled a group of admirers, Henri was struck not so much by her distinctive beauty as by the horrible certainty that although she was not yet forty, she was fatally ill. News of her death eighteen months later did not surprise him.

Mostly Monsieur Rostand's patrons were the cream of Paris society – or so they liked to think. For Henri, imbued with a fair measure of Maude's cynical sense of humour, his customers were a never-ending source of amusement.

Occasionally, very occasionally, the couples were actually married to each other. More often, however, middle-aged men brought their mistresses; mature beauties were flamboyantly squired by virile young men. Henri looked after them superbly: no *maître d'hotel* had more gravitas or man-of-the-world understanding of every couple's unique secret. His clients loved it and tipped generously. Soon he had a substantial deposit account, and, in the same bank, Maude's birth certificate, prayer book and the 1929 newspaper cutting were lodged in a safe box. Henri had no idea why he took this unusual step with material of little obvious value; he simply felt a compulsion to treasure his tenuous connection with Cannings Ambo, the mysterious village in England.

Barely a week passed without Henri receiving offers of other jobs. He declined them all, conveying the impression of infinite sorrow at doing so; those whom he refused regarded him with even greater affection thereafter, giving him even bigger tips.

Financial security was one reason for staying. The other was Marie-Claire, Monsieur Rostand's daughter.

Marie-Claire, three years older than Henri, was beautiful and had an aura of excitement and experience. Her tongue was cutting, especially with those men whose attentions she resented, yet she was kind to Henri from the start. Hopelessly in love with her, he kept heroically silent as she conducted a series of affairs with the few men who did not incur her derision or anger.

For Henri, looking at another woman, or going away from Marie-Claire, was unthinkable.

On his twenty-first birthday in 1938, she gave him a spectacular reward for his five years of devotion. At two o'clock in the morning, when Café Rostand was closed and the house quiet, she came up to his room in the attic, climbed into his bed and set about furthering his education with breathtaking *élan*.

They were both surprised by the excellence of his performance. Momentarily exhausted after the third passionate fling, Henri paused to declare his undying love, half afraid that she would laugh at him.

Marie-Claire's reply, however, was as staggering as her purposefully naked entry into his room.

"But, of course! Soon, we shall be married! You will make the café prosper when Father retires and I shall make you the happiest man in France."

The date of the wedding, a mere month away, was fixed the following day, giving immediate proof of Marie-Claire's intentions. Henri was indeed happy, ridiculously so. But one night, as they relaxed over a glass of cognac after closing up, he saw into their future.

"Legendre and that actress were in again this evening," Monsieur Rostand said.

"I saw them!" Marie-Claire looked as black as thunder. "They were with Dufresne and the Palmieri whore."

"Ah!" Monsieur Rostand looked troubled. "That woman is a Fascist."

"She's a Nazi!" Marie-Claire said angrily. "They all are."

Henri nodded. "I listened to them talking. They are looking forward to the day that Hitler comes."

"The Saviour of France!" Marie-Claire mocked, repeating a phrase that she had heard many times from their wealthy, highly-placed clientele.

"That's exactly what Legendre called him," Henri said. "What's wrong with these people, for God's sake?"

"They're shit-scared of Communists," Marie-Claire said contemptuously. "They think that the only way they can save their necks and hang on to their privileges is to have Hitler running the country."

"He must conquer us first!" Henri declared grandly.

"That may not be so difficult," Monsieur Rostand said in a grave voice. "We are not ready to fight. Look at the Army!" He paused. When he continued, it was in the whispered tone of a frightened man. "There is talk that when they come, we might throw Paris open to them."

Henri and Marie-Claire bristled with anger.

But in the weeks that followed, many of their customers developed the treacherous theme in huddled conversations over candlelit tables, while Henri, his face expressionless, listened.

The first months of 1939 saw the happiness of his marriage clouded by an increasing breakdown in French public life against a sinister background that reeked of betrayal.

When Leander sat with William after dinner on the evening of 17 February, she found him detached, no longer a complete part of the real world. A visit from Matthew and his grandsons, William and John, during the afternoon had tired him. After a sleep, however, he became more lucid than at any time during the past week.

As was their habit, they reminisced.

"What was the name of that awful woman?" William asked.

"Which awful woman?"

"The one that came here to complain to Father about the way you dressed and carried on."

"Oh, yes, Mrs Dallow!" Leander chuckled. "Father sent her packing."

"He threatened to set the dogs on her and we hadn't got any," William smiled. "What was it you said about Bellerophon?"

"Oh, William, I must have said hundreds of things," Leander replied. "Deep down, I still think he's the best horse we've ever had."

"What about Hyperborean?"

"Yes, she's wonderful."

"And The Atheling . . . he was very good. What was it you said about Bellerophon? You said it *before* he won the Derby. I know!" Suddenly William was alert and bright-eyed. "It was, 'He can do it, I'm sure he can. And if he does, everything will be in our grasp.'"

"Oh, yes, I remember!"

"And you were right, weren't you, Lea?"

"We've done pretty well." Leander sounded almost dissatisfied: she was becoming notorious for raising her sights repeatedly, so that each outstanding performance became the accepted standard for the future. "And we've been very lucky, William. Some wonderful people have helped us enormously."

"Horatio."

"*Especially* Horatio. We couldn't have done it without him."

"And you," William said. "You've done a fair bit to put us on the map." His gaze became penetrating. "One way and another, I think you've pulled some pretty hair-raising stunts over the years, Lea."

"What *do* you mean, William?" Her smile concealed a twinge of anxiety: how much did he know?

"That doping business. You sorted that out."

"Yes."

"I've always thought that Joe Symes was mixed up in that."

"Have you? Whatever gave you that idea?"

"And who was behind it? Maude and George were bad enough to think of a scheme like that and they certainly hated us."

"That really is fanciful, William," Leander laughed.

He looked doubtful, but pressed on. "And what about that affair after the War when Rothwell put it about that our horses weren't trying?"

Leander was sufficiently surprised to let her guard down. "I never realised you knew about that."

"Didn't know!" Very briefly, William looked quite cross. "The Stewards at Newbury had a go at me, and I was expecting to get dragged in front of the Jockey Club at any minute."

"It was fairly serious," Leander agreed.

"Then what happened? All of a sudden, *The Clarion* starts going on about Rothwell's buttocks and he was done for."

"Pure coincidence, William," Leander said airily.

"Coincidence my foot! That's a Timberlake paper for a start."

William chuckled. "So you see, Lea, I'm not completely green. I don't know how you did it, but you did. There must have been lots of other things, too."

Having worn himself out, William lapsed into a shallow sleep and Leander tiptoed from the room, smiling at his perspicacity.

Although he was still asleep two hours later when she returned, his breathing was very bad and he was in distress. Kathleen Stanton came at once.

"Well?" Leander asked. "Tell me the truth, Kathleen."

"Not long," Kathleen replied sadly.

Matthew hurried up from Rose House and settled down in a chair at his father's side with Leander opposite him.

Shortly after midnight, William woke. There was an unworldly serenity about him. He smiled at Matthew, then turned to Leander.

Her hand reached out to grasp his, they smiled at each other and together they said, "Thank you, my dear. For everything."

William Flamsteed, the man who had never completely conquered his shyness, who had always looked to his sister for support and approval, even when founding a company that was to earn a priceless reputation for quality, closed his eyes and died. In nearly seventy-eight years he had never deliberately made an enemy and scores of people had been the better for knowing him.

Despite the lateness of the hour, Leander went to the library and set to work on the Big Book.

They opened up Ruth's grave to bury William beside her on a freezing-cold day of wind and snow showers. Of all the mourners, many of whom had braved the weather to travel long distances, none looked sadder than Fred and Tish Cartwright. At The House afterwards, they wept openly, saying that they owed everything, most especially the priceless gift of their own happiness, to William.

"Please don't be upset," Leander begged them. "William knew how much you all cared for him and he was very pleased. He wouldn't want you to get so miserable." She paused, and there was a sparkle in her eyes. Fred, reminded of the enchantment that could shine out so suddenly, was startled. "And he was very lucky, you know, right to the end."

"How's that?" Tish asked.

"My dear, what if I'd popped off first? William would have been lost, utterly lost!"

Fred, now sixty-five and as strait-laced as he had once been radical, was momentarily taken aback by the remark, but soon joined Tish in smiling acceptance.

"She never lets anything get her down, does she?" he whispered, once Leander had moved away to talk to another group.

"What do you expect?" Tish asked. "You've known her long enough!"

Leander's cheerful attitude was, Steven thought, the finest tribute that she could pay to William, who, unlike so many men in this precarious century, had lived out his life fully, dying in the comforting presence of the two people dearest to him.

The one period of deep melancholy and unease that Leander experienced came when she was thanking John Shepherd for the funeral service.

After thirty-nine years of caring for the spiritual needs of Cannings Ambo, John was nearing his sixty-fifth birthday. Age was yet to present him with difficulty, but the day when his retirement had to be considered could not be far away. There was no question of a repeat of the miracle by which John had taken over from his own father, the Good Shepherd: unhappily, John and Mary were childless. Long since reconciled to this misfortune, they were a devoted, if slightly fussy and introverted couple.

Leander viewed the prospect of an outsider replacing John with something close to distaste.

An outsider! It was a dreadful way of looking at things and Leander did her best to shake herself out of it.

But on the day her beloved William was laid to rest, what dear Aunt Elisabeth used to call 'the right sort of people' seemed more important than ever.

When the blow finally fell, Leander admitted that she had allowed herself to drift into a fool's paradise after William's death. Aided and abetted by the Duchess of Laverstoke, who was at a loose end with the Duke increasingly away in London, she did, however, have a marvellous time while she was doing it.

"Your grandmother and my mother are becoming a menace," Charles joked to Rachel one evening in June. "It seems they were cutting a hell of a dash at Ascot yesterday. Dear Mama gave 'Grauncher' Ormesby a fearful going-over in front of half the Royal Enclosure."

Rachel spluttered with laughter, well able to imagine the scene in which a minor peer, who was far too susceptible to involvement in financial scandal, had received a comprehensive mangling.

"Actually, I'll bet Leander egged her on," Rachel said. "She's always had it in for Ormesby. I think he once tried to do the dirty on a Timberlake."

"Crikey!" Charles whistled. "I thought that carried the death penalty."

Rachel's guess was right. Although the Duchess was seventeen years younger than Leander, with an established reputation for controversy, it was the older woman who usually took the lead in creating mayhem.

Leander led the umbrella-brandishing assault on a bunch of idiots who attempted to launch a pro-Fascist demonstration in Chippenham Market Place, and Leander it was who set about a bookmaker on Bath racecourse whom she suspected of trying to fiddle an old gentleman whose first-ever bet was a winner. The servants' hall at Eaton Mandeville was invariably agog when the Duchess's chauffeur returned after a day out with the increasingly notorious pair.

The havoc contained a few calm interludes. Sometimes, prompted by the ever-worsening state of Europe, they exchanged apprehensive confidences. The Duchess confessed her concern over the Duke's health and Leander found herself worrying about George.

"You were pretty drastic with him, weren't you?" Clementine Prideaux asked, accompanying the question with a searching gaze that half persuaded Leander she knew much more than the essentials of the Celia Blennerhasset scandal.

"Yes, I was." Leander looked sad.

"Hubert has always insisted that George was a thorough wrong 'un," the Duchess said sympathetically.

"I'm afraid he was, Clem. We could have lost everything because of him, and I've always thought he had a lot to do with Steven's death." She paused, with a faraway look in her eyes. "I had to be *terribly* hard. Such a shame! And I'd like to know how he is."

"You don't hear from him?"

"Not for years."

There were also many moments of quiet pleasure.

At Newbury in July, Leander and the Duchess spent a blameless afternoon when two young Latimer's Barn representatives made a winning début.

Isocracy was a two-year-old colt belonging to Claude Timberlake; Sammy Thorn, who rode him, was something of a stop-gap emergency measure.

During the winter of 1938–39, Steven had been shocked by the realisation that Mark Pilgrim was fifty. There was no diminution in his ability to act as first jockey other than the relentlessly increasing problems of keeping his weight below eight and a half stone. His son, Michael, with burning ambition to keep up the family tradition, had already proved that he was a rider of great talent. There was one massive fly in the ointment: because of Mark's comparatively late marriage to Rhona, Michael was only eleven, at least seven years away from being granted a jockey's licence.

Sammy had volunteered to fill the gap. He was eighteen, had been with Steven for nearly four years and always caught the eye when he was riding work on Cannings Down. Steven accepted the offer thankfully and arranged for Sammy to start with three rides for which Mark could not do the weight.

"What about this boy?" the Duchess asked Leander. "Is he good enough?"

"Definitely! He's got tremendous nerve and style. He'll do us proud once he has the experience."

"And what's this Isocracy like?"

"He might turn out to be useful." Leander looked round furtively to check that no one was near the deck-chairs in which they were taking their ease. "As a matter of fact, Clem, he could be a Classic prospect for next year. He's by Agamemnon out of Pennycomequick, so it's all there."

"And he can go a bit, can he?" the Duchess asked.

"Clem, I promise you, he's been catching pigeons at home!"

Cyril Osgood, their driver for the day, was sent off with ten pounds. "Remember, Osgood," Her Grace warned, "find an honest-looking bookie. We don't want a repetition of that fiasco at Bath!"

Isocracy and Sammy were established friends who knew exactly what was expected of them and how to do it. For the first three and a half of the six furlongs, they were content to stay at the back, away from the trouble caused by the four inexperienced front-runners. When Sammy shook Isocracy up, he displayed the speed and power to move effortlessly round the bumping and boring: better still, when Isocracy hit the front, he lengthened his stride and went away like a champion in the making. Urged on by Sammy, with showmanship that was unnecessary but thrilling, Isocracy came home by five lengths.

The Duchess was delighted, not least because of the odds of six to one, a reflection of most punters' lack of faith in the novice pair. Sammy was subjected to a paean of praise which he bore with manful modesty. By contrast, Leander's few quick words came as pure gold to the young man who knew that few of his future rides would be as easy.

Afterwards, as they enjoyed tea and cream cakes, the Duchess was deep in thought until Leander pulled her out of it.

"What's up, Clem? Not going broody, are you?"

"Good God no!" The Duchess found the suggestion funny. "No, I was thinking what a lot you'd got to be proud of."

"In what way?"

"Look at young Sammy and that colt: neither of them have ever raced before, yet they come out and do that! They were a credit to you."

"To Steven," Leander corrected.

"And where did he get his ideas from, eh?"

"I suppose I haven't done badly," Leander admitted.

"Can you think of anyone who's done better?"

"If only it could go on for ever," Leander said with a sadness in her voice that caused the Duchess to react sharply.

"Why shouldn't it? You've built a system that can keep going indefinitely."

"Everyone is convinced there's going to be another war."

"Leander, they may well be right, but there's no reason why it should involve us."

"Surely we'd get dragged in?"

"Not if Chamberlain can help it. Believe me, my dear, there's no earthly reason why we should get mixed up in all these European squabbles. They're nothing to do with us."

Leander was so desperate to accept her friend's opinion that she disregarded everything else, even all that William had said. It was the only time in her life that she did such a silly thing.

Five weeks later, Leander returned to The House after putting fresh flowers on the grave of Ruth and William to find Amelia frowning at a newspaper.

"What is it, darling?" Leander asked. "You look awfully worried."

"I think I am." Amelia reconsidered the information she had been absorbing. "Germany has signed a pact with Russia."

"Oh." Leander was puzzled. "Is that bad?"

"I think so. Russia has promised to stay neutral if Germany is involved in a war."

"That sounds like *good* news," Leander said doubtfully, as though she was trying to convince herself. "It's one less to worry about. Russia's awfully big and powerful."

"It also means that Hitler can do what he likes about Poland," Amelia said grimly.

For nearly six months, Germany had been demanding sovereignty over the Polish port of Danzig. The Poles were defiant; England and France, pledged to support them, were catastrophically ambivalent.

Rather than jolting Europe into awareness, the announcement of the pact produced the inactivity of the rabbit petrified by a weasel. What diplomacy there was took place in secret and was ineffective. Chamberlain used a Swedish businessman called Birer Dahlerus to tell Hitler of all the good things that would be his if only he would refrain from war.

But the time had come, and the squalid last-ditch attempt to raise the stakes of appeasement to levels that would have caused most Englishmen to choke in disgust was brushed aside. The German Army launched a ferocious attack on Poland in the small hours of 1 September and by six the *Luftwaffe* was bombing Warsaw.

In one very dramatic way it was different from August 1914. This time there was the wireless to bring almost immediate news of what was happening. With that news came a terrible realisation: it was not only the Polish Army that was being mauled. The new concept of 'total war' meant civilian casualties, too, apparently in horrifying numbers.

Automatically, without anyone arranging it, The House became a focal point. When Steven finished work with the second lot at midday, he found more than twenty people in the large sitting-room where the wireless was pouring out a constant stream of bulletins, some of which, Steven instinctively felt, had to be misleading.

The gathering was mostly of villagers, although Charles, accompanied by a very pregnant Rachel and young Lord Henry, had come to stay for a few days.

"Mother's getting things organised on the estate," Charles explained. "She wants the West Wood fortifying because that silly old fool Brigadier Featherstone-Dudley has told her that Hitler is bound to drop a battalion of paratroopers in Hockley's Spinney."

Eventually, at midnight, people drifted home or to bed. Leander and Amelia, kept company by Rupert and Silas, made themselves comfortable in armchairs, dozing for some of the time, but mostly trying to enjoy what they were sure were the last few hours of peace and quiet.

Throughout 2 September, the talk was all of negotiation and compromise. Mussolini proposed a conference and the idea was strenuously supported by Georges Bonnet, Foreign Minister of France. Amelia deduced that their motives were similar.

"They want to play for time," she said. "They have to prepare for war!"

A statement issued from Downing Street said that the British Government insisted on the withdrawal of all German troops from Poland before negotiations started.

Steven spent a most frustrating morning attempting to discover whether that afternoon's racing at Salisbury was on or off. In the absence of definite information, he simply set off with the two horses that were entered.

At ten o'clock that night, the Duke of Laverstoke telephoned from London, asking most particularly to speak to Leander.

"What's going on up there, Hubert?" she demanded.

"The most awful kerfuffle!" he replied. "It's bedlam. Look, Leander, I'm leaving now to motor home. Shall I call in on the way down and put you in the picture?"

"That's very kind of you, Hubert. Please do!"

"Don't know how long I'll be."

"It doesn't matter, I shall be up and about."

In fact, when he finally reached Latimer's Barn at half past two, half a dozen people hurried out into the warm summer night to surround the car in which he had driven himself.

"You won't believe it," he said when Leander finally had him sitting down in the kitchen with a stiff whisky and a plate of sandwiches. "Neville went to the House at seven-thirty and waffled for over an hour. He's still blethering on about a conference."

"Did he get away with it?" Charles asked.

"No, my boy, he damned well didn't." The Duke paused to swallow a sandwich and most of his regard for Chamberlain. "When Greenwood got up to reply for the Opposition, Leo Amery shouted, 'Come on, Arthur, speak for England!' That got a tremendous cheer from both sides."

"And what was the outcome?" Leander asked.

"The sitting broke up in uproar. A Cabinet meeting started at eleven and the story is that some chaps were refusing to leave until an ultimatum is sent to Berlin."

"So it's war, then?" Amelia asked.

"No doubt of it, m'dear. With or without Neville, we shall be at war with Germany before any of us is very much older."

On Sunday 3 September, John Shepherd cancelled the morning service when he heard that the Prime Minister would speak to the nation at eleven-fifteen. Instead of going to church, he and Mary went to The House.

For the first time other than for a wedding or a funeral, the large sitting-room was full, but the fifty or more people perched on every seat and arm-rest were silent and tense in a way that no one had ever experienced before.

They were all there, the families that had turned Cannings

Ambo from an obscure backwater into a renowned producer of quality. Izzards, Pilgrims and Merriweathers rubbed shoulders with Hawksworths, Flamsteeds and members of the Goakes family. Rupert, Silas and Claude's wife, Lily, represented the Timberlakes, while Jeremy Dundas, rescued by the village from the last great man-made nightmare, was squeezed between a pregnant marchioness and Cyril Osgood, a soldier from the previous century.

At last it was time, and Neville Chamberlain's voice crackled from the loudspeaker. One thing was immediately apparent: the Prime Minister was a broken man near the end of his tether.

After explaining all the desperate attempts that had been made to preserve peace, he told of the ultimatum that had been sent to Germany at nine o'clock that morning. It concerned the violation of Poland and allowed only two hours for a reply.

Eleven o'clock had come and gone: no one in Hitler's Third Reich had bothered to send any form of reply.

"Consequently," Chamberlain intoned hollowly, "this country is at war with Germany."

After an uncomfortable pause, he continued:

"You can imagine what a bitter blow it is to me that all my long struggle to win peace has failed. Yet I cannot believe that there is anything more or anything different that I could have done and that would have been more successful.

"Up to the very last . . ."

Leander, sitting nearest to the wireless set, rose quickly to turn it off. The man was annoying her.

"Well, Rupert, my dear, we didn't make much of a job of winning the peace," she said and walked to a window without waiting for a response.

There was none, in any case: the silence in the room behind her was total.

For the first time in her life, Leander felt cast down and beaten. My God, she thought, after all we've been through, now this! Giles and Gerald and all the other lovely young men died for nothing. What *is* going to become of us?

Then her eyes, which had been unseeing, focused on the great expanse of immaculate lawn and Lord Francis Rashleigh's original stable and coach-house, both very nearly a hundred years old, as was The House. Turning her head slightly, she took in the two magnificent yards built during her lifetime. She thought of the elegant glory of her father's poplar avenue and the village, improved out of all recognition over the years. And she thought of all those who had worked so hard, especially James Munroe and Timothy Daniels, who died trying to save horses.

Turning, she found all eyes fixed on her, exactly as it was in The George on Armistice Night. They had seen her stiffen with indomitable resolve. The old woman, born in this very house seventy-nine years ago, now had white hair, but she had never fallen off a horse or received a hard knock; her body, without a single ache or pain, was ramrod straight and her chin was up.

"It isn't a scrap of use sitting around like that," she told them. "We must decide what we're going to do about this *bloody* man Hitler!"

It was the first time she had ever sworn: they all knew it and were electrified.

And her eyes were alight with a magic that had fire in it.

DEREK NICHOLLS

THE BLUE RIBAND

From Ireland to the rolling Berkshire downs and the bluegrass country of Kentucky, from sleepy country courses to the dazzle of Ascot and finally Epsom, winning the Derby had been his grandfather's unfulfilled dream.

When Edward Manning takes over the old man's racing stables in Ireland, he realises that the dream has become his own. But it could only ever be made to come true with the help of women — especially the beautiful Caroline.

HODDER AND STOUGHTON PA